"[An] unsettling, mind-bending apocalyptic novel."
—Caroline Leavitt

Mankind is the endangered species.

"This book is a vivid detour into hell...Scary good."
—Luis Alberto Urrea, author of *Queen of America* and *Into the Beautiful North*

"Joseph Wallace re-births an ancient terror with creepy, pulse-pounding plausibility. His tale is just a few mutations away from coming true."
—David Brin, author of *Existence*

continued . . .

INVASIVE SPECIES

JOSEPH WALLACE

BERKLEY BOOKS, NEW YORK

THE BERKLEY PUBLISHING GROUP
Published by the Penguin Group
Penguin Group (USA) LLC
375 Hudson Street, New York, New York 10014

USA • Canada • UK • Ireland • Australia • New Zealand • India • South Africa • China

penguin.com

A Penguin Random House Company

INVASIVE SPECIES

A Berkley Book / published by arrangement with the author

For information, address: The Berkley Publishing Group,
a division of Penguin Group (USA) LLC,
375 Hudson Street, New York, New York 10014.

ISBN: 978-0-425-26949-7

PUBLISHING HISTORY
Berkley premium edition / December 2013

PRINTED IN THE UNITED STATES OF AMERICA

10 9 8 7 6 5 4 3 2 1

Cover photos by Shutterstock/Getty Images.
Cover design by George Long.
Interior text design by Kelly Lipovich.

In memory of Dad, who shared his love of nature with me, and Mom, who put up with the consequences.

And to my brothers, Jonathan and Richard, my comrades in turning over countless mossy stones and rotten logs to see what wriggled and slithered beneath.

AUTHOR'S NOTE

When do you start writing a novel?

For me, that's a complicated question. My novels usually begin with a combination treasure hunt/rummage sale: I am always accumulating offbeat facts, long-lost stories, and memorable details, usually with absolutely no idea when—or if—I'll be able to use them in a book. Then one day, out of the blue, a story comes together in my mind, and I'm able to say, "Now, *that's* why I kept those knickknacks around!"

I remember the most important inspiration for *Invasive Species*. It was a riveting essay whose title and author escape me (maybe one of you out there can help), detailing the author's move from the familiar northeast to a Texas farm filled with snakes and lizards and other wildlife unlike any he'd ever seen before.

The vignette I remember most vividly involved a wasp: a two-inch-long tarantula hawk, named for the spiders it would paralyze to feed its young.

The author was lying on a deck chair, watching the enormous wasp drag its paralyzed prey toward its lair.

Three times, the author poked at the wasp with a stick, wanting to see if the tarantula, left alone, would revive.

The first two times, the wasp rose in the air and circled around before returning to its prey. The third time, however, it made a beeline straight to a spot three inches in front of the author's face. Lying back in his chair, he was helpless. If the hawk had wanted to unleash its excruciating sting or bite, he couldn't have stopped it.

Instead the wasp just hovered there, staring into his eyes. The message was clear: I'm giving you another chance. You do that one more time, though, and you're dead meat.

Then it flew back to resume its task. And the author, his heart pounding, left it alone.

Interspecies communication between two apex predators at its clearest: a smart, agile, venomous predator telling a human what was what, and the helpless human understanding—and heeding—the warning.

That was where *Invasive Species* began.

ACKNOWLEDGMENTS

You can't develop a long-remembered vignette into a novel without a ton of help. As always, my deepest gratitude goes to my wife, Sharon AvRutick, for many years now my first and most trusted reader. You would not believe how messy my books are before she sees them for the first time.

My children, Shana and Jacob, put up with my tendency to describe over dinner various fascinating, oft-disgusting things about bugs. Then again, they're used to me by now.

I'm grateful to my fellow members of the Marmaduke Writing Factory for gathering, renting the basement floor of a local historic house, and giving me access to the windowless conference room ("The Cave") where this novel was written. It's the best "writers' retreat" I've ever attended.

When you spend most of your time alone in a cave, though, you come to crave human company. Thank goodness for the existence of the Black Cow Coffee Company in Pleasantville and its manager and baristas, including Linton, Emily, Michelle, Danielle, Jianna, Mike, Natalie, Emma, Austin, and Steven. I'm grateful to all of them for putting up with me after my solitary stints writing about the end of the world.

Thanks also to my high school writing students, who always inspire me: Cary, Becca, Violet, and Benji. Special gratitude to Emmalisa Stangarone, who began the year as my writing student and (while also finding time to sing, act, study, and apply to college) ended it as my research assistant. You'll see the results of her investigations into various topics—ranging from terrifying emerging diseases to bizarre cargo cults—in my forthcoming follow-up to *Invasive Species*, currently called *The Slavemakers*.

You can see Emmalisa herself in the book trailer for *Invasive Species*, which can be found at josephwallace.com.

What would I do in these uncertain times without Deborah Schneider, my literary agent? For years now, she's been my sherpa through an ever-shifting publishing environment, putting up with my moods and the fact that I don't ever seem to write the same kind of book twice. My lifetime dream was to publish a novel; if not for Deborah, I doubt it would ever have happened.

I'm so glad that *Invasive Species* landed with Berkley. It's been a pleasure to work with my editor, Natalee Rosenstein, her assistant, Robin Barletta, and the rest of the team. Every journey to publication should be like this one.

If you're interested in learning more about me and *Invasive Species*, check my website (josephwallace.com), my writing group's blog (marmadukewritingfactory.com), and my YouTube channel. You can also follow me on Twitter @Joe_Wallace and find me on Facebook at facebook.com/joewallacewriter. Hope to see you!

ONE

Casamance Region, Senegal, West Africa

THE SINGLE-PROP BUSH plane sliced through the base of a towering cumulus cloud and emerged into the brilliant tropical sunshine. Sitting in the shotgun seat, Trey Gilliard took in the explosion of colors: golden light turning the base of the clouds silver, a sky of the deepest purplish blue, and below, the vast, rumpled green expanse of rain forest.

Malcolm Granger's voice came over Trey's headset. "Looks like broccoli."

Trey had heard this before. They'd sat side by side in this two-seater Piper PA-18 many times over the years, Malcolm fighting through wind shear and thunderstorms and clear-air turbulence and air currents that could slam you into the ground like a fist, all to help Trey find what he'd come to see.

"I effing hate broccoli," Malcolm said.

Trey had heard this, too.

"Lower," he said.

He saw Malcolm frown and glance over, his mirrored shades catching the sunlight. But Trey knew he wouldn't have to ask twice. This was what it was like, being Trey's pilot. You did what he said or you flew with him once, kissed the ground when you landed, and never let him near your airplane again.

Malcolm was one of the few pilots who'd come back. In fact, if Trey called, he'd cancel whatever else he had on his schedule and haul this little Piper—or one of the other bush planes he owned—over to whatever forest, desert, or mountainside Trey had staked out.

"What's the fun in life," Malcolm told anyone who asked, "if you don't try to end it every once in a while?"

The sound of the engine changed, grew rougher, as the plane slowed and dipped toward the forest canopy. From above, the carpet of leaves seemed as soft as a huge bedspread, but this was a fiction. Guide your plane into it, and you'd find out soon enough exactly how soft it was.

People in Trey's line of work—and there were a few— had found out. He didn't need to learn it for himself.

Still . . .

"Lower," he said.

Trey was his own boss. He chose when to work, where to work, what he wanted to do.

He knew how lucky he was to be able to live this way, since no one in their right mind would hire him full-time. There were only a few people left on earth who, like Malcolm, could put up with him.

Over the years, though, a few organizations had figured out a way to use what he offered: an aggressive intelligence untethered to common sense; a willingness to take whatever chances were necessary to achieve his goals;

and the ability, above all, to plunge into the wilderness, see everything there was to see, and report back on what he'd found.

Turn the wheel of Trey's personality just one or two degrees, and he might have ended up a mercenary, a soldier for hire. He'd met enough of them on his travels and could see the similarities—foremost, a disdain for staying in one place, for following the rules, and for most of humanity.

The difference was small, but crucial: Mercenaries liked to kill, and Trey didn't.

Instead he preferred to save. To preserve. Which was why he was here now, in this remote region of Senegal, just beyond the line where the savanna ended and the rain forest began.

To see what was here. To see what was worth saving.

The organization paying his bills this time was called the International Conservation Trust. ICT. When they could tolerate working with him, they'd send him to some remote region and gladly forget about him for a while.

He'd disappear into the wilderness, and when he emerged weeks later, gaunt, dirty, sometimes ridden with parasites or feverish from disease, he'd report on what he'd found. What birds were new to science. What endangered mammals were making their last stand. What bizarre eyeless salamanders writhed through pitch-black caves. What plants, whose blooms or seeds might give birth to medicines that could cure cancer, clambered for the light in untracked swamps.

In an age of massive destruction, Trey told them where they should spend their precious resources.

Then off he'd head to another wilderness.

Staying sane, barely, only because he could spend most of his time where no one else would go.

"What do you see?" he asked.

He heard Malcolm laugh. They were fifty feet, no more, above the canopy. The plane bucked and slewed in the warm currents rising from the breathing leaves.

"Trees, Thomas," Malcolm said. "One fuckin' tree after another."

Malcolm was the only person who called Trey "Thomas." Though it was his name: Thomas Hunter Gilliard III.

Trey.

Malcolm pointed with his chin. Trey nodded. He'd seen it, too: a small troop of colobus monkeys, their thick fur red and black against the green. Six of them perched in the canopy's branches, looking up at the plane roaring past them.

Before Trey would disappear into the forest, he and Malcolm would undertake this kind of survey from the air. ICT called them Emergency Assessments, and what they did was allow Trey to identify the least damaged areas. Only then would he return on foot and begin to inventory what was there.

He and Malcolm had been flying a grid here in the Casamance forests for five days. So far Trey had been disappointed. The forests seemed tainted to him, impure. Sure, there were giant kapok trees, monkeys, beautiful birds, an abundance of butterflies down there. But also fresh clearings made by human hands, smoldering fires, and other signs that the forest was being plundered for wood or cleared for farms and pastures.

Maybe he'd come too late. He should have been here five years ago.

He lifted his gaze and felt himself grow still inside. "The hell is that?"

Even over the headset, Malcolm heard the change in Trey's tone. Following the direction of his gaze, he turned the plane to the west. The sound of his low whistle reached Trey's ears.

Perhaps two miles ahead of them, a large expanse of forest was dying. Bare trees looked like contorted skeletons, their branches pointing to the sky like accusing bony fingers. The leaves that remained were yellowing, sickly. As Trey watched, a gust of wind whirled some of them into a dust devil, leaving another bare branch behind.

"Ugly," Malcolm said.

Trey was silent.

"I'll take us north and back east," Malcolm said.

"No." Trey took a breath. "Maintain course."

"But—"

Trey knew. The dying forest lay beyond the boundaries agreed to by ICT and the Senegalese government. It was outside the grid. Trey and Malcolm didn't have permission to fly over.

"Maintain course," Trey said again.

Malcolm kept the Piper flying west. The dying patch of forest, miles in extent, drew closer.

Trey leaned forward, his gaze unwavering. Trying to see, to understand. Was there any kind of industry here? Had some oil pipeline burst, some mining-operation tailings lake overflowed?

Trey couldn't understand how. He could detect no

roads leading from the edge of the inhabited land, five miles to the north, to this stricken forest.

Maybe when they were closer . . .

But they never got the chance. Trey caught a glimpse of a sudden dark form rising from the canopy directly in front of the Piper. The computer in his brain, the part that identified and categorized everything he saw, said: *Bird. Raptor. Black kite. Second-year male.*

Then it struck the plane's propeller and became nothing but chunks of meat and a burst of feathers. A dark penumbra that wreathed the windows for an instant before being whipped away.

The plane's engine coughed, choked. Died.

They flew, glided, in silence. The single propeller on the Piper's nose did not move.

Malcolm, his left hand fighting the yoke, his right reaching for the ignition, said, "Shit." Trey didn't need the headset to hear him.

The plane dipped toward the canopy. Trey braced himself for the impact.

I'll live, he thought.

I'm not done yet.

They were maybe twenty feet from the topmost limbs when the engine fired. The propeller spun, slowed, then sped into a blur. Malcolm pulled back on the throttle and the plane's nose rose. Just a little.

They hit an air pocket and dropped ten feet. Trey could see butterflies spinning amid the branches below. A tiny pool of water trapped in a bromeliad plant winked in a beam of sunlight.

Malcolm pulled back harder. Again they rose, the engine coughing and groaning. The plane swung north.

Trey lifted his gaze and saw, a mile or so ahead, the edge of the forest, the almost surgical line where the jungle came to an end and the savanna began.

The savanna. Flat land. Fields and pastures and roads, any of which could be used as a landing strip if you really needed one.

Trey knew that the pilot's thoughts were traveling the same track. Malcolm pulled back on the yoke one more time. The Piper fought its way upward, until the rumpled forest was a thousand feet below. Trey could see the yellow grasslands, the gleaming silver stripe of the Gambia River, the blue Atlantic.

The engine died again.

"Hang on," Malcolm said.

The plane glided on the hot, rising air, losing altitude faster and faster even as they came closer to the savanna and possible salvation. Trey looked down and saw the forest reaching for them as they fell. He could see the muscles on Malcolm's arms knot as he struggled with the yoke.

Their destination lay just ahead: a flat grassy field across the Massou-Djibo Road, which ran along the forest's edge. Trey's brain calculated distances and speed, and he knew they wouldn't make it. They were going to hit the trees.

But they didn't. Trey hadn't calculated for Malcolm's cussedness, or his understanding of his little bush plane. Through sheer willpower and physical strength, the pilot wrestled the dead plane over the last line of forest. Vines whipped the wings as they went past, and then suddenly they were a hundred feet over level, treeless ground. The dirt road sketched a red-earth line through the grassland below.

"Hang on," Malcolm said again. The Piper glided, the blurred ground racing just below them. A moment later they made contact, rose a few feet, and then touched down for good and were bumping across the field. Stones kicked up by the tires rattled off the fuselage.

Malcolm brought the plane to a halt. After a few moments' silence, Trey pulled off his headset. "Thanks."

Malcolm shrugged and stretched his arms. "No worries."

Then, scanning the empty landscape around them, he sighed. "Guess we'll have to walk out," he said.

Trey unsnapped his harness, swung open the door beside him. Hot air wafted in, along with the sound of crickets and the staccato call of a red-eyed dove.

"Won't be the first time," he said.

Malcolm laughed. "Or the last."

THEY STOOD ON the road. There was no sign of cars, or people, in any direction. A single cow stared at them from a nearby pasture. Clouds were piling up to the west, foretelling storms that afternoon. There were storms in the Casamance every afternoon.

"Gonna get wet," Malcolm said. Then he rolled his eyes. "Yeah, I know: Won't be the first time."

"Let's go," Trey said.

They set off, maintaining an easy pace that still ate up the distance. Both of them were tall, but after that the similarities ended. Trey, an American, was dark, olive complexioned, with deep-set eyes and a strong nose and chin. People said they could never tell what he was thinking, which was fine with him.

Malcolm, who'd grown up in Cape Tribulation, Australia, was more solidly built, with a broad, flat face and blue eyes. If he ever traded this life for a desk job, he'd be fat in a month. His unkempt blond hair was thinning, and his face and freckled arms were always either pink, sunburned, or peeling.

Trey was thirty-six. He'd never asked Malcolm's age, but guessed about fifty.

As if intuiting Trey's thoughts, Malcolm said, "This is where I s'pose I should say that I'm getting too old for this crap."

Trey didn't even dignify that with a response.

THEY'D WALKED FOR about a half hour when Trey stopped still in the middle of the deserted road. He leaned his head back, let his eyes scan the sky until they focused on a martial eagle circling, a black cross against the blue sky high above.

Malcolm had seen this behavior before. He wanted to get back to civilization so he could collect his tools and a vehicle, come back, and rescue his plane, but he knew there was no point in interrupting Trey's train of thought.

As they stood there in silence, thunder rumbled in the distance.

Finally Trey allowed his gaze to drop. "Malcolm," he said.

"Yeah?"

"Back then, right before we hit that kite, did you smell something?"

Malcolm blinked. This wasn't what he'd expected. "Did I what?"

"There was an odor rising from that dying forest, something I've never encountered before. Didn't you notice it?"

After a pause, Malcolm shook his head. "Sorry, but if I did, the memory's been wiped clean by the almost-dying stuff that happened afterward."

Trey frowned. Before he could speak, they heard the sound of an engine. Perhaps a mile up the road, a pickup truck was heading toward them. A plume of reddish dust rose in its wake and the sun reflected off its black metal cab. They were about to be rescued.

Trey said, "What's killing that forest?"

Malcolm had no answer.

But it didn't really matter. When Trey got like this, he wasn't really talking to you. He was talking to himself, and you just happened to be in the vicinity.

TWO

Mpack, Senegal

IF YOU SPENT most of your life in the wilderness, you learned to be a light sleeper.

Or maybe it was the other way around. Maybe only people who could awaken instantly chose to spend so much time alone in places inhabited by poisonous snakes, scorpions, and spiders, not to mention bigger creatures with sharp teeth and irritable dispositions.

Trey came alert in his one-room stone hut. For the briefest instant—as always—he was surprised to find that he was under a roof, not canvas, the forest canopy, or the sky. Then he was off his cot and getting dressed even as he registered what had woken him.

The sound of a man shouting, followed by a high and keening cry, a woman's voice, quickly cut off.

By the time Trey was out the door, into the damp morning air, there was little to see. A few young boys, already in their uniforms, were kicking a soccer ball around the town square as they waited for school. The doors to all the houses around the square were closed, which was unusual even at this early hour.

Trey knew these schoolboys. He'd caught their attention—and earned their laughter and catcalls—on the town's soccer field as soon as he'd arrived. And some real respect when he'd started to learn Kriol, their local lingua franca, right away.

Since then, they'd usually come running whenever they saw him, asking endless questions about America or showing him the latest lizard, frog, or insect they'd caught.

But now, as he walked into the square, they looked away, refusing to meet his eye. If anything, they seemed a little afraid.

This was interesting. Trey walked up to them, focusing on Moussa, the boy he knew was their leader.

Tall, thin, the most athletic of the group, Moussa held his ground as Trey approached. The other boys scattered, though all stayed within earshot. There was a hum of tension around them that Trey hadn't seen before.

"What was that shouting about?" he asked Moussa.

The boy said nothing, but Trey had expected no different. The unspoken answer, from several of the others, was just as clear as words would have been. They all looked at the medical clinic on the opposite side of the square.

The Diouf Health Center, a compact building of red stone erected within the past decade. A gift from the French government, complete with state-of-the-art scanning and surgical technology, as penance for two centuries of colonization and slavery.

Moussa followed Trey's gaze. "You cannot go in there," he said.

That was never the right thing to tell Trey.

THERE WAS A trail of blood, drying black in the warming sun, leading across the square toward the clinic.

As he approached, Trey saw a young man carrying a Kalashnikov rifle step out the front door. Dressed in a ragged camo uniform, complete with the square cap Senegalese soldiers all wore, he looked confused, shaken. Trey wondered if he'd been told to guard the entrance but wasn't sure exactly how. Was he supposed to shoot anyone who came in for Band-Aids or aspirin?

The blood trail led up three stone steps, between the soldier's feet, and under the closed door. Trey walked up the steps and said to the soldier, "Pardon me."

"It is closed," the soldier said. He was eighteen, maybe, with a child's smooth cheeks and no authority but what his gun gave him.

"Look," Trey said, pointing at the sign hanging beside the red wooden door. It read, *Toujours Ouvert.* Always Open.

The man stared at the sign without apparent comprehension. It was quite possible he only knew how to read Diol or one of the other local dialects, if he could read at all. When his gaze returned to Trey's face, Trey said, "Seydou Honso wants to see me."

The guard frowned. While he was pondering his response, Trey walked around him, opened the door, and stepped through into the waiting room.

The room was empty and dark inside. Someone had turned off the bright fluorescent lights that usually made everyone, pink skinned or brown, look jaundiced. The only light came from the blue-green glow of a computer monitor.

Trey took in a breath. The clinic was suffused with the smell of blood. And something else, too, a bitter, acidic odor.

A smell Trey had encountered once before.

The door leading into the examination room hung open, and through it Trey could see a single light burning. Four figures stood there, little more than backlit shadows clustered around the steel examination table.

There was something on the table. The light was focused on it, so Trey could see what it was.

As he made to step closer, two of the figures moved toward him. They came through the door, which they closed behind them.

Even in the shadowy light, Trey knew who they were. Seydou Honso, the physician who ran the clinic—and, according to legend, all of Mpack—and his daughter, Mariama.

Seydou was about sixty-five, with a face so lined and furrowed that it was easy to miss how clear his eyes were, how sharp his gaze. The people at the International Conservation Trust had urged Trey to stay on his good side or risk finding that no one in town, in the Casamance, would help him.

They'd also warned Trey to avoid Mariama Honso like the plague. Slightly built, with a square, determined face and the same piercing gaze as her father, she was no more than thirty. She had already made a name for herself in Senegal. Several names: Activist. Troublemaker. Agitator. She'd spent more than one stint in jail for speaking out against the government's treatment of the people of the Casamance.

Heeding ICT's warning as much as needed most, Trey had invited Mariama out for a drink the day he'd arrived. They'd gotten to know each other a little, and so far the world hadn't ended.

Now the two of them were looking at Trey, as if trying to figure out what he knew, what he'd guessed. How smart he was.

"You must leave," Seydou Honso said in French. "Now."

Trey didn't move. "What is that smell?" he said.

The old man's hands twitched at his sides. His daughter's chin lifted.

"I've smelled it before, you know," Trey said.

Neither spoke.

"Over a stretch of dying rain forest five miles south of the Massou-Djibo Road."

Trey never forgot the reaction this last statement provoked. Seydou Honso's face clenched, his eyes nearly disappearing behind the bunched ridges of his wrinkles. But Mariama's seemed to light up, her eyes gleaming even in the dimness.

"Papa," she said, "we have to—"

"No." The word rang out in the silent room. An instant later, Trey heard the front door open. Footsteps. The end of a rifle poking into his back.

Trey's arm rose to knock the gun away. Then, just barely, he restrained himself and allowed the soldier to push him toward the door.

Mariama's voice came from behind him. "Papa, listen—"

"No," said Seydou Honso again.

SOMETHING TREY HAD learned during his long solitary years in the world's last wild places: Pay attention to anything that doesn't fit. It's usually what's most important.

So as he crossed the square, the young soldier standing on the steps behind him, gun at the ready, he thought about what he'd glimpsed in the examination room.

The four figures: Seydou and Mariama Honso and two soldiers, both as young as the one who'd been guarding the door. The soldiers' faces, Trey had seen, had been filled with fear, even horror as they gazed down at what lay on the steel table.

Trey could understand why. They were looking at another soldier in uniform, lying on his back. Even at a distance, Trey had seen he was dead. His unmarked face had been frozen in its last expression of shock and horror, his eyes wide, his mouth pulled back to expose clenched teeth.

His face might have been untouched, but his midsection—everything from his waist to the middle of his rib cage—was an unrecognizable mass of shredded fabric and meat, glistening with black blood and bits of white bone.

As the Honsos came through the door and blocked his view, Trey had noticed one more thing: The fabric, and some of the man's flesh, was scorched. He'd been shot at closer than point-blank range. Someone had jammed a gun, something powerful like a Kalashnikov, into his belly and fired a burst from it.

Maybe the dead soldier had done it himself.

MOUSSA WAS CROUCHED in the center of the square, examining the splatter pattern of dried blood. Already tiny black ants and a beetle the color of an emerald had come to feast on it.

The boy stood when he saw Trey. "Phone," he said.

Trey thought about this. Mpack had no cell-phone service. The only public telephone was located in a concrete shack at the far end of the square, a building people called "the office," because it contained a desk, a chair, and that phone.

Who was calling? It was unlikely to be Malcolm Granger, who was fully occupied repairing the Piper. Anyway, Malcolm hated telephones as much as Trey did. If he needed to say something, he just showed up and said it.

Someone from New York, the closest thing Trey had to a home base? Equally unlikely. He had no family there, and not many friends, few of whom had any idea where in the world he was at any given time.

His brother, Christopher? No. Since Christopher had settled in Queensland, Australia, two decades earlier, he and Trey had spoken only once or twice a year. After their parents died, there hadn't seemed much reason to stay in touch.

Trey sighed, thanked Moussa, and walked toward the office, knowing before he picked up the receiver whose voice he'd hear and what she'd have to say.

He'd heard it all before.

* * *

"WE'RE PULLING YOU out," Cristina Kendall, his boss at ICT, said.

What Trey had expected. "No," he said. "I'm not done here."

"This is not a request." Cristina was calling from Dakar, the capital city, but she sounded like she was right there in the room lecturing him. "We got the order today," she went on. "You're not welcome in the Casamance, in Senegal, effective immediately."

Trey was silent.

Her sigh came clearly over the line. "So," she said, "who'd you piss off this time?"

He didn't reply. Some strange, clanging music rang down the line.

When Cristina spoke again, her tone had hardened. "Trey, it's—what, about a seven-hour drive from Mpack to Dakar?"

After a moment, he said, "Yeah."

"Well, throw your stuff in your car and start driving. I've told our staff to expect you by evening."

Trey was quiet.

"You hearing me?"

He said, "Yeah."

"Listen," she said, her voice now little more than a venomous whisper. "You're dancing on very thin ice this time, Trey. One of these days you're going to fall through, and no one's going to care enough to pull you out. Got that?"

Trey hung up the phone.

branches that
through pa
All th
appro
he

THREE

CRISTINA KENDALL HAD ordered Trey to return immediately to Dakar. Instead he drove his Land Rover three hours in the wrong direction.

First south from Mpack, then west back along the rutted red-dirt Massou-Djibo Road. He passed the field where he and Malcolm had landed—the plane had been hauled off to Ziguinchor—and seen that it was now populated with cows that, had they been there last time, might have defeated even Malcolm's ingenuity.

On past this landmark another twenty miles before finally reaching the junction of another dirt road. Nearly hidden behind the underbrush that grew at the forest edge, this one took him south again, into the rain forest itself.

Or maybe "road" was too generous a term. It was more like a wide path, a half-imagined thread winding this way and that between the forest's buttressed trees. Trey fought the wheel over ruts and exposed roots, past vines and shrieked as they scraped the car's body, ches of mud that grasped at the tires.

while, as he left the forest's edge behind and ached its heart, the trees around him gained in ght and breadth. The canopy rose until it formed a roof 150 feet above him, leaving the forest floor as dark as if night had fallen. Only his headlights and an occasional stray beam of sunshine illuminated his way.

The road petered out for good at the base of a giant kapok tree. Trey turned the ignition key and sat there for a moment, listening to the engine making snapping sounds as it cooled. Then he took a breath, opened the car door, got out, and started walking.

HE DIDN'T WORRY about getting lost. Trey had been born with an unerring sense of direction, as if there were some metal inside of him that could always sense the magnetic pole. He knew from the moment he set forth where his destination was, and how long it would take him to reach it.

Just as he was always aware of the world around him. Categorizing. Cataloging. It wasn't even a conscious effort. He registered the whooshing sound of a hornbill's wings as it flapped through the canopy, the distant peeping of the rain frogs, the low grunts of a troop of mona monkeys and the sound they made leaping from limb to limb, like surf crashing against a stony shore.

He saw a giant katydid stride on spindly legs across a leaf, a woodpecker creeping up a massive trunk, a Maxwell's duiker—a small forest antelope—crouching in a muddy depression, hoping he wouldn't spot it.

There was very little Trey missed.

He paused for a moment to squat beside a colony of slave-making ants in the midst of a raid. The attacking horde of big, red ants was routing the nest of smaller black ones. Corpses were strewn across the ground, and the victors were carrying off the eggs and larvae they would hatch out and enslave.

He wondered whether human slaves passing by here—Senegal had been full of them—had ever watched a slave-maker raid and thought: All life on earth is the same.

When Trey stood, the sudden movement brought forth a low, angry snarl from behind a nearby tree. A leopard was watching.

Trey was calm. Aware of his heart beating, the blood moving through his veins, the prickle of moisture against his skin. Aware he was alive.

But not the master here. Not the boss.

He had no primacy in the rain forest. He was just a package of meat and bone, a creature with remarkably few defenses. Soft and fleshy, with no hard shell. No sharp claws or teeth. No ability to run fast or climb effortlessly or leap from branch to branch.

How easy it was to kill a human, if you got one away from the big cities, the stone and steel structures the species built as defenses, as hiding places. As easy as killing a worker termite if you pulled it away from its hardened-mud mound.

The leopard snarled again, from farther off. Today, at least, it would let him live.

Trey smiled. Right then, right at that moment, there was nowhere else on earth he would rather be.

* * *

WHEN HE WAS five years old, Trey's family went on a trip out west. They visited four states and a half dozen national parks, but Yellowstone was the place he recalled most clearly, with its bubbling mud pits like something from Mars, its big geysers, its bison and elk and moose. One day there was a storm so violent that a hailstone came down from the sky and cracked the windshield of their car.

It was in Yellowstone that Trey first felt that pull, the desire to just walk away from the car, the road, his mom and dad and brother, to get *out* and just . . . see what was there.

They were picnicking in some rest area, surrounded by tall conical evergreens, a clear brook running down a nearby hill. Christopher, who was eight, was fascinated by the chipmunks that raced around the picnic area, standing up on their hind legs, chattering, begging for food.

But Trey found them boring. Why come all the way out here to look at *chipmunks*? They had chipmunks back home in New York. So these ones were bigger, with different patterns of spots. Chipmunks were chipmunks.

He was far more interested in the big gray-and-white bird that picked apart a pinecone with a thick, sharp beak. The salamander, longer than his foot, he found under a rock by the side of the brook. The grasshoppers that went whirring away from him like tiny toy helicopters.

And the enormous creature that moved cautiously among the trees, keeping out of sight of the picnickers.

Trey, who already had sharper eyes than anyone else he knew, was the only one to see it.

A bear. They'd spotted a few during this visit to Yellowstone, though Dad said that he'd seen many more—forty-eight, in fact—during a trip he'd taken here when *he* was a kid. Black bears, they were called (though one had been brownish red), with cute rounded ears and eyes like black buttons.

"Don't be fooled," Mom had said, as they watched one scratch its back against a tree. "They can be dangerous."

Trey had found that hard to believe.

Sitting as still as possible on the edge of the picnic area, Trey watched the bear move through the woods. He could tell that this one was different from the others they'd seen. Its gray-brown fur, tipped in silver, was thicker, longer. Its eyes, as it focused on Trey, were dark and deep. When it moved, the muscles rippled along its legs and its thick, humped shoulders.

Trey stood to get a better view.

Watching him, the bear made a low grunting noise that he could feel in his chest. He expected someone else to notice, to shout, to come running, but no one did. They were all too busy laughing and tossing peanuts to the begging chipmunks.

The bear backed away deeper into the shadows of the pine trees. Without hesitation, Trey followed.

Missing the caution gene. That was how his mother already described him.

The bear grunted again as Trey came up to it. He could feel the heat radiating from its body, smell its earthy odor when it blew its breath out through strangely delicate lips.

Then it reared up on its hind legs and peered down at him. To Trey, it seemed as tall as the pine trees, as massive as a hillside. It was unbelievably big and powerful, so Trey did what he would have done with anything whose existence he doubted, despite the evidence of his own eyes.

He reached out and touched it.

The bear's fur was coarse, thick, oily but still as scratchy as his dad's cheek when he didn't shave for a few days. It felt hot to his touch, though Trey never knew whether the heat was the bear's or his own.

But mostly what he sensed was the power radiating outward from beneath the fur. The incredibly strong muscles, and beneath them, the engine, the core of the beast beneath his palm. An unharnessed energy that he'd never sensed in his family, in any person, and for the first time he realized that the world was not a pyramid, with humans sitting on top.

The bear flinched and let out a strange, whining cry, but did not move.

Trey closed his eyes. The pure connection between the two of them did not require vision.

But apparently the bear's cry had been loud enough to attract the attention of others. After that, Trey's memories were blurred. He remembered screams, shouts, being knocked down—by human hands—his head banging against the ground. Being carried by someone running, then thrown into the backseat of the car, the feel of vinyl against his cheek.

His mom saying, "Oh, my God, oh, my Christ," over and over.

Both Mom and Dad touching him, lifting his shirt, holding his hand, checking his legs, again and again, as if trying to discover wounds they'd somehow missed the first twenty times they'd inspected him.

Or maybe they were just trying to make sure he was real, just as he'd done with the bear.

The grizzly. That was what Christopher told him it was called. A grizzly.

IT WASN'T UNTIL years later, when he found some newspaper clippings hidden in the bottom of his father's desk drawer, that Trey learned the fate of the giant bear.

Turned out it already had a criminal record, that bear, having previously been convicted of wandering too close to campgrounds and picnic areas. It had never been aggressive, had done nothing more than watch, but you never could tell with grizzlies, so twice it was anesthetized and taken to more remote parts of the park to be released.

Its encounter with Trey was the third strike. The National Park Service brought in a marksman with a high-powered rifle, and the curious bear was shot no more than a mile from the picnic ground.

Reading about the bear's death, alone in his quiet house, Trey felt his eyes prickle. And at that moment, at age eleven, he made himself a promise.

Not to avoid the presence of the wild creatures on earth, but to seek them out.

And to keep them safe by going alone.

TREY WALKED THROUGH the dim forest for nearly two hours. Then, when and where he'd known he would, he saw it:

a brightening in the forest ahead, as subtle as the first wash of light in the eastern sky an hour before dawn.

But nothing as natural as that.

Trey stopped for a moment, looked, listened, and went on.

FOUR

HE DREW CLOSE to the dying forest. The green, stained-glass light that glowed through the unbroken canopy behind him gave way to something brighter, harsher. The wind changed direction for a moment, blowing into his face, and with it came the now-familiar bitter odor.

Only then did Trey realize that the forest around him was silent. Even healthy rain forests can be surprisingly quiet, but this was different. He heard no birdsong, no frogs calling, not the midday shrill of cicadas or whisper of crickets. It wasn't the quiet of a vast natural engine concealing its secrets, but a stillness more like death.

Perhaps a hundred yards ahead he could see a tangle of underbrush. Inside a healthy forest, very few plants grow in the understory; not enough sunlight reaches the ground. Only where a great tree falls, creating a light gap, do vines and thorn bushes and saplings sprout.

Only where a great tree falls, or all the trees are stricken.

What the hell was going on here?

HE STOOD IN the angled afternoon sunlight beside peeling trunks, beneath bare, twisted branches. Every step he took, he was forced to kick through piles of leaves, sodden and rotting.

Something was out of whack, and Trey couldn't figure out what. This pissed him off.

He knew that people tended to think of natural landscapes as immutable, never-changing, but of course it wasn't true. Through time—eye blinks, really—glaciers had carved pathways across the world, forests had sprouted and withered, oceans had turned to desert. Nothing stayed the same forever.

And the balance was fragile, especially in the rain forest. Clearing for farmland or industry, the arrival of an invasive pest from elsewhere, humans hunting out keystone species—any one, or a hundred others, could doom an entire ecosystem.

So what was messing with this one?

Only one plant seemed to be thriving in the gap created by the blight: a kind of sprawling, woody vine that Trey had never seen before. Its leaves were a dark glossy green, and here and there he could see its tiny, fleshy fruit, red like a cranberry but smaller and more oval.

The vines spread from tree to tree, sometimes climbing five or ten feet up a trunk before reaching out toward the next. Examining the tree nearest him, Trey saw that the vine didn't appear to be the cause of its blight, at least not in any way he could see.

It gave off a spicy odor that reminded him of ginger.

A hundred feet ahead, directly in his path, lay a thick wall of half-dead brambles, yellow-green leaves and spiky branches interwoven like a cage. Again, this was something Trey had never seen in the healthy forests he'd explored.

Another unfamiliar plant taking advantage of light gaps in this forest. Though, unlike the glossy vine, the brambles didn't seem immune from whatever was killing the trees.

Something jumped near Trey, right at the periphery of his vision. His pulse quickened, but he did not flinch. With careful, slow movements, he turned his head. A pair of bright black eyes regarded him from the depths of a tangle of the vines. A squirrel, it was, a small forest squirrel, its fur mainly dark gray but with a rufous patch on its back.

It stared at him, curious but seemingly unafraid, for a good ten seconds before it turned, revealing a thick, bushy tail, and disappeared into the tangle. Unseen, a second one greeted it with a chuckling call.

Then the forest was silent again. Even the wind had died.

Silent . . . until Trey took two more steps forward. Then he heard it, a sound that made the back of his neck prickle.

Not a rustle like the one the squirrel had made. Not birdsong, or the crash of some large animal navigating the thicket of brambles ahead.

No: a low humming, almost beyond the reach of even

his exceptional hearing. He felt it, a vibration in his bones, in the tips of his fingers and deep in his skull, more than heard it.

Moving silently, he came up to the brambles. The thorny branches wrapped around each other and the trunks of the nearby trees. Though their leaves were yellowish, scraggly, sickly, they were thick enough to block the view.

Ahead, the humming sound rose in pitch and intensity, then quickly died away.

Trey glanced around for some way to climb over the wall of brush, but saw none. The only way through was . . . through.

He began to edge his way into the mass of thorns. One step at a time, clearing the tendrils away, letting them go when they were behind him. Feeling them tugging at him, restraining him, as if in warning.

The smell was much stronger here.

After a half hour, scratched and bleeding, he was almost through. Hidden by the ten-foot-tall stump of a dead tree, he stopped moving and, with great care, pulled away one last half-dead shoot and peered in.

Circled by the wall of thorn bushes was a clearing measuring about twenty-five feet in diameter. The sandy ground within the clearing, as clean and leafless as if someone had just raked it, was molded into strange little hills and hummocks. Atop each mound was a hole, perhaps two inches around.

For ten seconds, fifteen, Trey had no idea what he was looking at. Then something ejected a spurt of sand from the hole nearest to where he stood, followed by a tiny pebble and a piece of twisted root.

And he did know. Partly.

It was the home of a colony of some kind. But of what? The holes were far too big for any ants he knew of, any bees, any wasps. Maybe some minuscule mammal?

Too many questions.

He crouched down beside the stump to wait. Ten minutes later, the answers started coming.

IT BEGAN WITH a rustling on the opposite side of the clearing. At first little more than a slight, dry sound, like fabric rubbed between a thumb and forefinger. Then it grew louder, and a patch of brambles began to shake. Something big was coming through them, something that let loose with a moaning sound as it approached.

For a moment it paused, as if resting. Then, with a last squeal, it burst through the brambles and staggered across the ground into the middle of the clearing.

A monkey. A red colobus, and a big one.

There was something wrong with it. As Trey watched, it stumbled and fell, lying spread-eagled on the ground for a moment. Then it struggled back to its feet, its legs shaking, and turned slowly toward him. When it did, he could see that the skin over its stomach was hugely swollen, as if it were carrying a large tumor beneath its fur.

He drew a little farther behind the tree stump, then held his breath to stay as still as possible. He didn't know what to expect. Would it panic if it knew he was there?

When it turned its face toward him, he saw that its eyes were a silvery white. Was it blind? He couldn't tell.

The monkey took three wavering steps across the clearing before its foot caught on one of the mounds and it fell. This time it just lay there, its patchy fur rising and falling in time to its breath.

Again something moved at the edge of Trey's vision. He shifted his gaze to the nearest mound, the one whose hole he'd seen being cleaned out a few minutes before.

As he watched, a triangular head topped with bulbous, iridescent green eyes emerged. A freakishly thin, black, arched body topped by a pair of crimson wings followed, the wings flickering so quickly they seemed to leave a bloody smear in the air.

It was a wasp. An enormous wasp, maybe three inches long. Trey had never seen one like it before, of any size.

He felt something wriggle in his stomach. There was something about the way it tilted its head to regard the fallen monkey. Something alert, intelligent, calculating.

The wasp perched for a moment atop its mound, unmoving. Then it flew up on humming wings and swooped low over the colobus.

The monkey twitched. Perhaps it could see through its silvery eyes, or perhaps it sensed or heard the vibrations of the wasp's speed-blurred wings. It seemed, in an abject, helpless way, terrified.

The wasp returned to its perch, and only then did Trey notice that it was no longer alone. Others had emerged from their tunnels while he was watching the first. Six more, each seemingly identical, bloodred wings flickering like flags, green eyes turned toward the monkey.

The first one traced a few steps, changed the rhythm of its wing beats, and lifted three inches into the air before settling back onto its mound. When it was still, a second one took flight, streaking upward so quickly that Trey felt his stomach twist.

A moment later the wasp reappeared, plummeting toward the colobus, landing with an impact that came to Trey's ears as a dull, dead thud.

The monkey's eyes opened wide, and its mouth gaped as well. Its arms and legs flailed, as if it were trying to run, or fight back.

Moving on spiderlike legs, the wasp ran back and forth over the monkey's back. Then, without warning, it lifted the skinny black tube of its abdomen. Its stinger slid out, as white and sharp as a needle made of ivory, and plunged deep into the flesh of the colobus's neck.

The monkey cried out. Its eyes wide, its mouth hanging open, it grew still, and Trey wondered if the sting had killed it.

But then it stirred, the wasp still perched on its neck. Stretched its legs, drew in a deep breath, and slowly got back to its feet. It seemed, if anything, less shaky. Stronger than it had been. When it turned, Trey could see that red-tinged drool was dripping from its open mouth.

The wasp rose into the air, flew back to its mound, landed, and took a few seconds to clean its front legs with its mandibles.

Then it turned its head to look at Trey.

At that moment he realized that it had known he was there all along. All the wasps had. They'd just had more important business to conclude before dealing with him.

Trey stood as still as possible, but he knew it was hopeless. Wasps' eyesight was much keener than humans', and, unlike some lizards and other animals, they didn't rely on their prey moving to be able to see it.

The wasp leaped in the air and flew arrow-straight at his face. At the same moment, the colobus snarled and, moving with startling speed, rushed across the clearing toward him.

Even though Trey's brain was telling him he'd get trapped in the brambles if he didn't plan his escape carefully, his body wasn't listening. He recoiled and felt the thorns scratch the skin of his neck and arms and grab hold of his clothes. In an instant, he was trapped.

The wasp came on. Reared up. Hovered three inches from his face. Behind it, the monkey crouched to leap. Then it paused, silvery gaze on him, froth bubbling around its mouth, as if waiting.

Waiting for orders.

The wasp's green eyes stared into Trey's. Its thin abdomen, the sheath for that needlelike stinger, pulsed.

Any second, Trey expected to see the stinger slide out, expected the hovering wasp to swoop forward the last three inches, expected to feel the needle puncture him, expected . . . what?

Agony.

For five seconds at least, however, the wasp made no move toward him. Instead it stayed virtually still, swinging just a little this way and that in the air, its triangular head swiveling so that its multifaceted eyes never left his face.

Almost, Trey thought, as if it were figuring something out.

Making up its mind.

Then it did. Swinging upward, it paused for a moment at its apogee, then swooped down like a dart.

Trey closed his eyes.

And heard a crashing sound in the brush behind him. He opened his eyes to see the wasp draw back. It swung away, made a big loop around the clearing, and vanished down its tunnel. The others, too, had disappeared. The colobus was clambering through the tangles at the farside of the clearing.

The crashing got louder. Now Trey could recognize it: the sound of a blade meeting wood. A moment later, he felt the brambles tear away from his hair and clothes.

A hand grabbed his arm and pulled. Half stumbling, he fought his way out through the brush, then stood there, his legs shaking.

A slightly built woman in black pants and a ragged, long-sleeved white shirt stood before him, machete hanging by her side. Its blade was stained with thick sap that pooled and dripped from its sharp edge.

She was looking away, toward the clearing, but when she turned her head Trey knew who it was. Mariama Honso, her eyes wide, her expression filled with alarm mixed with a kind of exultation.

Before he could say anything, she stepped forward and hugged him. Enveloped him in her arms for a moment before letting go.

It wasn't a hug of relief, he knew, or affection, or any emotion he recognized. He didn't have any idea why she'd done it.

He said, "What—"

But Mariama was listening to something else. Trey heard it, too: the humming of wings.

Her gaze found his.

"You fool," she said. *"Flee."*

FIVE

THE PLAN HAD seemed simple when Mariama hatched it. She'd go after Gilliard, that brave, foolhardy, strange American visitor. Arriving in time, she'd prevent him from getting himself killed, then bring him back. On the way, they'd stop someplace quiet, private.

Mariama had thought the Etoile Bar in Ziguinchor would serve. There her father, Seydou, would join them. Together, they would explain to Gilliard what it was he'd seen, and what it meant.

What it meant for the world.

Soon. If not this month, then next, or the one after. They were sure of this, Mariama and Seydou. It had already begun.

And then, once he believed, they would tell him what he needed to do.

And pray that he understood.

* * *

MARIAMA WAS YOUNG, but already she knew many ways that a seemingly foolproof plan could go wrong.

This one began to go wrong with the phone call. The call Trey had received after visiting the health clinic and seeing the dead soldier. Mariama and her father, still at work in the clinic, didn't learn of the phone call for more than two hours. By then Trey was gone, heading on his suicidal mission to the forest.

Already almost beyond her reach, and very likely doomed.

Still, she had to try.

Too much depended on his staying alive.

THEN HER CAR, her beloved 1983 Peugeot 305, ran over a sharp stone on the Massou-Djibo Road and had a flat tire. Thirty miles from her destination. Listening to the flapping of the slack rubber against the washboard dirt as she guided the car to the edge of the empty road, she almost despaired.

In her mind, she saw Trey moving in his strange, cat-like way through the forest. She'd followed him once, and thought he was quicker and quieter than anyone she'd ever seen, besides herself.

She'd even thought he might have spotted her, and *no one* ever saw Mariama if she didn't want them to.

She imagined him now, following the hints, the clues he'd picked up these past few days. The dying forest. The dead man on the clinic table. The smell.

Using his unusual skills to race to his death.

And she wouldn't reach him in time. It was hopeless. She knew that. She hoped his pain wouldn't be too overwhelming before the end came.

But Mariama Honso had never given up on anything, hopeless or not. She was as hardheaded as a rhino.

All life was hopeless, but you kept living anyway.

She changed the tire, got the car back on the road, and drove.

SHE FOUND GILLIARD'S Land Rover where she'd thought she would: where some long-vanished logger had given up his foolish attempt to build a drivable track to the giant, immensely valuable hardwood trees that grew deep in the forest. The end of the road.

Mariama climbed out of her car, bringing only her recently sharpened machete with her. As she went past the Land Rover, she placed her palm against its hood. It was cool to her touch.

More evidence that she was too late.

She went on.

TREY HAD LEFT few signs that he'd passed this way, but still Mariama was able to follow. A broken branch, flower petals scattered where he'd brushed against them, half a footprint in a patch of mud. She knew where he was going, into the part of the forest that no outsider should ever enter.

And then, at the very heart of the forbidden place, she saw him. Standing there on the edge of one of the colonies, trapped in the thorns of the volor plant. But alive. Still alive. She was amazed.

As she drew closer, she could read his expression. A mix of fear . . . and fascination.

That was unusual. Most people, facing what he was, showed only pure, unadulterated terror.

She felt like shouting at him, but that was the worst thing she could do. He would jump, struggle, become so enmeshed in the volor that it would take hours to extricate him.

Worse, *they* would be startled by her voice as well. And when they were startled, they attacked. They bit and stung. Paralyzed or killed.

They. The thieves.

So, even as her brain screamed at her to hurry, to run, to yell, she moved slowly, carefully. Coming up behind Gilliard, she cut through the brush with her sharp blade. Clearing a path for him, if he would only take it, if he would only notice.

Beyond him, the thieves retreated. They knew her. They knew Mariama.

But this still might not be enough.

Finally he was free. Waking as if from a dream, he turned to look at her. His eyes were wide. She could see that he understood what had just happened, how close he'd come.

He took a couple of steps away from the colony. Mariama went up on her toes and wrapped her arms around him, just for a moment. He stiffened, pulled away from her, but she held on a little longer before letting go.

He had no idea why. Of course he didn't.

It was one of the things she needed to tell him.

Only not now.

"You fool," she said, to make sure he was listening, but also because it was what she thought of him. *"Flee."*

When he was gone, she turned to face the thieves, hanging in the air, watching her through those green eyes that seemed to understand everything.

But then again, she did, too.

EVEN THEN, EVEN after Mariama had saved him, her luck was bad. She hadn't thought to tell him to wait for her where they'd left the cars—and he hadn't. She shouldn't have been surprised. She'd already seen that this odd American spent as little time with other adult human beings as he possibly could.

Then a storm struck as she was driving back. The Peugeot had to fight through grasping mud, where Gilliard's fancy Land Rover had undoubtedly plowed right through. It took her twice as long to get home as it had taken to reach the forest.

Still, Mariama wasn't worried. There was plenty of time for Trey to hear what she and her father had to tell him.

Only there wasn't. By the time she made it to Mpack, her white car now a spattered reddish brown from the drying mud, he was gone. Gone forever.

The village children were waiting to fill her in. When Gilliard had arrived, he'd been met by a group of soldiers who had flown down from Dakar. Soldiers and a woman, a skinny American woman who'd shown up burning with anger.

Standing where everyone could see them, she'd yelled at Gilliard. Her voice was as high-pitched as a fish eagle's (she also resembled one, the children said), and she talked so fast that even those who understood some English couldn't follow her.

When she'd taken a breath, Trey had turned and walked away from her. He'd gone into his hut. Five minutes later, he'd emerged, carrying his pack and some other things, and climbed into the car with some soldiers and the angry woman.

"Do you think he'll come back?" the children asked. They liked Gilliard. He was strange and generous, two things they appreciated in outsiders.

"No, I'm afraid not," Mariama said. "I think he's gone for good."

As she spoke the words, she felt a black space open in her chest, just around her heart.

"HAVE THEY PUT him in jail?" she asked her father that night. They were in the empty clinic. It was clean, scrubbed down, disinfected. You could only detect the thieves' odor if you sat still and breathed deeply.

Seydou Honso shook his head. There might even have been a glint of amusement in his eyes.

"No," he said. "The government has no interest in keeping him. They just want him out. The soldiers were the lady's idea."

"That was Kendall? The one who was always calling?"

He nodded. "I think she believed the only way to get him to listen was to bring men with guns."

Mariama said, "That was probably true."

They sat in silence for a while. Now there was no expression on Seydou Honso's face except for a kind of grim certainty.

"I fear we have missed our chance," he said.

Mariama had known he would feel this way. She said, "No."

"But who else will listen? Who else will understand what is taking place?"

"There are others," she said. "But Gilliard is the one to tell them."

She thought about his expression when she found him in the forest. Yes, he would understand.

"But how?" Her father turned his palms up. "He's gone, and he won't be welcomed back. Ever."

"I know," Mariama said.

"And calling him on the telephone won't work, no more than it did for that Kendall lady."

"No."

"Then what?"

"I will go see him," she said.

Seydou's eyes widened. "But how? You have no passport."

This was a fact. Mariama's outspokenness had led to her losing her right to travel anywhere outside Senegal. She even required permission to leave the Casamance region.

Legally, that was.

"You know how," she told her father.

He stared at her. Then he said, "You cannot."

"I can. I must." She reached out and put a hand on his strong arm. "Papa, I have no choice."

He argued with her. Finally, almost breathless, he said, "You'll die."

She smiled. "Perhaps I won't," she said. Then, "Or perhaps I will. You know I have never feared death."

Nor had he, not for himself. She knew that. Every day he risked malaria, dengue, river blindness, and a hundred diseases that had no name, in order to treat the clinic's patients.

He had no fear for his own life. For hers, though, yes. Of course.

Mariama said again, "I have no choice."

In the end, he knew it was so. "But not right away," he said. "There are people I can talk to, people who will help you."

She nodded. Though she didn't speak, she knew he understood her gratitude.

"If I'm lucky," she said, "how long will it take to reach him?"

"Weeks." He grimaced. "If you're very lucky."

"Will they get there first?"

He flicked a hand eastward, toward the vast rain forests of Central Africa and the savannas and deserts beyond them. Then west toward the Atlantic Ocean and the New World.

All the places the thieves had already reached, or soon would.

"First, second," he said. "Does it matter?"

Mariama said, "I have to believe it does."

Seydou Honso smiled at his daughter, his expression full of love and grief.

"I know you do," he said.

SIX

Ujiji, Tanzania

THE FIRST THING Sheila Connelly's gaze always sought out, every time she rode the Lake Tanganyika ferry from Kalemie, Congo, to Ujiji Port, was the mango avenue beyond the marketplace.

The mango trees had been standing for two centuries or more. By now they were bent and twisted, their branches hung with weaver birds' nests, their trunks riddled with holes where the ravages of time and weather had rotted them out. But still surviving, still flowering each year, their boughs still heavy with fruit in the right season.

Ujiji's mango avenue had long provided shade for the caravans of goods that crossed the lake from the vast, untracked forests of Central Africa and headed east. Sculptures and tapestries and weapons of many kinds, and foodstuffs, and slaves.

Countless thousands of slaves. Men and women captured in the forests of the Congo, carried across the lake in the bilges of ferries like the one Sheila was riding now, then driven on a death march across the plains and deserts of East Africa to their ultimate destination: Arabia.

Sheila wondered if the captives had known, as they stumbled, bound and whipped, past the fruiting trees, that these mangoes would be the last reminders of their tropical home they would ever see. Did any of them ever reach up and pluck a ripe, sun-warmed fruit as they passed, or had they been too terrified that they'd be punished if they did?

The hulking steel ferry, the *Uhuru*, let loose with a blast from its horn and, spewing dirty white water, approached the wharf. Sheila dragged her eyes and thoughts back to the present and scanned the harbor area. There were plenty of people there waiting for the ferry, but her mother didn't appear to be one of them.

This was typical. Undoubtedly Megan Connelly was somewhere in the crowded marketplace, haggling over something she'd decided she had to own, picking up some last-minute supplies for Sheila's visit, or merely shooting the breeze with vendors she'd known for years.

Sheila couldn't blame her. The markets were still the lifeblood of a port city, of a society. Even now, you never knew what you might find: bins full of tiny bananas, totems wrought of rosewood by artists from some barely known rain forest tribe, wooden spears with stone points.

And, instead of slaves, disease. Mystery pathogens. Unnamed viruses and bacteria brought on the ferry from their birthplaces in the heart of Africa.

Sheila knew more about the diseases than anything else at the Ujiji Market. She was a physician, out of her residency just five years, who'd signed on to work in the overflowing refugee camps of the war-torn countries of Central Africa. She'd thought it important to repay some of the debts owed by the world's wealthy societies to those who'd been dealt a worse hand.

But standing by the rail as the ferry docked, Sheila wondered if this part of her life was reaching its end. She was wearing out, losing interest.

She knew the signs of burnout. She'd seen enough of it.

MEGAN CONNELLY SEEMED tired, too. Worn.

"What's wrong?" Sheila said as they hugged. "You look awful."

That was Sheila. She always said what was on her mind and had no patience with those who didn't. This had tended to make her life noisy and tumultuous.

Pulling away a little, Megan smiled up at her. "There's this thing that happens, love," she said. "Experts call it 'getting old.'"

She had a point. How old was she now? Sixty-one? -two? Old enough that the years were beginning to take a toll, laying down lines across her forehead and around her mouth, turning her fair skin papery, bringing out spots on her hands. Megan had been too active throughout her life to ever develop severe osteoporosis, but she seemed a little more stooped than she had six months earlier, the last time Sheila had seen her.

Still. There was more. A gray undertone to her skin. Something odd about the whites of her eyes.

"I'll examine you later," Sheila told her.

Megan laughed. "Oh, you flatterer," she said. "You'll have me in my grave before lunch."

Then she returned to her daughter's inspection. "I like your hair," she said. "What there is of it."

Since they'd last seen each other, six months earlier, Sheila had gotten tired of her long coppery ponytail. So she'd cut most of it off, giving herself something approaching a pixie cut.

"How about this?" she asked, half turning to reveal the new tattoo on the back of her left shoulder, peeking out from under her sleeveless white shirt. A regal sunbird with wings spread, all glittering green and yellow and red.

Megan's eyes widened. "How many is that?"

"Just three."

"I remember," her mother said, setting off toward the market, "when Ariel stickers were enough for you."

"Long time ago," Sheila said.

"Seems like yesterday to me."

THEY STOPPED AT the stand run by the same old woman who'd been selling fried corn cakes with cane sugar sprinkled on top for as long as Sheila had been coming to the market. Twenty years it was now, ever since her mom and dad moved here on a three-year mission with the Presbyterian church, fell in love with the place, the people, the African light, and decided to stay.

Twenty years out of Sheila's twenty-nine. She could hardly imagine what it felt like not to live in Africa, which was another reason why, after graduating from medical school, she'd come back.

She'd also wanted to be close to her parents, though not too close. On the same continent, at least.

"A *shilingi* for your thoughts," her mother said.

Sheila smiled.

"I'm still hungry," she said.

The market stalls sold corn cakes, wooden carvings, textiles, weapons . . . and bushmeat.

The bodies of wild animals taken from the vanishing forests to the west and denuded savannas to the east. Hunted with bows and arrows and wire snares and Kalashnikov semiautomatics, then brought back to the towns and cities.

Too many Africans still considered the eating of wild game a birthright, and would do so until all the game was gone.

The crowd around the bushmeat tables was large and boisterous. Sheila, pausing, saw whole baby crocodiles; rain forest rats, piled four to a stick, with their mouths pulled back into rictus grins; civets smelling like swamp water; tiny antelopes with legs as delicate as green sticks; a sliding pile of algae-scummed river turtles, still barely alive.

On the next table over were piles of smoked monkey meat, brown and dry like old leather. The guenons had been transported whole, their heads bent back over their bodies by the smoking process, while the larger mangabeys and colobuses had been hacked into steaks and burned-fur-covered limbs.

Sheila had lost her appetite.

Her mother's hand touched her arm. "Let's go, honey."

Sheila hesitated. Then, just as she made to turn away, the crowd stirred, parting before something new. Three living baby chimps, tied together with ropes, pulled by a slab-faced man in dusty cotton pants, a shirt that had once been white, and a faded old baseball cap with what looked like a bullet hole just above the brim.

Orphans of the bushmeat trade, these babies were. Worth more alive to zoos or medical laboratories than for the meat on their bones. Two of them seemed merely exhausted and terrified, clinging to each other and staring up at the faces in the crowd. They were making little moaning sounds, calls to their family that would never be heard.

The third had had a rougher time. Its eyes were glassy, its arms and legs quivering. Its stomach was swollen, Sheila saw, most likely from malnutrition. It wouldn't last long now.

"Sheila," her mom said, more insistently, "I've seen more of these than I'd like, these past months. Let's go."

The sound of the baby chimps' cries followed them almost to the edge of the busy marketplace.

"OKAY," SHEILA SAID.

Dinner over, they were sitting with their coffee on the porch of the compact house Megan and Scott had built here, outside Ujiji. The sun was dipping toward the horizon, and the cool evening breeze was chasing away the afternoon's huddled storm clouds. It would be another gorgeous starlit evening, perfect for the kind of companionable quiet that Sheila craved.

But first there was something they needed to take care of.

It was a ritual. Her parents hadn't believed in visiting doctors except in emergencies. There had been a few of those over the years, a fracture here, a kidney stone there, that had necessitated the hour-long drive to the nearest hospital, in Kigoma. Since Sheila had become an M.D., the Connellys had waited for her occasional visits for more routine checkups.

This system had worked fine until Sheila's father had died of a sudden heart attack two years earlier. Sheila had always wondered if waiting for her visit had cost her father his life.

Megan, face a blur in the encroaching darkness, said, "Can't we do this tomorrow morning?"

Sheila knew that if they waited, some obstacle would come up in the morning, another in the afternoon, and soon enough she'd be back on the ferry and Megan would have escaped her checkup.

"I don't want to know" was Megan's mantra.

"Nope," Sheila said. "Now."

With a sigh, her mother got to her feet.

"You're not going to find anything, you know," she said.

Sheila thought, *I hope not.*

MEGAN'S BLOOD PRESSURE was low, as were her pulse and temperature. None of them outside the normal range, but all lower than usual.

Sheila sat back and thought about this. Her mother stayed silent.

They were in the small room, once a study, that Sheila had insisted they turn into an examining room and storage area for medical supplies. Clamps, scalpels, forceps.

Splints and bandages. Antibiotics to ward off infection, epinephrine in case of allergic reactions, rabies vaccine, gamma globulin. Pills for fever, for stomach disorders, for Megan's migraine headaches, for whatever other treatable malady Sheila could think of.

Nothing to treat a sluggish pulse and heart rate, though. Not until she knew what was causing it.

"Diagnosis, doc?" Megan said lightly.

Sheila shook her head. "I'm thinking we'll have to pay a visit to Nyerere."

The hospital in Kigoma.

"No need. I'm fine."

Sheila didn't bother to argue. "Off with your shirt," she said. "I want to listen to your lungs."

With a shrug, Megan unbuttoned her blouse. Slipped it off. Half turned to drape it across the table beside her. Turned back and gave her daughter a bright-eyed look, as if to say, "Can we get this over with?"

But Sheila barely noticed. She was staring at the exposed skin between the bottom of her mother's white bra and the top of her blue cotton pants. And trying to breathe.

Megan's belly was swollen, round, as if someone had surgically implanted an inverted bowl under her skin. Dead center in the swelling was a round black hole, perhaps a third of an inch across.

Tumbu fly larva, Sheila thought. *It must be a tumbu fly.*

Anyone who lived in tropical Africa for any length of time had encountered tumbu flies. The adults were innocuous, just one among a billion small winged creatures that infested the tropics. But they had a clever survival trick: They were parasites. And they used large mammals to host their young. Horses, cows, antelopes, and gazelles. Dogs.

And humans.

The eggs, laid on the ground or in wet laundry, would hatch into tiny larvae. As soon as one came into contact with a potential host, it would grab hold and then eat its way through the skin and into the flesh.

It was a perfect home, the mammalian body. Warm, safe from predators, providing abundant food and moisture as the larva matured.

The first sign of tumbu fly infection was usually a myiasis, a tumorlike swelling that indicated where the tunnel lay. A round opening in the skin, which the larva used as an airhole, confirmed the diagnosis.

But tumbu fly myiases were tiny, since the larvae rarely exceeded a few centimeters in length. This swelling was different. Judging by the size of the swelling and the airhole, the larva within would have to be huge, a couple of inches long. The biggest Sheila had ever seen.

As she watched, something wriggled just below the surface of her mother's skin.

"Sheila?"

She raised her eyes. Megan was staring at her curiously.

"Sheila, what's wrong?"

Sheila wet her lips, but still her voice was a croak when she spoke. "Mom," she said, "why didn't you tell me? You should have gone to the doctor days ago!"

Megan blinked. "Tell you what?"

Sheila ground her teeth so hard she could hear them. "This," she said, pointing. "This!"

Her mother's gaze followed the direction of her finger.

For a long moment she stared at her swollen belly, but when she lifted her head her face showed no comprehension.

"I don't know," she said.

Sheila felt a kind of cold fear spread outward from her heart. But she had to set it aside. There would be time for more questions later. She had a job to do.

"Well," she said, "let's get this thing out of you. I'd guess you've got an allergic reaction going on there, too. I'll put you on prophylactic antibiotics and an antihistamine. The swelling should go down fast once it's out."

Talking to herself, that was what she was doing. Her mother was simply staring at her, as if she hadn't understood a word. There was definitely something strange about her eyes.

Sheila stood, stepped over to the supply cabinet, found two ampules of lidocaine hydrochloride. The first she injected near the airhole, to anesthetize the area.

"Don't."

Surprised, Sheila glanced up into her mother's face. Megan had always been a stoic. Once, though gray-faced from the pain of a broken arm, she hadn't protested as Sheila had rigged a field splint, nor during the long, bumpy ride to the hospital.

"Almost done," Sheila said, trying but failing for the same light tone she used with her young patients. "Just sit still."

Megan said, "No. Please. *Sheila*."

Sheila wanted to put her hands over her ears. Without responding, she squirted the second dose of lidocaine through the airhole to calm down the larva. It was a lot easier to pull out a sleeping worm than a wriggling one.

As the anesthetic sluiced into the burrow beneath the skin, she saw a flash of writhing white come to the surface of the airhole, then something black, and then white again.

Her mother spoke no more. Nor did she make a sound when Sheila reached in with her sterilized thumb forceps, got hold of the larva, and slowly pulled it out of the hole.

She could see at once that this grub came from no tumbu fly. Those were oblong, resembling white kidney beans.

This larva, however, was two inches long, with an opalescent white body; big eyes like pearls made of onyx; soft, half-formed legs; and curved black mandibles. Even as she stared, it twisted its body into a U shape and, seemingly unaffected by the lidocaine, bit viciously at the end of the forceps.

Sheila felt her heart thud against her ribs. Over the years, she'd evicted her share of scorpions from various bedrooms, bathrooms, and tents, often using forceps much like this one to transport them safely. She'd always marveled at the tensile strength of the armored creatures, an inherent will to survive that she both admired and feared.

But she'd never felt anything like the strength that seemed to course through this writhing larva. It mashed away at the forceps with its powerful mandibles, creating a vibration that Sheila could feel through her fingers and all the way up into her forearm. Without thinking, she tightened her grip on the handle.

And then, just like that, the larva died. Some grayish goo came out of its jaws, and suddenly it was just a limp wormy thing hanging from the forceps' metal tips. A bitter smell filled the room.

"Christ," Sheila said. "Mom, what the hell *is* this?"

But Megan didn't respond with words, only with a low, guttural groan.

Alarmed, Sheila looked up, but even as she did Megan's eyes rolled up so only the silvery whites were showing. Her mouth stretched wide.

Sheila had barely dropped the forceps and begun to reach out when her mother toppled sideways and fell to the floor.

SEVEN

Manhattan

THERE WAS A big cockroach in Trey's subway car, a water bug like the ones you see scattering from the light in the bathrooms of third-rate hotels all over the world. Not a native New Yorker—an invader of a species from the forests of Asia—but it didn't seem to care. To a roach, one warm, dirty, food-rich environment is as good as another.

Trey watched it scuttle over to investigate some sticky yellowish stuff, maybe spilled soda, on the orange plastic seat across the car from his. Tan in color, flat as something that had been stepped on, it looked alert, energetic, fully alive.

And alien.

Somewhere in our nervous system is an inherent belief that all other creatures are in some way like us, that we can relate to them, understand their thinking, get inside their heads. We make cats, dogs, parrots, even lizards human in our eyes, ascribing our emotions to our pets to justify the food, housing, and love we offer.

But the truth is, if you got inside a cockroach's head, you'd find plenty of nothing. No brain, no control tower for the central nervous system. In fact, if you decapitate a roach, it doesn't die. It doesn't even take a break from running around. True, it can't see, but the only severe damage you've done is to deprive it of the ability to eat. A headless roach will live on until it starves to death.

This is not a creature we can relate to, no matter how hard we try.

The train pulled into the 81st Street station. As it jerked to a halt, the cockroach hustled across the seat and inserted itself into a crack that Trey doubted he could have slid a dime into. He got to his feet and saw, as he stepped out of the car, a young woman sit down right in front of where the roach was hiding.

Most likely the bug was now going to hitch a ride home in the woman's Coach bag or in a pocket of her North Face jacket or snuggled in the fleece lining of her Uggs.

It was perfectly adapted to life in this big city.

Certainly better adapted than *he* was.

"HEY, HAMLET," JACK Parker said. "What are you pondering?"

"Cockroaches," Trey said.

Jack stared at him for a moment. "Well," he said, "you're in the right building, the right floor, but the wrong office. Cockroaches are down the hall."

He laughed. "Cockroaches *and* the men who love them."

Jack was a senior scientific assistant in the Department of Entomology at the American Museum of Natural History. Short, squat, bearded, with a bald head and a barrel chest, he looked like a battering ram and had a personality to match.

The two of them were sitting in Jack's office on the fifth floor, where most of the museum's staff scientists worked. Its anthropologists and paleontologists and ichthyologists and experts in biodiversity and extinction, all laboring away here, mostly hidden from the public.

And entomologists, too. The people who studied insects, bugs, and spiders.

There were more entomologists at the museum than scientists in any other field. This made sense, since at two million species (give or take thirty million), there were more insects, bugs, and spiders than all other creatures in the animal kingdom combined.

"They should make a permanent exhibition about cockroaches," Trey said.

Jack growled. This was a sore subject for him.

No visitor to the museum would realize the abundance—or importance—of entomology at a glance, since there wasn't a single permanent exhibit anywhere in the public areas dedicated to bugs. Dinosaurs, of course. African mammals, sure. Meteors and gems and ancient peoples and even New York trees. But no cockroaches or butterflies or walking sticks or rhinoceros beetles. When it came to arthropods—insects and spiders, basically—no nothing.

Jack had a simple theory about why this was: People were idiots.

"They fear what they don't understand," he said. "And you don't go to museums to see things that terrify you. You make horror movies about them."

Jack would know. He could recite the dialogue from just about every grade-Z movie ever made.

The people who were terrified of bugs would have fled screaming from Jack's office. It had originally been a non-descript room like so many others in the building: four peeling walls, linoleum floor, grime-streaked windows overlooking Central Park West and the park across the way. Just another chamber in the hive, until Jack had decorated it with mementos of his own area of expertise: the order Hymenoptera. Bees, wasps, and ants.

Specifically: wasps.

On his big oak desk were trays of specimens borrowed from the collections room, each containing rows of little yellow-and-black hornets whose black-eyed gazes seemed filled with rage even in death. The bookcases were filled with everything from reference books to penny dreadfuls ("Attack of the Wasp Woman!"), and every other surface was covered with sculptures, postcards, beer cans, and other knickknacks, all variations on the theme.

"What have arthropods ever done to deserve their evil reputation?" Jack asked.

"I'm about to tell you," Trey said.

THE TWO OF them had met more than a decade earlier. Trey, emerging from four weeks assessing a vast, empty stretch of foothill thorn scrub in northern Peru, had encountered a multidisciplinary museum expedition that included Jack. No one there ever forgot the contrast between Trey's dirty, ragged, half-starved condition and the opulently equipped expedition.

Unexpectedly, the chance meeting had also marked the beginning of a friendship. Just about the only lasting friendship Trey could claim, and one that most people didn't understand. How could the explosively, unstoppably enthusiastic and talkative Jack have anything in common with Trey, who spent so much time observing and analyzing the world around him that sometimes you forgot he was there?

Trey had wondered about that himself.

Jack's thick arms were crossed over his chest. "What are you talking about?"

Trey didn't answer.

After a moment, Jack said, "People are whispering about you, you know."

"Yeah?"

"Yeah. They're saying you had your butt kicked out of Senegal and got fired by ICT."

Trey was quiet.

"They basically disappeared you, except you ended up here instead of Guantánamo."

This was true enough. A short flight on a military airplane and Trey had been in Dakar, three hours after that he'd left Senghor Airport on a Senegal Airlines 747, and less than seven hours later he'd disembarked at JFK.

Feeling disoriented. More disoriented than he'd ever felt before, and he'd been traveling his whole life.

And also curious. When he'd gotten into trouble before, he'd always known why. But not this time.

He brought himself back and looked at Jack. "ICT can't fire me, since I don't work for them."

"They can stop giving you assignments."

This was true as well.

Jack blinked. "Jesus," he said. "Jesus, Trey, you're, like, famous. You're the guy who always does whatever the hell you want, and always gets away with it."

Trey closed his eyes. He saw the wet gleam of the ivory white stinger. The agonized monkey. The wasp hovering just in front of his face, deciding whether he should live or die.

He opened his eyes again to find Jack staring at him. "Shit, Gilliard," he said, "what the hell happened out there?"

Trey said, "Get your pencils."

JACK WAS A brilliant draftsman. Two centuries earlier, he might have been an itinerant artist-scientist, traveling the world with paints and collecting jars. Producing works like those that now hung on the office walls. A John James Audubon of the insect world.

But those times had passed. In the modern era, his artwork was known only to those who read his journal articles. And to his friends, who were often faced with the challenge of finding the perfect place in a small apartment to hang a portrait of, say, a tarantula-hawk wasp attacking its prey.

Over the years, Trey had often seen—but not captured—insects that didn't yet exist in the scientific literature. Jack's crystal-clear reproductions based on his descriptions had existed long before actual specimens were collected, when they were at all.

Knowing the drill, Jack sat down behind his desk,

rummaged, pulled out his case of artists' pencils and a sketch pad. Then looked up and said, "Okay. A bee?"

"Wasp."

A gleam in Jack's eye. He loved wasps. "How big was it?"

Trey held his thumb and forefinger three inches apart.

Jack's mouth turned down at the corners. "Come on, Trey."

Trey's fingers didn't move.

"You sound like a civilian, the kind who mistakes a housecat for a mountain lion."

Trey said, "But I'm not, am I?"

"Not what?"

"A civilian."

Jack stared at him, and now there was a kind of desperation in his expression. "Trey, the largest known wasp on earth, *Scolia procer*, isn't that big!"

He made a gesture over his shoulder at one of the old prints hanging on the wall. It showed a fat black-and-yellow wasp whose wings extended from its back like an airplane's.

"That's not what I saw," Trey said.

"I know! But—"

"The ones I saw were bigger," Trey said. "Can we get started?"

Jack drew in a breath. His face was a little red. After a moment, though, he lifted a hand and held it over the pencils. "Okay," he said. "Color and shape of the body?"

"Black," Trey said. "Skinny like a mud dauber. Arched abdomen."

Sitting in an old armchair across from the desk, he spoke. For twenty minutes, the only sounds other than his voice were the distant hum of traffic down on the street, the scratch of the pencils, and Jack's questions making sure he was getting the details right. The color of the wings. The angle of the head. The size of the mandibles.

When he was done he held up the picture, a nearly perfect representation of the wasps Trey had seen. All that it was lacking was the sense of menace, of calculation, of intelligence that came to Trey whenever he closed his eyes.

The soul.

"You *saw* one of these," Jack said, as if he still couldn't quite believe it.

"I saw a colony of them." Trey sat back a little in the chair. "In a forest that was dying."

Jack stared down at the drawing, and when he raised his head his eyes had a different look. Trey had seen it many times before. It meant his friend's mind was engaged. It meant he was ready for the hunt.

"The whole story, please," Jack said.

AGAIN TREY TALKED. It was a requirement of his occupation, talking—if someone was paying you to go look, they expected you to tell them what you'd seen—but one he hated. Usually when he was done being debriefed, done talking to fund-raisers and scientists and whatever press was interested in his explorations, he'd disappear into the wilderness again. Making up for a few days of noise with weeks of silence.

Jack was quiet, looking down at his desk, at the drawing. For someone who loved the sound of his own voice, he knew how to listen, too.

Only when Trey was done did he look up. "That smell," he said. "Was it formic acid?"

The characteristic odor of ant colonies, the acid found in their stings . . . and wasps', too.

Trey frowned. "No. Not quite. It was . . . stronger."

He was much better describing what he'd seen than what he'd smelled.

"And the dead man you saw had the same odor."

"The room did, at least."

"And you think the wasps were going to kill you."

"I think they were considering it."

Jack frowned. Opened his mouth as if there was something he wanted to say, then shook his head as if he'd changed his mind. What he finally said was, "But the sting didn't kill the monkey. You said being stung made it . . . more alert. Aggressive."

Trey said nothing, just turned his palms up.

"Do you think they attacked that woman after she rescued you?"

Trey shook his head. "I tried calling the village to ask about her," he said, "and no one there will speak to me. But—"

"But she didn't seem afraid?" Jack widened his eyes. "Suicidal?"

"No. Determined." He struggled to find the right word. "Powerful."

Jack grimaced. "I hate this shit."

"What?"

"Having a few pieces of the puzzle, but not enough. And not having access to the rest of the pieces."

"I know." Trey felt weary. "But I'm not getting back

into Senegal anytime soon, and I don't know how else to get the other pieces."

Jack stared at him for a few seconds. Then he gave a sudden grin. "You're so clueless, you make me seem like Stephen Hawking. I admire that in you. You really don't know what to do next?"

Trey shook his head.

Jack's eyes flicked over to the laptop computer that sat open on his desk. The screen saver showed not wasps but, unexpectedly, a litter of golden retriever puppies.

"Well, I do," he said.

EIGHT

Nouadhibou, Mauritania

THERE WAS NO space on the dhow for Mariama.

She'd spent days with the Ndoye family, hiding from officials amid the donkey carts surrounding the marketplace and among the villagers mending fishing nets down near the beach. Waiting, just waiting, for someone to sell them transport out of the country.

The Ndoye family: an old father and mother, both of them thin, tired, and gray before they'd even left the shore. Their grown children and younger ones, too, along with some cousins, or maybe they were friends, or simply people they'd met along the way as they'd met Mariama. A dozen in their group at least, maybe more, including one girl, perhaps fourteen, who stood out for her quick smile, friendly manner, and unquenchable optimism.

The girl reminding Mariama of children she'd known in Mpack, children she doubted she'd ever see again.

None of them here expected ever to see again the places where they'd been born. All that mattered now was that they'd scraped together the thousands of francs needed to commission an old fishing boat and its captain. A boat like the dhow the Ndoyes got, so rusty in the fittings and wormholed around the hull you marveled that anyone would trust it beyond the ocean's blue edge.

Mariama wanted to warn them, to tell them to wait for a sturdier craft. But it would have been useless. You took what you could get, and if hunger and thirst and storms and those European Union patrols—ships from Portugal and planes from Italy and who knew what else— if they weren't going to stop you from trying, then a leaky old boat wouldn't, either.

If the Ndoyes hadn't taken the dhow, then the next group would have. The next group being Mariama and other men and women she'd met here in Nouadhibou. The next batch of the uncounted refugees who came here every year from Senegal and Morocco and Mauritania itself, all with a single goal in mind.

To reach the Canary Islands.

Islands that for some reason were part of Spain, even though they were located right off the western coast of Africa. Once you made it to the Canary Islands, the refugees had been told, it was easy to reach the real Europe, where there were jobs, food, a new life.

For most of them, this was their first trip from home. Not for Mariama, who had visited Paris, Johannesburg, and New York with her father. A few years earlier, when she still had a passport, she wouldn't have had to travel this way. She would be stepping aboard a comfortable jet at Senghor Airport.

Instead she'd come to this little port town, just another body hoping for passage out. Carrying with her nothing but a few pieces of clothing in a cloth satchel, extra money in a leather belt under her shirt, and just one memento from home: a locket containing a photo of her father, hanging on a tarnished silver chain around her neck.

MARIAMA ENDED UP on the *Sophe*, a twenty-foot wooden boat that she thought seemed sturdy and strong enough. There were twenty-two of them on board, packed tightly against the rails and across the slippery wooden deck. Twenty-two plus the captain, who had a sharp face and quick eyes that didn't miss anything.

They departed from an unlighted dock on a pitch-black night speckled with cold rain. Staking a place by the rail near the back, Mariama helped an old man and a mother with a little daughter settle beside her.

Prayers rose and tears fell as they left shore, but Mariama stayed silent and dry-eyed.

DURING THE FIRST two days, they saw three EU patrol boats and one spotter plane. None were close, and none noticed their little boat amid the waves.

On the third morning they came upon the old dhow carrying the Ndoye family. It had set off two days before them, but there it was, foundering in a patch of choppy ocean under a slate gray sky. They could hear the engine grinding, but it wasn't making any progress.

"It's taking on water," someone said.

They could all tell that.

"What do we do?" someone else asked.

They were only a few hundred meters away. Some of the dhow's passengers had noticed them as well and had begun waving cloths and shirts to get their attention. Mariama thought she saw the teenage girl she'd met onshore.

"We must rescue them," said the old man beside Mariama. "Otherwise they will all die."

Their captain shrugged. "That is not our concern." His canny eyes were cold. "Look at us," he said. "Look at our boat. Can we take on more passengers? Even one more? No. We would just sink as well."

Everybody looked. He was right: There was no space.

"We will make room for some," the old man insisted. "We cannot leave them all."

Already they could see that the captain was guiding their boat away from the dhow. "Which ones?" he said. "Which will we choose? No. They will all try to climb aboard, and we will all die."

Behind them they heard a splash, another. Two of the young men had abandoned the dhow and were swimming toward the *Sophe*. But they were too far away, much too far, and how much strength did they have? If they were like Mariama, they had been eating little but rice and plantains for days—weeks—on their journeys.

The captain didn't look back, though Mariama saw his mouth tighten at the sound of the splashing. The old man's gaze caught Mariama's, but he did not speak again, and nor did anyone else.

Behind the swimmers, beyond their pumping arms and kicking legs, Mariama could see the ones that had stayed behind. Some were bailing, throwing water off the dhow's deck with their cupped hands. But others, the old and the children, were still waving, and some were just sitting there, staring at the departing *Sophe*.

It happened quickly. First the two swimmers gave up. One turned back, but the other, perhaps the victim of cramps or dizziness, began to splash around in circles. Soon he was thrashing in one place, and then, as they watched, he slipped below the surface, leaving behind only a tiny crease in the water, and then nothing at all.

The boat itself followed just a few moments later. Echoing over the water came a dull cracking sound, followed by a puff of black smoke that rose a little way into the air before being blown away by the wind. The front of the boat rose from the water, as if it were being pushed upward by a hand. It stood still for a moment, looking like the fin of some sea creature. Then it slid down and back, smoothly as a blade, and was gone.

Mariama had twisted around to see small forms leaping into the water before the dhow disappeared. Now she turned away and looked up at the captain.

But he stood straight, staring at the western horizon.

AS THE SUN sank, the swells grew larger, the clouds thicker, the winds sharper. The boat labored forward against the confused currents. Even the ocean itself was fighting to keep them in Africa.

The old man beside Mariama had fallen into a kind of wordless trance after the sinking of the dhow. On her other side, the mother, a tough, wiry woman from Mauritania, tended to her daughter, who looked about six.

The girl seemed unwell. She'd spent most of the journey with her eyes closed, and her dark skin seemed underlain with gray.

"She does not like the motion of the boat," the woman said. "She will be fine when we reach land."

Mariama did not speak. She knew the truth, but there was no point in sharing it.

The woman said she was headed to London, where she had family. She shook her head as she said it: In this small boat, miles and miles from land, it was hard to imagine a place like London even existing.

"And you?" she asked Mariama.

"New York."

"So far away. Why?"

Mariama hesitated for a moment before saying, "There is a man I need to find."

"In that whole big city?" The woman laughed at her. "Good luck!"

It seemed impossible to Mariama as well.

ON THE AFTERNOON of the fourth day, as they shared the last of their water, Mariama spotted a brown stripe on the horizon to the north. "Fuerteventura," the captain said.

Their destination.

No. Their way station.

As the sun headed toward the horizon, the stripe grew larger, longer, became the coast of an island, a distant beach. Behind the beach they could see a jumble of houses painted in bright colors and, farther away, the gleaming white and pink towers of tourist hotels.

The captain pulled back on the engine, left it rumbling just strongly enough to keep the boat in place, bumping in the gentle swells flowing out from the island. "We will make land after dark," he said.

So they waited, watching the sun sink and the big jet planes coasting into the airport.

Mariama sat with the mother and daughter. The little girl was worse. Though she seemed to be awake, and would nod or shake her head when asked questions, she rarely opened her eyes.

When the sun dipped below the horizon, the captain aimed the *Sophe* at the beach. The houses and hotels were lit like stars, constellations, and still the jets came in from Portugal and England and Italy. The same countries that supplied boats and planes to keep Africans out of the Canary Islands sent thousands of their own citizens to the same place.

The woman looked down at her daughter, then back up. "Will you help us get to shore?"

Mariama paused and then said, "Yes. Of course."

The woman's smile reflected the light of the hotels, the silvery water. "Then we will finally be safe."

Mariama thought, No.

No, we won't.

WHEN THEY WERE perhaps fifty feet from the beach, the captain brought the boat to a halt. Over the subdued mutter of the idling engine, they could hear music. But the beach itself seemed deserted.

"The tide is low, and the water is shallow," the captain said. "I cannot go in any farther."

One by one, stiff on their feet, the men and women

clambered over the side of the little fishing boat and splashed into the water. Some made little sounds of fear as they went, but none hesitated. They could see their goal just ahead.

No one said good-bye.

Soon just the three of them and the captain remained on board. "Hurry!" he said. "Or I will take you back with me."

Mariama went over first, landing in warm, calm water that reached barely to her waist. The woman, struggling, lifted her daughter over the railing and into her arms. Getting a grip on the limp figure, Mariama felt the girl's rounded, swollen belly bump against her side.

She thought: *If I were truly brave, I would drop you now. I would swim away and let you drown.*

It would be a blessing.

Instead she kept the girl's head above the surface as the mother splashed into the water. Then, together, they made their slow way through the placid ocean and up onto the beach.

TWO HOURS LATER Mariama had showered and changed into a colorful print skirt and a dark blue blouse and was sitting in the living room of a small house in Fuerteventura. The house's residents—mother, father, and five daughters—perched on chairs and the sofa and stared at her.

They were making sure she was eating well, as they'd promised Mariama's father they would.

Seydou Honso might have been confined to Senegal, but he still had plenty of friends elsewhere, including here.

People who owed him allegiance (or favors) and were willing to hide his refugee daughter from the authorities and make sure she was dressed and fed.

Especially if Seydou paid, which he had. Money needed no passport to travel.

Mariama was grateful, but impatient. She wanted to move on right away. The sick girl on the boat had shown her how much she needed to hurry.

But the family told her that her transport onward wouldn't be departing for three days. There was nothing they could do to speed it up. And anyway, as the mother pointed out, she would do no good if she died from exhaustion or starvation on the way.

So she stayed, and she rested, and she ate well. The fish-and-tomato stew they called tieboudienne, the baobab drink bouyi, and other Senegalese specialties that made her miss Mpack with an ache that filled her chest.

She spent most of her time thinking about the enormity of the task that lay ahead. Every once in a while, when no one was looking, she took the locket from around her neck and popped it open.

Just looking at it gave her strength.

LATE THE THIRD night, she was woken by a knock on the door of her bedroom. She'd been dreaming of the boat, and even when she awoke, disoriented, she felt like her bed was rocking on treacherous swells.

One of the daughters leaned in through the doorway and said in an apologetic tone, "You asked to be called if there were any messages for you."

Mariama said, "Of course. Thank you. I will be right there."

After washing her face, she followed the girl into the kitchen. A computer sat on the table, its screen bright in the dimness. Without a word, the girl turned and left. They were willing to shelter her, these nice people, but they didn't want to know a thing about her plans.

She sat down in front of the computer, marveling. Just days ago, on the boat, she'd been dangling like a puppet over the very edge of the world. How easily she could have fallen off, sharing the fate of the people in the doomed dhow.

And yet here she was, all the miracles of the modern age at her fingertips.

It was absurd.

She bent over the screen. The name of the person who'd sent the message was unfamiliar, but the code she and her father had agreed on was there. The message was from him.

Only there was no message. Just a link. Compressing her lips, Mariama clicked on it.

At first it *still* didn't make any sense. It was just an article about the death of some American expatriate in Tanzania. Only when Mariama read through did she begin to understand what it meant and what its consequences might be.

She felt cold. While she sat here, events were spinning on—and out of control—without her.

She took in a long breath to calm herself. Then leaned forward over the keyboard and began to compose a message of her own.

NINE

Manhattan

TREY COULD BLAME his relentless yen to travel on his parents.

His father, Thomas, was a specialist in respiratory diseases, but unlike most doctors he'd never chosen a sedentary life at a hospital, HMO, or university. Instead, as if something were chasing him, he stayed on the move, spending a few months here, a year there.

He'd had a willing conspirator in Trey's mother, Katherine. She was a writer, and her ongoing series of columns for *Adventure Travel* magazine, detailing life on the run with a husband and two young sons, had proven very popular.

By the time he was fifteen, Trey had visited more than thirty countries. If his family never stayed put long enough for him to make friends, to learn what it was like to live in human society instead of just skim over it, he didn't mind. He was sure that the trade-off was worth it.

His brother, Christopher, disagreed. "You just don't know any different," he told Trey when they were teenagers. "You've never learned how satisfying it is to grow roots."

"You haven't, either," Trey pointed out.

"That's true." Christopher thought about it. "But there's a difference. As soon as I can, I'm going to. Deep roots."

And then Christopher went out and did it. Grew roots. When he reached the age of eighteen, he went back to Australia, always his favorite among the places they'd visited, got a job, and settled down in Port Douglas, Queensland. Eventually he fell in love with a woman there and got married.

Just like normal people did.

Christopher and Margie still lived in Port Douglas and had produced two children. Twin girls, whom Trey had seen only a handful of times over the years.

On his most recent visit, three years earlier, he found himself driven to explain himself to his brother. They were sitting on the porch of Christopher's house at dusk, drinking Fourex Gold and watching a steady stream of flying foxes winging past, dark silhouettes against a celadon sky.

In halting words, he tried to describe why he couldn't stay still. How the world seemed like such a fragile place, and that by going where it was most fragile, most endangered, he might be able to make a difference.

Christopher smiled at him over his beer. "Dad used to use exactly the same excuse when he dragged us around."

Trey was struck silent.

"But that's okay." Christopher leaned his head back and looked up at the darkening sky. "He was who he was, and you are what you are." He laughed. "At least you're not inflicting your compulsions on your own kids."

Right then, the twins came home from a play date, and Christopher's face lit up. He looked happy in a way that made Trey feel ashamed of himself.

But not for long. The next morning he was off again, spinning round the world, just as his father had.

WOULD THOMAS AND Katherine have been proud of him? He liked to believe so, but he'd never know for sure.

Early in his career, Thomas had seen the field of respiratory medicine morph into something almost unrecognizable. Every year seemed to see the emergence of a new or resurgent respiratory disease. AIDS-associated pneumonias. Legionnaires' disease. SARS. Bird flu. Even tuberculosis, once considered nearly eradicated, came roaring back, more deadly than ever.

Not all the diseases sprouting like vile mushrooms all over the world had names. Some unidentified ones were so ferocious—and so little understood—that the physicians hurrying to study and treat them knew that doing so might be suicidal.

When Trey was in his second year of college, Thomas Gilliard was summoned to Guangdong Province in China to investigate one such newly hatched disease. Katherine went along, as she always did.

Three days after seeing his first patient, Thomas fell ill. His lungs filled with fluid, then with blood, and less than forty-eight hours later he was dead.

Katherine had been warned to stay away from him, but ignored this advice. Even before Thomas died, she'd begun to experience the same symptoms. Her death came three days after his.

And Trey, world traveler, just nineteen, found himself accompanying his parents' bodies back to the United States.

Back home. As if they'd ever truly had a home.

"YOU LOOK LIKE a poster for Reading Is Fundamental," Jack said.

Trey looked up. The open books before him bore titles like *A Young Man's Grand Adventures in Afrique Ouest Français* (Colonel Fitzwilliam Wallis, First Bengal Lancers, Ret., 1878) and *Into the Jungles of the Camerouns with Gun and Knitting Needles* (Lady Mary Maurice Smith, Women's Goodwill Society, 1904). Books that were mirrors of a time when the world was an empty map, where grand adventures were still possible.

"Found nothing, huh?" Jack said.

Trey shook his head. No mention of monkey-killing wasps in the rain forests of Senegal or anywhere else the peripatetic Victorian authors had traveled.

He lifted the book by Lady Mary and watched as fragments of the deteriorating, yellow-orange pages drifted down onto his lap. Books like these were another thing in the process of vanishing, unnoticed and unmourned. When they were gone—and libraries were relentlessly clearing shelf space to make room for computer terminals—they'd be gone forever.

If something wasn't at the tip of your keyboarding fingers, it wouldn't exist.

Jack, who considered Trey sentimental about such things, moved easily back and forth between the two worlds. Entirely comfortable in the wilderness, chasing after new species on mountaintops, in swamps and forests, he was equally content traveling across time and space on the Internet.

He saw Trey looking at the paper dandruff on his lap and said, "Get used to it. Scientists can't survive without technology."

"Then I guess it's lucky," Trey said, "that I'm no scientist."

"Lucky for us, at least." Jack's gaze moved to his computer. "Come here."

When Trey stood behind him, he gestured at the screen.

"Here's what I've done," he said. "Should I send it out?"

He'd created a kind of garish advertisement, like something that might have touted an old-time Coney Island sideshow. At its center was Jack's drawing of the wasp. Above the illustration were the words "Have You Seen This Bug?" in big red-and-white letters, and the space below contained a description of the wasp's size and where Trey had seen it, a smaller sketch of one of the colony's mounds with a wasp perched on top of it, contact information, and a warning ("Dangerous! Do not approach.") that Trey was sure would be ignored.

"Who will receive this?" he asked.

"Well." Jack took a second to think about it. "I'll send it to every bug hunter I know, for starters. Every entomology department in every university, of course. Nature-travel and bird-tour companies. I'll also be posting it on my bug blog, Facebook and Twitter of course, my Tumblr and Pinterest—"

He grinned at Trey's expression. "Social-media sites

where not only scientists, but real people, will see it. That's the key, I think. I want someone I'll never meet to tell someone else I'll never meet, 'Hey, doesn't this look like the wasp you stepped on when we were playing tennis at Club Med this spring?'"

Trey was silent.

"Gotta look for help," Jack said. "Way of the world."

After a moment, Trey nodded. You couldn't always do everything yourself. He understood that.

Hated, but understood.

"Send it," he said.

SOON AFTERWARD, HE headed back to his apartment in Brooklyn's upscale Park Slope neighborhood. His parents had bought it once he and Christopher grown, a place on the ground floor of a four-story yellow-brick building just a few blocks from Prospect Park. Worth a fortune these days because of the neighborhood, but it was nothing glamorous: one bedroom, one bath, a foldout couch in the living/dining room, separated by a counter from the tiny kitchen.

More a place for stopping off to do laundry between trips than a real home.

After they'd died, Trey and Christopher had inherited it jointly. Christopher, just twenty-two but already settled in Australia, had wanted nothing to do with it, even refusing Trey's offer to buy out his half.

"You sell it, give me my share," he'd said. "Till then, feel free to live there."

So that was what Trey did, as much as he lived anywhere.

*　*　*

HE SAT AT the little table in the dining area and powered up his laptop. Despite Jack's jibes, he knew his way around the Internet.

He had no choice. The ability to use a computer was nearly as essential to his (tenuous) relationship with his employers as his skill at returning from the wilderness with data no one else could obtain.

He got no pleasure from computer literacy. But all Jack's talk about social media had reminded him that days had passed since he'd been online. With a sigh, he logged on.

And then, right away, almost deleted the most important e-mail of his life because it looked like spam.

It had come from a travel company in the Canary Islands. Unsurprisingly, Trey had ended up on countless travel e-mail lists, and at first he assumed this one was just another advertisement.

Except for the subject heading. It didn't advertise cheap vacations in Majorca, time shares on Grand Canary, easy hops to Casablanca.

It just said: "This time . . ."

Trey looked at it and thought, *What does* that *mean*?

So instead of deleting the e-mail unread, he opened it.

It contained three short lines of text. The first said, ". . . you don't have to flee."

The second: "Sheila Connelly."

And the third: "Find her."

Trey sat looking at the screen. Thinking.

Then he reached for his phone and called Jack.

TEN

DESPITE THE HOUR, Jack was still in his office. No surprise to Trey, who knew that Jack frequently stayed at work long after the museum closed, even through the night.

This had always been true, but even more so since his divorce had eliminated his main reason for setting foot outside.

Not that he was ever alone in the vast building. Jack was far from the only museum scientist at work during the dead of night, when the streets outside were quiet but for an occasional bus or taxi, and even Central Park itself seemed to sleep. You could concentrate better, they believed. Gain perspective that was impossible in the glaring light and endless noise of the city day.

Trey didn't need convincing. It was his favorite time at the museum as well. With only scattered emergency bulbs casting a feeble glow, the tigers and gorillas in their darkened dioramas, the shadowy dinosaur skeletons, the great blue whale dominating its ocean room, all managed to capture some of the magic—some of the awe—of the living creatures they evoked.

Plus, when he visited at night, the place was deserted. That was always a good thing.

ONLY THE COMPUTER screen and a bumblebee-shaped child's night-light illuminated the office. Jack had opened a window, and Trey felt the night's cold, damp exhalation as a prickle on his skin. Taking a breath and holding it, he could detect, at the very edge of his hearing, a series of staccato, high-pitched cries: the contact calls of a flock of birds—he heard orioles, tanagers, and grosbeaks—migrating north over the city.

Trey had forwarded the e-mail to Jack. Now they stood looking at it again, though they'd both long since memorized the brief message.

"It's Mariama," Trey said.

Jack frowned. He'd been frowning since Trey arrived. "And you're sure of this how, Sherlock?"

"The word 'flee,'" Trey said.

Jack's frown deepened into a scowl. "But why go through"—he gestured at the screen—"this gobbledygook? Why use someone else's account? Why not just say, 'Hey, Trey. It's Mariama. How ya doin'?"

Trey said, "I don't know. Maybe she's protecting herself . . . or someone else."

"And maybe you're grasping at straws, Scarecrow."

Trey just looked at him, and after a moment Jack sighed. "I argue with you," he said, "because it feels so good when I stop."

Sitting down at his computer with a thud, he muttered,

"Sheila Connelly, huh. There must be a ton of people with that name out there."

He tapped at the keys. "No. I was wrong. Most of them use a second *o* instead of an *e*. At least we're not looking for a single ant in a hill."

A moment later, he said, "This one? Tanzania Sheila? The one whose mother died?"

"I think so."

Jack swung around to look up at him. "You searched this yourself, didn't you? Before you came in?"

Trey nodded.

"And?"

"I didn't find anything that meant a thing to me." Trey hesitated. "I thought you might have better luck."

"Because I live in this century? Or just because I'm awesome?"

Trey didn't bother to say anything. Grinning, Jack went back to the computer. "Still, don't expect too much. I think it's a snipe hunt."

Trey said, "Just look."

MEGAN CONNELLY'S DEATH had received a burst of attention in Tanzania's tabloids, mostly because it involved an American who'd been living in the country for decades. The death of an American anywhere on earth also seemed to warrant a few lines in the wire services, which had meant a bit of international newspaper and cable news website coverage as well.

Long or short, though, the articles all said basically the same thing, and it wasn't enough.

Connelly, who had come to western Tanzania as a

missionary, had—along with two Tanzanians—died in a suspicious fire that consumed her house in Ujiji. Her daughter, Sheila, a physician working for the nongovernmental organization Les Voyageurs, had been hospitalized due to distress. And also (several of the articles hinted) because officials suspected that she might have had something to do with the fire.

"When did this all take place?" Trey asked.

Jack looked. "The fire, five days ago. The most recent article is dated yesterday."

"And Sheila is still hospitalized?"

"As far as we know."

Trey said, "For 'distress.'"

"Yeah. Sounds more like detention than treatment to me." Jack gave a sympathetic grunt. "Though I'd be distressed, too, if my mother had just died and I was being held in a Tanzanian hospital."

He shrugged. "But I still don't see anything here about wasps."

"Keep looking," Trey said.

NOTHING. JUST THE same few details regurgitated again and again.

Damn. Trey hated when he couldn't find what he was searching for. When he couldn't *see.*

"Told ya," Jack said. "Snipe hunt."

"No." Trey found that his hands were clenched. "We're missing something."

Jack shrugged. "We've read every word of every story."

"Then why did Mariama point me here?"

Jack opened his mouth, then closed it again. *Maybe she didn't,* he'd begun to say. *Maybe it wasn't even her.*

Trey said, "Could there have been a story up when Mariama looked, but that's gone now?"

Jack went still for a second. Then he said, "Sure."

"Can it be retrieved?"

Again a pause. Then, "Maybe."

Jack went to Google, typed, clicked. A page of results unfurled. The first four led back to articles they'd already read, but the fifth took them to a page that, under the heading of a newspaper called the *Kigoma Dart*, said, "Error 404: The article you are looking for no longer exists."

"Huh," Jack said.

"We need more than a dead link," Trey said.

"Yeah, I know. Let me see if this article's been cached." A few more clicks. "Damn. No."

He sat back in his chair and pulled at his beard. Then he leaned forward again. "Let's try the Wayback Machine."

The name awoke vague memories of cartoons Trey's father had shown him on DVD when he was young. A dog and a boy who traveled back in time to famous historical events.

"The what?" he said.

"The Wayback Machine." Jack was tapping at the keyboard as he spoke. "This site that stores deleted Web pages." He laughed. "Everything on the Internet lives forever, if you know where to look. Just ask any politician."

Ten seconds later he said, "Bingo." And there the article was, as if it had never been taken down, under the title "New Details in Tragic Ujiji House Fire."

Trey scanned it, finding nothing unexpected until the next-to-last paragraph. There, directly beneath the sub-head "Daughter Speaks" were the only words from Sheila Connelly he'd seen in any of the articles he'd read.

Even these were not direct quotes, just a paragraph written as if the reporter had actually talked to Sheila. "Miss Connelly claims to have no knowledge of the fire," the passage said. "She claims that her mother was ill from a tumbu fly larva, which she extracted. During the minor operation, her mother died, she believes of an allergic reaction. The body of Mrs. Connelly was too badly burned to confirm her daughter's statements. Police hope to question Miss Connelly further as she recovers."

"Claims this," Jack said. "Claims that. They've as good as convicted her of arson and murder."

Trey said, "Sure. But that's not what's important."

"Yeah." Jack pulled at his beard, which by this time of the night stuck out in wiry tufts. "But her story doesn't add up, either. No one's ever died of an anaphylactic reaction to a tumbu larva."

Trey was quiet. It was late, and Jack's mind wasn't working as quickly as it usually did.

He'd get there eventually, though.

Trey watched it happen. First, Jack closed his eyes. Then he said, "Wait a second. Wait."

Then his whole body grew still. His intense concentration made him resemble a statue, a monument. A figure from Easter Island, flesh captured in stone, but not flesh itself. He didn't seem to be breathing.

As commanded, Trey waited. In the silence, he heard a car honk down on the street. He glanced over at the bee clock hanging on the wall. Four thirty. Already traffic was beginning to build toward rush hour. The freedom, the wildness, of the New York City night was retreating. Soon the city would be filled with human voices once again, sounds as meaningless to Trey as the gabble of flamingos.

Jack opened his eyes. They were dark with comprehension. "That colobus monkey you saw," he said. "You don't think it got stung because it was threatening the colony. You don't think it was there by chance. You think it was . . . a host."

"I saw the swelling, but thought it was a tumor."

"And that man in the clinic, the one who was shot in the stomach. You think he was, too. A host."

"Yes."

"And Sheila's mother as well."

Trey let him work it out.

"You're saying that your wasps are parasitic. That they use primate hosts to hatch their young." Only Jack's mouth moved. The rest still seemed rooted to his chair, to the earth.

"And not just lower primates," he said. "*Homo sapiens* as well."

"We need to know what Sheila Connelly saw," Trey said. "We need to know what that larva looked like."

Jack stared at him, unblinking. Then, drawing in a huge breath, he shook his shoulders like a bear or a dog. In that moment, he was flesh again.

He turned back to his computer. Within a few seconds he'd called up a website for booking airline reservations.

"Today or tomorrow?" he asked.

Trey stood, stretched, walked over to the window. The predawn light made the leaves on the trees across the way look like fog, like smoke. It reminded him of mountain forests he'd visited, the clouds wafting through, the deepest of mysteries made briefly tangible.

A familiar feeling pierced him, stabbing like a blade. The thrill of the hunt.

You are what you are, his brother had said to him. Meaning: *You'll never change.*

Trey might never know whether it was a curse or a blessing, or both.

"Today," he told Jack. "Now."

ELEVEN

Kigoma, Tanzania

TREY HAD NEVER worked in Tanzania. The reason: The country was too well trodden. With the exception of a vanishing patch of forest here, a remote mountain range there, all the wild areas had been extensively studied by scientists before he was even born.

For Trey, that was a deal breaker. Nothing was more boring than walking in somebody else's footsteps.

He'd visited, though. Just once, with his parents and Christopher when he was fourteen. In and around the tuberculosis conference Thomas and Katherine were attending, the four of them had followed vast herds of wildebeests in the Serengeti, witnessed lions bringing down a zebra in Ngorongoro Crater, and climbed Mt. Kilimanjaro.

It was this last that Trey remembered most vividly. Even now, he could bring back the breathless thrill of standing amid ice fields at nineteen thousand feet on the summit at dawn, all of Africa at his feet, the fading stars above close enough to touch, brilliant meteors tracing across the purple sky.

He remembered his parents flanking him, his mother's arm around his waist, his father's draped across his shoulders.

TREY WALKED DOWN the stairs and onto the tarmac at Kigoma Airport a little after noon two days after his departure from New York. The atmosphere was noticeably wetter, more tropical, than in the savannas to the east. Clouds piled up on the horizon, replete with moisture picked up over the Congo rain forests to the west.

To the first European explorers, Africa had been an unimaginably vast continent. More than a single place, it was a thousand that didn't even overlap or intersect. Trackless swamps, endless forests, sourceless rivers. Going in, you knew you were going to get lost.

You could disappear for years, or forever. As David Livingstone did before being found by Henry Morton Stanley in Ujiji, only a few miles from where Trey was standing right now.

But that was then. Nothing was far enough apart anymore. You could move from desert to forest, from mountain to savanna, in just a few hours. The mystery was all but gone, the teeming plains little more than gigantic zoos filled with semidomesticated animals, idling minibuses, and clicking tourist cameras.

The taxi stand outside the terminal building was starved for business. Trey chose a canny-eyed young man from among the dozen importuning drivers and climbed into the backseat of his 1970s-era Peugeot. It had once been red, most likely, but the sun and rain had turned it a grayish brown.

The driver glanced at Trey in the mirror. "Yes?"

"Nyerere Hospital."

Without a blink, the driver pulled away from the curb. If he had some idea why Trey was here—and Trey thought he did—he didn't show it.

The hospital was located on the outskirts of town. It was a relatively new building, rectangular, made of whitish stone and steel. The polished sandstone floor of the lobby had ammonite fossils in it.

As he walked in, Trey saw a squarish young white man in a gray suit, blue tie, and sunglasses sitting in the waiting area. Instead of going to the reception desk, he walked over to the man, who looked up at him (or at least in his general direction) without taking the sunglasses off.

Trey had seen a thousand just like him in a hundred countries. It didn't matter to them if they were walking clichés: Embassy men, CIA officials, and (increasingly) private contractors almost always dressed like this.

Trey read this one as embassy.

"You're making sure that Sheila Connelly gets out of here with no fuss," Trey said to him, not phrasing it as a question.

Embassy was a little softer than Trey had expected, with a round face behind the dark glasses. His sandy hair was thinning on top, even though his smooth cheeks marked him as no more than thirty.

Trey guessed he was unhappy to have been posted here, and Trey couldn't blame him. Since the end of the cold war, East Africa's global importance had dwindled. Tanzania was far from being prime territory.

Finally Embassy shifted in his seat. "You a friend of

hers?" His voice, too, was unexpectedly soft, the accent showing South Carolina origins.

Trey said, "Hope to be."

He introduced himself, then sat down opposite and said, "Didn't think she'd need protecting by you guys."

Embassy's sunglasses were trained on him. Trey waited, giving the man the chance to decide how much he was willing to say.

CIA agents were never worth talking to. They were always looking to dump you in some secret prison and forget about you. Nor did embassy men open up when their mission was dangerous or high profile.

But this kind of mind-numbing assignment? Babysitting a hospital waiting room? There was a chance.

Eventually Embassy shifted a little in his seat and said, "Well. There's been some rumblings from the families of the other people who died." He paused. "We're just making sure she gets on her way safely."

He licked his dry lips. His forehead gleamed with sweat. The lobby wasn't air-conditioned, and it must have been hot inside that suit.

Trey got to his feet. "I'm getting myself something to eat and drink," he said. "Want anything?"

"Not allowed to eat while I'm on duty," Embassy said darkly.

Trey waited.

"Cafeteria here is under renovation."

Trey smiled. "I'll figure something out."

FIFTEEN MINUTES LATER, he was back from a market down the street, carrying Cokes, coffee, sandwiches, and a paper bag full of passion fruit. Keeping a chicken sandwich, coffee, and the passion fruit for himself, he handed the rest of it over.

Embassy dug into a sandwich, then said through a mouthful, "Nice try. But I still can't tell you anything."

Trey said, "'Course not."

The man took another bite, followed by a gulp of soda. His sunglasses were a little fogged up. "Real good," he said.

Trey said, "No one really believes that Sheila burned down her mother's place, do they?"

Embassy lowered his sandwich and looked across at Trey. "People who set fires go to jail," he said.

"And?"

"We're putting your friend on an airplane today and waving 'bye. Then everyone's happy and I can go back to my place in Dar."

Trey said, "What killed Sheila's mother?"

It was worth a shot. But the sunglasses were as blank as blacked-out windows. Trey knew he wasn't going to get any more.

He stood. Embassy looked up at him and said, "She gets no visitors. Sandwiches won't get you through the door."

"I know." Trey hesitated. "She goes home today, you said."

Embassy nodded.

"Can you tell me about what time?"

Trey watched him think about it before saying, "The last flight back to Dar."

Trey said, "Thank you."

Looking down again at the remains of the food Trey had brought, Embassy added, "And the first flight tomorrow to Rome, and then New York."

At the door Trey turned and said, "You going to be here when I get back?"

Embassy sighed. "Yeah."

"Okay."

"But they won't let you talk to her then, either."

TREY CLIMBED INTO the taxi and handed over a passion fruit, which the driver accepted without comment. Getting a knife out of the glove compartment, he sliced off one end of the purple fruit's tough skin. Then he handed the knife to Trey, who did the same with one of his own.

The driver slurped up some of the seeds and pulpy fruit, then said, "Yes?"

Trey said, "Ujiji. The house that burned."

The man shook his head. "Nothing left there."

Trey took a moment to eat some of his passion fruit, sour enough to make his eyes half close.

"The house," he said. "Please."

The driver seemed to be considering whether to say no. But it was a quiet day, Trey had hired him for hours—and was paying well—so eventually he sighed, finished sucking out the innards of his fruit, engaged the gears, and pulled away from the curb.

THE FIRE HAD done a thorough job. Where the house had stood, all that remained was sodden rubble. Even the nearby trees had been scorched.

But it didn't really matter. Trey knew what had happened here, or at least most of it.

He stood in the midst of the rubble and breathed in

deeply through his nose. Nothing but the odor of smoke and wet wood.

He turned and walked past the scorched trees to the edge of the clearing. Breathed in again, but smelled only the forest itself.

Somewhere in the distance, a trumpeter hornbill let loose with its raucous call.

He went back to the waiting taxi. Climbed inside, slamming the door behind him. Before he was even settled in his seat, the car had pulled out and was leaving the ruin behind.

"Ujiji Market," Trey said.

The driver grunted.

THEY PASSED BENEATH an avenue of mango trees lining the road. People were clustered in the shade, eating lunch or sleeping or just sitting in twos or threes, talking. Some of them looked up at the passing taxi, but without much interest.

"It's not a market day," the driver said. "No ferries today."

Trey didn't reply. In silence they headed past the mango trees and toward the market, the docks, and the shore of Lake Tanganyika, its surface ridged with whitecaps under a looming sky.

AS THE DRIVER had said, the market was quiet. But not deserted. Many of the stalls and tables were open, selling piles of bananas, stacks of brightly colored textiles, or wooden sculptures of elephants and giraffes.

Trey bought a little carved warthog made out of

rosewood, then walked over to a woman selling *kanga*s, traditional garments made from cotton. She was wrapped in one herself, blue with a pattern of big gold leaves on it.

Trey knew that *kanga*s always came with a *jina*, a kind of motto or aphorism, stitched into the fabric. From a distance, he couldn't make out what hers said.

She was an old woman, somewhere between seventy and eighty, with a wrinkled-nut face and white hair cropped close to her scalp. Her eyes were sharp, though, watching Trey approach. Sharp and suspicious.

He was used to that.

"*Habari*, Mama," he said.

She inclined her head. "*Mzuri.*"

Now he could read her *kanga*'s *jina*. It said, *Majivuno hayafai*: "Greed is never good."

He smiled, and again when she bargained fiercely with him over a red-and-blue *kanga* patterned with fanciful birds and a motto that read, "Humanness is better than material things."

Finally he handed over twenty thousand *shilingi*— about ten dollars, more than the woman had asked—and made a "keep it" gesture when she looked at him with raised eyebrows.

The money disappeared into her *kanga*, and she handed over his purchase. Then, with a sigh, she lit a cigarette and said, "Yes."

Yes. Ask your questions.

Trey said, "Mama, what killed the missionary lady and those other people?"

"Fire," she said at once.

When he didn't reply, argue, push, she watched him.

"Have there been other such fires," he said after a while, "in Ujiji and Kigoma?"

After a pause, she nodded.

"Many?"

She shrugged and made a back-and-forth motion with her hands. "Some here. Some there. Not so many."

She looked up to the sky, where only a pair of vultures circled.

"Not yet," she said.

Trey leaned against her table, looking out at the quiet marketplace before turning back to her. "Have you seen them?" he asked. "The wasps?"

She nodded.

"I have as well."

Her eyes were very dark. "I was . . . afraid."

"Yes. Me, too."

"Yet we both still live," she said.

He looked back at her. "Mama, why burn the house? Why blame the daughter?"

For a long time, many seconds, she didn't answer. Then she said, "They do not want anyone to know what happened."

"They?"

"If people learn about this, who will be blamed?" she said. "We will. Tanzania. Aid will stop. Tourists will no longer come here."

"And everything depends on tourists."

"Yes." She looked down at her pile of *kangas*. "We will go hungry."

Again they were silent for a while. Then Trey said, "The wasps. Have they always been here?"

"The *majizi*? No. Of course not. Four months. Five, maybe." She gestured at the oily lake beyond. "They came across. With the bushmeat and the live animals. The monkeys. And the hunters, too."

Trey took a breath. "What did you call them?"

"*Majizi.*"

Thieves.

Trey said, "What is it they steal?"

But the old woman only shrugged.

Then, as she looked over his shoulder, he saw her face set. "Enough questions," she said. "Go now."

A young man in a military uniform was standing at the other end of the uncrowded market. He was chatting with one of the vendors, laughing.

"Just tell me," Trey said. "The thieves, are they still here?"

"Yes, of course," she said. "They will never leave. But not only here."

"Where else?" Trey asked, although he knew the answer.

She opened her arms wide.

Out there.

In the world.

AS HE'D SAID, Embassy was still at the hospital. He looked around hopefully to see if Trey had brought more food, then shrugged in a resigned way.

"You almost didn't make it in time," he said. "They'll be down in a minute or two."

"Sheila and who else?"

"My boss and this lady from the NGO."

"Les Voyageurs?"

He nodded. Then, for the first time, he reached up and took off his sunglasses. His eyes were very pale blue underneath sparse lashes.

"I told you," he said. "You're not allowed to talk to her."

Trey was quiet.

"Yeah. You can follow her like a lost puppy from here to Dar to Rome, but you can't interact with her till you're at JFK. Ignore that and you'll be grabbed."

Trey didn't even bother to ask on what grounds. When did that ever matter?

Across the lobby, the elevator door opened and four people came out: two more embassy men (one of whose gray hair and more expensive suit indicated his seniority) and a fiftyish woman in an expensive suit. And Sheila Connelly.

Tall, skinny, her skin pale, her short copper-red hair ragged. Dark hollows under her eyes. She was wearing black pants over hiking boots and a cheerful flowered blouse that she'd buttoned wrong.

The woman from Les Voyageurs was holding on to Sheila's arm, guiding her. Both embassy men had seen Trey immediately and were looking at him hard as they shepherded the two women toward the front door.

Trey got to his feet and walked toward the group. Behind him, he heard Embassy sigh and rise as well.

Sheila's gaze shifted his way, but she showed no interest. Her eyes, which were large and an unusual dark blue-green, had a blankness that might have been drug induced or might not.

Trey reached a decision. *Hell.* He hated being forbidden to do something.

"Sheila," he said.

Her gaze sharpened a little as she looked at him.

"I know that larva wasn't from a tumbu fly," he said.

Already the two younger embassy men had him by the arms. But Sheila said, "Wait!" And her voice had so much authority that everyone stopped still.

She took a step closer and stared into his face. Her eyes, irises so dark as to be almost black, seemed enormous in her gaunt face.

"Do you know what it was?" she asked. Her voice was deep, hoarse.

"I think so."

Red spots rose to her ashen cheeks. "Why did my mother die?"

"I don't know yet," Trey said. "But I'll find out."

"Okay," the senior embassy man said. "That's enough."

The two others spun him around. Trey twisted in their grasp. "Wait for me at JFK," he called out as they yanked him toward the door. "Don't leave there without me."

"I won't," she said.

Her voice was little more than a breath, but he heard it.

TWELVE

DURING HIS CAREER, Trey had stalked rare birds, elusive frogs, poisonous snakes, a scorpion nearly the size of a lobster, even a shadowy, half-glimpsed pack of bush dogs in Suriname that he eventually realized was also stalking *him*.

Never a human, though.

Not until now.

HE SAT ON a blue plastic seat amid hordes of tourists in the spacious waiting area of Nyerere Airport in Dar es Salaam. Every once in a while, he'd raise his eyes from the battered paperback he was reading—a novel by Lee Child—and look across at Sheila Connelly.

She was sitting beside the gate for the overnight Emirates Air flight they'd both be taking to Rome. From what Trey could see, she was dressed in the same clothes she'd been wearing earlier in the day.

Beside her was the elegant woman from Les Voyageurs. Her outfit had probably cost more than a typical Tanzanian earned in a year.

On Sheila's other side was another embassy man, one Trey hadn't seen before. He wore a gray suit and a white shirt and a red tie and sunglasses.

Sheila and the Les Voyageurs lady seemed oblivious of Trey's gaze, but not the embassy man. Every time Trey looked in his direction, he turned his head and gazed back, the lenses of his glasses like two distant blacked-out windows.

Trey felt a lot like a stalker.

He didn't like it.

HE KILLED THE time by watching the tourists. Tanzania's lifeblood. The only thing preventing the Serengeti, the Selous, the Ngorongoro, and the other fabled wilderness areas from being plowed under and converted to cattle pasture. The last thing keeping its famous herds of wild game alive.

The tourists on their way into the country wore freshly bought khakis and were excited, anticipatory. The tourists on their way out looked exhausted, bug bitten, and deeply satisfied. They'd seen giraffes and wildebeests and lions and, if they were lucky, leopards and rhinos. Now they could head home, their adventures over, and get back to whatever they did with their lives.

Trey felt a sense of dislocation a lot like sorrow. For a moment he envied those who could look upon the wilderness—or what was left of it—as a temporary break from real life, not life itself. For all the joy he got from hopscotching around the globe, from taking his life in his hands while sitting beside Malcolm in rattletrap prop planes, from trekking through disease-ridden and rebel-haunted forests, sometimes he wished that he could un-learn what he knew.

That he, too, could dress up in adventurer's clothes and choose to be blind.

THE HOURS PASSED. Trey read his book. Lee Child's pro-tagonist, Jack Reacher, was enormous: six-and-a-half feet tall and 250 pounds of pure muscle. He was smart and clever and relentless, but in the end he tended to solve problems with his fists. No one had fists like Reacher's.

Trey thought of his parents. His father had been tall and slender, nonviolent, gentle to the core. His mother, short and compact, had possessed a strength and volatil-ity that made those around her instantly treat her with respect. Trey had never seen her lose her temper, not fully, but he always knew she would be a force to be reckoned with, to be feared, if she did.

Still, neither she nor his father could have survived a single blow administered by any of the villains Jack Reacher shrugged off in a typical day's work, much less by Reacher himself. There was something comforting in that superman's strength, a sense that the world could be measured, controlled. That all it took was smarts and brawn to make things right.

On the other hand, all of Reacher's power would do him no good at all if he happened to run into the kinds of enemies Thomas and Katherine Gilliard had faced in *their* typical day. Their enemies, the villains in their stories, didn't aim at you with a gun or stand toe-to-toe with hands clenched into fists.

They attacked you as you sat eating dinner, as you drove to work, as you talked to a friend, as you made love, as you slept. They bit you or stung you—you might not even notice—or they simply entered your body in a mouthful of food or a breath of air. Then they got into your bloodstream and killed you before you even knew you'd been attacked.

Jack Reacher could make the world right because all of his enemies were human.

And humans were easy.

SHEILA AND HER chaperone were among the first to board. The embassy man watched them as they went through the gate and down the walkway. Then he spun on his heel and came over to Trey. His mouth was a line as he looked down through his sunglasses.

"Not a word to her until you get to JFK," he said.

Trey smiled. "Yeah, I've been told."

"There'll be an air marshal on board. You won't know who he is, but he'll be keeping an eye on you the whole flight."

Trey didn't say anything.

"He's got orders to restrain you if you so much as approach Sheila Connelly. You'll be detained in Rome, and you'll never see her again."

That sounded like a threat, but not necessarily aimed at him. Trey said, "Why do you have your pants in such a bunch over this?"

Of course the embassy man, scowling at the question,

didn't explain. But Trey knew anyway. It was obvious. They—the Tanzanian government, the U.S. Embassy, and Les Voyageurs—wanted her out of the country. They wanted Trey out of the country. And they wanted no complications in the meantime.

He thought about the old woman in the marketplace, her gesture when she'd indicated where the thieves had gone. *Out there. Into the world.*

All the cover-your-ass on earth wouldn't be enough if she was right.

"Don't worry," Trey said to the embassy man. "I'll stay away from her."

The truth this time.

He could wait a few more hours.

TREY WAS ONE of the last to board the 777. Already some of the tired tourists were asleep under mounds of blankets, while others were frowning at their iPads or getting ready to watch movies on their seatback screens. The atmosphere had a festive feel, as was typical of the onset of these long flights. A "we're all in this together" vibe that would last for a while, until everyone started getting bored and cranky.

Trey's seat was on the aisle about halfway down the plane. He looked back and saw Sheila leaning against a window near the back, her pale face peaceful in sleep. Her chaperone, sitting next to her on the aisle, watched Trey, an unreadable expression on her face. He raised his hands in a placatory gesture, and after a moment she nodded.

Trey took another quick look around.

It took him about fifteen seconds to identify two plain-clothes air marshals, one male, one female. The way they peeked at him reminded him of meerkats popping up from their burrows.

He made sure not to let the marshals know they'd been spotted. He didn't want them to feel bad.

TREY HATED SLEEP. Hated how much time it sucked up that could be better spent doing more productive things. Hated how it eventually won every battle, no matter how strong you were, no matter how hard you fought it.

He hated being . . . *away*.

But there was one thing he'd learned after hundreds of flights: If you didn't sleep on airplanes, you were an idiot. Whatever else you could do on a plane, you could do better almost anywhere else. Sleep was the most productive thing you could get out of the way while strapped to a seat.

So on both flights, all the way till the announcement came of their final approach to JFK, Trey read his book and ate airplane food, but mostly he slept. Knowing that when they arrived, and the important work began, he'd be ready.

HE GOT OFF the airplane in New York before Sheila and her chaperone. Waited by the gate as the hordes made their way past, faces bleached gray by the barren lights of the terminal. It was only eleven at night here, but most of these travelers' bodies were stuck in the timeless limbo of jet lag.

The two women finally came through the door. Sheila's face was slack, but her eyes were alert. Beside her, despite her expensive clothes, the older woman just looked worn out.

They came up to Trey. He said to Sheila, "I almost thought they'd spirit you away. Make you disappear."

The chaperone straightened and stared at him. "Are you nuts?" she said, her incredulity sounding funny expressed in such a crisp, cultured tone. "I'm handing her over to you, and now I'm *done*."

She brushed her hands together, the age-old gesture of dismissal. "One night in the airport hotel for me, and back home tomorrow."

Then, unexpectedly, she switched her gaze to Sheila, and her expression softened. "Are you sure of your decision, dear?" She looked back at Trey. "We were supposed to be met by someone from the New York office, but she didn't want to."

"I'm sure," Sheila said. "You can go."

The woman looked at Trey. Her expression said, *Are you sure?*

No, Trey wasn't. But he knew he had no choice. He nodded.

"Thank you," she said.

Which really meant, *Better you than me, pal.*

THE EX-CHAPERONE WAS barely out of earshot, her heels clicking away down the quiet terminal, when Sheila said to Trey, "Tell me what it was."

He reached into his pocket and pulled out a copy of Jack's drawing.

Sheila stared down at it. "You've seen these?"

Trey nodded.

"Where?"

"In southern Senegal."

He watched her take in the new information. It seemed she hadn't been completely undone by her days of confinement, by exhaustion and grief. He shouldn't have been surprised: You had to be strong to work with ill and dying refugees.

"That's where they're native?" she asked.

"We think so."

She blinked. "Who is 'we'?"

Trey looked around, saw a café still open at the far end of the terminal. He pointed to it and said, "Let's sit, and I'll tell you what I know."

First at the café and then, when it closed, on adjacent seats at a deserted gate, they talked. By the time they were done, it made no sense to try to find her a hotel room.

"People coming through the city stay in my place all the time," he said.

Her gaze was unblinking. "'People'?"

"Folks I've met along the way. Scientists. Field researchers. Aid workers. People like you who have business here but can't afford the rates."

"People like me," she said.

Trey waited.

"Okay." She paused. "Thank you."

Her acquiescence came a little quicker than he'd expected. He wondered whether it was because she already trusted him or whether she didn't much care whether he was a friend or a psychopath.

He thought she hadn't quite decided, not yet, whether she had anything left to lose.

THIRTEEN

Aboard the MV Atlas

HIS NAME WAS Arjen. He was tall, at least a foot taller than Mariama, and as skinny as a fig sapling, with big knotty hands and a prominent Adam's apple that moved up and down when he laughed. Which he did often.

And a thin, bony Scandinavian face that lit up whenever he saw her. Green-blue eyes that glinted with amusement as he told tall tales of his years aboard freighters like the *Atlas*. Stories of sea monsters, ancient as dinosaurs, rising from the calm surface of the horse latitudes at dawn. Of a wooden house floating a hundred miles from the mouth of the Amazon River, a family of monkeys clinging to its roof. Of a flying saucer hovering over Hong Kong harbor, illuminating thousands of upturned faces on the boats below before ascending and disappearing at unimaginable speed.

Laughing when Mariama mocked him. Saying, in his thick and joyful accent, "Yes, you doubt me. But can you *prove* I am lying?"

Arjen, the *Atlas*'s first officer, knocking on Mariama's

cabin door when his shift was over. Sometimes this was at 4:00 A.M., but Mariama was always waiting for him.

Sweet Arjen. Doomed, she thought, like all those others who spent their lives on ships like the *Atlas*.

The coal mine's canaries.

WHEN HER HOSTS in Fuerteventura told her about the next stage of her journey, Mariama sighed and shrugged.

"The slow boat," she said.

But she wasn't surprised. With no passport, she could not fly. When you couldn't fly, and governments knew who you were, the world became a huge place once again. A huge place where you had to move slowly, quietly, to avoid notice.

For enough money, though, you could always find a freighter that would take you aboard. No passport necessary, and entry to any of a hundred port cities. It was hardly even a risk. No one would be paying attention.

Mariama's hosts chose the MV *Atlas*. They knew the captain, knew that he and the crew would look the other way. They'd done it many times before.

But it could just as easily have been another ship. The port of Las Palmas, where Mariama embarked, was overrun with freighters. At least half would cross the Panama Canal, the next step on Mariama's slow journey.

And then? As the ship made its transit across the Atlantic, and she laughed with Arjen, and shared her bed with him, and talked with the other passengers aboard the *Atlas*, Mariama allowed herself to dream.

To dream of cold, and the safety cold could bring.

* * *

"VALPARAISO," ARJEN SAID to her one night, close to dawn. He stretched in her little bed, years of experience somehow allowing him to lie comfortably without crowding her. Too much.

She wasn't sure she'd heard of it.

"In Chile. A beautiful city on the Pacific Ocean. All hills. Staircases and outdoor elevators and these little trains that take you up and down."

He grinned in the dim light that came through the porthole of her cabin. "And the *curanto*! The best seafood stew you will ever eat."

"Where is it?" she asked.

"I told you. In Chile."

"No. I mean the latitude."

He turned his head to look at her across the pillow. "Thirty-three degrees south, more or less."

"Not far enough."

Not cold enough.

Arjen stayed silent for a few moments. Mariama was still, feeling the motion of the boat across the Atlantic's long swells as a pull on her bones. The first night or two, the unceasing movement had bothered her, but now she only noticed it in quiet moments like this.

Then he propped himself up on his elbow. "Every day," he said, "you walk the decks, even going places you should not. Some of the crew believe you are a terrorist, but I don't think so."

"Thank you," Mariama said.

"Me, I just think you are strange."

She smiled. "Thank you very much."

But now his expression was serious. "When you walk, Mariama," he said, "what are you afraid of?"

She felt her chin lift. "I am afraid of nothing."

He didn't smile. "All right. Then what are you searching for?"

For a long time she just looked into his eyes. Then, deciding, she reached out and took his rough, callused hand in both of hers.

"Listen to me," she said.

WHEN SHE WAS done, he was silent for a long time. Then he said, "I have seen birds, rats, spiders, snakes on board. But never one of these—"

"We call them thieves."

"No. Nor smelled them."

Mariama sighed. "Not yet."

"But I will?"

"I don't know," she said. "Maybe not on this ship, but others, certainly. Airplanes, cars. Any place they can hide."

"This is happening already?" he asked. "Now?"

She said, "Oh, yes." Then paused. "I am standing still, and they are not."

"But you know of a way to stop them?"

She was silent.

He thought for a while. Finally he said, "Valparaiso. I know why you asked where it is."

She waited.

"You wondered if you would be safe there, because it is cold. Those . . . thieves could not live there."

Mariama shook her head. "No. Not there. It would need to be farther south."

"Magallanes?" he said. "Tierra del Fuego?"

She did not reply.

Again he thought. Then he said, "Would you do this? Know what you know, and run away?"

Again Mariama was silent.

Gatun Locks, Panama

SHE SMELLED IT soon after she stepped off the ship. Drew in a single breath and felt her heart flip inside her chest.

Arjen was there, walking her past the Customs officials who met every ship, but who also looked the other way if provided with the proper inducement. The *Atlas* was in dock for two days, maybe three, and his plan was to enjoy all the delights Panama City offered for every minute he was free, starting immediately. He'd asked Mariama to come along, but hadn't seemed either surprised or disappointed when she'd smiled and shaken her head.

Now he was looking at the expression on her face. "What?"

She breathed in again, then said, "Come with me."

They walked past the visitors' center, the big concrete-and-glass building that overlooked the locks, the carts and trucks selling candy and Coca-Cola and batteries for your camera. Beyond lay a row of ramshackle stone and wood buildings that, like thousands of others throughout the Canal Zone, had belonged to the Americans before they handed over control of the canal to the Panamanians in 1999.

Mariama told Arjen to stay where he was, then walked up to one building, another, a third. She rattled doorknobs, looked inside when the doors were unlocked, stood still and breathed in.

At the sixth building she tried, a one-story stone structure little larger than a shed, she saw what she knew she'd find. Closing the door again, she gestured for Arjen to join her.

"Stay beside me," she said as he came up.

She swung the door open. Inside were jugs of cleaning fluid, bottles of bleach, mops, brooms. The bitter odor she'd detected was stronger, making Arjen wrinkle his nose.

"There," she said.

The thief moved forward, out of the shadow and into the rectangle of sunlight that splashed through the open door. Seeing it, Arjen cursed.

Mariama saw at once that there was something wrong with it. With its wings, which twitched and whirred but did not lift it off the concrete floor.

The injured thief crawled toward them. Mariama knew it could have been close to death, missing half of its body, and it still would never think to hide. Thieves attacked.

Its head was tilted, and its shining green eyes were focused on Arjen. She sensed his anxiety, his desire to run, and did not blame him for it. There was something about the intensity of a thief's gaze that terrified even the bravest men.

But Arjen stood his ground.

When it was about two feet away from him, it reared up on its long legs like a demonic spider. Arjen gave a sudden gasp, as if awakening from a daze. He took one quick step forward, shifted his weight onto his left leg, and lifted his right boot into the air.

The wasp's eyes were like multifaceted mirrors, but somehow they still conveyed . . . fearlessness. Rage.

Arjen brought his boot down.

In the last instant, he altered his aim. The wasp's long body was the obvious target, but all its venomous intelligence seemed to radiate from the creature's head. So it was the head he crushed with his heel.

His foot hit the stone floor with a crack. Instantly the bitter odor intensified a thousandfold. Mariama heard Arjen gag, but again he held his ground. When he lifted his foot, they looked down at the black-and-green pulp smeared across the floor.

Beside the remains of the wasp's head, the nearly intact body writhed, first on its belly, then its back. The long black legs stretched and twitched, grasping at air. The abdomen pulsed, and as they watched, the needlelike white stinger emerged from its tip, then withdrew, leaving a drop of black liquid gleaming like an evil jewel on the floor.

"Let's go," Mariama said.

Arjen didn't move. She had to say it again, and then put a hand on his arm, before he allowed himself to be led away.

OUTSIDE HE SPENT more time than he needed scraping the bottom of his shoe in the dirt. "The smell is all over me," he said.

"It just seems that way," she told him. "It will fade, I promise."

Eventually he straightened and looked at her. His face was pale. "You were not afraid," he said.

Mariama didn't reply.

"You said you did not fear anything, and you were telling the truth."

She made a gesture of frustration with her hands. "I am standing still," she said. "And soon they will be everywhere."

Arjen didn't seem to absorb what she was saying. Again he stared at the shed's closed door. "That thing," he said, "it wanted to kill me."

Mariama laughed. He gave her a surprised, nearly offended look.

"Yes," she said. "Of course it wanted to kill you. I told you. That's what the thieves do."

Then her amusement ebbed.

"One of the things they do," she said.

AS THEY PARTED, he asked, "You need a place to stay?"

She nodded.

"For how long?"

A shrug. "A few days."

Every stop just another way station.

His eyes had cleared, though his gaze was still troubled. "And when you move on, will you be heading south like you said? To Magallanes? Tierra del Fuego?"

She shook her head. "No. That was just a dream. I have a job I must do."

"You alone?"

Mariama closed her eyes for a moment.

"I hope not," she said.

FOURTEEN

FIVE MINUTES AFTER they pulled away from the airport, Sheila fell asleep in the taxi. Trey had to shake her awake when they reached his apartment, and though her eyes were open he had to keep his hand on her arm to make sure she didn't crash into any walls.

Most visitors who stayed at Trey's place used the sofa, but he let her take his bed. He knew at least some of what she was going through. Knew that it was more than jet lag. What she was seeking, embracing, wasn't sleep, but freedom from consciousness, and the comforts of a bed might help, at least a little.

He remembered his own experiences too clearly. It had felt like he'd slept for days after his parents died. But he always woke up, which was a blessing and a curse.

The blessing was that for an instant or—if you were very lucky—a few, you did not know who you were or what had happened to you. The curse, of course, was that you remembered, and then had hours to wait until you could sleep and forget again.

There were other alternatives, of course. Trey had never been tempted to go to sleep after making sure he wouldn't awaken, but he could understand why others were. He'd known a few over the years, people who craved the kind of timeless freedom the waking life could never provide.

He could understand it, but not sympathize with it, not much. Humans were the only species with the inclination to commit suicide, and he thought it was a strange evolutionary quirk. A herd that culled itself.

Sitting at his table, wide awake, Trey wondered what kind of person Sheila was.

HE SHOWERED, PUT on clean clothes, stayed up the rest of the night. He'd had enough sleep on the airplanes.

Every once in a while he stood to stretch and to check on Sheila. Though she never seemed to change position, he could see the lightweight sheet that covered her rising and falling.

It was strange, having her in his apartment. Strange having anyone there. Most visitors used it when he was on the road. It was little more than a hotel to them, and to him, too.

HE WOKE HER at eight. But instead of retreating beneath the covers, trying to hold on to oblivion, as he'd expected, she merely opened her eyes and looked at him. Her eyes, that strange blue-green, were at once clear, alert, though her face was so gaunt that the tendons along her jaw stood out. The hollows under her eyes were bruises.

She sat up. "We'll go see your friend at the museum." Then, looking down at the dirty, rumpled clothes she'd slept in: "Soon as I have a shower."

Trey nodded. "Okay." Then, "There's coffee."

He hesitated. What else? He had little experience as a caretaker, and no particular desire to learn how.

"We'll stop for something to eat on the way," he said finally.

Sheila's mouth compressed. "I'm not hungry."

He suppressed an unexpected flash of anger, though from her expression it must have shown on his face. "What's the first rule for you guys, the aid workers in the refugee camps?" he asked.

She stared at him but didn't answer.

"Stay healthy, right? Something like that? Stay hydrated and well nourished." He stood and walked to the bedroom door, then turned back to her. "Otherwise you'll just get sick, too. Die. Be of no use to anyone, only make more work for the others. Right?"

Sheila's eyes were still on his. Her face was stone. Trey thought he might not be grading out to an A in this caregiving thing, but he didn't much care.

"We have a lot of work ahead," he said. "Jack and me. With you, if you want, or without. But the one thing you're not going to do is slow us down. You want to walk away, do as you please. Prove a point. Starve yourself. You want to help, then we'll stop to eat on the way."

Before she could say anything, he pointed. "The shower's that way," he said and went back to the living room.

*   *   *

SHE EMERGED FIFTEEN minutes later, scrubbed, her hair in place, the application of soap and shampoo only making her look more fragile and unhealthy. Trey felt a moment's regret for his sharp words, but only a moment.

"Coffee's over there," he said.

She nodded, went to the coffeemaker, and poured herself a mug.

"Cream?" he said. "Sugar?"

"This is fine."

Taking a sip, she looked around the apartment. "None of this looks familiar. Guess I didn't notice much on my way in last night."

"Yeah. Hard to see much with your eyes closed."

She glanced into his face, away. Her expression softened, and suddenly she seemed almost embarrassed.

"Well," she said, "you know . . . all this? Thanks."

Trey said, "You're welcome."

After a moment, she walked over to the bookshelves that lined the interior walls. The mystery stories that his father had read almost exclusively (the last chapter invariably first, because he didn't like surprises). The complete collections of Dickens and Twain that his mother had inherited from her mother. And Trey's own contribution: row upon row of nature books, travel books, field guides, and explorers' and scientists' memoirs.

Sheila picked up an Inuit sculpture of a grizzly bear carved from green serpentine, looked at it, put it down. "Your place," she said. "It's nice."

Something in her tone caused Trey to say, almost without realizing, "It belonged to my parents."

"Yeah?" She looked over at him. "Where do they live now?"

It was a casual question, but he couldn't mask his reaction, the tightening of the skin across his cheekbones. And she noticed.

"They died," he said.

Her hand went to her mouth. "Oh! I'm sorry."

"It was a long time ago."

She nodded. Then he saw something in her face change. "Wait," she said.

Trey sighed. He hated when this happened.

"You're *that* Trey Gilliard."

"Never met another one," he said, as he had before.

"The doctor's son."

"Yes."

She looked at him. He held her gaze, waiting. Knowing what she'd say.

The repertoire was limited. People always said one meaningless—or even cruel—thing or another. Some said, *Your father was a real hero.* Others, *What was your mother thinking? I'd never take risks like that if I had kids.*

Trey had a gracious, meaningless response to each. He never rose to the bait.

But Sheila said, "Do you ever get over feeling like an orphan?"

After a long pause, he shook his head.

JACK WAS WAITING impatiently when they walked into his office. Jaw set, beard bristling, he was standing behind his desk, and Trey could see that he already had his pencils and sketch pad ready.

He'd probably been standing like that, waiting in that exact position to make sure they saw and felt guilty, for an hour.

"You ready?" he said. "Or maybe you want to go to a movie first."

Sheila didn't seem to be listening. She was looking around the office, taking in the ramshackle furniture, piles of old books, and Jack's collection of wasp-themed junk.

"Cool," she said. Then, "I got stung sixteen times before I was twelve years old."

Jack blinked, then looked at her with something approaching respect. "Thirty-seven times by the age of ten," he said. "But thirteen of them came at one time."

Sheila walked to the streaked windows and looked out at the park. "I used to love this museum," she said, as quietly as if she were speaking to herself. "Especially the Hall of African Mammals."

"You from New York?" Jack asked.

When he met someone new, Jack usually had one polite question in him before he got impatient. Trey thought this was probably it.

Still looking out the window, Sheila shook her head. "When I was little, we lived in Boston. After that, Tanzania."

She paused. "Shit," she said. "Where do I live now?"

"I heard Trey's place." Jack's eyes gleamed. "Knowing him like I do, I'm sure he'll welcome you there for as long as you need. Stay a year!"

Both Trey and Sheila looked at him, and he laughed. "Now that we've settled *that*," he went on, "can we get to work?" He looked down at his pad and pencils. "I fucking hate a blank piece of paper."

As Sheila sat down across the desk from him, he looked at her out of the corner of his eye. "Heard about your mom," he said. "Sorry."

Sheila said, "Thank you, Jack."

SHE DESCRIBED THE larva she'd extracted and Jack scratched away with his pencils and erased and asked questions. Trey did not look. He wanted to see it fresh, complete, not as a work in progress.

While they worked, he sat in an armchair across the room. Taking an old book from the pile he'd gathered, he paged through another tale of adventure, discovery, and high tea among the itinerant aristocracy of nineteenth-century Europe.

He found descriptions of everything from white ants to elephants, but nothing that even resembled the wasps he'd seen.

As he put the book down, a thought struck him immobile for a moment. Something he'd forgotten to mention to either of them.

"A woman I talked to called the wasps *majizi*," he said. "Thieves."

"What woman?" Jack asked.

"A vendor at Ujiji Market."

"And she sounded like she knew what she was talking about?"

Trey nodded. "Yeah. She'd seen them."

"Huh." Jack pulled at his beard. "Thieves. Interesting. So what do they steal?"

The question Trey had asked the old woman, who hadn't answered.

"Maybe . . ." Sheila sounded unsure. "I think maybe . . . your awareness."

They looked at her. Color rose to her pale cheeks, but she didn't waver. "My mother couldn't recognize that she'd been"—a breath—"parasitized. Even when she was looking right at the spot where the larva was, she didn't seem to see it."

There was silence as they all thought this through. Then Jack gave a shake of his head as strong as a wet dog's. "Wait. You're saying that these wasp larvae can . . . *disguise* themselves? Cloud men's minds?"

Sheila didn't answer.

"Like *stealth babies*?"

Sheila's expression hardened. "I'm just telling you what I saw."

"Could it be," Trey said, speaking carefully, "that you're putting two different things together? Maybe your mother had something else, a second condition, that prevented her from seeing clearly."

"You mean like a stroke?" Sheila was shaking her head. "I wondered about that, but I'd seen no other signs. We were together for hours. No symptoms of stroke. Just . . ." Her certainty seemed to vanish. "Just that she didn't seem to understand she'd been infected."

Even Jack looked uncomfortable with the direction the conversation was taking. "A stroke might also help explain why she—passed away so suddenly."

Again Sheila shook her head. A muscle in her jaw jumped.

"All we know for sure," Trey said, "is that we don't know enough."

"You're right, Yoda." Jack picked up the half-finished drawing and shook it. "So let's get this done with."

* * *

FIFTEEN MINUTES LATER Trey heard Sheila say, "Yeah. That's it."

He looked up just as Jack lifted the drawing so he could see it.

Trey looked at the elongated white body, eyes like pearls, black mandibles. "There's no reason to believe that's *not* the larva of what I saw," he said.

"Yeah." Jack scowled. "You know what fucking sucks? I'm the only one sitting here who actually gives a damn about wasps. And I'm also the only one who's never seen one of these guys in the flesh—larva *or* adult."

Sheila sighed.

"I wish it had been you," she said, "instead of me."

THEY SHOWED SHEILA the poster Jack had e-mailed around the world. "Any response yet?" Trey asked.

Jack said, "No. Just mostly people asking if I missed April Fool's Day."

For a moment he looked disconsolate, but then his face brightened. "But it's early yet. Most of the people likely to see these beasts aren't spending all their time on the Internet. They'll get to it."

He walked over to a cluttered table in the corner of the room beside the windows. "Meanwhile: Look!"

They looked. He was holding a multicolored map of the world mounted on corkboard. Poster sized, at least three feet by two. Big enough to illustrate all the world's countries and plenty of cities and geographic landmarks.

He pointed at a red pushpin stuck into the Casamance area of Senegal. As they watched, he moved a poster of the movie *The Wasp Woman* off the wall and hung the map there instead. Then he stuck a second red pin into western Tanzania, right at the edge of Lake Tanganyika.

"The story thus far," he said.

Sheila said, "Two pins."

Trey thought again about the old woman, the gesture she'd made that had encompassed the whole world.

"Just wait," he said.

FIFTEEN

Canal Zone, Panama

IT WAS A dance.

That was what Mariama decided. A long, involved dance, with everyone following the steps that had been assigned to them. Even Mariama herself.

Maybe Mariama especially. She was learning that you could be aware of the dance and still be trapped by your role in it.

By now, every stage of her journey here, from the surreal trip on the fishing boat all the way through her nights with Arjen aboard the freighter, seemed as if it had been preordained. Choreographed. All her forward movement, all her plans, all her cleverness and good fortune, seeming to exist at the whim of some master puppeteer she could not even visualize, much less see.

Standing in the fat man's office, Mariama wondered: Is this how the dreaming ones feel?

She didn't know. No one had figured out how to ask them.

* * *

THE FAT MAN'S name was Bannerjee. He looked at her across the desk and said, "And why should I help you?"

Mariama suppressed a sigh. Arjen had sent her here, telling her that this Bannerjee was the best in the Canal Zone if you needed a passport. He'd also told her to watch out for him, this man. She hadn't needed to be warned.

"Because I can pay," she said.

He appeared to think about it. Yet she knew that Arjen had gotten word to him as well. He had been expecting her.

He would do what she wanted, when they'd completed their portion of the dance.

"Your friend," he said now, "he has told you that I am the best."

"How much?" She kept her eyes on his. "For the best?"

"Two thousand."

"And I will get . . . ?"

"A Panamanian passport and a valid visa to the United States. They will get you into New York. After that—" He shrugged and pooched out his lips, as if to say, *You will no longer be my problem.*

"Fifteen hundred," Mariama said.

They settled on seventeen, five hundred now and the rest when she got the passport. She retrieved the cash from her money belt, counted it out, and handed it across the desk. Bannerjee counted it for himself, then bent over and put it in a safe or lockbox somewhere near his feet.

In a back room furnished only with a wooden chair and a big camera, he posed her against a white wall and took her picture. "Don't smile," he said before pressing the button. "Since September eleventh, it makes them suspicious when they see people smiling in their passport pictures."

Mariama wondered if this was so, and why, but didn't question it. She didn't feel like smiling anyway.

"When do I come back?" she asked.

"You don't," he said at once.

"Then where?"

"I will send someone to deliver it in three days. Just tell me where you are staying."

She told him.

He blinked but didn't comment, saying only, "Have the rest of the money ready."

She was staying in a place Arjen had told her about, a stone building that had once been a one-room school-house built and used by the Americans. It was part of a subdivision of structures that had boasted houses, shops, and restaurants, but now contained only ruins.

Although it was only about fifteen miles from downtown, when you were there you felt a thousand miles from anywhere. The hum of distant traffic was often obscured by the calls of crickets or the wind rattling through the empty buildings.

In the schoolhouse itself, there were still blackboards and the smells of chalk dust and the sweat of children. Spiders in the corners and mice squeaking at night. But a cot, too, and a functioning well outside, not far from the door.

More than Mariama had expected.

Best of all, the windows had long since been bricked up. The only way in and out was through a reinforced steel door. The outside walls were crumbling, leaving chunks of stone scattered across the ground. But the long, slow ruin still had a ways to go: The interior walls still stood. There was no way in through the cracks, not even for something small and clever and determined.

With care, she could be safe there.

Safe as you could be anywhere. Each night, she checked every inch of her windowless chamber, her schoolhouse tomb. And then lay sleepless for hours on the sagging cot. Thinking. Planning.

When she was outside, she watched the skies. But saw, heard, smelled no sign of them at all.

She knew this meant nothing. Less than nothing. But she did it anyway.

TREY GILLIARD WAS so near. It was infuriating. She could almost reach up from the Canal Zone and touch him in New York City. Almost shout loud enough for him to hear her.

But not close enough. And she couldn't risk contacting him from here.

No one knew she was in Panama, she was almost sure of it. It was possible that the government of Senegal did not even know that she'd left the country.

But they hadn't forgotten who she was and what she knew. And since they'd expelled Trey, too, they must be aware of what he knew as well.

Someone would be watching him, she was certain of that. Listening in on his calls, reading his e-mails. It was legal for the government to do that in the United States these days, or so she'd heard.

No, it wasn't worth the risk. The message she'd sent him from the Canary Islands had been her one shot.

Had he understood?

Phone calls, e-mails, they were close to useless now anyway. She needed to see him. Needed to be in the same room with him, telling him what he didn't know. Showing him. In person.

The three days she had to wait for her passport felt like years.

ON THE SECOND day, she had a revelation. She couldn't risk calling Trey, but she could learn more about him.

She went into town, bought an international phone card, and paid for private access to a phone in a downtown real-estate office whose owner was on vacation. Alberto Castro would never know she'd been there, and no one else would think to be listening in on Castro's line.

She sat at his big steel desk. Alongside piles of paper sat a photograph of a cheerful-looking young man with a serious-faced wife and two smiling children, a girl of about ten and a boy of perhaps seven.

Mariama felt an unexpected jolt of something like sorrow. She wasn't sure what caused it. Maybe it was the fact that she would never have a life like the Castros'.

Or maybe it was that the Castros' dream of a life would too soon come to an end.

Swiveling around in her chair, Mariama picked up the phone and dialed the international operator. When someone picked up, she said, "Rockefeller University in New York City, please."

Mariama had never visited Rockefeller University or even seen a picture of it. She imagined a gigantic apartment building filled with geniuses and their technology.

Winners of the Nobel Prize. Inventors of new machines to replace failing organs, of new medicines, of new ways of looking at the world.

The sort of people who would laugh at the health clinic Mariama's father ran in the Casamance.

To the receptionist she said, "Elena Stavros's office, please."

Elena Stavros, the one person in the building full of geniuses Mariama knew wouldn't scoff at her.

MARIAMA AND ELENA had met just once, two years earlier, at a conference in Cape Town, South Africa. Mariama had attended with her father, back when they were allowed to travel.

Mariama remembered Elena Stavros vividly. How could she not? Elena, a microbiologist, was small, like Mariama, and just a few years older, but in all other ways so different that people had laughed when they saw the two together.

Mariama was self-contained and slow to smile, with a quiet voice and a face whose expressions were hard to read. Elena, on the other hand, flaunted a great mass of black hair, expressive eyes, and a face that always seemed to be gripped by one rampant emotion or another.

She was also loud. In fact, she was so loud that three times during symposia and panel discussions she'd been warned to keep her voice down.

Somehow the two of them had decided they liked each other. They'd spent hours one night sharing experiences and memories, and among the topics of conversation they'd touched upon was Trey Gilliard.

Mariama had mentioned that the International Conservation Trust was planning a months-long mission in the Casamance rain forest. Elena had blinked and said, "Hah! That means you'll meet Trey. Lucky you!" She'd paused. "Unless they've gotten sick of him by now and fired his ass."

Elena's face had reddened as she spoke, something Mariama had pretended not to notice. She'd just said, "How do you know him?"

"Oh, our paths have crossed." Then, as if acknowledging her discomposure: "He's absolutely brilliant about nature. With people? Not so much."

Later, as the future's path became inexorably clear, Mariama had thought of those words often. Brilliant with nature, that was important. She didn't care how he was with people.

"When you see him, tell him I said hi." Then Elena's gaze had sharpened. "And also tell him that the door to room 33 is shut."

Mariama had promised. But by the time Trey had finally shown up in Senegal, ICT's mission delayed again and again, Mariama had become persona non grata, warned to stay far away from all visitors.

The times she'd managed to get close to Trey, they hadn't had the chance to exchange pleasantries, jokes, or cryptic references to the past.

Or anything important, either.

"STAVROS," THE VOICE on the other end of the line said. "Who is this?"

Her voice instantly familiar. Mariama found herself

smiling. "My name is Mariama Honso," she said. "From Senegal. We met in Cape Town. Do you remember me?"

There was a brief pause. Then the voice came again, louder. "Mariama! For God's sake. Of course I do! The lion kill!"

Mariama remembered the lion kill. It had been on a field trip to Kruger National Park and the victim had been a zebra.

"Where are you?" Elena went on. "Here? In the city? Let's get dinner. There's this great Ethiopian place—wait, do you like African food?"

Mariama laughed. It was amazing she could still laugh.

"I'm not in the city," she said. "Not yet. Soon, though, and then—dinner."

"But I'm hungry for injera bread *now*." Elena's sigh came down the line. "Okay. Deal. Why are you calling?"

"I have a question."

"Shoot."

"Are you still in touch with Trey Gilliard?"

Elena was silent for a few moments. Then she said, "No. Not recently." She made a sound that might have been a laugh. "People don't stay in Trey's life for very long, you know. But I do keep an eye on him from afar."

"You do?"

"When I can. God knows why."

Mariama took a breath. "Do you know if he's there? In New York?"

"To the best of my knowledge." A pause. "I heard he was in Tanzania recently, but I think he's around again. Him and some woman he met there."

Mariama felt something loosen inside her chest. This was good. This was better than she could have prayed for.

Elena was saying, "That's not typical of Trey. He doesn't often bring anyone home."

When Mariama didn't speak, Elena laughed. "Sweetie, why do you want him?"

Mariama said, "I'll tell you when I see you."

"You want me to give him a call, tell him you're coming to town?"

Mariama kept her voice calm. "No, thank you. I'll get in touch with him myself."

When it's time.

Once she hung up, Mariama sat for a while in the unfamiliar office, beside the photograph of a family she would never meet.

She'd taken a risk, but it had been worth it.

Maybe, just maybe, there was still a chance.

SIXTEEN

ONE MAN CAME through the door. She had expected two at least.

They'd underestimated her, as people always did. Thought she was merely a girl, and therefore easily handled.

And thank the gods they had, because one man was almost more than enough. She'd been so consumed with her plans that she'd lost some of her instincts, some of her alertness.

The knock on the schoolhouse door came when she expected it. But as soon as she unlocked the door, it swung open so violently that she didn't get out of the way in time. Next thing she knew, she was on her knees on the floor, dazed, looking up at the man who came striding in.

He was a brute, a huge white man with a scowling face and thick legs and bare arms like slabs. Quick on his feet, though, grabbing the front of her blouse and yanking her up, his left hand already under the shirt and against her bare skin.

When she tried to knee him in the groin, he turned his hips just far enough to take the blow on his thigh. If it hurt him, he showed no sign.

He wasn't reaching for her body. She heard the latch of her money belt click. A moment later, he'd tossed her across the room as effortlessly as she might have tossed a cushion.

Waking up finally, she protected her head when she crashed onto the stone floor near the cot. Still, she lay there, breathless, for long seconds while he inspected what was inside the belt's zippered compartment.

When she struggled to her feet, he pointed at her, a casual warning to stay still. He didn't seem to be paying much attention to her, but she knew how quickly he would respond if she went for him.

Not that it mattered. She barely was able to get enough air into her lungs to say, "My passport—"

"Shut up," he said.

He was holding a big wad of bills in one thick hand. Almost all her money.

"Here's what happens," he went on. His accent was American. Not all of them had gone home.

"I'll take this," he said. "You want the passport, you find another thousand. Give it to my boss, and you can have your passport."

"But how—"

He shrugged. His face rearranged itself into something that appeared to be a grin. "Who cares? Fuck for it, kill for it, whatever you need to do. But the price is another thousand. You don't have a choice."

Eyes still on her face, he jammed the bills into his pocket, tossed the belt onto the floor. Then his gaze dropped a little and he focused on something.

"That, too," he said.

For an instant Mariama thought again that he meant her body. Then she realized it was her silver necklace, her locket, that had captured his attention.

"Give," he said, holding out a beefy palm.

Mariama shook her head.

He wasn't much for explaining himself or asking twice. She was learning that. He came across the room at her, again much faster than she'd anticipated, his hand grabbing for the chain, clearly not caring if he yanked her head off with it.

He was fast, but this time she was faster. His hand had not yet reached her neck when she brought up a chunk of rock that had come from the crumbling wall outside. One of several she'd brought in and hidden.

She swung her arm in a short arc and banged the stone against his temple. That stopped him in his tracks, but he didn't go down. Instead, his face took on a thoughtful expression, his eyes suddenly vague. She could feel the tips of the fingers on his outstretched right hand brushing her neck and the links of the silver chain.

She hit him again, harder, and this time he did fall. Onto his knees, at first, and then all the way, toppling onto his side. His eyes closed.

She studied him for a few moments, waiting to see if he would awake and leap at her, whether he might be pretending. But he didn't seem like the kind to engage in subterfuge. He was unconscious.

There was already a huge purple bruise on his swollen

forehead, and some blood seeped out of the abrasions where the rough stone had broken the skin. Nothing gushing, though. Good.

Kneeling over him, she searched his pockets. She took back the money he'd stolen from her, but found nothing else. No wallet, no identification, no money of his own.

There was one thing: a knife with a spring-driven folding blade. Mariama tested it a couple of times, pushing the button that released the blade and folding it back in again. Then she slipped it into her pocket.

When she was done, she walked over to the door, which was still open, and looked out. Heard no one. Light pollution from Panama City brightened the western sky, and a half-moon and smeary stars cast some light on the falling-down buildings and patchy brush of the old subdivision. Somewhere out in the darkness, a dog or coyote yapped.

His car was parked out front. She knew the keys must be in it. And why not? He'd assumed that he would be the only one going in, the only one coming out.

Returning to the fallen man, she took both his wrists in her hands, pulled his arms over his head, and dragged him to the door. He snorted and once his right foot kicked, setting her heart racing, but he didn't awake.

It was hard work. She was dripping with sweat well before they reached the spot she'd chosen. Behind a pile of rubble a hundred feet from the school, a spot that no one would likely ever visit, but for the dogs and carrion birds and insects.

When she had him lying there, illuminated only by the moonlight, she paused to catch her breath. Then she squatted beside him and reached out with both hands.

One pinched his nose shut while the other covered his mouth.

He fought back. Or, rather, his body did, flailing its arms and kicking its legs. But the organizing principle, the conscious mind that would have resisted her in some specific way, that would have gone for her eyes or her throat in return . . . that was missing.

All that was left was the organism's inherent desire to live. And that wasn't enough.

Soon his movements grew weaker, more sporadic. Then they ceased entirely. When she was sure, she stood one last time, stretched her weary arms, turned away, and walked over to his car.

In the past, she might have spared his life. Tied him up and later, when she was safe, told someone where he was.

But they were living in a new world, one that permitted no unnecessary risks.

SHE HELD THE edge of the blade against Mr. Bannerjee's neck. His mouth opened and some saliva dropped out of it and onto his desk.

She knew she must have looked like a creature from a nightmare to him: sweaty, disheveled, bloodthirsty, fierce. He must have guessed what had happened to the man he'd sent for her.

"Where is it?" she asked him.

A few minutes later, she was holding a green Panamanian passport issued to Maimouna Wade, complete with her photo and a U.S. tourist visa. After looking it over, she put it in her belt and squatted beside Mr. Bannerjee, who was again sitting slumped behind his desk.

"You're very lucky," she told him. "I'm letting you live. But if you tell a single person about any of this, I *will* send someone to correct that error."

He looked at her but said nothing.

"Do you understand?" she said.

He nodded. His mouth and chin were quivering.

She wasn't satisfied, but it was as much as she could expect. She couldn't afford to leave this man's body behind where it might be found.

Some chances you had to take.

THE FLIGHT TO New York City was uneventful. Not crowded, so Mariama had a two-seat row to herself. She'd brought a book to read, just like the other tourists (though most of them spent their time staring at their laptop computers), but she looked out the window for much of the flight, her mind far away.

She still had so much planning to do.

The plane landed on time. The passengers disembarked and headed to Immigration. In her modest skirt and flowered cotton blouse, Mariama looked like any other West African woman coming to the world's melting pot city.

She waited on the line, and soon enough it was her turn. Somewhere deep inside she could feel a flutter of nerves, but on the surface she appeared completely calm. Compared to everything she'd been through, this was easy.

The young man in the Immigration booth looked tired. He glanced at Mariama's face, then at the passport. Typed something into his computer. While he was waiting, he asked her if she was there on business or pleasure.

"I'm visiting my family," she said.

"So some of both, eh?" he said.

Mariama smiled. She wondered how often he made that joke.

He stamped her passport and handed it back to her. "Enjoy your visit."

"Thank you," she said.

Done. All she had was a carry-on bag, so she wouldn't even have to wait for a suitcase to come trundling out on the baggage loop. Nothing left to do but to disappear into New York City, get in touch with the people whose apartment she was going to share, and—at last—go see Trey Gilliard.

SHE WAS STILL a few feet from the door labeled *Ground Transportation* when she felt the tap on her shoulder. "Excuse me, ma'am."

Her first instinct was to run, but she knew that would be disastrous.

Instead she turned to see two men in uniforms with black pants and bright blue shirts. They were big, strong, polite. In the way of security officials everywhere, they stood a little too close to her.

On their blue shoulders were labels saying *TSA*. Mariama knew what that stood for: Transportation Security Administration.

"Yes?" she said.

"Come with us, ma'am, please," said the one who had spoken first.

And the other said, "We have a few questions to ask you."

Mariama went with them. What choice did she have?

ALL THIS TIME, with all the dangers she'd faced, she had never truly believed that her part in the dance would end so soon.

SEVENTEEN

" 'NATIVE SUPERSTITIONS RUN wild in this fever-ridden black heart of the Dark Continent, where God has never smiled and people worship the spirits of the teeming forest whose grasping tendrils they never escape.' "

"Is that purple prose getting all over your fingers?" Jack asked.

Sheila said, "Go on."

By now, Trey had become sure he'd never find what he was looking for in the old travel memoirs. So sure that when he did find it, in a book called *Beasts, Bugs, and Bedouins: A Journey through the Slavelands*, he turned the page before what he'd read filtered through to his conscious mind.

Then it got his full attention.

" 'The native witch doctors tell tales of pythons large enough to eat a young hippopotamus—or a large man— whole, then retiring to digest their meal for two full years before stalking a new victim,' " he read out loud. " 'Of strange doglike creatures, seen only in the shadows, that howl outside a village the night before the wretched victim of a mystical curse perishes. And of a winged demon that, in the guise of a wasp, preys on monkeys, and even on the most unfortunate of men.'"

"Hey," Jack said.

Sheila was standing very still and straight in her spot by the window. "Keep reading," she said.

"'Once they find you,'" Trey went on, "'your life is forfeit. There is no surcease, no restitution, no cure. Neither escape: These demons act in unearthly concert, as with a single intent. There is only the summoning, the long dreaming days, the last terrifying madness, confronted only at your own mortal peril, and then the inevitability of death.'"

He stopped reading. Very quietly, almost under her breath, Sheila said, "Long dreaming days."

"The last terrifying madness." Jack grunted. "Anything else?"

Trey shook his head. "No, that's it."

"I guess it would've been too much to expect an illustration." Jack turned his palms up. "I don't know. It all sounds like a Victorian flight of fancy." He grimaced. "I mean, in the same passage we have hippo-eating snakes and mystical doglike creatures that foretell your death with a woof."

No one spoke for a while. Then Trey stirred. "No," he said. "I don't think so. If I hadn't seen the thieves myself, I'd agree it was myth, legend. But the thieves do exist, so we can't assume there's no truth at the heart of this description."

Jack was still frowning. "Then tell me: What are 'dreaming days'?"

"Something we haven't seen yet."

"That's helpful." Jack leaned back in his chair and stared at the ceiling. "Okay, let's go through this methodically. The madness is last—"

"The inevitability of death is last," Sheila said.

"Well, besides that. But 'summoning' comes before. What's that?"

Trey said, "I wonder . . ."

"Silent wondering not allowed," Jack said. "Spill."

Trey was remembering. The colony. The thief hovering in front of his face, deciding.

Even here, even after all this time, the memory made his skin feel cold.

"At the colony," he said. "That monkey I saw."

Seeing again the colobus's terror, its white-rimmed eyes and desperate cries as it staggered into the clearing.

"You think it was going . . . against its will," Sheila said. "Not that it was just disoriented?"

Trey said, "Yes."

"But how? Who was summoning it, and how?"

Jack brought his feet back down to the floor. "Well, I could come up with a theory about *that*." He seemed suddenly more cheerful. "Fungus," he said.

Sheila said, "What?"

"Fungus," Jack said again. "Specifically, *Ophiocordyceps*."

Trey was nodding. "Yes, that could be it."

Sheila looked at the two of them and frowned. "Please tell me what you're agreeing about."

"Various species of *Ophiocordyceps* fungi are found in tropical forests all around the world," Jack said. "They have a diabolical way of dispersing themselves, colonizing new territories."

He was enjoying himself. "It all starts when an ant, a grasshopper, or another bug breathes in some of the fungus's spores. The spores lodge in the bug's lungs and the fungus starts to grow, to spread through the body. At the same time, it releases chemicals that affect the insect's brain. Basically, it turns its victim into a zombie."

Sheila said, "You're making this up."

Jack grinned. "Nope. The bug's behavior suddenly changes. It finds a bush and climbs to the top, a place it would never normally go. An ant that has never left the ground, for example, might climb six or eight feet up. Then, with its last strength, it grabs hold of a branch with its strong mandibles. And dies."

Sheila was staring at him. "Why on earth does it do that?"

"So when the fungus sprouts through the dead ant's eyes, mouth, and other openings, it can release its spores out into the breeze, to drift down and be breathed in by another ant, or a hundred, or a whole colony."

They waited while she absorbed this. Then Trey said, "In some forests, you can find them pretty easily. The remains, I mean. These white fungus stalks and sprouts catch your eye—they gleam among the green leaves—and there, clinging to the bush, is something that was once an insect."

"Oh, did I mention?" Jack was grinning at Sheila's expression. "The fungus liquefies the host's innards and converts them to sugars. Food!"

Again they waited. After a while Sheila said, "Okay. I have a few questions."

Her voice crisp, like she was taking a patient's history.

"Are mammals ever infected by these fungus spores?" she asked.

Jack looked a little less happy and said, "Not that anyone's found yet, no."

She nodded. "What you described to me is a pretty straightforward parasite-host relationship. But do these fungi ever work with other species to their mutual benefit? Are the relationships ever symbiotic?"

Jack scowled.

"And if the thief-fungus relationship is symbiotic, the fungus has to get something out of the deal. Unless the infected monkey climbs to a treetop before it dies." She looked at Trey. "Does that seem likely to you?"

Silence. Then Jack, looking a little disconsolate, shook his shoulders. "Okay," he said. "As a theory, it needs work."

"We don't have enough of the pieces yet." Sheila paused, the corners of her mouth turning down. "And if something *was* 'summoning' the monkey Trey saw, yours is a much better theory than I could have come up with."

For a moment her eyes went out of focus. She pointed at the old book Trey was still holding. "If she'd lived, would my mother have been summoned as well?"

Neither Trey nor Jack spoke. It didn't matter. Sheila went on without waiting for an answer.

"And was Mom going to experience the dreaming days?" she said. "The madness? Was her death inevitable?"

Her voice shook a little on the last sentence. Then it firmed.

"I *hate* not having the answers," she said.

THE PHONE RANG about an hour later, a loud, clattery sound in the silence. Jack answered on the third ring and said, "Yeah?"

And then, "Yeah."

And then, straightening, his face lighting up, "Yeah?"

He listened for another second, then said, "Hang on. Let me put you on speaker. There are people here who'll want to hear this."

He pushed a button. The speakerphone kicked in just in time for Trey to hear a voice say, "—Gilliard there?"

"Yes, I'm here," Trey said.

"Gilliard! Hey. Remember me?"

A familiar British accent, nasal voice. Trey could see the storklike frame, the long, indolent face, the blue eyes like chips of glass.

"Sure," he said. "How you doing, Ranny?"

Randolph Whitson, one of the countless field biologists whose paths had crossed Trey's over the years.

"You still at La Tamandua?" Trey asked.

"Always. That's why I'm calling."

La Tamandua Tropical Research Station, set amid the cloud forests below the peak of Monte Blanco in Costa Rica. Trey remembered it well from his single visit a decade earlier. The dense, wet forest had been filled with jewel-like poison dart frogs, iridescent birds, and foliage of more shades of green than even Trey had ever seen before.

Ranny, a mammalogist associated with the University of London, had built the research station, beam by hardwood beam, and since then he'd rarely left. His specialty was bats, but by now he knew everything that lived in those forests.

"Finally got a phone in there?" Trey asked.

The crowing laugh came down the line. At the beginning, Ranny hadn't allowed a radio or satellite phone to be installed on La Tamandua's premises. Word was he'd chosen the station's site, in a little valley, because cellphone service didn't penetrate there.

"No effing way," Ranny said. "I'm calling from Rio Viejo."

The small town an hour's drive from the station.

"And you drove all that way just to chat?" Jack asked. It was time to get to the point.

"You kidding? We were running low on beer, and anyway it's Graciela's time of the month, so she needed some shit."

Over by the window, Sheila gave a quick blink and an unmistakable roll of the eyes.

Trey didn't bother to ask who Graciela was. With Ranny, there was always a girl. Always a different girl.

"But I figured, long as I'm here, why not call? 'Cause I think I caught one of those buggers you've been looking for."

Jack rose onto his toes. "You just told me you'd *seen* one!"

The laugh. "Saw it and caught it. Hang on."

Garbled noises over the line before Ranny returned. "Last time I was in here, somebody showed me that Wanted poster you sent around on the computer. Ugly bugger. Give me a bat any old day.

"But then damned if I didn't find your beast chewing through one of my mist nets maybe three mornings later." A pause. "Most bats give up once they're tangled in the net, but not this guy. He had determination, that one."

"And you collected it?" Jack looked like he couldn't believe what he was hearing.

"Yeah." Ranny seemed to hesitate, and when he spoke

again his voice had a different tone. "Yeah. Tell you the truth, I didn't want to go near it. Wanted to leave it alone, let it get away and go back to wherever it came from. But I knew you were on a kick for these guys, so I maneuvered around and squeezed it till it gave up and died."

A sound, maybe a cough, came down the line. "You didn't mention the smell in your ad, I notice. That thing effing stinks. It's bothering Graciela. So when are you going to come pick it up?"

Jack said, "What? Send it to us."

"Yeah?" Ranny was laughing. "Sure. No prob. I'll just stick it in a box and courier it up your way."

Jack growled at his tone.

"Sorry, pal," Ranny went on. "Maybe that's how it works at your museum, but not here. Here we carry out our specimens. I'm not leaving for six more weeks, and there's nobody else around."

When no one spoke, he said, "The way this thing smells, if you don't come for it in the next two days, I'm putting it outside. And you know how long it'll last in the wet here."

Trey was remembering how he'd felt the first time he'd encountered the thieves. He said, more quietly than he'd intended, "I'll go."

Then, louder, "Ranny, I'll be there by tomorrow night."

Sheila said, "Trey, no."

At the same time, Ranny was saying, "Great. If I remember right, there's a direct flight to San José from Kennedy at around six in the morning. Drive fast, and you'll be here before nightfall."

"I'll drive fast," Trey said.

Ranny laughed. "My man. Bring more beer."

He disconnected. Jack was already sitting behind his computer, clicking the mouse. After a few moments, he looked up. "Six twenty-five on LACSA. From Kennedy, like he said."

Trey nodded, but he was looking at Sheila. "What's the problem?"

"Those things," she said.

Jack raised his eyes from the screen. "Only one of them, and it's dead."

"Come on, Jack," she said, her voice suddenly harsh. "Give someone else credit for a little intelligence. We all know that where there's one, there'll be more."

Jack stared at her. His mouth moved, and Trey was sure—certain—that he was about to say something like, *I guess it's your time of the month, too, huh, Sheila?*

Trey didn't let that happen. "Both of you," he said, "pipe down."

Their eyes went to him. Neither of them looked happy to be interrupted, but it was Sheila who spoke. "Trey, you'll be walking into too many unknowns. I don't think it's worth the risk."

Jack said, "As opposed to his usual M.O.? We need that specimen."

Trey saw the wasp hovering just before his face, the others staring at him from the mouths of their burrows.

"I'll be back as soon as I can," he said.

EIGHTEEN

Costa Rica

TREY DROVE FAST.

He'd gotten an old black Jeep Cherokee at the airport rental counter in San José, dented and dinged and with chipped paint and a touch of rust. The agent had been apologetic. It was all they could find for him on such short notice, in a country filled with tourists seeking shiny SUVs equipped with air-conditioning and powerful sound systems to keep the smells and sounds of the tropics out.

But it was just what Trey wanted, with plenty of power and four-wheel drive. These were the only requirements for a region whose roads were composed of mud, rutted dirt, turtle-backed all-weather gravel, and—worst of all—pothole-ridden asphalt that hadn't been resurfaced in twenty years.

Under dripping skies, he left San José behind and, weaving in and out of traffic, made his impatient way through the capital's suburbs and onto the Pan-American

Highway. Driving north past steaming volcanoes and lowering clouds punctuated by flocks of circling vultures.

Trey had once planned to drive the entire extent of the Pan-American Highway. He'd begin up in Prudhoe Bay, above the Arctic Circle, and not end till he reached Ushuaia, Argentina, just north of Tierra del Fuego. Along the way, wherever he found something interesting, he'd stop. For a day or a year, he didn't know, but always knowing he'd eventually get back on the road.

At the Darién Gap in Panama, where for fifty miles the highway didn't exist, he'd abandon his car and hike through the jungle to Colombia. There he'd buy a new junker, get back on the road, and keep going.

That was the plan, but even as he made it, he knew it was impossible. What about the rest of the world? The Americas weren't enough. He couldn't drive everywhere he wanted to go. He'd miss too much.

The whole way to La Tamandua, Trey drove faster than anyone should. The cautious tourists goggled at him and swerved out of his way. Locals, keeping up on the rutted highway for a while in their old pickup trucks, laughed and honked their horns as they fell back. For twenty or thirty miles, a pair of men on Harley-Davidsons accompanied him, effortlessly keeping pace, a convoy, a motorcade, before peeling off.

Why so fast? He wondered about this later. Because Ranny had told him to, threatening to destroy the specimen if he didn't arrive by nightfall? Or because after days of sitting still in New York, he gloried in the chance to *move*?

Yes. Those were both true. But not the whole truth.

The other part: He was afraid.

And when something frightened you, your only option was to confront it. To race toward it, not to hide.

He sped past farms and villages and factories, leaving the highway and ascending on ever-smaller and rougher roads into the Tilarán Mountains. The Jeep bucking and plowing, sending up sprays of mud but staying on the road.

Two thousand feet. Four. The old Jeep's engine beginning to protest from lack of air. The clouds descending, billows of gray mist blown by a cold, fitful breeze.

He drove through the town of Rio Viejo, where Ranny made his phone calls. Then turned onto the all-weather road that ended at the lip of the forested valley where the field station was located.

The ten-hour drive had taken him barely seven. It was time for him to confront his fears.

THE CLOUD FOREST as dusk neared. Low, gnarled trees whose branches hung heavy with mosses, and air plants. Philodendrons and vines climbing up moisture-slick trunks. Clouds sweeping through, coating every surface with droplets that caught the light and gleamed like gems.

A forest out of Middle-earth.

Trey parked the Jeep beside a battered Nissan—Ranny's, he assumed—in the little dirt lot carved out of the brush beside the road. If you wanted to visit the station, you left your car here and hiked down a wet, muddy trail for two miles. If this felt like too much, you were welcome to turn around and go home.

Ranny didn't want it any other way. His goal, he said, was to keep the riffraff out.

Trey climbed out of his car, then reached back in for

his daypack. Before he'd taken ten steps, his skin, hair, and clothes were slick with moisture. As he walked, sure-footed as always on even the wettest, steepest trails, he heard a distant bellbird give its ringing "tonk" call from a treetop and a troop of black howler monkeys welcoming nightfall with their roars.

Eventually he spotted a brighter patch ahead: the clearing where La Tamandua stood. As he approached, he realized that the station was silent, its generator off. No music, no voices. Through a mist-streaked window, he could see a lamp burning inside, but no sign of movement.

Shifting his flashlight to his left hand, he walked forward and pulled the door open.

A puff of warmer air wafted out. Trey breathed it in. It was stale, carrying the odors of overripe fruit, cigarette smoke, and bug repellent.

And the bitter smell of the thieves.

Trey would always know, would always hate, that smell.

THE THREE ROOMS—a dormitory-style bedroom, a den/office/living room, and a laboratory—were empty, of humans and anything else living. But they hadn't been empty for long. No more than six or eight hours.

The light Trey had seen from outside came from a goosenecked lamp that craned over Ranny's desk. Even as Trey looked at it, it flickered, reaching the end of its battery backup. He turned it off.

The dirty plates in the sink had once held rice and beans. What was left was congealed, but not yet petrified. Yesterday's dinner or today's breakfast.

There were two plates. One had held more food, eaten more messily, the second a smaller, neater portion.

In the station's dorm room, containing a half dozen cots, two had been pushed together. The room smelled of perfume and sweat and sex.

Ranny's clothes were piled haphazardly on shelves and slung over a rack in the corner of the room. A woman's clothes—Graciela's clothes—were more carefully folded or hung neatly on the rack. She'd brought a large variety of short skirts and colorful slacks, halter tops and sleeveless blouses.

Trey left the laboratory itself till last. It was modest, one of the smallest Trey had seen, but that made sense. All Ranny needed here was a ready supply of collecting equipment and the materials to preserve the specimens. More in-depth study could wait for his occasional trips back to better-equipped laboratories in England.

A half dozen bats in various stages of preservation sat on a work table. Amid specimens of insectivorous leaf-nosed and foxlike fruit-eating bats, Trey recognized a vampire bat, its size, oily fur, and squinting grin distinctive even in death.

None of the bats occupied pride of place on the table, though, the spot right in front of the chair. A small wooden box, perhaps a foot long by six inches wide and the same again deep, sat there. It was open. Its top, waiting to be nailed on, lay beside it.

But there was nothing inside, amid the white-foam packing material that would protect the specimen in transit. Just a depression in the foam, about three inches long. Skinny. Insect shaped.

What had happened to the specimen?

Trey took some air into his lungs. Somewhere outside in the forest, a large branch cracked and fell to earth. It made a sound like a gunshot or the breaking of a mast just before the ship goes down.

Looked at one way, all he'd learned from his search was that the two of them were out. It was nearing dusk, the time that Ranny would have been stringing his mist nets between the trees of his study area. Setting his traps for the bats he hunted and studied. Graciela could well have accompanied him.

Trey could just wait here, and in an hour or so they'd return.

That was the fantasy. But Trey knew better. He knew the reality was different.

He was going to have to go look for them.

He found the station's first-aid kit and put it into his daypack. Near the front door was a row of pegs, three of them holding hard hats with attached headlamps. He took one and put it on.

Last, he went looking for the weapon he knew would be there. It was standing in the shadows by the laboratory door: a shotgun, unloaded, cleaned, oiled, not recently used. The ammunition—a box of #9 birdshot shells—was in a supply closet in the corner of the room.

Trey took the gun and a handful of shells with him and walked out into the cold, dripping forest.

NINETEEN

THE ABRUPT TROPICAL dusk had fallen while Trey was inside. Rain pattered on the leaves above his head, and every once in a while a bigger drop struck his hard hat with a thump.

The bellbird had fallen silent, but in the wet darkness crickets and glass frogs had started calling. A gigantic beetle, nearly as big as Trey's hand, buzzed slowly past. It had two bright green lights shining like headlights from the front of its thorax.

The air was growing even colder. Trey knew that temperatures here could dip into the forties at night, a far cry from the sticky heat of the lowland rain forest.

Trey remembered the trails from his previous visit—he never forgot a trail he'd hiked—but, radiating out like spokes from the field station, they would have been easy enough to follow anyway. The shotgun under his arm, he searched one trail, then retraced his steps and headed down the next.

When full darkness fell, he had no choice but to turn

on his headlamp. He hated using lights. They were like neon signs: For everything you spotted, a hundred things spotted you.

The beam turned green leaves gray. Shadows moved at the corners of the light, and small, unseen creatures rustled through the wet foliage at his feet. The howler monkeys roared again.

Staying patient, he moved slowly along each trail, looking for evidence that anyone had been there. Recently crushed leaves or bent stems, kicked-up leaf litter. And on the fifth trail, as he stepped into a small clearing caused by a tree fall, he caught just a whiff of the thieves' odor. That was all, and then it was gone, chased by the breeze.

He turned the lamp's beam this way and that, but could see nothing in the harsh light. Lifting his gaze, he saw that the mist had risen and a half-moon had emerged from hurrying clouds. That was enough. He reached up and turned off the lamp.

At first the darkness seemed absolute. He was blind.

Amid the forest's rustles and calls, he waited as his eyes gradually adjusted to the diffuse light of the moon and stars. When he could see the movement of a small gray salamander across the trail ten feet away, he knew he was ready.

He turned slowly in a circle in the middle of the clearing, searching for anything unusual, anything out of the ordinary. At the same time, he listened beyond the sound of the night insects and the whisper of the breeze through wet leaves.

Three times he turned before he saw it: the tiniest glimmer, detectable only through the corners of his eyes.

Not the light cast by the stars or moon or the cold luminescence of a colony of forest mites. A gleam from the ground at the far end of the clearing.

And movement, too. A brief, flickering shadow obscuring the light.

Trey walked toward it.

The glow grew brighter as he approached, but only slightly. The feeble illumination it cast revealed drooping leaves, a gray-brown tree trunk, a vine twisted around the trunk like a snake. And a large, slumped form he couldn't make out yet.

He knew what it was, though.

The light he'd glimpsed was a flashlight's beam. Like the lamp in the field station, it must have been burning for hours, because by now it was so weak that he could see the coil itself flickering inside the bulb.

Ranny was lying on the ground, the flashlight attached to his belt.

Trey reached up and turned on his headlamp. The scene before him sprang into full relief, black shadows erupting. A great curassow, unseen in the foliage above, gave a harsh croak and lifted off from its roost, heavy wings making a rushing sound like the wind. The diamond-bright pinprick eyes of dozens of spiders gleamed from nearby trunks.

Ranny lay on his back beside a small tree, his collecting gear—rolled-up mist nets, cloth bags, the harness he used to climb—scattered around him. His eyes were closed, his face gray.

Trey squatted beside him, felt for a pulse. Found it after a moment, just a slight, delicate throbbing in the throat. Ranny's skin was warm, but it had a strange, waxy consistency to it, as if in some strange way it had been molten and was now firming again.

Trey called out his name, shook his shoulder, but Ranny didn't stir.

The long dreaming days.

Trey aimed his beam and saw what he'd expected to: the telltale swelling on Ranny's stomach, pressing against the inside of his shirt. Unblinking, Trey watched it. Half a minute, a minute. Nothing. Nothing.

Then . . . something moving beneath the cloth. A sinuous flutter, quickly gone.

Something coming to the surface of the skin for a gulp of air, then twisting and diving deeper once again.

Trey stood. He let the beam describe a wider arc. Knowing what he was looking for and soon finding it.

The girl lay perhaps eight feet away, on her side, back to him. Under the clear plastic rain poncho, her tight blouse, white with a pattern of flowers stitched in it, was untucked from the waistband of her short ruby red skirt. Her long brown legs were bare and slick with mist. So was her left foot, though she wore a white sneaker on her right one.

Graciela.

Looking at that one bare foot, Trey felt his fear dissipate. It was replaced by a kind of burning determination, the ice-cold certainty that always took the place of anger deep in his core.

He knew that, whatever happened, he would never be afraid of the thieves again.

As he took his first step forward, the shadows shifted. A thief moved, spiderlike, into view on Graciela's hip, then stood there, staring at him. Slender black body shining with dew, wings flickering.

"There you are," Trey said.

The thief tilted its head at the sound of his voice, but did not otherwise react. It was waiting, Trey thought. Waiting to see what his next action would be.

He wondered if it knew what a gun was. Whether it understood what the birdshot could do to it.

Trey tilted his head so that the beam shone directly into the thief's eyes. It merely turned away from the light, watching him instead from the corners of its eyes.

For a minute, maybe more, the standoff continued. Just as Trey knew—knew!—that it was dying to come for him, he wanted nothing more than to pull the trigger and blast its body into rubble and ichor.

He lowered the beam a little. The wasp turned back to stare at him. What was going on in its insect brain? Conscious thought or only the primitive neuronal firings of a simpler species?

There was one way to find out.

He swung the shotgun down and poked the barrel into Ranny's stomach. One twitch of his finger and the larva beneath the skin would die.

Did the thief understand what he was threatening to do?

The wasp sprang a foot into the air. Before Trey could shift his aim, it landed on Graciela's bare leg, closer, facing him head-on. Its mandibles twitched and its wings made a strange chittering sound on its back.

Trey had long since learned not to ascribe human emotions to other mammal species, much less insects. Still, he couldn't help it. In this thief, he saw rage and something more: anxiety, even horror. Yes, it understood.

Trey poked the barrel of the rifle deeper into Ranny's stomach. Up the barrel and into his hand came a quivering motion from within the flesh.

The thief came for him. As he'd known it would.

Even so, even though he'd expected it, the attack was so fast, so unerring, that the wasp almost reached him. He barely managed to raise the shotgun, and if it had contained a single bullet instead of a birdshot-filled cartridge, he would have been dead.

In the headlamp's beam, he caught a glimpse, a snapshot, of the creature. Its reaching legs, green eyeshine, white stinger.

Then he pulled the trigger. The gun kicked against his shoulder. The sound of the shot echoed through the forest. The familiar odor hit his nostrils before mixing with the smell of smoke. And the thief disintegrated before him.

Trey stood still. Even over the thudding in his ears, he could hear the grunting roars of the howler monkeys his shot had startled.

Jacking another shell into the chamber, Trey put his back against a tree and waited. Ten minutes, fifteen, as his hearing returned, the howler monkeys quieted, and the dead wasp's smell hung in the air.

Nothing. Maybe the two thieves—the one Ranny had caught and the one Trey had just killed—were the only ones here. The pioneers. The colonists.

It was time to go. There was nothing he could do for Ranny and Graciela.

Go.

Only . . . he couldn't.

ABOUT A MILE back to the research station. Another two up to the Jeep. All along treacherous, muddy trails, illuminated only by his headlamp.

Trey was strong, but strong enough to drag or carry Ranny—who looked to weigh about 180 pounds—all the way, and then return for Graciela? He didn't think so.

Still, he had to try.

Propping the shotgun against a tree, he bent over, got his hands under Ranny's arms, and lifted. His plan was to use some version of the fireman's carry, but he never got a chance.

As he lifted, Ranny let out a cry, a sound of intense pain. Then he said, "No!"

Trey, shocked, almost let him fall, but managed to return him gently to the ground. Only then did he see that Ranny's eyes were open.

Sightless eyes, slicked with an odd silvery sheen. They reflected the headlamp's beam, gleaming like mercury as they shifted this way and that. Random motions, as if Ranny were looking at something no one else could see.

As if he were dreaming.

"Ranny," Trey said, his voice a hoarse whisper.

Ranny's mouth moved. The sheen over his eyes faded a little. "Trey?" he said.

"Yes. I'm here."

Ranny was looking at him. "Trey," he said again.

Trey said, "Yes?"

"*Kill me.*"

TREY COULDN'T SPEAK for a moment. Then he said, "I'll get you to a doctor. I promise. He'll help. I'll—"

"*No.*" Only Ranny's mouth moved. "You can't. It hurts. . . ."

"Then I'll bring someone back here—"

"No." Ranny blinked, and when his eyes opened again the silvery shine was stronger. "They're . . . here. In here. Forever."

He drew in a breath. "Trey," he said. "*Please.* Kill me." Another breath. "And . . . her."

His eyes gleamed, and he was gone again. Back inside his dreams.

Trey sat there.

Kill me.

He couldn't do it.

COULDN'T PULL THE trigger, at least. Was what he did instead any different? Any better? He never knew.

But what other choice did he have? He was out of options.

Unzipping his daypack, he pulled out the first-aid kit he'd taken from the station. Snapped it open and saw, amid the usual gauze pads and antibiotic creams and antihistamines, the scalpel he'd expected to find.

These kits always included a knife or scalpel, a holdover from the days when people believed the first, best response to snakebite was to cut open the spot and suck out the poison-laced blood. Now, even though that theory was long out of fashion, habits hadn't changed.

Trey searched through the kit until he found a pair of forceps. Then, squatting over Ranny's still form, he shoved the man's heavy, wet shirt halfway up his chest. A couple of moves of the knife, one quick snatch with the forceps, and he was holding the larva up to the light.

It was as Sheila had described: long, white, tensile, with black mandibles and large eyes and an almost unbelievable strength for something its size.

Beneath him, Ranny stirred, drew in a ragged, gasping breath, and died.

TREY KNEW THAT he should keep the larva. Kill it and preserve it and bring it home.

It was important. It might tell them things they had to know.

But . . . no chance. With a movement that was like a spasm, he threw it to the ground. It writhed and twisted and bit at the earth until he ground it to pulp with the stock of his gun.

For long minutes he stood there, not moving, hearing nothing but the roaring in his ears. Then, carrying the scalpel and forceps, he walked over to where the girl lay. Graciela, with her brown legs and bare foot, her face turned away as if she'd chosen to avert her gaze from what lay ahead.

Trey rolled her onto her back, then pushed her shirt up, exposing her swollen belly.

Under her skin, something moved.

* * *

"NO SPECIMEN?" JACK said.

Trey was calling from the airport in San José. He was still covered in mud and sweat, and smelled of rotting vegetation and a bitter stink he thought would never leave him.

He knew he looked like a madman. Felt like one, too.

"No," he said. "It was gone."

"And Ranny and the girl?" Sheila said. He hadn't known that he was on speakerphone, that she was listening.

"Gone."

Nothing but the crackling line. Then Sheila's voice, closer. "Trey," she said, "did you see them?"

He didn't answer.

"Shit," she said.

Still he didn't speak.

"There was nothing you could do." Her voice was strong. "Remember that. Remember what you told me. Whatever happened, whatever you had to do, you had no choice."

He was silent.

"Trey," she said. "Come home."

TWENTY

Marco Island, Florida

KAIT HAD BEEN watching for days.

As soon as school ended each afternoon, she'd leave Mrs. Warren's fourth-grade class at Tommie Barfield Elementary and hurry home. Once there, she'd barely pause for a snack before heading out the kitchen door and down to the boat slip.

"You give it a name yet?" Ma had asked one time, when she had Kait's attention for more than thirty seconds.

Kait had just shaken her head. Inside, though, she'd thought: That was stupid. You didn't name wild creatures.

They had their own names, she was sure of it, names they used for each other. Names you'd never know. You could decide to give them any name you wanted, but it wouldn't mean anything.

Now that she thought of it, maybe that was true for your pets, too. Their two dogs, for instance. Their setter, Fire (named by Da because in some lights his coat looked almost like flames), and their mutt, Chester (Ma had named him because she said he looked like a Chester). Maybe they called each other something completely different and wondered why people used such strange sounds to call them.

Anyway, when Kait went down to their boat slip and looked at the dolphin, she decided not to give it a name. It was just the dolphin. Her dolphin.

If it felt like telling her its true name, it would.

It had first come to the slip two years before, when Kait was eight. Almost every day, the dolphin had been there, lazing in the warm water near Da's boat. Sometimes it would dive for something to eat, but mostly it would just lie on the surface, its breath coming through the hole in its head like little explosions, surprising Kait every time.

She would sit there for hours after school, watching the dolphin until dinnertime. Watching and drawing. That was what Kait did best, draw. She didn't like to talk that much, but she loved to draw what she saw.

Often the dolphin would look at her with its bright eye. She wondered what it thought when it saw her.

"Is it sick?" she'd asked Ma and Da.

They'd smiled at each other, who knew why, and Da had said, "No, it's not sick."

"Then why is it always there?"

Ma had given her a hug. "Keep watching, sweetie, and you'll see."

And just a few days later, she *had* seen. She walked down to the slip early one Sunday morning and saw that now there were two dolphins, hers and a tiny little one, no bigger than some of her stuffed animals, lying in the water beside it.

* * *

NOW, ALMOST EXACTLY two years later, it was back. The mama dolphin. Alone again, but looking just the same and acting just as she had the first time. Lolling around in the calm blue-green water between their boat slip and the one next to it. Looking as happy as any creature on God's green earth. (As Grandma Mary put it.)

"Is she going to have another baby?" Kait had grown a lot in the past two years, and had a better idea what kinds of questions to ask. Actually, it was hard to believe how little she'd known, back when she was eight.

"Sure looks that way to me," Da said.

So Kait spent every moment she could down there, by the slip, hoping to see the birth. Over the years she'd witnessed her share of rabbits and hamsters being born, chicks hatching from eggs, and even, once, a garter snake delivering itself of a mass of squirmy black-and-yellow babies that formed themselves into a knot before heading their separate ways.

But never a dolphin. Kait wondered how many people in the whole world had seen a baby dolphin being born. Especially in the wild. Ones in aquariums or SeaWorld didn't count. She didn't think you should ever keep dolphins in a big tank of water, or orcas, either.

But a wild one? Maybe she'd be the first ever.

So, sitting on the edge of the dock, her legs dangling over the water, she watched and watched. And drew, of course. She might have changed a lot in two years, but she hadn't lost her love of drawing.

Sometimes other kids would come and stay for a little

while, but Kait didn't have that many friends and didn't care when Amanda or Isabelle would drift away to do something they thought was more fun. Watching a lazy dolphin wasn't their idea of how to spend a warm spring Saturday, and that was fine with her.

She kept it company after dinner every night till dark, when Ma called her for bedtime. Then she'd pretend not to hear until Da came down, hoisted her up—laughing and complaining at the same time—and carried her back to the house. (She was ten now, and much too big to be carried. That was her opinion, at least, but Da didn't share it.)

She'd always known that she wouldn't be able to watch every minute—even if her parents had let her camp out on the dock, she would've had to sleep sometimes. So she wasn't especially surprised when she ran down to the water one morning before school and saw, floating at the mama dolphin's side, a new baby, even smaller and more perfect than the one from two years earlier.

With a rush of emotion that squeezed her heart, Kait instantly fell in love with the rubbery, gray creature, with its tiny beak and bright eyes. If she'd spent a lot of time at the slip before it was born, now she was there every single possible minute.

Watching and drawing.

FOR THE FIRST week, the baby grew in leaps and bounds. Every day it seemed stronger, more active, following its mother farther from the shore and dock, diving a little deeper. Still it stayed mostly at the surface, happy, comfortable, the water rolling off its shiny skin.

Then, one morning, something was different.

No one else noticed, not the neighbors who stopped by to take a look every day, not the sea kayakers who put slip 173 on their regular route, not even Ma and Da.

Only Kait saw. The baby dolphin stopped growing. It spent more time sleeping. Its dives were less deep, and it no longer ventured as far as it had just a few days earlier.

The mama dolphin pushed it with her nose, urging it away from the dock. She looked around for the baby as she dived, rocketing to the surface out in the channel as if trying to capture its attention.

But the baby just drifted.

"Is it sick?" Kait asked Da as they sat side by side on the edge of the dock late one afternoon.

"I'm sure it's not," he told her, though the look on his face said something else.

THE NEXT DAY Kait noticed the swelling. A bump on the baby dolphin's back, a few inches from its blowhole. There was a round black mark in the middle of the bump, like a second, tiny blowhole.

"Huh," Da said when she called him to see. "Maybe it's got an infection."

"Call the doctor." Kait hated how her voice almost squeaked over the words. If ever she had wanted to be bigger, stronger, it was now. So Da would listen to her.

"Please," she said.

Da listened. He called. But it didn't make a difference.

"Bunny," he said, "they won't come. If it was abandoned, maybe, but not if the mother is still with it."

"But it's sick."

Da looked unhappy. "They say dolphins aren't endangered. They say it's just the cycle of life."

Kait heard: the circle of life. She'd seen that movie, *The Lion King*, on the Disney Channel. She understood what it meant. Despite what the movie said, it didn't seem very noble to her.

"So he'll die," she said. "Fish will eat him."

"Maybe you should stop watching," Da said.

Kait felt her chin lift. She crossed her arms over her chest and stared into her father's eyes.

He knew that expression of hers and didn't argue.

THE SWELLING GOT bigger. The baby dolphin grew weaker. It was spending all its time on the surface now. It didn't nurse as often, or for as long.

Its mother stopped trying so hard to teach it. Kait thought she was giving up.

Nobody else came to watch now. The neighbors were busy, and the kayakers paddled right on past.

Kait didn't sleep well at night. She picked at her food at breakfast and dinner and gave away most of her sack lunch at school. Her parents looked at her, and frowned at each other, and suggested movies, dinner out, a trip across the state to see Harry Potter at Universal Studios.

But they didn't push. They knew Kait had to see this through.

EARLY ONE MORNING the baby dolphin wasn't floating anymore. It was half pulled up on the flat wooden platform that bobbed off the end of the dock. Da had built this platform when Kait was littler so she could step from it straight into their canoe to go paddling with him.

The baby looked as if it had been on the platform for hours. Its skin was all dry except for its tail, which hung unmoving in the water. The one eye she could see was a strange silver-white color.

At first Kait thought it was already dead. Then it gave a long, slow breath through its blowhole.

Kait looked down at the swelling on its back and saw movement beneath the baby dolphin's skin.

She ran to get Da.

SOMETHING WAS COMING out of the black hole in the swelling.

Da said, "What the hell?"

He scrambled down the wooden steps to the floating platform. Kait followed.

The baby dolphin flinched a little at their footsteps, but made no effort to push off, swim away. Right then, Kait realized that its mother was gone. She'd abandoned her baby.

The thing was about halfway out of the hole now. Kait saw red wings, a head that looked to be too big for the black, wormlike body. Everything about it was droopy, wet. Drops of some liquid ran off it and speckled the baby dolphin's back.

Kait's hands covered her eyes, but then she spread her fingers. She had to look.

"What is it?" she asked.

"The damnedest thing." Da squatted down. "Some kind of bee? No, a wasp. One heck of a big wasp."

Kait had watched plenty of yellow jackets and cicada

killers, even caught some in her butterfly net. She knew what a wasp looked like. This wasn't a wasp. Or . . . it wasn't *only* a wasp. It was also something else, some other kind of thing.

She could see its mouth parts moving. A whitish drop formed; with a twitch of its big head, it flung the drop away.

"Shit," Da said, forgetting that Kait was there, speaking to the wasp-thing instead. "Where the hell did *you* come from?"

The baby dolphin breathed. The wasp-thing dragged itself farther out of the hole. With one last pull, it was free.

The baby dolphin's body quivered, all the way up and down. Its blowhole gaped open, and its sad little droopy beak twitched. Then it was still, and Kait knew it was dead.

The wasp-thing raised its heavy body high on its skinny black legs. It stood still for a moment, and then a stream of the whitish liquid began to pump out of its rear end. It turned its big triangle head and looked at them, at Kait and Da.

It's deciding what it wants to do to us, Kait thought.

Da made a funny gulping sound. His hand whipped out, faster than Kait could follow, and the next thing she knew the wasp-thing was flying through the air. It landed on its back in the water beside the dock.

Kait watched it struggle, its legs waving around, its wet wings twitching. A mackerel came to look at it, but swam away again.

Just a few seconds later it was dead, bumping against the pilings alongside some seaweed and a bit of newspaper.

Kait looked back at the baby dolphin. Already its eyes were glazed over, like the dead fish you saw at the market.

Everything was dead.

Da put his hand on top of Kait's head for a second, just like he'd done when she was little. "I'm sorry, Bunny," he said. "I wish we hadn't seen that."

Kait didn't say anything.

GRANDMA MARY WAS at the house. Ma must have called her while Da and Kait were down at the slip.

Da went upstairs to take a shower.

"You and me, we're going out for breakfast," Grandma told Kait.

"I have school," Kait pointed out. The first words she'd spoken in a while.

"Hang school!" Grandma talked like that. She wasn't that much bigger than Kait, but she could be a lot louder.

Ma said, "I already called to tell them you'd be late."

"I'm not hungry," Kait said.

Grandma gave a big shrug. "Okay, fine, you can watch me eat, and after that we can do a little shopping."

Grandma Mary loved shopping.

"Go," Ma said.

So Kait went. They ate at Breakfast Plus (Kait ended up getting French toast, and even eating some of it), then went off to Marco Walk, where they visited every store. At Richard's Reef, Grandma insisted she buy some earrings. Kait was quiet, but Grandma didn't make her talk.

By the time they got back home, it was almost noon. "We'll make sandwiches," Grandma said. "And then, if you feel up to it, I'll take you to school."

Kait didn't say anything, but she thought she might be able to manage school.

While Grandma went in the front door, Kait squatted down beside the front step to watch a small lizard that was sunning itself. An anole. When it saw her looking, it puffed out a pretty red pouch under its throat.

"You don't scare me," Kait said.

That was when she heard it. At first she thought it was the sound of a bird, a gull or maybe even an eagle. But then she realized it was coming from inside the house, a high sound unlike any she'd heard before.

And then she figured out what it was: someone screaming. A kind of scream she'd never heard before.

Grandma Mary.

MEN. DOZENS OF men. Maybe hundreds. A couple of women, too, big women with fake smiles, at least one of them sitting with her at all times.

Grandma Mary was in the hospital, they told her. But she would be fine. Fine.

They promised.

It took them a long time to say anything about Ma and Da. But Kait knew. She'd known from the moment she'd heard Grandma start to scream. That sound she'd never heard before, but which still echoed in her ears.

The men asked her a thousand questions, or maybe it was the same question in different words a thousand times. Kait didn't say anything. She didn't feel like talking.

But she *knew*.

TWENTY-ONE

IN THE TWO days Trey was gone, some kind of floodgate seemed to have opened. Or perhaps there was an algorithm for how long it took people to notice Jack's alert on the Internet, go out looking for thieves, and report back on what they'd seen.

Or maybe, Trey thought, the algorithm was a darker one. Maybe the first people to go out looking for thieves didn't make it back to their computers. Maybe there was some magic number of searchers that overwhelmed the wasps' ability to stay hidden or to kill, and what the three of them were seeing was the overflow.

Whatever the equation, he returned to Jack's office to find pins sprouting from the map on the wall. Each pin marked a spot where a sighting had been reported, and the pins steadily clustered more thickly and spread more widely.

Some of the reports were sketchy, others likely hoaxes. But enough were certain—a scrap of video taken from

Ivory Coast, a photo from Thailand, a detailed description from an entomologist in southern Italy, a series of images from somewhere in South America, showing a thief standing astride what looked like the still form of a capybara—to make the overall picture clear. To make the conclusion inescapable.

The thieves had spread across the world. More than that: Their spread was explosive. They were moving like the Spanish influenza had in 1918, like malaria-carrying mosquitoes before that, like countless other pests and epidemic diseases throughout human history.

But even more easily than those of the past. "They're fucking turbocharged," Jack said. "There's, what, tens of thousands of airplane flights taking off and landing every day? How many have these beasts on board, hitching a ride?"

Trey stayed silent. Sheila, sitting at Jack's computer, didn't appear to be listening.

"And not just planes," Jack went on. "Planes, trains, and automobiles. All we're missing is Steve Martin and John Candy."

"No reports from the United States yet?" Trey asked. "That's strange."

"Must be that border wall they've been building in Texas." Jack rolled his eyes. "The president should give a speech touting its success. It might help him win reelection."

He gave a dismissive shake of the head. "Nah. It's just a blip. Nobody's reported it to us yet, but they will. Soon."

He looked at the map, at the scattering of pins in South

and Central America. "Put it in the books. The thieves are already here."

Sheila merely raised her gaze from the computer screen.

"You're right," she said. "Look at this."

SHE HAD A series of windows open on the screen. Most showed variations on the same headline: "Bee Attack Leaves Florida Couple Dead."

"Already saw that," Jack said. "'Africanized Honeybees Claim Another Victim.' 'Killer Bees on the Prowl.' 'Young Couple Stung to Death.' 'Family Dogs Victims, Too.'"

He scowled, as if not proud of his tone, then shrugged. "Killer bees have been spreading throughout Florida and Texas for decades. These aren't the first deaths."

Trey was reading the first paragraphs of the different stories. "They all say the same thing."

"Not this one," Sheila said.

She clicked the mouse and brought a new page to the front.

The *Marco Island Sunrise*, a local online newspaper filled with stories about shopping deals and fishing charters and a new real-estate development. And the deaths of two island residents.

Trey read the sad details. The attack on the parents. The daughter surviving due to being out shopping with her grandmother. The grandmother being kept overnight in the hospital after discovering the bodies of her son and daughter-in-law.

"Look here," Sheila said.

It was a link to a video, a black rectangle in the middle of the page. The heading was, "Orphaned Daughter Speaks."

"Yuck," Jack said.

Sheila clicked on it, and after a few moments the video began. It showed a reporter, a slim young woman, standing in front of a Florida scene: white houses with red roofs, palm trees, blue water shimmering in the distance. She was holding a black microphone.

"In a *Sunrise* exclusive, we were able to talk with Kaitlin Finneran, daughter of the couple whose tragic death is the talk of Marco Island," the reporter was saying. Under her suitably solemn expression, she looked thrilled. "Kaitlin's story will shock you."

"Double fucking yuck," Jack said.

The camera focused on two figures sitting on a bench: an exhausted-looking seventyish woman with white hair and a ten-year-old girl with fair skin dusted with freckles, black hair pulled back into a long ponytail, and big dark eyes. She had a hollow, thousand-yard expression in her eyes that Trey had seen too often before.

And too recently. He glanced at Sheila, who was leaning forward as if she wanted to climb through the screen.

"It's too soon," she said. "The grandmother should never have allowed this."

"She's in shock herself," Trey said. "I doubt she knows what's right."

Sheila grunted.

"So, Kait," the reporter was saying, "you've said that you don't believe killer bees killed your parents."

Kait shook her head.

"Then what did?"

Kait stared into the camera. As Trey watched, some banked flame lit behind her eyes, and suddenly she seemed completely focused and aware.

"The wasp-thing," she said.

The reporter said, "The what?"

Kait didn't blink. "I watched it hatch out of the baby dolphin," she said. "Da killed it." She bit her lip, and when she spoke again, her voice was choked. "That's why they killed him and Ma."

"So you're saying—"

But Kait's grandmother had had enough. She stirred and put her hand on the girl's arm. "We're tired," she said. "Do you think you can leave us alone now?"

The scene went back to the reporter in front of the island scenery. "We talked to Derek Franks of the Collier County Sheriff's Office about Kait's extraordinary claims. Should the residents of Marco Island be afraid of wasps, as well as killer bees? His response: 'Residents should not be afraid of either.'"

Sheila clicked the mouse, freezing the reporter with her mouth open. They were silent for a few moments, and then Jack said, "The little girl must not have understood what she was seeing."

Trey said, "Why?"

"Because wasps don't parasitize dolphins."

Neither Sheila nor Trey spoke. Jack's face turned red. "Okay," he said. "Fucking sue me for being scientific, okay? Wasps are *not* such generalists."

"They are in their diet, aren't they?" Sheila said. "I mean, some are."

"But not in their breeding methods."

Sheila shrugged. "Yeah, and viral diseases couldn't

jump from species to species. It was a natural law . . . until this one virus took the leap from African chimpanzees to humans a few decades back. You know, the one transmitted during sex. That rule breaker has managed to spread pretty well through the population. What was it called again?"

Jack's beard bristled. "I love it when you condescend to me," he said. "Makes me feel all tingly inside. Still . . . a *dolphin*?"

"It's not impossible," Trey said. "A newborn dolphin stays at the surface. It's not strong enough to dive yet. A larva needing only an occasional breath of air could grow inside one, hatching out before it would be in danger of drowning."

"So these things can parasitize any mammal," Jack said.

Neither Trey nor Sheila answered.

Jack was looking at the map. "We're going to need more pins."

"**ONE THING I** don't understand," Trey said a while later.

Jack said, "Only one?"

"Kaitlin says her father killed a thief. If there had been any others around, wouldn't they have attacked right away? Why wait?"

Jack turned his palms up. But Sheila said, "No. You're looking at this the wrong way."

They waited for her to explain.

"If there'd been any other thieves in the area when Kaitlin's father killed the hatchling, he and Kaitlin would have been dead at once," she went on. "The ones that attacked—they came later."

"Later?" Jack asked. "Like, for tea?"

"Jack—"

"No, tell me. Why?"

"That's obvious," Sheila said. "For retribution."

"Retribution?"

"Revenge," Sheila said.

TREY TOOK A breath and watched Jack carefully. He knew what was going to come next.

Jack's eyes narrowed and red spots rose to his cheeks. He raised both hands and rubbed his face. The air whistled through his nose as he gave an explosive breath out, like a whale clearing its lungs through its blowhole.

All as expected.

Less expected was the wiry, snarling tone in his voice as he said, "Sheila, shut the hell up."

Sheila blinked. "What?"

Jack's face was dark. "Listen to you. 'Revenge.' Don't be an idiot."

She stared at him.

"You know where revenge comes from?" he went on. "Conscious thought. Calculation. *Human* attributes."

"Okay," Sheila said, her voice flat. "I misspoke."

"No," Jack said. "You didn't misspeak. You're ignorant. And you still don't understand."

Trey said, "Jack, you've made your point—"

"No," Jack said again. "Both of you. *Listen*. It's simple. Wasps, like all insects and most living things, are motivated by two things: the instinct to survive and the need to procreate. *That's all.* Nothing else."

"I know that," Sheila said.

"No, you don't." Jack's voice was quiet now, but no less fierce. "No . . . you . . . don't. You're watching me freak out, and you want me to stop, but inside you haven't learned a thing."

He ran his hands again over his face. "You know what intelligence is? Let me tell you: It's the ability to ponder, to think things through, to see both sides of an issue. To change one's mind."

He paused for a moment, but when Trey began to speak he raised a hand in warning. "Shut up, Trey," he said. "I'm not done. You still don't get it. Neither of you. 'Intelligence' is the greatest weakness afflicting the human species. We insult the thieves when we attribute it to them."

He took a breath, and when he went on, his voice was calmer. "Worse than that, we underestimate them. Because lacking intelligence sets them free. They don't ponder, equivocate, mull things over. They act. They survive. They procreate. That's all. But it's enough."

He looked back and forth from Sheila to Trey. Neither spoke.

"Wasps evolved more than a hundred million years ago, and they're still going strong. They haven't much missed being 'intelligent,' have they?"

TREY THOUGHT THAT would be the end of the discussion, but apparently Sheila didn't. She crossed her arms over her chest and said, "So tell me: How did they do it?"

Jack blinked. "How did who do what?"

Sheila didn't answer his question directly. Instead, she stood very still, and when she spoke again there was a wondering tone in her voice. "And I'll bet it was the same thing at my parents' place, too."

Her gaze sought Trey's. "Listen. I killed the larva. My mom died. I was taken to the hospital. I've been trying to figure out: Why did the house burn down, and who were the other people who died there? No one would ever tell me."

Trey said, "Well, we know that the local governments in Kigoma and Ujiji have been aware of the thieves for a while. Weeks or months."

"Yes." She paused. "Here's what I think happened: Someone was in my house when the thieves came back. Maybe some policemen investigating the scene. Maybe looters or squatters who knew I was gone. Whoever it was, the thieves killed them."

"And you're still alive because you weren't there," Trey said.

She nodded. "Like Kaitlin Finneran."

"Then who burned down the house?" Jack asked.

"The authorities, I'd guess."

Trey thought of the old woman in the market. "Killer wasps being bad for tourism and foreign aid."

Sheila nodded, frowning. "But the question still is: How did the thieves know to come back to the house? How did they *know* I'd killed one of their young?"

"Oh, that's easy," Jack said, his good mood restored.

Sheila looked at him.

"The hive mind."

* * *

SHEILA KEPT LOOKING at him, adding a minuscule shake of her head.

"Come on, you must have heard of it," he said. "Consciousness shared instantly within a population of a social species."

"Well," Sheila said slowly, "yes, I'm familiar with the term, but I always thought it was kind of science fiction. You know, pod people? *Invasion of the Body Snatchers*?"

Jack smiled, pleased with the reference. Then he shook his head. "Haven't you ever seen those nature documentaries, *Planet Earth* or something, that show a flock of sparrows or school of anchovies when a predator comes along?"

"Of course," she said.

"Well, watch them again. They're brilliant. And listen to what David Attenborough says in the narration. When the flock or school tries to escape, what happens? They all make the same decision at precisely the same instant."

After a pause, Sheila said, "But that's because they all read the situation the same way. They all receive and process the same information, and react identically. That doesn't seem very 'hive-mindish' to me."

"That's because it isn't." Jack smiled at her. "It's also not what's going on here. You're doing it again, you know, forcing your feeble human theories on something far more beautiful and profound."

Sheila compressed her lips but didn't say anything.

"Listen. The fish in a school don't all react the same way to the same information . . . because they're not all *receiving* the same information. Think about it. Not every member of the school is under the same threat. If they were each reacting to what they were seeing, the ones on the edges of the school would flee in opposite directions, while the ones closest to the predator would plunge or head for the surface. No coordination. Every fish for itself."

Sheila nodded, beginning to understand. "But that's not what happens."

"No, it's not. The movement of the school is exquisitely—and instantaneously—coordinated. And the goal is for the most members of the flock or school to survive, not any one individual. In fact, you could argue that some individuals sacrifice themselves for the greater good."

Sheila was quiet.

"*Invasion of the Body Snatchers* wasn't the half of it," Jack said. "*That's* the beauty of the real hive mind at work."

There was a long silence. Then Sheila looked at Trey. "You know about this?"

Trey nodded. "You spend as much time out in the woods as I do, you see it in action."

"Okay. I buy it." She paused. "But that leads to the obvious question."

The corners of Jack's mouth turned down. "I know," he said. "'How does it work?'"

"Yes, that's the one."

Now Jack was scowling. "I fucking hate obvious questions."

"Why?"

"Because the answer to this one is: We have no idea."

* * *

"GEORGE SUMMERS IN Ag," Jack decided.

They'd been figuring out what their next step should be. No one wanted to sit around, sticking pins in the map.

"Ugh," Trey said. "The government?"

"I know. But Agriculture is in charge of keeping track of invasive species."

Sheila didn't look impressed. "Things like wood-boring beetles and aphids."

"George is kind of an asshole, but he's not stupid. He might listen." Jack looked Sheila up and down. "Especially if it's you doing the talking. He likes a bit of skirt."

"'A bit of skirt,'" Sheila said.

Jack grinned.

"Anyway, forget it," Sheila went on. "Despite such inducements, I'm not going."

Jack looked surprised, but Trey had seen this coming. "You're planning to go see Kaitlin," he said.

Sheila nodded.

Jack thought about it. "Makes sense," he said. "We might learn something."

She frowned. "I'm not going to learn, but to teach."

Jack said, "What?"

Sheila was looking at Trey. "You came halfway across the world," she said to him, "to tell me that I wasn't crazy. That I hadn't killed my mother." She paused. "You saved my life."

Trey could think of nothing to say in return. But Sheila wasn't looking at him anymore. She was facing the computer screen.

"This poor little girl," she said. "Kaitlin. She deserves someone to do the same for her, doesn't she?"

TWENTY-TWO

Washington, D.C.

"LET ME GET this straight," George Summers said. "You rode the Acela all the way down here to tell me about a bug."

He was sitting behind his desk on the fifth floor of the Department of Agriculture building. A disgruntled-looking man in his late forties, with a face like a hatchet, narrowed eyes, a permanent five-o'clock shadow, and a mouth with a lifetime's experience in turning down at the corners, as it was doing now.

Jack was looking back at him. It wasn't a friendly look. "The Metroliner," he said. "On our own dime. You're forgetting that not everybody's lucky enough to have the American taxpayer springing for his travel."

Trey stayed quiet. As far as he was concerned, the best thing you could do when dealing with government officials was keep your mouth shut.

Especially when you were skew data like Trey. Someone who went off the grid, traveled for a living, got in trouble.

Governments hate skew data.

"I don't know," George Summers was saying to Jack. "The American Museum still pays you, don't they? Seems to me they use plenty of taxpayer money, too."

Jack's mouth was a grim line behind his beard. "I took a vacation day."

"Well, then, I'm afraid you wasted one. We should have just wrapped this up on the phone." Summers pointed to a stack of thick files on his metal-topped desk. "And then I could have added your report to the pile without wasting time with this lunatic social call."

After a moment Jack sighed and said, "George, if you'll just listen—"

But Summers didn't seem to be in the mood for listening. It got in the way of his talking.

"Tell me something," he said, his eyes on Trey. "How many foreign insects and plants do you think make it into the U.S. each year? Let's just say each year since 2001. A rough guess will be fine."

Trey just shook his head. But Jack shifted in his seat and said in a whiny approximation of a child's voice, "Papa, tell us about the effects of September eleventh again!"

Summers's mouth turned down, but the jibe didn't stop him. "One of the first things the new Department of Homeland Security did after 9/11," he said, "was reassign hundreds of Ag scientists who'd been focused on stopping the spread of invasive insect and plant species. Overnight, presto, they became members of Customs and Border Protection."

"He always forgets," Jack said, "that I was there."

Summers stared at him. "Were you? Funny, I don't recall that. I don't recall seeing your face back then, when people who'd spent their whole lives fighting troublesome bugs suddenly found themselves being told to learn the twelve signs of a suicide bomber." His face darkened. "Know what? Surprise! Most of our people didn't want to become cops. You should have seen them heading for the doors. Homeland Security didn't get its new border protectors, and we didn't keep our inspectors."

Summers took a deep breath, and when he went on his voice was calmer. "After that, the pests went wild. Our borders were closed to anyone with swarthy skin, but they were wide open to *them*. Chilli thrips. Emerald ash borers. A thousand others. *They* didn't need passports—"

"Oh, for God's sake," Jack said, "shut up."

Summers stared at him.

"If you don't stop living in the fucking past and start paying attention," Jack went on, "you're going to be dreaming of the days when chilli thrips were your biggest problem."

This was the part of the conversation where, in other countries Trey had visited, he and Jack would have been spun around and frog-marched to the nearest windowless room with bars on the door.

Here though, George Summers merely sat back and gave them a grim-eyed look.

"Why should I listen?" he said. "I already know what you're creaming your jeans to tell me about."

Jack blinked. "Yeah?"

"Yeah. A wasp. A big black wasp."

"YOU THINK I didn't hear?" Summers said. "With all the noise you've been making? You're as bad as cicadas in August, you two."

Jack looked disgusted. "Then why are you jerking us around?"

Summers's dark gaze was unyielding. "Because I don't buy it. I think you're lumping a few truths together with a bunch of guesses and suppositions and wild surmise. With the result that, like all paranoiacs, you're seeing bogeymen everywhere."

Jack said, "We think—"

"I know what you think. And I know how it went." He pointed at Trey. "*You* encountered a new species of wasp in Senegal, along with a lot of mumbo jumbo." Now at Jack. "When Gilliard came back to New York, having screwed his reputation even more than before, *you* took his slender thread of evidence—though that's an insult to slender threads—and ran with it."

He sat back. "And then the two of you hijacked that poor young lady doctor whose mother had been killed. Encouraged her delusions. She's the alcoholic and you're the 'friends' who keep refilling her glass. You two should be ashamed of yourselves."

His expression was bleak. "And where is she now, your damaged friend? Heading to Florida, so she can spread your delusions to another vulnerable victim. Disgraceful."

He stopped, and for a few moments the room was silent. Then Jack reached down for his laptop. "Watch the videos—"

"I've seen them. I watched them all after you called. You think I don't do my homework? Yes, there's a wasp. Hooray."

"And—" Jack said.

Summers ran over him. "And the population is spreading. Surprise! Welcome to the world. Species move around, especially these days, or hadn't you noticed?" He gestured again at the pile of folders on his desk. "What do you think I work on every single frackin' day?"

"They've made it here to the U.S.," Jack said.

Summers's face tightened for a moment. "First of all," he said, and now his voice was quiet, icy. "First of all, I don't believe you. You're doing it again, taking every tragedy you can find and claiming it for your wasp. Leave that poor little girl in Florida alone."

He fixed his gaze on Trey, who stayed silent.

"What killed those people on Marco Island was Africanized bees, one of the pests that fell through the cracks after 9/11," Summers said. "They're not part of your story. But say you're right about the rest. Your wasp's here. The point is: *So what?*"

He looked again at his stack of files. "That just makes it like thousands of other invasive species. Those killer bees we've been talking about. Anacondas. The giant African land snail. You want more? I could go on all day."

His eyes went back to Trey's face. "You want reassurance, Gilliard? Here it is: We'll get to your wasp, I promise, just as soon as we've dealt with all those others."

Trey said, "Wasn't my idea to come here. Fact, I bet Jack ten dollars you'd be completely useless."

Now Summers was quiet. Trey held out a hand, and after a moment Jack, scowling, got out his wallet, extracted a bill, and handed it over.

"Easiest money I've made in months," Trey said.

Summers stood. "Okay, you two clowns. We're done here. I have actual work to do. You know, important work in the *real* world." He pointed. "Close the door on your way out."

Trey stayed where he was. "Three days ago, in Costa Rica, I saw 'my wasp' in action," he said. "I saw it kill two people."

Something flickered in Summers's gaze. "Explain."

Trey explained. When he was halfway through, Summers sat down again.

He didn't speak until Trey was done. Then, his voice hoarse around the edges, he spoke four words.

"I don't believe you."

And five more.

"Get out of my office."

JACK AND TREY left the enormous Agriculture building, wended their way through the concrete barriers strewn along the sidewalk to prevent a car bombing, and crossed Independence Avenue to the Mall. The day had grown hot, the afternoon sun hanging heavy in a smeared sky.

They had time to kill before catching their train home. At a food truck that was still selling lunch, each bought a falafel and a can of soda wrapped in a wet napkin. Then they sat on a bench amid purposeful men and women in business suits, meandering tourists in shorts and T-shirts, and runners whose neon shoes shone like beacons as they went past.

Jack took a bite of his sandwich, then wiped a hand across his mouth and said, "Think they've made it here yet?"

Trey shrugged. "Maybe. Only a matter of time."

"They'll love it." Jack watched the oblivious crowd. "Perfect weather and so many hosts to choose from."

They ate in silence for a while. Then Jack said, "What's your take on our friend George?"

Trey finished his sandwich before answering. Then he said, "He was trying too hard."

"You think?"

"Yeah. You could hear it in his voice."

Jack nodded. "Agree. Overrehearsed, right? And all those pat phrases: 'Disgraceful.' 'You should be ashamed.' Yadda."

"He didn't expect to hear about my face-to-face at La Tamandua, though."

"Yeah. That shook him."

A busload of Chinese tourists passed, heading toward the Capitol Building. Eyes on them, Jack said, "Question is, why try to throw us off?"

"That one's easy," Trey said.

He was thinking about his taxi driver in Kigoma, who'd been reluctant to take him to see the Connellys' torched house. The old woman in the marketplace, wary about talking to him, always watching to see who might be listening. And Sheila's guards at the hospital, making sure no one talked to her.

He thought about governments and what they would do to protect their investments. The money they made from tourism, foreign trade, imports-exports, and other markets that would crash if word of the thieves got out.

He thought about the way governments made the same mistakes over and over again. It was what they did best.

"They're going to try to keep the lid on," he said.

Jack's mouth tightened, making his beard bristle. "For how long?"

Trey shrugged. "Forever?"

"Least till Election Day."

The two of them looked out at the passing crowd. All the government workers chatting as they walked by. All those moving mouths. Over on Constitution Avenue, a TV news truck was setting up a remote shoot. Another news camera was set up in front of the Reflecting Pool, the Capitol Building in the background.

"Election Day or forever," Jack said, "I don't think it's gonna work."

TWENTY-THREE

Marco Island

ON A TRIP to the United States when Sheila was a child, her parents had brought her to Florida. She had only the vaguest recollection of Disney World and the various restaurants and beaches they'd visited. Only one memory remained vivid two decades later.

They'd taken a walk at dusk from their hotel in one of the cities on the North Coast. Daytona, maybe, or Jacksonville. Their path had taken them down street after street filled with small, newly constructed wood-frame houses built on plots of what until recently had been wetland. Every single square foot of the natural world had been filled, leveled, cleared, and "reclaimed" for humans to develop.

Reclaimed. Killed, was how Sheila had thought of it. People had killed Florida.

But then they'd come to a single undeveloped plot, one that still contained trees and brambly bushes and muddy water. There was a big white sign saying *Land: For*

Sale, and Sheila guessed that within a year there would be a house there, just like the ones that stood on either side.

For the moment, though, a remarkable abundance of wildlife was using this tiny stretch of unspoiled land as a refuge. A dozen white egrets perched in the branches, their nighttime roost. Turtles were stacked on a log, catching the last warmth of the day, and butterflies and dragonflies flitted here and there.

The For Sale sign was streaked with bird shit.

That was when Sheila had the thought she still remembered two decades later. People could—and would—do everything they could to kill Florida, to kill the world, but that it was ridiculous, hubristic, to think they'd succeed. Nature would find a way to survive.

These birds, turtles, butterflies would have to move when this land, too, was cleared, but they'd find someplace to go. Some would probably die, but not all.

The rest might even return to the plots where the first houses had been carved out of the swamp. Sheila had noticed that some of the buildings were already overgrown, sagging, their wood rotting in the relentless humidity and heat.

THE FINNERAN FUNERAL was at a Catholic church that looked like it had been built the week before. Hot white light poured through the clear windows up near the top, cooler blue and green through the stained glass lower down.

Sheila saw that the beams running across the ceiling showed signs of termite damage.

The sad, shocked crowd had too many young parents

in it, and far too many children. Girls, mostly, dressed in whatever dark clothes they owned, their faces sallow under permanent Florida tans. Short skirts were in style here, rows of bare legs swinging in the pews.

A young priest spoke of seasons, of forgiveness, of love. Sheila didn't bother to follow what he was saying. She was looking at the two simple wood coffins that sat before the priest and thinking about her own parents.

Then her gaze sought out the gray-haired woman in the front pew and the girl in black beside her. Mary Finneran and her granddaughter, the child of the deceased. Kaitlin.

Kaitlin was bent over, focused on something in her lap, her right hand moving. Writing? No. Sheila thought she was drawing.

AFTERWARD, SHEILA WENT to the end of the line to pay respect to the mourners. At the head, Mary Finneran was pale, red eyed, but she seemed calm and composed. Strong. Beside her, Kaitlin looked thinner than she had in the video, with her grandmother's sharp chin and a watchful gaze.

Hanging from her right hand was a piece of white paper with a drawing on it. In her left was a ziplock bag containing a few colored pencils.

Sheila couldn't make out what the drawing showed, just its range of colors. It seemed that the girl had mostly used silver or gray, with a little blue as well.

The line moved slowly forward. Nobody was speaking until they reached the Finnerans, not even the children shuffling along. It was quiet. Silent as a church.

Eventually Sheila's turn came. Mary Finneran locked eyes with her. "Dr. Connelly?"

Sheila nodded. "I'm so sorry," she said.

"Thank you." The older woman looked Sheila up and down, as if deciding whether to trust her. Kaitlin's quick glance held the same cautious judgment.

Mary looked over to where the hearse, the limousine, and the diminished crowd of family and friends waited for the trip to the cemetery. The priest and a man in a dark suit stood nearby, exuding mournful impatience.

"We have to go," she said, still indecisive. Then, sighing, she reached into her black handbag and withdrew a square slip of paper. "Come to this address at five o'clock," she said. "Can you find it?"

Sheila said yes.

Without another word, Mary Finneran put her hand on Kaitlin's shoulder. Together they walked out the door and into the light.

As the girl turned, Sheila caught a glimpse of what she'd been drawing during the service. It was a dolphin. No, two: an adult and a baby, pearly blue-gray and alive in the gleaming silver water.

SHEILA HAD CALLED the day before. Without giving any details, she'd told Mary Finneran that she thought the official story of the Finnerans' death was wrong.

"Why should I believe you?" Mary Finneran had said. "Why do I need you in my hair? You can't imagine the number of calls I've gotten, and plenty of them have been from cranks. Why should I trust you're any different?"

Sheila had thought it over before saying, "You were

the first"—struggling with the words—"on the scene, right?"

"Yes."

"Did you see any dead bees?"

"*What?*"

Sheila, certain that the grief-stricken older woman was about to hang up on her, had hurried on. "Listen," she'd said. "Africanized bees are deadly, but they're still honeybees. When they sting a person, they leave their stinger behind. Then they die almost immediately. Someone who's been attacked will be surrounded by dead bees."

There'd been a long silence over the line. Then Mary Finneran had said, "You're telling me Kait was right."

Before Sheila could answer, she'd gone on. "No! No, I need to hear it face-to-face. Can you come here?"

And Sheila had said, Yes. Yes, of course.

FIVE O'CLOCK. THEY were sitting on Mary's back porch, the hot day edging into a cooler evening.

Mary went to get something to drink. Sheila leaned back in her chair and watched first a white egret and then a small flock of ibises flap past.

Unkillable Florida.

When Mary returned, she was carrying a tall glass filled with ice cubes and a light brown liquid. "Iced tea," she said, "with a kick."

"Thank you." Sheila took the glass, cool and sweaty in her hand. She sipped it. There was gin in it.

"Where's Kaitlin?" she asked.

Mary sat across a glass-topped table from Sheila, sipped her own drink, and said, "She goes by Kait. She's inside drawing something, I imagine, but I'm sure she'll be out soon."

Then her mouth firmed. "Which makes it a good time now to spit out what you came down to tell me."

Sheila nodded. Before she could speak, though, the door slid open. Kait stood there, wearing yellow shorts and a red T-shirt with some restaurant's name on it, her face without expression. All coltish arms and legs, unruly mop of hair, and dark eyes staring into Sheila's own from across the deck.

She was holding something in her hand: a sheet of paper.

Mary said, "Kait, what have you been drawing?"

Still the girl hung back. As Sheila watched, she saw her body gradually grow rigid. When she finally moved, it was on stiff legs. An angry stride. She slapped the drawing facedown on the table in front of Sheila.

"They won't believe me," she said, almost spitting out the words. "They say I'm making it up."

Sheila turned the drawing over. It was what she expected it to be, but even so the sight made her heart pound.

A portrait, almost scientifically accurate, of a thief. The head, the bloodred wings, the aggressive posture, triangular head tilted, the way it stood high on its legs—all were unmistakable.

Only its abdomen was too thick, but the whitish liquid Kait had drawn dribbling from the end explained that, too. This was a newborn thief, still attaining its final adult shape.

"Well?" Kait was staring at Sheila. "Do *you* believe me?"

Instead of replying, Sheila bent over, reached into the shoulder bag at her feet, and withdrew a copy of Jack's drawing.

She placed it on the table beside the other. The two thieves stared up at them.

"My God," Mary said. Her hand was over her mouth.

"Yes," Sheila said to Kait, "I believe you."

Kait stared down at the drawings. "The wasp-thing," she said.

THEY TOLD THEIR stories. Only once, as Kait described watching the life and death of the baby dolphin, did she grow teary. The rest of the time, she spoke in a sober voice that betrayed, Sheila thought, too little emotion. As if the girl had already spent too much time thinking about what she'd seen. Or had already dissociated herself from it.

The same way Sheila sounded as she described what had happened to her mother.

Mary mostly listened. By the time the two of them were done, she looked older than when they'd begun.

"You say these creatures started in Africa," she said.

Sheila nodded. "As far as we know, yes. West Africa."

"But now they're here."

"Yes."

"Why?"

Sheila gave a shrug. "You must know how easy it is for invasive species to spread in this day and age." She paused. "They used to have to hitch rides on the wind or on islands of floating vegetation. These days it's effortless."

Mary was frowning. "That's not what I meant." She gestured at the drawings. "These creatures were happy to live—and stay—in their forests for, what, thousands of years. Millions. Why are they spreading *now*?"

"We don't know yet," Sheila said. "Declines in population of food and host species in their home range? A change in their biology, some evolutionary leap that's led to increased aggressiveness? Pure chance? Any answer is just a guess."

"It doesn't matter why," Kait said.

Sheila said, "You're right."

"It just matters that they're here." Kait looked up at her. "They're in Africa. They're here. Are they everywhere else, too?"

Without thinking, Sheila put a hand out and brushed a lock of hair out of Kait's eyes. The girl flinched a little, but didn't pull away.

"I'm afraid so, honey," she said.

WHEN KAIT WENT inside to get ready for bed, Mary said, "Why were they attacked? I mean, my son and his wife. Was it just a coincidence?"

Sheila looked at her, trying to decide how much speculation to share. Finally she said, "That's possible, but I think it might have been something else."

"What?"

"Retribution."

Mary stared at her. "You mean, like payback? They come back and punish you?"

"Yes."

"Sounds like a crackpot theory to me."

Sheila thought of Jack's similar—though less temperate—response and didn't say anything.

"But how would the other ones know?" Mary's gaze shifted toward the sky, where a big heron was winging in front of darkening clouds. "Are they always watching?"

Sheila opened her mouth to say something like, *We have no idea,* when she heard Mary say, "Oh, God."

Sheila lowered her gaze.

The older woman's face was contorted. "Kait was there," she said. "When Tim killed that one. *She was there.*"

Sheila understood. Somehow the idea hadn't occurred to her. The idea that Kait might still be in danger.

"I think," she said and hesitated. "I think that, if it was going to happen . . . it would have already."

"But you don't know, do you?" Mary was on her feet. "You're just guessing."

She stopped beside the door. "I have a friend with a place in Charleston," she said, half to herself. "I'll call her from the road."

Then she paused, her eyes widening. "But will that be enough? These creatures. You said they're everywhere." She seemed almost to be begging. "Sheila—tell me where to go that will be safe."

But Sheila had no answer.

Fifteen minutes later Kait was sitting in Mary's car. "Grandma," she was saying, "we'll be fine."

Mary, ignoring her, made sure Kait's seat belt was securely fastened.

When Sheila had loaded two suitcases into the trunk, Mary handed her another square piece of notepaper. There was a phone number written on it in green ink.

"Call me when you know it's safe," Mary said. "When you're sure."

Sheila just looked at her, and after a moment Mary, amazingly, laughed. It was a bitter, self-mocking sound, but still, it was a laugh.

"All right," she said. "Don't wait *that* long."

TWENTY-FOUR

Manhattan

BURUNDI. MADAGASCAR. FIJI. Ecuador. Mexico.

Trey stuck the last of the morning's pins in the map, then stood back to look at the ever-thickening and growing clusters.

"Useless," he said under his breath. Then, more loudly, "I'm useless."

Jack looked up from his desk. After their encounter with George Summers at Ag, he'd admitted that he had to get back to work. To his real work, the kind the museum paid him for. He was still gathering data on the thieves, but an increasing amount of his attention was focused elsewhere.

In front of him lay a tray from Entomology's collections room. Rows of black-and-yellow wasps stuck on pins, a yellowing card scrawled with ornate fountain-pen handwriting identifying genus and species beneath each one. *Philanthidae*, the drawer was labeled. And the English, too: *Beewolves*.

Beewolves, wasps that preyed on bees, were Jack's specialty.

"What did you say?" he asked.

"I said that I'm useless here." Trey wriggled his shoulders. "Looking at YouTube videos, reading blogs, checking out the latest picture pinned on—"

"Pinterest," Jack said.

"Whatever. A million people could do all that better than I can."

"Look on the bright side," Jack said. "Your girlfriend will be back soon. She can take over the job of sticking pins in the wall, and you can go back to staring out the window. You're a ninja master at that."

His eyes widened a little at Trey's expression. "Okay, don't bite me. Ix-nay on the ins-pay. What are you going to do instead?"

Trey was silent for a few moments, but he'd already thought it through. He'd known for days where his path was leading.

"I have to find out what the thieves are doing," he said, "and I can't do that here. Not via computer. Not with—" He held his hands out. "Not with *pins*, real or virtual."

Jack gave a half grin. " 'Obsessive Traveler Flies the Coop,' " he said. "I read it in the paper, just below 'Dog Bites Man!' "

His expression grew more serious. "How, though?" he asked. "How do you know where to go?"

Trey had been figuring that out, too. He looked at the telephone, a technology even he was comfortable with, though he hated it, too.

"I know where to start," he said.

Kinyare, Uganda

"EIGHT WEEKS," THOMAS Nyramba said.

Fortyish, thickly built, with a shaven head shaped like a bullet, he was sitting behind the desk of his wood-paneled office in the Kinyare police station. Trey occupied a wooden chair opposite him.

The sunlight coming in through the windows was tinted green by the surrounding forest. Over the rattling of the ceiling fan, Trey heard the nearby shrill of crickets and, farther off, the loud calls of a great blue turaco, a dinosaur-like bird that lived only in these African rain forests.

"Eight weeks, or a little more." Nyramba shrugged. "That was when we first saw them. How long were they here before that?" Another shrug. "Who knows?"

Trey nodded. Yes: Who knew? He'd spent four months in this region some years back, surveying the area for ICT, and he knew that the dense, wet forests guarded their secrets closely. The people of Kinyare might have detected the thieves just two months earlier, but that didn't mean the wasps had just arrived. They could have been hiding out for years, picking off a colobus here, a golden monkey there. A chimpanzee. A human.

"But it does not matter," Nyramba said. "They are here now, and they will stay."

Another cry echoed through the room. Not the call of a turaco this time, or any other bird. A man's shout.

Thomas Nyramba tilted his head. "John Ndele," he said. "Do you remember him?"

Trey did. A loud drunk, with small, yellow-shot eyes and a propensity for using his fists. You couldn't have spent much time in Kinyare without knowing John Ndele.

"He finally killed his wife," Nyramba said. "So now he is down the hall."

In a cell, that meant. In many villages, in many countries, killing your wife was not much of a crime. But in Kinyare, Thomas Nyramba's rules applied. You broke them at your peril.

Ndele shouted again.

"That would wear on my nerves after a while," Trey said.

"Yes. It does." Nyramba's sudden, wolfish grin showed white teeth against dark skin. "But not for much longer."

JOHN NDELE LOOKED up from his cot when the cell door swung open. His expression said, *About time!*

But then, as he pushed himself into a sitting position, he saw who had come for him. His squinty eyes widened, and his face paled.

Along with Trey, Thomas Nyramba had brought his two deputies, beefy young men in khaki shirts and sunglasses. "You thought we would let you walk free?" Nyramba said. Then, "Stand up."

His voice prickled the hair on the back of Trey's neck.

Ndele didn't move. The deputies looked at Nyramba, saw him nod, stepped into the cell, and hauled the prisoner to his feet.

For a moment Trey thought Ndele would faint. He slumped in the deputies' grasp, and his eyes rolled, showing the yellowish whites.

Nyramba took a step forward and slapped his face. That woke Ndele up. He began to weep.

Trey stood still and did not speak.

* * *

"HOW MANY IN your village have died?" Trey asked.

They were heading down the Nkuru Trail, which led south away from town and into an undisturbed stretch of forest. The deputies went first, pushing Ndele, his hands cuffed, before them. Trey and Nyramba followed, far enough behind that they could talk.

"Too many, before we learned." The police chief sighed. "Our doctor. A nurse. Others. Five of our hunters never returned from the forest."

Trey grimaced. "I think hunters are always among the first," he said. "They're alone. Unprotected."

Nyramba walked a ways without answering. Then he gave Trey a sidelong glance. "That is not the only reason."

Trey waited.

"The *majizi* and the hunters, they want the same things. Bushmeat. Monkey meat."

Still Trey was silent.

"They will not accept anyone else in their territory," Nyramba said. "Unless—"

"Unless what?" Trey said.

Nyramba gave him an amused glance. "You know the answer," he said. "You've figured it out."

He was right.

THEY WALKED. THE forest grew darker. The trail was a muddy, winding stripe alongside a lowland stream strung with waxy white flowers and mushrooms that smelled like rotting meat, like death. Ndele, stumbling, struck dumb by his fate, needed more encouragement from the deputies, so progress was slow.

"Not so much farther," Nyramba said. "Twenty minutes, perhaps."

"How many have you brought here?" Trey asked.

"Fourteen. So far."

Trey kept his face a blank, but Nyramba smiled anyway.

"That many," Trey said finally, "from Kinyare alone?"

The police chief laughed. "No, only one from the village before this. Mattias, who assaulted women, and would not stop."

Trey said, "From where, then? I don't understand."

"Why must all bad men come from our village?" Nyramba was still smiling. "The world is full of those who deserve to be condemned."

When Trey was silent, he went on. "The first four came from the Lord's Resistance Army. Together, they had probably killed a thousand people here in Uganda and in Sudan. Another was a member of Al Qaeda, plotting against our president. Fool! Another, from the town of Inomo, has not been able to stay away from young boys. Children, I mean."

He stopped and faced Trey. "Tell me," he said. "What else should I have done? They had to die. Should I have let them die without purpose? Without use?"

Trey didn't answer.

"And, at the same time, let the innocent get taken by the *majizi*?"

THE END OF their trail was a small clearing not far from the stream. Ndele was only half conscious by now.

There was the stump of a fallen kapok tree beside the trail. Someone had plunged a large spike deep into the stump and attached a chain to the spike. The deputies attached the end of the chain to Ndele's manacles, shook them so the chain clanked, then stepped back. The prisoner didn't even test the strength of his bonds, merely lay back with his eyes closed.

Their job done, the deputies went past Trey and Nyramba and back down the trail. Their faces were expressionless, and they were walking fast. They didn't look back.

Trey watched until they were out of sight, then said, "How did you choose this place?"

"It is where I first saw the *majizi*." Nyramba sighed. "Emmanuel, a bushmeat hunter, he was here."

Trey drew in a breath through his nose. He thought he might have caught the slightest whiff of the familiar scent.

"Are they here now?" he asked.

"Yes." Nyramba looked around. "Somewhere. They always stay downwind. And you only see them when they want you to."

Then he stiffened. "There."

Trey followed his gaze. Saw one thief, two . . . four of them. Two moved to hover over the trail, right at eye level, perhaps fifteen feet away. Two others flanked them, one on a small bush to the right, the other half hidden in the foliage on the left.

Standing guard. That was what those two were doing. Cleverly, too, using a formation that didn't allow you to keep your eyes on all of them at once. You couldn't kill them all with one shot—not even with #9 birdshot—or strike them down with a single blow.

If you killed one, or even two, the others would reach you before you had time to adjust or protect yourself.

Trey stood still. The two that were hovering seemed to be looking straight into his eyes.

"You interest them," Nyramba said. There was an edge to his voice that might have been alarm. "We must go."

Trey didn't want to take his eyes off the wasps. Most of all, he wanted to see what would happen next to the prisoner, cowering beside the stump.

"Now," Nyramba said.

Still Trey was reluctant to leave. The same reluctance that had pulled at him when he stood beside the thief colony in the Casamance. Looking over his shoulder as he walked, he watched as the thieves swooped toward Ndele. One landed on the prisoner's shoulder and skittered around behind his neck, while the second perched on his ragged white shirt just above his belly.

The trail curved and Ndele was out of sight. Still Trey hesitated, wanting to go back, to see it through till the end.

He felt a hand on his arm. "No," Nyramba said. "They do not like to be watched."

Trey turned away, listening as intently as he could for any sign from the hidden scene behind them.

But he heard no sound at all.

"NOW I WILL show you something else," Nyramba said. "If you think you are strong enough to see it."

Trey didn't reply, just followed as the older man led the way back up the trail. This time, though, they turned onto a smaller path that headed west through wet, silent forest.

Less than a quarter of a mile down the path, Trey heard the clanking of chains ahead and some deeper, grittier noises he couldn't identify. Sounds that grew louder as the two of them approached a bend in the trail.

"Slow," Nyramba said, his voice and expression both grave. "Take care."

Trey nodded and stepped around the bend. Then he stopped where he was, his heart giving a convulsive leap in his chest.

Ahead stood another stump, another spike, another chain. Another prisoner. Two adult thieves guarded it from low-hanging branches, alert but not alarmed by Trey and Nyramba's appearance.

But the similarities to the last scene ended there. This prisoner was a naked man, his body filthy, his skin covered with oozing cuts and scrapes, his stomach grotesquely swollen. He was standing in the middle of the path and staring directly at Trey with a silvery gaze. His chin was slicked with blood—maybe his own—and his breathing came in tortured grunts.

The last terrifying madness, the old book had said. *Confronted only at your own mortal peril.*

Trey thought about the colobus monkey at the thief colony in the Casamance. The way it had gotten to its feet after being stung. Its bared teeth as it had come across the clearing at him.

"What is in the venom," he said, "that causes this?"

"You have seen it before?" Nyramba asked, stopping a stride behind him.

Trey didn't reply. Calculating the length of the chain, he stepped forward to get a closer look.

"Any farther," Nyramba said, "and I will be returning to Kinyare alone."

Trey said, "How near is he to the end?"

Before Nyramba could answer, the prisoner straightened and, without any warning, leaped forward to the limits of the chain. Gasping and growling, more blood spilling from around bared and broken teeth, he reached for Trey's throat with his right hand.

Trey, holding his ground, saw that the prisoner's left arm, the one attached by the chain to the stump, was dislocated at both the elbow and shoulder, turned nearly inside out. But the man—the host—seemed to feel no pain.

"At this time," Nyramba said, "they will kill you if you try to harm the young. And sometimes even if you do not."

As if called, the wormlike creature nesting inside the snarling man came to the surface. Trey saw a flash of white in the black circle of the airhole before it retreated deeper into the tunnel of flesh.

The host ground his teeth, yanking at the chain, grasping with clawlike fingers. Pink froth dripped to the ground.

Trey turned away. Nyramba was watching him closely, something in his expression that might have been amusement.

"You asked a question," the police chief said. "After the final sting, the convicted grow worse and worse, but they only become like this at the very end. This man's punishment will likely end tonight, and then he will have peace."

Trey didn't speak, just walked past him and back along the trail. Behind them, the prisoner howled at the sky.

"SO . . . FOURTEEN."

Thomas Nyramba smiled. "Fifteen now."

They were back in his office, drinking Nile Specials.

"And the thieves, they stay away from the people of the village?" Trey said.

A nod. "We have made a treaty, and both of us respect it."

Trey listened to the language, the choice of words, and thought of what Jack's response would have been. It was all about survival and procreation.

He said, "But what happens when you run out of . . . offerings?"

Nyramba laughed. "What? Run out? People are bringing us"—he paused, searching for the word—"*troublemakers* from every town that the thieves have left alone so far. Four more will come tomorrow from Fort Portal."

He sat back in his chair, still smiling. "We will never run out."

"Is the same thing being done in other towns?"

"Of course. Where it is needed." He gave a shrug. "But none of us will ever lack for people who, like Ndele, deserve what they get."

Trey was silent.

"And you in the United States?" Nyramba said. "In New York? What is your response?"

Trey shook his head. "There've been very few reports so far anywhere yet, and none in New York."

"There will be."

"I know."

"And when there are, when the *majizi* come," Nyramba said, "you Americans will do the same things."

Trey was silent.

Or worse, he thought.

"Or worse," Nyramba said.

TWENTY-FIVE

Jabiru Wetland Preserve, Queensland, Australia

"YOU LOOK OLDER," Christopher Gilliard said.

Trey looked at him. He'd been thinking the same thing: Some last spark of youth in his brother had been extinguished since they'd last seen each other. He'd always been more solid, more settled, than Trey, but now time had thinned his sun-bleached hair, broadened his paunch, and lent his face the solidity of encroaching middle age.

He was thirty-nine. Trey was thirty-six. Neither of them were kids anymore.

Only one of them had chosen a life that allowed him to pretend he was.

Christopher said, "When were you last here?"

Trey thought back. With all the traveling he'd done, all the countries he'd visited, he'd made it to this corner of northern Australia just a handful of times, most recently three years ago. Actually, closer to four.

"Too long," he said.

"And it took all this to bring you back here."

"Yeah."

Christopher turned his head to look over the wetlands he'd been hired to preserve, to protect. He breathed in through his nose, and though there was no smell other than that of damp earth and waterweed and, from farther away, dust carried by the wind from the Outback, Trey guessed what odor his brother was searching for. He'd been searching for it himself.

"You can't stay here," he said. "You and Margie and the girls."

Christopher didn't reply at once. Trey saw the corner of his mouth twitch upward and caught a glimpse of the boy he'd adventured with in a dozen different countries while their parents were otherwise occupied.

Still without looking at Trey, he said, "Yeah? How about you? You don't stay anywhere. You spend your whole life running. Do *you* feel safe?"

Trey was silent. After a few moments, Christopher did turn his head. There was affection in his expression, and amusement, too. Even after all this time, he was still the big brother, Trey the child. And they both knew it.

"The world's too small," Trey said at last.

"For you. For most of us, it's just right." Christopher smiled. "And anyway, I think you're missing something: I'm safer from those bugs than you are, no matter how far or fast you run."

Trey blinked. "You are? Why?"

"Because they need me."

THEY WERE STANDING on a grassy bank, the freshwater marsh at their feet stretching toward a row of forested hills in the distance. The calm surface was green with algae, silvery where the sun caught it. Black swans and Australian teal and magpie geese paddled across the water and dabbled in the weeds, while lily-trotters ventured across giant lily pads on long-toed feet.

Not just swans and geese relied on the marsh for water and food. Driving in, Trey and Christopher had passed a big gang of gray kangaroos near the preserve entrance. Honeyeaters and other small birds flitted in the underbrush, and a flock of cockatoos clad in graveyard black circled overhead, letting loose with mournful honking cries.

The wetlands were a human creation, kind of. They had been here for thousands of years until the Europeans colonized the area during the nineteenth century. In an eyeblink, the flow of water was diverted, put to other uses, and the wildlife died out or went elsewhere.

On Trey's last visit, Christopher had explained the system of damming and water diversion that had restored the original marshes. Now he said, "These days, we need to keep pumping or the wetlands will dry out again." He snapped his fingers. "Like that."

He gestured again, this time taking in not only the green hills that bordered the marsh, but what Trey knew lay beyond. The vast Outback, hundreds of thousands of square miles of searing heat and spiny grassland and redrock desert, where wildlife was scarce and water almost nonexistent.

"These bugs of yours, they value the wetlands," he said. "Like every living thing, they need water. Also food and hosts for their young, both of which congregate here. This is an oasis for them, too."

Trey saw where he was going.

"If it weren't for me and my team," Christopher said, "the oasis would vanish. The bugs don't want that."

Trey thought about Thomas Nyramba, so certain that he and the *majizi* understood each other. That, like two warring societies, they'd reached a deal.

Trey had seen nothing to prove Nyramba wrong, or Christopher, either. Not exactly. What neither of them seemed to understand, though, was that the deal wasn't between two equal partners. It wasn't a treaty, signed and witnessed and understood, that happened to exist between two different species.

No. It was the same deal as the one enslaved ants made with their captors: We'll do what you command. In return, you'll let us live.

For now.

"How do you know this?" he said to Christopher. "How can you be sure?"

For a long time his brother didn't answer. He stood without moving, and when he finally spoke his eyes stayed fixed on the glimmering surface of the marsh.

"Brian Pearce," he said. "He managed the preserve along with me. They killed him—or, I guess you'd say, used him. When he died, I sent the rest of the staff home and shut this place. Two days later, the pumps broke down."

He watched a heron stalk along the shallows, hunting for fish. "I couldn't stand it, to let it all go to hell. So I came back, just me, and fixed what was broken."

His expression bleak, he waited long enough that Trey said, "And?"

"And they watched me, the whole time I was here

working. Six of them, maybe, or eight, when I was out-side, at least two whenever I went in."

Trey made a sound in his throat.

"Yeah." Christopher managed a grin. "I'd prefer not to live through another day like that one, ta very much."

He shook his arms and shoulders. "Anyway, they fig-ured out what I was doing, or at least that I was necessary to this place, and since then they've left us alone. All of us. I can tell they've taken a few of the kangaroos, and who knows how many smaller mammals, but they're hands-off the humans for now."

He tilted his head and laughed. "I guess I owe my life to these waters, just as much as the lily-trotters, ducks, and herons do."

Then he turned his back on the wetland. "Let's go," he said. "There's something I want to show you at home."

Trey said, "Okay."

Christopher paused and added, "And also, Margie and the girls would love to see you."

Trey smiled and nodded, but Christopher looked a little embarrassed.

He was embroidering the truth, and they both knew it.

MARGIE GILLIARD WAS tall and willowy and blond, with a firm jaw, blue eyes, and a no-nonsense manner. She greeted Trey with wariness, her behavior reminding him why: She'd always worried that whatever wanderlust infected him would spread to his brother. But she seemed pleased enough to bring him a beer and insist that he stay for dinner and the night.

He accepted the offers. "Thank you."

Her eyes betrayed a glimmer of amusement. "Well, we could hardly make you stay in a hotel, could we? You're Kit's brother."

"I hear unspoken words," Trey said, smiling. "'Even if not much of one.'"

She laughed. "You'll do," she said, "until someone better comes along."

In the living room the seven-year-old twins, Jaida and Nicole, long limbed and tan in shorts and T-shirts, stopped playing a video game to look him over. They claimed to remember him and proved it by recalling the time he'd dropped a pitcher of water that had shattered all over the deck outside.

Despite the years, they seemed comfortable with him in about thirty seconds. Trey found himself remembering—with the same surprise he always felt—that he enjoyed being around children. He often found it easier to talk to them than to adults.

Regardless of anything else, the fact that he lived in New York City part-time made him golden to the two girls. They asked him endless questions about shopping on Fifth Avenue, celebrity sightings, and other subjects he knew nothing about, and thankfully forgave him his cluelessness.

When they'd relinquished him, Christopher jerked his head toward a door off the living room. Trey followed, and they entered a small, dim study containing a desk, a bookshelf, and a computer.

"'Kit'?" Trey said.

Christopher smiled. "Got a problem with that, Thomas the Third?"

Then his expression darkened. "You need to see this,"

he said, sitting down at his computer. "An old friend of mine in the Southern Highlands sent it to me."

The Southern Highlands were on New Guinea, the enormous island that lay just a short flight north of Port Douglas. Before settling in Australia, Christopher had worked on water projects in that area.

Trey had visited him there only once. He retained vivid memories of the Huli Wigmen, with their painted faces and elaborate wigs of human hair twined with flowers and the feathers of birds of paradise. A proud, warlike people, they'd been more than willing to show off their ceremonial dress to outsiders, but had kept their age-old ceremonies a secret.

"The video was raw when I got it," Christopher was saying. "I've done a little editing, but it's still pretty rough."

It began with a close-up on a man's face. An old man with dark skin and fierce eyes, staring straight into the camera. "I am Isaac Agiru," he said. "Listen to what I am about to tell you."

"Agiru. I've known him for years." Christopher gave a snort of amusement. "He was a rebel until the government changed. Now he's a member of the National Parliament. Tough old bugger."

"He's speaking English," Trey asked. "Not New Guinea Pidgin."

"Agiru wants this to be seen and understood."

"Two months ago," the old man went on, "the *stilmen* came to the highlands."

"*Stilmen* is the Pidgin word for thieves," Christopher said.

Trey knew.

"We did not understand how to fight them, and at first many died throughout the district." Agiru's expression turned fierce. "But soon we learned."

"Look at him!" Christopher's voice was admiring. "Don't cross the Huli. Don't even steal a pig from them."

"Today we will go to war," Agiru said.

For a moment the screen went black. "How does he know?" Trey asked.

"Watch."

The screen lit. It showed two men lying on their backs on a grass mat on the floor of a hut. When the camera came in close, Trey could see that their eyes were half open. Light from offscreen caught a silvery sheen.

He took a breath. Beside him, Christopher said, "Seen this before, too, have you?"

Trey nodded. "Too often."

"Today we will take out the worms that live inside these men," Isaac Agiru was saying, though the camera remained focused on the dreaming men. "Later, the *stilmen* will come. They will want revenge, as they always do, but we will defeat them."

Trey thought about Sheila, about the little girl Kait and her parents, and about revenge.

The video's view shifted to a dusty village square ringed by wooden huts and an elaborately ornamented longhouse, the building where all the important—and secret—Huli rituals took place. A steady stream of men was emerging from the front door. Sixty, or perhaps even more.

They were dressed for battle, with painted faces beneath their large, triangular wigs. They looked powerful, unafraid.

Trey could see a pile of wooden and metal objects in the corner of the screen. He leaned in closer to inspect the image.

"I've studied that," Christopher said. "They had guns, clubs, nets, and canisters and sprayers of what I imagine is DDT."

DDT, the pesticide banned for forty years in the United States but still available in other countries.

"You can't see when the battle starts, but I think they rigged mist nets to arrows, and shot them over the first wave of *stilmen*."

Trey nodded. It was a clever strategy. Still . . . "How many attack?" he asked.

Christopher shrugged. "A lot."

The screen showed the closed door of the hut where the two infected men lay. After a moment, the door opened, and a young man came out. He walked up to the camera and showed what he held in his hands: the limp white bodies of two thief larvae.

Agiru's voice. "And Jonathan and Tiken?"

The young man shook his head. His face was grim. "It has been too long," he said.

The camera returned to the old man's face. "Now we will wait," he said. "They will come."

"How do the thieves know?" Christopher asked. "I'm guessing they have a sentry that goes and warns the colony. Something like the ones who were watching me."

Trey said, "Maybe."

There was a jump in the video. When it focused again, Trey could see that hours had passed. Dusk was approaching. The longhouse cast black shadows across the ground.

Whoever was carrying the camera put it down on a

wall or other structure, aimed at the plaza and the waiting men.

Most of the warriors had been sprawled on the ground, but now they got to their feet and went to the pile of weapons. A moment later they had moved out of sight of the lens, some heading to the front of the plaza, some to the sides.

"They come," Isaac Agiru's voice said.

Trey leaned forward, his ears straining to hear the hum of wings, his nose prickling as if somehow he could smell the thieves' odor.

A moment later, someone screamed, a sound of agony. There was a flurry of movement on the right side of the screen—a man staggering, his hands clutching at his face as he fell to the ground. This was followed by disordered shouts, the twang of unseen bows, the sound of gunfire, the sharp crack made by birdshot shells.

And then someone knocked into the camera. The view jolted and spun, coming to rest aimed upward at a patch of treetops.

Trey said, "Don't tell me—"

Christopher sighed. "Sorry, yes."

More shots, more cries, another scream. The hum of wings close to the camera's microphone. A glimpse of a thin black body. Nothing else. No one reset the camera's aim.

All Trey could make out were the trees against a darkening sky. He wanted to climb inside the screen. He needed to *see*.

The scene leaped forward again. Hours had clearly passed, and now it was nighttime. It seemed the battle was over.

"That's it?" Trey said.

Christopher nodded.

The camera was again focused on Agiru's face, just as it had been at the beginning. Illuminated by the harsh light of an offscreen lantern, the old man was still wearing his full Huli regalia. His face was painted yellow, with red slashes under each eye and beneath his mouth; a white line ran down his forehead and nose. His beard was blue, his wig ornamented with brilliant red-and-yellow bird-of-paradise feathers.

"It is done," he said. *"Mipela I paitin ol stilmen na killim olgeta."*

We fought the thieves and killed them.

His eyes glinted. "Seventeen of our warriors are dead. But the *stilmen* will not return."

"How can he say that?" Trey said.

"Listen."

"We are not the first to fight them. The first to defeat them. The *stilmen* attacked the people of the lowlands and islands, Kambaramba and Karkar and Imbonggu and Margarima, first. The warriors of those places fought back. They drove the attackers away, although many men died.

"The lowland peoples warned us, the men of the Southern Highlands, the Huli and the Duna. They told us to watch the forest, to watch the skies. And we did. So when the *stilmen* came here, we were ready. We knew what we must do.

"And, like them, we are victorious. The *stilmen* will be gone from here. This was the last big battle, and we defeated them.

"Together, the people of Papua New Guinea have discovered: The *stilmen*, they like to kill, but they do not like to die."

He leaned toward the camera, his face a totem of strength and certainty. "If you are watching this," he said, "this is what we have taught you."

He sat back and made a dismissive gesture, a flick of one hand.

"Remember," he said, "they are still just *binatang*."

Bugs.

"And they do not like to die."

THE VIDEO CAME to an end. Christopher stood, stepped away from the computer. "Plenty to ponder in that," he said.

Trey said, "Yeah."

"Mostly, it makes me think that in New Guinea, on the islands and in the mountain valleys, victory is possible," he said. "But here in Oz, we don't have a chance."

Trey looked at him.

"Think about it. We're a huge, empty country. Not very many people, most of us clustered in a few areas, and hundreds of millions of rabbits and other potential hosts. We couldn't be more outnumbered."

He shook his arms and shoulders, the same gesture he'd made when overlooking the wetlands. Trey recognized it as a sign of acceptance.

"No, this war is over," Christopher said again, "and we've already lost."

"Then leave," Trey said, the words emerging almost before he'd thought them. "Take your family and go to the Southern Highlands."

Christopher smiled. "I've been in touch with Agiru. He said they will welcome us when the time comes."

He looked into Trey's face. "Come with us."

Trey was quiet.

Christopher took a breath to calm himself, a familiar habit Trey had forgotten. When he spoke again, his tone was lighter.

"I know. What was I thinking? You'll race around, trying to save the world, until the last possible minute. Beyond."

His gaze burned into Trey's. "But then what?"

Trey was silent.

"We'll be safe in New Guinea. Where will you go?'

TWENTY-SIX

Dry Tortugas, United States

WHEN THE MEN from the U.S. Department of Homeland Security met her at Kennedy Airport, Mariama assumed her counterfeit passport had tripped her up. Perhaps the fat man back in Panama City had alerted the authorities. Maybe this was his revenge.

Or maybe her number had just come up. She *had*, in fact, entered the United States illegally. No matter how porous the borders were, sometimes you just got caught.

As she sat across the table from the three men who would question her, her mind was racing. She had to be able to keep going. They had to allow her to go on. What could she say that would make them unlock the door and set her free?

But then it turned out not to matter. As soon as the questioning began, she realized she had it all wrong. They didn't give a damn about her passport.

The leader, a man with a strong jaw and unblinking

gray eyes, said, "You are from Mpack, in the Casamance region of Senegal."

Not a question.

Mariama recalculated. "I am."

He reached into a briefcase and pulled out a single sheet of paper. Laid it down on the table between them. "And you are familiar with these."

She looked down at the paper and saw a drawing of a thief.

Mariama laughed. All three men, their careers built on unflappability, showed their surprise in subtle ways: a blink, a slight clenching of the jaw, the fingers of a hand flexing for an instant.

"Yes," Mariama said. "Quite familiar."

"Do you know how to stop them?"

Getting to the point more quickly than she expected. *They must be very afraid,* she thought.

Yet she was unsure how to respond.

She could say yes, she knew. But what would happen then? She'd get absorbed. Become merely a cog.

Disappear into the machine.

Or she could say no and . . . perhaps complete the task she'd traveled across the world to accomplish.

The three men's eyes were fixed on her. Even with the lag she demanded due to a (feigned) difficulty with English, she had barely a second left before her hesitation became obvious, before their suspicions were raised. And once that happened, there would be no turning back. They'd break her to find out what she knew.

Decide.

"Of course not," she said. "I came here to escape them."

She saw the disappointment on their faces. And, for a moment, she almost weakened, told the truth.

But she'd never been much for playing on a team. Her philosophy: A team was only as strong as its weakest player. And in Mariama's opinion, almost every player was weaker than she was.

IT WAS THE wrong decision. Catastrophically wrong.

She'd thought at worst they'd send her home. Then she could start trying again.

But they didn't. After two days in New York they flew her here, to this rock in what had to be the Caribbean Sea, with its old fort and manicured lawns and boatloads of tourists coming to see the ruins and watch the seabirds circling above, white against the blue sky.

None of them knowing there was a small prison on the island, too, a featureless building a stone's throw from where the crowds wandered, and a world away.

For the first few days, Mariama expected to be interrogated. To be tortured. Why else would they bring her to a prison off the mainland?

But as the days passed, Mariama realized that she was here just so they didn't have to worry about her. But why? She was no threat, was she? Why had they neither sent her home nor questioned her further?

She was treated well enough. A cell to herself, with a cot, a small table, and a barred window overlooking a patch of scrubby salt grass, a stretch of sky, a single palm tree, and one end of the small paved runway used by the airplane that had brought her here. The window admitted, along with sunlight in the late afternoon, the sounds of the wind and birds calling, and even sometimes the crash of waves.

Between the window and the overhead electric bulb, the light in her cell was always strong enough to read by. That was most important of all. As Mariama had long known, the greatest punishment a jailer could inflict was to take words away from her.

They wouldn't let her read newspapers or magazines, or listen to the radio or watch television. Instead, they brought her books. Novels, books about ancient history, mystery stories.

But nothing that would give her a clue about what was going on in the real world.

She asked. Of course she did. She asked the people who brought her meals. She asked those who accompanied her during her two hours outside every day, the walks she took within the courtyard, under the brilliant blue sky and circling white birds. She asked the guards who stood outside her cell day and night.

No one would tell her a thing, so eventually she stopped asking them. And there was no one else to ask. If she wasn't alone in this jail, they kept her separate from any of the other prisoners.

Whenever she was outside, the trade winds would be blowing. Every day, she'd take in a deep breath, searching for the familiar smell but detecting nothing.

Not yet.

SHE STOPPED ASKING, but not wondering.

Why am I here?

It wasn't the foundation for a philosophical disquisition. She wasn't questioning her place in the universe. No. It was:

Why am *I* here?

Why am I *here*?

That led to another question: Who had condemned her? In the darkness of her solitude, Mariama even allowed herself to believe it might be the thieves themselves. That somehow they'd infiltrated the highest reaches of the United States government and commanded that Mariama Honso must be neutralized.

Even in the darkest moments, her essential sanity made Mariama laugh. Even at her maddest, she would never believe herself to exist at the center of the world.

No, not the thieves.

Who, then?

There was only one answer that made sense.

THE WEEKS PASSED. She told the guards she'd changed her mind, that she wanted to talk, that she had important things to reveal. But it didn't help. No one ever responded.

The guards, young men and women in uniforms she didn't recognize, brought her food. Maids cleaned her cell while she was outside.

Summer turned to fall. Even here, the air had a chill to it in the late afternoon.

One day she had a revelation: She'd been forgotten. She'd slipped into the system, but now no one remembered she was here, why she'd been sent, why requisition slips were still being signed and manpower still being allocated to guard her and keep her alive.

Late at night, sleepless, she thought: I will know when

the world comes to an end. On one sunny day the tourists will stop coming to visit the fort. Then the guards and those who keep me fed will disappear.

And then it will be only me, me alone, the last person left on earth.

The last untainted human. Until the thieves find me, too, as they someday will, and pollute me, and finish the job they've already begun.

THAT WAS THE worst day.

The beginning of the worst days.

TWENTY-SEVEN

Washington, D.C.

"THIS CAN'T GET out," the chief of staff said. "Not a whisper, not a breath."

Harry Solomon didn't bother to stifle his laugh. How often had the old guy called with something desperate that needed fixing? How many assignments had he prefaced with this same tired demand?

It was dumb on so many levels. If Harry or his people had ever let a story leak, even a whisper, even a breath, then the COS wouldn't ever have called again.

So why did he always say it? Harry thought he knew. The point was to make the old guy feel better about himself, to help him justify going ahead and telling Harry what he needed done.

What the Big Man needed done.

Okay. Thought about that way, it made some sense.

"'Course," Harry said. That wasn't enough, so he added, "You know me and my guys. We don't talk."

Harry knew he'd still have to wait while the COS wrestled with his fears and needs. Usually after about fifteen seconds, the latest tale of woe would come pouring out.

This time, though, the hesitation lasted longer. Much longer. Long enough that Harry actually found himself saying, "Hey, you still there?" over the secure line.

"Yeah." The old guy's voice sounded different, like he was having second thoughts.

"Then talk." Now Harry's curiosity was piqued. Usually the call involved some brushfire that needed extinguishing before it could bring the Big Man down. Harry would listen and roll his eyes. Only in public life, and only in this country, would the sort of thing he was asked to clean up require much more than a laugh or a shrug.

Squashing some figure out of the past with a new claim of presidential drug use. (Regardless that the Big Man had been open about his "youthful indiscretions.") Stoppering up some new embarrassment perpetrated by the First Lady's alcoholic brother. Infiltrating and sterilizing some group of fringe nuts killing time by developing theories that the Big Man was a Manchurian Candidate.

Easy stuff.

"Call me back when you got the cotton wool out of your brain," Harry said and made to disconnect.

"Wait—"

Harry waited. He'd always intended to wait. He was interested.

Then, as the chief of staff finally began to explain, more than interested. As the stream of words, delivered in a rush, went on, Harry felt sweat prickle on his neck. A muscle jumped in his jaw.

When the COS took a breath, Harry said, "Where, again?"

"Fort Collins."

"At the DVBID?"

The Centers for Disease Control's Division of Vector-Borne Infectious Diseases.

"CDC was involved, yes. Under the auspices of the MRIID."

The United States Army Medical Research Institute of Infectious Diseases, that was. Did someone actually get paid to come up with these names?

"But not at Fort Detrick?" Harry said.

The main offices and labs of MRIID were housed in Fort Detrick, Maryland, a lot closer to Harry than Fort Collins, Colorado.

"No."

"Why not?"

"There were reasons."

Meaning, *You don't need to know the reasons.*

Harry could feel his blood pulsing in his throat. This was no DUI to be kept out of the newspapers.

"How many are there?" he asked.

A pause. Then, "Six."

Shit, Harry thought. "What happened?"

Silence.

"Listen," Harry said. "I'm not going into something fucked up by the MRIID without knowing what I'm stepping into. I read *The Hot Zone*, yeah, and saw *28 Days Later.* You want to expose a crew to Ebola or the rage virus, find somebody else."

Even then, a couple of extra seconds of silence over the line. Then the COS said, "No virus. No pathogens. These men were . . . stung."

Harry couldn't believe it. *"Stung?"* he said. *"Bit?* You

mean, like bees? I think I saw a movie once about that, too."

The old guy wasn't laughing. When Harry was finished, he just said, "Yes. Stung. And you're going to clean it up. Tonight."

Then he explained how.

As he did, Harry felt his unease return. Whatever it was, it sounded like an emergency. An F5. A 9.1.

Harry didn't ask why. Didn't ask what it was about. Those weren't the kinds of questions he could ask, especially not in an election year.

They weren't even the kinds of questions he was supposed to wonder about. But by the end of the conversation—the COS's monologue, really—he felt, for the first time in a long while, a little shaken. He'd never show it, of course, but there you were.

He had only one question left. Only one he could ask.

"Whatever stung those six men," he said, "is it still there?"

"Of course not."

Meaning: *We hope not.*

Okay, one more question. "You killed it?"

Silence.

Meaning: *No.*

Fort Collins, Colorado

IT WAS THE damnedest government laboratory Harry had ever seen.

He'd been in others, and they were all basically the same. Squat buildings on university campuses or in office parks. Concrete or brick on the outside. On the inside, linoleum, fluorescent and halogen lights, glass and steel. Disposal boxes for sharps and other hazardous materials in every room. Plenty of bottles of Purell.

People in white coats and eyeglasses hurrying around clutching pads and clipboards and cell phones and little handheld computers.

But the building where Harry and his team were sent late that night was none of these things. It was a two-story shingled house way out toward Horsetooth Mountain, in the shadow of Roosevelt National Forest. On the outside, just a house, out of sight of any neighbors, hidden away in the forest. The kind of thing a family might use for ski weekends in another season.

The nodding leaves of the aspens caught the panel truck's headlights when they pulled to a stop at the end of the long dirt driveway. Beyond the dark house, the surface of a stream glinted silver, reflecting a high, cold three-quarter moon.

Harry felt uneasy out here. He wasn't used to being spooked. It pissed him off.

The man in the seat beside him, Trent, craned around. "Too bad I forgot my fly rod," he said.

Harry didn't bother to reply. He swung the door open and climbed down. The breeze was cool—it felt like fall here already—and he could hear the stream trickling over pebbles and, farther off, an owl hooting.

No people talking, no cars, no dogs barking. The officials who'd chosen this location had wanted solitude, isolation, and they'd gotten it. Harry didn't like how dark it was.

Why at night? he'd asked.

There were advantages to working at night, he knew. Fewer eyes watching, for one. But also disadvantages: If some eyes happened to be open, they'd be more likely to notice you, to notice the truck labeled *Central Moving & Storage* rumbling past.

And also, when you got to the site, no matter how isolated it was, at night you had to bring lights. Lights where people didn't expect to see them often meant local police where you didn't want to see *them*.

Why at night?

Getting back the usual bullshit.

Why else?

A last long pause, and then the chief of staff had spoken. One more sentence.

We think they mostly come out during the day, he'd said.

That hadn't made Harry feel any better.

THE FIRST TWO were lying in the front hallway.

"Holy fuck," Trent said.

The dead men were wearing the same white lab coats government scientists always wore. But their lab coats were no longer white. They were red. Red shading to black in the beams of the men's flashlights.

Their coats and the floor around them, too. The smell of blood was very strong, and so was another, less familiar odor.

"What the fuck *is* this?" Trent said.

Harry hadn't told them, any of them, what they were going to see here. That was how it worked: No one knew any more than they had to.

Not that knowing in advance made the sight much

easier to take. Harry had heard *stung* and had looked up the after-effects of bee stings on the computer. People who died of shock, who gasped and clutched their throats, who died, eyes popped out, when they swelled up and choked to death.

That would have been bad enough, but this was worse. Much worse. These men's eyes weren't still, protruding, staring, as Harry had expected. They were gone. Torn out of the sockets. Nothing left but white flecks and globules across their cheeks.

The other four, scattered across the floor of the lab itself, were the same. Eyeless, with every exposed portion of skin—faces, necks, hands, shins above their socks—covered in red, swollen speckles and slashes. And some deeper gouges where, Harry thought, something had fed.

The crew's flashlight beams kept returning to the eyes. "What the hell did this?" someone asked.

"Some kind of bee," Harry said.

Knowing he shouldn't have said anything, but feeling shook up. His tongue a whole lot looser than it should have been.

"A *bee*?"

"A shitload of them, I guess."

The beams went this way and that, crisscrossing, intersecting, as everyone looked in every corner of the room. Harry saw that, regardless of the building's modest, deceptive exterior, the laboratory was well equipped with scanners, scopes, centrifuges, who knew what else. Important research had been going on here, until the bees came.

"Get to work," Harry said, "and let's get the hell out of here."

He didn't have to say it twice.

* * *

HE AND TRENT put the dead men into body bags, carried them out to the truck, hoisted them into the coffin-shaped coolers that ran half the length of the truck. When they were done, they'd drive to the rendezvous point halfway to Denver. There they'd find a car waiting for them, and the truck and its contents would no longer be their responsibility.

While he and Trent lugged the bodies, the other two were focusing on their area of expertise. This involved a lot of careful carrying of liquids, some precise wiring, and plenty of quiet cursing.

Harry often dismissed what they did as no harder than splashing lighter fluid on charcoal, but he knew the two men earned their pay. A few hours from now, when they were all safely far away, this isolated little house would erupt. By the time it was done burning, there would be nothing identifiable left.

Nothing to make the story blow up, costing Harry his job.

Or worse than just his job. He was under no illusions.

Not in an election year.

IT WAS TIME to clear out.

First, though, and as he always did, he took one last walk through the premises. One time there'd been a body in a closet that he hadn't found till that last moment. He would've had a lot of bad days if he hadn't thought to open that closet door.

But he also had another goal for walking through the

scene one last time, alone. He was always on the lookout for something, anything, that he might find useful later.

Did anything here qualify? He wasn't sure. But he did find something: an index card, on the floor near where one of the workers had fallen.

Harry picked it up. There was blood on it, but it was still readable. Four short lines, half typed, half handwritten in black ink.

Beside the typed word *Family*, a handwritten *Philanthidae?*

Beside the word *Genus*: *Philanthus*???

Beside *Species*: ????

And beside *Type Specimen*: *Patagonia, AZ*.

Harry said, "Huh," tucked the card into his pants pocket, and went out to join the rest of his crew.

TWENTY-EIGHT

Manhattan

"WE'VE LOOKED AT this video, like, twenty-seven times since your brother sent it," Jack said. Slumped in the chair at his desk, he was scowling. "And it pisses me off just as much this time as the first."

He wasn't happy that the camera had mostly been aimed at the sky.

"The people who shot it had other things on their minds," Sheila said.

"Yeah? Well, next time, hire a cinematographer. I heard there's quite a crowd of them in PNG."

Sheila looked at him. "You of all people should know that we make do with what we've got."

"Yeah." He glowered. "Doesn't mean I can't piss and moan about it."

Sheila had returned from Florida the day before. Trey had come straight from the airport to the office after his flight back from Australia, not even stopping at home to drop off his bag and change clothes. Now here they were, the three of them: Jack at his computer, Trey in a chair beside him, Sheila looking over their shoulders at the screen.

Together again, as if that made a difference.

Trey thought about his visit with his brother. At the airport in Cairns, Christopher had smiled and said, "Things go the way I think they will, you won't be able to spin around the globe so easily anymore."

Trey had shrugged off the words, but now he was seeing the truth in them and wondering how he'd react. How would he handle waking up every day in the same place?

Sheila was looking at him. "You okay?"

He nodded. "Sure. Why?"

"You seem tired."

Jack laughed. "The mighty Trey Gilliard with jet lag? After just eighty hours on airplanes over five days? You must be getting old."

He looked up at the clusters of pins on the map. "I'm getting pisssed off. Those things are everywhere, and we still know damn-all about them."

He grasped the arms of his chair. "We fucking need to get some fucking specimens of this fucking species, and fucking soon."

"Yeah," Sheila said. "But until then, what have we learned?"

Trey, who had been slumped in his seat, straightened. "Agiru says that the people of the Southern Highlands weren't the first in PNG to fight off the *stilmen*."

"Makes sense," Jack said. "Look at the map. The first arrivals to PNG most likely came by boat to the islands and ports, or via airplane to Port Moresby, which is also on the coast." He shrugged. "Those are the places the thieves would colonize first, before moving up into the mountain valleys."

"Plus the lowlands are hot and humid, friendlier turf for them," Sheila said. "It must get cold in the highlands."

"Though they seem able to withstand the cold pretty damn well." Jack waved a hand. "Look at the fucking map. They can survive almost everywhere."

Trey had only been half listening. Now he said, "My point is, how could those islands and villages have been battling the thieves, and no one has noticed?"

Jack went still for a second. Then he was bending over his keyboard. A moment later he said, "Here's how."

It was a little article on CNN.com dated about a month earlier. Just two paragraphs under the headline, "Papua New Guinea Violence Flares Anew."

Trey bent closer to look at the tiny type. The story was datelined Kambaramba, East Sepik Province. "'This long-restive region was riven again by battles among different factions of the Kambot people,'" he read out loud. "'Twenty-two were reported dead, local authorities said. The outbreak of violence follows others in Madang, Karkar Island, and elsewhere. Authorities blame the violence on heightened tensions following disputed parliamentary elections.'"

Jack looked impressed. "That's actually kinda brilliant," he said. "If PNG is famous for anything, it's for tribal violence. Nobody would think twice about a report like this, and nobody would double-check."

Sheila was nodding. "Another government wanting to hush up bad news."

"Until the chief sent around this half-assed video and spilled the beans."

"If it wasn't him, it would've been someone else." She

shrugged. "Governments always think they can hide things, and they're always wrong."

"I have an idea," Jack said. "They could pull their heads out of their asses and fight back, like the villages did."

"Not all people are as fearless as the Huli, and governments are cowardly by nature. Most would prefer to ignore a problem and hope it becomes someone else's."

Trey took a deep breath and said, "My brother believes that, in Australia at least, humans have already lost that war."

Or at least he *thought* he said this. He saw both Jack and Sheila staring at him, and then Sheila was taking his arm and pulling him to his feet.

"I'm bringing you home," she said.

He tried to shake her off. "I'm fine."

"Sure you are." Jack was standing there, too. "You look like one of the zombies from *Night of the Living Dead*, and not one of the handsome, debonair ones, either. And that last thing you said? It made zombie sense."

He looked at Sheila. "Malaria?"

She shook her head. "He's cold, not feverish."

"Home or hospital?"

She hesitated, then said, "Home first. Then we'll see."

"Go."

They went.

By taxi, or at least that was what Sheila told him later. But Trey couldn't have said one way or another, since as far as he could tell, he wasn't there.

HE ROUSED A little when they went through the front door of his apartment. He was aware, at least. Aware of lying down, really more like falling. Of someone—Sheila—taking off his shoes and pulling a sheet up over him as he shivered and shook.

Then he lost some more time, with no idea whether it was minutes or hours. When he awoke, he was a little more alert and realized where he was. His bed.

But not his. It was Sheila's bed now. Its contours didn't match his body's anymore.

He was supposed to sleep on the sofa.

He saw that she was sitting on a chair beside the bed. He caught the expression on her face. Concern. Worry, rearranging itself into a smile when she saw he was awake.

"Hey," he said.

She seemed to understand that. "Hey."

He saw her stretch, as if her muscles were stiff and cramped. "I'm going to get myself a cup of tea. I'll get you one, too. You'll be okay for a minute without me?"

He nodded, watched her leave the room.

His room. Hers.

Why was he in here?

He'd ask when she came back.

BUT BY THE time she did reenter the room a few minutes later, carrying two mugs and a steaming teapot on a tray, he'd forgotten what he'd been thinking about.

Her eyes were on him as she came through the door. He saw her stop so suddenly that the mugs clattered against each other, nearly toppling.

"What are you doing?" she said, in a tone of voice he hadn't heard before, hoarse, twisting upward in pitch at the end.

"Doing?" he said. His mouth felt fuzzy, his words indistinct in his ears. "I'm not doing anything."

She put the tray down on the floor—another clatter—and was sitting on the bed beside him before he could move. He felt her grab his right hand, and only then did he realize that he'd been scratching his stomach under his shirt.

Sheila's face was a mask of horrified realization as she pushed the shirt up. He lifted his head off the pillow and looked down at his body.

They both saw it. The small swelling. The tiny black airhole.

Something moving beneath his skin.

"Oh, God," Sheila said, her voice a gasp. "Oh, no. *Trey.*"

TWENTY-NINE

Albuquerque, New Mexico

JEREMY AXELSON SIGHED.

Here they were again. How many nights had been spent this way since the campaign started? A thousand? Ten thousand?

It felt like a million.

Axelson could probably have figured it, the real number, or close, if he'd wanted to. But why bother? It would just depress him, and right now his brain was fried extra crispy anyway. The last thing it needed was a math problem to solve.

A million nights. A million hotels. Not that it made a difference. Wherever they stayed, it always felt like the same room. You could only tell where you were by the subjects of the paintings hanging on the walls.

In Iowa the paintings showed towheaded kids among ripening fields of corn. Vineyards or the Golden Gate Bridge in northern California. Leaping dolphins in Miami. Here in Albuquerque? Mountains and canyons.

Of course, you didn't ever get the chance to see the actual scenery. Just the paintings.

The three of them were watching four televisions. Or not watching. The speech was over, and now it was time for the political consultants to offer their opinions, the spinners to spin, and the panelists in the studios to sit in middle-aged rows and pontificate.

The TVs were muted. Not that it mattered: Each of them, two men who'd pushed past fifty and a woman a decade younger, could have recited the words being spoken on-screen. No need to hear them.

"Guy puts me to sleep," the rumpled, bearlike man sitting across from Axelson complained.

He wasn't talking about the anchors, the consultants, the spinners, or the panelists.

He was talking about the man who'd just given the speech. Sam Chapman.

The president of the United States.

"You say that every time," Axelson pointed out.

"He does it every time."

The woman—tiny, sharp-eyed—stirred in her chair. "If he does it another ninety times between now and November," she said, "he's going to win."

The three of them stared at the silent screens, and for a while nobody said anything.

Ron Stanhouse, the campaign manager. Chief pollster Melanie Hoff. And Axelson himself, tall, angular, with a narrow face and a beaklike nose and a general air of geniality belied by the glitter of intelligence and calculation in his eyes.

Axelson was the communications director. Which meant it was his job to make the world think that the smell arising from their campaign was imminent victory, not flop sweat.

Not their campaign. Tony's.

Senator Anthony Harrison, the man who, in two weeks, would be nominated to run for president against Sam Chapman.

And who, eight weeks later, was going to lose.

"Give me today's numbers," Stanhouse said.

Hoff sighed. "Nationwide, likely voters, we're behind 49–43–8. Make them choose, it's 53–47. Likeliest screen, a little closer: maybe 52.2 to 47.8. Not good enough." She grimaced. "You know all this. The numbers haven't budged in weeks."

"Think they'll budge a little after tonight," Axelson said.

Tonight the president had delivered what amounted to an out-of-season State of the Union speech from his desk in the White House. The supposed excuse was to reassure America over instability in the Mideast. The truth was that Sam Chapman knew that whenever he demonstrated the trappings of the presidency, his numbers went up.

The results of the first instant poll appeared on one of the screens.

More likely to vote for: 31%.
Less likely: 13%.
No difference or no opinion: 56%.

"Tomorrow's numbers will be worse," Hoff said.

At the beginning of the cycle, Chapman had seemed vulnerable. The unemployment rate had risen in his first year and had stayed stubbornly high, gas prices had been spiking, the housing market continued in its endless stay in the doldrums.

And though he was still seen as likable—it was one of the things that had gotten him elected in the first place—nobody had ever claimed that the earth shook when he spoke. Support for him had been broad, but only an inch deep.

Almost by definition, Chapman was the kind of incumbent who might fall to a strong challenge. And among the usual gaggle of senators, ex-governors, and hopeless gadflies, Anthony Harrison, former governor of Colorado, had an excellent shot at the nomination.

That was why Stanhouse, Hoff, and Axelson had signed on with him.

Almost immediately, though, the breaks had started going the incumbent's way. None of the potential challengers, including Harrison, had emerged unscathed from a long, tedious, and expensive primary season. The recent laws allowing for nearly unlimited anonymous corporate donations had given even the fringiest wannabes life and staying power.

Another ex-governor had, as was her wont, gobbled up far more than her share of media oxygen before declining to run.

Now, at the end of the circus, as Harrison was finally emerging with the nomination, a skeleton or two had been unearthed from his closet. Nothing the campaign hadn't known about, and nothing they couldn't deal with, but still, the news had occupied too many cycles.

The point was: To defeat a sitting president, you had to get all the breaks. Or just one, if it was big enough.

But neither was happening for Harrison. For them.

"Swing states?" Stanhouse said.

Hoff shrugged. "Today we'd win Florida, Georgia, North Carolina. Colorado, of course. But we'd lose most of the others: Pennsylvania, Virginia, the industrial Midwest—maybe even Missouri."

She switched her gaze to Axelson. "Your guys better write him one hell of a convention speech."

When he didn't reply, she drained her drink, mostly just ice and water now, and got to her feet. Stretched, yawned, and walked to the door.

"Figure out a way to change the game," she said, "and I'll give you better news."

A KNOCK ON the door.

Axelson didn't move. It was late, dark-night-of-the-soul late, but he was still up. He hadn't moved since Hoff and Stanhouse left, except once to freshen his drink and turn off three of the TVs. The television that was still on, tuned to TCM, was showing an old Bob Hope–Bing Crosby movie, the one where they went to the North Pole.

The Road to Utopia. Axelson laughed and drank. Could he go along? Utopia was sounding pretty good right about now.

The knock came again. For a moment Axelson considered ignoring it. But he knew he wouldn't be able to hide from whatever news lay on the other side of the door. Not forever.

With a groan, he got to his feet, walked over, and swung the door open.

A young man stood in the hall. He was wearing a

pinstriped gray suit, a crisply pressed sky blue poplin shirt, and a patriotic red tie. With his fair skin, open expression, and studious black-framed eyeglasses, he lacked only an American flag pin to be ready to appear on camera.

No, wait. He *was* wearing a flag pin, on the lapel of his suit jacket.

Perfect.

"Do you sleep in that getup?" Axelson asked him.

The young man smiled. "Gary Kuster, sir," he said. "Can I talk to you?"

Axelson knew who he was. A member of the field staff, an advance man whose job it was to lay the groundwork for campaign appearances.

He was good at it, too. A rising star, keen minded, and not nearly as guileless as his fair-haired-boy looks would have you believe.

Axelson didn't move. "What about?"

He was tired. He didn't want to hear any more complaints. Nothing that this irritatingly bright-eyed boy had to say could possibly be of any interest, not tonight.

"Sir," Kuster said, "I need to show you something." He looked Axelson straight in the eyes. "Something that will win us the election."

Axelson sighed. He'd outgrown dramatic pronouncements from underlings twenty-five years ago. They always thought they'd found the faux pas that would sink the opposition, the angle that no one else had seen. And they were always wrong.

He swirled the Scotch in his glass. It needed more ice. "Do I have to go somewhere to see this 'something'?"

Kuster lifted his left hand. He was carrying an iPad. "No. Here's fine."

Finally Axelson moved out of the doorway. As he fished the last shards of ice from the bucket, he watched Kuster push a button. The iPad lit up, revealing a YouTube page.

"What are you going to do," Axelson asked, "show me rock videos?"

HE COULDN'T BELIEVE it.

The guy *was* showing him videos. And not stuff of any interest, either. Not even old Allman Brothers performances, Bugs Bunny cartoons, or trailers for the movies that Axelson would miss this fall, when every minute would be spent staving off electoral humiliation.

Not even the cute amateur shit that he'd watched during the endless down hours every campaign had to endure. Cats running on treadmills, monkeys pulling dogs' tails, the guy who traveled all around the world dancing. (Axelson would have traded jobs with *that* guy in a heartbeat.) That old one, with the little kid biting the finger of the other little kid.

No. None of that. Videos of wasps.

Big wasps. Axelson had grown up in Texas, not that far from the Rio Grande, and the wasps down there, the cicada killers, they could be huge. But these ones looked different, skinny and black, with legs that made them look like they were half spider. These ones were spooky.

One of them crawled over a branch and stared at the camera. Axelson felt like it was looking right into him.

Damn spooky.

"What's the point?" he said.

Kuster didn't reply. The camera zoomed in so that the wasp's face filled the screen. Watching, Axelson could have sworn that he could see intelligence in its gaze. The way its mouth moved, it looked like it was licking its chops.

When the video ended, he said, "Okay, you've put me off my feed. Now tell me why the hell I should be interested."

Kuster smiled at him. "I told you. These bugs are going to win us the election."

Then he began to explain. His voice staying calm, but with an edge of excitement, of triumph, behind it. Euphoria.

Sometimes he paused to show Axelson evidence. Proof. Another video, a newspaper article, notes he'd made on a legal pad.

At first Axelson remained skeptical, out of sorts. Then his attention sharpened. He found himself leaning over Kuster's shoulder, peering in at the screen or down at the neat handwriting on the pad. His heart thumped, and again.

And then, finally understanding, seeing exactly where this was going, Axelson felt his legs get weak. He sat down, his drink forgotten. But he still didn't say anything. He just listened. Listened for more than an hour, until Kuster was finally done.

At last the young man said, "That's it. What do you think?"

Axelson cleared his throat. He wondered what his face looked like.

"Who else knows?" he asked. His voice was scratchy. "Who else knows the whole story?"

"No one," Kuster said. "No one else has put it together yet, much less figured out the White House's role. Just you and me."

Axelson was already reaching for his phone. "Let's fix that," he said.

He knew what he'd just heard. He understood what it meant.

He punched a button and said, "Ron? Wake up and get back in here. Melanie, too. Everybody. The whole senior staff. Roust 'em."

Normally Stanhouse would have bitched about it. It was late, it'd been a bad day, and why the hell was it his job to track everyone down? But he merely said, "Okay," and disconnected.

He recognized that tone in Axelson's voice.

Soon enough, no more than fifteen minutes later, everyone was there. In rumpled clothes, some of them still rubbing their eyes, but ready. Eager. It was amazing how fast a staff's morale could turn around, if they sniffed a change in the wind.

Axelson surveyed the room. A dozen faces. His team.

Then he looked back at Kuster, who was still sitting in the same chair, and said, "Go over it again."

Kuster smiled and began.

THIRTY

"TAKE IT OUT," Trey said.

His heart was hammering, as if he'd just climbed a mountain and was standing at twenty-seven thousand feet. But he hadn't moved. Couldn't move.

Understanding at last what had happened to him. His mind clearing for an instant, just an instant, then clouding over again. Like a tide sweeping in, obliterating everything in its path, before being sucked back out, leaving only ruins behind.

A battle. A war.

His heart was his enemy. With every beat, every liquid leap inside his chest, every surge of blood in his veins, his consciousness dwindled.

Sheila stood beside the bed. Frozen. Stunned. He could see that. As if through a smeared window, he could see the anguish on her face.

His heart thudded. He was disappearing inside his poisoned blood.

"Take it out," he said, or thought he said. *"Now."*

Only knowing he'd actually said the words, and not just dreamed them, when Sheila, her bloodless face half obscured by the hand over her mouth, shook her head. Hard. In terror.

"I can't," she said.

Trey reached out and grabbed her arm. He could still feel it. It was cold.

"Sheila," he said, "there's no time. It's . . . taking me."

His blood rushed. Something was chewing at the edges of his consciousness, dropping crimson veils over his vision. Winning the battle. Winning the war.

"Trey." She was sitting on the edge of the bed, holding his hand in both of hers. "You'll die."

Her voice tiny through the roaring in his head, the rattling of his heart.

"No." His tongue felt swollen in his mouth.

In some remote, untouched corner, he thought, *It's trying to stop me. It knows that if we wait just a little longer we'll be too late.*

It.

With an effort almost beyond his imagining, he wrenched his shattered thoughts back into an approximation of something whole. His vision cleared. A little.

"Sheila, no," he said. His voice wasn't his own.

"You don't die," he said. "Not—yet."

He squeezed her hand. *Listen to me.*

Save me.

Her face was a mask of grief and indecision. Tears streaked her cheeks and dripped from her chin. "My mom—"

"Sheila," he said, "I don't know—when this happened. *I don't remember.* But not long. Look—"

He couldn't breathe. His lungs were filling.

"Look." He was speaking underwater. "It's so small."

Still she did not move.

"Agiru—" he said. His words tumbling out in gasps. "The old man. He said they weren't in time—"

Was she listening? Would she *understand*?

"Do you see—" Despairing. "That's why you don't remember you were infected. Not at first. Because you won't die . . ."

It was hopeless. She would not go. She would not try.

It was already too late.

He felt something flutter inside him. A tiny wriggle within his flesh.

For one last instant, everything was silent, calm. He sat in the eye. The center of the vortex.

He could see. He could hear.

He could breathe. He inhaled and said, his own voice, his own words, "Sheila. *Kill it.*"

The creature wriggled again, more strongly. Diving deeper. Releasing its poison.

Saving itself.

Sacrificing him.

Trey's mind burst apart. His mouth moved, he could feel it moving, but the roaring of his heart kept him from knowing if he spoke words or if the words made any sense.

With his bloodred gaze, he saw Sheila put her hands over her face. Then she took them away, and, when she did, her expression had changed.

She got up from the bed. He saw her, could still see her, as she ran for the bedroom door and out of view.

The creature dug.

The veil fell, and he was blind. No: blind on the outside. Inside, he could still see.

Seeing, he glimpsed . . . something.

Huge. Monstrous. Shapeless.

At that last instant, Trey knew what it was.

And what it wanted.

FAR IN THE distance, he felt . . . something new.

Pain.

A dart of pain as clear as crystal.

Light danced before his eyes. The aurora borealis. The height of a migraine's aura. Twisting, whirling fragments of light, but through them he could again glimpse the real world. The world outside, the one that the monster deep in his brain could not yet control.

The tide pulling back.

He looked down at his body. It lay on the bed. Still. Waxen. Someone else's body.

Sheila sat on a chair, leaning over it. Leaning over the body. She was wearing latex gloves from the first-aid kit he kept in his bathroom.

Trey could see the side of her face, see that she was calm now. A doctor. Doing what she had to do.

She held a small knife in her right hand. A paring knife from the kitchen. In her left hand, rubbing alcohol in a brown bottle.

The bottle spilled. The liquid was cold on the body's pierced skin.

Somewhere in the center of his brain, Trey felt something new rise. Something jagged.

Fear. Rage.

Not his own.

Trey watched as Sheila swabbed first the knife blade with the alcohol, then the body's bare belly. Her face intent, she bent over him. The blade caught the light as it sank into his swollen flesh.

In the moment before the two warring worlds inside his brain collided, merged, burst apart again, Trey saw the larva wriggle in the parted lips of the cut. He glimpsed its black head, saw its mandibles reaching in vain for something to attack.

Sheila lifted it from the body. It twisted on the points of a gleaming pair of forceps.

Trey felt terror erupt inside him. Something shrieked inside his head.

Who was it?

What was he?

The world inside flew. Shattered.

He was gone.

THIRTY-ONE

ONE MOMENT WAS a dreamless blank, and the next Trey was lying in his bed, aware of the sheets against the bare skin of his back and arms, the pillow against his head. The body he'd been watching from a distance was once again his own.

He lay there, unmoving. His eyes were closed, but the shadows projected on them came from the yellowish light illuminating the bedroom.

He could feel himself breathing, his lungs pushing the bellows of his chest up and out, down and in. He could feel his heart beating, but more gently now, set free from its adrenaline frenzy.

He could feel the pain in his stomach. In the skin of his stomach.

Still he didn't move. These sensations were all reassuring. He was alive. He'd been right. Sheila had gotten the larva out in time. Whatever poison it had released to stop his heart, it had not yet possessed in sufficient quantities to succeed.

It had tried. It had done its best, and he still lived.

But . . .

Somewhere deep inside his brain, something had changed.

Something was different.

He explored, like you search for a missing tooth with your tongue. He probed, and found . . .

Something gone?

Something new?

He didn't know.

Maybe both.

TIME PASSED. THEN he awoke again and, this time, opened his eyes.

Sheila was sitting in a chair beside the bed, elbows on knees, head propped on her hands. The latex gloves were gone, her hands scrubbed clean. But she'd neglected to wash her face. Tearstains had left tiny streaks on her cheeks, like the paths the first raindrops leave down a dusty windshield.

No tears now, though. Just an echo of terror in her eyes. Trey could see it. It was still there. He wondered if it would ever leave.

Her gaze found his face. "There you are," she said, and it sounded casual until her breath caught on the last word.

She reached out and took his hand. Just as she had done before, when he was falling. Before she pulled him back.

Her hand still felt cold in his, and she didn't want to

meet his eyes. He could only imagine the horror she must have gone through as she made that first incision, as she removed the writhing larva from his flesh. She must have been sure, certain, that he would die.

That she would kill him, as she believed she'd killed her mother.

But she'd gone ahead anyway. She'd done what he'd asked, what he'd pleaded for.

Trey moved his mouth. Making words seemed strange, as if he didn't quite know the language anymore.

"Thank you," he said.

Now she was looking directly at him. "If you ever make me do that again," she said, "*I'll* die."

He shifted his gaze to the window and saw that night had fallen. The light he'd seen through his closed eyelids had come from the bedside lamp, not the sun.

He realized he didn't even know when—or how— they'd come back to the apartment. The entire day seemed obscured, covered in fog.

Was that what every victim felt? Every host? Was that the preamble to the dreaming days, and death?

"I was asleep," he asked, "for how long?"

Sheila looked at her watch. "About four hours."

"God," he said, remembering his dreams. No. They hadn't been dreams.

He'd have to tell them about what he'd seen, what he'd felt. Sheila and Jack. Even though he didn't want to. Even though something inside him, inside the part of him that had changed, fought against the telling.

Sheila raised her eyes to his. "Once you'd survived the initial procedure," she said, only the slightest quaver in her voice betraying her resolve, "I wondered if you'd live, but never awake." Her mouth turned down at the corners. "Whether all I'd done was turn your dreaming days into dreaming years."

She rolled her shoulders, winced. "I thought about calling an ambulance, taking you to the hospital." Both her voice and gaze sharpened. "But Jack's right. We don't understand *anything* about this. Maybe moving you would have killed you. I didn't know."

Her mouth twisted, a grimace, not a smile. "So I kept you here and stayed beside you." A pause. "And . . . *prayed*."

Trey drew in a breath, remembering the maelstrom inside his head. His fear. All the pain. Dimming now in the memory, becoming surreal, as pain always did.

"I'm . . . glad you stayed with me," he said.

Her hand tightened in his. "After about two hours, you began to give the signs of someone emerging from deep sedation. That's when I thought you might be all right. But still . . . it took so long."

Trey tried to push himself up into a sitting position. He couldn't stop himself from making a sound in his throat.

Sheila frowned. "Stay where you are. I rigged up a butterfly bandage for the incision, but you really need a couple of stitches."

He shook his head and kept trying. Finally, with her help, he propped himself against the headboard. He was sweating, light-headed.

Sheila said, "Oh, so you're *that* kind of patient."

He reached for the water bottle that stood on the bedside table and took a drink.

His belly hurt. He looked down and saw a large white

sterile pad—a little stained with yellowish red—covering where the swelling had been and, underneath it, the edges of the butterfly bandage.

Seeing it made the bile rise in his throat. That was where it had been. The invader. The parasite.

Sheila said, "I'm sorry if it's a mess." For a moment her gaze turned inward again. "You're not exactly equipped for surgery here."

Trey nodded. He felt cold.

"But if we keep it clean, I don't think there'll be much risk of infection. Since the larva was"—she struggled for the word—"comparatively undeveloped, it hadn't gotten in very deep."

Deep enough. Trey could remember the sensation as it dove beneath the surface. It had felt like it was digging into his center, his core.

He made to swing his legs over the edge of the bed, to get to his feet. Sheila put a hand on his shoulder and, without effort, kept him where he was.

"Overruled," she said. Then, more gently, "Give yourself a little time. You're still clearing all that junk out of your system."

She frowned. "I wish I had some way of measuring your kidney function. Don't be surprised if your pee comes out some strange colors the next few days. Your blood is likely full of debris."

"I'm fine," Trey said.

She kept her hand on his shoulder. "Then why are you shivering?"

After a moment, he lay back down.

"Better," she said.

For a moment he thought he might drift off again.

Then, almost before it became a conscious thought, the question was out of his mouth. "Where's the larva?"

Sheila's mouth turned downward. "In a jar, in the bathroom." She gave a little grin. "I didn't want to be in the same room with it."

"Is it—"

She nodded. "As a doornail, about thirty seconds after I pulled it out. And I didn't squeeze it." She widened her eyes. "I don't think those things can live long away from their hosts. Not until they're ready to hatch."

She got to her feet and walked out of the room. Trey watched her go, that strong stride on long, slender legs causing her knee-length skirt to swish back and forth as she moved.

Her skirt. Had she been wearing a skirt earlier? Trey didn't think so, though his dreaming hours made him unsure of what he knew and what he didn't.

She came back in carrying a little jam jar. Trey noticed that she was wearing a white sleeveless blouse with a network of small flowers around the neck and down the sides. She'd washed the tearstains off her face.

"You look beautiful," he said, surprising them both.

Sheila's face colored. Then she gave him an askance look. "Calm down, cowboy. I'm still telling you to stay in bed till tomorrow."

She sat down in the chair and showed him the jar. At its bottom lay the dead larva, a limp white tube with oversized head, staring black eyes, and those familiar, vicious mandibles.

Trey had seen two of them before, alive and then dead, in the cloud forests of Costa Rica. Bigger, those had been, and more deadly. But seeing this one made his heart pound again, as if it were still inside him, still spreading its poison.

The top of the jar was screwed on tight. Sheila saw him looking. "Can't hurt to be sure." She gave a little laugh, shaky around the edges. "I would have glued it shut if I'd found where you keep the glue."

"Jack will be happy," he said.

She frowned. "I've been trying him, but for once he's not at the office, and his cell phone's off."

Trey leaned closer, but the larva had nothing else to tell him.

Or maybe it did. Finally his head was clear enough for something else to occur to him. Something he should have thought of as soon as he awoke.

His gaze shifted to the window, which was closed, the shades drawn. To the door of the room, closed as well. To the shadows cast across the ceiling by the lamp at his bedside. To the dark closet and shelves in the corner.

Sheila, watching him, nodded. "I wondered when you'd think of that."

"But—"

"Nothing." There was something blurred in her expression. "Let me tell you, Trey, I wanted to lock myself in the bathroom, the minute I was done." She closed her eyes for a moment, then turned her gaze on him once again. "But I couldn't. Not with you here."

Trey didn't say anything. "Thank you" was not enough for everything he owed her.

She leaned over, reaching down out of his line of vision. When she straightened, she was holding a kitchen knife, a claw hammer, and a big hardcover book.

"The place needs more weapons," she said. "And better ones."

Trey looked at her armaments and said, "Yeah. Pretty pathetic."

Sheila's gaze shifted to the door. "Still," she said, "sometimes they don't come for hours for . . . revenge."

Trey nodded but didn't speak.

"It could still happen at any moment," she said. "Couldn't it?"

Trey raised his eyes to look at her. "Yes. It could. But I don't think it will."

"Why not?"

"Because it's a lot easier for a thief to plant a larva in me than to hitch a ride here."

"I don't know," Sheila said. "They seem like pretty caring parents to me."

Trey shook his head. He was missing something, some revelation that lay just beyond his conscious mind.

Something he'd learned from the creature, the *presence*, inside him.

He was reaching for this knowledge when he heard Sheila gasp. He focused on her and saw that her face was bloodless.

"What?" he said, alarmed. "What's wrong?"

"Trey," she said, "where's your suitcase?"

He looked around, as if he expected to see it on the floor. Even as he did, though, he felt a tide of horror rise inside him.

"I went straight to the museum," he said, his voice a whisper. "It's still there."

But Sheila was already standing, half turned toward

the door. Reaching into her bag, pulling out her cell phone, dialing.

Saying, even before Jack's phone began to ring, "Answer me this time, you idiot. *Answer.*"

THIRTY-TWO

ONE RING OVER the speaker. Two. Three.

Trey remembered reading that the first few rings you hear when making a call on a cell phone are phony. They're generated by your phone to keep you occupied while the signal is bouncing off various satellites and cell towers. The person you're calling doesn't hear them.

Five rings. Seven. By now Jack's cell phone would be ringing.

Trey could see that Sheila's eyes were growing frantic and knew his own expression must be a mirror of hers.

The squawk of Jack's voice. "Yeah?"

"Where the hell have you been?" Sheila's voice was breathless. "I've been trying to reach you all afternoon."

"At the movies."

Sheila rolled her eyes. "Where are you now?"

"Walking down Eighty-first Street. Heading back to the office."

"Turn around."

"Say again?"

"Just listen to me." Sheila took in a breath. "Trey was infected. I removed the larva—"

"Holy shit—"

"Jack, he's okay."

She held up the phone. Trey called out, "I'm fine. Now shut up and listen to her."

"So the old man was right," Jack said. "If you remove the larva early enough, it can't set off a sufficient immunocascade—"

"Yes," Sheila said. "We'll tell you everything when we see you. Now—"

"Trey, what did you see while you were dreaming?"

"Jack—"

"'Cause I have some theories about that, too."

Sheila was holding the phone tightly. "Wait—are you still walking?"

"Sure. Told you: I'm heading to the office."

Sheila squeezed her eyes shut for a moment. Then she opened them and said, spacing the words out as if she were speaking to a child, "Jack, listen. Trey left his bag, the one he took to Australia, there. In your office."

That shut him up for a moment. Then he said, "Ah."

"Yes," Sheila said. "Ah."

After a pause he said, "Trey, do you have any memory of seeing the adult? In your rental car in Port Douglas, maybe?"

Trey worked through his dim memories of the past few days. Or were they visions? Created by the presence he could still feel shifting at the edges of his consciousness?

Finally he said, "I don't know."

"Doesn't matter." Even over the phone, Jack's excitement was evident. "This is so fucking cool. Come right in so we can talk."

"Jack, that's not—"

They heard his muffled voice speaking to someone else.

"Jack!" Sheila's voice was like a whip crack. "Where are you?"

No answer for ten seconds. Then Jack's voice: "Inside. Now I'm waiting for the elevator to the fifth floor."

"Are you listening to me?" Sheila said.

"What? Oh, hang on, I'm getting on the elevator. Cell service sucks in here."

"What are you doing? Stop!" Red spots had risen to Sheila's cheeks, and her left hand had, unbidden, risen to pull at her hair.

In other circumstances, Trey might even have found it funny: Sheila's powerful force meeting the immovable object that was Jack Parker.

But not here, not now.

Jack's voice came over the line, clearer.

"On five. What were you saying?"

Sheila's voice was despairing. "We're saying there might be an adult thief in your office."

They heard him laugh. "Yeah, I got that part."

"So don't go in."

"Don't go in my office?" He sounded disgusted. "The hell I won't."

Trey said, "I've seen those bugs, Jack. They're fast, and they know what they want. If one's in there, even if you think you're ready, it could still get the jump on you."

"Blah," Jack said, "blah blah. Trey, could you keep it down? I'm listening at the door here."

Trey stopped talking.

Jack said, "I don't hear any angry buzzing coming from inside."

"They're pretty close to silent, Jack," Trey said.

"It was a joke."

Trey said, "Ha."

"There you go." Static on the line. Then, "I'm going to put the phone down and go in."

Sheila closed her eyes. "Oh, Jack."

"I know. You don't know what you miss till it's gone."

A clunk as the phone was placed on the floor. The creak of a door swinging open. Footsteps.

Sheila said, *"Shit."*

They could hear Jack's voice in the distance: "That smell—"

Sheila's eyes opened wide. Trey was sweating.

Jack said in a singsong tone, "Oh, *ladrón*, where are you?"

Then, in a different tone: "Hey!"

A crash. Another.

"Hulk, smash!"

A hissing sound.

Silence.

Thirty seconds of silence that felt like forever to Trey. What was he doing here in bed? He should have been there with Jack.

He was supposed to be on the front lines. He was *always* supposed to be on the front lines.

A rustling sound over the phone, and then Jack's voice, much closer. They could hear his breath. He was panting.

"Got her," he said, "before she got me. She's dead."

Unmistakable triumph in his tone.

"You're okay?" Sheila asked. Her voice was strained.

"Told you, I'm fine." A laugh. "More than fine. I'm great."

"Hulk smashed it?" Trey said.

"No. That was a joke. We need it undamaged."

"You sure it's dead?"

"Oh, I'm sure. It's dead. It is no more. It has ceased to be. It is an ex-thief."

"How did you do it?"

"Come in and I'll show you."

Sheila said, "Trey can't travel yet."

But Trey was already swinging his legs over the side of the bed. He still felt shaky, but far stronger than he had when he'd first awoken. "I'm fine," he said, getting to his feet. "Just give me a minute and we'll go."

"Good," Jack said. "Get a move on."

"TAKE OFF YOUR shirt," Sheila said the moment they walked into the office.

Jack looked at her. Opened his mouth to make a joke, then quailed a little at her expression. "I told you, I'm fine. She didn't get near me."

Sheila crossed her arms. Jack's beard bristled. Then he caught a look at Trey, all sallow skin and shaky legs, and his expression turned thoughtful.

"Okay," he said.

It was hard to see the skin of Jack's round belly underneath its generous covering of black hair. After a close inspection, though, Sheila pronounced him unmarked.

"For now," she said.

"Told you," Jack said.

"Yeah, well, that doesn't mean we can be sure. We'll check again every few hours."

"Can't get enough of me, huh?"

He walked up to Trey and gave him a once-over. For a moment his expression turned serious.

"I feel better than I look," Trey said. "A little. I'll feel even better when my pee isn't dark brown, though."

"I want every detail." Jack paused. "Well, except the pee part."

Trey nodded.

"But first—look."

It was Trey's bag, where he'd left it on the floor near the windows. There was a ragged hole just beside the zipper, where the thief had chewed its way out.

Trey drew in a deep breath. How many hundreds, thousands, of other thieves had already traveled the same way?

"Here she is," Jack said.

The dead adult lay on her back on Jack's desk, her bloodred wings folded, black legs crossed in death like any insect's. Her body seemed undamaged.

"How did you kill her?" Sheila asked.

"Take a breath and guess."

Trey breathed in deeply. Under the harsh smell of the thief, he could detect another odor. After a moment, he figured out what it was.

"Pyrethrum," he said. Then, to Sheila, "What they use to fog trees and plants when they're collecting bugs. Deadly, but only to its targets. Plus it breaks down fast and doesn't harm the specimens."

"Kills them without harming them, a neat trick." Jack

nodded toward a half-full plastic plant sprayer sitting on the corner of his desk. "Mixed up a little of my own solution before walking in here, and knocked her out of the air when she came for me."

He frowned. "She was damn strong, I'll give her that. It took a couple of shots."

"Still, they can be killed," Sheila said.

Trey said, "They're just *binatang*."

"It's easy to forget," Jack said, "but it's true. Individually, they're easy enough to defeat."

"Individually," Sheila said.

Trey's hand crept up to his shirt. He touched the sterile pad on his belly and felt something stir deep inside his brain.

Sheila reached into her shoulder bag and took out the jar containing the dead larva. Opening the jar, she tipped it out onto the desk beside its parent.

In silence, they all looked at the two still forms.

"That's all they are," Sheila said in a wondering tone.

"Smaller creatures than these have brought civilizations crashing down," Trey said.

Jack shrugged. This sort of conversation didn't interest him.

He brought his face close to the two thieves, larva and adult. "Okay," he said to them, "tell us everything you know."

That was what interested him.

THIRTY-THREE

Charleston, South Carolina

MARY FINNERAN SAT in the shade under the live-oak trees in White Point Garden and looked out at Fort Sumter. The hazy summer sun, high in the sky at midday, had turned the harbor shimmering silver. The ferryboats and yachts left meteor trails across the choppy water, and farther out a cruise ship heading for land caught the sunlight and flashed white like a semaphore flag.

The skies were nearly as crowded. Wide-bodies brought tourists from all over the world, corporate jets carried executives for a round of golf or festivities at a plantation, and fighter jets and huge, creeping C3 cargo planes, which seemed as unlikely to achieve flight as snails, shuttled back and forth between nearby military bases.

Whenever Mary looked at these airplanes, *any* of them, she wondered whether they were carrying stowaways. What was aboard that no one knew about.

She let her gaze fall, come to rest on her hands. They looked like claws to her. She knew she'd lost weight since they'd come here, which was ironic in a town where you couldn't walk twenty feet without tripping over a place that served shrimp and grits, mac and cheese, barbecue, and gallons and gallons of sweet tea.

She felt her lips compress. She knew exactly what happened to you when you were old and lost too much weight. You got shaky. Your mind started to wander. You fell, breaking wrists as fragile as dry sticks and hips as sharp as bone knives. You lay in bed for weeks, as one system after another—heart, kidneys, brain—gave out, shut down.

You died.

If you wanted to live, if you wanted to be there to protect your granddaughter, who had nothing and no one without you, you kept eating. You kept the weight on. You made sure that you didn't waste away.

Maybe later they'd stop by Jestine's for fried okra and fried chicken. Hush puppies and Co'Cola cake. You couldn't waste away at Jestine's.

In the meantime, Mary rummaged for the plastic bag of pretzels she carried around. At the same time, her eyes sought out Kait, who was sitting perched on one of the shiny black cannons that aimed so bravely out toward the water.

Mary rarely took her eyes off her granddaughter, even though she knew full well that watching never saved anyone. It was magical thinking, but still you fell for it. A kind of deal with God: If I never look away, she will never come to harm.

And if the worst happened anyway, Mary was going to be there, right beside her. The last thing Kait was going to see was the face of someone who loved her more than life itself.

Kait put her cheek against the rough, freshly painted metal of the cannon's barrel. There was something about powerful weapons that drew kids, even girls. Even Kait, who usually just wanted to stay home reading or drawing pictures.

Pictures that she kept in a folder that resided deep in the back of a dresser drawer.

Mary ate a pretzel, then sighed and sat back against the bench, sweating in the shade. It was a hot day. They were almost all hot days in Charleston in the summer, hotter even than down on Marco Island. The kind of wet, unmoving heat only gulls and pelicans could love.

She wasn't complaining. It was nice here. The people were friendly enough. Mary's standards were based on how they treated Kait, and most of them—guessing that there was some tragedy in the story somewhere, but far too polite to ask about it—were unfailingly kind to the near-silent ten-year-old.

There had been more open arms than Mary could count, more attempts to bring Kait together with other children her age. Failed attempts so far. Kait preferred her own company. She always had.

"Grandma! Look!"

Mary's old heart pounded. She'd allowed her attention to wander.

But Kait's voice held no fear. She was standing balanced halfway down the barrel of the cannon. A tightrope walker, a high-wire artist, arms out, face split by the wide grin that used to come so often, and now so rarely.

The slippery barrel. Even as Mary swore she wouldn't, she found herself calling out, "Be careful, Bunny."

Damn. Let the girl have some fun.

Kait frowned. "I will." Then she took another step, wobbling a little before setting herself again. The grin returned, unbidden, as she concentrated and reached out for her next toehold.

A movement at the edge of Mary's vision. Her alarms went off. Again. Adrenaline flooded her poor worn-out system. Again.

As Kait reached the end of the barrel and jumped back down to the ground, Mary forced herself to turn her head. A man was coming in their direction, moving with purpose through the sunstruck tourists and moseying dog-walkers.

A tall, shambly sort of man wearing an expensive gray suit and carrying a leather briefcase. Perhaps fifty, the length of his legs and the way he held his head reminding Mary of an egret. On the street behind him, at the curb outside the building where Mary and Kait had rented a one-bedroom apartment, a black limousine idled.

Somehow she knew immediately that he was coming to see her. She looked back and saw that Kait was standing still, her face a blank but her hand up near her mouth. Her position and expression of stress, worry, not so different from when she was little and sucked her thumb.

The man stopped, far enough away not to be seen as a threat. Mary had the sense that he'd chosen the distance carefully.

"Mrs. Finneran?" he said. It was a question, barely. He knew who she was.

There was something familiar in his stance, in his face, as well. "I am," she said.

Kait hopped down and came trailing up to them. Using that hesitant way of moving she'd developed, every stride containing an escape clause.

"My name is Jeremy Axelson," the man said.

A familiar name, too, but she couldn't remember where. "Can I help you?"

He said, "Perhaps I could sit and explain?"

Again, not really a question. Mary frowned. "If I said no, would you sit anyway?"

He smiled at her. There was kindness in the smile. Or maybe he was just wooing her.

"Most likely," he said.

"Then go ahead and sit."

He folded his skinny frame onto the bench. Close enough that their talk would be intimate, private, far enough away that she didn't feel crowded.

The man was good at what he did, Mary realized. Whatever that was.

Kait dipped past them, picking up her Totoro backpack and taking it to a bench across the path. In Mary's sight lines, but far enough away to be separate. A moment later, she had her sketch pad and colored pencils out and was bent over, drawing.

Mary hoped she wasn't drawing another picture of those creatures. She'd sneaked a look at Kait's hidden trove. Almost all of them were of the wasp-things.

The man was sitting there, patient. Mary had the unsettling feeling that he'd been able to read her thoughts while her attention was elsewhere.

She looked into his calm face. "I do know you," she said. "From somewhere."

"Television, perhaps. I show up on the news shows a lot, since I work for Anthony Harrison." He paused. "The presidential candidate."

"I know who Anthony Harrison is," she said with asperity. "And now I know who you are. You're his . . . mouthpiece."

He seemed unoffended. Rummaged in his pocket and pulled out a photo ID.

"Communications director," he said. "So, yes: mouthpiece."

"You," she said, taking a moment before finding the word, "spin."

He smiled. "I prefer to put it another way: It's my job to make sure my candidate's thoughts and views are presented properly to the press and understood fully by the public."

She tilted her head. "Q.E.D."

He laughed.

"You're convincing on TV," she said, "but I don't envy you trying to spin your man's chances."

Axelson looked into her eyes. There was something in his expression beyond the calm intelligence he projected. Something eager, electric.

"Oh," he said, "there's plenty of time for things to change before Election Day."

It was in his tone, too. Mary felt a spiderlike sensation creeping across her stomach. Dread.

She said, "Speak your piece, Mr. Axelson."

"I will. But first let me show you something." Yet even as he reached into his briefcase and pulled out a small sheaf of papers clipped together, she knew. Maybe she'd known from the first moment she'd laid eyes on him.

The first page showed a photo. A lousy one, most likely captured from a computer screen. Lousy but recognizable.

Mary didn't even have to look at the rest, but she did, paging quickly through them. The last was a drawing, stiff and far from lifelike. A drawing done by a bureaucrat, not an artist.

"You want a halfway-decent picture of one of these creatures," she said, "get my granddaughter to do it."

Axelson nodded, but didn't directly respond. "You know what really killed your son and daughter-in-law, don't you?"

Yet again a statement couched as a question. Spoken in a quiet voice, but Mary knew that Kait had heard. People always underestimated how well she listened.

"You know what's going on," Axelson said.

Mary said, "Why are you here?"

Again instead of replying, Axelson reached into his case and withdrew another pile of papers, a thinner stack. Not a hodgepodge of photocopied photos and drawings this time. A memo. A briefing.

He handed it to her. Across the way, Kait put her art materials into her backpack, stood, and came over to stand beside Mary. One hand rested lightly on her grandmother's back, as much physical contact as she granted these days. Mary moved the papers on her lap so she could read them, too.

Axelson shifted a little in his seat, but didn't intervene.

The title of the briefing was "Spiderweb." Below this heading was a series of bulleted paragraphs, each beginning with a location and date in boldface. Patagonia,

Arizona, in May. Anza-Borrego Desert State Park in California, and Galveston, Texas, early in June. Later the same month, Biloxi, Mississippi.

This data was followed by a few words of description. "Two seen by birders at Falcon Dam." "Found dead inside town hall." "Host: Rhesus monkey." "Possible human involvement."

Possible human involvement. Mary raised her eyes.

Axelson gave a tiny nod.

"Look," Kait said. "There's us."

Marco Island, Florida. "Host: Bottlenose dolphin. Emergence? Yes."

On the next line: "Probable human involvement."

Mary felt sick to her stomach. She said to Axelson, "These witnesses, survivors—are you visiting all of them?"

"Someone on my staff is, yes. I wanted to see you two myself."

He pointed at the papers. "Keep reading."

The locations on the first two pages were almost all from the southern tier of states. Nothing north of Georgia or Oklahoma or New Mexico.

"Any in South Carolina?" Kait asked. Her face was a shade paler than usual, but mostly she looked merely interested. Unlike Mary, she'd always liked lists.

"Nothing that's risen to a level of certainty," Axelson said.

She looked at him as she worked out what his words meant. "You're saying," she said at last, "that you've heard they're here, but you don't know if the stories are true."

His look was thoughtful. "Yes, that's exactly what I'm saying."

"But they are," Kait said. "If they're in all those other places"—she pointed one slim forefinger—"they're here, too."

Axelson said, "Read a little further."

Mary turned a page. More reports. More sightings. More "human involvement."

In northern California. Baltimore. Portland, Oregon, and Portland, Maine.

Outside Chicago.

In Davenport, Iowa, and Sioux Falls, South Dakota.

More than two dozen reports from nearly as many states. Southern, northern, coastal, and landlocked.

A C3 rattled the ground as it cruised overhead. Mary raised her gaze to watch it, then met Axelson's eyes.

Kait got it, too. "They're everywhere," she said.

Axelson nodded. "Two dozen reports might not seem like that many," he said, "but those are only the ones we know about, only the ones we've confirmed. How many others have gone unreported? And how many more will we hear about today? Tomorrow?"

Mary and Kait were silent.

"It's an invasion," he said. "Our country's being invaded, right here, right under our eyes, and nobody's doing a thing about it."

Mary gestured at the papers. "So many reports—why aren't the newspapers and TV all over this?"

"Two dozen reports over many weeks in a country as big as ours—well, that's not quite an avalanche," Axelson said. "Especially not when the deaths are reported to be from 'natural causes,' allergic shock, or killer bee attacks."

Now there was an edge of anger in his voice. "But the government should know what's going on. The question we need to ask is, Are they asleep at the switch? Or is it something else?"

Mary said, "What do you want from us?"

He gazed at her. Calculated sincerity and hope and compassion mixed in his expression, and beneath them, excitement. Avidity.

It was the look of a spinner who's seen the opportunity of a lifetime.

"Come with me," he said. "Come meet Governor Harrison, and he'll tell you."

THIRTY-FOUR

Rockefeller University, Manhattan

CLARE SHAPIRO WAS a biochemist and a lab rat, which wasn't hard to guess when you met her. She was tall and thin, with knotty hair pulled back in an unfashionable "I don't give a shit" ponytail and unsettling, pale-gray eyes that looked at you as if you were wasting her time before you ever uttered a word.

Maybe because you were.

Trey and Jack hadn't come to Rock U to analyze the limitations of Clare Shapiro's charm. They were there because she was better than anybody else on earth at one thing: analyzing the chemicals in wasp venom.

Trey knew that scientists around the world were working to develop new antivenins, new drugs, even potential weapons, from wasp venom. But before they could get to work, they had to understand what they were working with. For that, they went to Shapiro and her team.

Trey and Jack had done the same a week before, when they'd sent the two thief specimens to her.

After getting a call that she was ready to talk, they'd come to her dingy little office on Rock U's fourth floor. It had a view of an airshaft and pigeons promenading around on the windowsill. Trey doubted that Clare cared. She probably never even looked out.

As they entered, she said, "Parker."

"Hello," Jack said. Trey could have sworn he looked a little shy.

Her gaze shifted. "And you're Gilliard? The one who served as a host to a larval wasp?"

"Yes, that one," Trey said.

She regarded him with interest. "Mind if I get a blood sample from you?"

"Sure." He began to roll up his sleeve.

She gave a hint of a smile. "When you leave will be fine. I'll tell you where to go."

Trey wondered if a blood sample would reveal the changes in him. The presence, the other, that he was beginning to think would be with him forever.

He was most aware of it when he awoke in the dead of night, when there were no distractions. At those times it felt most like a being, a *consciousness*. Half formed, incomplete, but there, living inside him.

Trey had gone through every detail of his experience with Jack and Sheila, except this one. He wasn't sure why he was keeping it a secret.

Maybe it was telling him to stay quiet.

Shapiro's cold gaze held him. "Gilliard, how much do you understand about the chemistry of wasp venom?"

"Let's assume I understand nothing," he said.

Her expression tightened, and he thought she was biting back some choice words. Instead, she said, "You know we have the tools to decode genomes across the animal kingdom, right?"

He nodded. Beside him, Jack said, "I'm still getting asked if there's any dinosaur blood in our amber-trapped mosquitoes, so we can unravel the dino DNA and clone new ones."

Shapiro ignored this. "A few years ago, we successfully decoded the genome of *Nasonia vitripennis*—that's a parasitic wasp, though not closely related to yours," she said. "We were able to map out the constituents of its venom and compare it to the venom of other wasps."

Her expression had lightened a little. This was no surprise. Trey knew that even the most contrary people liked to talk, as long as you stuck to what interested them.

"So we used a two-dimensional liquid chromatography electrospray ionization Fourier transform ion cyclotron resonance mass spectrometer—"

"Assume I understand nothing," Trey said again.

She looked at him, sighed, put her hands flat on the desk. "It's a device for analyzing the chemical constituents of substances like wasp venom. Will that do?"

"Yes."

"Good. What its analysis showed us was that *N. vitripennis*'s venom contains at least seventy-nine different proteins—half of which were never previously associated with insect venoms, and nearly two dozen of which weren't similar to *any* other proteins we'd ever seen. They were complete mysteries to us."

She stared at him with her unearthly gray eyes, making sure he understood. "These proteins are as alien," she said, "as ones we might find in insects discovered on Mars."

Silence spread in the room. Then Trey sighed. "You're warning me that seven days hasn't been long enough for you to solve all the mysteries of thief venom."

"No," she said. "Not quite enough."

Her eyes brightened. "But I wouldn't have called if we'd found out nothing about your beast." She blinked like a cat. "Logically, first we used a bioinformatic approach, employing amino acid sequences of known venom proteins to search for transcripts—identifiable patterns—of proteins in your wasp's venom."

"Let me guess: The problem with that approach," Trey said, "is that it only recognizes previously known proteins, not any 'Martian' ones."

"Yes." Shapiro gave a quick nod. "But it's a useful first step."

"And the next one?"

"A combination of two techniques: The ion cyclotron resonance mass spectrometer I mentioned and—" A glint of amusement in her eyes. "And an off-line two-dimensional liquid chromatography matrix-assisted laser desorption and ionization time-of-flight mass spectrometer as well."

Trey said, "You had enough venom for all these analyses?"

"Just. We're lucky that your beasts have exceptionally roomy venom sacs and that this adult specimen hadn't stung anyone recently."

"I'm the luckiest!" Jack said brightly.

Trey and Shapiro both ignored him. "What did you find?" Trey asked.

"Mass spectrometry showed the presence of more than one hundred proteins—significantly more than we uncovered in *N. vitripennis*. Again, about a third were unrecognizable—we don't yet know *what* they do. We'll keep working on those."

"And the rest?"

"Some, like an allergen 5 protein, are quite familiar. They represent well-known venom constituents that appear in many different wasp species."

She gave her quick smile. "Which tends to indicate that your wasps did not, in fact, originate on Mars. They evolved here."

Another blink. "Of the rest, some are merely translational or transcriptional." She noticed his expression and said, "Proteins that help the venom gland function. They're the grease in the machinery."

Trey was beginning to learn what Shapiro's expressions meant. He could see that even as she spoke, her mind was on to the next thing. The next six things. She was like a chess player who can see the forced checkmate fifteen moves ahead.

And now Trey could tell that she had something else to tell them, something more important. "But that's not all, is it?" he said.

"No." Suddenly her face was alight. "In our tests, we kept finding the same protein, again and again. In some ways it resembled ones we've seen in other parasitic wasps, but with significant differences as well."

Her eyes widened a little. "It is highly unusual to see any protein appear so often."

"What does it mean?" Trey asked.

"It means it's important. Crucial. It means that the beast has put the most energy, the most evolutionary effort, you might say, into producing this constituent."

Trey thought that over. "And which known proteins does it resemble?"

She tilted her head and looked at him, then at Jack. "Most closely: phospholipase A1."

Jack sat up straighter in his chair. *"Shit,"* he said.

Trey waited.

"That's a major venom allergen in the genus *Polistes* and others," Jack told him. "When people die of anaphylactic shock from wasp stings, phospholipase A1 is often the culprit."

Trey looked at Shapiro. He had one more question to ask, the most important one. "That same protein," he said. "Did it also turn up in the larva?"

"Yes," she said. "Repeatedly." Again the widening of the eyes. "It's unprecedented to find the same venom in an adult wasp and its larva, but that's what we discovered."

Trey thought about the poison he'd felt pumping through his bloodstream. "Disturb the larva, and it releases the venom."

Shapiro nodded. "Yes."

"Any chance of an antivenin?"

She grimaced. "That's a long way off."

But her gaze was still bright as she looked at him. She had something else to tell him, but was waiting for him to figure it out first.

"You also found," he said slowly, "an explanation of why I didn't realize I'd been . . . infected." He looked over at Jack. "Or Sheila's mother, either."

Jack's eyes were still on Shapiro. "The chemical that clouds men's minds?"

She nodded. "Yes. In a gland in both adult and larva that, as far as we know, is also unique among wasps."

"What does the gland contain?"

"A benzodiazepine."

Jack said, "Jesus."

At last something that was familiar to Trey, too. He knew that benzodiazepines were a class of drugs used as muscle relaxants, to control seizures, as sedatives, to battle anxiety.

And to make patients forget what they'd just gone through. To create amnesia.

"Every symptom of early infestation you've described—the lethargy, the dreaminess, and the inability to remember being implanted—can be caused by benzodiazepines," Shapiro said.

Jack was frowning. "Okay. Phospholipase. Benzodiazepine. You're drugged to the gills. Why?"

"I think I know," Trey said.

They both looked at him.

"Let's tie this together." He paused, marshaling his thoughts. "The fact that I'm sitting here shows that removal of the larva isn't necessarily fatal to the host."

Jack said, "Not when the larva is small."

"A mammal that's been infected," Trey went on. "Especially a primate—and we know that primates are the preferred hosts—when it notices the swelling. Sees the airhole, figures out there is a larva underneath. How does it respond?"

Jack answered. "It worries at the wound. Even non-primates will try to get the larva out. A dog will scratch, a cat will chew, and a monkey will have a friend or family member pick it off."

"Yes. But only if it's aware that it's been infected. Only if it *notices*."

"Which the amnesic properties of the benzodiazepine prevent," Shapiro said.

"That's how it worked on me," Trey said.

"Until Sheila noticed, and even then it was almost too fucking late." Jack sat up in his chair. "You're right. That's it. That's the point. When the larva is implanted, your mind is fogged so you don't mess with it. Then, by the time it's big enough that someone notices it and tries to get it out—well, by then it's almost certain to kill you."

Trey nodded. "Could another sting, late in the process, influence the host's brain to bring on the protective rage response I've seen?" He paused. "Is that even plausible?"

Shapiro gave a shrug. "I don't see why not. The human brain is easily influenced, and there are many known compounds that antagonize the ionotropic glutamate receptors, which mediate rage. Phencyclidine is just one well-known example, but it's far from the only one."

"Phencyclidine?" Trey said. "PCP?"

She nodded. "Angel dust. No, phencyclidine didn't show up in our assays, but there's something there. Now I just have to find it."

This seemed like a cue. Trey and Jack stood. "You've done amazing things," Trey said, holding out his hand. "Thank you."

An eyeblink of a smile, and then she stood and shook his hand. Hers felt like it was made entirely of tendons.

"My team is very skilled," she said.

Then she frowned. "Want more? Want that antivenin? Get us a supply of new specimens. There's only so much we can get out of a single venom sac."

Jack made a sound through his nose. A laugh.

"Soon enough," he said, "that shouldn't be a problem."

* * *

THEY HEADED TO the fifth floor, where Trey would leave a blood sample. At the elevator he said, "Hold on. I forgot to ask her something."

When Jack made a move to go with him, Trey shook his head. "Wait here."

As Jack's curious gaze followed him, he went back to Clare Shapiro's office. She was still standing where they'd left her, peering down at some papers on her desk.

She raised her eyes as he entered the room. "Yes?"

"Are there any substances in wasp venom," he said, "that can permanently change the chemistry of the human brain?"

She tilted her head, thinking, then said, "None that I'm aware of. Theoretically, of course, it's quite possible. Why do you ask?"

Trey shook his head and answered her question with another of his own.

"Clare," he said, "what do you know about the hive mind?"

THIRTY-FIVE

"I GOT A voice mail from Mary Finneran," Sheila said as they walked in the door.

Something in her tone made Trey stop and look at her. Jack, oblivious, sat down at his computer and said, "Who's Mary Finneran?"

Before she could answer, Trey said to Sheila, "The woman you visited in Florida. The one whose son— daughter?—was killed."

"Son and daughter-in-law." Sheila frowned. "She and Kait are living in Charleston now."

"I remember. What did she say?"

Sheila crossed her arms, hugging herself as if she were cold. "She said to make sure we watch Anthony Harrison's acceptance speech tonight."

Jack looked up from his screen and said, "The hell does *that* mean?"

Trey stood still, his mind working. Then he figured it out and felt a hole open somewhere deep inside him.

"It means the deluge," he said.

* * *

THE PRESIDENTIAL CONVENTION hall looked like any other. Strung with bunting and red-white-and-blue banners, it was brightly lit but carefully calibrated not to make the audience look corpselike. The seats were filled with banner-waving delegates, politicians, reporters, and perhaps even some regular people.

Jack, Sheila, and Trey had met in Trey's apartment because Jack's apartment was always a disaster area, and Trey wanted to watch on a full-size screen, not a computer monitor at the office. He didn't watch much television, but when he did, he needed to *see*, to be able to understand and interpret what he was seeing.

"Can they get to the point?" Jack said after two hours. "Or should I just shoot myself now?"

But still the speeches went on and on, all lauding Anthony Harrison's merits for the presidency. The audience rose to its feet for repeated scripted ovations. Delegates pledged their support to the candidate and showed off their crazy hats and buttons and waved their banners.

Trey barely listened. He was watching the faces and seeing, under the cheers, the laughter, the shouts and ovations, something different: worry.

They were worried because none of them—not delegates, reporters, pundits, viewers—knew what was coming when Anthony Harrison took the stage. Unlike every nominee for decades, he'd declined to release a transcript of his speech ahead of time, or to give even the slightest hint what it would contain.

"This is the most important night of Harrison's

political career," said an offended talking head on MS-NBC, "and we have no idea what he's about to say."

"Well," replied a pundit, "he may be on his way to a crushing defeat, but he certainly has kept our attention tonight."

Jack pointed at the screen.

"Here he comes," he said.

ANTHONY HARRISON LOOKED like a politician. He was tall, broad shouldered, and wore his pinstriped steel-gray suit and red tie comfortably but not ostentatiously. His hair was thick and touched with gray at the temples.

As he acknowledged the ovation from the crowd, smiling and waving at this ally and that supporter, Trey watched his face. Harrison didn't have the shifty, angry look of so many career politicians. Nor was he a handsome blank. There seemed to be some intelligence in his gaze, some awareness of the absurdity of the theater he was engaged in.

"This guy was a governor, right?" Trey asked.

Both Jack and Sheila turned their heads to look at him. "Uh, yeah," Jack said. "Of Colorado? For eight years?"

Trey said, "Was he good?"

Jack snorted, but Sheila said, "I think he was okay. Honest enough. Not the brightest or dimmest star."

"How do you know this?" Jack asked. "Didn't you live in the Congo or something?"

She shrugged. "Sure, but I'm still American. This is still my country."

Trey thought about it. Was it still his country? Sometimes he didn't feel like he even belonged to the same species as the people cheering and waving banners on-screen.

FINALLY THE CROWD restrained itself and sat down, and Anthony Harrison began to speak. His voice was deep, relaxed, confident. Trey could see how he'd come so far.

The nominee's expression was serious, even grave. "As I'm sure most of you have heard," he began, "I recently discarded the speech I'd planned to deliver tonight. In it, I talked about many of the challenges facing our nation, and why I am the man to confront them."

He looked around the hall. "All of it is still true. But just in the past few days, I've learned about a situation— a crisis of monumental proportions—that demands my immediate attention, and yours. A crisis that my opponent has known about far longer than I have, but has chosen to ignore. *That* is what I must talk about tonight."

The camera panned the confused, apprehensive crowd before returning to Harrison. "My fellow Americans," he said, "I am with you tonight to tell you that our great nation is under attack."

A frightened murmur from the crowd.

"More than an attack," Harrison said. "An act of terrorism."

So that's his angle, Trey thought.

"Give me a goddamn fucking break," Jack said.

"We are a strong nation," Harrison went on. "We've faced terrorism on our shores before, and we've overcome it. We've triumphed because we've stood together, proud, strong, united. That's who we are as a people. Nothing can bring us to our knees."

He gazed into the camera. Now he looked angry. Righteously angry.

"Nothing can bring us to our knees," he said again, "except an administration that hides a grave threat to our lives, our freedom, merely so it can win an election."

Though the cameras stayed on Harrison's stern face, Trey could hear sounds of dismay from the audience.

"The lives of your neighbors, your coworkers, your parents, your *children*, are in peril. Too many have died already—and how many more will die before Election Day?"

"Careful, asshole," Jack murmured, "or you'll have them fleeing the hall."

"How many thousands will die?" Harrison said, his expression now one of controlled rage. "Ask the president. Ask the president—and then ask why he is covering up this crisis, this invasion, this terrorist act."

Harrison's voice rose. "Or don't. Don't ask. All you'll hear is what I heard when I contacted him, offering to do everything I could to help confront this new enemy. All you'll hear are lies and obfuscations and denials. Because he doesn't know what to do. He doesn't have any idea."

An accusatory finger. "Instead, our president is trading the lives of American people for votes." His eyes looked into the camera, into the eyes of the American people. "Hoping to keep the news of this invasion out of the newspapers until after he has been reelected."

Harrison's face was red. "I'm sure my opponent and his staff are scrambling for a response as I speak. Well, let me tell you what they're going to say. They'll tell you I've gone off the deep end. They'll say I'm desperate, making it all up, lying. They'll tell you not to believe a word I say."

He took a breath. "And, you know, I can understand that. Why should you believe me? I am, after all, a politician, and though I've been an honest one throughout my career, I certainly wouldn't blame you for being skeptical. We folks don't exactly have the most sterling reputation, and a lot of that reputation is deserved."

A slight ripple of uneasy laughter from the unseen audience.

"But if you won't believe me," Harrison said, "will you believe Enrique Montero?"

The cameras focused on a young man in the front row of the balcony. He had an oval face, dark eyes with circles under them, and straight black hair. He looked very nervous, glancing back and forth at the older woman and man who flanked him—his parents, Trey assumed.

"In many ways, until recently Enrique lived the American dream. The son of legal immigrants who, through determination and hard work, were able to open their own grocery store in Chico, California. While his older brother, Gonzalo, worked at the store, Enrique attended college . . . until two months ago."

The camera came back to Harrison's face. "Two months ago, Gonzalo was killed. And you know who was arrested for murder? Who spent weeks in jail before being released? Yes, Enrique. Yet he was innocent—he *is* innocent. The real culprit? The invader, the terrorist. The threat the president doesn't believe we deserve to know about. But we do. Enrique and his parents do."

The camera went back to the family's faces. They were crying.

"Jesus Christ," Jack said. "Why don't you pick their bones while you're at it?"

Now the camera focused on a pretty young woman with sandy blond hair. She looked angry.

"This is Elizabeth Keaton," Harrison said. "Six weeks ago, she was a newlywed, married just eight months to her high school sweetheart, James. They'd just bought their first house together, in Davenport, Iowa. They were planning on having four children—four, at least."

On camera, Elizabeth Keaton glanced at someone to her left and nodded. Then she faced forward again, and now her eyes were red.

"Then James disappeared. You know what the authorities told Elizabeth? That he'd probably run away with another woman!"

Harrison's face filled the screen. "I am not blaming the Davenport police. They are good at what they do, and we should all be proud of them and grateful for their service. It's not their fault that they weren't given the information they needed—information that might have saved James's life, or at the very least brought an end to Elizabeth's uncertainty. For, yes, James, too, was a victim of these terrorists. Tragically, his life, too, came to an end—and with it, Elizabeth's dreams."

Harrison lifted a hand. "I'll give you just one last example, although I could share a dozen more if I wanted to. No, just one more, to show you how this is a tragedy, a threat, that spans generations."

Sheila made a sound in her throat.

And there were Kait and Mary on-screen. Kait, her thick black hair held back by a headband, wore a blue dress with a big belt around the waist. Her dark eyes stared out from a face that was ghostly pale under the freckles.

In her own simple red dress, Mary, her white hair standing out in the crowd, looked just as resolute. Together, grandmother and granddaughter cast an indelible image, as they'd been intended to.

To Mary's left sat a long-jawed, blue-eyed, blond-haired woman of about forty-five. Her face was perfectly made up, her hair was piled up on top of her head, and her diamond earrings and necklace sent little gleaming stars across the screen.

"Harrison's wife," Jack said. "Samantha."

Two children, a boy and a girl, sat to Kait's right. The boy was perhaps twelve and had the candidate's olive complexion. The girl, maybe eight, was a small, blond replica of Samantha. As the camera focused on them, the girl took Kait's hand in her own and squeezed it.

"On July twenty-third, Kait spent the morning with her father—and Mary's son—Tim, on the dock behind their home on Marco Island, just as she'd done countless times before," Anthony Harrison said. "Together they were watching a baby dolphin who had been born in their boat slip just a few days before—a sick little dolphin Kait hoped to save.

"But the dolphin died. It was killed." Now Harrison's voice rose and became accusatory once more. "A sad story, but not one I would be talking about right now . . . if the same killers hadn't then visited Tim and Joanna Finneran's house and murdered them as well."

Cries from the crowd.

"Yes," Harrison said. "These innocent young parents died without knowing the dangers they were facing. Why didn't they know? Because our government, our president, didn't tell them."

His expression was ferocious. "Tim and Joanna Finneran, James Keaton, Gonzalo Montero—*none* of them had to die. But they did. Now the American people—the voters—*you and I*—need to know why."

He rocked back a little behind the lectern. "You've been very patient," he said. "I know you've long been wondering what I'm talking about. Invaders, I say. Attackers. I can imagine you're all thinking of soldiers in uniforms, of rebels, of people with bombs strapped to their bodies.

"But no. That's not it. What's been attacking us, killing Americans, leaving people like Enrique and Elizabeth and Kait alone in the world is . . . this."

Trey was never sure whether people in the convention center saw the image on a theater screen or television monitors or somehow projected in 3-D into thin air, but what viewers at home saw was the face of a thief projected so suddenly and so large that even Trey jumped. Whatever the audience saw must have been just as dramatic, because loud gasps were mixed with shouts and muffled screams.

The camera focused on the crowd. Some were staring upward, some were averting their eyes, and many were crying.

On-screen, Harrison raised both hands in a quelling gesture. "Ladies and gentlemen," he said, "hear me out. This is not a monster I'm describing, not some ancient beast out of Jurassic Park." He held his right thumb and forefinger apart. "They are wasps, the biggest on earth, but still just this big. That's big enough. Big enough to kill with a single sting."

The screen showed the vicious-looking thief again, then went back to Harrison. "This wasp, this creature," he said, "is hunting us. It wants to kill us. It will not be stopped by locked doors and shut windows. And if you kill one—well, more will come, and more, and more."

He paused for a beat, then said, "And I haven't even told you the worst part of this story."

Jack groaned.

"The worst part—the part that we will never forgive the president for hiding from us—is that these creatures' larvae, their young, are parasitic. They must grow inside mammal hosts to survive. Mammals . . . including humans."

His voice rang out. "One grew inside the baby dolphin that poor Kait tried to save," he said. "One grew inside Gonzalo, Enrique Montero's brother. And one grew inside James, Elizabeth Keaton's husband. Grew inside them, and killed them."

The camera went back to the crowd, which looked shell-shocked.

"Yes," Harrison said. "I am sorry, so sorry, to be the one giving you this news. It should have been the president. This is the president's job, but he won't do it. He's too busy running for reelection."

A breath before he delivered the next blow. "And if, tomorrow, one of these creatures begins to grow inside *you*, you know what he'll do? He'll hide, just as he always does."

His fist struck the lectern. "But *I* won't hide. As soon as I am finished here, my staff—including a team of brilliant scientists and doctors—will be providing detailed instructions on how best to stay safe in these dangerous times. Check our website for fact sheets, videos, and links to important information and advice. Keep watching the station you're tuned to—after my speech, we'll have experts on every network.

"Now and in the coming days, my staff and I will do everything we can to prepare you to face what scientists are calling the most serious crisis of our lifetimes. Perhaps the current administration does not think you are worth it, but I do."

Again his voice grew quieter. "At the beginning of this speech, I spoke of terrorism. I spoke of invasion. Some of you may be thinking, 'All right—he's scared us. But this doesn't sound like terrorism to me. It sounds more like an epidemic. Frightening, yes, but just bad luck. Nobody's fault.'

"Yes, that's how it sounds . . . but it's not how it is. Until recently, no one had ever heard of these creatures—not even the nation's leading scientists. But now the wasps are here. Here, in America, killing our citizens. Where did they come from? How did they get here?"

He leaned forward. "I believe they were sent by our enemies. By those who envy our freedoms, who hate us for our democracy. I believe—I *know*—these creatures were created and hatched in a laboratory and sent here, just as surely as anthrax spores, a dirty bomb, or any other bioweapon would be. And with the same goal: To terrify us. To destroy us."

"Brilliant," Sheila said.

Her eyes were wide.

"This *is* terrorism," Harrison said. "Pure and simple. Who is behind it? We don't know yet. But we will find out." His eyes were fierce. "Elect me, and I guarantee *I* will find out. Find out who has targeted us, and if we have to scour the earth we will make sure they *pay*. Just as we will make sure that every last one of these creatures has been driven from every corner of our great country."

Trey felt something stir deep inside him. An awakening.

"When Election Day comes, and you're deciding how to cast your vote, remember that you face a stark choice," Harrison said. "My opponent, the man who is willingly putting your lives at risk, or me: the one who promises—who *swears*—to clean up the mess President Chapman has left behind and restore our great nation to the strength and honor it has always proudly held.

"Thank you. And may God bless America and protect us in the trials to come."

THIRTY-SIX

THE DELUGE.

They kept the television on for most of the night. Jack sat on the sofa and wielded the remote, flicking back and forth among the networks and cable news stations. Sheila had taken over the apartment's one comfortable chair, while Trey, unable to stay still, sat at the kitchen table or on the edge of the sofa, but spent most of his time leaning against various walls.

They watched pundits and commentators and party members spin the political implications of Harrison's speech, as if this were the story of the night, not the threat itself, not the deaths. Scientists—whoever the shows had found willing to pontificate in the middle of the night—offered their learned opinions. Bloggers who had posted videos of the thieves blinked in the harsh light of the movie cameras. Conspiracy theorists weighed in. Instant polls measured the consequences.

And driving it all was the Harrison campaign's carefully

planned publicity blitz. Compelling, sober, terrifying spokespeople were everywhere, on every channel, all reinforcing the same message: This is serious. This is scary. The president has dropped the ball. Trust Anthony Harrison.

Having watched this routine a dozen times, Jack started to growl. "Next they're gonna start sending people door to door," he said, "and I'm gonna slug the first one who rings the bell."

Hospitals and police stations reported being flooded with calls and visits. Hordes of people thinking they'd been stung. Further hordes fearing they were now hosting larvae. False alarm after false alarm.

"Therapists all over the world are thanking Harrison and making down payments on their dream homes," Jack said.

"Hush." Sheila ran her hand through her hair, which had grown out from its pixie cut. "You know what's interesting," she went on. "They all keep going over the same list of attacks, but nobody's managed to come up with any fresh footage of the thieves, or even of someone who's been infected."

"Huh," Jack said. "Well, it hasn't been very long. We'll start hearing shit soon enough."

"I don't think so."

It had been a long time since Trey had spoken. Jack and Sheila both turned to stare at him, as surprised as if a chair had decided to join the conversation.

"Don't think so?" Jack asked. "Don't think so what?"

"I don't think we'll be hearing of many attacks," Trey said. "Not now."

Sheila was watching him closely. "Why not, Trey? You think they're hiding?"

Trey thought about it, then shook his head.

"Then what?"

"Waiting," he said.

AT SOME POINT in the evening the president sent his press secretary, a rumpled-looking man who looked like he hadn't slept in a week, out to meet a crowd of reporters. He stood before a microphone in front of a cluster of cameras and tried to convey outrage.

"He looks terrified," Sheila commented. "I think the first he heard of this was tonight."

"No," Trey said. "He's terrified because he *did* know—they all did. But they weren't prepared for the secret to leak."

Sheila's eyes were on him. "How do you see that?"

Trey shrugged. How did he understand anything he saw? Tone of voice, posture, stresses, intonations, expressions in the eyes.

He just did.

"With his reckless, irresponsible speech, Governor Harrison has proven himself unfit for public office," the press secretary declaimed. "He is using family tragedies for personal benefit, something President Chapman—or any person with an ounce of morality—would never do."

Reporters shouted questions. The press secretary said, "Our hearts go out to those who have lost family members and friends, just as we express sorrow over those who die too soon from so many other maladies. We take this new threat very seriously and are utilizing all resources at our disposal, including the Centers for Disease Control and, if necessary, the military, to repel it."

Then, to a cacophony of shouts, he turned and walked away.

"Not enough," Sheila said.

Jack shook his head. "Not close."

Trey felt something move inside him, somewhere near his core.

And stayed quiet.

TWO IN THE morning. "It's weird," Jack said.

"What is?" Sheila asked.

"I feel ripped off." He gave a little smile. "I mean, for a while there, this was all . . . ours. We were, like, the only ones who knew. And now, just like that, we're not."

Sheila looked at him. "I wish it had never been mine."

His mouth twisted. "Yeah. And I'm sorry. But you know what I mean." He opened his arms. "As long as it was just us, there was a chance it wouldn't all blow up and go to shit. Now—no."

"I don't think there was ever a chance." Sheila sighed. "People were going to find out, and things were going to start spiraling anyway."

"I guess so."

"It's what people do," Sheila said. "They ruin everything."

"'People ruin everything.'" Jack's voice was approving. "I think I'll make a T-shirt with that."

"Tell me something," she said to him. "*Could* someone weaponize wasp venom?"

"I told you," Jack said. "No. It's bullshit."

He took a gulp of coffee. "Listen," he went on. "Sure, you could make the venom more potent, more deadly—at least, someone like Clare Shapiro could. I'm sure those busy bees at the Defense Department are 'efforting' that as we speak."

He turned his palms up. "But when it's still inside the wasp? Creating a new breed of superwasps? Come on. Crapola."

"But thief venom is so powerful," Sheila insisted. "Powerful enough to kill a human—and much more than would be needed for smaller hosts. Why would it evolve that way?"

Jack grinned at her. "Black widow spiders," he said.

"What?"

"Sheila," he said, "what do black widow spiders eat?"

She shrugged. "I don't know. Crickets? Beetles?"

"Yeah. Stuff like that. Yet their venom can kill a human. Hell, it can kill a horse or a cow. Why?"

Sheila opened her mouth to answer, then closed it again.

Jack was enjoying himself. "The widow's venom is thousands of times more powerful than it 'needs' to be. In fact, if anything, its potency is an evolutionary *disadvantage*."

Sheila thought this over, then nodded. "Because people who see a black widow are likely to kill her, where they might ignore a less venomous spider."

"Exactly. And not only people—other animals will go out of their way to kill widows as well." He crossed his arms over his chest. "We all fall into the trap of seeing nature as infallible, of seeing every evolutionary step as an improvement, an aid to species survival."

"But it's not true?" Sheila said.

Jack shook his head. "Of course not. Evolution isn't a

straight path. It's filled with dead ends, wrong turns, mistakes."

His shrug was eloquent. "Sometimes Mother Nature just deals a wild card."

"And the rest of us pay the price," Sheila said.

SOON AFTER, JACK started yawning so widely that they could see where his wisdom teeth had been yanked fifteen years earlier. Eventually he started eyeing Trey's sofa. "At night, I think better prone," he said.

"I certainly hope so," Sheila said.

Groaning a little, he lay back on the sofa. Three minutes later his eyes were closed and his mouth was open, though he wasn't quite snoring.

"Down for the count," Trey said.

Sheila, who'd come over to sit opposite Trey at the table, regarded Jack's sleeping form with something like affection. "How come I feel like we've acquired a teenage son?" she asked.

Trey said, "He'll still be a teenager when he's sixty."

"That's true for most of you research types, isn't it?" Her voice was light. "Heading off into the field, leaving your lives behind, staying forever young?"

"Right now," Trey said before he could stop himself, "'forever young' is about a million miles from how I feel."

Sheila looked at him. There was something new in her expression.

"Talk to me," she said. "Tell me what's happened to you."

Meaning: *Since you were infected. Since I cut that thing out of you.*

Trey took a deep breath. He'd been waiting for her to ask. He'd known she suspected something.

What he hadn't figured out was how he was going to answer. Whether he was going to lie to her—say, "I'm fine," and change the subject—or trust her to understand. Open himself up.

Looking at her pale, beautiful face, the intensity and intelligence of her gaze, he knew he couldn't lie. Subterfuge wasn't in her makeup, and tonight he couldn't summon it, either.

"When you took out the larva," he said, "something got left behind."

Her gaze strayed to where she'd performed the surgery, then back up to his face. "The site was clean," she said.

He smiled. "Yes, you did a beautiful job for someone who expected her patient to die. It's almost healed already—but I didn't mean there."

"Then where?"

Slowly Trey reached up and pointed to his head. "Here," he said.

Then he hesitated and spread his hands over his chest for a moment. "Or here." He shook his head. "I don't know exactly. Just somewhere *inside*."

Sheila's eyes were narrowed. "Left . . . what?" she asked.

"The hive mind," he said.

She kept her eyes on his, steady, unblinking. But the faintest flush rose to her cheeks.

"I asked Clare Shapiro at Rockefeller about it," he went on. "She agrees with Jack that such a thing exists—that the minds of bees and wasps stay connected somehow.

That they can communicate over great distances in ways we don't understand."

Trey paused, remembering Shapiro's unrestrained impatience at having to explain something so simple to a neophyte. "Listen," she'd said. "*Of course* apocritids are capable of communication between members of the colony—that's because each bee or wasp isn't really an individual. Each is a separate part of one superorganism that incorporates data from thousands—or millions—of different viewpoints and makes a decision based on that data.

"A million units," she'd said, "but one controlling mind."

Now Sheila said, "Tell me."

He struggled to answer, as he'd known he would. "I feel like it's watching me, and also looking out through my eyes," he said finally. "Though not always. Not every minute. Sometimes it's quiet." He paused. "Like now."

"It's looking elsewhere?"

He shrugged. "Maybe that's it. But even then, I can sense it. A heaviness. An *awareness*." He raised his hands from the table in frustration. "It kind of . . . moves inside me."

She was silent.

"And when it's fully present," he said, staring down at his coffee mug, "it does more than watch. I feel like it's *taking*."

"Oh, Trey," she said. He looked up to see that her expression was full of sorrow. She reached across the table and took his sweaty hands in her cool ones. Over on the sofa, Jack stirred but didn't awaken. Somewhere in the distance, a car downshifted, its engine roaring, falling silent, then roaring again, much farther off.

Still holding his hands, Sheila broke the silence with a single word. *"Taking,"* she said, her gaze sharpening. The scientist reasserting herself. "That makes me wonder."

"Yes. Me, too."

"We got the larva out early."

He nodded.

"So what does the hive mind take from the rest of its victims?" she asked. "The ones where it stays until the end?"

Trey stayed silent.

"What is it learning about us?" she said.

Still he didn't speak.

"And what will it do with what it learns?"

AT AROUND FOUR Sheila started rubbing her eyes, a childlike gesture. "I can stay up with you," she said.

Trey smiled and shook his head. "No. You'll be of more use to all of us if you get a little rest."

She stood, then leaned across the table and kissed him. Just a quick kiss, her lips warm on his, before she pulled away.

Something in her expression made him say, "What?"

"I kiss . . . multitudes," she said and headed off to bed.

TREY WAS DEEP in his own thoughts when the phone jangled. It was just past six. After two rings he got to his feet and walked over to the kitchen counter. Jack hadn't moved on the sofa, but his eyes were open.

The call was coming from a blocked number. With a sigh, Trey picked up the receiver and said, "Yeah?"

"Gilliard?" said the voice on the other end. "George Summers." Then, after a brief pause, "Department of Agriculture."

Trey said, "Yeah. I remember you."

"Is Parker there?" Summers's voice sounded stretched, tense, and Trey wondered if he, too, had spent a sleepless night.

"Guy should check his cell phone every once in a while," Summers added.

Trey said, "Yes, he's here." He glanced at Jack, who was sitting up, alert now. A movement at the periphery of Trey's vision showed that Sheila had come to the bedroom doorway and was listening as well.

Trey held the phone out to Jack. "It's Summers."

Jack took it, then pointed and mouthed, "Speaker."

Once Trey had pushed the button, Jack leaned back on the sofa and said, "You knew. All that time bullshitting us in your office, and you knew."

"Jack, I don't have time for this," Summers said.

But Jack did. "And know what else? Trey and me, we saw it right away. But you had to pretend that we were idiot conspiracy theorists, but now that your boss is being hit with a pile of—"

"Fuck you, Parker." Summers's tone was venomous. "First of all, he's not my boss—I'm career here, you know that. Second, fuck you anyway."

Jack was grinning. "Very nice. I'll do anything you ask now."

"We need you to come in. Right away."

"Oh, now you want me? Well, fuck you, too."

"Could you put a lid on it for, like, two seconds, and just listen?"

Jack grinned, but kept quiet. When Summers spoke again, his tone had changed. "You know this is a shit-storm," he said, "and we need your help."

Some of the pleasure drained from Jack's expression. "I don't know, George. I saw the *Bourne* movies. 'Coming in' isn't always such a hot idea."

"We need to know what you know. You're doing nobody any good sitting in your little office in that big stone building filled with rocks and old bones."

Again, a pause and a change in tone. "I mean it. We want to hear what you have to tell us."

Jack moved his mouth around, as if testing arguments, but in the end he just sighed. "Okay," he said. "Say I say yes, what do I do?"

"How fast can you get out to LaGuardia? We have a plane waiting for you."

"Wow." Jack's eyes widened. "You sure know how to woo a boy. Let me just go back to my place for my clothes—"

"We'll buy you some when you get here."

"And I have to tell the museum."

"We already did that."

Jack scowled. "Let me just check with—"

"No," Summers said.

"What?"

"Not your friends. Just you. You're the expert."

Jack said, "You're wrong about that. They know things I—"

"Just you," Summers said again. "Those are my orders, and that's the way it has to be."

Jack looked at Trey. Now he just looked weary.

"You know that part of the movie where someone says, 'You're making a big mistake'?" he said. "Well, we've reached that point. You're making a big mistake."

They heard Summers make a sound. It was probably a laugh.

"I wouldn't bet against it," he said.

FRESHLY SHOWERED BUT his hair still a mess, Jack watched the TV as he got dressed.

"Call when you can," Trey told him.

"Sure, if they don't bump me off as soon as they pump me for everything I know."

It came out sounding like a joke, but Trey didn't think he was kidding. Those *Bourne* movies must have made a strong impression.

Jack ran his hands through his hair, then said, "Look, it's that guy again."

"That guy" being Anthony Harrison's communications director, Jeremy Axelson, whom they'd seen on every network the night before. Somehow he still looked awake, alert, ready to face the new day.

As they watched, he looked straight into the camera and pointed. Jack got the remote and raised the sound.

"One piece of advice for the president and his staff," Axelson was saying. "You're in deep already. Don't dig yourself any deeper. Don't obfuscate, don't hide, don't destroy. It's not the crime—or not only the crime—it's the cover-up. Whatever you try, it won't work. We'll find out. It's a guarantee. *We'll find out.*"

The doorbell rang. "Your taxi's here," Trey said.

Jack was still staring at the TV. Then he turned his head and gave them a wide-eyed look.

"Summers is an asshole," he said, "but he's right about one thing."

"There's a storm coming," Sheila said.

For once Jack looked completely serious.

"I don't believe," he said, "that *any* of them—on either side—has the slightest clue how bad this is going to be."

THIRTY-SEVEN

IT WAS THE same crew as the other time, Harry Solomon realized. Fort Collins. Trent and the two young guys, the ones who knew how to make things burn.

Harry wondered what here in Vermont needed burning.

He wasn't sure he'd gotten over Fort Collins yet. It had left a bad taste in his mouth, and in his brain, too.

At least this time they weren't going to have to carry away any corpses. The chief of staff had assured him of this. Harry doubted the COS's word, but the car left for them in this gravel parking lot beside a long-closed factory was a late-model Subaru Forester. Not big enough for the four of them and a stiff, much less multiple stiffs.

Harry didn't know exactly what their job would be. That was new. Ever since Anthony Harrison had made his first speech about those bugs, the COS—the whole White House—had been in full-on panic mode. Harry, and who knew how many others, had been working double-time, calling in favors—and offering money or threats when favors didn't work—from newspaper reporters, police departments, and the general public, all to keep the story from boiling over.

The panic had led to increased security, which meant Harry now got his orders in stages. Today, for instance, he and the rest of the crew had been told to meet here in Springfield, and then drive the Forester to some house a couple of towns away. There they would learn their ultimate destination and what they were expected to do.

It was a pain in the ass, not knowing in advance, but Harry could see why the COS was crapping bricks. Just a few weeks left till Election Day, and their guy's best chance was to convince the voters that the story was being overhyped by the Harrison campaign.

Harry wasn't so sure he believed it. That the story *was* being overhyped. He'd seen the dead guys in that house, and now he knew what had killed them. A few more attacks, someone filming the wasps chewing the eyeballs out of somebody, and all the bribes and threats in the world weren't going to win Sam Chapman the election.

Harry's phone buzzed. He peered down at the screen: the coordinates of their first stop. Pain in the ass.

He looked back up at his waiting crew. "Let's go."

HARRY DROVE. THE GPS guided them west on a small highway, northwest on a smaller one, and then onto a dirt road heading due north. They passed dairy farms with black-and-white cows. A pond with people rowing on it. Cabins set back from the road, surrounded by maples and oaks that were already losing their leaves, and some pines and firs, too.

Then three more turns—east, north, east—and onto a small dirt road marked with No Thru Traffic signs. At the end of this road, in a small clearing at the end of a winding driveway, lay their initial destination.

It was a wooden cabin, hand-built a half century or more ago, now weathered to gray. Harry stopped the car and they got out. Other than the pinging of the cooling engine and the whisper of a breeze through the trees, there was no sound. No human voices, no birdcalls, not even the chirp of crickets.

Later, Harry knew he should have understood what this silence meant, but he didn't. He wasn't paying the right kind of attention.

Instead, he was looking around. He guessed this was someone's hunting or fishing cabin. Not a telephone pole or power line in sight. The kind of place you'd come to *because* there was no phone service.

"I could like it here," he said.

Beside him, Trent opened his mouth to say something. Whatever it was, it went forever unspoken, because instead of talking he went flying backward. Flung through the air like some huge hand had flicked him away.

His arms spread out as he flew. He had a surprised expression on his face.

As Harry threw himself to the ground, he heard the muffled snap of a silenced .457, sound traveling more slowly than death, as always. Rolling, twisting, getting back to his feet, he hurled himself toward the edge of the clearing, as far as he could from where the bullet had come from.

Knowing exactly what was happening.

More muffled shots. The other two men dead in five seconds: a cutoff cry and the thump of a body hitting the ground, followed by one last crack of a gunshot, another thump. A wet, hopeless moaning.

Just as Harry made it to the edge of the clearing and dove into the brambles that surrounded it, he felt something riffle through his hair. A moment later, he heard the shot that had barely missed him.

He scrambled forward, feeling the thorns scratch his face and pull at his clothes. It was more like swimming than running. With every passing second—and there were too many of them, far too many—he imagined the gunmen approaching to finish their task. He knew, *knew*, they were drawing near, standing there, aiming.

But somehow he made it through the brambles into more open forest. His skin shrinking away from the expected impact of the bullet, he got to his feet. Stumbling, tripping, falling, pulling himself upright, stumbling forward again. So slow. Someone in a wheelchair could catch him. How could he outrun a bullet?

Fighting for breath, half blind, he didn't see the stone wall snaking through the forest until he nearly fell over it. Stopped in his tracks, he raised his head and saw, perched atop the wall a few feet away, a little girl.

No more than six, she was dressed in blue denim overalls and a pink-and-white-checked shirt. A beam of sun made it down through the canopy and glinted off her blond hair.

"Run!" Harry yelled. Or rather, gasped. Thinking only of what a .457 round would do to her.

She stared at him, mouth open, not moving. Almost immediately, she was joined by three other people: a boy of about nine and an adult man and woman, all standing on the other side of the wall. They were wearing denim and flannel and carrying colorful daypacks. The man held a walking stick.

A young family hiking through the Vermont woods, coming upon this wild-eyed old guy with torn clothes and scratched-up face.

But they didn't run away, as Harry had thought they would. They didn't leave him alone again in the woods. Instead, as he came up to the wall and half climbed, half fell over it, they clustered around him, helping him to his feet, brushing him off, their voices sounding like birdcalls in his ears.

The people pursuing him were still there. He knew it. Right now they had their weapons trained on him, on all of them, as they decided what to do next. Harry's only chance was that they hadn't been cleared to take out any other targets or to kill in front of witnesses.

Maybe, at this moment, the chief of staff was deciding whether Harry—and this innocent family—would live or die.

Maybe it was the president himself making the decision.

The family was staring at him, all four of them. He knew he had to answer their questions, had to say something. But what? What? He'd never been in this position before. He'd never been the prey.

Finally he came out with, "Someone in the woods. A hunter. Took a shot at me. More than one shot."

The boy and little girl seemed to think this was pretty exciting news, worth investigating further. But the mom gasped and put her hand to her mouth, and the man dropped his walking stick and swept his daughter off the stone wall and into his arms.

"Come on," he said to his reluctant son. "Let's go. Now!"

After taking a few steps, the woman looked over her shoulder. "Come with us," she said.

A nice lady. She had no idea that if Harry went with them, the threat of death came, too.

THEY MOVED THROUGH the woods for fifteen minutes. The father tried and failed repeatedly to get cell-phone service. Harry found himself noticing the golden and orange leaves spinning to the ground in gusts of wind, the sun gleaming on dew-soaked spiderwebs, a white-tailed deer stopping to stare at them before trotting away, its tail lifted in warning.

He began to understand that the gunmen weren't going to kill him. Not here, not now.

The forest thinned. They climbed over another stone wall and reached a road, a different one than Harry and his doomed crew had arrived on. Dirt, but graded and graveled, with SUVs and a scattering of cars parked along the edges. On the other side of the road a small lake glinted in the sun. A Volvo with a pair of kayaks on its roof came down the road, slowed, and turned onto a muddy track that led down to the lakeshore.

The father was on his phone, presumably with the police, reporting the presence of a dangerous hunter in the woods. When he finished the call, he turned his eyes on Harry. The man wanted to be rid of him, it was obvious, but he only said, "Did you park along here?"

Harry shook his head. "No—my car's back in there, near where you found me." He widened his eyes. "I'm not going back for it, not yet, no way."

The father frowned, but couldn't argue with this. "You have someone you can call? Who can rescue you?"

Rescue you. Harry almost laughed. "Sure."

Then he patted at his pockets. "Oh, hell," he said. "My phone's back with my stuff."

Gone, along with everything else his team had brought. His team itself. Their bodies long gone by now. By the time the police arrived, there would be no sign he and his men had ever been there.

No, that wasn't true. An expert forensic team would surely be able to find evidence that people had been shot there, but who was going to call out a forensic team after a report of some hunter mistaking a hiker for a deer? The cleanup would be good enough to fool the forest ranger or low-level badge the state of Vermont would send to check out the scene.

"Listen," Harry said, "is there any chance you could give me a ride to someplace with a phone?"

Thinking, *Someplace with lots of other people around.*

The man frowned again and exchanged glances with his wife.

"Don't worry about it," Harry said, starting to turn away. "I can walk or hitchhike."

But the wife was shaking her head. "Of course we'll take you," she said, smiling. "We can't abandon you here after you almost got shot. We're going to Ludlow. Is that okay?"

"That's just fine," Harry said.

He had no idea where Ludlow was, but it didn't matter.

Anyplace was better than here.

LUDLOW WAS CARS, cafés, art galleries, a ski mountain gearing up for the season, and hordes and hordes of leaf-peepers wandering around.

Perfect.

Thank God for Vermont, Harry thought. All these tourists, and still old-fashioned enough to have a line of pay phones outside a supermarket. Someone had even scratched *Worship God* on the silver coin boxes, just like they used to do in New York City back when there were pay phones everywhere.

Harry had memorized the number he was about to call. He'd been thinking about using it for days, ever since Anthony Harrison had given that speech. Telling Axelson about the stiffs, about the secret lab that had been operating all those weeks ago. Showing him the card he'd had found, the one that said, *Philanthus*???

Proving that Anthony Harrison was right: The president's men had known about the bugs for weeks or months and hadn't told anybody.

Of course, back then Harry had been interested in the financial side of things. He'd thought his information would be worth a fortune.

Now it was all about survival.

He dialed the number. It went to voice mail, a calm voice saying merely, "Axelson."

When the beep came, Harry said, "My name is Harry

Solomon. You know who I am. I got something to tell you you'll want to hear. Call me within ten."

He read out the number, then hung up and stood there. Years ago, you had to guard your pay phone from all the other people who needed to use it, but no longer. Now half the crowd milling past were stuck to their cell phones, the rest patting their pockets to make sure theirs were still there.

He didn't think the COS's men would kill him in public, not now. But he knew they'd have no qualms about muscling him into a car, driving him away, and making sure no one ever saw him again.

It was just a matter of time.

Call me back, you bastard, he thought.

The phone rang.

THIRTY-EIGHT

THE FOUR OF them sat in a corner booth in a chocolate restaurant down below Union Square. Until Mary Finneran had said that Kait wanted to eat at one, Trey hadn't even known that such a thing existed.

To him, a restaurant that came equipped with bubbling vats of chocolate near the entrance, napkins made to look like milk, dark, and white chocolate, and a menu offering little but chocolate foods seemed like a sign of a civilization about to crumble. Then again, a lot of things did.

The four of them: him, Sheila, Mary, and Kait. Uncharacteristically, it was Sheila who was doing most of the talking. Sheila and Mary. Trey guessed that Mary did her part to keep any conversation going, but it was strange to see Sheila so relaxed and animated.

Or maybe "relaxed" was the wrong term. "Comfortable" would be more accurate. In between sips from a nonalcoholic chocolate martini, she was describing everything she and Trey had been doing these past days. Every once in a while she'd ask Trey for a detail, or for backup on some assertion she was making, but mostly he was extraneous to the conversation.

This was fine with him. He was all talked out. If he never had to utter a word again, it would still be too soon.

For two weeks, he and Sheila had done what they could to bring reality—or at least a touch of it—to the media coverage of Anthony Harrison's blockbuster speech. They'd called the networks, CNN, MSNBC, public radio, positioning themselves as experts, offering to describe the process, the risks, the way those risks could be minimized.

When you could safely remove an implanted larva, and when you couldn't.

At first they'd been a hot item, in demand, but soon attention had begun to drain away. Trey wasn't surprised. Absent some new infusion of energy, some new headline, no story captured the public's attention for long. Not an epidemic, a tsunami, a terrorist attack. Nothing. Not these days.

When reports of new attacks fell off, then stopped almost entirely, he had known their time was up.

They were sitting in the chocolate restaurant waiting for a science reporter from the *New York Times*. Trey hadn't put it into words, but he had the sense that this interview would be the last big one, a postmortem for all of their efforts.

He missed Jack. But Jack was gone, in some secret research lab in Florida. Since the government had spirited him away, they'd heard from him just once, a voice-mail message saying he was fine and working hard.

"Not that it's gonna make the slightest bit of difference," he'd added.

*   *   *

WAITING, TREY DRANK his coffee—at his insistence chocolate-free—and watched Kait, who was sitting opposite him by the window, taking sips from a cup of hot chocolate filled with melting marshmallows (and served in a marshmallow-shaped white mug) and working on a chocolate pizza. She was a neat eater, cutting the gooey brown crust into bite-size chunks before transporting them, one by one, via fork to her mouth.

"When I was your age," Trey said, "I would have been wearing that thing by now."

Kait's eyes flickered to his face for an instant. "Grandma told me to keep it off my blouse," she said. Her quiet voice matched her solemn, oval face, dark eyes, and fair skin. Her blouse was white and dotted with little yellow, blue, and red flowers.

Mary, in the midst of her own conversation, heard and said, "You're darn tootin' I did. That shirt is new, and I'm not made of money."

She turned back to Sheila. Trey and Kait looked at each other, and Trey said, "Grandmas are always listening, aren't they?"

"They sure are," Kait said.

Her gaze strayed over his shoulder. He turned to look and saw that there was a TV perched above the restaurant's counter. It was tuned to ESPN, which was showing highlights from a soccer game. A player in a white uniform scored a goal with his head.

"I play soccer on my school team," Kait said. "My new school. In Charleston."

Trey nodded. "What position?"

"Striker," she said. Then, hesitating, she added, "I score a lot of goals."

"That was my position, too," Trey told her.

Kait's brow knit. "Really? But—" She closed her mouth again.

Trey thought he knew what she'd been about to say. "You're surprised that I played soccer, because most people my age didn't."

Kait nodded. "That's what my da told me."

"Your da was right. Most kids in the United States didn't. Not back then. But I didn't spend all my time in the U.S. when I was a kid."

She thought about that. "Where, then?"

"Brazil," Trey said. "Kenya. England. Other places, too. My dad was a doctor, and we traveled a lot. But the places all had one thing in common."

"Football."

Trey smiled. "Yes, their football. Soccer. I knew when I was, like, six, that if I was going to fit in, I had to play."

"Me, too," Kait said. "Now."

Her eyes growing distant.

"Is it helping?" he asked. "Soccer?"

She hesitated, then said, "Yes. I think so. But—"

Again the words cut off. Trey said, "But what?"

She compressed her lips, her gaze reaching his eyes, then quickly away. "It's just," she said, "you know? The other girls? They're like, you know, all really . . . blond."

Trey smiled. "Well, you can't blame them for *that*. Some people are just unlucky."

She stared at him for a moment, then actually laughed. Beside her, Mary looked startled.

"Being different is only a problem," Trey said to Kait, "if you *want* to be just like everyone else. And who wants that?"

He saw her working it through. After a while she gave a considered nod. "I never did . . . before," she said.

"Then why start now?" He pointed at himself. "Look at me—I'm doing fine, and I'm not like *anybody* else."

"You can say that again," said Sheila, who'd apparently also been listening.

THE *TIMES* REPORTER was named Becca Shaw.

Seeing her curly blond hair, Trey glanced at Kait. She gave him a wide-eyed look, and when he raised a finger to his lips, she let loose with a small, stifled giggle.

Becca Shaw was smart, serious, interested. Pulling a chair up to the head of their booth, she withdrew a tiny digital recorder and a well-used notebook from her black shoulder bag and began to ask pointed, relevant questions. She worked through the history of Trey's discovery, touched on Sheila's tragedy without crossing any lines, made sure she got every detail right about the thieves' life cycle.

She also took advantage of the Finnerans' presence to ask about their own encounter with the wasps. Answering, both Mary and Kait were clear-eyed and coherent. Trey wondered if he'd have been capable of as much, if he'd been in their shoes.

"I just wish I hadn't agreed to sit there on TV during Harrison's speech," Mary said, repeating something she'd said to Sheila. "This isn't about politics. It's a health issue."

Becca Shaw opened her mouth to say something, then closed it and, frowning, shook her head.

It's both, Trey knew she'd almost said.

It's always both.

"LOOK," KAIT SAID. "On the TV. It's Mr. Axelson."

"Oh, joy," Mary said.

Trey and Sheila turned to look at the television above the counter. Someone had switched from ESPN to CNN, and on the screen the familiar figure stood in some scrubby field behind a cluster of microphones and a scroll that read, "Breaking News: Statement from the Harrison Campaign."

Becca Shaw was already standing beside the counter, asking a waiter to turn the sound up. He was working the remote as the rest of them joined her.

It was a press conference, and Axelson was listening to a question when the sound came up.

"Look at his face," Mary said.

Kait tilted her head. "He's . . . happy."

It was true. At first glance, Axelson's expression seemed to convey nothing more than his usual interest and intelligence as he listened. But if you looked beneath, you could see more. If you knew what to look for—his posture, something gleaming in his eyes, the way his hands grasped the edge of his lectern—you saw a kind of fierce joy.

"He looks like he's afraid he'll fly right up in the air if he lets go," Mary said.

"Shhh." Becca Shaw was leaning forward, as still as a dog pointing toward the hunter's prey.

On the screen, Axelson nodded. "Yes, that's exactly what I'm saying. President Chapman and his administration have known for weeks—months, maybe—that these creatures pose a deadly threat, but have gone to great lengths, *criminal* lengths, to hide their knowledge."

"Do you have proof?" someone called out.

"Yes, we have proof," Axelson said, pausing between each word and enunciating very precisely. "Incontrovertible proof of a cover-up."

Even through the screen, it was impossible to miss the excitement that rippled through the crowd of reporters at the press conference. Voices shouted out. Axelson let them go on for a few seconds before raising his hands.

"Sorry," he said. "I can't explain yet."

Beside Trey, Becca Shaw was holding her breath.

More shouting voices, angrier now. The communications director was unfazed. "In the Harrison campaign, we believe in doing what's right for America, not just what's right for us," he said. "Or the press."

"As opposed to the Chapman campaign," Mary said in a low voice.

"At this moment," Axelson continued, "our campaign manager, Ron Stanhouse, and other members of our team are meeting with their opposite numbers at the White House. Until we learn the results of this meeting, we consider it unwise—unpatriotic, even—to detail what we've learned in the past days."

He leaned forward, the camera coming in close to his face. "But let this be understood," he said. "I am here today to tell you that the president's reckless actions have led to American deaths. Instead of protecting us—his sworn duty—he has put us, as a nation and a people, in harm's way."

Axelson stared into the camera. "Let it be understood, President Chapman," he said. "Anthony Harrison will keep America safe. And you will be held accountable."

With that, he turned and walked steadily away from the microphones.

When the scene returned to the studio, one of the anchors said, "The White House has just released a statement." She gave the camera a strange look, a kind of half smile. "The statement says, in full, 'The White House will have no statement at this time.'"

"Uh-oh," Becca Shaw said, her voice little louder than a breath. Reaching into her bag, she pulled out her smartphone and glanced at the screen. By the time she lifted her gaze, she was already far away.

"Thanks for all your help," she said. "You'll hear from us with any follow-ups, and we'll let you know when the story will run." Her eyes flicked up to the screen. "I'm guessing sooner rather than later."

Then she was gone, out the door, moving fast.

Mary and Kait headed back to their booth. Sheila, though, was still looking up at the television. The guy behind the counter had switched back to ESPN. A golf ball, shining white against deep green grass, rolled toward a hole. It teetered and then fell in. A golfer pointed his club at the sky.

"'The president's reckless actions have led to American deaths,'" Sheila said, then turned her eyes toward Trey. "What on earth do they know now," she said, "that they didn't before?"

Trey didn't answer. Somewhere deep in his brain, in his gut, in the tips of his nerve endings, something was shifting. Rousing. Coming closer to consciousness than it ever had before.

Flooding him with . . . anger? Fear?

No.

Anticipation.

THIRTY-NINE

"I'M SORRY," SAID the gatekeeper at Rockefeller University's security desk, "but Dr. Shapiro is on leave."

The man didn't *sound* sorry. Trey was silent for a moment. Then he said, "When is she expected back?"

A trace of impatience in the return look. "Dr. Shapiro's leave is indefinite."

"Do you know where she's gone?"

The gatekeeper's mouth tightened. His body language caught the attention of a guard standing near the front door, who fixed his gaze on Trey.

"Never mind," Trey said. He began to turn away, then stopped. "How about Elena Stavros? Is she gone, too?"

"Do you have an appointment?"

Trey shook his head. "Just tell her Trey Gilliard is here to see her."

With a frown, the gatekeeper punched a few numbers into the phone. After a moment, a squawk came across the line.

"Security," he said in a precise tone. "There's a man named Trey Gilliard here to see you, but he's not in the system."

The squawk got louder, so that Trey could make out the words. "Gilliard? Arrest him at once!"

The gatekeeper said, "What?"

"No, no. Send him up."

A loud crunching sound as the phone clattered into its cradle.

The gatekeeper looked at Trey, then bent to print out his security pass. He muttered something with his head down.

Trey thought it was "I hate this goddamn job."

TREY AND ELENA Stavros had first met on the Rio Roosevelt, the River of Doubt, in Brazil nearly ten years earlier. He'd been doing his usual thing: walking into the wilderness, then emerging weeks later twenty pounds lighter, engraved with dirt, festooned with bug bites, and brimming with an encyclopedic knowledge of the area's fauna.

Meanwhile, she'd been heading downriver, the microbiologist on an interdisciplinary team studying a new form of leishmaniasis. They'd met, taken measure of each other, and grabbed the chance to share a tent for the nights before their paths diverged.

You took your opportunities where you found them, and you didn't waste time with preliminaries.

In the year that followed, they'd spent two weekends together—one in Bangkok, one in Rio. Both had been memorable, filled with laughter and cigarette smoke (hers) and various other kinds of pleasure and release. Neither Trey nor Elena had asked for or expected anything more.

And then, one day, Stavros had stepped off the carousel. The grapevine said that she'd gotten married. True or not, Trey hadn't seen her again, though he'd heard she'd taken what was basically a desk job here at Rock U. The wheel had spun them to different places.

This, too, was how it worked, most of the time.

WHEN HE WALKED into her office, she was standing behind her desk. She looked him over, the same frank assessment she'd given him a decade earlier.

He did likewise. She was almost as he remembered: short, a little stocky, with olive skin and dark eyebrows and all that irrepressible black hair. And eyes that had the amazing ability to actually sparkle. She was the only person Trey had ever met whose eyes did that, and they were doing it now.

It was she who broke the silence, as usual. "Bastard," she said. "You've stayed thin while I've gotten fat."

Her voice exactly the same: deep, a little scratchy from years of cigarettes and retsina. And talk.

Before he could reply, she came around the desk and across the room and hugged him. That was familiar, too, her soft, compact body belying her arms' stranglehold.

Then she pulled away from him and looked up into his face. Up close, he could see that the years had added some lines around her mouth and across her forehead. The hair might now be getting some help staying black. On the other hand, she didn't smell like cigarette smoke anymore.

"You look great to me," Trey said, and he wasn't lying. "For an old married lady," he added.

He'd noticed the photo on her desk, an eight-by-ten showing Elena with a tall, dark-haired man and two young girls.

"Can you imagine?" she said. "Boring old homebody me, making cheese sandwiches for school lunch every morning."

Trey smiled. He'd seen this so often. The population of itinerant scientists, doctors, and field researchers was always being thinned by those who tired of the constant motion, who sought a more settled life.

Or who thought they did. Plenty then discovered that they couldn't tolerate the lack of stimulation, new sounds and smells, changing colors of light. Who missed the geography of unfamiliar bodies, another kind of terra incognita, as well.

Trey wondered whether Elena ever yearned for her old life.

She went back to her desk and sat down. "You came to see Clare," she said. "To talk about all this foolishness."

Trey sat down in a chair opposite her. "Foolishness?"

"This . . . hoopla." She glanced down at her desk, and Trey knew that she was searching for a cigarette. With a grimace, she raised her eyes to his. "Making it into a political football. Making it about who wins an election."

Trey said, "Because the thing itself, the thieves, that's not foolishness. Regardless of the hoopla, it's real."

She stared at him. He recognized the expression. It meant: Do you remember who you're talking to here?

"Real?" she said. "Christ, Trey, it's more than real. It's the end of everything."

TREY SAID, "WELL . . ."

Elena sat up straight in her chair. "Oh, come on. You know more about these beasts than anyone. Don't you see it?"

She ticked the evidence off on her fingers. "A new threat we don't understand. A clever, resourceful enemy. An attack we have no comprehensive defense against—and no time to develop one."

She shook her head. "That empty suit Harrison is right. It's an invasion, a war. What he doesn't understand is that we've already lost."

The same words Trey's brother had used.

"Come on," Elena said. "I've seen you on TV. You've been out front on this. You've seen what those creatures are capable of. You know I'm right."

It was true, he thought. He had known, almost from the start, but hadn't allowed himself to face it. Too busy taking one step at a time, just as he'd always done, and not looking at the whole picture.

"Look," Elena went on, impatient as always with a slow pupil. "Let me give you a hypothetical."

Her words awakening a powerful memory in him. Elena had always said, "Let me give you a hypothetical."

Sometimes her hypotheticals were devastatingly true. Other times they were ridiculous. But they always got her point across.

"Listen," she was saying now. "Hurricane Sandy."

Trey said, "What about it? I wasn't here."

"But you remember what it did."

Trey said, "Sure. It knocked out power to millions of people, overloaded satellite circuits, flooded the subways, destroyed entire towns. Hundreds of people died."

Elena nodded.

"That's not quite the end of the world."

She drew in a breath through her nose. "Trey," she said. "All that destruction was caused by a single Category Two hurricane. Now tell me—"

The hypothetical.

"Tell me what would happen to the region if there'd been another hurricane a week later, only this one a Category Five, and another one the next week, and one the week after that? And what if, at the same time, a storm of the same size hit Florida and one hit California, followed by another, and another. And not just in the United States . . . Europe. Japan. China. *Everywhere*, one blow after another, for weeks. What would happen?"

Trey said, "That couldn't—"

"Imagine," Elena said.

Trey took a long time before answering. In the silence, he heard—felt, really—an electric hum, a vibration through his bones. It was Rockefeller University's power supply, the whale song of hundreds of powerful computers and the rest of the hungry machinery the university's brilliant scientists needed to do their work.

Trey wondered if the university had generators to provide emergency power in case of a blackout. Most likely. But how long would the fuel for these emergency generators last?

And how brilliant would Rock U's scientists be without their machines?

"It would take months—years—to get back to where we'd been," he said.

She made a dismissive gesture with her hands. "And if those months, years, were characterized by repeated hurricanes, earthquakes, tsunamis? Destroying crops, making huge areas uninhabitable, tearing apart our power grid?"

Trey was quiet.

"The five-hundred-year drought," she said.

This was also Elena. Announce what she was talking about, and leave it to you to catch up.

"I have a friend who's a paleobotanist," she said. "He was studying ancient pollens in Nevada—remnants found along old trade routes—and he uncovered evidence of a drought that lasted half a millennium."

"Droughts don't last that long," Trey said.

"That's what I told him, and he said, 'Why not?'" Elena widened her eyes. "He said just because we haven't seen one during the pitifully short time we've been recording history doesn't mean it's not possible."

Trey was quiet.

"That drought did some serious damage, as you might imagine. Entire civilizations disappeared into the dust. So tell me: In a world that now holds seven billion people, what havoc would a five-hundred-year-long drought wreak?"

Now there was no sparkle in her eyes. "And weather? Drought? They're just blunt instruments. Bad luck helped along by climate change. The threat posed by these thieves of yours is a whole lot more . . ." She searched for the words. "Direct. Clever. *Real*."

Still Trey didn't speak.

"Think about it," she said. "What happens when there's no one willing—or left—to oversee our communications satellites? Man our hydropower plants? Open the locks in the Panama Canal? What happens when there are no firefighters willing to quell a fire before it goes out of control, or ambulances and tow trucks to tend to car crashes on the highway?"

The words hung in the air for a few moments.

"All you have to do to end our world," she said, "is make people terrified to go to work."

Her expression was bleak.

"And it will take about five days, not five hundred years."

THEY SAT. TREY could hear a machine grinding away somewhere down the hall, a phone ringing, cars honking on York Avenue below.

He said, "Where is Clare?"

"Oh, I imagine you've guessed. The government thing." A waggle of her hands to signify meaningless hysteria. "They're working to shut the barn door."

She saw his expression and sighed. "Okay. They enlisted her in some ultra-high-security effort that required her to drop contact with everyone she ever knew. Thereby solving two problems at once: confronting the threat and keeping her from blabbing to the public, which she certainly would have done."

"They did the same with Jack Parker up at the museum," Trey said.

"Yeah?" She flicked a glance at him. "Can't really understand why you and your girlfriend—" Her eyes gleamed. "Why you and your *skinny, gorgeous* new girlfriend are still being allowed to make noise in public. I guess because all you're doing is talking about public health."

"She's not my girlfriend."

"Whatever." Her expression turned serious. "Speaking of which, where is she?"

"Sheila? She's heading down to the Chesapeake Bay to see some friends."

A frown. "Trey," she said, "from now on . . . keep her close."

He looked at her. She was staring at the photograph on her desk.

"Don't be caught too far apart when the end comes," she said.

THERE DIDN'T SEEM like much else to say. Trey stood.

Getting to her feet as well, Elena said, "By the way, what did Mariama want?"

Trey wasn't sure he'd heard her correctly. "Who?"

"Mariama. Honso? She said you'd met when you were in Senegal."

"Yes," Trey said. Then, "Elena, I have no idea what you're talking about."

His tone got her attention. She looked into his face, and her eyes went round.

"Mariama called me looking for you," she said. "This was at least two months ago—over the summer. She called from—from Panama, I think it was. Said she'd be arriving in the States in a couple of days and needed to find you. I told her where to look."

She took note of his expression and lifted her hands, an uncharacteristically defensive gesture. "Trey, she asked me not to say she'd called. She wanted to find you herself, show you something in person."

Trey said, "I never heard from her."

Elena's hand went to her mouth. *"Shit."*

He thought about the last time he'd seen Mariama, standing beside the colony of thieves. Saving him. "Did she say anything else? Give any clue at all?"

"No. Nothing." Her mouth twisted. "I'm sorry, Trey."

After a moment, he shook his head. "No. Not your fault. How could you have known back then?"

Still, Elena looked angry at herself. "Damn. I wonder what happened to her."

Trey drew in a deep breath.

"I can guess," he said.

AT THE DOOR to her office, she put her arm around his waist. She'd always liked physical contact.

"Listen to what I'm telling you," she said.

"I will." He hesitated. "But I'm beginning to wonder if we've been wrong. Why so few attacks? Everyone's running around, hysterical, but where's the evidence?"

She released him, looked up into his face. "Slave-making ants."

"What?"

"You know, ant species that raid other ants' colonies, bringing back eggs and pupae and making the newly hatched adults into slaves."

Trey said, "I know what they are."

Remembering the raid he'd watched in the Casamance forest, just before that first encounter with the thieves.

"I used to watch them back in Greece when I was a child, and I saw how their strategies worked," Elena went on. "They always attacked the biggest, strongest nearby ant colony, but they never began until they were ready. Until they had enough fighters. Until they *knew* they would win."

Trey nodded.

"Before then?" she said. "When they were preparing? They didn't even allow themselves to cross paths with their chosen victims. They left no sign, no scent, no nothing, until the moment they attacked.

"And by then, the battle was as good as over."

There were sudden tears in her eyes. Trey hugged her, allowing his gaze to stray back to her desk, to the photo with the tall man and the two little girls.

"When it happens," he said, "you can't be here."

Still holding on to him, she laughed. It was a joyless sound.

"Oh! Sweetie," she said. "If I knew of anyplace to go, we'd be long gone already."

IF I KNEW of any place to go.

When Trey got back to his apartment, he did something he knew he should have done long ago. He made a series of phone calls.

Getting through in some cases, leaving messages in others.

Starting the process.

The last call was to Kenya. He hadn't even bothered to figure out what time it was there. It didn't matter.

A click on the second ring. "Granger."

Malcolm Granger. They hadn't seen each other since that day in the Casamance when Malcolm had landed the Piper in the field. The day they'd first spotted the thieves' dying forest.

"It's Trey."

"Gilliard!" Malcolm's voice was loud over the line.

"Malcolm," Trey began. "I need—"

"I know exactly what you need," his friend said. "Christ, I've been expecting this call for weeks."

Trey said, "And?"

"What the hell do you think?" Malcolm said.

FORTY

Washington, D.C.

"WHAT DO YOU want from me, Gilliard?" George Summers asked.

Trey looked across the desk at him. "That's easy," he said. "I want you to get out of my way, so I can talk to someone who gets things done."

Being obnoxious on purpose to gauge the depths of Summers's worries, which he assumed were plentiful and multiplying.

Even career bureaucrats with no fear of getting fired didn't like it when their boats got rocked. And nothing rocked the boat like an incumbent president losing his bid for reelection. New department chiefs got named, new patronage posts were handed out, and even those who kept their heads down could find their lives suddenly very unpleasant.

Summers's boat was already rocking. Ever since the revelations that the Chapman administration had known about the thieves for months—but hadn't told anyone—

the possibility of a Harrison victory had grown exponentially. Issues like unemployment, health care, and foreign policy seemed to have been almost forgotten—and when they *were* discussed, it was always in the context of the thieves' impact. That didn't do much for the incumbent's chances, either.

Only the fact that the number of thief attacks had declined nearly to zero gave the president any chance at victory.

A confident Summers, having been insulted, would have tossed Trey out of his office. The Summers who answered, though, merely said, "You have someone specific in mind?"

He was scared.

"Nathan Holland," Trey said. "The president's chief of staff."

Summers gave a bark of a laugh. "Clap harder, Gilliard."

"Here's what you're going to do," Trey said. "You're going to work your way up the food chain until you find someone who has Holland's ear. And then you're going to tell him that if he wants even the slightest chance of saving his man's presidency, and his own butt, he'd better sit down and meet with me. Today."

Summers's mouth hung open.

"I'd ask to see the president himself," Trey said, "but I don't have the time to spell everything out for him."

TREY HAD ASSUMED he'd be sent over to the West Wing, but as it turned out the chief of staff came to see him. An hour after Trey made his demand, Nathan Holland was sitting across from him in a room down a long hall on the third floor of the Ag building.

A desk, a few chairs, a dead plant, two lighter-colored squares on the walls where paintings had once hung. Someone's corner office, before all the antigovernment shouters and the bad economy had brought downsizing even to D.C.

Sitting in a chair off to the side of the room was another man, youngish, thick bodied. Trey didn't know whether he was an assistant or some kind of security, or both. Not that it mattered.

The men in the hallway outside were definitely Secret Service.

Holland was wearing a suit that had no doubt cost more than Trey had spent on clothes in the past ten years combined. His gray hair was trimmed into a near buzz cut, and despite the furrows of age, his clean-shaven face had the toned, cared-for look that spoke of expensive skin treatments.

None of it mattered. Nothing could hide the fact that the chief of staff looked old, exhausted.

Burdened.

"So here I am," he said. His vowels bore the trace of his Chicago roots. "Now tell me why I should listen to you."

"How's *not* listening to me working out?" Trey asked.

Holland grimaced. "Don't fence with me, Gilliard."

"Okay. No fencing," Trey said. "So tell me: How many reports have you read with my name on them?"

"What?"

"Seems like a simple enough question. I was the first American to see the thieves—or at least the first to live long enough to talk about them. I'm the guy who's been tracking their spread. The guy who's been traveling around the world learning everything I can about them, as I'm sure you already know. So I'm asking you: How often has my name popped up these past months?"

After a few moments, Holland said, "Often enough. Why?"

"Well, shouldn't *that*, by itself, be enough to get you to listen to me?"

The words hung in silence. Holland's steel gray eyes stayed on Trey's face, but it didn't matter. Trey could return gimlet stares all day if he had to.

"And anyway," he added, "you came here today. *Of course* you're going to listen."

Holland's frown deepened, but when he spoke it was to say, "All right. So what do you want to ask?"

Trey laughed, an unexpected sound in the gloomy corner room. "Ask? I'm not here to ask anything."

"Why, then?"

"To tell you what you're going to do for me."

NATHAN HOLLAND SAT across from him, huffing and puffing at his presumption. Apparently Trey had neglected to use the proper tone. Hadn't paid the respect the office of chief of staff was due. Hadn't been a supplicant.

Only . . . Trey didn't do supplication. He never had, and he wasn't about to start now. Human beings were the only species that spent so much time begging, and though this might generally be a successful tactic for an erratic, violent species occupying a crowded world, so far Trey had survived without it.

Often enough, his unwillingness to kowtow had gotten in his way, but it wouldn't this time. Holland would come around. Trey knew it, and he thought the chief of staff knew it, too. They just had to go through this ridiculous little dance first.

Eventually Holland settled back a little and said, "Tell me that name again."

Trey thought Holland remembered it just fine. But he repeated, "Mariama Honso."

"I have no idea who that is," Holland said.

"Sure you do," Trey said. "She was coming to see me back in July, and you stopped her."

"Did we?"

"Yes. You stopped her, arrested her, and stashed her somewhere."

An instant's cloudiness in the chief of staff's eyes was the giveaway. The tell.

"Or maybe you didn't even bother to arrest her," Trey said. "You're still doing that 'indefinite detention' thing, aren't you?"

Holland didn't answer.

"I don't care. We can talk about the morality of that another time. The point is: Mariama's staying somewhere on the government's dime, and I know why."

Holland, his mouth pursed, waited for him to go on.

"Somehow you learned she was coming here," Trey said. "Maybe you'd been tracking her progress all the way from Senegal, or maybe she pinged a watch list when she tried to enter the U.S."

He leaned forward in his chair. "That doesn't matter,

either. What matters is that you put it together—where she was from, what she was going to do. And the last thing you wanted, just a couple of months before the election, was some modern-day Paul Revere stirring up the populace . . . and the media."

Holland looked toward the third man in the room and said, "Kyle, would you please wait outside?"

Without a word, the man got up and joined the agents in the hall, closing the door behind him.

"Go on," Holland said.

"You cared more about shutting her up than learning what she knew. All that mattered was keeping a lid on the story. Making sure it didn't bite your guy until after the election, when you'd have four more years to deal with it."

The chief of staff's eyes were as translucent as old sea glass.

"When you *thought* you'd have four more years," Trey went on. "But now everything's gone to hell anyway, right before the election. Mariama is the least of your worries. She can't possibly have anything to say that will make things worse for you—especially if you make her sign something promising she'll stay quiet or go back to jail. Which I know you'll do."

Holland looked at him, and something changed in his expression. Some life, some spirit, drained away.

"Mariama Honso," he said.

"Where is she?" Trey asked.

"I don't know," Holland said. "But I can find out."

"And bring her here?"

Holland's silence meant, *What do* you *think?*

"Today," Trey said.

Holland's lips twitched.

"You don't ask much, do you?" he said.

DON'T BE CAUGHT *too far apart when the end comes,* Elena Stavros had said.

Trey stood outside with the Secret Service while Holland made some phone calls. Leaning against the wall, he thought about Sheila and Kait and Mary Finneran stashed by the Harrison campaign in a safe house on the Chesapeake. Jack and Clare Shapiro. Elena and her family. Mariama.

Christopher.

And about his plan. The one he'd begun to put into place only the day before.

Something moved sluggishly inside of him.

He wondered if he'd have enough time to see it through.

"WE'VE LOCATED HONSO," Nathan Holland said.

His tone struck Trey as odd, but he didn't pursue it. "You'll bring her to me today?" he said.

The chief of staff shook his head. "There are procedures, and she hasn't been staying next door," he said. "Tomorrow."

"Where?"

Holland looked around, gave a tiny shrug. "Here will do."

Trey said, "I'll have to talk directly to her. Just me, at least at first."

The chief of staff sighed. "You'll get to talk." Then his

eyes sharpened. "Anyway, tomorrow we'll be . . . otherwise engaged."

Again there was something in the chief of staff's tone. Trey felt his heart give a single thud in his chest.

"Engaged doing what?" he asked.

The chief regarded him with an unreadable gaze.

"Tonight," he said, "the president will tell you."

FORTY-ONE

Higgins Island, Maryland

THEIR WOODEN HOUSE, like most of the others they'd passed on the way, stood on sturdy stilts anchored by solid blocks of concrete. The man who'd brought them had told Kait that, come a flood tide from Chesapeake Bay, you could sit on the front deck and look down at the water flowing harmlessly under the house.

"Sometimes," the man had said, "you can even see schools of bluefish and striped bass swimming past!"

Kait had guessed this was just a story, but she'd liked hearing it anyway. The man and the others with him, who'd been wearing suits but had seemed more like policemen, had been nice enough. At least, they'd tried to be nice. They hadn't ignored her, like so many adults, like so many of the new people, did.

Mr. Axelson, who'd arranged for them to spend a few days here, in this house on the edge of the marsh, didn't ignore her, either. Even when she asked the wrong questions, and she could tell he wished she'd pipe down, he was polite and friendly. Only his eyes gave him away.

Wrong questions, like when the policeman-in-dress-up-clothes told her about watching the bluefish. Kait had said, "Can I ask you something?"

"Of course." He'd smiled at her. "Anything."

"What happens to this house if there's a hurricane?"

That had made his smile go away. His mouth had moved for a second without any sound coming out. What he'd said finally was, "No hurricanes in the forecast, sweetie," which both of them knew wasn't really an answer.

After this conversation, she'd planned to draw a picture of the house being swept away, stilts and concrete moorings and all.

But then, last night, she'd heard something that had made her change her mind. So when she did sit down and draw, the result didn't show them being whisked away by the wind or swamped by a giant wave. No. The house was being borne on the backs of a school of silvery fish. Big, strong fish carrying them to safety.

When she showed her grandmother the drawing, Mary smiled and said, "That's because Sheila's coming for a visit, isn't it?"

No one was smarter than her grandmother.

AND NOW HERE she was. Sheila. Sitting out on the deck under a blue sky, a glass of iced tea "with a kick" in her hand. Her and Mary and Kait, just like the first time back on Marco Island, just after Ma and Da died. The day of the funeral.

It felt like a million years ago to Kait, that day. Though not at night. Not when she dreamed.

She hadn't known she would do it, but the minute she saw Sheila stepping out of her car in the driveway, she'd gone hurtling down the wooden steps and leaped into her arms. She'd heard Sheila gasp, then laugh, and then for a long time they'd just held each other.

But now that she was looking at Sheila from across the deck, Kait could see how skinny she looked. Skinny and sad, and maybe even a little scared. And that made Kait scared, too.

"What have you heard from Trey?" Mary was asking.

"Not much. He's over in D.C., tracking down someone he thinks might be able to help."

"Help how?"

But Sheila just turned her palms up.

Kait said, "You miss him. You wish he was here."

Sheila said, "Stop looking inside my head, Kaitlin Finneran!" Then she smiled. "Yes, of course I do. But if he thinks this is important . . . well, it is."

Her smile vanished. "I also heard from Jack. A text."

"What did it say?" Mary asked.

"'Worst-case scenario. Batten down.'"

Kait wasn't sure she knew what that meant, but this time she didn't ask. Sometimes you could learn more from staying quiet.

"Is it what we guessed?" Mary asked.

Sheila sighed. "I think so, yes."

She was so thin, Kait thought again.

Almost as if hearing her thought, Sheila looked at Kait again. "We think the president is planning to attack the thieves," she said. "He's giving a speech tonight, and we think that's what he'll be announcing."

"I know," Kait said. She looked at her grandmother. "That's why he wanted us to be with him, right?"

Sheila said, "Who did?"

"The president. One of his lackeys called last week." Mary's eyes had that look they got only when she was angry. "I don't know whether he wanted us *there* at the speech—we didn't get into details. They definitely wanted us available to answer questions from the press after he was done. And then—"

She paused. "And then what?" Sheila said.

"And then I think he wanted us to join him while he watched the attack."

Kait could see that her grandmother's lips were almost the same color as the rest of her face and that the wrinkles on her forehead were standing out. This was how she looked when she was *very* angry.

"We said, "No, thank you.' We're not going to be a Ping-Pong ball anymore, are we, Kait? We're tired of bouncing around and being looked at, right?"

Kait nodded. Did anyone like being looked at? Maybe some of the blond girls in her class. But not her.

A shadow passed overhead. She looked up and saw that it was an osprey, almost near enough to touch. When they'd first gotten here, she'd gone down to explore the marsh. There had been deer among the little stands of pine trees and muskrats in the more open water, and gulls and terns. Though no dolphins.

It had all reminded Kait of home, which had made her cry. But she'd been dry-eyed by the time she returned to the house.

Now Mary was saying, "That's when Jeremy Axelson had us brought here. One of Harrison's fund-raisers owns this house, I believe."

Sheila said, "And then, when the president's speech is done, Axelson will announce that you are not available for comment—implying that you disagree with the decision. He'll use your absence to push public opinion."

Mary nodded. "Most likely. We can't stop that." She sighed. "We brought this on ourselves, I'm afraid. But at least we don't have to participate anymore. This Ping-Pong ball is now retired."

Kait stirred in her seat. "I don't understand something."

"What, Bunny?" her grandmother asked.

"The president is going to attack the wasp-things?"

"Yes, that's what we think."

"Where?"

Neither Mary nor Sheila answered. Some bird in the marsh gave a high-pitched, piping call.

"And what will happen . . . after?" Kait said.

When the grown-ups still didn't speak, she stood and walked out to the edge of the deck. Leaning over the railing, she looked out toward the marsh.

Her nose prickled from the faintest taint of a familiar bitter odor. And she thought she could detect, at the very limits of her hearing, the sound of wings.

FORTY-TWO

MARIAMA'S LAST DAY in limbo was her sixty-eighth.

She knew this because she asked the guard who brought her breakfast what day it was. The date. Not for Mariama, scratching marks in her cell's stone wall to help her stay sane. She had no fear of losing her sanity.

Nor did she think marking the passage of time was a way to keep in touch with reality. Quite the reverse, in fact.

She supposed that, if you had a cast-in-stone sentence, this many days, weeks, years, watching the marks in the wall multiply might give you hope. You'd be filling in the blanks, knowing that when you got to the last one, you'd walk out.

But for her, scratches in the wall might only mark the last days of her life, whether there were ten thousand of them or only a handful.

Why, then, on this day, her sixty-eighth, did she ask her guard, the yellow-haired Carla, for the date? Why did she expect an answer? She was never quite sure. Maybe on some unconscious level she knew that something had changed. That this day was different.

Anyway: She'd asked. And Carla had glanced back at the second guard, the stoical young man who had never volunteered his name.

Mariama expected him to shake his head. But he shocked her by giving a little shrug.

"Sure," he said. "Go ahead. She'll find out soon enough anyway."

Mariama felt her blood warm, as if she'd been hibernating all these weeks and was now awakening.

"What are you talking about?" she said.

But before either guard could speak, Mariama felt rather than heard the sound. Something new. A vibration, a thrumming in her breastbone before spreading out along the pathways of her skeleton until she could even feel it in her fingers and toes.

"A plane," Mariama said out loud.

Carla was smiling as she put the tray down on the table beside the cot. "It's October fifteenth," she said. Behind her, the other guard allowed himself a small smile as well. He looked like a man who realized that a deadly dull assignment was finally coming to an end.

Mariama counted at last. Sixty-eight days since she'd arrived.

Sixty-eight days lost.

The sound of the plane, props whacking against the trade winds, grew louder. "You have time for breakfast," Carla said. "They won't be ready for you for a couple of hours."

Mariama had no appetite for the eggs and toast congealing on the plate. "Tell me," she said. "Why am I leaving?"

The male guard looked at her with an expression she hadn't seen from him before. Respect?

"All we know," he said, "is somebody told them to jump, and they jumped."

Mariama said, "Who?"

The guard just shrugged. She'd gotten all from him she was going to.

But Mariama didn't care. She knew who it was. Who had told the authorities to jump and set her free.

For the first time in weeks, she felt something that could have been called hope.

PAPERWORK.

She'd just learned it was the fifteenth of October, and now she had to write it again and again, like a punished student forced to write the same sentence over and over on the blackboard.

Each form had different words, but they all required her to say the same thing. *I will not tell anyone where I've been these past sixty-eight days. I will not tell anyone where I've been . . . I will not . . .*

America was such a strange, schizophrenic mix. It could hide you on a rock for months at a time, not answering or apologizing to anyone. But when it finally let you out, the paperwork still had to be in order.

Maybe that was why scandals like Abu Ghraib made such headlines. Too much evidence left behind. America hadn't yet learned that if you wanted to behave like the rest of the world—most of the rest of the world—you had to jettison your love of record keeping, your need to document all your actions.

Mariama sighed and signed another form.

SHE WAS SITTING in an office. A wooden desk held a metal tray, a couple of waterlogged-looking books, and a computer whose background showed a snowy mountain scene. Mariama wondered if this was a joke for whoever usually sat behind the desk, or a dream.

Windows on two sides, the sun spilling in through one, the breezes rattling the blinds in both. Seabirds called somewhere nearby, liquid yelps and shrieks.

All of this a hundred yards from her cell. And now she was free. It was hard to comprehend.

The man in charge was dressed in a military uniform. She couldn't guess at his rank, but she could tell he had some seniority, some power. His close-cropped hair was shot with gray, and in his tanned face his eyes, so dark as to seem black, possessed a kind of canny intelligence that worried her.

Still, she had to speak, had to ask. Looking up from signing the last form, she said, "You will be sending me back to Senegal?"

He looked into her eyes. She found his expression hard to read, another worry. But after a moment he shook his head and said, "No, Miss Honso, you're not going home, not yet."

Relief and worry mixed. "Where, then?"

He didn't reply, looked down at the papers on his desk.

She took a breath. One more question left to ask, the most important one.

"You will give me my possessions back, won't you?" she said.

Instantly he raised his head and fixed her with those knowing eyes. "Why do you care? You had hardly anything with you when you were apprehended."

In that moment, Mariama changed tactics. She had no choice. He was the enemy, and a clever one. Supplication wouldn't work on him. Nor would pretending that she barely spoke English.

Her chin lifted. "I remember exactly what I had with me. A small overnight bag with a change of clothes, a toothbrush, and a tube of toothpaste. A money belt containing more than a thousand U.S. dollars, a paperback book, a bag of pretzels, a watch, two silver bracelets, and a locket I wore on a silver chain around my neck."

He was still staring into her eyes. She knew she couldn't afford to look away. "And you care about which of these things?" he asked.

"The bracelets were made by a friend of mine," she said. "And the locket—that was given to me by my father, whose photo is inside. As I'm sure you know." She kept her eyes on his. "I doubt I will ever see him again, my father, so of course the locket is most important to me."

He stared at her for a little longer. She held his gaze, unwavering. Everything she'd said was the truth.

Finally he nodded. Took the papers she'd been signing and banged them against the desk to make the edges even. Mariama wondered if anyone would ever look at them again.

"You'll receive your personal items when you reach your destination," he said.

Mariama looked down, allowing her immense relief to show as gratitude. "Thank you."

He grunted and got to his feet. "Let's go."

MARIAMA FLEW.

The little prop plane was a four-seater. The pilot and one guard beside him, Mariama and a second one in the back. The whole flight, she looked at none of them, just down at the ocean below. Staring at the blue-green water, waves looking like ripples, brilliant white flecks showing where the fishing boats and yachts were out.

Blue, green, white.

Freedom.

And more than freedom: a goal, a purpose, renewed.

Mariama flew.

THEY SWITCHED AIRPLANES at a small airport in what the guards said was Florida. The new plane was a small jet. It took Mariama and her watchers—ones she hadn't seen before, in suits this time, not uniforms—north.

"Where are we going?" she asked. No one answered.

Down below, the land was gray and green, split by highways and cars that, when they caught the sun, looked like the gleaming carapaces of rain forest beetles. Expanses of savanna and marsh. Lakes that winked in the sun.

Mariama stared at it. All the joy had drained out of her. Already. Her happiness had been so fleeting.

She knew what was down there.

* * *

WASHINGTON, D.C., THAT was their destination.

The terminal was huge and cavernous, like the mouth of a whale or a sea monster. No, not a mouth. A stomach. Mariama felt like she'd already been eaten.

She felt dizzy. She'd been alone for so long.

They put her in a big black car and drove her into the city. She was silent, looking out the window at the squadrons of honking taxis and trucks, at the battalions of people going about their business.

In front of an enormous grayish white building with a front lined with columns, within view of the White House, they handed her over to yet another pair of guards. Only then did they give her a manila envelope that contained her belongings.

She looked inside: the belt, the paperback book, the bracelet, and the locket.

She took a deep breath and, with a guard on either side, went into the building.

TREY WAS THERE.

She'd thought it must have been him behind her release, but still she'd doubted. All her hopes, all those days of solitude, hanging from such a slender thread.

Yet here he was. Standing in a darkened hallway outside a half-open door. Beyond him, inside the room, she could see the shadowy forms of a crowd, perhaps twenty people, seated before a large, flickering television screen.

"Got your e-mail," he said.

A lifetime ago.

"Sorry it took me so long to figure everything out." He shook his head. "Too long."

She said, "I thought I would be there forever."

They hugged. Stepping back, she looked up into his face and noted how haggard he was. Even in the poor light, she could see that time and worry—and something else—had taken a great toll since they'd last met.

She looked at the silent crowd. "What is this?"

He didn't speak, just gestured toward the television. Mariama followed his gaze. It took her no more than a few seconds to understand what she was seeing.

"Oh, no," she said. "They can't."

"Of course they can."

Mariama put her hands over her mouth.

"I'm sorry," he said.

She couldn't take her eyes off the screen.

"We're too late."

FORTY-THREE

THE PRESIDENT OF the United States, surrounded by a dozen members of the senior staff, military officers in uniform, and other guests, sat in a plastic box.

Trey might have found it funny if his stomach hadn't been clenched in a knot. It was like a gigantic version of one of those cubes that held autographed baseballs, the ones that kept dust and moisture out as your prize sat on your mantelpiece.

"Have you seen my Ted Williams? He hit a home run with this ball in 1941."

"Have you seen my president? He's afraid he might lose the next election."

A box, a chamber. Perhaps seven feet high and as deep, and twenty feet wide, with a door on each end. Perched on a newly poured concrete platform, about ten feet up, connected to the ground by two staircases and two ladders. Set high, Trey guessed, to provide a good view of the action.

Mariama stood still beside him. He could hear her

short, controlled breaths over the muttering of the newsman on the TV and the occasional comment from the subdued group sitting here in the sweaty darkness. He'd expected her to be emaciated, hollow eyed. But she looked the same as she had in Senegal: compact, muscular, her sharp gaze never seeming to miss a thing.

On the screen, Secret Service agents and uniformed personnel arrayed themselves on the concrete platform around the president's enclosure. Then the screen split to show a group of six military helicopters, big Apaches, on a muddy, gray-green field a couple hundred yards away.

Mariama said, "Where is this?"

"South Florida," Trey said. "Old sugarcane land on the edge of the Everglades."

"Why there?"

"Visibility." Trey shrugged. "Doesn't hurt that it's a swing state."

She looked at him.

"One that could go either way in the election next month. At this stage in an election year, it's all political. Beat the thieves in Florida, win Florida."

Mariama opened her mouth to say something, then closed it again.

"Mostly, though," Trey said, "they chose it because thieves are abundant there."

"But aren't they abundant everywhere?" Mariama asked.

JACK WAS IN the room, too, leaning against a wall to the side of the television. He'd arrived early that morning, out of sorts and uncharacteristically terse. All he'd said, when Trey asked why his project had been shut down, was, "We didn't give them a magic bullet fast enough."

"So?"

"Any old bullet will do if you're shooting yourself in the foot."

On the screen, Marines and members of the National Guard were hustling around, battling a gusty wind. A reporter leaned against the breeze, his slick shiny hair flying around as he shouted into the camera.

The president, sitting in the box, looked at his watch. The chairman of the Joint Chiefs of Staff, wearing a medal-hung uniform, leaned in close to say something into his ear.

Jack, looking back, saw Trey with Mariama, pushed himself away from the wall, and came over. Trey introduced them, and for the first time since he'd resurfaced, Jack's face showed some animation.

"Took your sweet time getting here," he said to her.

She gave a small smile. "I left Senegal to come here two days after Trey did."

"What did you do, walk?"

"I walked, yes. And rode cars, a fishing boat, a freighter, airplanes. And then I sat."

"Three months to get here," Jack said, shaking his head.

She nodded. "And just in time for this."

THE HECTIC SCENE on the television screen stilled. The president, looking stoic and determined, was waiting to give a signal.

The people in the room all leaned forward. Everyone seemed to be holding their breaths.

Except for Mariama. She was full of questions. "Insecticide?" she asked. "Defoliant?"

"From what we heard, both," Jack answered. "And, for all we know, flypaper and bug zappers."

"And when they're done?"

"Declare victory. Go home. Win election."

Mariama looked at Trey. "Did you tell them this is madness?"

"In Senegal," he said, "does your president listen to you?"

She was silent.

"We argued, all the Avengers they'd assembled," Jack said. "No one listened. They just told us they understood what we were saying, but would make the decision they considered 'right for our great nation.'"

"They understand nothing," Mariama said.

ON THE LEFT side of the screen, the president and his guests watched the final preparations.

On the right, Marines climbed into the helicopters. Solid metal doors slid shut. Heads topped with helmets appeared in the glass bubbles of the Apaches' cockpits. Support staff hurried away.

One after another, the rotors started to chop, sending dust clouds spiraling into the air.

In that unreachable place deep inside Trey's core, something awoke.

THE PRESIDENT GAVE a nod. A moment later, the first of the Apaches lifted into the air, powerful and ponderous. The rest of the squadron followed. Below them, the dust flailed upward like grasping hands, then fell back.

The president was standing, staring through the plastic.

"Those helicopters," Mariama said, her voice a breath. "And that box."

"What about them?" Trey said.

"Are they airtight?"

IT WAS OVER sooner than even Trey had expected.

Spread out in formation perhaps two hundred feet above a scrubby marsh, the helicopters released plumes of poison. A strange oily, glittery white, the clouds drifted outward and down.

Trey caught a quick glimmer of movement amid the low underbrush, a gleam of sunlight off dark scales. A big rat snake searching futilely for safety.

He found himself thinking of everything there on the ground, in the water and low bushes, that wasn't a thief. Rare birds. Florida panthers.

The first of the plumes reached the ground. The helicopters flew on.

Trey knew what was coming, knew for sure, before anyone else did. The hive mind told him, spreading the heat of its anger through him in a wave that threatened to stop his heart.

Then everyone knew. Everyone could see. The lead helicopter seemed to stutter in the air, as if it had run into some thicker, denser patch of atmosphere. For a moment it jittered in one place, the two behind it swinging off to the sides to avoid a collision.

And then, as if piloted by intent instead of merely obeying the laws of gravity, it plunged straight downward. In an instant it had passed through the chemical fog and slammed into the ground. The image on the screen shook from the impact. A billow of flame blew upward, white at the center, tongues of green around the edges.

Someone in the room screamed.

Inexplicably—unless you understood what you were seeing—a second Apache flew straight through the fireball. A moment later, it exploded in midair.

In the center of the neon blaze, the helicopter's skeleton showed, laid bare by fire. A human figure twisted like a black wire within it as it, too, fell to earth.

In the room, people sobbed. At a great distance, voices on the television shouted in hysteria.

Trey could not breathe. His mind seemed to blur, then split apart. Part was still here, in the room, but the rest was . . . somewhere else. Among the men dying in the disastrous assault. Among the wasps that were killing them. He was witnessing the destruction as if he were there. And somehow he *was*.

He brought his hands to his face. For an instant it almost seemed as if his alarm, his distress, was being *broadcast* there, to the thieves. He had the fleeting sensation of . . . indecision. Concern.

He felt a touch on his arm. When he lowered his hands, he saw that Mariama was staring up at him. Somehow her gaze seemed to bring him back together again. His muscles quivering, cold sweat drying on his body, but his mind reunited.

For now.

On the screen, a helicopter accelerated and tilted to

the left. It was nearly on its side when its rotor caught the tail of another. Metal flew in strange smoking arcs, one jagged piece hurtling straight toward the camera but falling short, as the remains of the two craft plummeted. Trey never learned whether the pilots of the last two Apaches received an order to return to base. Perhaps they did. Perhaps someone had the presence of mind to order them out of there, back onto the ground.

Or maybe they just followed the most basic animal instinct. Flee. Survive.

But they were far too late. One had completed only half a turn before his craft tilted, righted itself, tilted again, and went down.

The second pilot didn't even make it that far. One last explosion shook the camera and sent a fountain of smoke skyward.

The screen switched back to the president in his box. He was still standing. His eyes were wide, his mouth wrinkled and pursed. He looked dumbstruck. Uncomprehending.

Beside him, the chairman of the Joint Chiefs of Staff was shouting. Others in the group inside the plastic enclosure were staring around, looking as stunned, as lost, as witnesses to calamity always do. The camera zoomed in to focus on a Secret Service agent, sunglasses gone, eyes and mouth stretched wide, yanking on the door from the inside.

"Fucking idiot," Jack said. "Don't open that."

The screen went black.

Someone turned on the light in the room. People scrabbled for their phones, ran for their offices, tapped on their tablets. Desperate for information that would be no different from what they'd just seen for themselves, for reassurance that wouldn't come.

One of Mariama's two guards was turned away, listening over his earpiece. A moment later both turned and, at a run, headed down the hallway, as if she no longer existed.

Trey was calm again. His mind his own. The sweat was drying on the back of his neck. "It's over," he said.

Mariama's eyes were again on his face. She opened her mouth to say something, but before she could speak, his telephone buzzed.

He took it out of his pocket. Saw it was Sheila calling. He hit a button.

"Trey," she said. Her voice a whisper.

His heart thudded. "What?"

"They're here."

FORTY-FOUR

TREY SAID, "WHERE are you?"

"With Kait and Mary. In the safe house."

"I know that," he said. *"Where?"*

"In the bathroom."

"Are there any windows?"

"No." He heard her take a breath. "We jammed a towel under the door. But there are dozens of them inside the house. Hundreds. Kait saw them coming."

A pause. Then, her voice shaking for the first time, "Trey, we don't know what to do."

Trey didn't, either. A call to the police would be sending unprepared cops into an ambush. And how could they make their own rescue attempt into anything more than a suicidal gesture?

Jack had disappeared, but Mariama was standing close, looking up into Trey's face.

"My friends," he said to her. "The thieves have them trapped."

"Yes." She seemed unsurprised. Calm. "Do you have a car?"

Trey said, "No."

At the same moment, Jack came back down the hall. "Sure," he said, spinning a key chain on one finger.

They looked at him. He shrugged. "I called in a favor."

Trey said into the phone, "Sheila, we're on our way. Two hours, tops."

"But—"

"Trust me. We'll figure something out."

"Okay." He could have kissed her for not asking questions. Then she said, "Damn! My phone is almost dead."

By such slender threads our lives hang, Trey thought. "Just hold on, okay?" he said.

"We will." Again her voice caught. "Trey—"

"On our way," he said again and disconnected.

"WHERE ARE WE going?" Jack asked, handing Trey the keys as they moved down the hall.

Trey said, "Higgins Island on the Chesapeake."

Jack nodded. "You have the address?"

Trey said yes.

"Good. I'll plug it into my GPS. If you drive fast—"

Trey didn't let him finish his sentence.

"I'll drive fast," he said.

JACK HAD BORROWED an Audi A3, which had no problem breaking the speed limit. Driving fast was even easier since Route 50 was nearly deserted. Only a few cars aimed out of town, and almost no one was heading in. The late-afternoon sky was a flat blue-gray and nearly empty as well, though near its apogee a jet caught the sun and seemed to catch fire.

"Humans," Jack said from the backseat, "are so fucking predictable."

Trey knew what he meant. When the world turned upside down, the eternal human tendency was to stay put. Hunker down.

Better to die at home, in your bed, than on unfamiliar turf.

"I'll bet the supermarkets are out of bottled water already," Jack said. "The people who make spring water, they just love catastrophes."

Mariama, sitting in the passenger seat beside Trey, grimaced. "What's the point in buying water in bottles?"

"So you have enough to drink before the water comes back on."

Mariama laughed. "I guess that depends, no? On how long before the water starts to flow again?"

Trey thought about droughts that lasted five hundred years.

But Jack just grunted and said, under his breath, "Talk about your major buzzkill."

TREY DROVE. THE D.C. suburbs fell away, and the landscape grew more rural. They passed open fields, farmhouses, interspersed with stretches of minimalls. The color of the light flattened as they drew nearer the coast, and they caught glimpses of rivers and bays, slate gray in the late-afternoon sun.

The few people in sight all seemed to be in a hurry as

well. A hurry to get back home. Trey wondered how many of them would spend their last minutes or hours or—perhaps—few days in the houses they'd retreated to. In their castles. Cowering in windowless bathrooms or broom closets, or stepping forward to fight back, brave, foolhardy, doomed.

"So, when we get there," Jack said, "what's the plan?"

Trey said, "Any ideas?"

"Me?" Jack snorted. "Do I really look like a guy with a plan? You know what I am? I'm a dog chasing cars."

Then, after a pause, "That's a quote. From *The Dark Knight*. The Joker said it first."

"When we get there," Mariama said, "I'll tell you what to do."

THEIR ROUTE TOOK them across the Chesapeake Bay Bridge. There were ducks on the water below and cormorants drying their wings on rocks close to shore.

"Oh." Jack had been looking down at his phone, giving directions when necessary, but now he caught Trey's eye in the rearview mirror. "They rescued the president." He touched the screen. "Our republic is saved."

Trey kept his attention on the road ahead.

"He's in some bunker while the White House and residence are being"—Jack made a sound that was probably a laugh—"bug-proofed."

At another time, Trey would have had plenty to say about this, starting with the impossibility of "bug-proofing" any building. Instead, he just shook his head.

"It wasn't a rescue," he said. "The thieves backed off."

"Trey is right," Mariama said.

Jack made a dissatisfied grunt. "Why? It's their Sabbath? They have a prohibition against eating elected officials?"

"No. They weren't ready for war," Trey said.

Feeling Mariama's gaze on his face.

"They're still . . . building their strength," he said.

Slave-making ants before a raid.

THEY LEFT THE highway and followed a series of smaller, winding roads heading south and back west toward the bay.

Approaching dusk, the light was watery, the air still and heavy. They drove through a small town, wooden buildings, empty streets, tourist shops closed for the season. Beyond it, the houses were bigger and set farther from the road, more isolated from each other. Sometimes all that was visible was a gate and a long driveway disappearing into the woods. No sign of the building itself.

"Yeah," Jack said. "Sure. I'd hide people here, too."

He checked his GPS. "Make the next right." Then, "About fifteen more minutes."

Something different in his manner. The ever-present good humor draining away as they drew closer.

Trey said, "Why are they there? Why are they threatening Sheila and the rest now?"

Mariama stirred. "When they're attacked, the thieves grow more . . . brazen."

Jack grunted. "The attack happened in Florida. They'd get brazen a thousand miles away?"

"Everywhere," Mariama said. "At once."

Jack made a sound in his throat.

Trey said, "Sheila killed two larvae. Is that why they came? More revenge?"

"Yes. When they're at sufficient strength, they go after anyone who harms them. You know this."

"And anyone who happens to be in their vicinity."

Mariama didn't seem to think that worthy of an answer.

They drove in silence for a few moments. Then Jack said, his voice very quiet, "The thieves. They're like Horton? They never forget?"

Mariama grunted.

"It's not a matter of forgetting," she said. "It's in their blood. To them, it is always happening right now."

Jack looked out the window. "Hell of a way to live," he said.

"SHEILA'S PHONE BATTERY must be dead," Jack said. "But her voice mail sounds cheery."

"She said it was dying," Trey said.

"Doesn't matter. We're almost there." Jack pointed. "Next right. That's it."

They entered a curving gravel driveway. In the encroaching darkness, the trees seemed to huddle over the drive, blocking any view but the one directly ahead.

The two-hour drive from Washington had taken an hour and a half. It felt like they were nearing world's end.

"The house is at the end of this drive," Jack said. "About another third of a mile."

Mariama draw in a deep breath through her nose.

"I hate that smell," she said.

* * *

THE CHARACTERISTIC BITTER odor prickled Trey's nostrils.

He could hear them, too. A familiar sound: the hum of wings, so high-pitched it seemed pure vibration, tickling somewhere in the center of his head.

But in this case multiplied a hundred times. A thousand.

The house, wood with weathered shingles, stood in front of them. It had been built on concrete posts and raised on stilts, with a wraparound deck overlooking the water beyond. Eight wooden steps led up to the front door, which hung open.

And then he saw movement on the lawn, on the drive, on the stairs.

A blur in the gloom. Glimpses of crimson. Flashes of black and green.

Jack said, his voice cracking a little at the edges, "Everyone's window closed?"

And, "Would you shut the air vents up there, please?"

Hundreds of thieves, crawling here, flying in short loops there. Dozens whirling into the air like malevolent dust devils as the car crept up the driveway. Others swooping close to the windshield before spinning away again.

Those on the front walk, on the stairs, on the patchy gray lawn, had all turned to watch. A thousand compound eyes staring, or one eye divided into a thousand?

The voice inside Trey awoke. He'd been expecting it to all along the way, but it had waited until now.

He wondered if that had been its intention. To lull him into a trap. Because now, exerting its will, it seemed to drag him toward the car door. His brain seemed to split, half of it here, inside the car, and half outside among the creatures.

He brought the car to a stop beside a gas lamp atop a metal pole, ten feet from where the wooden stairs led up to the open door.

A dozen thieves settled on the hood and stared in at him. Trey shivered, a convulsive movement of his shoulders.

Inside, the voice radiated happiness. Wholeness.

Mariama put her hand on Trey's arm, and after a moment he was able to pull himself back.

Behind them, Jack was staring out the window, his face a pale blotch in the darkness.

"Anybody got a spare Terminator?" he asked.

FORTY-FIVE

"I'LL GO IN, of course," Mariama said.

Jack leaned forward and stared at her. "What? That's insane. You won't make it three steps across the yard."

Mariama's expression contained a trace of amusement. "They won't attack me," she said.

Jack shifted his gaze to watch thieves moving lightly along the outside of the window. "And why is that?"

"Listen." Mariama's voice hardened. "I have lived among these creatures all my life. I know more about them than you do. They will not sting me."

Jack blinked. "Okay."

Her expression softened a little. "In the Casamance, Trey saw that I was unharmed. I will explain why later, after your friends are safe."

Trey said, "I'm coming with you."

She began to shake her head. Then she stopped and looked up into his eyes. In a sudden, unexpected move, she placed her right palm against his shirt, below his rib cage.

"When did it happen?" she asked.

He knew what she was asking, knew he had to tell the truth.

"In July," he said. "In Australia. Sheila—" He gestured at the house. "That was one of the larvae Sheila took out."

Mariama's eyes were still on his. "Trey," she said. "You feel it, don't you? The . . . consciousness."

After a moment, he nodded.

"That's good." Her eyes brightened. "Right now, that's good. Yes, you can come with me."

"Without, you know, dying?" Jack asked.

Mariama looked back at him. "People like Trey—they confuse the thieves." She switched her gaze to Trey. "It is hard for them to tell what you are—whether you are still a host."

"And how about me?" Trey said. "Will I always be able to tell?"

She grimaced but did not answer.

"STAY WHERE YOU are," Mariama told Jack. "Don't do anything foolhardy, and you shouldn't be in danger. The thieves are much more concerned about Trey and me."

Jack gave a nod, but he didn't seem reassured. He was breathing heavily, and Trey could see sweat on his face.

"The thieves will move away when Trey and I leave the car," she went on. "Then they will come back, but no closer than they are now. Because of me, the inside of this car will seem . . . dangerous to them."

"Okay," Jack said.

"Just don't provoke them."

"Ha!"

She looked at Trey. "I will get out first and walk around to your side. That will give the thieves a chance to understand about me. When I reach you, come out. But do not move too fast."

Trey said, "Got it."

She swung open her door and stepped outside.

IN THE LIGHT of the gas lamp, Trey saw a cloud of wasps rise around Mariama. He waited for them to descend again and envelop her. For her to fall, to be dead before she hit the ground.

But it didn't happen. The thieves rose, yes, but to escape. In an instant, the car hood and the windshield were wiped clean.

"Holy shit," Jack said. "She *is* the Terminator."

From his position behind the wheel, Trey caught a glimpse of Mariama's expression. There was relief there, but a kind of fierce joy, too. The joy you take in learning that your power over an enemy is undiminished.

After a moment, she began to walk around the car. The thieves hovering within five feet of her retreated. The ones farther off, either in the air or on the ground, stayed where they were, but there was a tension in their posture that Trey hadn't witnessed before.

He knew that he shouldn't ascribe human emotions to them, but Trey thought he was seeing fear. The thieves were afraid of her.

Mariama reached his side of the car and looked in at him. When he nodded, she swung his door open and took a step back.

Trey breathed in. The voice of the hive mind had receded, and he could hear only his heart thudding and the hum of wings.

Steadily, but not too fast, he stepped out of the car, slammed the door behind him, and straightened.

Beyond Mariama, a cloud of wasps whirled. As Trey watched, one detached itself and flew directly at him. A blur. If it had tried to sting him, he would have had no defense. But it paused, hovering just in front of his face, dipping a little closer, pulling back.

He saw its abdomen pulsing as it spun away.

"We must hurry," Mariama said.

TO TREY IT felt like being inside a dome. A shaken globe filled with black and crimson snow. Every step, the cloud whirled around them, up above, to the side, never closer than a half dozen feet. Taking a single glance behind him, he saw that a multitude of thieves had fallen again upon the car.

The sinking sun had disappeared behind a screen of haze near the horizon, turning crimson wings the color of dried blood. Somewhere not far away, a dog gave a sudden series of high-pitched yelps before falling silent.

Trey and Mariama walked. The wasps that had been staking out the pathway to the house and the stairs made way as they approached. Farther away, others rose on their spidery legs, twisting their heads to mark the humans' progress.

The voice inside Trey stayed silent.

Mariama reached the foot of the staircase, Trey a step behind. Most of the stairs were now clear, but at the top a battalion of thieves held their ground. Others moved around the edges of the dark rectangle made by the open door. Farther inside, unseen wings hummed.

A group, five, or maybe ten, came from somewhere off to the side, swooped low over Trey's head, and sped away. The sight of them flickered at the corner of his vision like the aura that precedes a migraine.

"Stay close to me," Mariama breathed into his ear. "You're in danger."

"I had no idea," he said, just as quietly.

Her indrawn breath might have contained a laugh.

"Listen," he said, his eyes on the thieves staring down at him from the top step. "If they decide I'm worth killing, you have to get the others out. You have to save them."

He heard her sigh. "I will do my best," she said. "I promise."

Then she said, "All right. Let's go in."

But even as Trey lifted his right foot onto the first step, he heard a sound that froze him as if he'd been staked to the ground.

A long, drawn-out scream.

He twisted around. The front passenger door of the Audi hung open. Jack lay writhing on the ground beside it, facedown, his arms up near his head, his feet kicking at the grass. Floundering forward in an attempt to escape that he must have known was hopeless.

Nearly every exposed patch of skin—his arms, his hands, his calves where his jeans had hiked up—was covered in wasps.

Especially his face. His eyes. A riot of legs and wings and mandibles.

As Trey watched, pinned in place, Jack's head turned

toward them. His mouth stretched wide open. He gave a wet, choking cry that must have begun as another scream.

Finally Trey awoke from his shock. But before he could move, before he could run back to try to save his friend, Mariama's hands grasped his arms. Her fingers were as strong as manacles.

"No!" Her voice a whip crack, designed to grab his attention. "Trey—it's too late!"

He tried to wrench away from her, but she hung on to him with strength born of desperation. "Trey," she said, each word like a gasp. "Trey! They'll kill you, too. Look at them. Look!"

He pulled his gaze away from Jack's quivering form. All around, the thieves had risen into the air. Their spinning flight, with him and Mariama at the center of the vortex, seemed to Trey to have an edge of hysteria to it. Joy or rage or some alien mixture of both.

Emotions mirrored in the awakening consciousness within him.

"Come on!" Mariama said.

Trey turned his back to the car and, together, he and Mariama ascended the wooden steps.

From behind them came the sound of Jack's last, shuddering breath.

SILENCE INSIDE THE house. Stillness.

Green eyes watched them from the dark corners where the walls met the ceilings. From the shadowy edges of paintings showing sailboats raising colorful spinnakers on bright blue oceans. From behind the DVD player, the rims of vases, and especially amid the leaves of the potted rain forest plants arrayed to catch the sun through a big, cheerful bay window facing south.

Only there was no sun now.

Trey and Mariama stood in the center of the living room. To the right was an open kitchen separated by a granite counter. Sitting on the counter were half-full glasses of what looked like iced tea, a newspaper folded in half, and a plate holding a peanut butter sandwich with one bite taken out of it. A thief stood on top of the sandwich. Not moving, just watching, like the rest of them.

The odor here was very strong, but Trey barely noticed it. He breathed, in and out, until he felt his heart begin to slow, his vision clear.

Then he pointed. "There."

A short hallway led to three doors. Two were open, showing glimpses of bedrooms beyond. The third was closed. Trey could see part of a blue towel jammed in the gap between the bottom of the door and the wooden threshold.

Trey took a step toward the closed door but felt a hand on his arm. Mariama said, "Wait," then gestured toward the kitchen.

They took a detour around the counter. Reaching up into one of the glass-fronted cabinets above the sink, she took down a tall plastic glass. From the counter she grabbed a section of the newspaper.

Turning to look at Trey, she said, "Now we're ready."

FORTY-SIX

"SHEILA," TREY CALLED out.

"Trey!" Disbelieving.

Then Kait's voice. "Are the wasp-things gone?"

Trey's gaze strayed to the end of the corridor. Wings flickered in the shadows.

"No," Mariama said. "But we won't let them hurt you."

A pause. Then Sheila said, "Trey, who is that?"

Trey said, "Mariama." He took a breath. "A friend. Listen to her, and we'll get you out of there."

Let it be true.

Mariama seemed to have no doubts. She called, "Unlock the door, then go to the far end of the room."

"It's small," Sheila said.

"As far as you can."

After a moment, they heard the ratchety sound of a bolt sliding. Mariama put a hand on Trey's arm for five seconds, ten, before giving him a nod. He reached out, turned the knob, and, pushing against the jammed towel's resistance, swung the door open.

The three of them stood arrayed against the opposite wall of the small room, where the white and blue tiles met the edge of the glass-walled shower. Mary, pale, exhausted, her arm protectively over Kait's shoulders, Sheila a stride in front of them.

Trey stepped quickly into the room. Behind him, Mariama twisted around in a circle, scanning for thieves—or warning them—then swung the door shut and jammed the towel back in the gap.

Trey let his eyes search the room for any other possible entry point. Someone had covered the vent in the ceiling with a towel, carefully pushing the cloth as deep as she could into each open slot. They'd even thought to jam washcloths into the faucets and drains.

Kait broke from her grandmother's grasp, ran forward, and threw herself into Trey's arms. "I *told* them you would come," she said.

As Trey hugged her, he lifted his gaze and looked at Sheila. Her face was pale, her eyes bloodshot, but she looked focused. Intent. Determined.

She opened her mouth to speak, then saw something in his expression that closed it again.

"Where's Jack?" she asked.

Trey said nothing, just kept his gaze on hers. After a moment her hand went to her mouth. She closed her eyes, and when she opened them again they were red.

"Well, we're certainly glad you're here," Mary said. Trey saw dark circles under her eyes and a crepelike texture to her skin that he hadn't noticed before.

Looking back at him, she seemed to read his thoughts. Her mouth firmed. "Now tell us how we get out of here."

Trey deposited Kait back onto the floor. She looked up at him. "The wasp-things are all over the place," she said. "Why didn't they sting you?"

"Bunny, we'll find out later," Sheila said. She looked from Trey to Mariama. "Yes—what do we do?"

Squatting under the overhead light, Mariama put the plastic glass on the floor and laid the newspaper flat beside it. Then her hands went up and behind her neck. She undid the silver chain and lowered the locket.

But it wasn't the photograph of her father that she was interested in. With quick motions of her nimble fingers, she pressed on the sides of the locket. And it was the back, not the front, that sprang open, revealing a hidden compartment.

Beside her, Trey looked inside and saw three tiny red spheres. Seeds. He'd seen ones like them before. Fitted into the space next to them was a minuscule plastic pouch containing a brown powder.

The hive mind inside released a flash of pure white light inside his head. Some violent sensation ran along his spine and made him shiver.

Mariama pointed at the glass with her chin. "Trey, please fill it. All the way."

When he returned, she was holding the pouch between the thumb and forefinger of her right hand. As he held the glass, she opened it and then, with infinite care, poured the powder in.

A pungent, spicy odor rose from the glass. Like ginger, with a trace of cinnamon mixed in. Trey recognized it, too, although he'd smelled it just once before. Months before, in the Casamance.

It was the smell of the vines, the only healthy plants in the dying forest. And those were the red seeds that the vines produced.

After a moment, Mariama straightened. "All right," she said. "Now the three of you will drink some of this. You first, Sheila. A sip at a time until I tell you to stop."

Sheila was suspicious. "What about Trey?"

Mariama's gaze glimmered in his direction. "There is only enough for the three of you. Anyway, Trey is already protected."

Sheila was unconvinced. "What is it?"

Mariama opened her mouth as if to dismiss the question, then took in a breath. "I'll explain fully later," she said, "when we're—free. We make this powder from a plant, the one Trey saw. It contains a substance that protects us from the thieves, and it will protect you as well."

"What kind of substance?" Sheila said.

Mariama compressed her lips, but again she answered. "An alkaloid. Or a combination of them. We don't know."

Sheila's face darkened. "An alkaloid? You mean a poison."

Mariama just looked at her. It was Kait who spoke. "A poison that makes the thieves sick?" she said. "But not us?"

Mariama smiled. "Yes. That is exactly right. Only it does more than make them sick: It kills them. Then it spreads. They pass it on, one to the next. Maybe through the air, or maybe when they touch each other. We're not certain."

She looked back at the closed door. "What we do know

is that this poison, this alkaloid, can kill entire colonies, whole populations of thieves. They will not expose themselves to it unless they have no choice." Her eyes flashed. "Here, today, they have a choice. They will leave you alone."

Trey said to Kait, "Have you heard of poison dart frogs?"

After a moment, she nodded. "Yes, I saw them on a TV show once. They were beautiful." She paused. "I should draw them."

"Well," Trey said, "alkaloids are the chemicals they keep in their skin."

Mariama nodded. "Plants contain alkaloids. Insects eat the plants. Frogs eat the insects—and end up with the poisons inside them."

"Anything that eats the frogs will die," Trey said. "But the frogs themselves are fine."

"And you will be fine, too," Mariama said.

Sheila was still looking skeptical. "How did you discover this miracle cure?"

"It's not a cure," Mariama said. "It's a protective weapon, just like the frogs have."

"And you came upon it by chance?"

"No." Now Mariama let a flicker of anger show, and Sheila's eyes widened. "Not by chance. The furthest thing from chance."

Mary stirred and spoke. "I don't understand."

Mariama closed her eyes for a moment. When she opened them she was calm again. "Trey knows this: that everything in nature is a battle, a contest."

"Yes," Trey said. "Endless rounds of one-upmanship over the generations."

"Over millions of years." Mariama nodded. "For example: Insects eat plants, so plants evolve poisons to ward off the insects. Then the insects learn how to eat the poisonous plants, and the plants evolve even more poisons."

"Like milkweed, which is as toxic a plant as you can imagine," Trey said. "It's like eating latex. Poison. Yet monarch caterpillars eat it, and wasps and spiders eat monarchs."

Mariama said, "If a plant was ever going to evolve a toxin poisonous to the thieves—and if animals were ever going to discover and utilize that toxin—it would be in the Casamance, where both the wasps and the plants evolved. My homeland."

She turned her palms up, letting her frustration show. "Please, let us talk more later. Now drink."

Sheila said, "One last thing."

Mariama waited.

"There's no way that we can infect—or inoculate—ourselves with this poison immediately. It will take far longer than that."

Mariama said, "That is true."

"But we'll be safe anyway?"

"Yes. The thieves, they can't tell. They can sense, *smell*, when we've been exposed, but not how long the toxin has been inside. Soon after you drink, they will do almost anything to avoid you."

"How do you know all this?" Kait asked.

Mariama's gaze turned toward her. "I told you," she said finally. "My people have lived among the thieves for a long time. They have learned how to kill us, but we have learned how to kill them, too."

Kait nodded. It made sense. She was convinced.

"Sheila," she said. "Grandma Mary. Drink."

AFTERWARD THEY SAT, mostly in silence, for about a half hour. Then Mariama said, "All right. It's time."

Kait wriggled her shoulders. "I am *so* ready to get out of here."

"Me, too," Mariama said.

She explained what they were to do. She would lead the way, followed by Kait, Mary, and Trey. Sheila would take the end of the line.

"No," Trey said. "I'll go last."

Mariama's eyes flashed. "You'll do as I say, please."

Then, without waiting, she yanked the towel out and swung the door open.

SOMEHOW TREY HAD expected there to be a waiting horde just outside the door, but the house seemed deserted. Nothing left but the thieves' scent.

"The alkaloid," he said.

"They don't like to be in enclosed spaces with it, no," Mariama said. "But they are not gone."

She was right. Even as she stepped out the front door and into the darkness, Trey could hear the sound of movement.

Kait darted back behind Mary and leaned in close to Sheila, who put her arm around the little girl's shoulders. If Mariama noticed the change in order, she made no protest.

Without thinking, Trey turned back and touched Kait's hair. She looked up at him.

"You're an amazing girl," he whispered to her.

And got, from this amazing girl, the ghost of a smile.

THE NIGHT AIR was cold and damp. Wisps of fog swirled through the circle of yellow light cast by the streetlamp.

There was no sign of anything living—no birdsong, no dogs barking, no human conversation or laughter— except the relentless presence of the thieves that still besieged the house.

The five humans stood atop the stairs that led down to the lawn, to the pathway, to the car. Trey could tell that the effect darkness has on the deepest roots of the human nervous system was spreading its tendrils even into this intrepid crew.

Kait's smile had long since vanished, and her short breaths were almost gasps. Mary was leaning heavily on the railing. Sheila's head was turning this way and that, as if she were trying to see through the darkness, as if seeing the thieves coming would protect her.

Only Mariama seemed unmoved. "All right," she said. "Trey, give me your car keys."

She put them in her pocket and then took a step forward, her head tilted. They all listened to the responding whirl and hum of the invisible horde.

For an instant, the hum grew louder, broke apart. Trey felt something ripple through his hair—the current of air created by unseen wings.

Mariama felt it, too. "All right," she said again, her

tone a degree grimmer than it had been. "Let's try something else. Trey, you carry Kait."

"I don't need to be carried," Kait said at once.

"I know." Mariama's voice was firm. "I know you don't. This isn't to protect you, but him."

"Forget it," Trey said. "I'm not using her as a human shield."

For a moment Mariama didn't reply. Then she said, "Trey, they are beginning to understand what you are. If you refuse, I think you won't reach the bottom of the stairs."

Kait pulled away from Sheila and stepped over to him. Like a little girl, she raised her arms.

"Up I go," she said.

After a moment, Trey hoisted her up onto his right hip. He felt one of her arms drape along his shoulder, her other hand touch his shirt just above his heart.

He said, "Thank you."

"It's okay." Then, "Sorry I'm so heavy."

He looked into her face, just a blur in the shadows close to his, and hoped she could see or hear his smile. "Are you kidding?" he said. "I could carry you for miles."

She shifted a little on his hip and said, "Just to the car, please."

Mariama led them down the stairs.

MARIAMA, MARY, TREY and Kait, Sheila.

Eight steps to the ground, ten down the path. Unseen multitudes of thieves watched them from the darkness. The occasional green-ice gleam when multifaceted eyes caught the light.

An overwhelming *awareness* all around them.

As they drew closer to the car, Trey could see the humped shape lying near it. Eyes that were holes of infinite blackness, bared teeth gleaming in the light.

At the same moment, he heard Sheila draw in a breath, understanding what she was seeing.

Trey shifted his grip on Kait, who had stiffened. With his left hand, he turned her head so that she was facing in toward his shoulder.

"Sweetie, don't look," he said. "Just . . . don't."

She put both arms around his neck and buried her face against his collarbone.

Trey saw that Mariama had taken Mary's arm. They walked the last few steps to the car. Mariama, keys in her hand, said, "Kait, get down now. But stay close to Trey."

When Kait was standing beside him, her arm around his waist, Mariama said, "I'll go in first. The rest of you wait until I tell you."

She swung open the back door, then the driver's one, and slid in behind the wheel with an eel-like quickness. A moment later, the engine roared and the headlights went on. Trey saw moving shadows, harsh in the brilliant light, recede from the beams into the more impregnable darkness behind.

But Mariama wasn't concerned with anything outside the car. Trey saw her turn on the overhead lights, saw her twist around in her seat. Wasps rose from all around her, fleeing through the open doors.

She climbed into the back, checking under the seats, in the storage compartments and seatback pockets and cup holders. Trey could see she'd done this before.

Once, then a second time, she paused. Her hand darted with the speed of a snake striking, and a moment later the smell of the thieves rose more strongly.

"Next time," Mariama said, "leave when your friends do."

She turned her head. "It's clear."

Kait scrambled into the backseat beside her. Trey helped Mary in as well and slammed the door. Once the two of them were inside, Sheila climbed quickly through the driver's side into the passenger seat. As Trey got behind the wheel, he saw her look down at the ground, at Jack. She took a deep breath but said nothing.

Trey closed his door, put the car into reverse, and sped down the driveway, the tires kicking up gravel. Looking back one last time at the house, he saw movement at the edges of the headlights' beam, a last huge swirl in the darkness as the thieves rose to leave the abandoned building.

Pulling out into the quiet street, he aimed them back toward the mainland. A quarter of a mile ahead, at the intersection with a bigger road, he could see traffic. It seemed surreal, that people were still living their lives out here.

"Where to?" he asked.

"Someplace to eat," Mariama said. "We all need some food. We have to be able to think."

"I couldn't eat," Mary said.

"You must."

Kait was twisted around in her seat, looking back the way they'd come. "But won't they be following us?"

"No, I don't think so. Not as we are now."

"Then we're safe?"

When no one answered, she frowned and shook her head, as if disappointed in herself.

"I won't ask that again," she said.

FORTY-SEVEN

THE FIRST PLACE they found was a diner, with harsh fluorescent lighting, Formica tabletops, a white caddy containing little plastic containers of jams and jellies, paper placemats adorned with ads from local businesses, and a little can of worn crayons that Kait immediately reached for.

Even as she drew, her face turned away, Trey could tell that she was alert to every word they spoke.

The rest of them were quiet, numb, as they studied the menu, merely mentioning out loud what they might order. Yet even through his haze of shock and sorrow, Trey realized he was hungry. Mariama had been right: They were running on empty. They needed fuel.

Jack would have ordered half the dishes on the menu. He also would have filled the quiet with jokes, observations, *words*. He'd hated quiet above all else.

Sheila had been dead-silent throughout, her face clenched, her eyes dark. After they'd ordered, she looked up and said to Mariama, "I don't care how much of that potion you had. You should have saved some for Jack."

Mariama, calm as always, returned the fierce gaze. But she seemed troubled as well.

"Jack shouldn't have mattered to them," she said.

"But he did."

"Yes, and I don't understand it." She paused. "The last place the thieves would have wanted to be was in the car—not after I'd been there. The smell should have terrified them. Since he was just another human to them—of no special concern—he should have been safe."

At that moment, Trey realized the truth. Understood it and felt a deep swerve toward sorrow.

"Oh, God," he said. "It's my fault."

Everyone looked at him. Taking a deep breath, he said, "Jack was of 'special concern.' Mariama, he killed one, too. An adult. Back in July."

He saw Mariama's face set.

"The one that came back with me from Australia, when I was infected."

"I see," she said.

Trey's voice sounded harsh in his own ears. "That means Jack was doomed, wasn't he? The moment we left the car, he was doomed."

Mariama did not reply.

He looked down at the tabletop, at the pattern in the brown Formica, designed to mimic wood. Somewhere, most likely in China, there was a factory built to fabricate fabricated wood. Was it still open? Or were the workers hiding at home, and were the plastic molds crawling with wasps?

"I always thought when Jack went, he'd go down fighting," he said. "With some grand, noble gesture, something brave and stupid. Not . . . this."

"Trey," Mariama said, "you're missing something."

Sheila said, "Yes, you are."

Trey raised his eyes.

"*You* might not have realized that the thieves would target Jack, but I am sure that *he* did," Mariama said.

Trey was silent.

"And I think he knew what might happen to him." She leaned toward him. "He knew that some thieves might get in when we opened the car door, or through the vents. He knew that it's nearly impossible to keep them out if they want to get in.

"He knew, but he kept quiet, because he wanted you to save the others. Because he understood that there was no other way: We couldn't bring him with us, we couldn't protect him when we went into the house, and you wouldn't have been willing to leave him to die. So he did what he had to do."

Very softly from beside him, Sheila said, "She's right, Trey. That was Jack."

She leaned closer. "A grand, noble gesture," she said. "Something incredibly brave . . . but not stupid."

Mariama nodded. "We should each have such an honorable death."

THEY ATE IN near silence. Burgers for Trey and Mary, gumbo for Mariama ("It reminds me of some of the soups we have at home," she said), Caesar salad for Sheila, and chicken fingers with honey mustard for Kait. "I eat it everywhere," she told them, "and compare."

There was a television on the wall in the corner, but it was shut off. When they asked the waitress what news they had missed, she shrugged.

"The president will be back in the White House tomorrow," she said. "He's gonna speak again then, but it'll just be words. And what good do words do?"

Besides that, she said, the news was filled with reported sightings of the wasps in places they hadn't been seen before. Only a few reports of attacks, virtually none confirmed, but people were staying inside, stores and schools were closed, businesses were shuttered.

The waitress looked around the diner. Only about a half dozen seats were occupied in a space that could have fit eighty.

"Some of us have to work, though," she said. "What choice do I have? Bugs or no bugs, I bet the government is still planning to take its chunk out of my paycheck."

When she was gone, Trey said, "All these reports. Are people just noticing them now, or are the thieves really showing up in new places?"

"The latter," Mariama said without hesitation. "I told you they'd become more brazen, and that's what they're doing. They're testing us."

"And next?" Sheila asked.

"Next? They're in no hurry. They'll wait to see how we respond."

"CAN I ASK you something?" Kait said to Mariama near the end of the meal. She had folded up her drawing and stowed it in a pocket and was now looking down on a huge piece of red velvet cake with gloppy icing and a scoop of melted ice cream.

The rest of them were drinking coffee.

"Of course," Mariama said.

"How do you know that the poison is going to protect you?"

Mariama looked thoughtful. "As I told you, back in Senegal we have lived with these creatures for a long time. We could hardly help but learn something about them."

Kait put her fork down with a little clatter and sat up straight in her chair.

"No," she said. "That's not what I mean. I mean, *every time* you go where the thieves are, how do you know it will save you? How can you be sure it will work?"

Again a pause. Then Mariama said, "I can never be sure."

"The wasp-things must hate you," Kait said.

Mary said, "Kaitlin!"

"It's all right." Mariama paused. "I don't know if they feel 'hate,' but they definitely know who I am—and that I have killed many of them."

Kait thought about this. "So you are being brave, too, whenever you go outside." Her eyes widened. "Whenever you go *anywhere*."

Mariama just smiled at her and didn't reply.

Mary stirred cream into her coffee. After saying little through the meal, she seemed to be regaining some focus.

"So, inside that locket of yours," she said.

Mariama tilted her head. "Yes, what about it?"

"You brought the powder from Africa. Did you come all this way to save us? To save the world?"

Mariama's smile turned rueful. "I suppose," she said. "I suppose that was what I was hoping to do—bring the sample to Trey, have him take it to the Centers for Disease Control. I thought they'd listen to him, the way they wouldn't to some unknown lady from Senegal. I dreamed they'd synthesize it, produce it in large quantities, and—yes—save the world."

The amusement had left her face. "But it was a hopeless dream. Even if I hadn't been imprisoned, I would have been far too late. Bureaucracies don't work fast enough."

She shrugged. "And now it doesn't matter anyway."

Trey said, "Were the seeds going to save us, too?"

"Yes." She reached up and took off the locket. Popped open the false back and carefully dropped the three red seeds onto the table. One of them rolled a few inches away, but Kait corralled it with two fingers and pushed it close to the others.

"You harvest the alkaloid from these seeds?" Sheila asked.

"It is also found in the leaves, but, yes, it's most concentrated in the fruit and the seed coverings."

Trey thought it over. "So some mammals eat the fruit. The alkaloid doesn't harm them, and they absorb enough of it to protect them while they disperse the vine's seeds."

Mariama nodded.

"I saw squirrels in those vines," Trey said.

"Yes. They eat the fruit, are unharmed, and disperse the seeds. All a balance, with everyone getting what they need."

"Except the wasps," Sheila said.

Mariama shook her head. "It worked for them as well,

historically. In a forest with so many mammals, so many primates, there've always been enough that didn't carry the poison. And the vine only grows in light gaps, so there were vast stretches of forest without it." She grimaced. "Until about twenty years ago."

"When logging arrived," Trey said. "And hunting for bushmeat."

"Yes. Fewer mammals and more light gaps. More vines. The balance was destroyed."

Sheila said, "And presto, the thieves need to move to more hospitable turf. So they start to search."

Mariama nodded.

"Only to find a world filled with hosts—and no vines. No alkaloids. No defense."

Mariama said, "That's right."

Trey looked down again at the seeds. "You brought the seeds so we could grow the plants here."

"Yes, that was my plan. To help people grow their own protection."

"Mariama Appleseed."

Her smile turned into a sigh. "Now we must depend on our other plan."

Trey thought: Yes.

The only one left that made any sense.

HE WAS WAITING for the waitress to bring his credit card back, imagining the worldwide chaos that would ensue in the first ten minutes after the computers that approved credit-card transactions crashed, when Sheila said to Mariama, "There's one thing we're still not sure about. The 'summoning.'"

A spasm of something that looked like disgust crossed Mariama's face. "You haven't encountered that?"

"No, not yet."

Trey said, "Jack thought it might be a fungus."

Mariama gave him a curious look.

"Like the fungi that infect the brains of ants and other insects—make them crawl to the top of bushes before dying. You must have seen them."

"Of course." Mariama's expression was bleak. "No, it's not a fungus. You will see."

That was all she would say.

IT WAS KAIT who broke the silence that followed. Her eyes on Mariama, she said, "You're a butterfly."

Mariama smiled at her and said, "Thank you."

The corners of Kait's mouth turned downward. "No. Listen. I read a story this year. What was it called, Grandma?"

"Which story?" Mary rolled her eyes. "You read so many."

"The one about the dinosaurs. And the big gun."

Trey said, " 'A Sound of Thunder,' by Ray Bradbury?"

"Right!" Kait looked back at Mariama. "Have you read it?"

Mariama shook her head.

"This man travels back in time to hunt dinosaurs. It's like a safari. You have to stay on a boardwalk and you're not allowed to kill anything there except a dinosaur, because all dinosaurs went extinct anyway. You understand? If you killed something else, it might change the future."

Mariama, a little wide-eyed, said, "Yes?"

"Well, this man, he gets scared and runs off the boardwalk. When they get back to the future—" Her hands grasped at air. "I mean, their *present*, they find everything's different. The world is different. The man looks at his shoe and sees that when he went off the boardwalk, he'd stepped on a butterfly. That's all it took to change the future—one butterfly!"

After a moment, Mariama said, "Why is the story called 'A Sound of Thunder'?"

"Because at the end this other man, the one who took him to hunt dinosaurs, he shoots him." Again Kait frowned. "But that's not the point. I was talking about the story with my—"

She took in a quick breath, almost a gasp, and her eyes filled with sudden tears. Scowling, wiping the back of her hand across her face, she went on.

"I was talking with Ma about the story, and she said that with most things, it doesn't matter whether they live or die, it doesn't change anything." Her chin lifted. "They matter to the people who love them, Ma said, but not to the future. Not like the butterfly in the story did."

"I think I agree with your mother," Trey said. "We're like—" He hesitated. "Like molecules of water in the ocean. Individually, we're just not that important."

"Oh, but you are," Kait said.

Everyone looked at her. Red spots appeared on her fair cheeks, but she went on.

"People like me and Grandma, we might only be important to each other—"

"And to us," Sheila said.

Kait shook her head. "But you—" She pointed at Mariama. "You." Sheila. "And you." Trey.

"You three," she said. "You're the butterflies."

None of them knew what to say.

"So don't die," Kait said. "Okay?"

FORTY-EIGHT

BRAZEN.

That was the word Mariama had used, and that was what the thieves had become. Brave. Fearless. Brazen.

It had begun immediately after the failed helicopter assault in Florida. ("A disastrously ill-conceived October Surprise whose only lasting impact may be the end of a presidency," as one prestigious newspaper put it.)

Now, less than two weeks later, it seemed like they were everywhere. Spreading through nature preserves and city parks. Occupying rent-controlled apartment blocks and expensive suburban developments. Establishing colonies in beachside dunes and golf resort sand traps.

Far more visible than ever before. And why not? Why should they worry about being seen? People were terrified of them. No one would go near an adult thief, much less try to kill it. Everyone knew you couldn't fight them without risking an overwhelming attack in response.

The media, as always, stoked terror in the guise of

providing information. You couldn't watch the cable news networks without seeing endless replays of the Florida catastrophe, along with footage of several other large attacks in different parts of the world.

Trey had seen one filmed in Russia. The screams had echoed in his head all day. After that, he stayed away from the coverage. It had nothing to teach him.

He did see one newspaper chart that was updated each day. With colorful graphics, it tracked the thieves' progress across the world.

"Just like our old map," Sheila said.

She was right. The chart showed how the wasps had followed trade and travel routes, radiating outward from Africa to ports, canals, and big cities around the world. From there, blessed with abundant food supplies and hosts for their offspring, they'd undergone an enormous population explosion, colonizing new territory in all directions and at breakneck speed.

By now, they'd established themselves on six continents. Only Antarctica had remained untouched, though one thief, dead of some unknown cause, had been found aboard a supply ship heading to McMurdo Station.

Mariama had shrugged at this news. "I do not think they'll try to populate Antarctica."

"Too cold?" Trey had asked.

She'd sighed. "I used to dream of living in a cold climate, because it would make me free of them at last. Now I think no place is safe. The thieves are opportunistic and hardy. If they have to live inside in the coldest regions, in corners, in attics and storerooms, they will."

"Then why is Antarctica exempt?"

"I didn't say it was." Mariama had looked directly into

his eyes. "The thieves won't bother with it because it is doomed. Those few humans at McMurdo pose no threat, and they will die off on their own soon enough after the end comes."

That was what conversations with Mariama were always like. Not if. Not even when.

After.

AFTERNOON SHADING INTO dusk in Central Park. Some late-season softball players were trying to get a game together on the Great Lawn, but there weren't enough of them to make two teams. The thieves had been staying away from the park's big open expanses, so far, but so were most people. Coming out here, as these young men and women were doing, was itself an act of defiance.

"This feels strange," Sheila said.

Trey said, "Well, yeah."

She gave him a sideways look. They were sitting on a splintery bench under the cold autumn sun, side by side, facing the empty gray grass.

"I mean," Sheila said, "where's Jack?"

"I knew what you meant." Trey sighed. They were here in the park because they'd gone to the museum to clear out what they'd left in Jack's office. Books, mostly. And memories.

Sheila slid down on the bench a little, leaning her head against the back, stretching her long legs out in the dirt. Her eyes were closed.

Trey thought she looked like she was made of some pure, icy substance: porcelain, maybe. Or unforged silver. Incomparably beautiful but untouchable as well.

"My mother's mother was one of twelve children," she said. "Nine of them died before they reached their sixth birthday."

She opened her eyes and stared down at her hands. "Can you imagine losing a brother or sister every year or two? Or burying your own children?"

Trey said, "We're the first generation to think we have the right to live forever."

The small group of softball players left the empty field and trailed past them.

"We were," Sheila said. "But that's finished."

Trey looked at her. After a moment, she sensed it and turned her head. Then, in an instant, her arms were around his neck and she was kissing him. Her lips were warm and soft, not porcelain, but there was something hungry, even desperate, about her grasp.

She broke away, loosened her grip, but kept her face close to his. "You," she said.

"What about me?"

"What Kait said: *Don't die.*"

THEY WALKED PAST Turtle Pond, its fringing brown cattails rattling in the breeze, to the area called the Ramble.

This hilly, densely wooded expanse had once been popular with two groups: gay men seeking rendezvous out of the public eye and birders seeking rarities. Today, though, it was the sort of place where only the insane would willingly venture.

The insane or the protected. Sheila had nothing to fear from the thieves. And Trey, though his safety was more equivocal, had decided not to hide, especially when he was in the company of one of the immunes.

They left the quiet park road, ghostly without its usual myriad of cyclists and joggers, and headed into the woods. Neither of them spoke, but they both knew what they were looking for.

It took only a few minutes. As always, the smell alerted them, at first just a harsh whiff carried away by the chilly breeze. Then stronger. A smell so omnipresent now, so familiar, that if they weren't searching they sometimes didn't even notice it.

The man lay on his back at the bottom of a small gully overgrown with bittersweet, mile-a-minute, and other invasive vines. He was wearing black pants, the right leg ripped to the knee, a Hannah Montana T-shirt, and an unzipped down jacket that had once been cream colored but was now caked with dirt.

He looked like he'd been homeless long before the thieves summoned him.

It took Trey a minute to find the wasp guarding its larva. The creature gave itself away with movement among the vines, a quick, agitated back-and-forth. As thieves always were, it was disturbed to be close to the poison and, perhaps, to Trey as well. To the corrupt, half-finished remnant of the hive mind he contained.

The wasp's head twisted as it kept them in view. There was likely another one or more somewhere in the vicinity. Staying hidden, watching, waiting to see if they presented a threat.

Sheila was looking at the man. No one would try to help him, they both knew. No one would go near.

And his death would make as little impact as the deaths of the homeless men who perished out in the streets whenever the city was gripped by a deep freeze.

Beside Trey, Sheila shuddered. They'd made it a practice to stop, pause, wherever they found a human host, to seek them out in parks and vacant lots and beneath underpasses and abandoned piers.

It had been Sheila's idea, her insistence, to seek out the infected. "Someone has to acknowledge them," she'd said. "Someone has to remember that they were once human."

Though each time she saw one, each time she witnessed the inevitable, she seemed sadder, more haunted.

"Let's go," Trey said and took her arm.

But at that moment they heard a rustling in the brush beside the trail. A man emerged, another host. Walking with purpose, his head turning this way and that. Trey wondered what he was seeing through that silvery gaze.

"Trey," Sheila said in a sudden, tortured whisper. *"Look."*

Trey had already seen it: a thief clinging to the back of the man's neck. Its slender abdomen was arched, and as the man passed they could see that it had plunged its needlelike stinger deep into his flesh, just between the second and third cervical vertebrae. Its head turned to watch Trey and Sheila, twisting to stay on them as the man moved down the trail.

Trey and Sheila both understood what they were seeing. The summoning.

He should have guessed. He'd seen wasps do this before, riding their victims, guiding them to their doom with chemicals administered directly to their brains. Only their victims had been cockroaches and spiders and other wasps, not primates. Not human beings.

That colobus monkey he'd seen in the Casamance, staggering into the thief colony's clearing, it must have had a rider as well. Trey had missed it. He hadn't known what to look for.

The man followed a curve in the path and moved out of sight. Again Trey said, "Let's go," and this time Sheila didn't resist.

THEY WALKED EAST and then up to Eighty-sixth Street and met Mariama at a Starbucks. She was staying with some old acquaintances in a Senegalese neighborhood in Brooklyn, but every day she and Trey talked, made plans, prepared.

Got ready for *after*.

The Starbucks was reasonably crowded. Logically or not, people felt more secure indoors, especially in crowds. Anyway, no matter what, they still needed their coffee. The last human force in the final battle would be fueled by Starbucks.

Sheila's mind was still on the latest victims she and Trey had seen. "Nobody was looking for them," she said. "They had no one."

Mariama shrugged. "That's how predators hunt. You know that. They choose the weak. The vulnerable."

"They cull the herd," Sheila said.

Trey breathed in. Someone had left a newspaper on their table, the *Times*. The headlines were all about the ongoing plunge in the stock market, factories closing because not enough workers were showing up, oil prices skyrocketing.

The president counseled patience. But Anthony Harrison promised that, when *he* was elected, things would change, and fast.

"This herd won't put up with being culled," Trey said.

Mariama gave another shrug. "Then they'll be overwhelmed."

"**WHY DO I** have it inside me?" Trey asked. "The . . . mind?"

Mariama had hinted around, but until now he'd refused to talk about it. Suddenly, sitting here, he knew he was being ridiculous. After, there would be no room for anything but complete honesty.

She gave him a considering look, as if debating with herself how to answer.

"You saw," he went on. "You knew right away."

She nodded.

"That means you've seen it before."

After another moment, another nod. "Of course I have. There is nothing about the thieves that we haven't seen." She widened her eyes. "Except for their poison, they're not very complex."

"Complex enough to bring down a civilization," Sheila said.

Mariama shrugged. "A one-celled organism could do that."

She turned back to Trey. "How long had you been infected when Sheila removed the larva?"

"Two days, I think." He hesitated. "More. Closer to three."

She raised her hand and touched the side of his head. "And how did you feel . . . in here? Before the worm was removed?"

"Like my mind was being eaten from the inside."

"Yes." She dropped her hand. "Yes. Others have used similar words."

Sheila moved in her chair. "How much longer before he would have died from the surgery?"

"A few hours. Perhaps less. It is . . . not predictable."

"So that's what happens even if you live?" Trey found this hard to say. "Some of it gets left behind?"

"Or it causes some kind of permanent changes in the chemistry of the brain." Mariama frowned. "We do not know. In the Casamance, our scientists have not had the tools to study such things."

Sheila's gaze had turned inward. "I should have noticed sooner," she said. "And when I did, I shouldn't have hesitated."

"No." Mariama reached across the table and touched her gently on the arm. "You were brave. Even in the Casamance, many would not have been as brave as you."

Sheila didn't reply, but Trey thought she looked a little calmer within herself.

"And by waiting, we've gained something, too," Mariama went on.

Trey thought of the white light that had filled his brain as the Florida assault had begun, as the helicopters had burst into flames.

"Awareness," he said. "Knowledge."

Mariama nodded.

"But what has Trey lost?" Sheila said.

Mariama didn't reply at once. Trey glanced over at the

table next to theirs. A woman was huddled over her laptop with the news on the screen. She was watching a clip of Anthony Harrison giving a speech in front of a huge crowd. He was gesturing as he talked, pointing, his face alight with anger.

Trey looked back at Mariama. "What's inside me . . . it's never going away, is it?"

She tilted her head as she looked at him, her silence an answer.

"This—illness." He struggled to find the right word. "This condition. Does it get worse over time?"

After a moment, she said, "Yes. Most often . . . quite slowly. But, yes, it's progressive."

Sheila made an impatient movement. "Progressive," she said, spitting out the word. "I guess that leaves me only one option."

Trey said, "Which is?"

"To be the doctor who develops the cure."

THEY STOOD OUTSIDE the subway station. Eighty-sixth Street had always been a little shabby, but now it was virtually abandoned. Small groups of people, in threes and fours, headed into one or another of the electronics stores or fast-food restaurants, but the street had none of the market-day bustle it had once possessed.

"Five days till the election," Mariama said.

Sheila wrapped her coat closer. "What will happen?"

Trey said, "Harrison's going to win."

Mariama said, "And then—"

And then.

"Mary and Kait and I are seeing Jeremy Axelson and the Harrison campaign team tomorrow," Trey said.

"Will they listen?" Sheila asked.

"I doubt it."

Sheila said, "Is it worth it? Mary's worn out. I don't know how much help she'll be."

Trey said, "I don't think the greatest orator on earth could change their minds. And I'm no orator."

The wind gusted, blowing some old papers down the street and up into a brief messy whirlwind.

"But I have to try," he said.

FORTY-NINE

TWO CONVERSATIONS.

The first took place in a hotel on Fifty-fourth Street between Madison and Fifth. Trey had never noticed it before: the Gaumont, a redbrick, five-story town house surrounded by restaurants and boutiques, with only a single modest sign hanging in front to announce its presence.

Inside, it was opulent but tasteful, all burnished oak and brocaded walls and oil paintings of handsome ladies and gentlemen in ornate gilt frames. As Trey and Mary and Kait waited outside the conference room door on the top floor, a man wearing livery pushed a wooden cart carrying silver-topped dishes down the hall.

Trey watched him go past and thought about the *Titanic*. Its maiden voyage had lasted—what?—four days and ended in two hours. Who was to say that the voyage of the human race couldn't last for millennia and end just as suddenly?

Kait said, "I didn't think Mr. Axelson would like a place like this."

Mary, who had been paging through a glossy magazine she'd found on a side table inlaid with mother-of-pearl, looked up. "I doubt he picked it."

"Then why is he here?"

"To celebrate," Trey said.

"But—"

"To celebrate quietly," he said, "since he has to pretend he doesn't know what will happen on Election Day."

He looked at Kait. She was wearing Uggs, purple tights, a red skirt, and a white sweater, all obviously new.

"You look nice," Trey said. Then, surprising himself, "Actually, make that *beautiful*."

She stared down into her lap and blushed.

Mary managed a smile. "A Fifth Avenue shopping spree," she said and shrugged. "Heck, it's only money."

Trey nodded.

"Meaningless slips of paper," she said.

THE HEAVY DOOR to the conference room swung open, reflecting the shaded light cast by sconces set along the walls. A young woman in a business suit stood there. Her expression revealed a certain measure of curiosity, carefully masked.

"Please come in," she said.

She led them through the door into a lush, dim, redcarpeted room scattered with small desks, sideboards, gleaming tables, and soft-cushioned chairs. Two Secret Service men stood in the center of the room. At the far end, close to where the curtained windows let in some light from outside, sat Jeremy Axelson and a scowling man Trey recognized as Ron Stanhouse, Anthony Harrison's campaign manager. Two younger men wearing identical impatient expressions sat a little farther off.

Axelson stood, shook Mary's hand, and then bent over to get closer to Kait's level. "How are you doing, sweetie?" he said.

She looked into his face. "I'm fine." Then, "Are you going to listen to what Trey tells you?"

He blinked, then laughed as he straightened. "Of course we will."

"I mean it. *Listen*."

Some of the humor drained from his expression, and he raised his eyes to look at Trey. "I guess we'll have to see what Mr. Gilliard says, won't we?"

Whatever Mr. Gilliard was going to say, he had no intention of addressing it to Jeremy Axelson. Stepping past, he walked over and stood above Ron Stanhouse, who had not gotten to his feet or even rearranged his slouch.

Stanhouse leaned his head against the back of his shiny, brown-leather-and-gold-button chair. There was amusement tinged with malice in his expression.

"Behold," he said. "The man who won us an election."

Trey was silent.

"Without all your work—and that of your friends—we would never have connected the dots," Stanhouse went on, his lips twitching behind his beard. "You couldn't have helped us more if you'd been on the payroll."

"Well, that's what I live for, helping you." Trey kept his voice calm, but there was something in his expression that made Stanhouse's eyes widen. Trey felt the brief, light touch of Kait's hand on his arm.

"What I live for," he said again. "Yeah. I get it. It's victory lap time—or it will be in a few days. Well, go ahead, pat yourselves on the back and keep all the credit. I don't want it."

He took a step closer. Stanhouse, looking uncomfortable, stiffened a little in his chair.

"The question is," Trey went on, "what happens then?"

Stanhouse's lips twitched again. "Well, he'll work with Congress on a jobs package, and—"

Trey just looked at him, and after a moment Stanhouse wriggled his shoulders. "Why are you here, Gilliard?"

"To tell you: Back your guy off."

Stanhouse knew exactly what he was saying. The malice in his eyes rose to the surface. "Now? Why should we do that? Pre- or postelection, it's a winning issue."

"And a losing battle," Trey said.

Stanhouse looked disgusted. "Come on, Gilliard. Stop being such a pansy. They're just *bugs*."

Beside Trey, Kait made a small sound.

Trey felt his hands form fists. He thought of Agiru, the old Huli warrior, who'd said the same thing. But Agiru had understood the *binatang*. These men didn't.

"And how many lives," Trey said, "will you be willing to sacrifice to these bugs?"

Before Stanhouse could answer, Jeremy Axelson stepped between them. "Look, Trey," he said, "Governor Harrison has run on a platform of strength, of determination, and he won't back away from that now, no matter what your fears may be."

"He has a choice," Trey said.

Stanhouse said, in a tone of complete disgust, "Like what? What Chapman tried? Stashing a bunch of scientists in a lab somewhere, then waiting around for them to come up with a solution? Sure."

Again, it was Axelson who played the good cop. "You must understand that showing weakness now—or early in the first term—would send just the wrong message to the American people, to our allies, and to our enemies themselves."

"You saw what happened in Florida," Mary said to him.

"The president's mistake in Florida was in thinking too small," Stanhouse said. "I can promise you, we won't make the same mistake."

But Trey was barely listening to him. He'd heard this boilerplate before.

Instead, he was thinking about what Axelson had said.

Our allies.

With a growing sense of horror, he said, "You're co-ordinating an attack on the thieves with other countries."

Stanhouse smiled at him. "You know only the president is allowed to do that . . . and our man isn't president. Yet."

Trey ignored this. "When is it going to happen, then? The attack. On Inauguration Day?"

Stanhouse didn't answer directly, but he didn't need to. Inauguration Day or soon thereafter, it didn't matter.

"Listen to me," Trey said. "*Listen*. It won't work. You'll lose."

We'll lose.

But Stanhouse was flapping a hand in dismissal.

"Those creatures," he said, "will not be allowed to rule our lives."

The meeting was over.

THE SECOND CONVERSATION, via telephone, was much shorter.

"Mr. Gilliard," Nathan Holland, the president's chief of staff, said. "What can I do for you?"

His voice, as gravelly as ever, echoed with exhaustion. He sounded a hundred years old.

Trey took a breath. "You need to tell President Chapman—"

"I have a better idea," Holland said. "Tell him yourself."

Trey said, "What?"

"Please hold," Holland said, bitter amusement in his voice, "for the president of the United States."

Waiting, Trey was struck by a vivid memory: sitting in various hotel rooms on his journeys into and out of the wilderness and watching repeats of *The West Wing* on television. How strange it always felt when the president talked to regular people.

There was a crackling over the receiver, and then a new voice, deeper than Holland's and more polished. Familiar.

"This is Sam Chapman," the voice said.

Trey plunged ahead. "Mr. President, you were on the right track. Your approach was on target, and it has to go on even if you lose. Somehow you need to convince Harrison of this."

"My approach?" There was an edge of amusement in the president's tone. "Which one?"

"The smart one. Calling together a team of scientists. Jack Parker from the American Museum, Clare Shapiro from Rockefeller—"

"I shut that effort down," the president said.

"Yes, I know, but you shouldn't have."

There was a pause, and then the president said, "You're right. It was a terrible mistake."

Trey was silent.

Chapman's voice was quiet. "You're far from the first to tell me this, of course. I should have had the will to see that effort through and not worried so much about losing the election."

His laugh was quieter than Holland's, but just as mirthless. "The election! I couldn't have done more to guarantee my defeat if I'd been working for the Harrison campaign myself."

Still Trey didn't speak.

"Be honest with me, though, Mr. Gilliard," Chapman went on. "Would it have made a difference, leaving that initiative in place? Would all my experts have figured out a way to defeat these creatures?"

"Defeat them?" Trey said. "No. Live with them? Co-exist?" He took in a breath. "Maybe not. But it was the best of a bad set of options."

Now it was Chapman's turn to be silent for a few moments. When he finally spoke again, his voice was very quiet. "As you may have noticed, we're not much for 'living with' in this country. We don't do coexistence well. I'm also afraid—"

He fell silent.

Trey finished the sentence. "That the next administration won't do 'coexistence' at all."

Chapman sighed. "Nor will they listen to a word I—or anyone in my administration—says. Reinventing the wheel is a longtime tradition in our political system."

"I know," Trey said. "But I had to call."

To try.

The president cleared his throat. "I told Nathan I wanted to speak with you," he said. "To thank you for everything you've done since this all started."

Trey said, "Done?"

"You and Dr. Connelly. Going on television, talking to magazines. Providing real information. Trying to help people stay calm."

Trey said, "For all the good it did."

"Trying to do good counts."

"Thank you." Trey took a breath. "Mr. President?"

"Yes?"

"That secure location where you went after . . . Florida."

"You mean where they bundled me off to after the disaster. What about it?"

"Just . . . keep it handy."

Again the president laughed. "Thank you, Mr. Gilliard. But I'm not going to hide behind locked doors while my countrymen die around me. Not this time. Not again."

Trey was silent.

"I'm still the captain. Win or lose, that's how I'll always think of myself. If the ship goes down, I'm going down with it."

FIFTY

ELECTION DAY.

Trey woke up pouring with sweat. Sheila, beside him in the bed, held him as he fought. "Trey—" she said. Then, when he focused on her, still half trapped by his dreams, she said, "What's it . . . saying?"

It.

Trey heard nothing but silence. It didn't matter. He was filled with cold certainty.

"It happens today," he said. "Not Inauguration Day. Today."

Her hand covered her mouth. "How can you be sure?"

Trey was quiet. How to explain the voice inside?

There was no explaining it. To understand you'd have to be like him. Not completely human anymore.

Sheila, watching, believing, took a deep breath and let her hand drop back to the sheets. Her chin lifted.

"If we have time," she said, "I still want to vote."

*   *   *

THE SILENCE ECHOING inside him, Trey made a series of telephone calls.

Everyone was ready. They'd all been ready for days.

Except one. The one who mattered most.

"Still waiting on that part," Malcolm Granger said, his voice over the phone as cheerful and easygoing as always. "You told me we had days. Weeks."

"I was wrong. Can you get it today?"

Malcolm laughed. "Okay. Gonna take some hours, though. We got hours?"

The hive mind was as quiet as if it had fled forever, though he knew it hadn't. Trey knew it was there, though. Hiding.

No, not hiding. Waiting.

"I don't know," he said.

"No worries." Malcolm's tone was light. "Doesn't matter."

Trey didn't say anything.

"Listen," Malcolm said. "Whatever it's like when the time comes, we've flown through worse, you and me."

SHEILA WANTED TO watch the news. The reporters said that voting was light across the country. This was especially true in rural areas, places that required long drives, long walks, visibility, in order to cast your vote. But in cities, too.

During these last few days, the thieves had nearly disappeared. Only a scattering of reports of new attacks had come in, and many of those were late accounts of incidents that had taken place days earlier.

An unusual number of absentee ballots had been requested and filled out, yet overall voting numbers were way down. Only a small fraction of the typical turnout for a presidential election was making it to the polls.

"Low turnout favors the challenger," Sheila said. "It's the people who want change who go to the polling place no matter what."

"America, you have a choice to make," Anthony Harrison had said in his speech on Election Eve. "A life lived in fear . . . or one filled with hope?"

Words. They were just words.

There was no longer any choice at all.

"LET'S GO."

Trey looked at her. She returned his gaze, and color rose to her pale cheeks. Without speaking, she got to her feet and picked up her fleece jacket from the back of a chair.

"No matter where I've been living, I've stayed a citizen of this country, and I've always voted," she said, slipping her arms into it. "I even changed my registration to be able to vote here. I'm not going to miss this one."

Trey didn't argue, just walked to the door and waited as she found her shoulder bag.

Don't be caught too far apart when the end comes, Elena Stavros had said.

He wasn't going to convince her to stay in the apartment.

And he wasn't going to let her out of his sight.

* * *

A BUS WENT by down on Seventh Avenue, a flash of blue-white light, a squeal of brakes that sounded like a distress call. Trey could see a couple of dark figures inside. A few cars, windows rolled tightly up against the chill—or in a hopeless gesture at safety—followed. Other than that, the avenue was empty.

Nearly empty.

Sheila said, *"Damn."*

The man walked past without seeing them. He was wearing suit pants, black socks but no shoes. No jacket or dress shirt, just a sleeveless undershirt.

His eyes gleamed silver in the streetlight.

As he passed, they could see the thief on the back of his neck, its stinger buried deep. A summoning, out in the open.

Trey caught a glimpse of the nightmare that had woken him that morning: Hundreds, thousands of people with their thief riders. Filling the streets. Filling the city.

The doomed man walked into a trash-strewn alley between a closed flower shop and an empty storefront that had once housed a pet store. Trey began to follow.

"Forget it," Sheila said. "Let's go."

Then, uncharacteristically, she added, "Trey, I've seen enough."

But he hadn't. He took a few steps into the mouth of the alley. "Come here," he said.

Still she hung back.

"Sheila."

She came up beside him. The man they'd followed had slumped back against the flower shop's crumbling brick wall.

A few feet farther down the alley lay a second man, and at their feet a woman was flat on her back. She looked as if she were staring up through the gap between the buildings, trying to see the stars.

"Three . . ." Sheila's voice was just a breath. "Together."

But this was only part of it. "Look," Trey said.

Sheila saw. These were no homeless people, no pierside prostitutes, no runaways. Not the ones so easily sacrificed while the rest stayed safe.

The second man's coat was open, revealing a dark suit, white shirt, a tie that might have been red but looked black in the faint light. The skirt of the woman's expensive suit was hiked up, revealing sheer hose that had run and legs bluish from the cold.

Trey raised his gaze, peering into the shadows. He knew what he was looking for, and in a few moments he found it. Two pairs of eyes. No, three, faceted gleams like green diamonds reflecting moonlight.

Darker than the shadows, the thieves moved forward to the mouth of the alley. Then stopped there, a half dozen feet from where Trey and Sheila stood. Staying far enough away to be safe from Sheila, but still sending a message as comprehensible as if they'd used words.

Don't come any closer. We'll sacrifice ourselves to save our young, but we'll kill you first.

"Let's go," Trey said. Sheila nodded.

But then a sobbing woman pushed past them.

SHE WAS BEYOND reach and down the alley before Trey or Sheila could do a thing to stop her. He took a step to follow, but Sheila grabbed his arm, hard, and yanked him back.

"No!" she said. Then, more quietly, "Trey, it's too late."

She was right. He took a breath and steeled himself to watch what happened next. The inevitable.

Only it wasn't what he expected.

He'd been sure that the thieves would make short work of the woman, but that was not what took place. Although they all rose high on their legs in the alarm posture, the wasps stayed where they were. Eyes on Trey, on Sheila, on the street beyond, as if expecting—guarding against—a further attack.

Leaving the woman down the alley . . . to what?

Half lost in the shadows, she knelt over the man Trey and Sheila had seen entering. Pulling on his arms, trying to get him to his feet, calling out to him, her voice almost drowned by her tears.

He lay there, dead weight, unresponsive. Lost to her, and even she must have known it.

But as Trey and Sheila watched, the other two hosts stirred. Stirred as if awakening, rose to their knees, and reached for the woman.

She screamed.

Even with his sharp vision, Trey could make out only a shifting in the darkness, a tangle of limbs. The blur of her face as she fell back, the white of her stretched-wide eyes. Her hands reaching up, grasping at air.

He heard a loud, dull impact, the crack of something—her skull—breaking. The woman's second scream turned into deep-throated moans, and then silence. Yet still the two hosts worked at her body.

Trey thought about the ravening prisoner Thomas Nyramba had taken him to see in Uganda. About what that man, his brain controlled as these ones were, would have done if he'd been able to break his bonds.

"Let's go," Sheila said. Her voice was harsh in the silence.

Trey looked at her, and though he didn't speak, she understood his question.

"Home," she said.

Still he didn't move.

She made a sound that might have been a laugh. "Voting!" she said. "Now? What a ridiculous dream."

TREY'S CELL PHONE sounded just as they walked through the apartment door. "Granger," the caller ID read.

"We'll be ready in an hour," Malcolm said. "Get your butts over here."

Trey opened his mouth to say okay, they were on their way, but he never spoke the words. At that instant, his brain filled, overflowed, burst with white light, and then the phone had fallen from his hand and he was lying on his back on the floor.

Sheila knelt over him, her eyes full of panic, but he could barely see her. Her mouth was moving, but he couldn't hear anything but the sound of wings.

Information poured into him. Messages from the hive mind, a torrent of them, like frames spliced together from a thousand, a million, different movies. Overwhelming him, drowning him, even as he understood what he was seeing, what was happening right now, at this moment, all over the world.

There was just enough of his mind left to understand that he and Sheila had waited too long.

FIFTY-ONE

TREY ZOOMED ABOVE a blood-tainted river, looking down at a mass of floating bodies. Every moment there were more, arms drooping and flapping in the current. Not waving, drowning. Drowned.

He flew amid a huge crowd, thousands of people, fleeing from a stadium. He saw them crushing, trampling, each other, witnessed those who escaped being picked off by the whirling cloud he was part of. One falling, then twenty, then a hundred. Clutching at their eyes, rolling on the ground, jerking and twitching.

He spun away from an oil tanker just as it broadsided a cruise ship. The resulting explosion caught him, killed him—he could feel his body shrivel in a wave of fire—but it didn't matter. He was instantly somewhere else, still alive, still part of the greater whole.

Such scenes and a thousand more, a million, flooding his brain. His human brain, not designed or equipped to contain, to survive this flood.

His human brain. He grabbed hold of that sense of recognition and used it to unite the shattered pieces that were still him.

I'm Trey Gilliard. I exist—

His vision cleared a little. He heard screams and shouts and knew they were coming not from within him but from the street outside the apartment. Sirens blared, then were cut off by the shriek of rending metal and a shattering crash. Another scream, a high-pitched sound of despair that seemed to go on and on.

Black smoke came around the door and through the windows into the apartment.

Sheila, still kneeling above Trey, was listening on his phone. She said, "Okay," snapped it shut, and bent close to him. Her face was bone white, but her expression was determined. Composed. Sheila the doctor, doing what had to be done.

"We have to go," she said.

Trey said, "No."

Or maybe he just mouthed the word. It didn't matter. Sheila understood it. "That's not a request," she said. "Come on."

Then, as his head spun from the immense keening hum, she got her shoulder under his arm and hoisted him up.

He worked, tried, to help. Somehow he got his feet under him. Not quite dead weight, though he would have fallen again if she'd let go of him.

"Where?" he managed to ask.

Sheila grimaced. He could see the tendons standing out in her neck, along her jaw, but she didn't waver.

"The park," she said.

Prospect Park. A block and a half away.

"Long Meadow."

Even farther. He shook his head. It was impossible.

Another siren blared in the distance and was cut off. He heard shouts, a loud rushing noise, what sounded like gunshots, and, farther off, an explosion. The apartment was filled with smoke.

Trey swayed on his feet, the images racing through his head joining with his own visions, his own memories. Every place he'd ever visited spun in the kaleidoscope. He could feel them being sucked out of his shattered brain and into the vast processor that was the hive mind.

The campsite where he'd lived for four months in the thorn forests of Peru, undiscovered temples rising out of jungles in Cambodia, the lion that had stood nose to nose with him at the mouth of a tent in Botswana. The grizzly bear in Montana.

His mother. His father. Christopher when he was a child. Past, present, real, or imagined, all part of the maelstrom.

It was as if time had no meaning, as if there was no place—no living thing—beyond the thieves' grasp.

Trey finally saw exactly how the hive functioned. The kaleidoscope shaking his mind free from its moorings functioned perfectly for them. They didn't need to ponder, to remember, to analyze. The wasps just saw everything at the same instant, saw and processed and acted.

It was his weakness, his humanity, that was driving him mad.

Sheila shook him. Coming back, he heard more crashes, three distant explosions in quick succession, and—most of all—the sound of wings. Not inside his head. Out there.

"We're going," she said. *"Now."*

They went, his legs maddeningly weak beneath him. Inside his head he was flying, but here he could barely walk. Yet somehow they made it across the floor to the front door and out onto the stoop.

The outside world was wreathed with black smoke billowing from the brownstone across the street. Red flames licked the sky, while white ones ate the building's heart. Already the inferno had spread to the buildings on either side.

Three fire engines, two pump trucks and one hook-and-ladder, blocked the street, engines on and lights spinning. Trey could see the bodies of three firefighters sprawled on the asphalt and one slumped behind the wheel of the hook-and-ladder. No one was left alive to hold the hoses, which writhed and danced like giant worms, vomiting streams of water first toward the sky and then in racing rivers down the street.

As they watched, the brownstone collapsed in on itself. A column of flame rose in the air. A landslide of rubble slid forward and, with a sound that shook the street, entombed everything beneath it: bodies, trucks, spewing hoses.

A blast of hot air blew past them. Thieves died in the collapse and in the burst of flames that followed. Trey saw them, felt them, *was* them. Again and again he died, but still he stood there, still he lived.

Trey saw how foolish, how weak, it was to be human. To care about something so inconsequential as a single life, when all that mattered was the whole.

Sheila pulled him forward, got him moving again.

Together they made it down the steps to the street. Then half ran, half stumbled toward the row of leafless trees that marked the edge of the park. Thieves flew freely all around them, buzzing in for the kill, peeling away when they sensed what Trey—and especially Sheila—carried.

Traffic was stopped at every corner, cars entangled like sculptures, like works of kinetic art. Stopped forever. The arteries of a city could be so easily blocked. A vast infarction, a heart attack New York could not survive.

Malcolm was just thirty miles away, but it might as well have been a thousand.

The contents of breached gas tanks spread across the streets. New fires were already erupting here and there, spreading, licking at the bases of the nearby buildings. Smoke came billowing upward from a subway entrance, carrying with it hopeless cries of terror and agony.

Trey knew that no one would be coming to fight any of these fires. By morning much of the city would be aflame.

How many other cities around the world as well?

Bodies lay here and there, but not as many as he had expected. The electricity was still on, and he could see faces in many of the windows. The horror-struck expressions of people who were terrified to stay where they were, but more terrified to go out.

He thought of the great tsunami that had struck Japan in 2011. Some people tried to flee and were swept away. Others chose to hunker down . . . and were swept away. Condemned to death, no matter which choice they made.

It went against the human belief system. There was always supposed to be an alternative. Survival was always assumed to be an option.

It was the same here. Some humans—the ones who fought back, who seemed like a threat—were being killed now, while others would be left alive to carry the thieves' young within them. Left alive for days, even weeks. But doomed nonetheless.

It was simple: Slave-makers never let anyone go free. One way or another, the only purpose in a slave's life was to serve.

FIFTY-TWO

THEY MADE IT to the park. The branches above their heads stretched like skeletal white fingers into a reddish sky filled with flowing flags of smoke. In the darkness ahead, footsteps thudded, people screamed and wailed, a dog barked hysterically, and ten thousand wings whirred.

Behind them, the staccato thud of explosions and the roar of another falling building.

A half dozen steps down the path, Trey broke away from Sheila, stopped, and bent over. The crescendo inside his head raged, a battle, a war between the dictates of the hive and his desperate attempts to keep himself from being conquered.

Sheila squatted beside him.

"Why are we here?" he said.

She didn't answer. Just reached for him, helped him straighten. Through the onslaught, he could see the mix of emotions in her expression. Compassion. Understanding. Love.

"Not much farther," she said.

They moved on down the trail, but Trey knew it was hopeless. Wherever they were going, whatever Sheila's plan, it was too late. He was losing the battle, becoming unmoored. Only Sheila, her strong body holding him up, kept him standing on the earth.

"You can do this," she said into his ear.

He thought, *Maybe this form can. This . . . shell.*

But not me.

BODIES LAY SPRAWLED across the path, cut down as they ran. Eyeless faces turned toward the sky.

The living cowered in the shadows, their gazes following Trey and Sheila's progress.

Others were here, too. Neither dead nor alive. As Trey and Sheila stepped onto the expanse of Long Meadow, they saw a dozen shadowy forms moving across the grass. Hosts in their final rabid stage.

Roused by the frenzy of the thieves' final assault, the hosts moved among the living. Killing those who fought back, holding down those who did not resist. Thieves arched their backs and plunged their ovipositors into the flesh of people who lay on the ground, unprotesting, paralyzed with fear.

Moving fast, three of the late-stage hosts came across the night-gray grass. A middle-aged man, a young woman, and a girl in a bloodstained white dress. Trey, barely able to move, merely watched as their hands reached toward him. But Sheila stepped forward, put herself between them.

Then a nearby thief relayed a warning to the hive mind,

which immediately assessed it and sent it back out again. *Beware!* It was like a shout inside Trey's head, and he knew that the jumbled remnants of the human hosts' dying minds heard it, too. The three of them hesitated, staring at Trey and Sheila through silvery eyes before turning away.

Sheila was scanning the sky. Then, making a sound in her throat, she pulled out her cell phone. Glanced at the screen, shook her head, and dropped the phone to the ground. Turned her eyes to the sky again.

And put her hands over her ears.

At first Trey didn't understand why. Then he did.

The sound, unrecognizable, penetrated his shattered brain. A horrendous clattering roar growing louder and louder, causing even the hive mind to give off a signal of distress. Something was coming, a light and commotion in the sky above the trees to the north.

It came into view: a huge passenger jet passing overhead, perhaps fifty feet above the ground. Upside down, its windows lit, figures glimpsed in the light. Flames spat from the engine in its tail.

Trey was inside the cockpit, looking through the eyes of the single wasp within. The pilots were dead, he could see that, lying facedown over the cockpit controls.

The screaming hulk disappeared from view. An instant later, there was a tremendous blast that turned the sky a brilliant white. The trees at the far end of Long Meadow ignited, casting dancing black shadows that stretched across the grass.

The hive-mind fragment aboard the plane died and was instantly sloughed off, as meaningless as a flake of skin.

Trey lay sprawled on the ground, Sheila beside him. He rolled onto his back, staring upward.

At first he didn't see the lights above him in the flickering sky. Lights that moved, seemed to stand still, and grew brighter again.

Sheila got to her feet. She pulled off her sweater and waved it in the air.

"TREY," SHE SAID to him, "get up." A catch in her voice. *"Please."*

Amid the rushing of wings, the shocks that made the ground beneath him twitch and spasm, the smoke that carried the smells of burning rubber, plastic, wood, flesh, Trey saw a small two-passenger helicopter land on the meadow just twenty feet from where he lay.

Malcolm sat behind the stick inside the plastic bubble.

"If we don't get over there," Sheila said, "they'll kill him."

Trey knew she was right. The thieves would soon investigate this new arrival, judge it a threat, eliminate it.

Even now, he was with the half dozen closest ones, all turning their attention to the helicopter and the enemy within.

Sheila was running across the meadow, but Trey knew that she was going to be too late. Feet could never compete with wings. Already the wasps were finding their way through the air vents and the gap beneath the rotor and roof. Only a few seconds remained before they fulfilled their assignment: to end one more human life.

Malcolm's life.

Trey never knew how he had the thought, or whether it was a thought at all. Maybe it was just another step in being absorbed by the hive mind. Maybe it was just part of the process of abandoning who he was, who he'd been.

But somehow at that instant, Trey understood something. Something he had only guessed at when his mind blurred, split in two as he watched the attack in Florida.

He was not just a witness to the hive mind. He was a participant. He, too, was part of the whole, adding his own shard of information to the vast data trove that forged a single organism from an entire species.

He didn't have to just watch as his friend died.

Lying on the ground, unmoving, he cast his own consciousness free. He was no longer trapped in the husk of his body. He was there, in the helicopter, alongside the wasps who had come to kill Malcolm.

He was there, sounding an alarm.

Danger.

Infection.

Death.

Adding his voice to the constant stream of warnings that ruled the organism's actions. The same warnings that sent a flock of pigeons hurtling away from the falcon's talons, a school of fish flashing away from the marlin's sword. A burst of information designed to be instantly processed and obeyed, not questioned.

You need intelligence to question.

The thieves inside the bubble hesitated for an instant. Then, as one, they pulled back, turned their entry points into exits, and were gone. Leaving Malcolm alone, still alive.

Trey saw Sheila reach the helicopter, saw Malcolm open the hatch, saw—and heard—her shout something. But he couldn't understand what she said. Human language no longer made sense.

A moment later Sheila and Malcolm were both running across the grass toward him. Toward his body. Then Malcolm had him in an embrace, a fireman's carry, and they were heading back toward the helicopter.

When they reached it, Sheila climbed through the hatch and then reached back for Trey as Malcolm clambered over them and sat behind the controls. As she hoisted him up, and he struggled to help, the helicopter lifted from the ground.

His legs were still dangling from the open hatch. He could hear Sheila's tortured breaths as he began to slip from her grasp. But then, with one last convulsive effort, she pulled him to her. Trey's head banged against the edge of the passenger seat, something whacked him in the stomach, stealing his breath, but he was on board, the hatch door slamming shut behind him.

On their knees, they clung to each other as the helicopter rose through skeins of smoke, wallowing in the heavy, wet autumn air. Malcolm, grim faced, fought with the controls, swinging the wavering craft around to face north. The engine groaned and complained, the rotors stuttered, but their tiny lifeboat stayed aloft.

Through a thousand eyes, Trey looked out over New York. Below, the city was going dark. One block, another, and then more, more, a cascade of failures of the grid that would never be reversed.

Going dark, but for the flames.

As they flew up the East River, the hive mind's ultimate triumph rose in a wave, a climax, inside him once again. The scene overlain with a hundred others, the effortless worldwide destruction of the most powerful species on earth. Its hugest metal and stone towers crumbling like a termite mound under an anteater's claws, leaving the people hiding within as soft and vulnerable as the white ants.

Seemingly impregnable species with no defense against such an attack.

The images spewing through Trey's brain were so horrific he would have done anything to avoid seeing them. But he had no choice. They were inside him. They *were* him.

As the helicopter flew past an Empire State Building lit only by fire, he gave up at last, let the remnants of his consciousness go. Surrendered and was at peace.

FIFTY-THREE

HE AWOKE TO a quiet, steady humming noise.

Not wings, neither inside nor outside his head. And not the frantic chop of a helicopter fighting its way through treacherous air. A steady, even sound, felt as much as heard.

He opened his eyes, tried to orient himself. First understanding nothing, but eventually attaining some kind of awareness. This strange shape was a body. His body, lying on its back.

His conscious mind still somewhere else. It was a tapestry so tattered you could see the light gleaming through it. A frayed flag hanging from a pole, pieces of it missing, gone forever.

He stared upward as his consciousness gathered itself. Above him was a curved surface, rows of yellow-green lights. He watched them for a while and then suddenly understood what he was looking at: the ceiling of an airplane. He was lying in the center aisle of a small jet. The hum was the sound of engines cruising through still, thin air.

His awareness sharpened. The shapes around him were faces. Sheila's face, upside down because his head was resting on her lap.

Then Kait's. Kait was squatting next to him, half in the aisle, half between two rows of seats. She had a white towel in her hand, an ice bucket at her feet, and as he shifted his eyes to look at her, she placed the cool, wet cloth against his forehead.

She saw him looking at her. Her expression was calm, only her bloodshot eyes showing any signs of emotion. "Hey," she said.

He moved his mouth, but no sound came out. Even that effort made her face blur, and he closed his eyes again.

Lying there in the dark, he thought: *At least the hive mind is quiet.*

He had that thought and realized at the same instant that he was capable of thought. That brought him part of the way back.

Listening inside, he heard only the most distant sound of wings, of screams. The thieves were still at work, but not here, and not with the intensity he'd witnessed—participated in—before unconsciousness had taken him.

For now, at least, he had been released.

He opened his eyes. Focused and tried again and managed to say, "Hey, you."

The corners of Kait's mouth turned upward. Before she could speak, though, Sheila tilted Trey's head and held a plastic cup before his mouth.

"Drink," she said.

He drank the cool water and felt his mind knit together

a little more. Taking a deep breath, he struggled to get up. At first, Sheila protested and tried to keep him where he was, but eventually she sighed and helped him sit.

He'd been lying near the back of the Citation X corporate jet that Malcolm had spent weeks refitting for long-distance travel. In preparation for this one-way journey that Trey and Sheila had almost missed.

Among the passengers, about a dozen in total, he recognized a handful. But he knew who—and what—they all were: Doctors. Scientists. Architects. Carpenters. Brilliant researchers and people who knew how to fix anything that broke.

More empty seats than had been intended, though. Trey and Sheila clearly hadn't been the only ones trapped by the thieves' sudden attack. They were just the only ones who'd been rescued.

He looked at Sheila. She was wearing the same clothes she'd had on in Brooklyn. She hadn't even washed her face, which was smudged with soot and streaked with old tears.

"That's twice now," he said, and he took in a long, ragged breath. "That you've saved me."

She tilted her head and looked into his eyes. "Just give me a chance to take a breath before you make me do it again."

Then she leaned forward and hugged him.

When they pulled apart, he said, "Where are we?"

She glanced at her watch. "About three hours out, four to go."

Trey had no memory of it, but he knew they'd left from Westchester County Airport. Now they were heading east over the Atlantic.

He looked around again, and his heart gave a sudden thump. "Where's Mariama?"

Sheila made a calming gesture with her hands. "Don't worry. She's here." A gesture toward the front of the plane. "In the cockpit."

"Help me up," he said.

"Trey . . ."

But already he was pulling himself to his feet. She helped him, and after a moment he stood, each hand on the back of a seat, propping himself up. All around, people were watching, but no one said anything.

Looking at him as if he were a walking corpse. Like he was still . . . the *other*.

He made his way forward. The cockpit door was ajar, the compartment beyond lit only with green and blue instrument lights.

With care, he pushed the door open, his eyes taking in the three figures within. Malcolm and a solidly built, blond-haired young man in khakis and a short-sleeved shirt sat at the controls. Both of them glanced back at him, then returned their attention to the black night that the jet was arrowing through.

Standing between them was Mariama, who turned. Her eyes widened and her mouth opened. Then she stepped forward and gave Trey a fierce hug.

"Don't break me, please," he managed to gasp.

She released him, stared up into his face. "You're very strong," she said.

"I don't feel strong."

Her eyes were still wide. "I didn't expect you ever to awaken."

Trey didn't reply. He looked out the cockpit window

at an icy half-moon hanging in the darkness, and then down at Malcolm sitting in the copilot's seat.

"You know," he said, "thanks."

Malcolm glanced back. "One-time offer, mate."

Trey said, "Deal."

"And if Nick here wasn't staying behind, ready to fly this bird without me, I would've left you and that brave girlfriend of yours to fate."

Trey, knowing it was the truth, shifted his gaze. "You, too, Nick. I owe you."

Nick said, "No worries."

"Christ," Malcolm said, a rough edge to his voice that Trey hadn't heard before. "Have to tell you, when those bugs were coming for me, I worried plenty."

Mariama said, "How did you protect yourself?"

"Protect myself?" Malcolm gave a laugh. "I 'protected myself' by sitting there and waiting for them to bite me." He shook his head. "Didn't do a thing. They just, like . . . disappeared on their own. Like they suddenly decided I wouldn't taste good. It must've been my lucky day."

Again Mariama turned to look at Trey. He returned her gaze but didn't say anything.

"Strong," she said again.

He was silent.

A FEW MINUTES later another piece of the fragile quilt of Trey's mind knitted itself back together. He remembered something new: a glimpse he'd gotten of LaGuardia Airport in the distance as they passed nearby in the helicopter. The runways blocked by abandoned airplanes and emergency vehicles. A jumbo jet broken nearly in half, flames belching from the passenger windows.

Trey said, "Your runway was clear?"

Nick said, "Clear enough."

"Man's being modest." Malcolm's voice held echoes of what Trey guessed had been a terrifying experience, even for him. "He got us off the ground with about three feet of clearance."

"I closed my eyes," Mariama said.

There was silence for a while. Then Trey asked, "Is air-traffic control still broadcasting?"

"What? Wake up, pal." Now Malcolm sounded uncharacteristically angry. "The last controller went off-air about fifteen minutes after we were airborne. You know the last thing he said before he started screaming?"

Trey waited.

" 'Don't land. Whatever you do, *don't land*.' "

The words hung in the quiet cockpit as the jet flew on, alone in the empty black sky.

A PALE SMEAR on the horizon ahead. Emerging from the smear, a darker line. The west coast of Africa.

The plane banked and headed south, staying over the water, skirting the coast.

"Is it over?" Mariama asked.

They were sitting in the back, where six seats faced each other. Trey, Mariama, Sheila, Mary, and Kait.

The core group, missing only one.

Trey went deep inside himself to seek an answer. "No," he said at last. Then, ". . . and yes. I think—" He struggled with the words. "I think it will take weeks or months before it's really over."

Weeks or months of unimaginable deprivation, of agony, for those humans who were still alive.

"But if you're asking whether the war is over, then I think the answer is yes. Over and lost."

"To the thieves, it's not a war," Mariama said, sounding like Jack. "They don't know the meaning of the word 'war.' To them, this was just another raid."

Trey thought about what New York City—what other cities—must look like now. "Whatever you choose to call it," he said, "we made it too damn easy for them."

"Yes."

Then Mariama's mouth firmed and her chin lifted.

"But never again," she said.

THE PLANE BEGAN a long, slow descent. Trey, sitting beside the window, looked out and watched as the land approached. Along the coast, a strip of white sand stretched out of sight in both directions, blue waves rolling to the shore. Beyond lay gray-green savanna, red earth, and the glistening silver stripe of a river. And, beyond that, the vast, rumpled green of the unbroken rain forest canopy stretching to the horizon.

Morning in the Casamance. Birds of prey—honey buzzards and black kites and a martial eagle—had already risen on the air currents and hung still, unmoving, as if pinned to the sky.

Beside him, Kait gazed at the forest and said, "It looks like broccoli."

Trey remembered that Malcolm had said the same thing. All those months ago, on the day they'd first glimpsed the thieves' homeland.

"One advantage to the rain forest," Sheila said from across the aisle. "You'll never run out of things to draw."

Below, a lighter streak at the edge of the forest resolved itself into a long paved airstrip. Trey recognized the field where he and Malcolm had almost crashed their plane, but it had been transformed.

Beside the airstrip stood a wooden hangar with a tin roof, a limp wind sock drooping from a pole, and, pulled out of the way, a two-seater Piper like the ones Trey and Malcolm had flown so often. Around the hangar stood a small cluster of figures.

The jet took a long swing over the forest, bumping a little on the air currents, and then aimed its nose at the runway. As they swung around, Trey caught a glimpse of buildings below. Wood and stone dormitories, storage facilities, a medical clinic, a bigger tin-roofed structure that he knew was a laboratory. People moved between the buildings or stood looking up at the approaching jet.

They'd made remarkable progress, but the hard work was just beginning. The work of keeping the human species from going extinct.

The jet made its final descent, touched the ground, bounced along, and pulled to a stop.

MARIAMA LED THE way down the stairs. Sheila and Kait helped Trey follow.

About a dozen people were there to greet them. Trey

recognized only two. One was Seydou Honso, who wrapped his arms around his daughter like he would never let go of her again.

Honso and others here in the Casamance had understood what was happening. Months before, they'd looked into the future, known what it meant, and begun to prepare.

The other familiar face belonged to Clare Shapiro, tanned and fit. She'd been one of the first foreigners to join the Senegalese.

The team she'd gathered—scientists from a dozen disciplines and as many nations—was already studying the alkaloid that provided the "vaccine" against the thieves. Unlocking its secrets. Looking toward the day when it could be synthesized, mass-produced, used to save whatever was left of the world.

Somewhere in the compound, Trey knew, he'd find Elena Stavros, a member of Clare's team. She was here with her husband and the two girls whose photo Trey had spotted on her desk. He was looking forward to seeing them.

If Elena hadn't told him about Mariama's phone call, none of them would be here today.

"You look like something the cat drug in, Gilliard," Clare said.

He summoned a smile. "And you look revoltingly healthy, Shapiro."

"I know. It doesn't suit me." She grinned, then stepped forward and, wonder of wonders, hugged him.

When she stepped back again, though, her expression was somber. "Once you're settled," she said, "come see me. We'll figure out what we can do for you."

He nodded.

She looked up into his face. "We've lost all contact with the outside. Did you see what happened?"

"I saw enough." He closed his eyes for a moment. "I'll tell you more later."

"But we're on our own now."

"Yes."

Clare drew in a long breath. "Then I'd better get back to work."

As she walked away, Trey felt someone nudge him. It was Kait, pointing over his shoulder.

"Look," she said.

Trey looked, noticing for the first time the wooden sign nailed to the side of the hangar.

Refugia, it read in drippy black letters. *Welcome!*

"*Refugia*," Kait said, sounding out the unfamiliar word. "What does that mean?"

Sheila came up to stand beside them. She linked one arm with Trey's, draped her other over Kait's shoulder. Her face was gaunt, pale, filled with sorrow but also fierce determination.

"It means home," she said.

EPILOGUE
Refugia

MY FATHER USED to talk about a book, a novel, he'd read when he was a teenager. It was about a society that had survived an apocalypse, but all they had left to remind them of what came before was . . . a to-do list.

With items on it like, "Drop clothes at laundry." Things meant to be forgotten ten minutes after they were written down.

But they weren't forgotten. Not by the survivors, who were so desperate to have something, *anything*, to remind them of the past, that they began to worship the list.

Dad said that the story didn't seem very believable to him even when he was a kid. But something about it must have stuck in his head. Because soon after we arrived here, he started to insist that those of us who had been there, in the Last World, had a responsibility to write down what we remembered. To leave a record for those who were too young back then, or who were born here, or who just chose to forget.

He said we had to make sure we never get stuck with shopping lists for memories.

So here I am, sitting inside and writing, even though I'd rather be doing almost anything else. But no one gets to opt out. We all take turns, writing down our memories and telling about the lives we live now.

So future archaeologists will know we were here, we were human, and we helped build the Next World out of the ashes of the last one.

YOU'RE SUPPOSED TO write an entry every six months. I confess: It's been more like two years. One of the reasons I get away with this is because I'm the colony's resident illustrator/art teacher. I usually tell Refugia's story the best way I can—through pictures.

Back at the very beginning, on the morning after the Last World ended, Mom told me I'd never run out of things to draw. She was right, of course.

Though all I had back then was the single pad and plastic bag of colored pencils I'd brought with me. As if, when I used them up, I'd only have to visit the local art supply store to get new ones. Sure. Uh-huh.

But I was lucky. During the early years, when Malcolm and Nick were heading out on their foraging expeditions, somehow they found me a huge supply in a warehouse in what used to be the Gambia: cases of pencils, reams of paper.

But still, it wasn't enough. Not to last forever. So one of the things my students and I do now is make our own paper, paints, and inks.

That's how our world works. For as long as they last,

you use the things mass-produced in the last one—whether they're colored pencils or internal combustion engines—and then you either do without or come up with replacements.

It's amazing how little we miss the things we used to take for granted. And how much we're capable of, as a species, when we use our hands and our minds.

BEFORE WE CAME to Refugia, I used to draw the thieves again and again. I can't really remember why.

I don't draw them anymore. There's no need. Anyway, it would be a waste of paper.

The wasp-things. *Philanthus parkeri*.

The first species to be given a scientific name in the Next World.

OTHER PEOPLE, THE ones who were alive a lot longer in the Last World than I was, have told its story much better than I ever could. I was only ten when it ended, and even though I have a good memory, most of that time seems fragmentary to me now. Surreal. A dream.

It's funny talking to those who were born here. It's hard enough to describe long-distance telephone calls, the idea that we could talk with someone on the other side of the world over wires. And when you try to describe how cell phones worked, they look at you like you're insane.

It seems pretty crazy now to me, too, actually. I mean, imagine it: To send a text message to someone in the next room, you needed the help of a satellite orbiting the earth.

Who ever thought *that* was a good idea? Who ever imagined that system would last?

I remember begging for a cell phone and being told I had to wait until I was thirteen. Of course, by the time I was thirteen, no one had them. They had become part of the dream. The dream of the Last World.

You know what satellites are to us now? A show. You lie on the beach at night, looking west over the ocean, watching for meteors, and every once in a while there's this huge one, a fireball tumbling across the sky. Those are satellites falling back to earth because no one is tending to them anymore.

When he was little, my brother, Jack, asked if anyone was ever hit by a falling satellite. Mom kind of laughed and said that, even in the Last World, sometimes satellites would fall. And, yes, people would worry, but she didn't think anyone was ever actually hit by one.

"Even then, it was a pretty empty world," she said.

"But emptier now?" Jack asked.

She said, "Yes, honey. Emptier now."

And the skies are so much clearer than they used to be.

SATELLITES. SPACESHIPS THAT went to the moon. Airplanes flying people every which way around the earth. The world is a whole lot quieter these days, especially since the last airplane, Malcolm's baby, broke for good. How long ago was that? About ten years, I guess.

Everyone was sure its final flight would end in a crash, and Malcolm would have to walk home. But the truth was, one day it just didn't work anymore. Some part he'd been patching with bubble gum finally gave up the ghost.

That was when he began to follow his next obsession. The one that's about to take flight tomorrow.

If I can be poetic for a second.

THE LAST TIME I wrote here, I talked a lot about my grandma Mary. I won't go over it again, but I wanted to make sure I mentioned her. She is not forgotten.

I visit her grave sometimes, but not so often as I once did. I've decided I want to remember her alive, protecting me, bringing Mom and Dad to me.

Mom agrees. "The world is full of memorials," she says. "Memories are more important."

Mom says things like that.

Mom, Sheila Connelly, is not my birth mother. You need to know that, and also that I do remember my real ma and da. They're in all the histories people have written about the Last World. Their part was important, even though they never knew it, because it brought Grandma and me together with Mom, and then with everyone else.

Everyone else: the names in every history of Refugia. Grandma Mary's, Mom's and Dad's, Mariama's. And Jack Parker, who died rescuing us from the thieves.

The graveyard here gets steadily bigger, of course. People die . . . but not as fast as babies are born. That's how it has to be, if we're going to survive.

The first step, at least.

It's been years since the thieves killed any of us. Clare Shapiro, Elena Stavros, and their group have made the vaccine work so well that the wasps don't dare come near.

Why should they? It's still a big world out there, and they don't like the way we taste.

I wish they had stayed here in the Casamance to begin with. I wish they had never figured out that humans made good hosts. I wish they had gone extinct without ever being discovered and named.

I wish I wish I wish. But here's the truth: I'm selfish. Because I would have accepted all the lives lost to spare just one. . . .

AS YOU ALL know, the last person killed by the thieves was my father. Trey Gilliard.

He was never stung. Once we came here, he was protected by the vaccine, just as the rest of us are. It just came . . . too late for him. Back in the Last World, the thieves poisoned him, and despite everyone's best efforts to find a treatment—Mom's and Clare Shapiro's most of all—there was nothing that could be done.

What you also need to know is that he wasn't in pain, those last years. His mind was quiet, and that was all that mattered. That and seeing us, Jack and me and the rest of Refugia, grow up. Thrive.

Near the end, he liked most to sit on the beach and watch Malcolm, Nick, and their team at work. To sit and dream of what was to come, even if he knew he wouldn't be part of it.

The next New World.

At his funeral, everyone cried. Even Clare, though she didn't want anyone to notice.

Me? I thought I'd never stop crying. I hadn't felt like

a little girl for a long time, maybe not ever, but I did then. When I think of it, I still do.

AS I SAID, the thieves have the run of a big world these days, but maybe it's not as comfortable for them as it used to be. When his airplane was still working, Malcolm reported that he saw fewer and fewer every trip. They'd killed or used up too many hosts in their last great raid, and too many possible other hosts (people, dogs, horses, cattle, even rats) had died off in the chaos that followed.

The thief population had to crash, and it did. That's how things work in nature. No one escapes unscathed.

They'll never go extinct, of course. They're here to stay. We're always going to have to live alongside them.

Dad said that the human race once believed it owned the world. No one thinks that way anymore. Now we consider ourselves lucky just to get to live on it for a while.

I MIGHT NOT be related to Dad by blood, but I seem to have inherited his love of exploration. (He called it his itchy feet.) So when Malcolm's baby, the obsession that kept him—and whoever else he could dragoon into helping—busy every waking hour for a decade, was finally done, I was the first to sign up.

Malcolm's baby: a gorgeous square-rigged sailing ship built from tropical hardwood and equipped for ocean travel. Modeled after the great expeditionary craft that crossed the seas in the Last World, before the steam engine and the silicon chip and nuclear power and satellites took over.

After Dad died, Malcolm named it the *Trey Gilliard*. I painted the letters on the bow.

We cast off tomorrow morning. As many as Refugia can spare are going: doctors and scientists and those who, like me, just want to see what lies on the other side of the horizon.

I'm bringing a pad and a bag of colored pencils along, so when we come back I can show you all what the New World looks like.

WE'RE PLANNING TO find out who else is out there. Because there *must* be others, somewhere, living in their own Refugias. Everyone is sure of it, even Clare Shapiro. We have to believe we're not alone.

Dad often spoke of one Refugia he was positive still survived in the highlands of the island of New Guinea.

"You have an uncle and aunt there," he told me and Jack, right near the end. "And cousins, too. I want you to meet them."

We will, Dad. I promise.

> —*Kaitlin Finneran Gilliard,*
> *Founder and Citizen of Refugia*

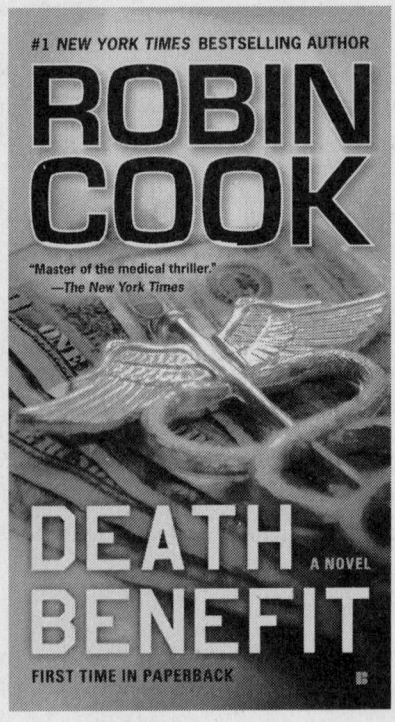

The novel of the fantastic unknown
by the Nebula Award–winning author
of *Time Travelers Never Die*

Jack McDevitt

ECHO

AN ALEX BENEDICT NOVEL

Eccentric Sunset Tuttle spent a lifetime searching in vain for forms of alien life. Twenty-five years after his death, a stone tablet inscribed with cryptic symbols is revealed to be in the possession of Tuttle's onetime lover, and antiques dealer Alex Benedict is anxious to determine what secrets the tablet holds. It could be proof that Tuttle discovered what he was looking for.

To find out, Benedict and his assistant embark on their own voyage of discovery—one that will lead them directly into the path of a very determined assassin who doesn't want those secrets revealed.

penguin.com

Step into another
world with

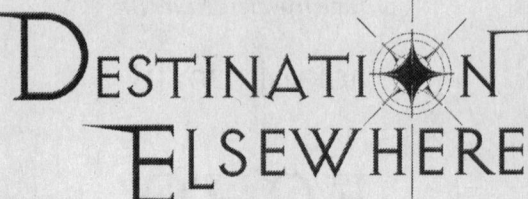

A new
community
dedicated
to the best
Science Fiction
and Fantasy.

Visit
 /DestinationElsewhere

M1160G0712

THE LAST TEMPTATION OF DR. DALTON

ROBIN GIANNA

 HARLEQUIN® MEDICAL ROMANCE™

Recycling programs
for this product may
not exist in your area.

ISBN-13: 978-0-373-06959-0

THE LAST TEMPTATION OF DR. DALTON

First North American Publication 2014

Copyright © 2014 by Robin Gianakopoulos

Printed in U.S.A.

Why did his mouth say one thing when his brain told him to shut up and walk out?

Until the slow blink of her eyes, the tip of her tongue licking her lips, the rise and fall of that tantalizing vee of skin beneath her robe obliterated all regrets.

"I don't think your sleep is my responsibility," she said. "You're on your own."

She swayed closer, lids low, her lips parted, practically willing him to kiss her. What was the reason he'd been trying not to? Right now, he couldn't quite remember. Didn't want to.

"Seems to me we agreed you were in charge of my life while I'm here." Almost of their own accord his feet brought him nearly flush with her body. Close enough to feel her warmth touch his bare chest. To feel her breath feather across his skin. "Got any ideas on a cure for insomnia?"

"Maybe a hammer to the head? I've got one in the toolbox in the closet."

He reached for her, put his hands on her waist. "I know you said you couldn't promise not to hurt me, but that seems a little drastic." His head lowered, because he had to feel her skin against his lips, touch them softly to her cheek, beneath her ear. "Any other ideas?"

Her warm hands flattened against his chest. When they didn't push he pulled her tightly against him, fitted her curves perfectly to his angles. Much as he knew he should back off right now, there was no way he could do it. He wanted her even more than the night they'd fallen into her bed together. And that night had knocked him flat in a way he couldn't remember ever experiencing before.

Dear Reader,

As I was writing my debut medical romance, *Changed by His Son's Smile,* I fell a little in love with a secondary character—charming playboy Dr. Trent Dalton. Writing a book about him and how a certain spunky woman turns his life upside-down was sure to be fun!

I chose Liberia as the setting for this story because of its unique ties to the United States, as well as its interesting West African culture. The civil wars the people of Liberia endured in the very recent past were horrific, with medical care nearly nonexistent during the worst of it. Mission hospitals and schools like my fictional ones in this story are an important part of the country's healing and growth. I hope you enjoy learning a little about Liberia, too, as you read the story.

Trent travels the world working in mission hospitals, careful never to get tied to one place—or one woman—for very long. Beautiful Charlotte "Charlie" Edwards certainly has to be determined and feisty to meet the challenges of running a mission hospital, and I knew she was the perfect heroine to tame him. But just when he finally realizes she's the one worth sticking around for, he finds out she just might have been playing him all along.

Please drop me a line through my website, www.robingianna.com, if you enjoy Trent and Charlie's story. I'd love to hear from you!

Robin

ACKNOWLEDGMENTS

Many thanks to:

Critique partner, writer friend and pediatric emergency physician Meta Carroll, MD, for spending so much time walking me through medical scenes and double-checking them for accuracy. I appreciate it so, so much!

My sister-in-law, Trish Connor, MD, for helping me figure out why my heroine had needed plastic surgery as a child.

Cynthia Adams, piano teacher extraordinaire, for the perfect music choices in the story.

A recent title by Robin Gianna:
CHANGED BY HIS SON'S SMILE

**Also available in ebook format
from www.Harlequin.com.**

DEDICATION

Mom, you always told me how important writers
are to the world.

This one's for you.

CHAPTER ONE

IT WAS ALL she could do not to throw her stupid phone out of the car window.

Why wasn't he answering? Charlotte Edwards huffed out a breath and focused on driving as fast as she possibly could—not an easy task on the potholed dirt road that was just muddy enough to send her sliding into a tree if she wasn't careful.

Thank goodness it was only May in Liberia, West Africa, and just the beginning of the rainy season. Her battered four-by-four handled the terrible roads pretty well, but once they were inches deep with mud and water all bets were off.

Adrenaline surging, Charlie cautiously pressed harder on the gas pedal. No matter how uncomfortable it would make her feel, she absolutely had to catch Trent Dalton at the airport before he left—then tell him off for not answering his phone. If he had, she'd have paid for a taxi to bring him back stat to her little hospital, instead of wasting time making this trek both ways.

The sudden ringing of her phone made her

jump and she snatched it up, hoping it was Trent, seeing she'd called a dozen times. "So you finally decided to look at your phone?"

"It's Thomas."

The hospital technician sounded surprised and no wonder. Her stomach twisted with dread, hoping he wasn't delivering bad news. "Sorry. You calling with an update?"

"The boy is still holding his own. I pray he'll be okay until Dr. Dalton gets back here. But I wanted to tell you that Dr. Smith has offered to do the appendectomy."

"What? Tell him no way. I'm not having a liar and a hack working on any of our patients—unless Trent's already gone, in which case we'll have no choice but to reconsider. I'll let you know as soon as I get to the airport."

"Yes, Ma."

She hung up and shook her head, managing a little smile. The word "Ma" was used as a sign of respect in Liberia, and no matter how many times she'd asked Thomas just to call her Charlie, or Charlotte, he never did.

Dr. Smith had been sent by the Global Physicians Coalition to work at the Henry and Louisa Edwards Mission Hospital for a one-year commission. But when his arrival had been delayed they'd asked Trent to fill in for the five days until Smith could get there. Though he'd just finished a stint in India, Trent had thankfully not minded his vacation being delayed until Smith showed up.

Not long after Trent had left to start his vacation, though, the GPC called to tell her they had discovered that Smith had falsified his credentials. No way would she have him work here now.

And, because problems came in multiples, they had a very sick little boy whose life just might depend on getting surgery pronto. If only John Adams, her right-hand man for everything to do with the hospital and school, hadn't been off getting supplies today. Charlie would've sent him to drag Trent back to take care of the little boy, saving her from enduring an hour's drive in close quarters with the man. That was, if he hadn't flown off to wherever he was going next.

Anxiety ratcheting up another notch, Charlie almost called Trent again, knowing there was little point. Then she spotted the airport in the distance. Shoving down the gas pedal, hands sweating, she slithered and bumped her way down the road, parked nearly sideways and ran inside.

Relief at seeing him still sitting there nearly made her knees weak. And, of course, that weakness had nothing to do with again seeing the gorgeous man she'd enjoyed a one-night stand with just hours ago. Memories of what they'd spent the night doing filled her cheeks with hot embarrassment, and she wished with all her being she'd known their last kiss this morning wouldn't really be goodbye. She wished she had known before she'd fallen into bed with him. If she had, she most definitely would have resisted the delicious taste of his mouth and the all too seductive smile.

He was slouched in a hard chair, his long legs stretched out in front of him, a Panama hat pulled over his face with just his sensuous lips visible. Lips that had touched every inch of her body, mortified heat rushed back to her face. Even sitting, his height made him stand out among the passengers sprawled everywhere in the airport. A battered leather bag sat next to his feet. His arms were folded across his chest and he looked sound asleep.

Dang it, this was all too awkward. She squirmed with discomfort at the very same time her nerve-endings tingled at the pleasure of seeing him again. Disgusted with herself, she took a deep breath, stepped closer and kicked his shoe. "Wake up. We need to talk."

She saw him stiffen, but other than that he didn't move, obviously pretending he hadn't heard her. What—he thought she'd come all this way just to kiss him goodbye again? Been there, done that and now it was over between them. This was about business, not pleasure. But with that thought instantly came other thoughts. Thoughts of all the pleasure she'd enjoyed with him last night, which made her even more annoyed with herself.

"I know you're not asleep, Trent Dalton. Look at me." She kicked him in the ankle this time, figuring that was sure to get his attention.

"Ow, damn it." He yanked back his leg and his finger inched up the brim of his hat until she could see the nearly black hair waving across his forehead. His light blue eyes looked at her, cautious and wary. "What are you doing here, Charlotte?"

"I'm here because you wouldn't answer your stupid cell phone."

"I turned it off. I'm on vacation."

"If you'd left it on, I wouldn't have had to spend an hour driving here, worried I wouldn't catch you before you left. We have to talk."

"Listen." His expression became pained. "It was great being with you, and moving on can be hard, you know? But going through a long-drawn-out goodbye will just make it all tougher."

"We can't say goodbye just yet."

"I'm sorry, Charlotte. I have to leave. I promise you'll be fine."

Of all the arrogant... Did he really think women had a hard time getting over him after one night of fun? Fabulous fun, admittedly, but still. She felt like conking him on the head. "Sorry, but you have to come back."

"I can't," he said in a soft and gentle voice, his blue eyes now full of pity and remorse. "We both knew we only had one night together. Tomorrow will be better. It will. In a few weeks, you'll forget all about me."

"You are so incredibly full of yourself." She couldn't control a laugh that ended in a little snort. The man was unbelievable. "Our fling was over the second you kissed me goodbye, tipped your hat and left with one of your adorable smiles and the "maybe see ya again sometime, babe" parting remark. What would make you think I had a problem with that? That's not why I'm here."

He stared at her, and she concentrated on keeping her expression nonchalant, even amused. She wasn't about to give him even a hint that she would think about him after he was gone.

"So why are you here, then?"

"I'm throwing out the new surgeon."

"Throwing him out?" Trent sat up straight. "What do you mean?"

"The GPC contacted me to tell me they found he'd falsified his credentials. That he'd had his license suspended in the U.S. for alcohol and drug use—over-prescribing of narcotics."

"Damn, so he's a loose cannon." He frowned. "But that doesn't mean he's not a good surgeon."

"Just because we're in the middle of West Africa doesn't mean our docs shouldn't be top notch. The GPC left it up to me whether I wanted him to work for us or not. And I refuse to have someone that unethical, maybe even doped up, working on our patients."

"So when is the GPC sending a new surgeon?"

"As soon as possible. They think they can get someone temporary like you were in a few days, no more than a week. Then they'll round up a doc who can be here for the year. All you have to do is come back until the temp gets here, or a day or two before."

"I can't. I just spent a solid year in India and I need a break before I start my new job in the Philippines. I have vacation plans I can't change."

She had to wonder what woman those plans might be with. "I don't believe your vacation is more important to you than your job."

"Hey, the only reason I worked twelve straight months was to pay for my vacation."

"Yeah, right." She made a rude sound in her throat. "Like you couldn't make tons more money as a surgeon in the U.S., paying for vacations and country club memberships and fancy cars. Nobody works in a mission hospital for the money."

"Maybe I couldn't get a job in the U.S." His normally laughing eyes were oddly serious.

"Mmm-hmm." She placed her hands on the arms of his seat and leaned forward, her nose nearly touching his. The clean, manly scent of him surrounded her, making her heart go into a stupid, accelerated pit-pat. But she wasn't about to back down. "So, I never did ask—why *do* you work exclusively in tiny hospitals all over the world, pulling up stakes every year? Most docs work for the GPC part-time."

"Running from the law." His lips were so close, his breath touching her skin, and more than anything she wanted to close that small gap and kiss him one more time. "Murdered my last girlfriend after she followed me to the airport."

She had to chuckle even as she watched his eyes darken, showing he still felt the same crazy attraction she felt. That she'd felt the first second she'd met him. "I always knew you were a dangerous man, Trent Dalton. I just didn't realize quite how dangerous."

Just as she felt herself leaning in, about to kiss his sexy mouth against her will, she managed to mentally smack herself. Straightening, she stepped back.

"So. We have an immediate problem that can't wait for you to think about whether playing golf or chasing skirts, or whatever you do on vacation, is more important than my little hospital."

"What problem?"

"We've got a seven-year-old boy who's got a hot appendix. Thomas is afraid it will rupture and says he doesn't have the skill to handle it."

"Why does he think it's his appendix? Even if it is, Thomas is a well-trained tech. I was impressed as hell at the great job he does on hernias."

"Hernias aren't the same thing as an appendix, which I think you know, Dr. Dalton. Thomas says he's sure that's what it is—that you're the only one who can do it. And to tell you that the last thing the kid needs is to get septic."

His brow lowered in thought before he spoke. "What are his symptoms?"

"His mother says he hasn't eaten for two days. He's been feverish—temp of one-hundred-point-four—and vomiting."

"Belly ache and vomiting? Maybe it's just the flu."

"The abdominal pain came first, then the vomiting."

"Has the pain moved?"

"From his umbilicus to right lower quadrant." She slapped her hands back onto the chair arms. Was the man going to ask questions all day in the hope of still getting away from here? "Listen, Trent. It's been thirty-six hours. If the appendix doesn't come out, it's going to rupture. I don't need to tell you the survival rates of peritonitis in this part of the world."

A slow smile spread across Trent's face before he laughed. "Maybe *you* should do the surgery. Why the hell didn't you become a doctor?"

"I can get doctors. I can't get somebody to run that hospital. So are you coming?"

He just looked at her, silent, his amusement now gone. The worry on his face touched her heart, because she was pretty sure it was on her behalf—that he didn't want to come back because she might get hurt, which she'd bet had happened often enough in his life as a vagabond doctor.

As though it had a mind of its own, her palm lifted to touch his cheek. "I've only known you a few days, but that's enough time to realize you're a man of honor. I'm sure you'll come take care of this little boy and stick it out until we can get someone else. A one-night fling was all it was meant to be for either of us—anything more would be pointless and messy. From now on, our relationship is strictly professional. So let's go before the boy gets sicker."

His hand pressed against the back of hers, held it a moment against his cheek then lowered it to gently set her away from him. "You're good, I'll give you that." He unfolded from the chair and stood, looking down at her. "But I can only stay a few more days, so don't be trying to guilt me into more than that. I mean it."

"Agreed." She stuck out her hand to seal the deal, and he wrapped his long, warm fingers around hers. She gave his hand a quick, brisk shake then yanked her own loose but didn't manage to erase the imprint of it.

It was going to be a long couple of days.

As the car bounced in and out of ruts on the way back to the hospital, Trent glanced at the fascinating woman next to him while she concentrated on her driving. The shock of seeing Charlotte's beautiful face at the airport had nearly knocked the wind out of him. The face he'd seen all morning as he'd waited to get away from it.

He stared at her strong, silky eyebrows, lowered in concentration over eyes as green as a Brazilian rainforest. Her thick brown hair touched with streaks of bronze flowed over her shoulders, which were exposed by the sleeveless shirts she liked to wear. He nearly reached to slide his fingers over that pretty skin, and to hell with distracting her from driving.

He sucked in a breath and turned his attention back to the road. How could one night of great sex have seemed like something more than the simple, pleasant diversion it was supposed to have been?

"The road is worst these last couple miles, so hang on to your hat," she said, a smile on the pink lips whose imprint he'd still been feeling against his own as he'd sat in that damned airport for hours.

"You want me to drive?"

"Uh, no. We'd probably end up around a tree. You stick with doctoring and let me handle everything else."

He chuckled. The woman sure took her role as hospital director seriously, and to his surprise he enjoyed it. How had he never known he liked bossy women?

"So, where were you headed?" Charlotte asked.

"Florence." But for once he hadn't known what the hell he was going to do with himself for the three weeks the GPC gave doctors off between jobs. Getting in touch with one of his old girlfriends and spending time with her, whoever it might be, in London, Thailand or Rio until his next job began was how he always spent his vacation.

"Alone? Never mind. Pretend I didn't ask."

"Yeah, alone." She probably wouldn't believe it, but it was true. He hadn't called anyone. He couldn't conjure the interest, which was damned annoying. So he'd be spending three weeks in Italy all by his lonesome, with too much time to think about the fiery woman sitting next to him. The woman with the sweet, feminine name who preferred going by the name of a man.

Charlotte. Charlie. If only he could have three weeks of warms days and nights filled with her in Florence, Rome and the Italian Riviera—with her sharp mind, sense of humor and gorgeous, touchable body. Last night had been… He huffed out a breath and stared out of the window. Not a good idea to let his thoughts go any further about *that* right now.

At least there hadn't been a big, dramatic goodbye. Seeing tears in those amazing green eyes of hers and a tremble on her kissable lips would have made him feel like crap. He had to make sure that during the next few days he kept his distance so there would be no chance of that happening. Which wouldn't be easy, since he'd like nothing more than to get her into bed again.

He looked out over the landscape of lush green hills and trees that led to the hospital compound and realized he hadn't got round to asking Charlotte how she'd ended up here. "You never did tell me how your family came to be missionaries in Liberia. To build all this."

"My great-grandparents were from North Carolina. My great-grandfather came from a family of schoolteachers and missionaries, and I'm told that when he and his new wife were barely twenty they decided to head to Africa to open a school. They came to Liberia because English is the primary language. Three generations later, we're still here."

"They built the whole compound at once?" The hard work and commitment so many missionaries had put into their projects around the world amazed him.

"The hospital came about twenty years after they built the house and school in 1932. I've always loved the design of that house." She gave him a smile. "Since Liberia was founded by freed slaves, my great-grandparents brought the Southern antebellum style with them. Did you know that antebellum isn't really an architectural style, though? That in Latin it means 'before war'? It refers to homes built before the U.S. Civil War. Sadly ironic, isn't it? That the same could be said for here in Liberia too." She was talking fast, then blushed cutely. "And you probably didn't want or need a history lesson."

"Ironic's the word," he said, shaking his head. "I've never worked here before. What the civil wars have done to this country is… Heck, you can't begin to measure it."

"I know. Unbelievable how many people died. What the rest have had to live with—the chaos and terror, the shambles left behind. The horrible, disfiguring injuries." Her voice shook with anger, her lips pressed in a tight line. "Anyway, nothing can fix the past. All we can do is try to make a difference now."

"So, your great-grandparents moved here?" he prompted.

A smile banished her obvious outrage. "Apparently my great-grandmother said she'd only move here if she could make it a little like home. They built the house, filled it with beautiful furniture and even got the piano that's still in the parlor."

"And Edwardses have been here since then? What about the wars?"

"The wars forced my parents to leave when I was little and go back to the U.S. Eventually we moved to Togo to start a new mission. The hospital and school here were badly damaged by gunfire and shrapnel, but the house was just in bad disrepair, stripped of things like the windows and sinks. John Adams and I have been fixing it up, but it's third on the list of priorities."

He couldn't imagine how much work—and money—it was taking to make that happen. "So what made you want to resurrect all this? It's not like you really remember living here."

"Just because I haven't lived here until now doesn't mean my roots aren't here, and John Adams's roots. They are. They're dug in deep through our ancestors, and I intend to keep them here. My plan is to grow them, expand them, no matter what it takes."

"No matter what it takes? That's a pretty strong statement." He'd met plenty of people committed to making things better for the underprivileged, but her attitude was damned impressive.

"These people deserve whatever it takes to get

them the help they need." Her grim tone lightened as they pulled in front of the one-story, painted cement hospital. "Let's get the boy fixed up. And, Trent…" Her green eyes turned all soft and sweet and he nearly reached for her. "Thanks for coming back. I promise you won't be sorry."

CHAPTER TWO

Thomas hovered in the clinic outside the door to the OR, looking anxious. "Where is the patient?" Trent asked. "Is he prepped and ready, or do you want me to examine him first?"

"I thought he should be examined again, to confirm my diagnosis. But he's in the OR. With Dr. Smith."

"Dr. Smith?" Charlie asked. What the heck was he doing in there? Hadn't she asked him to stay out of the hospital and away from patients? "Why? Did you tell him Dr. Dalton was coming back?"

"Said since he was here and the boy needs surgery fast he'd take care of it."

Anger welled up in Charlie's chest at the same time she fought it down. She supposed she should give Smith kudos for stepping up despite the circumstances, instead of being mad at her refusal to let him work there. "Well, that's...nice of him, but I'll tell him our other surgeon is here now."

"Give me a minute to scrub," Trent said as he grabbed a gown and mask and headed to the sink.

Charlie hurried into the OR to find Don Smith standing over the patient who was being attended to by the nurse anesthetist but not yet asleep. She stopped short and stared at the anxious-looking little boy. Could there be some confusion, and this wasn't the child with the hot appendix? His eyelid and eyebrow had a red, disfiguring, golf ball-sized lump that nearly concealed his eye completely. How in the world could he even see?

Her chest tightened and her stomach balled in a familiar pain that nearly made her sick. The poor child looked freakish and she knew all too well how horribly he must be teased about it. How terrible that must make him feel.

She lifted a hand to her ear, now nearly normal-looking after so many years of disfigurement. Her hand dropped to her side, balled into a fist. How wrong that he'd lived with this, when a kid in the States never would have. More proof that the project so dear to her heart was desperately needed here.

"Is this the child with appendicitis?" At Dr. Smith's nodded response, she continued. "I appreciate you being willing to take care of this emergency, but my other surgeon is here now. Help yourself to breakfast in the kitchen, if you haven't already."

"I'm here. Might as well let me operate. You'll see that I'm a capable and trustworthy surgeon. I want you to change your mind."

"I won't change my mind. Losing your license and falsifying your credentials is a serious matter, which frankly shows me you're *not* trustworthy."

"Damn it, I need this job." Smith turned to her, his face reddening with anger. "I told everyone I'd left to do humanitarian work. If I don't stay here, they'll know."

"So the only reason you want to work here is to save your reputation?" Charlie stared at him. "Hate to break it to you, but your drug addiction and loss of license is already public record in the States."

"For those who've looked. A lot of people I know haven't."

"I'm sorry, Dr. Smith, but you'll have to leave. Now."

"I'm doing this surgery and that's all there is to it. Nurse, get the anesthesia going." He turned to the patient and, without another word, began to swab the site while the child stared at him, his lip trembling.

Anger surged through her veins. Who did this guy think he was? The jerk wouldn't have spoken to her like this if she'd been a man. "Janice, don't listen to him. Stop this instant, Dr. Smith. I insist—"

Trent stepped between Charlie and Smith, grasping the man's wrist and yanking the cotton from his hand. "Maybe you didn't hear the director of this hospital. You're not doing surgery here."

"Who the hell are you?" Smith yanked his arm from Trent's grasp. "You can't tell me what to do."

"No, but she can. And I work for her." Trent had a good three inches on the man, and his posture was aggressive, his usually warm and laughing eyes a cold, steely blue. "I know your instincts as a doctor want what's best for this boy, which is immediate attention to his problem. Your being in here impedes that. So leave."

Smith began to sputter until his gaze met Trent's. He stepped back and looked away, ripping off his gown and mask and throwing them to the floor. "I can't believe a crappy little hospital in the middle of nowhere is too stupid to know how good I am. Your loss."

He stalked out and Charlie drew in a deep, slightly shaky breath of relief. She'd thought for a minute that Trent would have to physically take the guy out, and realized she'd completely trusted him to do exactly that. Then she pulled up short at the thought. She was in charge of this place and she couldn't rely on anyone else to deal with tough situations.

"Thanks, but you didn't need to do that. I had it handled."

Trent looked down at her with raised brows. "Did you, boss lady?"

"Yeah, I did."

He reached out, his long-fingered hand swiping across her shoulder, and she jerked, quickly looking down. "What, is there a bug on me?"

"No—a real big chip. I was wondering what put it there." His lips tipped up as his eyes met hers.

What? Ridiculous. "I don't have a chip on my shoulder. I'm just doing my job."

"Accepting help is part of being head honcho, you know." Those infuriatingly amused eyes lingered on her before he turned to the nurse. "Have you administered any anesthesia yet?"

"No, doctor."

"Good." He rolled a stool to the gurney and sat, that full smile now charmingly back on his face as he drew the sheet further down the child's hips. "So, buddy, where's it hurt?"

He pointed, and Trent gently pressed the top of the boy's stomach, slowly moving his hand downward to the right lower quadrant.

"Ow." The boy grimaced and Trent quit pressing his flesh to give the child's skinny chest a gentle pat.

"Okay. We're going to fix you up so it doesn't hurt any more. What's your name?"

"Lionel." The child, looking more relaxed than when Charlie had first come into the room, studied Trent. With his small index finger, Lionel pushed his bulging, droopy eyelid upward so he could see. "My belly will be all better? For true?"

"For true." Trent's smile deepened, his eyes crinkled at the corners as his gaze touched Charlie's for a moment before turning back to the child. "Inside your body, your appendix is about the size of your pinky finger. It's got a little sick and swollen, and that's what's making your belly hurt. I'm going to fix it all up while you sleep, and when you wake up it won't hurt any more. Okay?"

"Okay." Lionel nodded and smiled, showing a missing front tooth.

"But, before we take care of your sore belly, I want to talk about your eye." Trent gently moved the boy's hand before his own fingers carefully touched all around the protrusion on and above the eyelid. "Can you tell me how long it's been like this?"

Lionel shrugged. "I'nt know."

"I bet it's hard to see, huh?"

"Uh-huh. I can't see the football very well when we're kicking around. Sometimes Mommy has tape, though, and when she sticks it on there to hold it up that helps some."

"I'm sure you look tough that way. Scare your opponents." Trent grinned, and Lionel grinned back. "But I bet you could show how tough a player you are even more if you could see better."

Charlie marveled at the trusting expression on the child's face, how unquestioning he seemed as he nodded and smiled. She shifted her attention to Trent and saw that his demeanor wasn't just good bedside manner. The man truly liked kids, and that realization ratcheted the man's appeal even higher. And Lord knew he didn't need that appeal ratcheted up even a millimeter.

"Is your mother around? Or someone I can talk to about fixing it at the same time we fix your belly?"

"My mommy brought me. But I don't know where she is right now."

As his expression began to get anxious again, Trent leaned in close with a smile that would have reassured even the most nervous child. "Hey, we'll find her. Don't worry."

He stood and took a few steps away with a nod to Charlie. When they were out of hearing distance, he spoke in an undertone. "I want to take care of his hemangioma and we might as well do it while he's under for the appendix. There'll be a lot of bleeding to control, and I'll get him started on antibiotics first. After I remove the tumor, I'll decide if it's necessary to graft skin from his thigh to make it look good. In the States, you wouldn't do a clean surgery and an appendix at the same time, but I can do it with no problems."

"If it wouldn't be done in the States, we're not doing it here." Didn't he get that this was why she'd thrown Smith out?

"If you think mission doctors don't do things we wouldn't do in the U.S., you have a lot to learn." No longer amused, a hint of steel lurked within the blue of his eyes. "Here, I can follow my gut and do what's best for the patient, and only what's best for the patient. I don't have to worry about what an insurance company wants, or cover my ass with stupid protocol. You can either trust me to know I'm doing what's best for Lionel, or not. Your call."

Charlie glanced at the boy and knew better than anyone that they were talking about a tremendously skilled procedure, one that would require the kind of detailed work and suturing a general surgeon wouldn't be capable of. "I'm in the process of getting a plastic surgery center together. That's what the new wing of the hospital is for. How about we suggest to his mommy that she bring him back when it's operational?"

He shook his head. "First, there's a good chance they live far away and it won't be easy to get back here. Second, he's probably had this a long time. The longer we wait, the more likely the possibility of permanent blindness. Even if it is fixed later, if his brain gets used to not receiving signals from the eye that part of his brain will die, and that'll be it for his vision. Not to mention that in West Africa a person is more susceptible to getting river blindness or some other parasitic infection in the eye. What if that happened and he ended up blind in both eyes? Not worth the risk."

"But can you do it? Without him still looking… bad? The plastic surgery center will be open soon. And a plastic surgeon would know how to do stuff like this better than you would."

"You don't know who you're dealing with here." His eyes held a mocking laugh. "He'll look great, I promise."

She stared at him, at his ultra-confident expression, the lazy smile. Would she be making a mistake to let him fix the hemangioma when in just a few weeks she was supposed to have a plastics specialist on board?

She looked back at Lionel, his finger still poked into the disfiguring vascular tumor so he could see out of that eye as he watched them talk. She looked at the trusting and hopeful expression on his small face. A face marred by a horrible problem Trent promised he could fix.

"Okay. You've convinced me. Do it."

CHAPTER THREE

Hours passed while Trent worked on Lionel. Worry over whether or not she'd made the right decision made it difficult for Charlie to sit in her office and do paperwork, but she had to try. With creditors demanding a big payment in three weeks, getting that funding check in her pocket for the new wing from the Gilchrist Foundation was critical.

She made herself shuffle through everything one more time. It seemed the only things that had to happen to get the money were a final inspection from a Gilchrist Foundation representative and proof she had a plastic surgeon on board. Both of which would happen any day now, thank heavens.

So how, in the midst of this important stuff, could she let her attention wander? She was thinking instead about the moment five days ago when Trent had strolled into this office. Thinking about how she'd stared, open-mouthed, like a schoolgirl.

Tall and lean, with slightly long, nearly black hair starkly contrasting with the color of his eyes,

he was the kind of man who made a woman stop
and take a second look. And a third. Normally,
eyes like his would be called ice-blue, but they'd
been anything but cold; warm and intelligent,
they'd glinted with a constant touch of amusement. A charming, lopsided smile had hovered
on his lips.

When she'd shaken his hand, he'd surprised
her by tugging her against him in a warm embrace. Disarmed, she'd found herself wanting to
stay there longer than the brief moment he'd held
her close. She'd found her brain short-circuiting
at the feel of his big hands pressed to her back;
his lean, muscled body against hers; his distinctive masculine scent.

That same friendly embrace had been freely
given to every woman working in the hospital,
young and old, which had left all of them grinning, blushing and nearly swooning.

No doubt, the man was dynamite in human
form, ready to blast any woman's heart to smith-
ereens.

But not Charlie's. She'd known the second he'd
greeted her with that genial hug that she would
have to throw armor over that central organ. She'd
cordially invited him to join her and John Adams
for dinners, enjoying his intelligence, his amusing
stories and, yes, his good looks and sophistication.
She'd been sure she had everything under control.

But the night before he was to leave, when that embrace had grown longer and more intimate, when he'd finally touched his lips to hers, she hadn't resisted the desire to be with him, to enjoy a light and fun evening. An oh-so-brief diversion amidst the work that was her life. And, now that circumstances required they be in close contact for a little longer, there was no way she'd let him know that simply looking at him made her fantasize about just one more night. That was not going to happen—period.

Yes, their moment together was *so* last week. She smirked at the thought, even though a ridiculous part of her felt slightly ego-crushed that he, too, wanted to steer clear of any possible entanglement.

But that was a good thing. The man clearly loved women, all women. She'd known she was just one more notch in his travel bag, and he'd been just another notch in the fabric of her life too. Except that there hadn't been too many opportunities for "notching" since she'd finished grad school and come back to Africa.

She had to grin as she grabbed the info she wanted to share with the teachers at the school. Notching: now there was a funny euphemism for great sex if ever there was one.

She was so deep in thought about the great sex she'd enjoyed last night that she stepped into the hall without looking and nearly plowed her head into Trent's strong biceps.

"Whoa." His hands grasped her shoulders as she stumbled. "You late for lunch or something?"

Her heart sped up annoyingly as he held her just inches from his chest. "Is that a crack about how much I like to eat?"

"Not a crack. I've just observed that when you're hungry you don't let anything get between you and that plate."

She looked up into his twinkling blue eyes. "Hasn't anyone ever told you that women don't like people implying they're gluttons?"

"No negative implications from me. I like a woman who eats." His voice dropped lower. "I like the perfect and beautiful curves on your perfect and beautiful body."

As she stared up at him, the light in his eyes changed, amusement fading into something darker, more dangerous.

Desire. It hung between them, electric and heavy in the air, and Trent slowly tipped his head towards hers.

He was going to kiss her. The realization sent her heart into an accelerated tempo. A hot tingle slipped across her skin as his warm breath touched her mouth, and she lifted her hands to his chest, knowing she should push him away, but instead keeping her palms pressed to his hard pecs.

She couldn't let it happen, only to say goodbye again in a few more days. He'd made it clear he felt the same way. But, as she was thinking all that, she licked her lips in silent invitation.

His hands tightened on her arms as though he couldn't decide whether to pull her close or push her away, then he released her. "Sorry. I shouldn't have said that. I forgot we're just casual acquaintances now." He shoved his hands in his pockets, his expression now impassive, all business. "I wanted to let you know it went well with Lionel."

She sucked in a breath, trying to be equally businesslike, unaffected by his potent nearness and the need to feel his lips on hers one more time. "He's okay? You fixed the hemangioma? And he looks good?"

"You probably wouldn't think he looks good."

Her stomach dropped. "Why…? What, is it messed up?"

He laughed. "No. But right now it's sutured and swollen and would only look good to a zombie. Or a surgeon who knows what he's doing. We'll take the bandage off in a few days."

"Okay. Great." She pressed her hand to her chest, hoping to goodness it really had turned out all right. Hoping the hard beat of her heart was just from the scare, and not a lingering effect of the almost-kiss of a moment ago.

"Can you unlock your car for me? I need to get my stuff out and take it to my room."

"Of course. But I didn't tell you—even though I'm not happy with our Dr. Smith, I couldn't exactly throw him out on the streets until his flight leaves tomorrow. So he's going to be staying in the room you were in for just tonight."

"What? I'm not staying at your house again."

It was hard not to be insulted at the horror on his face. 'Goodbye, Charlie' took on a whole new meaning with Trent. "Sorry, but you're sleeping on a rollaway here in my office. I don't want you staying in my house, either."

"You do too." His lips quirked, obliterating his frown.

"Uh, no, I don't. Like I said before, you're an egomaniac. Somebody needs to bring you down a peg or two, and I guess it's going to be me."

"Thanks for your help. I appreciate it more than you know." That irritating little smile gave way to seriousness. "And it's good we're on the same page. Second goodbyes can get…sticky."

"Agreed. And you're welcome. I'll get my keys now before I head to the school." She turned, so glad she hadn't fallen into an embrace with the conceited guy. His long fingers grasped her elbow and the resulting tingle that sped up her arm had her jerking it away.

"Wait a second. You're going up to the school?"

"Yes. I have some things I want to go over with the teachers. I'm having lunch with them and the kids."

He was silent, just looking at her with a slight frown over those blue eyes, as though he couldn't decide something. He finally spoke. "Mind if I come along? I'd like to see it, and I'm not needed in the clinic right now."

"Sure. If you want." She shrugged casually. Did the man have to ponder whether seeing the school was worth being with her for a few hours? Or was she being hypersensitive?

She led the way down the short hall into the soupy, humid air, making sure to stand on Trent's left so her good ear would be closest to him. "The kids love visitors. But we'll be walking, so don't be surprised if you get a little muddy."

"Glad I'm not wearing my designer shoes today. Then again, I could've taken them off. Nothing like a little mud between the toes."

The thought of cool, squishy mud on bare feet, then playing a little footsie together, sounded strangely appealing, and she rolled her eyes at herself as they trudged up the road to the schoolhouse. Maybe she needed to try and find a local boyfriend to take off this edge she kept feeling around Trent. He reached for the binder of papers she was carrying and tucked it under his arm.

"So you were the boy who earned points by

carrying a girl's books to school? Why doesn't that surprise me?"

"Hey, I looked for any way to earn points. Carrying books was just one of them."

"I can just imagine. So what other ways did you earn points?" And why couldn't she just keep her mouth shut? "You know, never mind. I don't think I want to know."

"You already know some of them." He leaned closer as they walked, the scent of him teasing her nose. "But a few things got me more points than others. For example, my famous shoulder-rubs always scored big."

The memory of that shoulder rub came in a rush of clarity—them naked in her bed, sated and relaxed, the ceiling fan sending cool whispers of air across their skin. Her breathing got a little shallow and she walked faster.

"One of the ground rules is to stop with the references to last night. Got it?"

"I wasn't referring to anything but the shoulder rub I gave you at your office desk. Can I help it if your mind wants to go other places?"

She scowled at the bland innocence on his face. The man was about as far from innocent as he could be. "Mmm-hmm. So, when you mention back rubs, you don't picture me naked?"

His slow smile, his blue eyes dancing as he leaned closer, made her feel a little weak at the knees. "Charlotte, you can bet I frequently picture you naked." His gaze held hers, then slid away to the road. "Again, I'm sorry. That was inappropriate. Let's talk about the school. Did you open it at the same time as the hospital?"

Phew; she had to stop just blurting out what she was thinking, though he seemed to have the same problem. Good thing he changed the subject, or she just might have melted down into the mud.

"John Adams concentrated on getting the school open while I focused on the hospital. His daughter, Patience—I think you met her?—will be going to school next year, so he's been pretty excited about the project. They live in a small apartment attached to the school, so she'll probably be there today. She loves to hang out in the classrooms and pretend she can read and write."

"Patience is a cutie. She and I bonded over ice-cream." His eyes always turned such a warm blue when he talked about children; it filled her chest with some kind of feeling she didn't want to analyze. "So, is John from here?"

"Just so you know, he's always gone by both his first and last name. I'm not sure why." She smiled. "John Adams's parents both worked with my parents here. They left too when the war broke out. Their family and mine met up again in Togo and, since he's just a few years older than I am, he's kind of like a brother. And I love Patience like I would a niece."

"Where's her mother?"

"She died suddenly of meningitis. It was a terrible shock." She sighed. "Moving here with me to open this place has been a fresh start for John Adams and Patience, and hugely helpful to me. I couldn't have done it alone."

"I've been wondering where your funding is coming from. The GPC's been cutting back, so I know they can't be floating cash for the whole hospital."

"We've shaken down every possible donor, believe me. The school was as big a shambles as the hospital, and usually donor groups focus on one or the other. But we managed to get the building reasonably repaired and the basics in—desks and supplies and stuff. We opened with thirty primary-school-aged kids enrolled and have almost a hundred now." She shook her head. "It's not nearly enough, though, with half a million Liberian kids not attending school at all. And sixty percent of girls and women over fifteen can't read or write."

He frowned. "Is it as hard to raise cash for a school as it is for a hospital?"

"It's all hard. But I'm working on getting a donation from a church group in the States that'll help us hire a new teacher and have enough food for the kids' lunches. I'm excited. It looks like it's going to come through." Charlie smiled at Trent, but his expression stayed uncharacteristically serious. "We hate turning families away, but can't just endlessly accept kids into the program, you know? It's not fair to the teachers or the students to have classrooms so big nobody gets the attention they need. So I'm sure hoping it works out."

"How soon will you know?"

"In the next day or two, I think."

His expression was oddly inscrutable. "Be sure to tell me if the donation comes through or not, okay?"

"Okay." She had to wonder why he wanted to know, but appreciated his interest. "As for the hospital, I'm supposed to get a giant check from the Gilchrist Foundation as soon as the new wing is ready to go, thank heavens."

He stopped dead and stared at her. "The Gilchrist Foundation?"

"Yes. You've heard of them?"

"Yeah. You could say that."

CHAPTER FOUR

"Has the Gilchrist Foundation donated to hospitals you've worked at before?" Charlotte asked. "Did they come through with their support? I'm a little worried, because we're scraping the bottom of the barrel just to get the wing finished."

Trent looked into her sweet, earnest face before turning his attention to the verdant landscape—not nearly as vivid and riveting as the color of her eyes. "They're a reputable organization."

"That's good to hear." She sounded slightly breathless, her footsteps squishing quickly in the mud, and he slowed his stride. He resisted the urge to grasp her arm to make sure she didn't slip and fall. "I heard they were, but they're making us jump through some hoops to get it."

He almost asked *what hoops?*, but decided to keep out of it. The last thing he wanted was to get involved with anything to do with the Gilchrist Foundation. Or for Charlotte to find out his connection to it. "It'll be fine, I'm sure. So, this is it." He looked up at the one-storey cement building painted a golden yellow, the windows and door trimmed in a brick color. "Looks like you've done a nice job restoring it."

"It took a lot of money and manpower. It was basically a shell, with nothing left inside. The windows were gone and there were bullet holes everywhere. John Adams and I are pretty proud of how it turned out."

As they reached the wooden door of the school he saw Charlotte glance up at the sky, now filling with dark-gray clouds. "Looks like rain's coming, and I wasn't smart enough to bring an umbrella. Sorry. We won't stay too long."

"I'm not made of sugar, you know. I won't melt," he teased. Then the thought of sugar made him think of her sweet lips and the taste of her skin. It took a serious effort to turn away, not to pull her close to take a taste.

They left their muddy shoes outside before she led the way in. Children dressed in white shirts with navy-blue pants or skirts streamed from classrooms, laughing and chattering.

"Mr. Trent!" Cute little Patience ran across the room, the only one in a sleeveless dress instead of a uniform. "Mr. Trent, you bring me candy?"

"Sorry, Miss Impatience, I don't have any left." She wrapped her arms around his leg and the crestfallen expression on her face made him wish he'd brought a whole lot more. Too bad he hadn't known he'd be here longer than a few days.

"How about gum?"

He laughed and swung her up into his arms. "Don't have any of that left either." He lowered his voice. "But, next time you're at the hospital, I'll sneak some pudding out of the pantry for you, okay?"

"I heard that." Charlotte's brows lifted. "Since when are you two best friends? Dr Trent just got here a few days ago."

"Mr. Trent and me are good friends, yes." The girl's arms tightened around his neck, which felt nice. Kids didn't want or expect anything from you but love. And maybe candy too, he thought with a smile. There weren't too many adults he could say that about.

"Patience and I share a fondness for that chocolate pudding."

"Hmm." A mock frown creased Charlotte's face as she leaned close to them. "I didn't know you were stealing supplies, Dr Dalton. I'm going to have to keep an eye on you."

"What's the punishment for stealing?" His gaze dropped from her amused eyes to her pink lips. Maybe if he stole a kiss he'd find out.

"I don't think you want to know." Her eyes were still smiling and he found himself riveted by the glow of gold and brown flecks deep within that beautiful green.

"Miss Edwards!" Several kids ran their way. "You coming to see our play this Wednesday? Please come, Miss Edwards!"

Charlotte wrapped her arms around their shoulders in hugs, one after another, talking and smiling, making it obvious she wasn't a distant director around here; that she put in a lot of face time, truly cared about these kids. That impressed the hell out of him. He'd seen a lot of hospital directors in his day, even some in mission hospitals, who were more focused on the bottom line and making donors happy than they were about helping the patients they existed for.

Trent set Patience back on her feet. "Have you been doing any more drawing? You know I like to see your art." Nodding enthusiastically, her short legs took off running back down a hall.

He watched Charlotte with the kids. He'd never worked at a mission hospital that included a school in its compound. He hadn't been able to resist a chance to peek at it and see what they were accomplishing, even when he knew it wasn't the best idea to spend much time with Charlotte.

The whole reason he'd come was to see the school children, but he found it impossible to pull his attention from the smiling woman talking to them. He'd teased her about picturing her naked, but the truth was he couldn't get the vision of her out of his mind at all: clothed or unclothed, smiling and happy or ready to kick someone's ass.

Damn it.

Time to get his mind on the whole reason he was here—to find out what the kids were learning and how the school helped them. Charlotte patted a few of the children and turned her attention to him.

"Is this where we're going to eat?" he asked. The room was filled with folding tables that had seats attached, and some of the children were already sitting down.

"What, are you hungry? And you were making fun of me wanting lunch."

He grinned at her teasing expression. Man, she was something. A fascinating mix of energy, passion and determination all mixed in with a sweet, soft femininity. "I haven't eaten since five a.m. But I still wouldn't knock someone over in a hallway in search of a meal."

"As if I could knock you over, anyway." She took the binder from him and gestured to the tables. "Find a seat. I'll be right back."

Standing here, looking at all the bright-eyed and happy kids, he was annoyed with himself. Why hadn't it hadn't ever occurred to him to donate some of his fortune to this kind of school? He'd focused on giving most of his anonymous donations to the kind of hospitals he worked in. To those that medically served the neediest of humans in the world.

But that was going to change to include helping with education—a whole other kind of poverty. Not having access to learning was every bit as bad as having no access to health care.

"Here's my picture, Mr. Trent!" Patience ran up with a piece of construction paper crayoned with smiling children sitting at desks, one of them a lot bigger than the others.

"Who's this student?" he asked, pointing at the large figure he suspected just might be a self-portrait of the artist.

"That's me." Patience gave him a huge smile. "I sit in class sometimes now. Miss Jones said I could."

"I bet you're really smart. You'll be reading and writing in no time." And to make that happen for a lot more kids, he'd be calling his financial manager pronto.

"Yes." She nodded vigorously. "I go to read right now."

She took off again and he chuckled at how cute she was, with her little dress and pigtails flying as she ran. He sat at one of the tables and saw the kids eyeing him, some shyly, others curious, a few bold enough to come close. Time for the tried and tested icebreaker. He pulled a pack of cards from his pocket and began to shuffle. "Anybody want to see a card trick?"

Faces lit, giggles began and a few children headed over, then more shoved their way in, until the table was full and the rest stood three-deep behind them.

"Okay." He fanned the cards face down and held them out to a grinning little girl with braids all over her head. "Pick a card. Any card." When she began to pull one out, he yanked the deck away. "Not that one!"

Startled, her grin faded and she stared at him.

"Just kidding." He gave her a teasing smile to let her know it was all in fun, and she giggled in relief as the other children hooted and laughed. He held out the fanned deck again. "Pick a card. I won't pull it away again, honest. Look at it, show it to a friend, but don't let me see it. Then stick it back in the deck."

The girl dutifully followed his directions. He did his sleight-of-hand shuffling before holding up a card. "Is this it?" He had to grin at how crestfallen they looked as they shook their heads. "Hmm. This it?"

"No, that's not it." She looked worried, like it would somehow be her fault if the trick didn't work.

"Well, you know third time's a charm, right? *This* is the one you picked." He held up what he

knew would be the card she'd chosen, and everyone shrieked and whooped like he'd pulled a rab-
bit from a hat or held up a pot of gold.

"How you do that, mister?" a boy asked, cran-
ing his neck at the card deck as though the answer
was written there.

"Magic." One of the best parts about doing the
trick was showing the kids how to do it themselves. "How about we do it a few more times?
Then I'll teach you exactly how it's done."

Before Charlie and the teachers even got back to
the common room, the sound of loud talking and
laughter swept through the school's hall. Mariam,
the headmistress, pursed her lips and frowned.
"I'm sorry, Miss Charlotte. I don't know why
they're being so rowdy. I'll take care of it."

"It's fine. They're at lunch, after all." Though
she was pretty sure it hadn't been served yet. Curious as to what was causing all the excitement,
she walked into the room, only to stop in utter
surprise at the scene.

Looking ridiculously large for it, Trent sat at a
table completely surrounded by excited children,
like some handsome Pied Piper. He was holding
up cards, shuffling and flicking them, then handing them to kids who did the same, all the while
talking and grinning. As she came farther into
the room, she could hear the students bombard-

ing him with questions that he patiently answered more than once.

She hadn't seen this side of Trent before. Yes, she'd seen his gentle bedside manner with Lionel, his obvious caring for the boy. Still, she couldn't help but be amazed at the connection she was witnessing. So many of the children in this school had been traumatized in one way or another and a number of them were orphaned. Yet, to watch this moment, you'd think none of them had a care in the world other than having a fun time with whatever Trent was sharing with them.

She moved closer to the table. "What's going on here?"

One of the older boys waved some cards. "Mr. Trent is showing us card tricks, Miss Edwards! See me do one!"

"I'd love to." Her eyes met Trent's and her heart fluttered a little at the grin and wink he gave her. "But you should call him Dr Trent. He's a physician working at the hospital for a few days."

"Dr Trent?" Anna, a girl in the highest grade they could currently offer, looked from Charlie to Trent, her expression instantly serious. "You a doctor? My baby brother is very sick with the malaria. Mama Grand has been treating him, but we're worried. Would you care if I go get him and bring him here for you to see?

"Can your mommy or grandmother bring him to the hospital?" Charlie asked.

Anna shook her head. "Mommy is away working in the rice fields. But I can get him and carry him there if that is better."

"How old is he?" Charlie asked.

"Six years old, Ma."

Charlie knew many of these kids walked miles to get to school, and didn't want Anna hauling an ill six-year-old that kind of distance. Not to mention that she could hear rain now drumming hard on the roof of the school. "How about if I drive and get him? You can show me where you live."

Trent stood. "It's pouring outside. I'll go back and get the car and pick you two up, then we'll just see him at your home."

Charlie pulled her keys from her pocket and headed for the door. "It's okay, I'll just…"

In two strides, Trent intercepted her and snagged the keys from her hand. "Will you just let someone else help once in a while? Please? I'll be right back."

Charlie watched as he ducked out of the doorway into the heavy rain, all too aware of the silly surge of pleasure she felt at the way he insisted on taking on this problem, never mind that she could handle it herself. Well, not the medical part; she was thankful he'd be able to contribute his expertise as well as the nurses and techs at the hospital.

Her car pulled up in no time and, before she and Anna could come out, Trent had jogged to the door with an open umbrella and ushered Anna into the backseat. Water slid down his temples and dripped from his black hair as he opened the passenger door for Charlie. "You're riding shotgun this time, boss lady."

"It's my car. I know how to drive in this kind of weather."

He made an impatient sound. "Please just get in and stop arguing."

She opened her mouth to insist, but saw his set jaw and his intent blue eyes and found herself sliding into the seat, though why she let him tell her what to do she wasn't sure. It must have something to do with the man's overwhelming mojo.

She wasn't surprised that he proved more than competent at the wheel, despite the deepening mud and low visibility through the torrential rain. Even in good weather, this thinning road was barely more than a track through the bush. It couldn't really be called a road at all at the moment.

A group of crooked, heartbreakingly dilapidated zinc shacks appeared through the misty sheets of rain, and the distinctive smell of coal fires used for cooking touched Charlie's nose.

"It's up here. That one," Anna said, pointing.

The car slid to a stop. "Sit tight for a sec," Trent

said. He again grabbed the umbrella and brought it to their side of the car before opening Charlie's door.

"I'm not made of sugar, you know. I won't melt," Charlie said, repeating what he'd said to her earlier as she climbed out to stand next to him.

"You sure about that? I remember you tasting pretty sweet." Beneath the umbrella, he was so close she could feel his warmth radiating against her skin. The smell of the rain, mud, coal fires and Trent's own distinctive and appealing scent swirled around her in a sensory overload. His head dipped and those blue eyes of his met hers and held. She realized she was holding her breath, struck by a feeling of the two of them being completely alone in the world as the rain pounded a timpani concerto on the fabric above their heads.

Her heart did a little dance as his warm breath touched her face. Blue eyes darker now, his head dipped closer still until his lips slipped across hers, whisper-soft, clinging for a moment. "Yeah. Like sugar and honey."

His lids lowered in a slow blink before he straightened, turning to open Anna's door.

The child led the way as they trudged up to a group of metal shacks, giving Charlie's heart rate a chance to slow. Why had he kissed her when they'd agreed not to go there? Probably for the same reason she'd wanted him to—that overwhelming chemistry between them that had caught fire the first day they'd met.

They approached a shack that looked as though it must be Anna's home. A cooking pot sat over a coal fire with what smelled like cassava simmering inside. The shack's crooked door was partially open, and Anna shoved it hard, scraping it along the muddy ground until they could step inside the dark interior.

A young child lay sleeping on a mat on the dirt floor and another was covered with a blanket, exposing only his or her outline. An older woman with a brightly patterned scarf on her head sat on a plastic chair, stitching some fabric.

"Mama Grand, I bring a doctor to see Prince."

The woman looked at them suspiciously. "No need, Anna. I use more healing herbs today and Prince will be fine soon."

Anna twisted her fingers and looked imploringly at her. "Please. The doctor is here, so let him see if Prince is getting better."

Trent stepped forward and gave one of his irresistibly charming smiles to the woman. "I'm sure you're doing a fine job taking care of Prince. But the boss lady, Miss Edwards here, will be mad at me if I don't have work to do today. She might not even pay me. Can I please just take a look at your fine little one while I'm here?"

The woman's stern expression softened slightly,

and after a moment she inclined her head. Charlie had a hard time suppressing a smile. Trust Trent to turn it around to make Charlie look like the bad guy, and to know exactly how to twist it so his being there was no reflection on the older woman's treatments.

Trent crouched down and looked back at the woman. "Is this Prince hiding under the blanket? May I look at him?"

She nodded again, and Trent reached to pull the blanket from the small, huddled shape. He quickly jerked back when he saw the exposed child.

"What the…?" Trent's face swung towards Charlie, his eyebrows practically reaching his hair.

CHAPTER FIVE

THE LITTLE BOY looked like a ghost. Literally. He'd been covered head to toe in white paint. In all Trent's years of seeing crazy and unusual things around the world, he'd never seen this.

Charlotte covered a small smile with her fingertips, and he could tell she wanted to laugh at whatever the hell his expression was. Could he help it if it startled him to see the little guy looking like that?

"It's a common home remedy here for malaria. The sick person is painted white as part of the cure."

"Ah." Trent schooled his features into normal professionalism and turned back to the boy. He touched his knuckles to the sleeping child's cheeks, then pressed the child's throat, both of which were hot and sweaty. The boy barely opened his eyes to stare at him before becoming wracked by a prolonged, dry cough. When the cough finally died down, Trent leaned close to him with a smile he hoped would reassure him.

"Hi, Prince. I'm Dr Dalton. How do you feel? Anything hurting?"

Prince didn't answer, just slid his gaze towards his sister. She knelt down next to him and touched her hand to the boy's thin shoulder. "It's okay, Prince. Dr Dalton is here to help you get better."

"Have you had belly pain or diarrhea?" The boy still just stared at him, looking scared, as though Trent was the one who looked like a ghost. Maybe the child was delirious. "Anna, do you know about any belly pain? Has he been confused or acting strange?"

She nodded. "He did complain about his tummy hurting. And he has been saying silly things. I think he seems the same as when I had the malaria—shaking and feeling very hot and cold."

"Trent, how about I drive back to the compound and get the malaria medicine?" Even through the low light, he could see the green of Charlotte's eyes focused intently on his. "I'll bring it back here; maybe we won't have to scare him by taking him to the hospital."

He shook his head, not at all sure this was malaria. "If he has belly pain, it might be typhoid, which requires a different kind of antibiotic. Hard to tell with a child who's sick and obtunded like he is. The only way to know for sure is if we take him back to the hospital and get a blood test—see if it shows the parasites or not."

"No hospital." The older woman's lips thinned. "If de boy go, he will never come back."

Obviously, the poor woman had lost someone she loved. "I'll watch over him myself," Trent said. "I promise to keep him safe."

"Mama Grand, no boys are kidnapped any more. For true. The war is over a long time now."

Damn, so that was what she was worried about. He could barely fathom that boys this young had been kidnapped to be soldiers, but knew it had happened so often that some parents sent their children out of the country to be safe, never to see them again.

He stood and reached for the woman's rough and gnarled hand. "I understand your worries. But it's important that Prince have a test done that we can only do at the hospital. I promise you that I will care for Prince and look after him like I would if he were my own child, and return him to you when he's well. Will you trust me to do that?"

The suspicious look didn't completely leave the woman's face, but she finally nodded. Trent didn't want to give her a chance to change her mind and quickly gathered Prince in his arms, wrapping the blanket around him as best he could.

"You want to come with us, Anna? You don't have to, but it might make Prince feel more comfortable," Charlotte said.

"Yes. I will come."

"Are you going to hold Prince so I can drive, or do you want to take the wheel?" he asked Charlotte as they approached the car.

"You know the answer to that." Her gorgeous eyes glinted at him. "You're in the passenger seat, Dr. Dalton."

He had to grin. "You really should address this little controlling streak of yours, Ms. Edwards. Find out why relinquishing power scares you so much."

"It doesn't scare me. I just trust my own driving over anyone else's."

"Mm-hm. One of these days, trying to control the direction the world spins is going to weigh heavy on those pretty shoulders of yours. Drive on, boss lady."

Tests proved that Prince did indeed have typhoid, and after a couple days he'd recovered enough to return home. Charlie was glad that Trent's expertise had led him to insist the child be tested, instead of just assuming it was malaria, as she had.

She was also glad that, in the days that had passed since Trent had come back, she'd managed to stop thinking about him for hours at a time. Well, maybe not *hours*. Occasionally, the man sneaked into her thoughts. Not her fault, since she wasn't deaf and blind—okay, a little hard of hearing in that one ear of hers she was grateful to have it at all.

His voice, teasing and joking with the nurses and techs, sometimes drifted down the hall to her office. His distinctively tall form would occasionally stride in front of her office on his way from the clinic to the hospital ward until she decided just to shut the darn door.

She'd made a conscious effort to stay away from the hospital ward where she might run into him. She got dinner alone at home, or ate lunch at her desk so she wouldn't end up sitting with him in the kitchen. She spent time at the school instead of here, where thoughts of him kept invading her brain, knowing he was somewhere nearby.

It helped that Trent had kept their few interactions since the brief kiss in the rain short and professional. When the man said goodbye, he sure meant it, never mind that she felt the same way. Thank heavens he'd be leaving again in the next few days so she wouldn't have to suffer the embarrassment of thinking about all they'd done in their single night together.

Her door opened and her heart gave an irritating little kick of anticipation that it just might be his blue eyes she'd see when she looked up.

But it was John Adams standing there. "Any word yet on the funding for another teacher?"

She smiled and waved a paper. "Got the green

light. I'm sending the final forms today, and they said we should get a check in about a month. Is the woman you've been training going to work out?"

"Yes, most definitely." He dramatically slapped a hand to his barrel chest. "She is smart and beautiful and I am in love with her. Thanks to God I can officially offer her a job."

"You're starting to remind me of ladies' man Dr Dalton. No mixing business with pleasure." A flush filled her cheeks as soon as the words were out of her mouth, since she'd done exactly that, and the pleasure had been all too spectacular.

"Yes, ma'am." He grinned. "Anyway, I also stopped to tell you to come look at our little patient this morning."

"What little patient?"

"Lionel. The one with appendicitis and the hemangioma—or who used to have a hemangioma. You won't believe what Trent's done with it."

Alarm made Charlie's heart jerk in her chest. She'd worried from the moment she'd agreed to let Trent take care of such a delicate procedure. Had he messed it up? She'd checked on the child a couple of times, but a patch had still covered his eye. "What do you mean? Is it going to have to be redone when we get a plastic surgeon in here?"

"Just come and see."

She rose and followed him to the hospital ward, her fears eased a bit by John Adams's relaxed and smiling expression. Still, she couldn't shake the feeling that she might have made a big mistake.

Lionel's head was turned towards his mother, who sat by his bedside, and Charlie found herself holding her breath as they came to stand beside him.

"Show Miss Charlotte how well you're seeing today, Lionel," John Adams said.

The boy turned his head and she stared in disbelief.

The patch had been removed and, considering he'd had surgery only days before, he looked shockingly, amazingly normal.

The angry red bulge that had been the vascular tumor was gone. His eyebrow and eyelid, other than still being bruised and slightly swollen from surgery, looked like any other child's. His big, brown eye, wide and lit with joy, was now completely visible, just like his other one.

"Oh, my. Lionel, you look wonderful!" She pressed her hands to her chest. "Can you see out of that eye?"

"I can see! Yes, I can! And Mommy show me in the mirror how handsome I look!"

"You even more handsome than your brothers now, boyo, and I told them so," his mother said with a wide smile.

Tears stung Charlie's eyes as she lifted her gaze to the child's mother and saw so many emotions on the woman's face: happiness; profound relief; deep gratitude.

All because of Trent.

Where was the man? Had he seen the amazing result of his work? She turned to a smiling John Adams. "Has Dr Dalton seen him since the patch was removed?"

"Oh, yes. He took it off himself this morning."

"Dr. Dalton told me he gave me special powers, too, like Superman." The child's face radiated excitement. "Said I have x-ray vision now."

His mother laughed. "Yes, but Dr. Dalton was just joking and you know it. Don't be going and telling everyone that, or they'll expect you to see through walls."

"I can see so good, I bet I can see through walls. I bet I can."

"Maybe you'll become a doctor, Superman, who can see people's bones before you operate." Trent's voice vibrated into the room from behind Charlie's back. "That would be pretty cool."

"I want to be a doctor like you. I want to fix people like you do, Dr. Trent."

Trent's smile deepened as he came to stand next to Charlie. "That's a good goal, Lionel. If you study hard in school, I bet you can do anything you set your mind to."

Charlie stared at Trent, looking so relaxed, like all this was no big deal. Maybe it wasn't to him, but it was to her, and to Lionel and to his mother. A very, very big deal.

"I can't believe the wonderful job you did," she said, resting her hand on his forearm. "You told me I didn't know who I was dealing with and you were sure right."

"Now she learns this, just before I'm ready to leave."

The twinkle in his eyes, and his beautifully shaped lips curved into that smile, were practically irresistible. She again was thankful that he would be heading out of her life very soon before she made a complete fool of herself. "Good thing you don't have x-ray vision too. Hate to think what you'd use it for."

"Checking for broken bones, of course." His smile widened. "What else?"

She wasn't going where her mind immediately went. "Probably to decipher a bank-vault combination, so you could go on vacation without working a solid year. Speaking of which, the GPC says a general surgeon should be here in a matter of days, so you can have them schedule your flight out of here soon."

"Great."

The relief on his face was obvious and she hated that it hurt a tiny bit to see it. "I can't help but wonder, though, why are you working as a general surgeon when you can do things like this?"

His smile faded. "You think plastic surgery has more value? More than saving someone's life? I don't."

"It's a different kind of value: changing lives; changing the way someone is viewed, the way they view themselves. You have an obvious gift for this, a skill many would envy." Did he not see how important all that was? "Your focus should be on plastic surgery. On helping people that way."

"The way other people view a person, what they expect them to be and who they expect them to be, shouldn't have anything to do with how they view themselves." He took a step back and pulled his arm away from her touch. She hadn't known those eyes of his were capable of becoming the chilly blue that stared back at her. "Excuse me, I have a few other patients to check on."

She frowned as she watched him walk through the hospital ward. What had she said to make him mad?

"I have things to do too," John Adams said. But, like her, his gaze followed Trent, his expression thoughtful. "Bye, Lionel. See you later, Charlie."

"Okay. Listen, can you come have dinner tonight at my house? I'd like to talk to you about some things."

He nodded and headed off. Charlie watched Trent examining another patient and could only hope John Adams came up with a good idea for how she could accomplish her newest goal—which was to encourage Trent to perform surgery on a few patients in the day or two he'd still be here, patients who'd needed reconstructive surgery long before the plastic surgery wing had even been conceived.

She knew how desperately some of these people needed to have their lives changed in that way. Not to mention that it wouldn't hurt for her to have a few "before and after" photos that would impress the Gilchrist Foundation with what they were already accomplishing. And, really, how could Trent object?

As she headed back to her office, her cell phone rang and she pulled it from her pocket. "Charlotte Edwards."

"Hey, Charlie! It's Colleen. How're things going with Trent Dalton?"

"With Trent?" What the heck? Did the gossip vine go all the way to GPC headquarters? Besides, nobody here knew she and Trent had briefly hooked up…did they? "What do you mean?"

"Is it working out that he came back until the new temp gets there?"

Phew. Thank heavens she really didn't have to answer the first question, though their moment together was history anyway. "He's doing a good job, but I know he wants to move on. Do you have a final arrival date for the new doc?"

"Perry Cantwell has agreed to come and we're finalizing his travel plans. Should be any day now." Her voice got lower, conspiratorial. "Just tell me. I've seen photos of Trent that make me salivate, but is he really as hunky as everyone says? Whenever I talk to him on the phone his voice makes me feel all tingly."

If just his voice made Colleen feel tingly, Charlie hated to think what would happen if she saw him in person. She wasn't about to confess to Colleen that, despite his reputation, she'd fallen into bed with him for one more than memorable night. While she felt embarrassed about that now, she still couldn't regret it, despite unexpectedly having to work with him again. "He's all right. If you like tall, good-looking surgeons who flirt with every woman in sight and think everything's amusing."

"Mmm. Sounds good to me if the surgeon in question has beautiful black hair and gorgeous eyes." The sound of a long sigh came through the phone and Charlie shook her head. She supposed she should feel smug that über-attractive Trent had wanted to spend a night with her. But, since he likely had a woman in every port, that didn't necessarily say much about her personal sex appeal. "I actually have his new release papers on my desk to send out today. Are you going to hit on him before he leaves?" Colleen asked. "Might be a fun diversion for a couple days."

Been there, done that. And, yes, it had been— very fun. Keeping it strictly professional now, though, was the agreed goal. "I've got tons to do with the new wing opening any time now. And my dad called to say he's coming some time soon to see how things are going with that."

"Actually, I have some bad news about the new wing, I'm afraid." Colleen's voice went from light to serious in an instant.

Her heart jerked. "What bad news?"

"You know David Devor, the plastic surgeon we had lined up to work there?" Colleen asked. "He has a family emergency and can't come until it's resolved, which could be quite a while."

"Are you kidding me? You know I have to have someone here next week, Colleen! The Gilchrist Foundation made it clear we won't get the funding we need until I have at least one plastic surgeon on site."

"I know. I'm doing the best I can. But I'm having a hard time finding a plastic surgeon who wants to work in the field. I'm turning over every rock I can, but I can't promise anybody will be there until Dr. Devor is available. Sorry."

Lord, this was a disaster! Charlie swiped her hand across her forehead. The hospital was scarily deep in the red from getting the new wing built. It had to be opened pronto.

"Okay." She sucked in a calming breath. "But I have to have a plastic surgeon, like *now*."

"I know, but I just told you—"

"Listen. I need you to hold off a day or two before you send Trent's release papers. Give me time to talk to him about maybe staying on here. If he agrees, you can send Perry Cantwell somewhere else."

There was a long silence on the phone before Colleen spoke. "Why? Cantwell's expecting to come soon. And I can't just hold Trent's paperwork. He's already filled in for you twice and is way overdue for his vacation. I don't get it."

"I found out Trent's a plastic surgeon, not just a general surgeon." She gulped and forged on. "If Devor can't be here, I have to keep Trent here at least long enough to get the wing open and the funding in my hand. Otherwise I won't be able to pay the bank, and who knows what'll happen?"

"Maybe he'll agree to stay."

"Maybe. Hopefully." But she doubted he would. Hadn't he made it more than clear that he wanted to head out ASAP? The only reason he'd come back for a few days was because of how sick Lionel had been. "All I'm asking is for you to hang onto his release papers until I can talk to him."

"Charlie." Colleen's voice was strained. "You're one of my best friends. Heck, you got me this job! But you're asking me to do something un-ethical here."

"Of course I don't want you to do anything you feel is unethical." This was her problem, not Colleen's, and it wouldn't be right to put her friend in the middle of it. "Just send them out tomorrow instead of today, address them to me and I'll make sure he gets them. That will give me time to contact the Gilchrist Foundation and see if they'll make an exception on their requirements before the donation check is sent. If they won't, I'll try to get their representative to come right now while Trent's still here. I'm pretty sure the guy is close—somewhere in West Africa. I'll go from there."

Colleen's resigned sigh was very different from the one when she'd been swooning over Trent earlier. "All right. I'll wait until tomorrow to send the release papers and finalize Perry's travel plans to give you time to talk to Trent. But that's it."

"Thanks, Colleen. You're the best." Charlie tried to feel relieved but the enormity of the problem twisted her gut. "Hopefully they'll send the funding check even if we don't have a plastic surgeon here yet and we'll be out of the woods. I'll keep you posted."

The second she hung up, she searched for the Gilchrist Foundation's number. What would she do if they flat out said the conditions of the contract had to be met, which would probably be their response? Or if they couldn't send their representative here immediately? If the GPC couldn't find a plastic surgeon to come in any reasonable period of time, the whole hospital could fold. Every dollar of the GPC's funding, and all the other donations she'd managed to round up, had been spent renovating the nearly destroyed building, buying expensive equipment and hiring all the nurses, techs and other employees needed to run the place. And the money she'd borrowed to build the new wing was already racking up interest charges.

Adrenaline rushed through her veins as she straightened in her seat. The end justified the means. The hospital absolutely could not close and the plastic surgery wing had to open. It had to be there to help all the people who had horrible, disfiguring injuries left from the war. It had to help all the kids living with congenital deformities, like cleft palates, which they'd never have had to live with if they'd been born somewhere else. Somewhere with the kind of healthcare access she was determined to offer.

If the Gilchrist Foundation insisted on sticking with the contract stipulations, she had no choice but somehow to make sure Trent stayed on until the money was in her hand.

CHAPTER SIX

TRENT HAD BEEN relieved that Charlotte wasn't in the hospital commons for dinner. He hadn't wanted to make small talk with her while pretending he didn't feel insulted by her words.

The book he tried to read didn't hold his attention, and he paced in the sparse little bedroom until he couldn't take the confinement anymore. He headed into the humid, oppressive air and strode down the edges of the road, avoiding the muddy ruts as best he could.

When he'd first met Charlotte, he'd been impressed with her enthusiastic commitment to this place, to her vision of what she wanted it to become. And, as they'd spent time together, she'd seemed interested in his life. She'd asked smart and genuine questions, and he'd found himself opening up, just a little—sharing a few stories he usually kept to himself, nearly talking to her about things he just plain didn't talk about.

But, when it came right down to it, she was like anyone else: a woman who questioned who he was and why he did what he did. Who didn't particularly care what he wanted from his own life. Had she asked him *why* he didn't do plastic surgery exclusively? Expressed any interest in his reasons?

No. She'd just made the same snap judgment others had made. She'd told him what he should do, convinced she knew. Exactly like the woman in his life he'd trusted completely to have his back, to know him, to care.

A trust he'd never give again.

It was disappointing as hell. Then again, maybe this was a good thing. Maybe it would help him feel less drawn to her.

He needed to see this as a positive, not a negative. And, when he left in just a day or two, maybe the peculiar closeness he felt to her would be gone. He'd leave and hope to hell his world would be back to normal.

He kept walking, not having any particular destination in mind, just feeling like he didn't want to go back to that room and smother, but not wanting to chit-chat with people in the hospital either. Maybe he should call up a buddy on the phone, one of the fraternity of mission doctors who understood his life and why he did what he did. They always made him laugh and put any personal troubles in perspective.

As he pulled his cell from his pocket, he noticed a light up ahead. Had he somehow got turned around? He peered through the darkness and realized he was practically at Charlotte's doorstep. Had his damned stupid feet unconsciously brought him here because he'd been thinking of her so intently?

About to turn off on a different path, he was surprised to see little Patience bound out the door, holding a rope with a tiny puppy attached, bringing it down the porch steps. It sniffed around before doing its business, and Trent wanted to laugh at the look of distaste on the little girl's face as she picked up a trowel from the steps.

He didn't want to scare her by appearing out of nowhere in the darkness. "You have a new dog, Patience? When did you get it?"

She looked up at him and smiled. "Hi, Mr. Trent! Yes, Daddy got me another doggie. After my poor Rex was killed by that ugly, wild dog, I been asking and asking. He finally said yes, and my friends at the school like having her to play with too."

"What's its name?"

"Lucky—cos I'm lucky to have her. Except for this part." The look of distaste returned, replacing the excitement as she gripped the trowel. "I promised Daddy I would do everything to take care of her."

He scratched the cute little pup behind the ears,

chuckling at the way its entire hind end wagged in happiness before he reached for the trowel. A little doggie doo-doo was nothing compared to many of the things he'd dealt with. "Here. I'll do it for you this time." With a grateful smile, Patience let him dig a hole to bury the stuff. "What are you and your new pup doing here at Charlotte's house?"

"Miss Charlie fixed dinner for me and Daddy. They talking about work."

The door opened and the shadow of John Adams's big body came onto the porch. "Somebody out here with you, Patience?"

"Mr. Trent, Daddy. He's meeting Lucky."

"Trent. Come on inside. Charlie and I were just talking about you."

Damn. He didn't want to know what they were talking about and didn't particularly want to see Charlotte. But his feet headed up the steps, with Patience and the puppy trailing behind.

The warm glow of the quaint room, full of an odd mix of furniture styles and colorful rugs, embraced him as he stepped inside and he wondered what it was about this old house that gave it so much charm and appeal. An old upright piano against a wall had open sheet music leaning against the stand. Charlotte, dressed in sweatpants and a T-shirt, was curled on a sofa, and she looked up, her lips slightly parted.

The surprise in her green eyes gave way to a peculiar mix of wariness and warmth. As their gazes collided, as he took in the whole of her silken hair and lovely face, he was instantly taken back to earlier today. To their physical closeness beneath that umbrella. To the moment it had felt like it was just the two of them, alone and intimate. Despite all his promises to himself and to her, he'd found himself for that brief second leaning in to taste her mouth, to enjoy the sweetness of her lips.

Being in her house again sent his thoughts to the moment they'd sat on that sofa and kissed until both of them were breathless, ending up making love on the floor. Why did this woman make him feel this way every time he looked at her?

"Trent. I'm…surprised to see you."

Could she be thinking about their time together here too? "I was taking a walk. Then saw Patience and her new pup."

Patience ran to the piano and tapped on the keys, bobbing back and forth as the dog pranced around yapping. "Lucky likes to sing and dance, Mr. Trent, see?"

"She has a beautiful voice." As he smiled at the child, he was struck by a longing to go to the piano himself. To finger the keys as he'd done from the time he was six, until he'd left the U.S. for good. He hadn't realized until he'd first walked into this room with Charlotte a few days ago how much he'd missed playing.

"Miss Charlie has a very pretty voice," Patience enthused. "Please play for us, Miss Charlie. Play and sing something!"

Charlotte shook her head. "Not tonight. I'm sure Mr. Trent doesn't want a concert."

Her cheeks were filled with color. Surely the ultra-confident Charlotte Edwards wasn't feeling shy about performing for him? "Of course I'd like to hear you. What's your favorite thing she plays, Patience?" Surprised at how much he wanted to hear Charlotte sing, he settled himself into a chair, figuring there was no way she could say no to the cute kid.

"That song from church I like: *How Great Thou Art*. Please, Miss Charlie?" The child's hands were clasped together and for once she stood still, her eyes bright and excited.

As Trent had predicted, Charlotte gave a resigned sigh. "All right. But just the one song."

She moved to the piano, and his gaze slid from her thick hair to the curve of her rear, sexy even in sweatpants. Her fingers touched the keyboard, the beginning measures a short prelude to the simple arrangement before she began to sing. Trent forgot about listening to the resonance of the piano's sounding board and heard only the sweet, clear tones of Charlotte's voice, so moving and lovely his chest ached with the pleasure of it.

When the last piano note faded and the room became quiet, he was filled with a powerful desire for the moment to continue. To never end. Without thought, he found himself getting up from the chair to sit next to Charlotte, his hip nudging hers to scoot over on the bench.

"Let's sing a Beatles tune Patience might like," he said, his hands poised over the keys, his eyes fixed on the beautiful green of hers. He began to play *Lean On Me* and, when she didn't sing along, bumped his shoulder into hers. "Come on. I know you know it."

"Yes, Miss Charlie! Please sing!" Patience said, pressing her little body against Charlotte's leg.

John Adams began to sing in a slightly off-key baritone before Charlotte's voice joined in, the dulcet sound so pure it took Trent's breath away. When his hands dropped from the keyboard, he looked down into Charlotte's face, seeing Patience next to her, and he was struck with a bizarre and overwhelming vision of a life he hadn't even considered having: a special woman by his side, a family to love; the ultimate utopia.

"That was wonderful," she said, her eyes soft. "I didn't know you could play. Without music, even."

He drew in a breath to banish his disturbing

thoughts. "I was shoved onto a piano bench from the time I was little, and had a very intimidating teacher who made sure I was classically trained." He grinned. "I complained like heck sometimes when I had to practice instead of throwing a football around with my friends, but I do enjoy it." He hadn't realized how much until just now, shoulder to shoulder with her, sharing this intimate moment.

"Play something classical. Simple modern songs are about it for my repertoire."

He thought about what he'd still have memorized from long ago and realized it shouldn't be Bach or Haydn. That it should be something romantic, for her. "All right, but don't be surprised if I'm a little rusty. I bet you know this one: Debussy's *Clair de Lune*."

When the last notes of the piece died away, the softness on her face only inches from his had him nearly leaning in for a kiss, forgetting everything but how much he wanted to, and the only thing that stopped him was Patience's little face staring up at him from next to the keyboard.

"I liked that, Mr. Trent!"

"Yes." Charlotte's voice was a near-whisper as she rested her palm on his arm. "That... beautiful."

As he looked at the little girl, and stared into Charlotte's eyes filled with a deep admiration, the whole scene suddenly morphed from intimate and perfect to scary as hell. Why was he sitting here having fantasies about, almost a longing for, a life he absolutely did not want?

Abruptly, he stood. He needed to get out of there before he said or did something stupid.

Hadn't he, just earlier this evening, been annoyed and disappointed in her? Then one more hour with her and, bam, he was back to square one with all those uncomfortable and mixed feelings churning around inside. What the hell was wrong with him, he didn't want to try to figure out.

"You know, I need to head back to my quarters. I'm going to get most of my things packed up. I'm sure the GPC let you know the new temp is coming in just a day or two?"

"We need to talk about that." The softness that had been in her eyes was replaced by a cool and professional expression. He was damned if it didn't irritate him when he should be glad. "We have an issue."

"What issue?"

She glanced at John Adams before returning her attention to Trent. "Come sit down and we'll talk."

"I'm happy standing, thanks." Her words sounded ominous and he folded his arms across his chest, the disconcerting serenity he'd been feeling just a moment ago fading away like a mirage in the desert. He had a feeling this conversation had something to do with him staying longer, and that wasn't happening.

"The new temp is delayed. I'm not sure when he's going to get here." She licked those tempting lips of hers and, while her expression was neutral, her eyes looked strained and worried. As they should have.

"I told you not to try to guilt me into staying. I can't be here indefinitely." Except, damn it, as he said the words the memory of the comfort he'd felt a moment ago, that sense of belonging, made it sound scarily appealing.

"I'm not trying to guilt you into anything. I'm simply telling you the facts. Which are that, if you leave, there won't be another surgeon here for a while."

"The GPC does a good job finding docs to fill in when there's a gap. Especially when a place has nobody. Besides, you have Thomas here, and he does a great job on the hernias and other simple procedures."

"But what if we get another appendicitis case? Ectopic pregnancy? Something serious he can't handle?"

He shoved his hands into his pockets and turned to pace across the room, staring out the window at the heavy blackness of the night sky. Looking anywhere but into her pleading eyes.

"If there's one thing I've learned over the years, it's that one person can't save everybody who needs help, Charlotte. I'd be dead if I tried to be that person. Think about the ramifications of this for others, too: the longer I'm here, the more the snowball effect of docs having to fill in where I'm supposed to be next, which is the Philippines." He turned to her, hoping to see she understood what he was saying—not that the idea of staying here longer was both appealing and terrifying. "If the GPC hospital in the Philippines doesn't have anyone because I'm not there, is that okay? Better for patients there to die, instead of patients here?"

Her hands were clasped together so tightly her knuckles were white. "Just a couple of weeks, Trent. Maybe less, if it works out."

He shook his head. "I'm sorry, Charlotte. As soon as my release paperwork comes through from the GPC, I have to head out."

"Trent, all I'm asking is…"

The room that had felt so warm and welcoming now felt claustrophobic. He turned his attention to John Adams so he wouldn't have to look at her wide and worried eyes. "I have a few patients scheduled for surgery early, so I'm going to get to bed. If either of you know of patients needing surgery, you should schedule them in the next couple days before I leave." He scratched the dog behind the ears before he walked out the door, finding it impossible to completely stuff down the conflicting emotions that whirled within him.

As he walked through the darkness, a possible solution struck him that would assuage his guilt. Maybe a phone call to an old friend would solve all his problems and let him move on.

CHAPTER SEVEN

"How the hell are you, Trent?"

Trent smiled to hear Chase Bowen's voice on the phone. He'd worked with Chase for a number of years in different parts of the world, and the man had been the steadiest, most committed mission doctor he'd ever met. Until a certain wonderful woman had swept into the man's life, their little one in tow, and had changed him into a committed dad rooted in the States.

"I'm good. Decided to try to get hold of you during my lunch break before I see some patients in the clinic this afternoon. How's Drew doing?" When he'd heard the shocking news that Chase and Dani's little boy had cancer, it had scared the crap out of him. Thank goodness they'd caught it in time and the prognosis was excellent.

"He's doing great." The warmth and pride in Chase's voice came through loud and clear. "Completely healthy now, swimming like a fish and growing like crazy. So where are you working?"

"I'm filling in as a temp here in Liberia, hoping to head off on vacation soon, but there are some issues getting a new doc here." A problem he knew Chase was more than familiar with.

"So who's the lucky woman vacationing with you this time? Where are you going?"

"Still figuring all that out." No reason to tell Chase about his weird feelings, that he hadn't been able to find an interest in calling anyone. The man would laugh his butt off, then suggest he see a shrink. "How's Dani?"

"Wonderful. I haven't told you that Drew's going to have a baby brother or sister."

"That's great news. Congratulations." Of all the people he knew, Chase was the last one he'd ever have expected mostly to leave mission work to have a family. But he had to admit, the man seemed happy as hell. "You doing any mission stints at all?"

"Dani and I have gone twice to Honduras together, then I stayed for another week after she headed home. It's worked out well."

"You have any interest in coming to Liberia for just a week or so to fill in for me until the new doc gets here? The GPC needs me to head to the Philippines as soon as possible." Which wasn't exactly true, but he was going with it anyway, damn it.

"I don't know." Chase was silent on the line for a moment. "I'd really like to, but I'm not sure now's a good time. Dani's been a little under the weather, and I wouldn't want to leave her alone with Drew if she's not up to it. Let me talk to her and I'll call you back."

"Great. Give her a hug for me, and tell her I'm happy for both of you. And Drew too."

"Will do. Talk to you soon."

Trent shoved the phone in his pocket and headed back into the hospital. He'd known it was a long shot to think Chase might be able to fill in for him, but with any luck maybe it could still be a win-win. Chase could enjoy a short stint in Africa and Trent could shake the clinging dust of this place off his feet and forget all about Charlotte and her work ethic, spunkiness and warmth.

He thought about Dani, Chase and Drew and their little family that was about to grow. A peculiar sensation filled his chest and he took a moment to wonder what exactly it was. Then he realized with a shock that it was envy.

Envy? Impossible. He'd never wanted that kind of life: a wife who would have expectations of who you should be and how you should live. Kids you were responsible for. A life rooted in one place.

But there was no mistaking that emotion for anything else, and he didn't understand where the hell it had come from. Though Chase had never wanted that kind of life either—until he'd met a woman who had changed how he viewed himself.

The thought set an alarm clanging in his brain. He didn't want to change how he viewed himself. He'd worked hard to be happy with who he was and what he wanted from his life, leaving behind those who hadn't agreed with that view. Now wasn't the time to second-guess all that.

Resolutely shaking off all those disturbing feelings, he continued down the hospital corridor, hoping Charlotte's office door was closed, as it often was, since he had to walk by to get to the clinic. Unfortunately, the door was wide open and her melodic voice drifted into the hallway as she talked with John Adams.

"I'll be fine. I know how to use a gun, remember?"

"I'm not okay with that, Charlie. Patience and I'll pack a bag and move in for a few days until we're sure it was a one-time thing."

A gun? What was a one-time thing? He stopped in the doorway and looked in to see John Adams standing with his arms folded across his chest, a deep frown creasing his brow, and Charlotte staring back with her mulish expression in place.

"Except somebody needs to be at the school too, you know. After all the work and money we've put into the place, we can't risk it being wrecked up and having things stolen."

"What are you talking about?" Trent asked.

"This is not your concern, Trent. John Adams, please close the door so we can talk."

Trent stretched his arm across the door to hold it open. "Uh-uh. You want me to be stuck here for a while longer, you need to include me. What's going on?"

"Somebody broke into her house early this morning after she came to work. When she went there at lunch to get something, she found the door jimmied open and some things gone."

Trent stared at John Adams then swung his gaze to Charlotte. She frowned at him, her lips pressed together, but couldn't hide the tinge of worry in the green depths of her eyes. "What the hell? What was stolen?"

"A radio. The folding chairs I keep in a closet. Weird stuff. Thankfully, I had my laptop with me at work. It's not a big deal."

"It is a big deal." The protectiveness for her that surged in his veins was sudden and intense. "You can't stay there alone, period. The obvious solution is for John Adams to stay in their quarters at the school, and for me to stay with you until I leave."

Had those words really come out of his mouth? It would be torture to stay in her house with her, knowing she was close by at night in her bed. Bringing back hot memories of their night together. Making him think of the unsettling closeness and connection he'd felt while they'd sat at the piano together singing.

But there was no other option. Keeping her safe was more important than protecting himself from the damned annoying feelings that kept resurfacing.

"That's ridiculous, Trent." Her eyes still looked alarmed, but he was pretty sure it wasn't just about the break-in. "I'll be fine. Whoever it was probably just hit the place once and isn't likely to come back."

"You have no idea if that's true or not." He stepped to her desk and pressed his palms on it, leaning across until his face was as close to hers as hers had been to his at the airport. She smelled so damned good, and the scent of her and the lip gloss she was wearing made him want to find out what flavor gloss it was. "So, you never did tell me," he said, mimicking what she'd said to him at the airport. "What makes you so damned stubborn and resistant to accepting help when you need it? Except when it comes to the hospital, that is?"

"I'm not stubborn. I just don't think this is worth getting all crazy about."

"Maybe not. But it's not a hardship for me to stay at your house so you're not alone until we see if this is a one-time thing or not." So, yeah, that wasn't true. It would be a hardship to be so close to her without taking advantage of it, but no way was he leaving her at risk.

"Good." John Adams spoke from behind him. "Thanks, Trent. I appreciate it. I'm going back to the school now. See you both later."

He straightened. "I've got patients to see in the clinic then I'll get my things. See you back here at six."

"Seriously, Trent—"

"Six."

As he headed to the clinic, he was aware of a ridiculous spring in his step, while at the same time his chest felt a little tight. Obviously, his attraction to Charlotte was keeping the smarter side of his brain from remembering why he needed to keep his distance. And how the hell he was going to keep that firmly in mind while sharing her roof was a question to which he had to find an answer.

"So, Colleen, I'm all set!" Charlie forced a cheerful and upbeat tone to her voice. "Trent has agreed to stay on until the Gilchrist rep does his evaluation. So you can wait to schedule Perry Cantwell until then."

"That's great news for you, Charlie! So all your worries were for nothing."

The warmth in her friend's voice twisted her stomach into a knot. Lying to her felt every bit as bad as lying to Trent, but what choice did she have? "Yes, no worries." Oh, if only that were true.

"I'll let Perry know so he can plan his schedule. After the Gilchrist rep comes, give me a call to tell me how it goes."

"Will do. Thanks, Colleen." Charlie hung up and dropped her head into her hands.

How had her life become a disaster?

As if it wasn't enough to have the bank breathing down her neck, the plastic surgeon indefinitely delayed, Gilchrist insisting on the original stipulations of their agreement and having to skulk around lying to Trent and Colleen, she had a burglar who might come back and a gorgeous man she couldn't stop thinking about spending the night in her bed.

No. Not in her bed. In her spare bedroom. But that was almost as bad. Knowing his long, lean, sexy body was just a few walls away would be tempting, to say the least. But now there was an even better reason to steer clear of getting it on with him again for the days he was here.

She was pretty sure that if he knew she was delaying Perry Cantwell's arrival and had shoved his release papers beneath a pile on her desk he wouldn't take it lightly. In fact, she was more than sure that his easygoing smile would disappear and a side she hadn't seen yet would emerge—a very angry side— and she wouldn't even be able to blame him for it.

Her throat tight, Charlie took inventory of the new supply delivery, trying not to look at the big invoice that came with it. This whole deception thing felt awful, even more than she'd expected. But she just couldn't see another solution. Thank heavens the Gilchrist Foundation had said their representative should be here within the week. After they gave their approval and she got the check, Trent could be on his way. No harm, no foul, right?

The end justifies the means, she reminded herself again.

With a box of syringes in her arms, she stepped on a stool, struggling to shove the box onto a supply shelf, when a tall body appeared next to her. Long-fingered hands took the box and tucked it in front of another.

"Why don't you just ask for help from someone who's not as vertically challenged as you are?" Trent asked, his eyes amused, grasping her hand as she stepped off the stool.

Looking at his handsome, smiling face so close to hers, a nasty squeeze of guilt made it a little hard to breathe. She didn't even want to think about how that affable expression would change if he knew about her machinations.

"Just because I'm not tall doesn't mean I'm

handicapped. And I'm perfectly capable of getting off a stool by myself."

"I know. I only helped you to see those green eyes of yours flash in annoyance. Amuses me, for some reason."

"Everything amuses you." Except, probably, liars.

"Not true. Burglars don't amuse me. So are we eating here, or at your house to crack heads if anybody shows up?"

His low voice made her stomach feel squishy, even though he was talking about cracking heads. "Nobody's going to show up. And I still don't think you need to come. I have a gun, and I doubt you're very good at cracking heads anyway."

"Don't count on that." The curve of his lips flattened and his eyes looked a little hard. "Anybody tries breaking into your house, you'll find out exactly how good I am."

The thought of exactly how good she knew he was at a number of things left her a little breathless. "I just want to be clear about the ground rules—"

"Dr. Trent." Thomas appeared in the doorway and Charlie put a little distance between her and Trent, not wanting to give the gossip machine any more ammo than they might already have. "There's a boy in the clinic whose mother brought him in because he's not eating. I did a routine exam, but I don't see anything other than a slightly elevated temperature. He is acting a little odd, though, and his mother's sure something's wrong, so I thought you should come take a look."

"Not eating?" Trent's brows lowered. "That's not a very significant complaint. Did you look to see if he has strep or maybe tonsillitis?"

"His throat looks normal to me."

"Hmm. All right." He turned his baby blues to Charlie. "Don't be going home until I come back. I mean it."

"How about if I come along? I haven't had time to visit the clinic for a while." She might not be in medicine, but the way doctors and nurses figured out a diagnosis always fascinated her. And she had to admit she couldn't resist the chance to watch Trent in action again.

"Of course, Ma," Thomas said, turning to lead the way.

CHAPTER EIGHT

THE BOY, WHO looked to be about ten years old, was sitting on the exam table with a peculiar expression on his face, as though he was in pain. "Hey, buddy," Trent said, giving him a reassuring smile. "Your mommy tells us you're having trouble eating. Does your stomach hurt?"

The child shook his head without speaking. Checking his pulse, Trent noted that he was sweaty, then got a tiny whiff of an unpleasant odor. It could be just that the child smelled bad, or it could be a symptom of some infection.

"Let's take a look in your throat." Using a tongue depressor, he studied the boy's mouth, but didn't see any sign of an abscess or a bad tooth. No tonsil problem or strep. Once Trent was satisfied that none of those were the problem, the boy suddenly bit down on the stick and kept it clamped between his teeth. "Okay, I'm done looking in your mouth. Let go of the stick, please."

The boy didn't budge, then started to cry without opening his mouth. Trent gently pressed his thumb and fingers to the boy's jaw to encourage him to relax and unclamp his jaw. "Let me take the stick out now and we'll check some other things." The boy kept crying and it was all Trent could do to get him to open his mouth barely wide enough to remove the stick.

Damn. Trent thought of one of his professors long ago talking about giving the spatula test, and that sure seemed to be what had just happened with the stick. "Did you hurt yourself any time the past week or two? Did something poke into your skin?"

"I'nt know." The words were a mumble, the boy barely moving his lips, and Trent was now pretty sure he knew what was wrong.

"Thomas, can you get me a cup of water?"

"Yes, doctor."

When he returned with the cup, Trent held it to the boy's lips. "Take a sip of this for me, will you?" As he expected, the poor kid gagged on the water, unable to swallow.

"All right. I want you to lie down so I can check a few things." Trent tried to help him lie on the exam table, but it was difficult with the child's body so rigid. The simple movement sent the boy into severe muscle spasms. When the spasms eventually faded and Trent finally was able to get him prone, the child's arms flung up to hug his chest tightly while his legs stayed stiff and straight. He began crying again, his expression formed into a grimace.

Trent was aware of both Thomas and Charlotte standing by the table, staring with surprise and concern. He grasped the boy's wrist and tried to move his elbow. The arm resisted, pushing against his hand.

"What do you think is wrong, Trent?" Charlotte said, obviously alarmed.

He couldn't blame her for being unnerved, since this wasn't something you saw every day. It was damned disturbing how a patient was affected by this condition.

"Tetanus. I'm willing to bet he's had a puncture wound, probably in the foot, that maybe he didn't even notice happened. The infection, wherever it is, is causing his jaw to lock, as well as all the other symptoms we're seeing."

He released the child's arm and lifted his foot, noting it was slightly swollen. Bingo! There it was: a tiny wound oozing a small amount of smelly pus.

The poor kid was still crying, the sound pretty horrible through his clenched teeth. He placed the boy's foot back down and refocused his attention on calming him down. "You're going to be all right, I promise. I know this is scary and you feel very uncomfortable and strange. But I'm going to get rid of the infection in your foot and give you medicine to make you feel better. Okay?"

The brown eyes that stared back at him were terrified, and who could blame the poor little guy? With tetanus, painful spasms could be so severe they actually pulled ligaments apart or broke bones.

"What do you do for tetanus?" Charlotte asked. "Is it…?" She didn't finish the sentence, but he knew what she was asking.

"He'll recover fine, now that we've got him here. Thomas, can you get what we need for an IV drip of penicillin? And some valium, please."

"Penicillin?" Charlotte frowned and leaned up to speak softly in his ear. "Since he's so sick, shouldn't you give him something—I don't know—stronger?"

"Maybe it's a good thing you're not a doctor after all." He couldn't resist teasing her a little. "In the U.S., they'd probably use an antibiotic that costs four hundred dollars a day and kills practically every bacteria in your body instead of just the one causing the disease—kind of like killing an ant with a sledgehammer. But, believe me, penicillin is perfect for this. You can't kill bacteria deader than dead."

Her pretty lips and eyes smiled at him. "Okay. I believe you. So that's it? Penicillin? Do you need a test to confirm that's what it is?"

"No, his symptoms are clear. That's what it is." He found himself feeling pleased that she trusted him to make the right decision. Since when had he ever needed other people to appreciate what he did and what he'd learned over the years?

He reached to pat the child's stiffly folded arms. "Hang in there. I'll be right back." Grasping Charlotte's elbow, he walked far enough away that the boy couldn't hear them.

"Penicillin is just part of the treatment. We'll need to do complete support care. I have to get rid of the clostridium tetani, which is the bacteria in his foot that's giving off the toxin to the rest of his body. It's one of the most lethal toxins on earth, which is why it's a damned good thing his mother brought him in. He wouldn't have made it if it was left untreated."

She shuddered. "How do you get rid of the… whatever it was called…tetani toxin?"

"I'll have to open his foot to remove it and clean out the dead and devitalized tissue so it can heal. It'll give the penicillin a chance to work. I'll give him fluids and valium to keep him comfortable so he can rest. He'll have to stay here several days, kept very quiet, to give his body time to process the toxin."

She nodded and her eyes smiled at him again, her soft hand wrapping around his forearm. "Thank you again for coming back, Trent. I bet our lying Dr. Smith would never have been able to figure out what was wrong with this boy. You're... amazing."

He didn't know about all that. What he did know was that *she* was amazing. In here, looking at this boy, concerned and worried but not at all freaked out by the bizarre presentation of tetanus, despite not being in medicine herself. He'd bet a whole lot of his fortune that the women he'd dated back in the days of his old, privileged life in the States would have run hysterically from the room. Or, even more likely, would never been in there to begin with.

"I have to take care of his foot right now, which is going to take a little time. Promise you'll stay here in the hospital until I'm done?" He found himself reaching to touch her face, to stroke his knuckles against her cheek. "I know you think you're all tough and can handle any big, bad burglar that might be ransacking your house as you walk in the door. But, for my peace of mind, will you please wait for me?"

"I'll wait for you." The beautiful green of her eyes, her small smile, her words, all seemed to settle inside his chest and expand it. "Since it'll be past time for dinner to be served here, I'll fix something for us when we get there."

"Sounds great." He wanted to lean down and kiss her, the way he had in the rain the other day.

And the reasons for not doing that began to seem less and less important. Charlotte definitely didn't act like she'd be doing much pining after he was gone.

That was good news he hoped was really true, and the smart part of him knew it was best to keep it that way, to keep their relationship "strictly professional," and never mind that he'd be spending the night back in her house. The house in which, when the two of them *weren't* just colleagues, they hadn't gotten much sleep at all.

Despite the comfort of the double bed, with its wrought-iron headboard and soft, handmade quilt, Trent turned restlessly, finally flopping onto his back with his hands behind his head. The room was girly, with lace curtains, a pastel hooked rug and an odd mix of furniture. The femininity of it made him even more acutely aware that Charlotte was sleeping very close by.

Every time he closed his eyes, he saw her face: the woman who had fascinated him from the first second he'd walked into her office. That long, silky brown hair cascading down her back, her body with curves in all the right places on her petite frame and her full lips begging to be kissed were as ultra-feminine as the bedroom.

But her willful, no-nonsense personality proved

that a woman who oozed sexiness and femininity sure didn't have to be quiet and docile.

He'd guessed being here would be a challenge. How the hell was he going to get through the night keeping his word that their relationship would stay strictly professional? Get through the next few days?

Focusing on work seemed like a good plan. He'd tell her he wanted to head into the field to do immunizations, or whatever else patients might need, keeping close proximity to Charlotte at a minimum. The last thing he wanted to do was hurt her, and so far it seemed their brief time together hadn't negatively affected her at all. No point in risking it—not to mention that he didn't want to stir up that strange discomfort he'd felt at the airport when he'd tried to get out of there the first time.

A loud creak sent Trent sitting upright in bed, on high alert. Had someone broken in? Surely, lying there wide awake, he would have heard other sounds if that was the case?

Probably Charlotte wasn't sleeping well, either. He stared at the bedroom door, his pulse kicking up a notch at another creak that sounded like it was coming from the hall. Could she possibly be planning to come into his room?

He swung his legs to the floor and sat there for a few minutes, his ears straining to hear if it was her, or if he should get up to see if what he'd heard was an intruder. While it seemed unlikely someone could break in without making a lot of noise, he threw on his khaki shorts and decided he had to check the place out just to be sure.

He opened the bedroom door as quietly as possible and crept out in his bare feet, staring through the darkness of the hallway, looking for any movement. The scent of coffee touched his nose and he relaxed, since he was pretty sure no intruder would be taking a coffee break.

Charlotte was up; he should just go back to bed. But, before he knew what he was doing, he found himself padding down the narrow staircase to the kitchen.

"Did you have to make so much racket in here? I was sound asleep," he lied as he stepped into the cozy room. Seeing Charlotte standing at the counter in a thin, pink robe, her hair messy, her lips parted in surprise, almost obliterated his resolve to keep his distance. Nearly had him striding across the room to pull her into his arms, and to hell with all his resolutions to the contrary. But he forced himself to lean against the doorjamb and shove his hands in his pockets.

"I was quiet as a mouse. Your guilty conscience must be keeping you awake."

"Except for that 'murdering my old girlfriend' thing, my conscience is clean. I abandoned my vacation plans, didn't I? Came back here to work for you?"

She nodded and the way her gaze hovered on his bare chest for a moment reminded him why he hadn't been able to sleep, damn it.

"You did," she said, turning back to the percolator. "I'm grateful, and I know Lionel's family is grateful too. And the other patients you've taken care of since then." She reached into the cupboard to grab mugs. "Coffee?"

He should go back upstairs. Try to sleep. "Sure."

He settled into a chair at the table and she joined him, sliding his cup across the worn wood. His gaze slipped to the open vee of her robe. He looked at her smooth skin and hint of the lush breasts he knew were hidden there, pictured what kind of silky nightgown she might be wearing and quickly grabbed up his cup to take a swig, the burn of it on his tongue a welcome distraction.

Time for mundane conversation. "So, tell me about what you studied in school. Didn't you say you got an MBA?"

"Yes. I got a hospital administration degree, then went to Georgetown for my masters. I knew I'd be coming here to get the hospital open and running again, so all that was good." She leaned closer, her eyes alight with enthusiasm. "I met a lot of people who shared their experiences with me—about how they'd improved existing facilities or started from scratch in various countries. I learned so much, hearing the things they felt they did right or would do differently."

He, too, leaned closer, wanting to study her, wanting to know what made this fascinating and complex woman tick. "I've been surprised more than once how much you know about medicine. Tell me again, why didn't you become a doctor?"

"Somebody needs to run this place. Create new ways to help people, to make a difference. Like I said before, I can get doctors and nurses and trained techs. I focused my training on how to do the rest of it. My parents encouraged that; they've trusted me and John Adams with the job of bringing this place back."

A surge of old and buried pain rose within him and he firmly shoved it back down. It must be nice to have someone in your life who believed in you, who cared what you wanted. It must be nice to have someone in your life who didn't say one thing, all the while betraying you, betraying your blind trust, with a deep stab in your back.

"I've worked at a lot of hospitals in the world. That experience might come in handy if you have any questions."

"Thanks. I might take you up on that."

Her beautiful eyes shone, her mouth curved in a pleased smile, and the urge to grab her up and kiss her breathless was nearly irresistible. Abruptly, he stood and downed the last of his coffee, knowing that between the caffeine and her close proximity there'd be no sleep for him tonight.

"I'm going to hit the hay. Try not to make a bunch of noise again and wake me up. I don't want to fall asleep in the middle of a surgery to-morrow."

She stood too and the twist of her lips told him she knew exactly why he was awake. "Don't worry. The last thing I want to do is disturb your sleep."

"Liar." He had to smile, enjoying the pink that stained her cheeks at the word. "Anyway, you've already done that, so you owe me. Maybe you should disturb my sleep for a few more hours; help me relax."

Why did his mouth say one thing, when his brain told him to shut up and walk out? Until the slow blink of her eyes, the tip of her tongue lick-ing her lips, the rise and fall of that tantalizing vee of skin beneath her robe, obliterated all regrets.

"I don't think your sleep is my responsibility," she said. "You're on your own."

She swayed closer, lids low, her lips parted, practically willing him to kiss her. What was the reason he'd been trying not to? Right now, he couldn't quite remember. Didn't want to.

"Seems to me we agreed you were in charge of my life while I'm here." Almost of their own accord, his feet brought him nearly flush with her body. Close enough to feel her warmth touch his bare chest; to feel her breath feather across his skin. "Got any ideas on a cure for insomnia?"

"Less coffee in the middle of the night? Maybe a hammer to the head? I've got one in the toolbox in the closet."

He reached for her and put his hands on her waist. "I know you said you couldn't promise not to hurt me, but that seems a little drastic." His head lowered because he had to feel her skin against his lips. He touched them softly to her cheek, beneath her ear. "Any other ideas?"

Her warm hands flattened against his chest. When they didn't push, he drew her close, her curves perfectly fitted to his body. Much as he knew he should back off right now, there was no way he could do it. He wanted her even more than the night they'd fallen into her bed together. And that night had knocked him flat in a way he couldn't remember ever having experienced before.

Her head tipped back as he moved his mouth to the hollow of her throat and could feel her pulse hammering beneath his lips. "We have morphine in the drug cupboard at the hospital," she said, her voice breathy, sexy. "A big dose of that might help."

"You're a much more powerful drug than morphine, much more addictive, and you know it." Her green eyes filled his vision before he lowered his mouth to hers and kissed her. He drew her warm tongue into his mouth, and the taste of her robbed him of any thoughts of taking it slow. Of kissing her then backing off.

Her hands roamed over his chest, sending heat racing across his flesh, and he sank deeper into the kiss, tasting the hint of coffee, cream and sweet sugar on his tongue. Her fingers continued on a shivery path down his ribs, to his sides and back, and he wrapped his arms around her and pulled her close, the swell of her breasts rising and falling against him.

His thigh nudged between her legs and, as she rocked against him, he let one hand drift to her rear, increasing the pressure, loving the gasp that left her mouth and swirled into his.

The rattling sound of a doorknob cut through the sensual fog in his brain and Trent pulled his mouth from Charlotte's. They stared at one another, little panting breaths between them, before her gaze cut toward the living room.

"What the hell? Are you expecting someone?"

Her eyes widened and she pulled away from him. "No," she whispered. "Darn, I left my gun upstairs. I'll have to go through the living room to get it. Should I run up there? If he—or they—get in you could punch them or something till I get back down with it. Or maybe you shouldn't. Maybe *they* have a gun."

Metal scratched against metal then a creaking sound indicated the door had been opened, and Charlotte's hands flung to her chest as she stared out of the kitchen then swung her gaze back to Trent.

"The door was locked, wasn't it? Does someone have a key?" It hadn't sounded like forced entry to him. Maybe it was somebody she knew. And the thought that it could be a boyfriend twisted his gut in a way it shouldn't twist for a sweet but short interlude.

"No. The only other key is in my office at the hospital."

Her whisper grew louder, likely because she was afraid. He touched his finger to her lips and lowered his mouth to her ear. "Is there really a hammer in the closet?"

She nodded and silently padded to it in her bare feet, wincing as the door shuddered open creakily. She grabbed the head of a hammer and handed it to him, then pulled out a heavy wrench and lifted it in the air, ready to follow him.

What would she have done if he hadn't been here with her tonight? The thought brought a surge of the same protective anger he'd felt when he'd heard about the first break-in, which had made him more than ready to bust somebody's head.

"Stay here," he whispered. He slipped to the doorway and could see a shadowy figure with a bag standing near the base of the stairs.

"Who the hell are you? And you better answer fast before you can't answer at all," Trent growled.

"What the heck? Who are *you*? Charlie?" Her father's voice sounded scared and trembly and she tore across the room in a rush.

"Oh, heavens! Stop, Trent! It's okay. It's my dad." The wrench in her hand suddenly seemed to weigh twenty pounds and she nearly dropped it as she shook all over in shock and relief. She fell to her knees next to her father, placing the wrench on the floor so she could touch his chest and arms. "Dad, are you all right? Are you hurt?"

"I…I'm not sure." He stared up at Trent, who stepped off him to one side and lowered the hammer. "Next time I'll know to knock, seeing as you have a bodyguard."

"Sorry, sir." Trent crouched down and slipped his arm beneath her dad's shoulders, helping him to a sitting position. "You okay?"

"I think so. Except for the hell of a bruise I'm ing to have in the morning." He stood with the of Trent and Charlie and rubbed his hand s his chest, then offered it to Trent. "I'm Joseph rds. Thanks for looking out for my daughter."

, you're welcome. I guess. Though I think he first time I've been thanked for beat- body up. I'm Trent Dalton."

glanced at Trent to see that charming, ile of his as he shook her dad's hand.

CHAPTER NINE

Heart pounding, Charlie stepped close behind Trent, peeking around him as he stood poised to strike the intruder. Never would she have thought that the burglars would come back, especially at night when she was home. Thank goodness Trent was here. Much as she said she could look after herself—and she could; she was sure she could—having a big, strong man in the house definitely made her glad she wasn't alone as someone was breaking in.

She looked up to see Trent's jaw was t eyes narrowed, his biceps flexed as he hammer. He looked down at her, gave then burst across the room with surprise and overwhelm whoe

The man was shorter than his shoulder into the intr an American football landed hard, flat on over him, one leg on ei figure. With one hand cu Trent's other held the hamme

The shock of it all, and the worry of whether her dad was okay or not, had worn off and left her with a hot annoyance throbbing in her head. "What are you doing here, Dad? I thought you weren't coming for a couple more nights. Why didn't you call? You're lucky you don't have a big lump on your head. Or a gunshot through your chest."

"I tried to call but couldn't get any cell service. After I met with Bob in Monrovia, I decided not to stay at his house like I'd planned, because his wife's not feeling well. Then I got the key from the hospital so I wouldn't wake you—though that obviously wasn't a problem." He raised his eyebrows. "I won't ask what you're doing up in the middle of the night."

"That wouldn't be any of your business," Charlie said, glaring at Trent as his smile grew wider. His grin definitely implied something it shouldn't, and it sure didn't help that the man had no shirt on. Though, as she thought back to what exactly they were doing when her dad had arrived, it wasn't too far off. It had, in fact, been quickly heading in the direction of hot and sweaty sex and she felt her cheeks warm. "But if you must know, Trent is doing surgeries at the hospital for a few days and, um, needed a place to stay. We were just talking about the hospital and stuff."

"She obviously doesn't want you to know, but that's not entirely the truth," Trent said.

She stared at him. Surely the man wasn't going to share the details of their relationship—or whatever you'd call their memorable night together—to her *father?*

"What is the truth?" her dad asked.

"The reason I'm spending the night here is because someone broke into the house yesterday. I didn't think she should be alone until it seemed unlikely the guy was coming back. Which is why I knocked you down first and asked questions later."

"Ah." Her father frowned. "I have to say, it's concerned me from the start that you were living here by yourself. Maybe we should rethink that—have a few hospital employees live here with you."

"I've been here two years, Dad, and nothing like this has happened before. I'm sure it's an isolated incident. I like living alone and don't want that to change."

"Maybe you should get a dog, then—one with a big, loud bark that would scare somebody off."

A dog? Hmm. It might be nice to have a dog around and she had to admit she might feel a touch safer. "If it will ease your mind, I'll consider it."

"We'll talk more about this later." Her dad lowered himself into a chair and rubbed his chest again, poor man. Though she felt he'd brought it on himself by sneaking in. "I'm looking forward to hearing about how the new wing is coming along. Must be about finished, isn't it? When is the first plastic surgeon supposed to get here?"

"Um, soon." She glanced at Trent and saw his brows twitch together. This was her chance to ask him to stay until the Gilchrist rep got here, to do a few plastic surgery procedures, since the subject had come up. Maybe, with her dad there, he wouldn't be so quick to say no. She pulled the ties of her robe closer together, trying not to give off any vibes that said, *I'm desperate here.*

"Trent. Ever since I saw what a wonderful job you did on Lionel's eye, I've been meaning to ask." She licked her lips and forged on. "There are a few patients who've been waiting a long time to have a plastic surgery procedure done. Would you consider doing one or two before you leave?"

"You know, I'm not actually a board-certified plastic surgeon." His eyes were unusually flat and emotionless. "Better for you to wait until you have your whole setup ready and a permanent surgeon in place."

"You do plastic surgery?" Her father's eyebrows lifted in surprise. "I assumed you were a general surgeon, like the ones who usually rotate through the GPC-staffed hospitals."

"I am."

"Come on, Trent." Charlie tried for a cajoling tone that might soften him up. "I saw what you did for Lionel's eye. You told me, when you wanted to do it, that I didn't know who I was dealing with, remember? And you were right."

He looked at her silently for a moment before he spoke. "I'm leaving here any day now, Charlotte. It wouldn't make sense for me to perform any complex plastics procedures on patients, then take off before I could follow up with them."

"Please, Trent." Her hands grew cold. "Maybe you could even stay a few extra days, to help these patients who so desperately need it. When you see some of them, I think you'll want to."

"I can't stay longer. And it's not good medical practice for me to do a surgery like that, then leave. I'm sorry." He turned to her dad, the conversation clearly over by the tone of his voice. "Since you're here tonight, sir, I'm going to grab my things and head back to my quarters."

Charlie watched him disappear up the steps and listened to his footsteps fade away down the hall. Why was he so adamant about this? And what could she possibly do to convince him?

Trent managed to avoid Charlotte the entire following day. He took dinner to his room, and if she noticed she didn't say anything. When his phone rang and he saw it was Chase, a strange feeling came over him before he answered. A feeling that told him he'd miss this place when he left, whether it was tomorrow or days from now.

"So, I'm sorry, man, but it's just not going to work out," Chase said in his ear. "Wish I could sub for you. I'd love to head back to Africa for a week or so. But I'm pretty busy at work here and, like I said, Dani's not feeling great this month. Says she didn't have morning sickness with Drew, but she sure does now."

"Maybe it's you that's making her sick this time, and not her pregnancy," Trent said. "Which I could fully appreciate."

"Yeah, that could well be true." Chase chuckled. "Any chance you'll be coming to the States some time? Dani and I go to the occasional conference here. It would be great to catch up."

"No plans for that right now. I'll let you know if I do." He wouldn't mind a visit back to the States, so long as it wasn't New York City. It would be nice to see Chase and Dani, and maybe even cute little Drew and his new baby sibling. He hadn't been back for quite a while. "Who knows, maybe we can temp at the same time in Honduras when I'm between jobs. Let's see if we can make that happen."

"That would be great. Stay in touch, will you?"

"Will do. Take care, and give your family a hug for me."

Well, damn. He shoved his phone in his pocket. So much for that great idea. But he'd known it was a long shot that Chase would be able to fill in for him here in Liberia until the new doctor arrived.

The uneasy feelings he had about being stuck here were peculiar and annoying. It wasn't like it was a big deal if he went on his vacation all by his lonesome tomorrow or a couple weeks from now. The GPC was used to delays like this, so they probably had a temp lined up for him in the Philippines until he got there.

But this tug and push he kept feeling around Charlotte was damned uncomfortable. One minute all he wanted was to kiss her breathless, knowing that was a bad idea for all kinds of reasons; the next, she was bugging him about doing plastic surgery that he plain didn't want to do, which put the distance between them he knew they should keep in place. That he knew he should welcome.

There had been a number of times his plastics skills had come in handy over the years, doing surgeries on a cleft palate, or a hemangioma like Lionel's, that were important to how the patient could function every day. But actually working in a plastic surgery hospital? One dedicated to procedures that mostly improve someone's looks? No, thank you. He'd rather keep people alive than just make them look better to the world.

He sat at the tiny desk in his room and went through the mail that had arrived this week. One was from the GPC and he tore it open, wondering if it was finally his release papers, or if they'd had to relocate his next job to somewhere other than the Philippines because of this delay.

Perplexed, he read through the letter twice. Clearly, there was some mess-up here. How come the director, Mike Hardy, thought the new doctor was already at the Edwards Hospital? Mike's letter advised him that, because of the imminent arrival of this doctor in Liberia, a temp filling in at his new job wouldn't be necessary and he could still take his full three weeks off. His revised arrival date in the Philippines was exactly three weeks from today.

He picked up his phone to call Mike, but figured it would make sense to talk to Charlotte first. Maybe she knew something he didn't.

He left his room and strode down the long hallway from the residence quarters into the hospital. Dinner had been over an hour ago, so she very well might be back at home. And he wasn't about to follow her over there. If she'd already left, he'd forget about talking to her and just call Mike.

A glance in her office showed she wasn't there, so he went to the dining hall. Her round, sexy rear was the only part of her he could see. With her head and torso inside a cupboard as she kneeled on the floor, he stopped to enjoy the view and had to resist the urge to shock her by going over and giving that sexy bottom of hers a playful spank.

"Does anyone know if the rest of Charlotte Edwards is in here?" he asked instead.

Her body unfolded and she straightened to look at him, still on her knees. "Very funny. I'm just trying to organize this kitchen equipment. Too many cooks in here are making it hard to find anything when you want it."

"When you have a minute, I need to talk to you about the new doc coming."

He had to wonder why her expression was instantly alarmed. Was she worried there'd been an even longer delay? Thank goodness her dad was here now, so Trent wouldn't be spending any more tempting nights in her house.

She shoved to her feet and walked over. "What about the new doc?"

"I got a letter from Mike Hardy telling me all systems are go for my vacation. I'm wondering what the mix-up is. Or if someone is coming tomorrow and they somehow forgot to send my release papers."

She snatched the letter from his hand and looked it over, her fingers gripping it until they were practically white. "Um, I don't know. This is weird. Last I heard, there was nobody in place yet. Let me see what I can find out and I'll let you know. Believe me, I'm as anxious to get you out of here as you are to leave."

"Never mind." He tried to tug the paper from

her hand, but she held on tight. It pissed him off that she wanted him out of there so badly, which was absolutely absurd, since he wanted the same thing. "I'll call Mike in the morning. Give me my letter back."

"I'm the director of this hospital and staffing is my responsibility."

Her green eyes were flashing irritation at him, as well as something else he couldn't figure out. The woman was like a pit bull sometimes. "Why are you so controlling? Technically, the GPC employs me, you know. And this is my job, my vacation and my life. Give me my letter."

"Fine. Take the letter." She let it go and spun on her heel toward the doorway. "But I'm going home, then calling Mike. I'm asking you to let me handle this; I'll let you know what he says. Hopefully this means you're on your way very soon."

His hand crumpled the letter slightly as he watched her disappear into the hall. Why he wanted to storm after her and kiss her until she begged him to stay was something he wasn't going to try to understand.

CHAPTER TEN

CHARLIE HELD TRENT'S release papers in slightly shaky hands then shoved them deeper under the pile on her desk. She tried to draw a calming breath and remind herself that Colleen believed Trent had agreed to stay, so the new doctor wouldn't just show up on the doorstep and give Trent the green light to leave. But if Trent called Mike Hardy, who knew what would happen?

She prayed the Gilchrist representative would show up fast. Surely they'd be impressed with what a great job the hospital's plastic surgeon had done on Lionel's eye; they would never know the talented man would be out of there as soon as the rep left. Trent would charm them, even if he didn't know he was supposed to, because the man oozed charm just by breathing. And all would be well. It would.

Paying bills wasn't exactly the way to forget about the problem, but it had to be done. Charlie tore open the mail and grimly dropped every invoice into the box she kept for them. One thing she could do to relieve the stress of it all was work harder on other sources of funding besides Gilchrist. Her dad had always told her to never put all her eggs in one basket, so she tried to have multiple fundraising efforts going. Time to make some more calls and send more letters to previous donors. There was no way any of them would come close to what the Gilchrist Foundation had committed, but something was a whole lot better than nothing.

A letter with a postmark from New York City and the name of some financial organization caught her eye and made her heart accelerate. The Gilchrist Foundation was based in NYC. Could they possibly just have decided to send a check without worrying about the final approval?

She quickly ripped it open then sighed when she read the letterhead: not from the foundation. But her brief disappointment faded as she read the check that was enclosed with the letter. She stared, not quite believing what she was seeing.

Fifty thousand dollars, written to The Louisa Edwards Education Project. With slightly shaky hands, she scanned the letter that came with the check.

Please find enclosed an anonymous donation to provide supplemental funding for the Louisa Edwards School.

It was signed by someone who apparently worked at the financial firm it came from.

She stared at the bold numerals and the cursive below them. Fifty thousand dollars. Fifty thousand! Oh, heavens!

She leaped up and tore out the door of her office, about to run all the way to the school to show John Adams and her dad, who was there with him. To have John Adams plan to hire another new teacher. To think of all the supplies on their wish-list they'd decided not to buy for now.

And she ran, *kapow*, right into Trent Dalton's hard shoulder, just as she had before when he'd asked if she was late to lunch.

He grabbed her arms to steady her. "Wow, you must be extra-hungry today. Something special on the menu?"

"Funny." She clutched the check to her chest and smiled up at him. "But even you can't annoy me today. You won't believe what just came in the mail!"

"A new designer handbag? Some four-inch heels?" he asked, little creases at the corners of his eyes as he smiled.

"Way, way better. Guess again."

"A brand-new SUV?"

She held the check up in front of his face. "Look." She was so thrilled she had to gulp in air to keep from hyperventilating. "Somebody

acted like I want you to leave. I don't, really. I've just got a lot on my mind." And, boy, wasn't that the truth. "I spoke with Colleen, and apparently she does have someone lined up to come soon, but not today or tomorrow. I'm sorry about that also. I would greatly appreciate it, though, if you would stay just another few days." And all that was the truth, too, which made her feel a tad better. She wasn't being quite as deceitful as she felt.

"All right. Thanks for checking. I guess I can hang around for just a little while longer."

She drew a deep breath of relief, then glanced up at Trent's profile, at his prominent nose, black hair and sensual lips. It didn't feel like just over a week since he'd returned from the airport. As he walked next to her, not touching but close enough to feel his warmth, it seemed much longer. Oddly natural, like she should just reach over to hold his hand.

Which was not good. Not only would he be leaving in a matter of days, she didn't want to think about how shocked and angry he'd be if he ever found out about her little fibs. Okay, big fibs; the thought of it made her stomach knot.

Three figures, two taller and one small, along with a little dog, appeared up ahead on the road—obviously, her dad, John Adams, Patience and Lucky. Seeing them obliterated all other thoughts as Charlie ran the distance between them, waving the check.

"You're going to faint when you see this!"

Trent followed slowly behind Charlotte, not wanting to intrude on her moment, sharing her excitement with the two men and Patience. Though he'd been itching to leave, to move on with his life, he felt glad—blessed, really—that he'd still been here when she got the check. He'd never been around when someone received one of his donations, and it felt great to see how happy it made her. To know it would help them achieve their important goals.

He watched her fling her arms around both men, first her dad, then John Adams, just as she'd done with him. Well, not exactly the same. Her arms wrapped around their middles in a quick hug. That was different from the way she'd thrown her arms around his own neck, drawing his head close, giving him that kiss; her breasts pressing softly against his chest, staying there a long moment, her fingers tucked into his hair, sending a shiver along his scalp and a desire to kiss more than just her forehead.

"You don't know who the donor is?" her father asked.

She shook her head, the sun touching her shining hair as it slipped across her shoulders. "No.

I wish I did. I wish I could thank them. That *we* could thank them. Think there's any way to find out?"

"Not likely. But you could always contact the company it came from and ask."

"I'll do that," Charlotte said as they turned and headed back toward the hospital. "Maybe even ask if there's anything specific they want the money used for."

Trent knew his finance man was discreet and they'd get no information that could trace it back to him. "Whoever donated it stayed anonymous because they wanted to. I say just spend the money as you see fit and know they trusted you to do that," he said.

"Good point, Trent," John Adams said. "We do get the occasional anonymous donation, though nothing like this, of course. I think we should respect that's how they wanted to keep it."

"Okay." Charlotte's chest rose and fell in a deep breath, and Trent found his attention gravitating to her beautiful curves. "I'm feeling less freaked out. Just plain happy now. Why are you three leaving the school?"

"Daddy promised he would take me to the beach," Patience said. "He's been promising and promising, but kept saying it was s'posed to rain. But today the sun is shiny so we can go!" The little girl danced from one foot to the other, the colorful cloth bag on her shoulder dancing along with her.

"Mind if I come?" Trent asked. "I'll build a sandcastle with you." The kid was so cute, and he hadn't seen an inch of Liberia other than the airport and the road to and from the hospital and school. One of the things he enjoyed about his job was exploring new places, discovering new things. He turned to Charlotte. "Would that be okay? Thomas is taking care of a man needing hernia surgery, and I've already seen the patients in the clinic. The nurses are finishing up with all of them. I can check on everyone when I get back."

"Of course, that's fine. I'll see what's in the kitchen for you all to take for a beach lunch."

"Why don't you go along, Charlie?" her dad suggested. "You never take much time off to do something fun. I've been wanting to go through the information you gave me, anyway, so I can keep an eye on things while you're gone."

"Well…" Her green eyes held some expression he couldn't figure out. Wariness? Anxiety? "I'm not really a beach person, you know. And I don't want you stuck here doing my work, Dad."

"You may be the director, but I'm still a part of this hospital too, remember." Joseph smiled. "You need to get over this fear of yours. Go get your things together. John Adams and I will scrounge up some food for you all to take."

"What fear of yours?" Trent asked. From being around Charlotte just the past week or so, he couldn't imagine her being afraid of much of anything.

"Nothing. Dad's exaggerating."

"Exaggerating? The last time we were at the beach, I thought you were going to hyperventilate just going into the water up to your knees." Joseph turned to Trent. "When Charlie was a teenager back in the States, we didn't realize we were swimming where there was a strong rip current, like quite a few beaches here in Liberia have. She got pulled farther and farther out and I couldn't get to her. Her mom and I kept yelling at her to relax and not fight the current, to just let it take her. Then swim horizontal to the shore until she came to a place without a rip so she could swim back in."

"Rip tides can be dangerous." Trent looked at Charlotte and saw her cheeks were flushed. Surely she wasn't embarrassed by something that happened when she was a kid? "Scary for anybody. But obviously you lived through it."

"Yes. I admit I thought for sure that was it, though. That I was going to end up in the middle of the ocean and either drown or be devoured by a shark. So I just don't like going in the water."

"In the water? You don't even like getting in a small boat. Which has been a problem a few times," Joseph said. "You need to move past it and get your feet wet."

"Can we just drop this subject, please? I have a lot of work to do, anyway."

"Come to the beach, Charlotte," Trent said, wishing he could pull her into his arms and give her soothing kisses that would ease her embarrassment and the bad memory. "We'll work on getting you to move past your fear. You don't have to get in the water if you're not comfortable. But, you know, I did do a whole rotation in psychiatry at school. I'm sure I'm a highly qualified therapist." He gave her a teasing smile, hoping she'd relax and decide to come. Living with any kind of debilitating fear was no fun.

"Just go, Charlie," Joseph said. "It'll make me feel less guilty that I let you swim in that rip to begin with."

Charlotte gave an exaggerated sigh. "So this is about you now? Fine. I'll go. But I'm not promising to swim. I mean it."

"No promises needed," Trent said. "We can always just build a sandcastle so big that Princess Patience can walk inside."

"I like big sandcastles!" Patience beamed. "And In't care if we don't swim, Miss Charlie. Swimming isn't my favorite, anyway. We'll have fun on the beach."

"All right, then, that's settled," Joseph said. "John Adams and I will pack lunch while you get your things."

Trent grabbed swim trunks, a towel and his medical bag, which he'd learned always to have along on any excursion. Heading to the car, he had an instant vision of how Charlotte would look in a swimsuit: her sexy curves and smooth skin. Oh, yeah, he would more than enjoy a day at the beach with a beautiful woman; at the same time, he'd be glad to have chaperones to keep him from breaking his deal with her.

The thought of chaperones, though, didn't stop more compelling thoughts of swimming with Charlotte. How she'd feel in his arms when he held her close, trying to relieve her mind and soothe her fears, their wet bodies sliding together. How much he wished that, afterwards, they could lie on the hot sand and make love in the shade of a palm tree with the warm breeze tickling their skin.

Damn. His pulse kicked up and made him a little short of breath.

Chaperones were a very good thing.

CHAPTER ELEVEN

THE DRIVE THROUGH farms of papaya, mangoes and acres of rubber trees brought them to the soaring Grand Cape Mount, then eventually to the shoreline. Though John Adams had offered, Charlotte insisted on driving, of course. Trent had to wonder what made the woman feel a need to be in charge all the time. Didn't she ever want just to relax and go along for the ride?

Patience kept up a steady chatter until her father told her he'd give her a quarter if she could stay silent for five minutes. After she failed to manage that, Trent entertained her with a few simple card tricks he let her "win" that earned her the quarter after all.

They parked at the edge of the road and, as they unpacked their things from the car, Charlotte shook her head at Trent. "Is there a soul on the planet you can't charm to death?"

"To death? Doesn't exactly sound like you mean that in a nice way." Trent hooked a few beach chairs over his arm and they followed John

Adams and Patience, who carried their lunches and a few plastic pails and shovels.

"Okay, charm, period. Everyone in the hospital thinks you're Mr. Wonderful."

"Does that include the director of the hospital?"

"Of course. I'm very grateful you filled in here—twice—until we can get another doctor."

Her voice had become polite, her smile a little stiff. Was she regretting that her rare time off had to be spent with him? Or could she be having the same problem he was having—wanting to take up where they'd left off at her house, knowing it was a hell of a bad idea?

As they approached the beach, Trent stopped to soak in the visual spectacle before him. A wide and inviting expanse of beige sand stretched as far as he could see, palm trees swaying in the ocean wind. A few houses sat off the shore, looking for all the world as though they were from the Civil War era of the deep south in the United States.

"How old do you think those houses are?" he asked Charlotte.

"Robertsport was one of the first colonies founded here by freed slaves. I think it goes back to 1829, so some of the houses here are over a hundred and fifty years old."

"That's incredible." He looked back down the beach and enjoyed the picturesque lines of fishermen with their seining nets stretched from the beach down into the water, about ten of them standing three feet apart, holding the nets in their hands. Several canoes sat on the shore, obviously made from a single hand-carved tree. One was plain, but the other was splashed with multiple colors of paint in an interesting hodgepodge design.

He was surprised to see a few surfers in the water farther down the beach, not too far from a cluster of black rocks in the distance. The waves were big and powerful, but were breaking fairly far out.

"I didn't know the people here surfed. I know Senegal is popular for surfing, but didn't know the sport had made its way here."

"I'm told an aid worker was here surfing maybe six or seven years ago. A local was fascinated and gave it a try. It's starting to take off, I guess, with locals competing and some tourists coming now."

"You know, we could always borrow a board from them. Want to give it a try?" he teased. The waves were pretty rough, so he knew there was no way she'd even consider it. The water closer to shore, though, was comparatively calm. Hopefully, he could get her into the lapping waves without it being too scary for her.

"Um, no. I think I'm going to be happy just beaching it, thanks anyway."

He'd have to see what he could do about changing her mind. They stopped in the middle of the wide beach and Charlotte laid some blankets on the soft sand. Patience tossed her toys and plopped down next to them. "Daddy, come help me build the castle!"

"How about we eat first, li'l girl?" John Adams said. "Miss Charlie and I brought some jollof rice, which I know you like. I don't know about everybody else, but I'm starving."

"You always starving, Daddy." The child grinned up at her father and Trent saw again what a strong bond there was between the two. The same kind of bond he'd seen grow so quickly between Chase and his son, even though he hadn't met them until the child was a toddler.

That surprising emotion tugged at Trent again, just as it had when Chase had told him about having a new little one on the way. A pinch of melancholy, knowing he'd likely never experience that kind of bond—though he knew only too well that not every family was as close as it seemed. That sometimes the chasm grew too large ever to be crossed.

After lunch and some sandcastle building, complete with a moat, Trent decided it was time to push Charlotte a little, to encourage her to face her fear. She was on her knees smoothing the last turret of the castle, and he pushed to his feet to stand behind her, smacking the sand from his hands. "Come on, Miss Edwards. Time for your psychotherapy session."

Immediately, her back stiffened. "I'm not done with the castle yet. Maybe later."

"Come on. It's hot as heck out here. Think how cool and refreshing the water will be."

"I'm going to watch Patience swim first." She turned to the little girl. "Remember you told me you wanted to learn to float in the lagoon? I want to see you."

And, if that wasn't an excuse, he'd never heard one. Obviously, it was going to be tough going getting her in the water.

John Adams grasped the child's hand and pulled her to her feet. "Good idea. Come on, let's get in the lagoon and cool off."

The child's expression became even more worried than Charlotte's. "No, Daddy. I don't want to."

"Why not?"

She pointed at the lagoon water, separated from the ocean by about fifty feet of sand. "There's neegees in there. I don't want to get taken by the neegees."

"There's no neegees in there, I promise."

"For true, Daddy, there are. They talk about it at school." She stared up at her father with wide eyes. "The neegees are under the water and they grab people who swim. They suck people right out of the lagoon, and nobody knows where they go, and then they're never, ever seen again. Ever."

John Adams chuckled and pulled her close against his leg. "Sugar, I promise you. There's no such thing as neegees. Just like there's no witchcraft where someone can put a curse on you. All those are just stories. So let's get in the water and I'll help you learn to float."

Patience shook her head, pressing her face to her dad's leg. "No, Daddy. I'm afraid of the neegees."

Inspiration struck and Trent figured this was a good time to put those psych classes he'd teased Charlotte about to good use and solve two problems at once. "Patience, you know how Miss Charlie is afraid of the rip currents in the ocean? How she's afraid to go in the water too?"

The little girl peeked at him with one eye, the other still pressed against her father's leg. "Yes."

"How about if Miss Charlie decides she's going to get in the water even though she's afraid? Then, when you see how brave she is, and how she does just fine and has fun, you can get in the lagoon with your dad and have fun too. What do you say?"

Patience turned to look at Charlotte, whose expression morphed from dismay to serious irritation as she glared at Trent. He almost laughed, except he knew she was genuinely scared.

"I guess if Miss Charlie gets in the water and doesn't get bit by a shark then I can be brave too."

"Thanks for that encouragement, Patience. Now I really can't wait to swim," Charlotte said. She narrowed her eyes at Trent, green sparks flying. "And thank *you* for leaving me no choice here. I'll be back after I get my swimsuit on."

"I'll check out the rip situation before we go in." Trent jogged into the water and leaped over the smaller waves before diving into a larger one. The water felt great and the inside of his chest felt about as buoyant as the outside. Charlotte was trusting him to help her feel safe in the water and he was going to do whatever he could to be sure she did.

Swimming parallel to the beach for a little in both directions, he didn't feel or see any major rips in the sand, though he'd still have to pay attention. Satisfied, he bodysurfed an awesome wave into shore, standing just in time to see Charlotte emerge from the path that led to the car.

Her beautiful body wore a pink bikini that wasn't super-skimpy but still showed plenty of her smooth skin and delectable curves. His pulse quickened and he reminded himself this little swim was supposed to make her feel safer and get past her fear. It was not an excuse to touch her all over.

Yeah, right. It was a damned great excuse, and

The world had shrunk to just the two of them floating in the water. Intensely focused on all those thoughts, Trent forgot to pay attention to the waves. A large whitecap broke just before it reached them, crashing into their bodies and engulfing them.

Charlotte shrieked and her wide, scared eyes met his just before the wave drove them toward shore. He held on to her, crushing her against him so she wouldn't get flung loose, and her arms squeezed around him in return, tightening behind his neck. "Hold on!" he said as the surf took them on a long, rapid, undulating ride to shore.

Pressed tightly together, they rode the wave, and as it flattened Trent rolled to be sure it was his back and not hers that scraped along the sandy bottom. They slid to a stop in about five inches of water, just a short distance from the dry shore. With Charlotte still clutched in his arms, Trent rolled again so she was beneath him, shielding her from the surf. The last thing he wanted was for a wave to hit her from behind and startle her before she could see it coming. He looked into her eyes as water dripped from his face and hair onto hers. "Are you all right?"

"Yes. I'm all right." She dragged in some air. "Though I think I know how a surfboard feels now. Or a piece of seaweed."

He chuckled, then glanced up to see that John

not taking advantage of it was going to be nearly impossible.

"Ready?" He walked to her and stroked the pads of his fingers across the furrows in her brow, letting them trail softly down her cheek.

"Not really," she said under her breath. "But, since I'm now responsible for Patience not being afraid of the water for the rest of her life, I guess I have to be."

"I hope you're not mad at me. It's a good thing you're doing for her. And yourself." He grasped her hand and gave it a reassuring squeeze. "Don't worry. I'll be with you the whole time, and if you get really freaked out we'll head back in."

She nodded and gripped his hand tightly as they waded into the water, up to their knees, then her waist. In just another minute, the water was lapping at her breasts, which was so distracting he almost forgot to look for too-big waves that might be bearing down on them. He forced himself to look back at the ocean, making sure they weren't ending up in a dangerous spot, before returning his gaze to Charlotte's face. Her eyes were wide, the fear etched there clear, and he released her hand to put his arm around her waist, holding her close.

"I'm going to hold you now, so you feel more comfortable. Don't worry, I'm not getting creepy." He grinned and she gave him a weak smile in return. "In fact, why don't you get on my back and we'll just swim a little together that way until you feel more relaxed?"

"I admit I feel…uncomfortable. But I'm not a little kid, you know. Riding on your back seems ridiculous."

With that body of hers, there was no way she could be mistaken for a little kid. "Not if it makes you feel less nervous. Come on." He crouched down in the water up to his neck. "Get on, and wrap your arms around my throat. Just don't choke me if you get scared or we'll both drown," he teased.

To his surprise, she actually did, and he swam through the water with her clinging to him like a remora attached to a shark, enjoying the feel of the waves sluicing over his body. Enjoying the feel of her weight on him and of her skin sensuously sliding across his, just the way he'd fantasized.

"Okay?" he asked as a slightly bigger wave slapped into them, splashing water into their faces.

"Okay. I admit the water feels…nice."

"It does, doesn't it?" He grinned, relieved that this seemed to be working. "Ready to try a little on your own, with me holding your hand?"

"Um, I guess."

She slid from his back and, as she floated a foot or so away, her grim expression told him she wasn't anywhere near feeling relaxed. He took her hands and wrapped her arms behind his head, then placed his arms around her. Her face was so close, her mouth wet and parted as she breathed, her dripping hair glistening in streaks of bronze. He wanted, more than anything, to kiss her.

And, now that they were facing one another, pressed together, the sensuous feel of her soft breasts against his chest, of her legs sliding against his, was impossible to ignore. The sensation pummeled him far more than any wave could, and he battled back the raw need consuming him. He could only hope she couldn't feel his body's response to the overwhelming one-two punch that was delectable Charlotte Edwards.

"I…I'm not too freaked out, so that's good, isn't it?" Her voice was a bit breathless, but of course they were swimming a little, and treading water—though his own breath was short for a different reason.

"Yes. It's good." Holding her close was good. The feel of her body, soft and slick against his, was way better than good. He wanted to touch her soft satiny skin all over. Wanted to slide his hand inside her swimsuit top to cup her breast, to thumb the taut nipple he could feel poking again his chest. To slip his fingers inside her bikini b tom and caress her there, to see if she could sibly be as aroused as he was.

Adams and Patience were in the lagoon, the child's little body lying flat with his hands supporting her as she practiced her floating.

With a grin, he looked back down at Charlotte. "Looks like it worked. You being brave helped Patience be brave. You even rode a wave into shore!"

"Only because I was attached to you." A little laugh left her lips and she smiled at him. One thick strand of hair lay across one eye and clung to her face and lips. "I'm glad Patience got in the lagoon. Funny; I kind of forgot to be scared, too. Because of you."

"You're just a lot braver than you give yourself credit for. Hell, you're the bravest woman I know, living in that house alone, doing what you're doing here. Being afraid of a rip tide after nearly drowning in one is normal. Just a tiny, human nick in that feisty spirit of yours." He lifted the strand away from her face as he looked at the little golden flecks in her eyes, her lashes stuck together with salt water. "I'm proud of you for facing that fear. For getting in the water even though you didn't want to." Tucking her hair behind her ear to join the rest that lay flat against her scalp, he suddenly saw something he'd never noticed before.

Her ear was oddly shaped—not just different, slightly abnormal. Nearly invisible scarring appeared on and around it. Probably no one without plastic surgery experience would be able to see it at all, but he could. He pressed his mouth to it, touching the contours of it with his lips and tongue.

"What happened to your ear?"

Her fingers dug into his shoulder blades. "My... ear? What do you mean?"

He let his mouth travel down her damp throat and back up to her jaw, because he just couldn't resist any longer; across her chin then up, slipping softly across her wet, salty lips before he lifted his gaze back to hers. "Your ear. Were you in an accident? Or was it something congenital?"

She was silent for a moment, just looking back at him, her eyes somber until she sighed. "Congenital. I was born with microtia."

"What grade of microtia? Was your ear just misshapen?"

"No, it was grade three. I only had this weird little skin flap that didn't look like an ear at all. We were told that's often accompanied by atresia, but I was blessed to have an ear canal, so I can hear pretty well out of it now."

"When did you have it reconstructed? Were you living in the States?"

She nodded. "I think doctors sometimes do the procedure younger now. But mine wanted to wait until I was nine, since that's when the ear grows to about ninety percent of its adult size." A small smile touched her mouth. "I still remember, when I was about five, why he told me I should be a little older before it was fixed—that it would look strange for a little girl to have a big, grown-up-sized ear, which at the time I thought was a pretty funny visual."

He gave her a soft kiss. "So you remember living with your ear looking abnormal?"

"Remember?" She gave a little laugh that had no humor in the sound at all. "Kids thought it was so hilarious to tease me about it. Called me 'earless Edwards.' One time a kid brought a CD to class for everyone to listen to, then said to me, 'Oh, right, you can't because you don't have an ear!' I wanted to crawl under my desk and hide."

He shook his head, hating that she'd had to go through that. "Kids can be nasty little things, that's for sure; convinced they're just being funny. Now I know where you got that chip on your shoulder from."

He was glad to see the shadows leave her eyes as she narrowed them at him, green sparks flying. "I do not have a chip on my shoulder. I just believe it's more efficient for me to drive and do whatever I need to do than take ten minutes talking about it just to dance around a man's ego."

"Good thing I'm so full of myself, which you've enjoyed telling me several times. Otherwise you would have crushed my feelings by now."

"As though I could possibly hurt your feelings."

"You might be surprised." And she probably would be, if she knew how rattled he'd felt for days. How much he wanted to leave while somehow, at the very same time, wanting to stay a little longer.

Her palms swept over his shoulder blades, wrapped more fully around his back, and he took that as an invitation for another soft kiss. Her mouth tasted so good, salty-sweet and irresistible.

"Tell me more about your surgery." He lifted his finger to stroke the shell of it. "Did they harvest cartilage from your ribs to build the framework for the new ear?"

"Yes. I have a small scar near my sternum, but you can barely see it now. They finished it in three procedures."

"Well, it looks great. Whoever performed the surgery was very good at it. I bet you were happy."

"Happy?" Her smile grew wider. "I felt normal for the first time in my life. No longer the freak without an ear. It was…amazing."

Now it was all clear as glass. He pressed another kiss to her now smiling mouth. "I finally get why you built the plastic surgery wing, and why it's so important to you. You know first-hand how it feels to be scarred or look different from everyone else."

She nodded, her eyes now the passionately intense green he'd seen so often the past week; the passion that was such an integral part of who she was. "I know saving lives is important—more important than helping people view themselves differently, as you said. But I can tell you that feeling good about the way you look, not feeling like a freak, is so important to a person's psyche. And, even though I had to live for a while feeling like that, I know how blessed I was to have access to doctors who could make it better. You know as well as anyone that so many people around the world don't. And I want to give the people here, at least, that same opportunity to look and feel normal. Can you understand that?"

His answer was to stroke her hair from her forehead, cup her cheek in his palm and kiss her. From the minute he'd met her, she'd impressed him with her determination, and now he was even more impressed. She'd used a negative experience from her own life to try to make life better for others and worked damn hard to make it happen.

His tongue delved into her mouth, licking, tasting the ocean water and the flavor that was uniquely, delectably her. Tasting the passion that was so much a part of her. He was swept along by her to another place, deeper and farther and more powerfully than any wave could ever take him.

CHAPTER TWELVE

AS THE SURF lapped over their bodies, Charlie let herself drown in the kiss, in the taste of his cool, salty lips, his warm tongue deliciously exploring her mouth. Her hands stroked down his shoulder blades and back, reveling in the feel of the hard muscle beneath his smooth skin.

She tunneled her fingers into his thick, wet hair, wild and sexy and black as Liberian coal. His muscled thigh nudged between hers, sending waves of pleasure through every nerve. The taste of his mouth, the touch of his hands, the feel of his arousal against her took her breathlessly back to their incredible night of lovemaking.

"Charlotte," he whispered, his lips leaving hers to trail down her throat, to lick the water pooled there, then continuing their journey lower until his mouth covered her nipple, gently sucking on it through her wet nylon swimsuit.

She gasped. "Trent. That's so good. I—"

The sound of Patience laughing made her eyes pop open as he lifted his head from her breast.

His eyes— no longer the light, laughing blue she was used to seeing, but instead a glittering near-black—met hers. Everything about him seemed hard—his chest rising and falling against hers, his arms taut around her, his hips and what was between them.

"Charlotte," he said through clenched teeth. "More than anything, I want to make love to you right now. Right here. To wrap your legs around me and swim back into the waves; nobody would know I'm diving deep inside of you." His mouth covered hers in a steaming kiss. "But I guess that will have to wait until later."

If it hadn't already been difficult to breathe, his words nearly would have made her faint from the lack of oxygen in her brain. Even though she knew Patience and John Adams were fairly close by, she couldn't bring herself to move. The undulating water that wrapped around them was the most intimate cocoon she'd ever experienced in her life and she didn't want it to end. Couldn't find the will to detangle herself from his arms. "So I guess our deal is off."

"Our deal?"

"Not to start anything up again."

"Our deal has obviously been a challenge for me." His mouth lifted in a slow smile, his eyes gleaming. "Maybe we can come up with a slightly modified deal."

"Such as?"

His mouth traveled across her cheek, lowered to her ear. "We make love one more time. Cool down this heat between us and get it out of our systems. Then back to just colleagues for the last days I'm here so we won't have that second good-bye we both want to avoid."

The thought of one, just one more time with him, sent her heart into a crazy rhythm. "I agree to your terms. Just once."

"Just once. So—"

The sound of distant shouting interrupted him. They both turned their heads at the same time and saw a few of the surfers down the beach pulling what looked like an unconscious young man, or a body, from the water.

Trent sprinted down the beach with Charlotte on his heels.

Blood poured through the fingers of a young man sitting on the sand, holding his hand to his forehead. The group of surfers gathered around him looked concerned, and one shouted to another who was running to a mound of things they'd apparently brought with them. He returned with a shirt that he handed to the injured surfer, who pressed it to his head.

"Looks like you need a hand here," Trent said

as he approached the injured boy. "I'm a doctor. Will you let me take a look?"

"You a doctor?" The young man looked utterly surprised, and no wonder. There weren't too many doctors around there, period, and it was just damned good luck he happened to be on the beach when the kid was hurt.

"Yes. I work at the Edwards Mission Hospital. This lady is the director." He smiled at Charlotte, now standing next to him, before crouching down. "What's your name? Will you show me what we're dealing with here?"

"Murvee Browne," he replied, lowering his hand with the now-bloody shirt balled up in it. "I was surfing and, when the board flipped, I think the fin got me."

"Looks like it." Trent leaned closer to study the wound. It was one damned deep gash, probably five centimeters, stretching from the hairline diagonally across his forehead to his eyebrow. The injury appeared to slice all the way to the skull, but it was a little hard to tell while it was still bleeding so much. He'd let the kid know it was serious, but reassure him so he wouldn't freak out at what he was going to have to do to repair it. "You've got a pretty good one there. But at least it's just your forehead. I took care of one nasty surf accident victim where the guy's eyelid was slit open too."

Murvee grimaced while his friends gathered even closer to stare at the gash.

"You did it good, oh!" one friend said. "You so lucky the doctor is here today."

Murvee looked worried as he stared at Trent. "What you charge for fixing me up, doc? I don't make much. My mother makes money at the market, but she needs what I have to help take care of my brothers and sisters."

"Why don't you press that cloth against your forehead real firmly again and keep it there to stop the bleeding, okay, Murvee?" Chase said. "You don't have to worry about paying me. Miss Charlotte here pays me a lot, and she gets mad if I don't do any work to earn it."

He shot a teasing glance at her and she rolled her eyes in return, but there was a smile in them too. "We're going to have to have a little talk about your spreading rumors of what a tyrant I am," she said.

He chuckled and turned his attention back to Murvee. "Are you feeling okay? Not real dizzy or anything?"

"No. I feel all right."

"I'd like to take you back to the hospital to get you stitched up."

"No hospital." Murvee frowned, looking mulish. "I have to be home soon and I have to go to work. I can just have my mom fix it."

"Murvee..."

"How about stitching him in the jeep?" Charlotte suggested, giving him a look that said he was going to have to be flexible here. "I know you brought your bag with you. I'll help any way I can."

Trent sighed. He knew taking Murvee to the hospital and getting his wound taken care of there would take hours, and likely be tough on his family—if he could get the kid to go at all. "Fine. Since you seem okay other than the gash, I won't insist. Let's go to the car."

Murvee's friends helped him stand and the three of them headed down the beach. Trent kept an eye on the young man as they trudged to the car, and he thankfully did seem to be feeling all right, not shocked or woozy. Charlotte opened the back of her banged-up SUV and they worked together to get the kid situated inside and lying on a blanket with his feet propped up on the side beneath the window before Trent grabbed his medical bag.

"What do you need me to do first?" Charlotte asked.

"Did you bring any fresh water I can wash it out with? And are all the towels sandy, or do we have a clean one?" he asked.

"I brought extra towels. And I have water."

"Good." He turned to Murvee. "Let me see if

the bleeding has stopped." The young man lifted away the shirt; the bleeding had, thankfully, lessened. Trent got everything set up as best he could in the cramped space, putting his flashlight, gauze, Betadine, local anesthetic and suture kit next to the young man. Squeezing out some of the sanitizer he always kept in his bag, he thoroughly rubbed it over his hands and between his fingers then snapped on gloves.

"Here's the water and towels." Charlotte came to stand next to him, knees resting against the bumper of the car. "What else can I do?"

He looked at her, standing there completely calm, and marveled again that she took on any task thrown at her calmly and efficiently. Including dealing with a bleeding gash that would look so awful to most non-medical professionals, it might make them feel a little faint, or at least turn away so they wouldn't have to look at it.

"You want to wash out the wound to make sure it's good and clean before I suture it? Put the folded towel under his head. After I inject the lidocaine, I want you to pour a steady stream of the water through the wound." He drew the anesthetic into the syringe. "You still doing all right, Murvee? I'm going to give you some numbing medicine. I have to use a needle, and it'll burn a little, but you won't feel the stitches."

Murvee held his breath and winced a few times

as he injected it. "Sorry. I know this hurts, but pretty soon it will feel numb."

"I don't care, doc. I'm very grateful to you for helping me."

"I'm glad we were here today." He'd felt that way on many occasions in his life, since this kind of thing seemed to happen fairly often when he was working in the field, or even like today when he was touring and relaxing. Which was why he'd become convinced that whatever higher power was out there truly had a hand in the workings of the universe.

"Am I doing this right?" Charlotte asked as she continued washing out the wound.

"Perfect." He studied it, satisfied that it looked pretty clean now. "I think we're good to go. Thanks." He squeezed a stream of antiseptic on gauze then brushed it along the wound's edges.

Trent saw Charlotte reach for the young man's hand and give it a squeeze. "Tell me about surfing, Murvee. How long have you been doing it?"

"Me and my friends surf for a year now. A guy from the UK was surfing here a while ago and he was really good. He showed some people how to surf, and now many of us do. I want to get good enough to compete in the Liberian Surfing Championships, which has been around about five years now, I think."

Trent glanced at Charlotte again as he got the

suture materials together, smiling at the warm and interested expression on her face. He loved the many facets to her personality: the feisty fireball, the take-charge director, the soft and sexy woman whose love-making he knew would stay in his memory a long, long time and the person he was seeing now. She was nurturing and caring for this young man, distracting him with casual chit-chat so Murvee wouldn't think too hard about the time-consuming procedure Trent was about to do on him.

He nodded at his small but powerful flashlight and looked at Charlotte. "Will you shine that on the wound so I can see better?" They were parked within the trees and, while it was far from optimal conditions for suturing, the flashlight illuminated well enough.

She pointed the light at the wound. "Does that help?"

"Yes, great," he said as he began suturing. It was deep and would require a three-layer closure. The boy was lucky a medic was here today. While the injury would likely have healed eventually on its own, his scars would have been bold and obvious, not to mention there was a good chance the wound would have become infected, maybe seriously.

"You should see the way your head looks, Murvee. You want to check it out in a mirror, so you can watch what Dr. Trent has to do to repair that nasty gash?"

"I don't know about that, Charlotte." Trent frowned at her in surprise. Trust a non-medical assistant to come up with a wacky idea like that, though it was probably because, if she'd had a wound that required suturing, Ms. Toughness would have wanted to watch.

"I would like to see," Murvee said. "I want to tell my friends what you had to do, what it looked like."

"So long as you don't faint on me." He smiled at the young man, who gave him a nice smile in return that seemed pretty normal and not particularly anxious.

Charlotte held up a small mirror in a powder compact and Murvee took it from her, moving his head around so he could see himself.

"Please hold still, Murvee." When this was over, he was going to give Charlotte a few pointers on doctor-assisting. She'd done a great job helping the boy relax, but this wasn't helping *him*, though he had to appreciate the ingenuity in her distraction techniques. If the boy didn't get queasy, that was.

"What exactly you doing?" Murvee asked as he looked at Trent suturing his wound in the mirror, seeming fascinated, thankfully, instead of disturbed.

Since the kid asked, he figured he might as well give him the full details. "Your wound was so deep I could see some of your skull bone."

Murvee's eyes widened. "No kidding?"

"No kidding. I repaired the galea first—that's the layer that covers the bone. Now I'm sewing up the layer under the skin—we call it the subcutaneous tissue, or 'sub-Q.' You've got some very healthy sub-Q."

"Yeah, man. Fine sub-Q." He grinned, obviously proud, and Trent and Charlotte both laughed. "That's crazy-looking," Murvee said, staring into the mirror.

"The whole human body is kind of crazy-looking. One of the cool things about being a doctor is learning about how crazy it really is. And amazing."

Murvee looked at him then and Trent was glad the boy finally lowered the mirror. "Is my head going to look like this always, doc?"

"Not always." He gave Charlotte a look that she interpreted correctly, thank goodness, since she took the mirror from Murvee and tucked it into her purse. "After I finish, you'll look a little like Frankenstein, and your friends will be jealous of how cool and tough you look." He smiled, knowing from experience that boys and young men related to that and were usually amused. "But by sewing it in three steps using very tiny stitches it will heal well and, over time, the scar will become a thin line. You'll be as handsome as ever and all the girls will think you're great."

Murvee grinned at Trent's commentary, as he'd expected. "Girls think I'm great already."

The sound of Charlotte's little laugh brought their attention back to her. "I bet they do," she said. "And now you can talk to them about how you were hit by your board while you were surfing, which not many guys around here do, and ended up getting stitched up on the beach by a world-class surgeon."

"World-class?" Trent smiled, wondering if she'd really meant that, or if she was just talking to keep Murvee relaxed as he worked. Wondering why it felt nice for her to say it, when he'd always been sure he didn't need anyone's admiration or accolades.

"Are you kidding me?" Her green eyes met his and held, a brief moment of connection that warmed him in a totally different way than she'd warmed him in the water. "You're amazing. With technique like yours, you could be working as a plastic surgeon in Beverly Hills."

"Which would be your idea of having really made it, right?" Concentrating on suturing Murvee, disappointment jabbed at him that she apparently felt that way. He'd been there and done the Beverly Hills-type vanity plastic surgery and rejected it for a reason. A reason nobody understood or cared about.

"Is that a real question?" Charlotte asked, her expression one of annoyed disbelief. "If my idea of 'making it' was a Beverly Hills lifestyle, I'd have set my sights on a big hospital in the States after I got my degrees or gone to work on Wall Street. Not come to Liberia."

He looked back up at her. He should have realized her comment had just been intended as a light-hearted compliment. She was as far from a New York City or Beverly Hills socialite as a woman could be. "I know you haven't exactly chosen glamour over substance here. Except those pretty, polished toenails of yours could be considered pretty glamorous."

"Does that mean you like them? I changed the color last night." She smiled as their eyes met again and lingered.

"Yeah. I like them." He looked back down and continued the detailed suturing of Murvee's wound, trying to focus on only his work and not her lethal combo of femininity and toughness.

"Do you mind if I take a photograph of your injury, Murvee?" Charlotte asked.

When he agreed, she snapped a number of pictures and Trent wondered what she planned to use them for. Probably to put in a portfolio of the plastic surgery wing. Except it wasn't open yet.

Trent gave the young man some antibiotic tablets and instructions on how to take care of the wound.

"I know the hospital's a long way off. Any way you can get there in a week? I probably won't be there anymore, but there are several great techs who can remove your stitches. I'd also like you to have a tetanus shot."

"My family has a scooter, so I can come. Thank you again for everything." He pumped Trent's hand then reached for Charlotte's too, a smile so wide on his face you'd never have known the injury he'd just suffered if you hadn't seen the bandage on his head.

"You're very welcome. Like I said, I'm glad we were here today."

The young man headed back down the beach. Charlotte looked at Trent and the expression in her eyes made his breath hitch. He reached for her hand. "Ready, Miss Edwards?"

"Yes. I'm ready to head back."

He was pretty sure she knew that heading back to the compound wasn't what he'd been asking.

CHAPTER THIRTEEN

DARKNESS HAD NEARLY enfolded the hospital compound as Charlie pulled the car up to her house. When she'd dropped Trent off at his quarters, the look he'd given her before he'd walked away was sizzling enough practically to set her hair on fire.

Both excited and nervous, her insides felt all twisted around, thinking about her subterfuge with his release papers, the new doctor and all the things she was trying to manipulate. But all that worry wasn't quite enough to douse cold water on her plans. To keep her from wanting to relive, one more time, the passionate thrill of the night they'd spent locked in one another's arms the previous week.

Still sitting in her car with the engine off, she stared at a small impediment to that plan, all too clearly apparent in the lights that were currently burning in her house. Her dad was staying with her and wasn't leaving for another day or two.

Which meant that her house as a rendezvous for Trent and her to make love all night was out. Her mind spun with ideas of where else they might meet, though it couldn't be from now into the morning. The various possibilities, and the memories of their past love-making, had her ready to leap out of the car to run and pound on the man's door, despite the fact that she'd dropped him off only minutes ago.

Had she suddenly become a sex maniac? The thought made her laugh at herself, at the same time her anticipation ratcheted higher. For whatever reason, the secretiveness added a certain allure; why that was, she didn't know. But she wasn't going to fight the excitement she felt, because she knew she'd only get to enjoy it one more time.

The real question was, should she go inside and have dinner with her dad, take a shower to wash off the beach then find an excuse to leave again? Or just not come back until later? Her dad had encouraged her to take time off today, after all. Maybe he'd just assume they'd made a long day of it in Robertsport.

Except he'd know that wasn't true, because Patience had been with them and would be ready for bed very soon.

She shook her head at her ambivalence, reminding herself that she was twenty-seven years old and a grown woman. Her father wasn't naive or judgmental. Shoving open the car door, she decided she'd just go in and say hello, then tell him she had dinner plans with Trent; never mind that there couldn't be a candlelit dinner in a restaurant, just leftovers in the hospital kitchen.

The sound of her father's favorite jazz music met her as she opened the front door. He sat in one of the upholstered chairs she'd bought when she'd moved here, since little of the original furniture had survived the pillaging during the wars. The hospital files were open on his lap and he looked up with a smile as she entered the room.

"Did my girl get in the water today?"

"I did. I even rode a wave all the way in to shore. How about that?"

He clapped his hands. "Bravo! I'm proud of you. And not just for swimming today. For all you've done here." He gestured to the files. "I'm so impressed with what you've accomplished with the funding you have. You're making huge headway, especially considering the shambles you were left to work with."

"Thanks, Dad. That means a lot to me." When her parents had trusted her to bring the hospital and school back to life, it had been scary and admittedly daunting. But, with John Adams's help, they'd done a lot. And she had to admit she felt pretty proud of what they'd accomplished too.

"I know the plastic surgery wing is important to you, and of course I understand why." His expression was filled with both sympathy and pain. "You had to deal with a lot as a little girl."

"Things happen for a reason, Dad. You know that as well as anyone. I hope that experiencing what it feels like to look abnormal will end up helping people who have to deal with things a whole lot worse than my childhood embarrassment."

"I do know. And I'm excited about your project. But I have to ask some hard questions now, not as a father, but as a businessman. And this has to be treated like a business."

Uh-oh. She gulped, afraid she knew what was coming next. "What are your hard questions?"

"What happens if, by some stroke of bad luck, the Gilchrist Foundation money doesn't come through? Do you have a backup plan?"

She closed her eyes for a moment, wondering how she should answer. Should she tell him she'd known all along that it was a risk? That maybe it was a risk she shouldn't have taken? She forced herself to open her eyes and tell him the truth. "Honestly? No. I don't. If the foundation money doesn't come through, we're in serious trouble. I'm trying to solicit other sources of income, but none of it is for sure until we have it in our hands."

He nodded. "All right. So when will you know about the foundation money?"

"Soon. They're sending their rep here in the

next few days to see if we meet their requirements."

"And I see that you've met all those requirements except for one: a plastic surgeon on site."

"I *do* have a plastic surgeon on site—Trent. I just need for him to stay until their representative gives us the green light. Then we'll have the Gilchrist check and it'll all be good."

He looked at her steadily. "Except that something tells me Trent doesn't know about all this."

For once, she wished her dad wasn't so darned intuitive. "No. He doesn't. I don't see any reason for him to know."

"Why not? Seems to me he's an important part of the equation."

"Only for a short time. He performed a brilliant plastic surgery on a boy here in the hospital and another today on the beach that I can show pictures of." She sucked in a fortifying breath so she could continue. "He doesn't want to be involved, Dad. For some reason, he doesn't want to perform plastic surgeries. But I'm still hoping he'll agree to help a few patients with serious problems before he leaves."

"He seems like a good man. You should tell him the truth."

The truth? Her dad didn't know about the lies she'd told and her stomach twisted around when she thought about what his reaction would be if he did. If he'd still be as proud of her as he said he was. "I'm handling it, Dad. It will turn out okay; we'll get the funding." And she prayed that would really happen and every problem would be solved.

"I hope you're right. Now, there's something else we need to talk about, Charlie." Her father threaded his fingers together in his lap and looked at her. "Your goals are worthy goals. Your hard work is to be commended. But have you ever asked yourself if there's more you need to consider?"

"Such as?"

"Your own life." He stood and placed his hands on her shoulders. "Have you thought about exploring a relationship with a man who lives here? Or one of the single doctors coming through? Trent has impressed me, and I've met Perry Cantwell— who's coming soon, I think you said. He's nice enough, and good-looking to boot. I know it's damned difficult to meet someone when you live and work where there aren't too many folks around. I don't want to see you give everything of yourself for this place until there's nothing left of you to share with anyone else. I've seen it happen and I don't want it to happen to you."

"It won't. I promise. I just need to get that wing open and the place running smoothly then I'll think of other things besides work. I will."

And that was the truth. Even in the midst of

this serious conversation with her dad, and all the stress over the hospital's finances, thoughts of Trent were foremost in her mind, thoughts of meeting with him and finishing what they'd started this afternoon. All those thoughts sent her breathing haywire and her pulse skipping and she just wanted to end this conversation and be with him.

"In fact, Dad, Trent and I are going to have a late dinner over in the hospital. Are you okay here eating leftovers on your own?"

His serious and worried expression gave way to a big smile. "Of course. Leftovers are my favorite."

"Good." She kissed his cheek then gave him a fierce hug. She wouldn't tell her dad that the thought of giving up her freedom forever, her ability to live as she wanted and do as she wanted and run the hospital as she wanted, sent a cold chill down her spine. Or that one more wonderful night with Trent just might be enough to satisfy her relationship needs for a long, long time. "Thanks for the advice, Dad."

"Okay." He hugged her back just as fiercely. "Go on, now."

The night air embraced Charlie with a close, sultry warmth as she walked toward the hospital quarters. A huge gibbous moon hung in the sky, casting a glow of white light across the earth. Her feet moved in slow, measured steps, her dad's words echoing in her head.

Could there possibly ever be anything between her and Trent other than physical pleasure and friendship, a friendship based on both of their experiences working in developing nations and an appreciation of the tremendous need there?

No. She shook her head in fervent denial. What the two of them had experienced during their one night together was what anyone would feel after being focused on only work for months and months. What Trent no doubt felt for all the various women in his life, which if rumor was to be believed were many. He was famous in the GPC community for enjoying short and no doubt very sweet interludes until he moved on to his next job.

She could deal with that. After all, hadn't she known it from the start? Enjoying one more night of fantastic sex with a special man would be wonderful, just as it had been last week, without thoughts of tomorrows and futures and what any of it might mean.

The employee quarters loomed gray in the darkness, its roof lit by moonlight, and her steps faltered, along with her confidence. He'd said he wanted to be with her just one more time, hadn't he? She could only hope, now that they were on dry land and no longer only half-dressed, a knock on his door wouldn't bring the cool Trent who sometimes appeared. The one who had shown very clearly how little he wanted to be stuck with her in this little, forgotten place in Liberia.

A shadowy figure suddenly became visible in front of her and she nearly let out a small shriek at the apparition.

"Charlotte? Is that you?"

"Yes." She exhaled at the sound of Trent's low voice, blaming the surprise of his sudden appearance for her weak and breathy reply. "I was… coming to see if you wanted to find some dinner in the kitchen."

"Now there's a surprise—you being hungry again. Let's see what we can do about that." Through the darkness, she saw the gleam of his eyes for what seemed like barely a second before he moved fast and was there, right in front of her, his arms wrapping around her, pulling her close. Before she could barely blink, he was kissing her.

And kissing her. His mouth possessed hers in a thorough exploration that stole her breath. Not rushed, but intense and deep, giving and taking, completely different from his teasing, playful kisses of before. Every hard inch of him seemed to be touching her at once, his chest pressing against her breasts, his thighs to her hips, his taut arms against her back.

A small moan sounded in her throat as his

mouth devoured hers. She wanted this: wanted this sensory explosion; wanted his kisses and touch and the heat that crawled and burned across her skin.

His mouth left hers, softly touching her eyelids, her nose, her lips, stealing her breath. "You taste so good to me, Charlotte. Way better than any food, though I have a feeling that the more I taste you, the hungrier I'm going to get."

"Me too. Food is overrated." He tasted so delicious, so wonderful, so right. His lips and tongue returned to her mouth with an expertise that dazzled, so mind-blowing that her skin tingled, her knees got wobbly and, if he hadn't been holding her so tightly, they might have simply crumpled beneath her.

She flattened her palms against the firm contours of his chest, up to his thick, dark hair that was getting a little long, and the feel of its softness within her fingers was as sensual as the feel of his body pressed to hers.

The little moan she heard this time came from him, and he pulled his mouth from hers, his heartbeat heavy against her breasts. "Charlotte." His hands roamed across her back and down to her bottom, pulling her so close that his erection pressing against her stomach nearly hurt. "Do you have any idea how hard it's been for me to keep my distance this week? Not to come into your of-

with your plastics skills and magic skills and piano skills."

"And other skills." His lips curved and with a quick, deft movement, he flicked open her bra and slid it from her arms. "I'm looking forward to showing you some you haven't seen yet."

She wished her fingers were as magical as his as she struggled to get the last of the annoying buttons undone. Finally, finally, she was able to shove his shirt from his shoulders to see his muscled chest. She flattened her hands against it, loving the feel of it, thrilling in the quick, hard beat of his heart against her palms. "Oh, yeah? Like what?"

"Showing is always better than telling." He shucked his pants and underwear until he stood fully naked, the moonlight illuminating the broadness of his shoulders, his lean hips, his strong thighs and the powerful arousal between them.

"Hmm. Is this what you wanted to show me?" Desire for him nearly buckled her knees and she decided to take matters into her own hands, so to speak. She reached for him as she kissed him, stroking him, teasing him, and she felt him respond with a deep shudder. A low groan sounded in his throat. His hands tightened on her back and his fingers dug into her bottom until it nearly hurt.

"Not exactly. Oh, Charlotte." There was a ragged hitch to the way he said her name, and in the next breath he practically pushed her down onto the blanket, kissing her, covering her body with his heavy warmth that felt impossibly familiar, considering how short their time had been together the week before.

His fingers teased her nipples, glided slowly down, over her ribs, her belly, then lower. They slipped slowly, gently in and around the moist and slick juncture between her thighs; the sensation was most definitely magical. She couldn't control the movement of her hips as they reached for his talented fingers, sought more of the erotic sensation he gave her.

She needed more. Needed all of him. "Now, please, Trent. I want you now."

"If I could say no, not yet, I would. But, damn it, I can't wait any longer to be inside of you." Propped onto his elbows, he stared down at her. The intensity in his blue eyes held hers, mesmerized, as she opened for him, welcomed him. And, when he joined with her, it felt so wonderful, so familiar and yet so new all at the same time.

Rhythmically, they moved together, faster and deeper, until the earth seemed a part of them and the night stars seemed to burst into an explosion of light. And as she gave herself over to the pleasure of being in his arms, to the ecstasy of being at one with him, she cried out. He covered her mouth with his, swallowing the sounds of both of them falling.

For a long while, they lay there together as they caught their breath and their heart rates slowed. His face was buried in her neck. His weight felt wonderful pressing her into the soft earth, and she made a little sound of protest as he eventually rolled off her, keeping her hand entwined with his.

Still floating in other-worldly sensation, the sound of his laughter surprised her. She turned her head to look at him. "What's so funny?"

"Looks like we managed to lose the blanket." Despite the darkness, his eyes met hers, his teeth gleaming white as he grinned. "I guess we made love in the mud after all."

She looked down and realized that they were, indeed, squished down into the mud; how they hadn't noticed that, she couldn't imagine. Actually, she could. Her mind slipped back to how wonderful it had been to be with him again, and just thinking about it made her feel like rolling her muddy body on top of him.

So she did, and he laughed again as she smeared a handful of mud on his chest and stomach then wriggled and squished against him. "I think I like it. Don't people pay good money for mud baths?"

"They do. I'm pretty sure pigs like mud too."

"Are you calling me a pig?"

He gave her a lazy, relaxed smile as he stroked

more cool mud over and across her bottom, which felt so absurdly, deliciously sensual she couldn't help wriggling against him a little more. "I've been around enough women in my life to never, ever say anything that stupid."

The thought of all the women he'd had in his life shouldn't have had the power to bring the pleasure of the moment down, but somehow it did. Which was silly, since she knew the score, didn't she?

Something of her thoughts must have shown in her expression, because he wiped his muddy hand on the blanket then stroked her hair back from her face, all traces of amusement gone. "I have been to a lot of places and known a lot of people." He tucked her hair behind the ear her plastic surgeon had created for her then traced it softly, tenderly, with his finger. "But you're special. I've never met anyone who is such an incredible combination of sexiness, compassion and take-no-prisoners toughness. You amaze me. Truly."

"Thank you." Her heart swelled at his sweet words and she used her one not-muddy hand to cup his cheek as she leaned down to give him a soft kiss. "You amaze me too. Truly."

"And I can tell you that, if I was going to fund a school or a hospital anywhere, I'd trust you to run it." Through the moonlit darkness, his eyes stared into hers with a deep sincerity. "I'd trust you with anything."

Damn. His words painfully clutched at her heart and twisted her stomach, making her feel slightly sick. He'd trust her with anything?

She could only hope and pray he never found out exactly how misplaced that trust really was.

CHAPTER FOURTEEN

THE DELICIOUS PICNIC Trent had put together for them, complete with a bottle of wine he said he'd tucked in his bag for the right moment, was the most intimate and lovely meal Charlie had experienced in her life. It didn't matter that they'd both been curled up on his skinny bed, towels wrapped around and beneath their muddy bodies, and that the wine "glasses" had been plastic cups.

After they'd eaten, the pleasure of the shower they'd shared—laughing as they'd washed the mud off their bodies, then no longer laughing as they enjoyed making love again within the erratic spray of water—wasn't quite enough to make Charlie completely forget his words. To forget his misplaced trust in her. To remember her conviction that the end was worth the means.

She'd hardly slept after she'd crept into her house and fallen into her bed, tired, wired and worried. And still she ended up back at her desk as the sun rose. She stayed closeted in her office much of the day, contacting every potential donor, digging everywhere she could to possibly find some cash commitments in case the Gilchrist donation fell through.

Thankfully, the hospital and clinic had been busy too so she and Trent hadn't seen one another except when he'd passed by her accidentally left-open door, giving her a sexy, knowing smile and a wink.

Deep in thought, a knock on the now closed door startled her. "Come in." She readied herself to see a tall, hunky doctor with amused blue eyes, but relaxed when her dad appeared.

"Hi, honey. Have a second?"

"Of course."

He settled himself in the only other chair in her tiny office. "I've decided to head on home tonight, instead of waiting until tomorrow. Your mom called to say a church group has sent a few members to study our school, and I'd like to be there to talk with them when they get there."

"I understand, Dad. I'm planning to come see you and Mom soon for a few days anyway, as soon as…things are settled here." No point in starting up another conversation about the hospital funding and potential problems there. She stood and rounded the desk, leaning down to kiss his cheek. "But you should wait until tomorrow morning. Why in the world would you drive at night on these roads if you don't have to?"

"I'm stopping on the way. Do you remember Emmanuel and Marie? I'm going to visit them and check out their school, which is just across the border in the Ivory Coast. I'm staying there a day, then heading home." He threaded his fingers together like he always did when he had something serious to say, and she braced herself. "Will you remember what I said about not giving everything to this place? About being open to the possibilities that may come along in your personal life? Think about giving Perry Cantwell a fair shot."

"Does Charlotte have a personal life with Perry Cantwell?"

She swung around and stared at Trent leaning casually against the doorjamb, a smile on his face. But his eyes were anything but amused. They looked slightly hard and deadly serious.

A nervous laugh bubbled from her throat. The man was leaving in a matter of days. Surely he wasn't jealous of some possible future relationship with his replacement? "I've never even met Perry Cantwell. But seems to me you've been anxious for him to get here so you could leave. Maybe I'm anxious for him to get here, too."

It wasn't nice to goad him like that after what they'd shared together last night and she knew it. But her emotions were all over the place when it came to Trent: needing him to stay until the Gilchrist rep came; wanting him to stay because she'd grown closer to him than was wise, closer than she should have allowed. This looming good-bye was going to be so much harder than the first one, as she'd worried all along it would be. And added to that was the fear that he'd somehow find out about her machinations, destroying the trust, the faith, he said he had in her.

Which shouldn't really have mattered, since he'd be out of her life all too soon. But somehow it mattered anyway. A lot.

His posture against the doorjamb relaxed a little, as did the cool seriousness in his eyes. His lips curved as he shook his head, but that usual twinkle in his eyes was still missing. "Perry's a good surgeon, but I hear he cheats at golf. Talks down to nurses. Sometimes dates men. Not a good fit for you, Charlotte."

"I'm pretty sure you're making all that up." She stepped back to her desk and rested her rear end against it. "Dad's right that I need to keep all possibilities open—except maybe not men who date men."

Her dad chuckled, which reminded her he was there. "I've got to get going before it gets any later. Will you stay with Charlie tonight, Trent? I know we haven't had any sign of burglars since before I got here, but I'd feel better if we gave it a few more nights."

"Dad, I don't—"

"Of course I will. You didn't have to ask; I would've been there, anyway."

The smoldering look he gave her both aroused and embarrassed her, and she hoped her father didn't see it, along with the blush she could feel filling her cheeks. Though she had a feeling her dad wouldn't exactly be surprised to know that she and Trent were a little more than just acquaintances and colleagues.

Her father stood. The small smile on his face told her he'd seen Trent's look and was more than aware of the sizzle between them. She blushed all over again. "I need to grab my files before I go." He looked at the various piles on her desk and frowned, lifting up one or two. "I thought they were right here. Did you move them?"

"I put them—" Oh no; he had his hands on the pile she'd shoved Trent's release papers into, practically right in front of the man! Why, oh why hadn't she buried them deep in a drawer? She hastily reached to grab them. "Don't mess with that pile, Dad. Yours are—"

And because she was so nervous and moving too fast, and karma was probably getting back at her, the middle of the pile slid out and thunked on the floor, with some of the papers fluttering around Trent's feet.

He reached down to gather the mess and she feared she just might hyperventilate. Snatching them up and acting even stranger than she was already would just raise suspicion, so she forced herself to quickly but calming retrieve and stack the files. Until her heart ground to a stop when she saw Trent had a paper in his hand and was reading it with a frown. She couldn't think of anything else that would make him look so perplexed.

"When did this come?" His attention left the paper and focused on her. "This isn't my original release from the GPC. It's dated—" he looked down again "—three days ago. Why didn't you give me this? And why didn't they send it directly to me, like usual?"

She licked her dry lips. "Because Cantwell wasn't here yet, I guess. He was all scheduled to come, which is why they sent your papers, but then something went wrong, I don't know what." Except she did know. Colleen hadn't arranged for Cantwell's travel because a certain desperate, deceiving hospital director had lied and told her Trent had agreed to stay until the Gilchrist rep came.

The end justified the means, she tried to remind herself as she stared at the confusion on Trent's face. Except it was getting harder and harder to feel convinced of that.

"You still should have given them to me. Once the GPC releases me, my vacation is supposed to officially start. I need to find out when I'm expected in the Philippines now. That might have changed."

Her heart in her throat, she forced a smile. "I'm sorry if I messed this up. I'll call Colleen."

"Don't worry about it. I'll call."

His face relaxed into that charming smile of his, which somehow made the nervous twist in her stomach tighten even more painfully. The man really did like and trust her. Thank heavens the Gilchrist rep was due here any day, then this would all be over and he could be on his way.

And that thought made her stomach twist around and her chest ache in a whole different way.

"I've got my files here, Charlie. So I'm going to hit the road."

She turned to her dad, having nearly forgotten—again—that he was in the room. How was that possible since he stood only three feet from her? His expression was serious, speculative. Probably he, too, was wondering what was going on with her and why she'd buried Trent's papers deep within a pile.

"It's been nice to meet you, sir," Trent said, reaching to shake her dad's hand. "And don't worry. I'll take care of your daughter until I leave here."

"Thank you. I appreciate it."

"I'm standing right here, remember?" Relieved

to be back to a joking mood, Charlie waved her hands. "How many times do I have to tell you two? I don't need to be taken care of."

"We know." Her dad smiled, but his eyes still held a peculiar expression as he looked at her. "We just like to look after you. Is that so bad?"

She looked at Trent, horrified at the thought that filled her head. That she couldn't think of anything better than for him to stay here a full year, living with her and looking after her, the two of them looking after each other.

She could only imagine how appalled he'd be if he somehow read those thoughts in her face and she looked down at her desk as she changed the subject. "Can I help you get your things together, Dad? I'm about to head to the house anyway."

"Already done. My car's outside, ready to go." He pulled her into his arms for a hug. "We'll see you when you come visit next month."

"Can't wait to see both of you. Bye, Dad."

With a smile and a squeeze of Trent's hand, he disappeared, leaving the two of them alone in a room that now seemed no larger than a broom closet. She felt the heat of Trent's gaze on her, felt the electric zing from the top of her head to her toes, and slowly turned to look at him.

His hand reached out and swung the door closed, and that gesture, along with the look in his eyes as they met hers, made her heart beat hard at the same time as her stomach plunged.

She was crazy about this man. There was no getting around it, and she wanted so much to enjoy every last day, every last hour, every last minute she had with him. Surely he wouldn't find out about her lies? Maybe, even, he'd decide to stay longer on his own. It could happen, couldn't it?

She stepped forward at the same moment he did, their arms coming around one another, their lips fusing in a burning kiss that held a promise of tonight, at least, being one she'd never forget.

His warm palms slid slowly over her back, down her hips and back up, her body vibrating at his touch. The kiss deepened, his fingers pressed more urgently into her flesh and, when he broke the kiss, a little sound of protest left her tingling lips.

"You sure your desk is a little too small?" His eyes gleamed hotly, but still held that touch of humor she loved.

"Yes. We already had files all over the floor once tonight." The thought of why exactly that had happened took the pleasure of the moment down a notch, but she shook it off. She wasn't going to let anything ruin what could be one of her last nights with him. Reluctantly, she untangled herself from the warmth of his arms. "I'm going to head home. Join me for dinner about seven?"

"I'll be there." He leaned in once more, touched his lips to hers and held them there in a sweet and intimate connection that pinched her heart. "Don't be surprised if I'm even a little early."

She watched him leave, gripping the edge of her desk to hold herself upright, refusing to think about how, for the first time since she'd moved here, she would feel very lonely when he was gone.

The lowering sun cast shadows through the trees as Charlie approached her house, surprised to see Patience in front of the porch with little Lucky jumping around her feet.

"What are you doing here, Patience? Where's your dad?"

The little girl's smile faded into guilt. "Daddy was in a long, long meeting with Miss Mariam and I got tired of waiting. I came to show you the new trick I taught Lucky."

Oh, dear. John Adams was not going to be happy about this. "You know you're not allowed to leave the school and come all the way down here by yourself."

"I know. But it's just for a little bit. So I can show you. Then will you take me home?"

Charlie sighed. The child had the art of cajol-

.ing and wheedling down to a science. So much for getting showered and primped up before Trent came for their big date-night. "Okay. But promise me you won't do this again. You're not big enough to be running around all by yourself."

"I promise." The words came out grudgingly, but when Lucky yapped her eyes brightened again. "So, look! Sit, Lucky. Sit!"

The little pup actually did and Patience gave her some morsel as a reward, beaming with triumph as the dog began yapping and dancing again. "See Miss Charlie? She's really smart!"

"She is." She clapped her hands in applause, smiling at how cute and excited the child was. "And you being a good dog trainer helps her be smart."

"I know. I—"

A long, low growl behind her made Charlotte freeze, every hair on her scalp standing up in an instinctive reaction to the terrifying sound. She swung around and, to her horror, a large, feral and very angry dog stood there, its own hackles rising high on its back.

CHAPTER FIFTEEN

"PATIENCE." THE HARD hammering of her heart in her chest and her breath coming in short gasps made it difficult to sound calm. But the last thing she needed was for Patience to panic and make the situation worse. "Move very, very slowly and pick up Lucky, then quietly go up the porch steps and into the house. Don't make any sudden movements."

The child didn't say a word, probably as terrified as Charlie felt. The dog's lips were curled back in a snarl, showing every sharp tooth in its foamy mouth, and its jaws snapped together as it stared right at her. She couldn't risk turning around to see if Patience had done as she'd asked, because if it attacked she had to be ready. And it looked like it was about to do exactly that.

She glanced around for some weapon she could use to bash the dog if she had to. A sturdy stick was lying about five feet away and she slowly, carefully, inch by inch, sidled in that direction, her heart leaping into her throat as the dog growled louder, drool dripping as it snapped its jaws at her again.

Damn, this was bad. The animal had to be rabid; there was no other explanation for its aggression. That thought brought a horrified realization that this was probably the animal that had attacked and killed Patience's other dog. It was unusual enough to see feral dogs here and she knew the likely reason this one was still around was because it was very, very sick.

The sound of her screen door closing was a relief, and she prayed that meant Patience was out of harm's way. Should she try to talk soothingly to the dog? Or yell and try to scare it? She didn't know, and the last thing she wanted to do was something that would trigger it to attack her.

Sweat prickled at every pore, and her breath came fast and shallow as she kept her slow progress toward the stick, never taking her eyes off the animal. She was close. So close now. But how to pick it up when she got there? A fast movement to grab it and swing hard if the dog lunged? Keep her actions slow and steady, so she could get the stick in her hand and maybe not have to use it at all if she could just get back to the porch and in the house?

With her heart beating so hard it was practically a roar in her ears, she leaned down slowly, slowly, keeping her movements tight and controlled as she closed her fingers around the stick.

In an instant, the dog leaped toward her, mouth open, fangs dripping, knocking her to the ground, its teeth sinking deep into the flesh of her arm as she held it up in futile defense.

A scream of panic, of primal terror, tore from her throat. She tried to swing the stick at the dog, screaming again, but her position on the ground left her without much power behind the blow, and she realized the animal's teeth were sinking even deeper.

Some instinct told her to freeze and not to try to pull her arm from the dog's mouth, that it would just hold on tighter, shake her and injure her even worse. Its eyes were less than a foot from hers, wild eyes filled with fury above the jaws clamped onto her arm. It was so strong, so vicious, and a terrible helplessness came over her as she frantically tried to think how she could get away without getting hurt even worse, or maybe even being killed.

A loud, piercing gunshot echoed in the air and a split-second later the dog's jaws released her, its body falling limply on top of hers. Unable to process exactly what had happened, she grabbed her bleeding arm and tried to squirm out from under the beast.

"Charlotte." Trent was there, right there, his

foot heaving the lifeless dog off her, crouching down beside her. "Damn it, Charlotte. Let me see."

"Trent." Her voice came out as a croak. It was Trent. Trent carefully holding her arm within his cool hands, looking down at it. Trent who had saved her life.

Her head dropped to the ground and she closed her eyes, saying a deep prayer of thanks as she began to absorb everything. Began to realize that the danger was past.

"Charlotte. Look at me." His gentle hand stroked her hair from her forehead and cupped her jaw, his thumb rubbing across her cheekbone. "Let me see." He tugged at her wrist and she realized she was still clutching her arm. She loosened her grip, feeling the sticky wetness of her blood on her hand as she dropped it to the ground. "You feel faint?"

"Y…yes." Stars sparkled in front of her eyes as she stared at the jagged gashes. At the oozing blood.

"Hang in there with me, sweetheart." He looked only briefly at her wounds before he yanked his shirt open—a nice, white button-down shirt, she processed vaguely—and quickly took it off. He wrapped it around her arm and applied a gentle pressure then lifted her hand up and placed it where his had been. "Squeeze to help stop the bleeding. I'm getting you to the clinic."

She could barely do as he asked but she tried. The screen door slammed behind them and Charlie became aware of the sound of Patience crying.

"Mr. Trent! Is Miss Charlie okay?"

"She's okay, but I need to take care of her. You stay in the house and I'll call your dad to come get you."

"O…okay."

The door slammed again as Trent lifted Charlie into his arms and strode in the direction of the hospital. She let her head loll against his muscled, bare shoulder, at the same time thinking she shouldn't let him haul her all the way there. She might not be big, but she wasn't a featherweight either.

"It's too far for you to carry me. I can walk."

"Like hell. For once, will you let someone take care of you? Let yourself off the hook for being in charge of the world?"

"I don't…I don't think I do that. But I admit I'm feeling a little shaky."

He looked down at her, his blue eyes somehow blazingly angry and tender at the same time. "A little shaky? You were just mauled by a rabid dog. You've lost a lot of blood. It's okay for you to lean on me a little, just once."

"Yes, doctor."

He gave her a glimmer of a smile. "Now that's what I like to hear. Keep pressing on your arm," he said as they finally got to the hospital and he laid her on an exam table. He placed a pillow beneath her head then made a quick call to John Adams. She watched him pull the pistol from his waistband and place it on the counter, wash his hands, then move efficiently to various cupboards, stacking things on the metal table next to her.

"Thank you. I...don't want to think about what might have happened if you hadn't come when you did."

"I don't want to think about it either." His lips were pressed together in a grim line, his eyes stark as they met hers. "When I heard you scream, my heart about stopped."

"Why did you have a gun with you?"

"I work in plenty of unsafe places in the world, and always pack my thirty-eight. I had it with me because you left yours upstairs last time when you were supposed to be ready for a burglar, remember?"

She thought of how the dog had been right on top of her and shuddered. "How did you learn to shoot like that? Weren't you afraid you'd hit me instead?"

"No. Even though I was scared to death, I knew I'd hit the dog and not you." A tiny smile touched his lips as he placed items on the table. "I was on the trap and skeet shooting team at Yale. Rich boys get to have fun hobbies, and this one paid off."

Rich boys? She was about to ask, but he handed her a cup of water and several tablets. "What is this?"

"Penicillin. And a narcotic and fever-reducing combo. It'll help with the pain. I have to wash out your wounds, which is not going to feel good."

He lifted up her arm, placed a square plastic bowl beneath it and began to unwrap his poor white shirt from it, now soaked in blood. Those little stars danced in front of her eyes again and she looked away. "Tell me the truth. How bad is it?"

"Bad enough. I'll know more in a few minutes." His expression was grim. "Because that dog was obviously rabid, I have to inject immunoglobulin. I'm also going to inject lidocaine because—"

"I know, I know. So I won't feel every stitch. Do it quick, please, and get it over with."

He gave a short laugh, shaking his head. "You're something else." He pressed a kiss to her forehead, before his eyes met hers, all traces of amusement gone. "Ready? This is going to hurt like hell. Hang in there for me."

She nodded and steeled herself, ashamed that she cried out at the first injection. "Sorry," she said, biting her lip hard. "I'm being a baby."

"No, you're not. I've seen big tough guys cry at this. You're awesome. Just a little longer."

When it was finally over, she could tell he felt as relieved as she did. "That's my girl." He pressed another lingering kiss to her head. "This next part is going to hurt, too, but not nearly as bad as that."

He poured what seemed like gallons of saline over her arm. He was right; it did not feel good. She thought he'd finally finished until he grabbed and opened another bottle. "Geez, enough already! What could possibly still be in there?"

"Is there some reason you have to keep questioning the doctor?" His blue eyes crinkled at the corners. "With all the technology and great drugs we have, thoroughly washing wounds like this—any animal bite, but especially when the dog is rabid—is the best treatment there is. But this is the last jug, I promise."

"Thank goodness. I was about to accuse you of making it hurt as much as you possibly can."

"And here I'd been giving you credit for being the bravest patient ever." His smile faded and he gave her a gentle kiss, his eyes tender. "I'm really sorry it hurts. Good news is, it looks like there's no arterial damage and the bites didn't go all the way to the bone. I'm going to throw some absorbable stitches into the deep muscle tears to control the bleeding then get everything closed up."

Instead of watching him work on her arm, she looked at his face. At the way his brows knit as he worked. At the way his dark lashes fanned over the deep focus of his eyes. At the way he sometimes pursed his lips as he stitched. Almost of its own accord, her hand lifted to cup his jaw and he paused to look at her, his blue eyes serious before he turned his face to her palm, pressing a lingering kiss there.

"Are you going to use a bunch of tiny stitches so I don't have awful scars?"

"I can't this round, sweetheart." He shook his head. "This kind of wound has a high risk for infection. We have to get the skin closed with as few stitches as possible, because the more I put in the more chance of infection. After it's healed completely, though, I can repair it so it looks better."

Except he wouldn't be here then. Their eyes met as the thought obviously came to both of them at the same time.

"I mean, one of your plastic surgeons can when the new wing is opened." His voice was suddenly brusque instead of sweet and tender.

She nodded and looked down, silently watching him work, her heart squeezing a little. How had she let herself feel this close to him? So close she would miss him far too much when he was gone.

When it was all over and her arm was wrapped in Kerlix, taped and put in a sling, he expelled a deep breath. "How about we head to your house and get you settled and comfortable? I'll carry you."

"I really am okay to walk." She didn't trust herself not to reveal her thoughts and feelings if he carried her, folded against his chest. "I need to."

He looked at her a moment then sighed. "All right. So long as you let me hold you in case you get dizzy."

Trent held her close as they walked slowly toward the front porch of her house and she let herself lean against his strength. The dog's body was gone, thank goodness, though there were blood-stains in the dirt. John Adams must've taken care of it. She was glad she didn't have to look at it and remember its wild eyes; see again those teeth that had ripped her flesh and held her tight in their grip.

"I feel kind of bad for the dog," she said.

"You feel sorry for the dog?" He stared down at her, eyebrows raised.

"Rabies is a pretty horrible way to die, isn't it? You shooting it was the best way for it to go."

"Yeah. It's one hundred percent fatal after it's been contracted. It's a good thing we have the vaccine to keep you safe from the virus." He looked away, his voice rough when he spoke again. "After you get settled inside, I'll come out and rake up the dirt. Don't think you want to be looking at your own blood every time you come in and out of your house."

"No. I don't." She looked up him and marveled at his consideration. "Who knew you were Mister Thoughtful and not the full-of-yourself guy I was convinced you were?"

"I'm both thoughtful *and* full of myself—multi-faceted that way."

His eyes held a touch of their usual amusement and as she laughed her chest filled with some emotion she refused to examine.

CHAPTER SIXTEEN

TRENT KNEW THE narcotics would have worn off and Charlotte would be in pain again this morning. He'd slipped from the bed and gone downstairs to make toast and coffee for her, wanting something in her stomach before he gave her more fever medication, and the narcotic, too, if she needed it.

When he came back to her room with a tray, he had to pause inside the doorway just to look at her. Her lush hair tumbled across the pillow, the sun streaking through the windows highlighting its bronze glow. Her lips were parted, her shoulder exposed as one thin strap of her pretty nightgown had slid down her bandaged arm, leaving the gown gaping so low, one pink nipple was partly visible on her round breast.

He deeply inhaled, a tumble of emotions pummeling his heart as he stared at her. To his shock, the foremost emotion wasn't sexual.

It was a deep sense of belonging. Of belonging with her.

He wanted to stay here with her. He wanted to wake up in her bed, in her arms, every morning. He wanted to see her, just like this, at the start of each and every day.

Her eyelids flickered and she opened her eyes and looked at him. She smiled, and that smile seemed to reach right inside of him, pull him farther into the room. Pull him closer to her.

He managed to speak past the tightness in his chest. "Good morning, Charlotte." He set the tray on her nightstand and perched himself on the side of the bed. He stroked her hair from her face, wrapped a thick strand around his finger. "How's the arm feeling?"

"Not so great." She rolled onto her back, her lips twisting.

He ran his finger down her cheek. "I figured that. I brought you some toast and coffee and more meds."

"Thank you." Her good arm lifted to him and her palm stroked his cheek. He wished he'd shaved already, so the bristles wouldn't abrade her delicate skin when he kissed her. "But all I want is the fever stuff. I can't spend the day all doped up. I want to know exactly what's happening."

He nodded. "If you decide you need it later, you can always take it then. Why don't you sit up and have a little bit to eat first." He started to stand, but her hand grabbed the front of his shirt and bunched it up as she tugged him toward her.

"I am hungry again. But not for food—for you."

"Charlotte." He wanted, more than anything, to make love with her. But she was in pain and the need to take care of her, to keep her arm still so she wouldn't be in worse pain, took precedence over everything. "You need to rest."

"I've been resting all night. I slept very well, thanks to the drugs you gave me." She smiled at him and pulled harder on his shirt, bringing him closer still, and he could feel his resolve weakening at the way she looked at him. It was as though she was eating him up with her eyes and he knew he wanted to eat her up for real. "I do need to feel better. And you're very, very good at making me feel better."

"Well, I am a doctor. Took the Hippocratic Oath that I'd do the best I could to help my patients heal." He smiled, too, and gave up resisting. He gave in to the desire spiraling through his body. "What can I do first to make you feel better?"

"Kiss me."

Her tongue flicked across her lips and he leaned forward to taste them, carefully keeping his body from resting against her arm. It took every ounce of self-control to keep himself in check, to touch her and kiss her slowly, carefully.

"Does it make you feel better if I do this?" He

gently drew her nightgown down and over her bandages, then lifted her arm carefully above her head to rest it on her pillow. He traced the tops of her breasts with his fingertips, slowly, inching across the soft mounds, until he pulled the lacy nightgown down to fully expose her breasts.

The sunlight skimmed across the pink tips and his breath clogged in his throat as he enjoyed the incredible beauty of them. Of her. He lowered his mouth to one nipple then rolled it beneath his tongue, drew it into his mouth and lifted his hand to cup the other breast in his palm.

"Yes," she murmured. The hand on her good arm rested on the back of his head, her fingers tangling in his hair. "I'm feeling better already."

"How about this?" His mouth replaced his hand on her other breast, his fingertips stroking along her collarbone, her armpit, down her ribs, and he reveled in the way she shivered in response.

"Yes. Good."

He slowly tugged her nightgown farther down her body, gently touching every inch he could with his mouth, his tongue, his hands. He could feel her flesh quiver, felt the heat pumping from her skin, and marveled at how excruciatingly pleasurable it was to take it this slow. To think only of making her feel good, to feel wonderful, to feel loved.

The shocking thought made him freeze and raise his head.

Loved? He didn't do love.

But as he looked down at her eyes, at the softness, heat and desire in their green depths, his heart squeezed at the same time it expanded.

He did love her. He loved everything about her. He loved her sweetness, her toughness and her stubbornness and was shocked all over again. Shocked that the realization didn't scare the crap out of him. Shocked that, instead, it filled him with wonder.

He lowered his mouth to hers, drinking in the taste of her, and for a long, exquisite moment there was only that simple connection. His lips to hers, hers to his, and through the kiss he felt their hearts and souls connecting as well.

He drew back, and saw the reflection of what he was feeling in her eyes. Humbled and awed, he smiled. "Still feeling good? Or do you need a little more doctoring?"

"More please." She returned his smile, which changed to a gasp when he slipped his hand beneath her nightgown, found her moist core and caressed it.

"We need to lose this gown. I want to see all of you. Touch and kiss all of you." He dragged the gown to her navel, her hipbones, his mouth and tongue following the trail along her skin. He wanted nothing more than this. He wanted to help her forget her pain. For her to feel only pleasure.

She lifted her bottom to help him pull it all the way off, and he took advantage of the arch of her hips, kissing her there, touching and licking the velvety folds until she was writhing beneath his mouth.

"Trent," she gasped. "You've proven how good you are at making me feel better. But I want more. Why are you still dressed? I don't think I can strip you with only one hand."

He looked at her and had to grin at the desire and frustration on her face. "You want me to strip? I'm at your command, boss lady." He quickly shucked his clothes and took one more moment to take in the beauty of her nakedness, before carefully positioning himself on top of her as she welcomed him.

With her eyes locked on his, he moved within her. Slowly. Carefully. She met him, moved beneath him, urged him on. The sounds of pleasure she made nearly undid him and he couldn't control the ever-faster pace. There was nothing more important in the world than this moment, this rhythm that was unique to just the two of them, joining as one. And, when she cried out, he lost himself in her.

Curled up with Trent's body warming her back, his arms holding her close, Charlie felt sated, basking in the magic of being with him; wanting to know more about him.

"Tell me about being a rich boy. That's what you said you are, isn't it?"

He didn't respond for a moment then a soft sigh tickled her ear. "Yes. My family is wealthy and I have a trust fund that earns more money each year than most people make in ten."

"And yet you work in mission hospitals all over the world. Why?"

"For the same reason you live and work here— to give medical care to those who wouldn't have any if we didn't."

She turned her head to try to look at his face. "When did you decide to live your life that way instead of working in some hospital in the States? Or being a plastic surgeon for the rich and famous?"

The laugh he gave didn't sound like there was much humor in it. "Funny you say that. My dad and grandfather have exactly that kind of practice. I was expected to follow in their footsteps, but realized I didn't want to. When I was about two-thirds of the way through my plastics residency, I knew I wanted to do a surgical fellowship in pediatric neurosurgery instead."

Wow. She'd known he had amazing skills, but he did brain surgery too? "Did you?"

"No. I couldn't get into a program. Was rejected by every one I applied to. Then found out why."

She waited for him to continue but he didn't. "So, why?"

He didn't speak for a long time. She was just about to turn in his arms, to look in his eyes and see what was going on with him, when he answered. His voice was grim. "My mother was hell-bent on me joining the family practice. I didn't realize how hell-bent until I found out she'd used her family name, wealth and the power behind all of that to keep me out of any neurosurgery program. All the while pretending she supported my decision, when in fact she was manipulating the outcome. So I left. Left the country to do mission work, and I haven't been back since."

Charlie's breath backed up in her lungs and her heart about stopped. His mother had deceived him and lied? He'd obviously been horribly hurt by it. So hurt that he'd cut his family from his life. So hurt that he'd left the U.S. and hadn't returned.

It also sounded horrifyingly similar to what she'd been doing to him, too.

Her stomach felt like a ball of lead was weighing it down. "I'm…sorry you had such a difficult time and that you were hurt by all that."

"Don't be. It's ancient history, and it was good I learned what kind of person she really is."

The lead ball grew heavier at his words, making her feel a little sick, and she couldn't think of a thing to say. He kissed her cheek, his lips lingering there, and a lump formed in her throat at the sweetness of the touch.

"I'm going to fix you some brunch. Something better than the toast you didn't eat." He nipped lightly at her chin, her lips. "And, just for you, I'm going to perform a surgery today that I think will make you happy. But I'm not telling until after it's done."

She squeezed his hand and tried to smile. "Can't wait to hear about it." She drew in a breath and shook off her fears. He wouldn't find out. It would be okay. They'd get the donation check, the new wing would open and, when all that was behind them…then what?

She knew, and her heart swelled in anticipation. She'd ask him to stay, and not for the hospital. She'd tell him she was crazy about him, that she wanted to see where their relationship could go. The thought scared her and thrilled her; she was not sure how risky that would be. How it would feel to share her life and her world with someone. But she knew, without question, it was a risk she had to take.

By the way he'd made love to her, looked at her, taken care of her, maybe he'd actually say yes.

CHAPTER SEVENTEEN

TRENT LEFT THE OR, feeling damned pleased at the way the cleft palate surgery had gone for the child. He knew Charlotte would be happy too and couldn't wait to tell her.

The satisfaction he felt made him realize he'd been too hasty believing the skills he had were superfluous and not a good way to help people, and children in particular, as he wanted to. Working in his family's cosmetic surgery practice hadn't been what he wanted. But Charlotte had helped him see that those skills really were valuable in helping people have better lives.

While he'd done plastics procedures at many of his other jobs, it had taken her dogged persistence to make him see how important those techniques could be to those without hope of improving their lives that way except through a hospital like this one.

Striding down the hall, he couldn't believe his eyes, seeing the woman who was on his mind. There she stood, talking to John Adams, like it had been a week instead of a day since her ordeal. Hadn't he specifically told her to stay home and rest?

"What possible excuse do you have for being here, Charlotte?"

"I got bored. There's too much to do to just sit around."

"You're not just sitting around." He wanted to shake the damn stubborn woman. "Resting helps your body heal. Gives it a chance to fight infection. Which, in case you don't remember, is particularly important after a nasty dog bite." He turned to John Adams. "Can you talk sense into her?"

"Last time she listened to me was about six months ago or so," he replied, shaking his head.

Trent turned back to her, more than ready to get tough if he had to. "Don't make me drag you back there and tie you down."

She scowled then, apparently seeing that he was completely serious, gave a big, dramatic sigh. "Fine. I'll go rest some more. Though every hour feels like five. Can I at least take a few files with me to go over while I'm being quiet?"

The woman was unbelievable. "If you absolutely have to. But no moving around unnecessarily. No cooking dinner. I'll take care of that."

"Yes, Dr. Dalton."

He ignored the sarcastic tone. "That's what I

want to hear from my model patient." He noted the blue shadows beneath her eyes, the slight tightness around her mouth that doubtless was from pain she was determined not to show, and couldn't help himself. He leaned down to give her a gentle kiss, not caring that John Adams was standing right there. "I just finished the cleft palate surgery I promised you I'd do. Now I want you to give me a promise in return—that you'll take care of yourself. For me, if not for yourself."

Her eyes softened at the same time they glowed with excitement. "You fixed the boy's cleft palate today? That's wonderful! Did you take pictures like I asked you to? I need pictures to— Well, I just think we should keep a record."

"All taken care of. Now for your promise."

"I promise." She sent him a smile so wide, it lit the room. "I'll see you at home."

At home. That had a nice sound to it. He found himself admiring her shapely legs beneath her skirt, watching the slight sway of her hips all the way down the hall and out the door, and when he turned he saw John Adams eyeing him speculatively.

"So, is something going on between you and Charlie? I thought you were leaving in just a day or two. Speaking of which, did you go over everything Thomas needs to know about her stitches and the rabies vaccine course?"

He looked back at the door Charlotte had disappeared out of, and realized if he left it would be just like that—she'd disappear from his life and he'd likely never see her again.

With absolute conviction that it was the right decision, he knew he wasn't going to leave. He had to be here to take care of her, to improve the scarring on her arm after she was healed, to see exactly what a year with her would be like.

He turned back to John Adams. "I'm staying."

The man smiled and clapped him on the shoulder. "Good to hear. Welcome to the family."

Trent changed out of his scrubs, cleaned up and called Mike Hardy before going to Charlotte's so he could tell her his decision. He could only hope she'd be as happy about him staying as he felt about it. Thinking of the way they'd made love just that morning, the look on her face and in her beautiful eyes as they'd moved together, he had a pretty powerful feeling that she would be.

"Mike? Trent Dalton. How are you?"

"Good, Trent. Great to hear from you. Are you enjoying your vacation in Italy?"

"No." Had the man forgotten about all the delays? "I'm still at the Edwards Hospital in Liberia."

"You're still in Liberia?" The man sounded astonished. "Why? Perry Cantwell went there last week, so you should be long gone by now."

"Perry was delayed, so I had to stay on until he could get here." How could Mike not know all this? "I've decided I want to stay here for the next year. I'd like you to find a replacement for me in the Philippines and draw up a new contract for me."

"Trent, we never have two doctors at the Edwards Hospital. We just can't afford it."

He frowned. Mike usually bent over backwards if he had a special request, which he rarely did. Trent was one of only a handful of GPC docs that worked for them full-time, year-round. "I don't need another doc here with me. I'm sure Perry wouldn't care if he's here or in the Philippines. Ask him."

There was a silence on the line, which made Trent start to feel a little fidgety, until Mike finally spoke again. "I just found your file to see what's going on. Your release papers were sent well over a week ago. And I know Perry was about on his way when I had Colleen send them, so I'm confused. This is all a real problem, messing up your pay and vacation time and next assignment. I need to talk to Colleen and find out how these mistakes happened before we have any more discussion about you staying there. I'll call you back."

"All right."

The conversation with Mike left him feeling vaguely disturbed, but he brushed it off. He couldn't imagine there would be a problem. It probably would just come down to shuffling paperwork.

Since he had no idea when Mike would call him back, he went on to Charlotte's house. If he didn't find her resting, he was going to threaten her with something—maybe refusing to kiss her or make love with her would be a strong enough incentive, he thought with a smile. He knew that if she threatened him with something similar he'd follow any and all instructions.

He let himself in the door. Seeing her curled up in the armchair, her hair falling in waves around her shoulders, her expression relaxed, filled his chest with a sense of belonging that he couldn't remember having felt since before he'd left the States. Since before the betrayal by his mother. A cozy, welcoming old home with a beautiful and more than special woman inside waiting for him was something he'd never thought he wanted until now.

He stood there a moment, knowing he was beyond blessed to have been sent to this place on what was supposed to have been a fill-in position for just a few days. Another example of the universe guiding his life in ways he could never have foreseen.

"Hey, beautiful." He leaned down to kiss the top of her head, his lips lingering in the softness of her hair. "Thank you for being good, sitting there reading. I'm proud of you."

Her hand cupped his cheek, her eyes smiled up at him, and that feeling in his chest grew bigger, fuller. "I decided I should do what you ask, since you did that cleft palate surgery today like you promised. Not to mention that whole saving my life thing." Her voice grew softer. "I'm so lucky to have you here."

He was the lucky one. "I want you to eat so you can take some more pain medicine before that arm starts to really hurt again. Let me see what's in the kitchen."

His cell rang while he was putting a quick dinner together and he was glad it was Mike Hardy. "What'd you find out?"

"You're not going to like it." Mike's voice was grim and a sliver of unease slid down Trent's back. "Colleen's over here wringing her hands."

"Why?"

"She sent your release papers to the director of the hospital, instead of to you, because Charlotte Edwards asked her to. Apparently she's a good friend of Colleen's, and said she'd pass them on to you. Ms. Edwards also told her not to schedule Perry's travel yet because she claimed you'd agreed to stay on another two weeks.

"According to Colleen, the hospital has to have a plastic surgeon on site when the Gilchrist Foundation rep comes there in another day or so. If it doesn't, she won't get the donation she needs and won't be able to pay the bills. I guess they're pretty deep in the hole over there, might even have to shut the whole thing down. Charlotte Edwards's solution was to keep you there—get you to do some plastic surgeries she could impress Gilchrist with and pass you off as her new plastic surgeon. After that, Colleen was going to get Perry there and you could be on your way. But it's obvious you didn't know about any of this."

With every word Mike spoke, Trent's hands grew colder until he was practically shaking from the inside out with shock and anger. Everything Charlotte had said to him spun through his mind: praising his plastic surgery skills, begging him to do those surgeries and take photos, telling him there were problems with his paperwork, delays in getting Perry there. Coming up with a fake excuse when he'd found his release papers in her office.

Flat-out lying to him all along. Manipulating his papers, his life. His heart.

It was like *déjà vu*, except this was so much worse. Because she'd obviously only been pretending to like him. She'd obviously only had sex with him to keep him there, to tangle him up with her so he wouldn't leave until after the Gilchrist rep came.

And what had Mike said? After that, Colleen had the green light to get him out of there. *Bye-bye, have a nice life, I don't need you anymore.*

How could he have been so stupid, so blind? It was all so clear now, all the plastic surgery crap lines she'd fed him.

She hadn't cared when he'd left the first time and she sure as hell wouldn't care this time.

Balling his hands into fists, he sucked in a heavy breath, trying to control the bottomless anger and pain that filled his soul until it felt like it just might rip apart.

He had to get out of there. He'd already gone over with Thomas what had to happen with the rabies vaccine. She'd be all right. And the fact that the thought came with a brief worry on her behalf made him want to punch himself in the face.

Fool me once, shame on you. Fool me twice, and I'm obviously a pathetic moron.

"Thanks for telling me, Mike. I'm going to make my own arrangements to leave."

"All right. Perry's travel arrangements are being finalized this minute, so he'll be there soon."

Somehow, he managed to finish fixing Charlotte's dinner while he dialed the airline, relieved to find he could be out of there at the crack of dawn tomorrow.

He set her food on the table, placed two pain tablets next to it and forced himself to go into the parlor. The smile she sent him across the room felt like a stab wound deep into his heart. "Dinner's on the table. Come eat, then take your pills."

As she passed through the kitchen doorway, he stepped back, not wanting to touch her. Knowing a touch would hurt like a bad burn, and he'd been scorched enough.

"Where's yours?" She looked at him in surprise, her pretty, lying lips parted.

He'd play the part she'd once accused him of, so she wouldn't know he knew the truth. So she wouldn't know how much it hurt that she'd used him. That the pain went all the way to the core of his very essence, leaving a gaping hole inside.

It seemed like a long time since she'd told him he was full of himself and famous for kissing women goodbye with a smile and a wave. He'd do it now if it killed him.

"Colleen Mason just called to tell me I have a plane reservation in the morning, that I've been given the all-clear," he said, somehow managing a fake smile.

She sank onto the kitchen chair, staring. "What? I don't understand. I don't have... Perry Cantwell's not... I mean, that can't be right."

"It is. My vacation's been delayed long enough, and I'm meeting a...friend...in Florence." He leaned down to brush his lips across hers, and was damned if the contact wasn't excruciating. "It's been great being with you. But you know how I feel about long goodbyes, so I'll get out of here."

"But, Trent. Wait. I—"

"Take care of that arm." He turned and moved quickly to the door, unable to look at her face. To see the shock and despair and, damn it, the tears in her eyes. To know her dismay had nothing to do with him and everything to do with her precious hospital.

The thought came to him that he was running again. Running from pain, disillusionment and deep disappointment. And this time he knew he just might be running for the rest of his life.

CHAPTER EIGHTEEN

CHARLIE LAID HER head on her desk because she didn't think she could hold it upright for one more minute.

In barely forty-eight hours, her life had gone to ruin, and no amount of hard work and positive attitude was going to fix it.

She'd been a fool to think there had been any possibility of her relationship with Trent Dalton becoming anything bigger than a fling. It'd been foolish to allow her feelings to get out of control. To allow the connection she felt to him to grab hold of her—a connection that had bloomed and deepened until she could no longer deny the emotion.

She thought she'd seen that he felt it too. Had seen it in his eyes; seen it in the way he cared for her when she'd been hurt; seen it through his kisses and his touch.

Then he'd walked out. One minute he was sweetly there, the next he was kissing her good-bye with a smile and a wave, just like the first time. But, unlike the first time, he'd taken a big chunk of her heart with him.

How could she have been so stupid? She'd known all along it could never be more than a fling. Had known he was right, when he'd come back, that they should keep their relationship platonic—because, as he'd so eloquently said, second goodbyes tended to get messy.

Messy? Was that the way to describe how he'd left? It seemed like their goodbye had been quite neat and tidy for him.

Anger burned in her stomach. Anger that she'd let herself fall for a man who'd never hidden that he didn't want or need roots. Anger that the pain of his leaving nagged at her far more than the physical pain of her torn and stitched-up arm.

And of course, practically the minute he'd moved on, the Gilchrist rep had shown up. He'd been impressed with the wing but, gosh, there was this little problem of there not being a doctor there. She'd hoped the photographs of Trent's work would help, but of course it hadn't. After all, the man was long gone, and they'd made their requirements very clear.

A quiet knock preceded the door opening and Charlie managed to lift her head to look at John Adams, swallowing the lump that kept forming in her throat.

"I'm guessing things didn't go well," he said as he sat in the chair across from her.

"No. The Gilchrist Foundation can't justify giving us the check without meeting all their requirements. Which I knew would happen."

"What are you going to do?"

Wasn't that a good question? What was she going to do to keep the hospital open? What was she going to do to mend her broken heart? What was she going to do to move past the bitterness and regret that was like a burning hole in her chest?

"I don't know. I have to crunch the numbers again, see what can be eliminated from the budget. Lay off a few employees. See if any of the other donors I've approached will come through with something." Though nothing could come close to what Gilchrist had offered. To what the hospital needed.

"There is the money the anonymous donor gave the school." John Adams looked at her steadily. "I can put off hiring another teacher, hold off on some of the purchases we made."

"No." She shook her head even as the suggestion was tempting. "Whoever donated that money gave it to the school. It wouldn't be right to use it for the hospital. I'll figure something out."

"All right." John Adams stood and gently patted her head, as though she were Patience. "I'm sorry about all this. And sorry about Trent leaving. I've got to tell you, that surprised me. Especially since it was right after he'd told me he was staying."

"He told you he was staying?"

"He did. After he was irritated with you being in the hospital when you were supposed to be resting."

And his caring for her through all that was part of what had made her fall harder for him. "Well, he obviously didn't mean it the way most people would. Staying the night is probably what that word means to him." She tried to banish the acrid and hurt tone from her voice. After all, she'd known the reality. Regret yet again balled up in her stomach that she'd allowed herself to forget it.

Trent walked beneath the trees in Central Park to his parents' Fifth Avenue apartment on Manhattan's Upper East Side. He breathed in the scents of the city, listened to children playing in the park and the constant flow of traffic crowding the street and looked at the old and elegant apartment buildings that lined the streets.

It didn't seem all that many years ago since he'd been a kid roaming these streets, not realizing at the time how different growing up here was from the average kid's childhood in suburbia. But it had been great too, in its own way, especially when your family had wealth and privilege enough to take advantage of everything the city offered and the ability to leave for a quieter place when the hustle got wearying.

His mother had been more hands-on than most of the crowd his parents were friends with, whose full-time nannies did most of the child-rearing. He'd appreciated it, and how close they'd been, believing that the bond she shared with her only child was special to her.

Until she'd lied and betrayed him. The memory of that blow still had the power to hurt.

He thought of how his mother had tried to reach out to him during the years since then. She'd kept tabs on wherever he was working, and each time he moved on to a new mission hospital a Gilchrist Foundation donation immediately plumped their coffers. She'd sent him a Christmas card every year, with updates on what she and his dad were doing, where they'd traveled, asking questions about his own life. Questions he hadn't answered. After all, what he wanted to do with his life hadn't interested her before, so he figured it didn't truly interest her now.

She'd been shocked and seemingly thrilled to get his phone call that morning and he wondered what it would be like to see her after all this time. A part of him dreaded it. The part of him that still carried good memories wanted, in spite of everything, to see how she was. Either way, the need at the Edwards hospital was what had driven him here. Not for Charlotte—for all the patients who would have nowhere to go if the place shut down.

"Mr. Trent! Is that you? I can't believe it!" Walter Johnson pumped his hand, a broad smile on the old doorman's face.

"Glad to see you're still here, Walter." Trent smiled, thinking of all the times the man had had his back when he'd been a kid. "It's been a long time since my friends and I were causing trouble for you."

"You just caused normal boy trouble. Kept my job interesting." Walter grinned. "Are your parents expecting you? Or shall I ring them?"

"My mother knows I'm coming. Thanks."

The ornate golden elevator took him to his family's fourteen-room apartment and he drew a bracing breath before he knocked on the door. Would she look the same as always? Or would time have changed her some?

The door opened and his question was answered. She looked lovely, like she always had. Virtually unchanged—which wasn't surprising, considering his dad was a plastic surgeon and there were all kinds of cosmeceuticals out there now to keep wrinkles at bay. Her ash-blonde hair was stylishly cut and she wore her usual casual-chic clothes that cost more than most of his patients made in a year.

"Trent!" She stepped forward and he thought she was going to throw her arms around him, but she hesitated, then grasped his arm and squeezed. "It's just…wonderful to see you. Come in. Tell me about yourself and your life and everything."

Sunlight pouring through the sheer curtains cast a warm glow upon the cream-colored, modern furnishings in the room as they sat in two chairs at right angles to one another. One of her housekeepers brought coffee and the kind of biscuits Trent had always liked, and he felt a little twist of something in his chest that she had remembered.

"My life is good." Okay, that was a lie, right off the bat. His life was absolute crap and had been ever since he'd found out Charlotte had lied to him, that their relationship had been, for her at least, a means to an end and nothing more.

For the first time in his life, he'd fallen hard for a woman. A woman who was like no one he'd ever met before. Had finally realized, admitted to himself, that what he felt for Charlotte went far beyond simple attraction, lust or friendship with benefits.

And, just as he'd been ready to find out exactly what all those feelings were and what they meant, he'd been knocked to the ground by the truth and had no idea how he was going to get back up again.

"We've…we've missed you horribly, Trent." His mother twisted her fingers and stared at him through blue eyes the same color as his own. "I know you were angry when you left and I understand why. I understand that I was wrong to do what I did and I want to explain."

"Frankly, Mom, I don't think any explanation could be good enough." He didn't want to hash it out all over again. It was history and he'd moved on. "I'm not here to talk about that. I'm here to ask you a favor."

"Anything." She placed her hand on his knee. "What is it?"

"I've been working at the Edwards hospital in Liberia. They'd applied to you, to the Gilchrist Foundation, for a large donation to build and open a plastic surgery wing."

She nodded. "Yes. I'm familiar with it. In fact, I just received word that we won't be providing the donation now because they didn't meet the criteria."

"They're doing good work, Mom, and use their money wisely. I performed some plastic surgeries there and saw how great the need is. I'd appreciate it if you would still give them the donation."

"You did plastic surgery there?" She looked surprised. "Last time I spoke with you, when you stormed out of here, you told me that wasn't what you wanted to do. What changed your mind?"

"I haven't changed my mind. I didn't want to join the family practice doing facelifts and breast implants. I wanted to use my surgical skills to help children. But I've realized that I can do both."

"Are you working at the Edwards hospital full-time now? Permanently?"

"No." He'd never go there again, see Charlotte Edwards again. "It was time to leave. But I know they're getting a surgeon as soon as they can. I'd appreciate you giving them the funding check, which will help the rest of the hospital too. The people there need it."

"All right, if it's important to you, I'll get it wired out tomorrow."

"Thank you. I'm happy that, this time, what's important to me matters to you." Damn it, why had that stupid comment come out of his mouth? She'd agreed to do as he asked. The last thing he wanted was for her to change her mind, or dredge up their past.

"Trent." He looked at her, and his gut clenched at the tears that swam in her eyes. "Anything that's important to you is important to me. I know you don't want to hear it, but I'm telling you anyway—why I did what I did." She grabbed one of the tiny napkins that had been served with the coffee and dabbed her eyes. "When I went to college, all I wanted was to be a doctor. To become a plastic surgeon like my father and join his practice. I studied hard in college, and when I applied to medical schools I got in. But my father said no. Women didn't make good doctors, he said, and especially not good surgeons. I couldn't be a wife and mother and a surgeon too and needed to understand my place in our social strata."

He stared at her, stunned. It didn't surprise him that his autocratic grandfather could be such a son-of-a-bitch. But his mother wanting to be a doctor? He couldn't wrap his brain around it. "I don't know what to say, Mom. I had no idea."

"So I married your dad and he joined the practice. Filled my life with my philanthropy, which has been rewarding. And with you. You were… are…the most important thing in my life. Until I messed everything up between us." The tears filled her eyes again and he was damned if they didn't send him reaching to squeeze her shoulder, pat her in comfort, in spite of everything.

"It's all right, Mom. It was a long time ago."

"I want you to understand why, even though there's no excuse, and I know that now." Her hand reached to grip his. "I just wanted you to have what I couldn't have. I wanted that for you, and couldn't see, because of my own disappointment from all those years ago, that it was for me and not for you. That I was being selfish, instead of caring. I'm so very, very sorry and I hope someday you can forgive me. All I ever wanted was for you to be happy. You may not believe that, but it's true."

He looked at her familiar face, so full of pain and sadness. The face of the person who had been the steadiest rock throughout his life, until the moment she wasn't.

He thought about the fun they'd had when he was growing up, their adventures together, her sense of humor. He thought about how she'd always been there for him, and for his friends too, when most of their parents weren't around much. And he thought about how much he'd loved her and realized that hadn't changed, despite the anger he'd felt and the physical distance between them for so long.

He thought of how many times she'd tried to reach out to him through the cards she sent and through giving to the places he worked, places that were important to him.

As he stared into her blue eyes, he knew it was time to reach back.

"I do believe it, Mom. I'm sorry too. Sorry I let so many years go by before I came home. I don't completely understand, but I do forgive you. Let's put it all behind us now." He leaned forward to hug her and she clung to him, tears now streaming down her face.

"Okay. Good." She pulled back, dabbing her

face with the stupid little napkin, and smiled through her tears. "So I have a question for you."

"Ask away."

"Are you in love with the woman in charge of the Edwards hospital?"

He stared at her in shock. She had on her "mom" look he'd seen so many times in his life. The one that showed she knew something he didn't want her to know. He was damned if the woman hadn't always had a keen eye and a sixth sense when it came to her only child. "Why would you ask that?"

"Because you've been working in hospitals all over the world for years, and I know you donate money to them. There must be some reason you came here to see me and ask me to give the Edwards hospital the foundation money, and some reason you're not donating your own." She arched her brows. "If she hurt you, I'm taking back my agreement to give them the money."

He shook his head, nearly chuckling at her words, except the pain he felt over Charlotte's lies was too raw. "She worked hard to get the Gilchrist Foundation donation. I'd like it to come through for her and the hospital."

"And?"

He sighed. Sitting here with her as she prodded him for information felt like the years hadn't passed and he was a teenager again. "Yes, I'm in

love with her. No, she doesn't return my feelings."
Saying it brought to the surface the pain he was
trying hard to shove down.

"How do you know? Did she tell you that?"

"She lied to me and used me. Tried to keep me
there just to get your donation for her precious
hospital. Not something someone does to someone they love."

"I don't know. I love you but I lied and made
stupid mistakes. Have you told her how you feel?"

He stared at her, considering her words. Could
Charlotte have done what she did and still cared
about him at the same time? "No. And I'm not
going to."

"But you still love her enough to make sure she
gets the donation from my foundation."

"It's for the hospital, not her." But as he said
the words he knew it was for Charlotte as well,
and hated himself for it.

She regarded him steadily. "I think it's for both
the hospital *and* her. I made a bad mistake. Maybe
she did too. Don't compound it by making your
own mistakes." She stood and smiled, holding out
her hand like he was still a little kid. "Come on,
prodigal son. Your dad will be home soon. Stay
for dinner and we'll catch up."

"I'm sorry, Colleen. For everything. I hope Mike
wasn't mad that you sent the release papers to

me instead of Trent." Charlie studied her online bank statements as she talked to her friend, despairing that she'd find a way out of their financial problems. With everything else a total mess, getting Colleen in trouble would make the disaster complete.

"No, he's not. I wish you hadn't lied to me, though."

"I know. I'm so, so sorry. Everything I did was stupid and didn't even solve anything."

"I bet Trent was really angry about it." Her voice was somber. "I know he left there—I arranged his travel for when he heads to Europe from the U.S. What did he say?"

"He never found out, thank heavens." That would have been the worst thing of all. Despite the crappy way he'd left, she wouldn't have wanted him to know what she'd done.

"What do you mean? Of course he did. He was telling Mike he wanted to stay there in Liberia. Be assigned at your hospital for the year. And that's when Mike told him everything you'd done."

Charlie's heart lurched then seemed to grind to a halt. The world felt a little like it was tilting on its axis, and as she stared, unseeing, at her office wall, it suddenly became horribly, painfully clear.

Trent hadn't left because he was tired of her, ready for vacation, ready to move on. He'd left because he knew she'd lied and manipulated his paperwork. He'd left because of what she'd done to him.

"Oh my God, Colleen," she whispered. Trent had once told her that trying to control the direction the world spun would end up weighing heavily on her shoulders. Little had he known exactly how true that was. At this moment, that weight felt heavy indeed.

Numb, she absently noted a ping on her computer that showed a wire transfer from a bank. Mind reeling, she forced herself to focus on business. Any money would help pay a bill or two.

But when she pulled it up, her mind reeled even more dizzily. Air backed up in her lungs and she couldn't breathe. "Oh my God," she said again, but this time it was different. This time it was in stunned amazement. "It's the donation from the Gilchrist Foundation. All of it they'd committed to us. What…? Why…this is unbelievable!"

"Oh, Charlie, I'm so happy for you! This is awesome!"

"Yes. It is. Listen, I need to go. I'll call you later." Charlie hung up and stared at the wire transfer, unable to process that it had come through, beyond relieved that the hospital wouldn't have to shut down. Once the plastic surgeon showed, they'd be able to get the wing open and operating for a long time, helping all those who so needed it.

But knowing her project would now be complete didn't bring the utter satisfaction it should have. Didn't feel like the epitome of everything she'd wanted. And as she stared at her computer she knew why.

She'd ruined the sweet, wonderful, fledging romance that had blossomed between her and Trent. Through her adamant "the end justifies the means" selfish attitude, she'd no doubt hurt the most amazing, giving, incredible man she'd ever known.

He'd wanted to stay the year with her, which just might have turned into forever. But instead, she'd destroyed any chance of happiness, of a real relationship with him.

Her computer screen blurred as tears filled her eyes and spilled down her cheeks. How could she have been so stubbornly focused on the hospital's future that she couldn't see her own, staring her in the face through beautiful blue eyes?

She'd always prided herself on being a risk-taker. But when it came to the most important risk of all—risking her emotions, her life and her heart—she'd cowardly backed away in self-protection. Afraid to expose herself to potential pain, she'd tried to close a shell around her heart, hiding inside it like a clam. But somehow he'd broken through that shell anyway.

Why hadn't she seen she should have been honest with Trent, and with herself, about all of it?

Maybe the outcome would have been different if she had, but now she'd never know. Trent doubtless hated her now, and she had only herself to blame.

Her phone rang, and she blinked at the tears stinging her eyes, swallowing down the lump in her throat to answer it. "Charlotte Edwards here."

"Ms. Edwards, this is Catherine Gilchrist Dalton. I'm founder and president of the Gilchrist Foundation. I wanted to make sure you received our donation via wire."

"Yes, I did, just now." The woman was calling her personally? "I'm honored to speak with you and more than honored to receive your donation. I appreciate it more than I can possibly say, and I promise to use it wisely."

"As you know, your hospital was originally denied because it didn't meet our requirements."

"Yes. I know." And she hoped the woman would tell her why they'd changed their minds, though she supposed it didn't really matter.

"My son, Trent Dalton—I think you know him?—he came to see me, asking me to still provide the donation. Convinced me your hospital is more than worthy of our funding."

Charlotte nearly dropped her phone. Trent? Trent was the woman's son? She tried to move her lips, but couldn't speak.

"Hello? Are you there?"

"Y...yes. I'm sorry. I'm just...surprised to hear that Trent is your son." Surprised didn't begin to cover it. He'd called himself a rich boy? That was an understatement.

"Perhaps I'm being a busybody, but that's a mother's prerogative. Trent told me he'd wanted to spend the next year working at your hospital with you, but you made a mistake by lying to him which has made him change his mind."

"Yes, that's true." Her voice wobbled. "I was selfishly stupid and would give anything to be able to do it over again. To be honest with him about...everything."

"Would that 'everything' include caring for him in a personal way? Being his mother, I would have to assume you do."

The woman's amused tone reminded her so much of Trent, she nearly burst into tears right into the phone. "You're right, Mrs. Dalton. I do care for Trent in a personal way, because he's the most incredible man I've ever known. I'm terribly, crazy in love with him but, if he cared at all about me before, I don't think he does anymore. I don't think he'll ever forgive me."

"You won't know unless you try to find out, will you? I made a terrible mistake with him once, too, tried to manipulate his life and paid a harsh price for that. Our years of separation were very painful to me, and I should have tried harder to apologize, to ask him to forgive me. I suggest you make the effort, instead of wondering. And maybe regretting."

She was right. A surge of adrenaline pulsed through Charlie's blood. She'd find Trent and she'd make it right or die trying. "Thank you. Do you know where he is?"

"He's here in New York City, visiting with a few friends. He's leaving soon. I can try to find out his travel plans, if you like."

Colleen. Colleen had his itinerary. "Thanks, but I think I know how to get them."

CHAPTER NINETEEN

CHARLIE CAREENED DOWN the muddy road, hands sweating, heart pounding, as she desperately drove to the little airport, trying to catch the plane that would take her to Kennedy Airport in New York City, which Trent was scheduled to fly out of in about ten hours. And, of course, the rain had begun the moment she'd left, slowing her progress and making it nearly impossible to get there in time.

But she had to get there. A simple phone call wasn't enough. She had to find Trent and tell him she loved him and beg him to forgive her.

As she'd thrown a few necessities into her suitcase and tried to process the whole, astonishing thing about his mother being a Gilchrist, and the unbelievable donation and phone call, she'd realized something else.

The fifty-thousand-dollar donation for the school must have come from Trent. Who else would just, out of the blue, anonymously donate that kind of money to their little school? The incredible realization made her see again what she'd come to know: that he was beyond extraordinary. A man with so much money, he could choose not to work at all. Instead, he'd trained for years to become a doctor and a specialized surgeon. He helped the poor and needy around the world, both financially and hands-on. He was adorable, funny, sweet and loved children. And if she didn't get to the airport on time, and find a way to make him forgive her, she'd never, ever meet anyone like him again.

She loved him and she'd hurt him. She'd tell him, show him, how much she loved him and make right all her wrongs.

She jammed her foot onto the accelerator. She had to get there and get on that plane. And if she didn't, she'd follow him to Florence or wherever else he was going. If she had to, she'd follow him to the moon.

Trent stretched his legs out in front of him and pulled his Panama hat down over his eyes. His flight from Kennedy was delayed, so he might as well try to sleep.

Except every time he closed his eyes he saw Charlotte Grace Edwards. Never mind that there were five thousand miles between them, and that she'd lied and obviously didn't care about him the way he'd thought she did. Her face, her scent, her smile were all permanently etched in his brain and heart.

He'd broken his own damned rules and was paying the price for it. Knew he'd be paying the price for a long, long time.

He'd been happy with his life. He liked working in different places in the world, meeting new people, finding new medical challenges. Setting down roots in one place hadn't occurred to him until he'd gone to Liberia. Until he'd met Charlotte. Until she'd turned upside down everything he thought he knew about himself and what he wanted.

He hadn't gotten out fast enough. Their one-night fling had become something so much bigger, so much more important, so deeply painful. His vacation alone in Italy was going to be the worst weeks of his life, and his new job couldn't start soon enough.

A familiar, distinctive floral scent touched his nose, and to his disgust his heart slapped against his ribs and his breath shortened. Here he was, thinking about her so intently, so completely, he imagined she was near. Imagined he could touch her one last time.

Except the firm kick against his shoe wasn't his imagination.

He froze. Charlotte? Impossible.

"I know you're not asleep, Trent Dalton. Look at me."

Stunned, he slowly pushed his hat from his face and there she was. Or a mirage of her. He nearly extended his hand to see if she could possibly be real. He ran his gaze over every inch of her—her messy hair, her rumpled clothes, her bandaged arm.

She was real. The most real, the most beautiful woman he'd ever seen. His heart swelled and constricted at the same time, knowing what a damn fool he was to still feel that way.

"Why aren't you wearing the sling on your arm?"

She laughed, and the sound brought both joy and torment. "I nearly killed myself running off the road in a rainstorm to get to the airport, flew thousands of miles to find you, and the first thing you do is nag me?"

Yeah, she was something. He had to remind himself that single-minded ruthlessness was part of the persona he'd adored. "What are you doing here, Charlotte?"

She crouched down in front of him, her green eyes suddenly deeply serious as they met his. "I came to apologize. I came to tell you how very sorry I am that I lied to you. That I realize no hospital wing, no donation, no amount of need, could possibly justify it, no matter how much I convinced myself it did."

It struck him that she'd gotten the Gilchrist donation, and that his mother had probably meddled and spilled the beans about who he was. Charlotte must somehow feel she had to apologize, to make it right, because of the money, even though it was an awful big trek for her to catch him here. His chest ached, knowing that was all this was.

"No need to apologize. I know the hospital means everything to you."

She slowly shook her head as her hand reached for his and squeezed, and his own tightened on hers when he should have pulled it away. "No, Trent. The hospital doesn't mean everything to me. I know that now."

"Well, pardon me when I say that's a line of bull. Like so many others you fed me." She'd already proven he couldn't trust anything she said. "You've shown you'll do anything to make things go your way for the place. You've shown it's your number-one priority over everything."

"Maybe it was. Maybe I let it be. But it isn't anymore." She stood and leaned forward, pressing a kiss to his mouth, and for a surprised moment he let himself feel it all the way to his soul. He let it fill all the cracks in his heart before he pulled away.

"You're my number-one priority, Trent. You're

what means everything to me. Only you. I hated myself for lying to you. After you left, I hated myself even more for letting myself fall for you, because I was sure you'd just moved on to be with some woman in Italy. That I didn't mean anything to you but a brief good time."

"What makes you think that's not the case?" Though it was impossible to imagine how she could have believed that. That she hadn't seen the way he felt about her; hadn't known what she'd come to mean to him. But, if she didn't know, he sure as hell didn't want her to find out.

"Because I know you told Mike you wanted to be assigned to my little hospital for your year assignment." Tears filled her green eyes and he steeled himself against them; wouldn't be moved by them. "When I realized you'd left because of my stupid, misguided mistakes, I knew I had to do whatever I could to find you."

Obviously, she'd come because she still needed a plastic surgeon to get the hospital wing running. "You've found me. But my plane leaves in an hour, and I really don't want to go through a third goodbye. So please just go." The weight in his chest and balling in his stomach told him another goodbye might be even more painful than the second one in her kitchen, which he'd never have dreamed could be possible.

"No. No more goodbyes. I love you. I love you

more than anything, and all I want is to be with you."

She loved him? He stared at her, wishing he could believe her. But he'd learned through a very hard lesson that she lied as easily as she breathed. He wasn't about to go back to Liberia with the woman who "loved" him only as long as she needed him to do plastic surgery work, or whatever the hell else was on her agenda, then doubtless wouldn't "love" him anymore.

"Sorry, Charlie, but I'm sure you can understand why I just don't believe you."

Tears welled in her eyes again. "You just called me Charlie," she whispered. "You're the only person who always calls me Charlotte."

He shrugged casually to show her none of this was affecting him the way it really was. "Maybe because you're not the person I thought you were."

He had to look away from the hurt in her eyes. "I hope I am the person you thought I was. Or at least that I can become that person. And I do understand why you don't believe me. I deserve that disbelief. I understand you need proof that I mean every word." Beneath her tears, her eyes sparked with the determined intensity he'd seen so often. "You once asked me why I went to Liberia to rebuild the hospital and school. And I told you my roots were dug in deep there, and I wanted to grow those roots, and I'd do it no matter what it takes. But I've changed my thoughts about that."

"How?"

"I'm not willing to do whatever it takes for the hospital, because that attitude led to some terrible mistakes. But I am willing to do whatever it takes to convince you I love you. That I want to grow roots with you and only you—wherever you choose to grow them. I always told you I can find doctors to work at the Edwards hospital, but not someone to run it. But you know what? I'm sure I *can* find someone to run it, and I will if you'll let me travel with you, be with you, help you, wherever it is you're headed."

He stared at her, stunned. The woman would be willing to leave the Edwards Mission Hospital to be with him instead? As much as he wanted to believe it, he couldn't. Her lies and machinations had been coldly calculated, and he had to wonder what exactly it was she was trying to achieve this time around. "No, Charlotte. You belong in Liberia and I belong wherever I am at a given moment."

"I belong with you, and I believe that you belong with me. I'm going to work hard to convince you how sorry I am for what I did. To give you so much love, you have to forgive me." She swiped away the tears on her lashes as her eyes flashed green sparks of determination. "You said

I'm sometimes like a pit bull? You haven't seen anything yet. I'll get on the plane with you. I'll follow you wherever you go and keep asking you to forgive me and keep telling you how much I love you. I'm going to quit trying to control the world, like you always teased me about, and beg you to run it with me, for us to run it together. I want that because I love you. I love you and my life isn't complete without you."

He stared into her face. Would it be completely stupid of him to believe her again?

His heart pounded hard and he stood and looked down into her eyes focused so intently on his. In their depths, he saw very clearly what he was looking for.

Love. For him. It wasn't a lie. It was the truth.

He cupped her face in his hands and had to swallow past the lump that formed in his throat as he lowered his mouth to hers for a long kiss, absorbing the taste of her lips that he never thought he'd get to taste again.

"I love you too, Charlotte. I wish you'd just been honest with me but, standing here looking at you, I realize what you did doesn't matter if you really do love me. What matters is that I love you and you love me back." As he said the words, he knew with every ounce of his being it truly was the only thing that mattered. "Maybe if you'd told me, I would have left, I don't know. I do know that the way I felt about you scared the crap out of me."

"The way I felt about you scared me too. I knew you'd be out of my life in a matter of days, and it would be beyond stupid to fall in love with you. But I did anyway. I couldn't help it."

"Yeah?" Her words made him smile, because he'd felt exactly the same way. "I kept telling myself to keep my distance. But I found it impossible to resist a certain beautiful woman who tries to run the world." He tunneled his hands into her soft hair and looked into her eyes. "I've been running for a long time, Charlotte. I didn't really see it, until being with you made me look. But being with you made me realize that maybe, in all that running, I was really searching. And then I knew: I'd been searching for you."

A little sob left her throat and she flung her good arm around his neck. "Do you want me to come with you? Or would you like to go back to Liberia together? Will you live with me and work with me? Share my life with me?"

"I'm thinking heading back to Liberia is a good plan." He wrapped his arms around her, pressed his cheek to hers and smiled at the same time emotion clogged his chest. "So, is that a marriage proposal? Trust you not to let me be the one to ask."

"I'm sorry." She paused. "If we go back, I'll let you drive whenever you want."

He laughed out loud. "I'll believe that when I see it. And yes, Charlotte Grace Edwards, I'll marry you and live with you and work with you for the rest of our lives." He lowered his mouth to hers and whispered against her lips. "This is the last time you have to drag me back from an airport. This time, I'm staying for good."

* * * * *

WOLVEN

BAD WOLF RISING

From the Chicken House

I live in the exact place Di Toft sets these
amazing adventures and I've actually been
waiting for Cheddar Hell's Angels to ask me to
join them – I could really help in their struggle
against evil werewolf packs! I absolutely love
the climax to this heart-warming, hysterical
and howlingly hair-raising story of the most
unlikely pair of heroes ever to have changed
species overnight. It'll make you want to move
to Wookey, too.

Barry Cunningham
Publisher

DI TOFT

WOLVEN

BAD WOLF RISING

Chicken House

2 Palmer Street, Frome,
Somerset BA11 1DS

Text © Di Toft 2011
Cover illustration © Martin Simpson tweekhed.com
First published in Great Britain in 2011
The Chicken House
2 Palmer Street
Frome, Somerset BA11 1DS
United Kingdom
www.doublecluck.com

Cover and interior design by Steve Wells
Typeset by Dorchester Typesetting Group Ltd
Printed and bound by CPI Group (UK) Ltd, Croydon, CR0 4YY

The paper used in this Chicken House book is made from wood
grown in sustainable forests.

3 5 7 9 10 8 6 4

British Library Cataloguing in Publication data available.

ISBN 978-1-906427-54-2

To Dan and Frankie, with love

In memory of John Major 1932–2011

CHAPTER 1

THE BAKERLOO BEAST

NATIGOTSOMETHINK!
The intensity of Woody's mindhowl blasted through Nat Carver's brain like a freight train, threatening to knock him off the deserted Underground platform. They had parted company roughly five minutes ago and he could have sworn Woody had been in human form then. The fact that his best mate was using the two-way thing to communicate with him, instead of yelling from the top of the escalators, must mean that either Woody didn't want

1

to advertise his presence to the rogue werewolf they were hunting, or that he had wolfed out.

Of all the scary places Nat had found himself since he'd met Woody (and his life had been changed beyond his wildest dreams) the Oxford Circus section of the London Underground was one of the creepiest. It was old and filthy, the ticket offices and escalators were silent, the platform eerily draughty and deserted. Except for Nat, there wasn't a sign of life anywhere. Not *human* life, anyway.

Whereareyou? Nat sent back, as he ran towards the exit, glad to be leaving the claustrophobic Underground station. He had done his best to argue against Agent Alexandra Fish's plan to split up, but it was typical of her to assign each of them an area to search alone. Nat got the downstairs bit, the platform, which he wasn't very thrilled about.

'What about my claustrophobia?' he'd mumbled.

Fish shot him one of her looks. 'Don't be such a wimp,' she'd said, crisply. 'You're a *NightShift* agent now, remember. You can't go on being scared of closed-in spaces. Any werewolf activity has to be investigated in case it's connected with . . . well, you know who.'

Nat *did* know. Only too flipping well. Fish was right, and anyway, for tonight's exercise, she was the boss.

Since their first (unofficial) mission together, *The Case of the Black Widow Vampire*, when Nat and Woody had found themselves up against a deadly hive of thirsty vampires, Agent Alex Fish had proved to be a tough act: brave, shrewd and inventive in her fighting skills. A lot of people owed her their lives, Nat included. Tonight, Nat and Woody were working with Fish in a real assignment for *NightShift* (the ultra-secret agency working to uphold supernatural and paranormal law) and they were determined not to mess it up. When people using the London Underground had begun to disappear with alarming regularity, London's Metropolitan Police had suspected supernatural shenanigans and passed the case onto the agency.

Now it was up to rookie agents Nat Carver and Woody to find out what had happened. Meanwhile, not even the bravest of travellers risked the platforms on the Bakerloo line between Regent's Park and Oxford Circus, and although the line was still in service, trains no longer dared to stop there.

Despite Nat and Woody being equipped with enhanced supernatural senses and the ability to shape-shift, it was Agent Fish who had found a tiny scrap of human flesh deep in this deserted and lonely stretch of the underground. The grisly clue bore traces of saliva that was *not* human, and a simple test

3

back at the *NightShift* HQ showed it was 'lycan-thropic' in origin. Or to put it simply, the DNA belonged to a werewolf. But it was vital that the general public were not aware of the real source of danger. Supernatural acts of violence were still thought to exist in horror films only – and it was *NightShift's* job to keep it this way.

The investigation had been given a typically lurid name by Alex Fish, and **THE CASE OF THE BAKERLOO BEAST** had been scrawled across the front of the office file in thick black marker pen – the more sensational the name, as far as Fish was concerned, the better. Quentin Crone, *NightShift's* permanently worried and floppy-haired boss, thought that the investigating team was a match made in heaven, or hell, depending on whose side you were on. Who better to get their teeth into a werewolf case than the two new recruits? After all, they were no strangers to werewolf activity, as anyone who had ever witnessed either boy's own shape-shifting skills knew only too well. Crone had never actually seen it himself, but he had Fish's assurance that it was '*totally acers*', which Crone had interpreted to mean a 'spectacular phenomenon'.

At the top of the steep escalators, Nat scanned the immediate area. He felt vulnerable in his human form, and Woody's mindhowl had indicated he was on to something. Maybe he'd even caught a whiff of the killer. Nat's night vision hadn't detected anything unnatural lurking in the shadows, and he could feel Woody was near, which was a comfort. But if he needed to fight he would have to shift. In human form he wouldn't stand much of a chance against a werewolf, especially one who liked to eat his victims.

Nat squeezed his eyes tight shut and imagined himself looking in a mirror. It always helped him concentrate. *Come on, come on*, he urged himself, *chaaaaange.* He could see himself in his mind's eye – a thirteen-year-old boy, quite tall, with almost black hair and dark blue eyes that would soon glow with a soft topaz light.

Look out, his brain warned him, *'cos here it comes!*

This time it was so quick Nat didn't even have time to strip off his clothes. A familiar warm feeling stole through him, starting in his innards and filtering outwards to his skin and hair. He had willed his Wolven side to take over, and now his spirits leapt as his heart pumped the Wolven blood around his body. His muscles contracted, his bones lengthened, his face shimmied and shook in the imaginary mirror. *One, one thousand, two, one thousand* . . . as Nat counted the seconds his change was taking, his clothes threatened to suffocate him. *Ten, one thousand* . . . he flexed his muscles again and he could feel even the tough denim jeans give in and then split. *Fourteen, one thousand . . .* his T-shirt ripped all the way down his back as his spine lengthened. *Nineteen, one thousand . . .* still counting he could hear himself panting, ears stre-e-e-tching and growing pointed, snout puuuuushing and finally tongue lolling in a big Wolven grin. With the yellow glow in his eyes and his pupils dilated, his vision took on a supernatural clarity. He shook himself, a large silver-grey Wolven weighing around three hundred pounds, almost twice the weight of a natural fully grown *Canis lupus*, or wolf to you and me.

Twenty-two seconds! Oh, I am getting so *brilliant at this shape-shifting lark,* Nat thought to himself, rather smugly. *And it doesn't even hurt any more!*

In the station foyer, Woody had indeed got more than a whiff of their suspect. Not long after he had willed his own change (Nat wasn't the only one who felt more comfortable – and braver – in Wolven form), his nostrils had been assaulted by a familiar smell, the coppery, salty tang of fresh blood. He trotted to and fro across the upper level of the station, his long Wolven coat glowing so white it looked almost blue in the dim light.

When the smell became so strong it made his nose run, he stopped. He was standing by a door marked

Ticket Office, which looked as though it had been forced open sometime, either by someone hoping to find money, or the werewolf they were after. Woody nudged the door open to find a pile of broken furniture. Scrabbling around underneath it, he realised he'd come across a makeshift den, which was still warm. It felt like something had lain there only moments before.

Roguewolf, Woody thought to himself. It was evident from the den that this particular creature operated alone, unlike most werewolves who liked to run or hunt in packs. Woody growled. A werewolf who kills humans is thankfully a rarity, even in these troubled times, unless of course it has been corrupted by evil. Their orders from the boss were the same in any case; whenever possible *the suspect must be brought in alive.* Obviously this rule didn't apply to ghosts, who were already dead, or vampires, who were undead. *But,* shivered Woody, hoping that Nat or Fish would hurry up and appear, *if this rogue werewolf is responsible for stuffing its face with at least twelve people, I don't think it's gonna wanna come quietly.*

The werewolf (or lycan, as these shape-shifters are sometimes known) had once been a mild-mannered train driver named Martin Clough, and was indeed operating alone on the express orders of his maker.

Clough had been corrupted following an attack by a wolf in human clothing – a vile, hybrid creature, which had lain in wait for him at a small railway station in Somerset. The werewolf had told Martin Clough what to do and, dazzled by the creature's wonderful molten eyes, he had obeyed. He had gone to London and lived off humans in the London Underground ever since.

So when a large, white, Wolven creature pitched up uninvited in his private den, poking and prodding about, the thing that had been Martin Clough could *smell* it . . . all the way from the mouth of the Underground tunnel he now lurked in. The scent was puzzling. Whiffs of human and . . . what else? Not werewolf, but not really wolf either? But instinct screamed at him to avoid contact. There was something well dodgy about the intruder.

He was sure about one thing though. It hadn't smelt him yet. The lively draught from the Underground was drifting the wrong way for a start. Martin Clough licked his black lips with a snaking purplish tongue. *Would his hunger ever be satisfied?* He stifled a growl and slunk back into the tunnel, his crafty Halloween-coloured eyes glowing with malice.

Meanwhile, on platform three, agent Alex Fish had lowered herself onto the tracks, and was now walking gingerly towards the Underground tunnel. Even though she had personally ordered the electricity to be turned off, she glanced nervously across at the usually lethal third rail. She peered ahead, but her human eyesight was useless in these circumstances. Where were they? She hadn't seen Nat or Woody for at least ten minutes now, which was like, *way* too long.

'Come in, Woody. Over,' she said, hoping her throat mic was working. Nat and Woody had been under strict instructions to tell her if they were going to shift before they lost the power of human speech. Her earpiece remained eerily silent; there wasn't even any static.

She tried again. 'Come *in*, Nat. Over.'

Her voice sounded weak and puny in the near darkness, and although Fish was brave, she felt the first tiny fingers of unease tug at her fast-beating heart. *Now* she could hear something, but it wasn't a welcome sound. It was the sound of something snarling. And it was in the tunnel.

Alex Fish moved very slowly. She put her hands onto the cold slab of platform and hoisted herself up from the track, hating every second her back was turned towards what she guessed was coming for her with molten eyes.

'Oh man, oh man! Here it comes,' Fish muttered as she hauled herself to her feet, praying at the same time that Nat and Woody would come. She turned round, her mouth dry, her heart hammering in her chest. Loping easily towards her, orange eyes burning with hate (or hunger), came the thing they were looking for: the werewolf. And it was slavering.

'I don't know if you are capable of understanding me,' said Fish clearly, in her best agency voice, 'but I am arresting you on suspicion of murder by devourment. That means eating a human. You have the right to remain silent – on the grounds that you are unable to use human speech – and I have to inform you that I have the authority to use Ag compound on you if you resist arrest.'

'Grrrrrrggghhh,' growled the werewolf in reply, still advancing on Fish.

She swallowed. From her pocket she produced a silver object and raised its nozzle toward the werewolf.

'I have to inform you that resisting arrest is ill-advised,' she said calmly. 'If I pull this trigger, it will release a deadly stream of molten silver that will fry your old werewolf head like an egg.'

The werewolf hesitated slightly at the authority in her voice, then carried on, hackles raised, eyes glowing, and leapt up onto the platform.

'AAAAAAAhgggggggggggggggggggggggggggggr-rooooooooooooooooooh!'

The werewolf who had once been called Martin

Clough nearly jumped out of his rather scruffy fur as two Wolven, one brilliant white and one a silvery grey, appeared on the platform like smoke.

Finally! Fish's heart leapt at the sight of her two Wolven friends creeping slowly towards the werewolf.

'If you are unable to morph back to human state,' she continued, as though nothing had happened, 'I will have no alternative but to muzzle you and put you on a lead.'

Even as the last word left her lips, a confused Martin Clough leapt backwards, desperate to get away from the enormous white wolf-being whose lips were curled back on its muzzle to reveal sharp white teeth, and whose grey friend seemed to have matching sharp white teeth. Fish cried out as Martin Clough half-fell, half-jumped onto the track below, his four legs flying akimbo in his haste to get away.

Unhappily there was a loud cracking noise and a flash, followed by the sickening smell of fried, singed fur. Martin Clough was being electrocuted!

Fish stared at the smoking, twitching werewolf in horror and disbelief. *Blumming heck!* Hadn't she ordered the late trains to be cancelled and the line to be switched off? What if *she'd* touched it by mistake during her little trip along the tunnel? The werewolf would recover; it took more than a dose of electricity to finish off a lycan, after all.

Then, just when she thought things couldn't get any worse, they did. The midnight train for the Elephant and Castle came thundering through the tunnel at seventy miles per hour, taking the twitching, smoking form of Martin Clough with it.

'Well,' said Alex Fish, looking distinctly annoyed, 'that went well.'

Chapter 2

Furballs and Wedgies

When the 12:01 train to Elephant and Castle had roared through the station taking the unfortunate werewolf with it, Nat hoped they could all go home, but Alex Fish insisted they follow the train. At the next stop they found a small team of *NightShift* agents carefully peeling Martin Clough from the front of the locomotive.

Nat and Woody watched as the werewolf slowly reanimated, his rather squashed form shifting to human until he was sitting naked on the platform.

He looked harmless enough, thought Nat, as an agent snapped the cuffs on him.

Both Nat and Woody heaved a sigh of relief. They knew from bitter experience that unless the werewolf had been squished beyond all repair, soaked in Ag (liquid silver) or shot with a silver bullet (the traditional way to kill a werewolf), its supernaturally charged cells would be able to regroup and it would be as good as new, if a little more annoyed than before electrocution. At least now it was in custody. As the *NightShift* crew led him away, Martin Clough turned and gave them such an evil glare that Nat changed his mind about him being harmless. Too tired to shift, Nat and Woody escorted Fish through the dark streets back to Middle Temple Lane.

It was gone two o'clock in the morning when they slipped through the narrow alleyway into the *NightShift* HQ. Quentin Crone was sitting at his favourite place by the fire, a fine malt whisky in one hand and a copy of *Country Life* in the other.

Alex Fish stood in the middle of the room, spiky hair even spikier than usual, her expression one of extreme annoyance, bordering on fury. She was still bristling about the incompetence of the other team of agents who had neglected to turn off the power to the tracks. Nat and Woody stood on either side of her, eyes gleaming topaz in the dimly lit room, plumed tails wagging uncertainly.

'Very impressive,' muttered Crone, peering at the two Wolven over the top of his glasses. It was the first time he had seen both boys in Wolven form, and he felt a mixture of excitement and amazement.

'You will no doubt be interested to hear that our suspect's name is Martin Clough,' said Crone, without preamble. 'As soon as he was admitted to Battersea holding area, he named Lucas Scale as his maker.'

For Nat, there wasn't much chance of sleep following Quentin Crone's stark revelation, although Woody managed to drop off. They shared a suite of private rooms at the very top of the building. Each had their own bedroom with an overly bouncy four-poster bed (although Woody slept mainly on the floor even when in human form) and a large, chilly bathroom with an unreliable shower and a scratchy, old-fashioned, claw-footed bathtub.

The *Nightshift* HQ (just in case you ever need their help) is located somewhere in the EC4 area of London, but you need special instructions to find it. If you walk towards the Thames Embankment until you're roughly halfway down Middle Temple Lane, you'll see a silver plaque to your left, with *Scrote*,

Hanker & Whinge engraved on it. At the side of the building there's a tiny gap which looks too narrow to pass through, although in fact it's all part of a very clever optical illusion to discourage visitors. The entrance is behind a scruffy black door with badly peeling paint and no visible latch, lock or letterbox. Middle Temple is part of the ancient maze of buildings, passageways and courtyards near the Temple Church, the round church built by the famous Knights Templar. Nowadays, most of the buildings are used as barristers' chambers and lawyers' offices. The *NightShift* HQ contains both living and working space, a communal hall for dining and training, an enormous library and a fully equipped gym.

Still in Wolven form, Nat loped into his bathroom, stuck his great shaggy head in the toilet bowl and drank thirstily, glad that no one he knew could see what he was doing. He knew it was well out of order because Woody had once told him gravely that the lavatory was home to millions of unseen germs.

Nat chose to ignore this advice because:

a. Woody had got his information from a television advert, and;

b. everyone knows that adverts will say anything just to sell more bleach, which is also really bad for the environment.

Anyway, Nat's paws were useless for turning on

taps, and he was so thirsty his mouth felt as gravelly as the bottom of a cat-litter tray. Traces of fried were-wolf lingered in his nostrils and although he was absolutely cream-crackered (as his granddad would say) he knew he wouldn't be able to sleep just yet.

Now, as he stood in the moon-washed bathroom, he could hear Woody snoring. He took another guilty slurp from the toilet, trying not to think of the millions of scary germs lying in wait, then loped across to the small window that looked out onto the lane below.

Nat reared up on his hind legs, put his paws on the narrow sill and pushed the old-fashioned, mullioned window open with his snout. He poked his head out and looked down at the wet cobbles gleaming under the gas lights in the deserted courtyard. Woody had never been to London before, so when they had first arrived Nat and his parents had enjoyed showing him all the sights. The best bit (in Nat's opinion) had been when Woody had puked on the London Eye. Since his parents had left London, there had been precious little time for outings. It had all got rather serious, and he and Woody had been training hard.

Nat got down on all fours again, thinking he really should be going to bed, when he caught a fleeting glimpse of himself in the large, ornate mirror opposite. It suddenly struck him as odd that he had never seen himself in Wolven form before – he supposed it was because he was a whole lot scared of what he might see, and he wasn't at all sure he was ready for a proper look now. What would he see? *A big furry freak,* he thought to himself dolefully. But did he really believe that? No, if he believed it of himself, he would have to say that his best mate was a freak too, and Woody was no freak, he was a *legend.* An actual, real-life legend! And anyway, if he was honest, Nat liked being able to shift. He liked being able to communicate with his mind, he liked being able to run like the wind, and he liked it that he had Wolven blood.

Some stuff still struck him as inconvenient and weird. One day it might be helpful to write a self-help manual for shape-shifters. There were his feet, for a start. In Wolven form he probably spent more time than he should just sniffing his paws – they smelt lovely, just like cheese 'n' biscuits. But even when he was in human form, his toes had become embarrassingly hairy and it was now difficult to find shoes that fitted. He knew now why Woody rarely wore shoes. Then there was the furball thing. That was disgusting and it always happened after Nat had the urge to wash himself when in Wolven shape. Actually licking himself all over was surprisingly satisfying, not peculiar or unhygienic. But during the process, mouthfuls of fur would somehow get swallowed, and after a few hours – or days depending on the amount – there would be an eye-watering period of uncomfortable retching that made you go *HHRAAAAAACK* and *HUUURRKGH* and *YUUUUUUURKKK!* Then the fur would fly out of your mouth in a horrible half-regurgitated mess, along with what you had eaten for lunch. It was really bad.

Underpants were *hugely* problematic. Both Nat and Woody had suffered extremely painful wedgies when their pants had tightened during shifts. Usually an experienced shape-shifter can remove their clothes in seconds before a planned shift, but Nat, and especially Woody, knew from experience that this is not always possible. The extreme change in body shape would shred all other garments but, for some unfathomable reason, the pants stayed obstinately put, resulting in high-pitched howls and watery eyes.

The sound of Woody's snores brought Nat's thoughts back to the present. He went to reach for the toothpaste, forgetting he was still in Wolven form. For a moment he froze and stared at the enormous grey paw, which was roughly the size of a man's hand. He flexed his claws, fascinated by their deadly points. He pulled himself up to his full height and took a deep breath. Then he raised his head and looked squarely into the mirror for the first time.

Oh . . . oh my days . . . that's me! Nat stared at the enormous wolf creature in the mirror with its yellow Wolven eyes still glowing warmly despite the light from the moon. He opened his mouth and his tongue promptly unrolled and fell out of his jaws.

That was another thing. The Wolven tongue was way too long; either it was really badly designed or he just wasn't very good at controlling it, because it always seemed to be in the way, hanging out of the side of his mouth.

But apart from that, Nat thought to himself, he looked preeetty damn handsome. He made his fur puff up and lifted his lip in a ferocious snarl.

Aargh! Scared stiff of his own teeth, Nat backed hurriedly away from his reflection in shock, half frightened and half proud of how fearsome he looked.

No wonder the werewolf formerly known as Martin Clough had been terrified. Suddenly tired, Nat stretched and prepared to shift back to human form. He started the process. *One, one thousand, two, one thousand, streeetch, puush. Five, one thousand, come on!* Nothing was happening.

Nat pushed again, wondering if it was just taking so long because he was so tired. He counted all the way up to fifty, one thousand. Nothing. He looked down at his paws. Nope, still paws.

He gave himself a rest for roughly ten minutes and started again. After twenty whole minutes, his change began at last, and Nat felt the familiar heat take him over as his body transformed from a magnificent Wolven to a boy. But as he began an inventory to check all the parts of his body had changed, the hairs on the back of his neck (which a few minutes ago had been hackles) rose up as his Wolven senses took over. *Something's wrong!*

Nat's whole body went into red-alert mode. He looked in the mirror, relieved when he saw familiar navy-blue eyes and a mop of black hair. Check. Both ears, check. Nose, check. All present and correct, so what on earth was bothering him?

A horribly familiar voice sneaked uninvited into his head.

Whatlovelybigteethyouhavemydear!

Nat whirled round in panic, but the space behind him was empty, just a patch of shadowy moonlight. He shook himself.

Nothing there, he told himself shakily, *just a trick of the light*. But the voice in his head had been unmistakeable and if there was nothing there, why did he still feel uneasy? Why were his senses still jangling a warning?

He braced himself and looked in the mirror again. Nat's own human reflection had vanished and been replaced by the tall figure of a creature which was not quite wolf, not quite human – a hideous hybrid of the two species. Its ears were long and slightly ragged as though chewed, its eyes were the sick, feverish orange of Halloween pumpkins and dying planets.

Not real . . . you're not here, just in my head, Nat told the apparition firmly.

Lucas Scale's reflection licked its blackened lips, cocked its head to one side and leered with yellowy black teeth.

Not yet my dear, Scale's reflection giggled, *but soooooon, oh so soooooon!*

CHAPTER 3

THE APPRENTICE

Like a very large and very ugly homing pigeon, Lucas Scale had once more returned to the place he felt most comfortable, the twisted ruins of Helleborine Halt. It hadn't taken long for the nearby East Wood to creep into the grounds, sending its wild roots to reclaim the manicured lawns and smart flower borders. The history of Helleborine Halt reeked of evil, and as far as the shrinking population of Temple Gurney was concerned, the woods could keep it, thank you very much.

The Halt was the only place where Scale felt truly safe. The miles of labyrinthine caves under the building gave him the opportunity to come and go as he pleased, hidden from prying human eyes. The same corridors had once been home to a dozen or so doomed werewolves, and sometimes, on a cold and lonely night, Scale would swear he could hear their ghostly howls as they ran with the moon, forever in purgatory. *Ah,* he thought to himself, his raddled orange eyes growing moist with the memory, *what music they make!*

His black lips wrinkled and he snarled into the dimly lit cavern, pleased to hear how scary he sounded. It struck him again how clever he had been to make a deal with a demon (don't try this at home). Scale had studied the Black Arts at Cambridge, and he conjured the demon from its pit. The demon had kept its side of the deal by bringing Scale back to life when he had been shot through the heart with a silver bullet. Thanks to his demonic new best friend, he lived again, bent on revenge.

The demon had taught him well, and Scale had learned many things, including:
- possession (very tricky to get just right)
- awakening the dead (easy peasy, lemon squeezy)
- consorting with vampires (note to self – never work with the double-crossing, ungrateful, vicious blood-

suckers ever again)

- astral projection (an excellent way to avoid traffic and scare the pants off people).

It was this last skill that had just allowed Scale to visit Nat Carver. Admittedly, he didn't yet know where the Wolven actually were, but he had successfully projected himself into the Carver brat's consciousness, and he had no doubt that Nat was now whining about it to the other bane of Scale's life, the Wolven beast Woody, who had ruined his career.

Scale's ability to project his astral body was getting pretty damn good, even if he said so himself. How satisfying it had been to see the shock and horror on the Carver boy's face when he'd appeared in the mirror!

Of course the demon would eventually come and reclaim his soul. But in the meantime, there was chaos and revenge to be planned.

Now he slid back into his misshapen body and began rocking to and fro in his favourite chair.

'AAAAAAHHHHOOOOOOWAHHHH!' Lucas Scale screamed, tears of pain pricking his eyes. His tail was caught under the rockers! He shot to his feet and peered behind him expecting the worst. His poor tail looked as if it had been put through a wringer; Scale could almost see it throbbing. He whined self-pityingly and lifted his tail as gently as he could to inspect it properly.

After the pain had begun to subside, he consoled himself by imagining how lovely it would be to squash Nat Carver's head beneath the same rockers that had mangled his tail! Again he began to rock back and forth, back and forth, until the rhythmic action of the chair helped ease his mad mutterings.

Just before dawn the clouds drew back and the moon bloomed, casting its cold glow over the ancient woods. Inside Scale's lair the candles grew dim and his eyes became narrow slivers of orange light. A whimper made him snap to attention. He'd almost forgotten!

A wretched human shape lay writhing on the cold stone floor and Scale lurched towards it, snarling and showing his fangs. He aimed a kick at the creature, which howled as Scale's pointy, handmade boot connected with its ribs. *Treat 'em mean, keep 'em keen,* he thought with a satisfied grunt. *It's time.*

He watched with almost fatherly pride as his newest recruit transformed from a boy to a wolf. The first weeks are the worst for a new werewolf, and as the boy contorted in agony, Scale watched with warped happiness while light brown fur sprouted as if by magic all over his body. His ears grew long and pointed and then his face stretched, as if pulled by an invisible force, into the snout of a wolf. At one point the creature threw back its head and tried to howl, its frightened cry strangled and forlorn. Scale grunted again as he saw the despair and confusion that filled its eyes. He checked hastily that it was still attached to its shackles. He couldn't afford any accidents now. Finally, when the change was complete, Scale pulled the new werewolf roughly to its feet by its collar, taking care to dodge its deadly sharp fangs, *just in case*.

The werewolf had once been a boy called Josh Firkin, until he made the deadly mistake of riding his bike through the East Wood on his way back from youth club. A tall, shadowy creature had carefully stalked him, finally caught him and then spoken to him in beautiful, silken tones. Josh had felt himself relax as Lucas Scale explained gently what wild times they were going to have in the future and what wonderful rewards Josh would receive if he did as he was told. At the time Josh could happily have drowned in the orange depths of Scale's eyes. But when Scale had finished with him, he was no longer the boy whose simple hobbies had been riding his beloved BMX, playing his guitar and supporting Bristol City.

The human Josh Firkin no longer existed.

Later that morning, Scale was rocking backwards and forwards in his chair, scoffing a haunch of prime venison (freshly snatched from the deer park) with a side dish of pickled eggs, when the faint, but unmistakeable smell of sulphur started to drift up his nostrils. He wrinkled his snout and sniffed his pickled eggs suspiciously. He was sure he had checked the sell-by date on the jar. Nope, satisfyingly eggy-smelling, but not gone off.

But Scale began to lose his appetite when a reddish, smoky haze rolled into the cave and the temperature rose uncomfortably. Despite the heat, his mottled old flesh began to creep and he wondered if he had time to run. But it was too late.

An all-enveloping blackness was gathering in front of him, thick and cloying, darker than anything he had ever seen or imagined. Scale knew that within it floated a being that he had hoped he wouldn't see until he was ready. The dark matter cleared and left behind something that floated a few centimetres above the cave floor, moving towards Scale, who was now trying not to cringe in his rocking chair. The demon was not in his raw form, which was lucky for Scale, since his study of the Dark Arts had taught him that any human who sees a demon's true appearance will die mad. Although Scale wasn't completely human, he was happy not to take the chance.

The apparition hovering in front of him was curiously dressed in varying shades of red. It wore a pillar-box red duster coat and maroon cowboy boots, complete with vicious-looking spurs. A scarlet cowboy hat was pulled down low where its forehead should have been, hiding its eyes and casting a shadow over its face. Not for the first time, Scale was under the unsettling impression that it *had* no eyes, or indeed a face. The demon, whose name was too hard for Scale to pronounce properly because it sounded like claws being scraped across a blackboard, seemed to be waiting for him to say something.

'Er . . . w . . . welcome to my home,' grovelled Scale, trying not to stammer too much. 'To what do I owe the immense pleasure of your presence?'

Imagine hearing someone scraping a plate with a fork. Or the way tin foil feels on your fillings, or brain-freeze after eating ice cream. Then imagine all those things increased a thousand times and you'll understand how the demon's voice sounded to Lucas Scale.

'You will do something for me,' it screeched.

Scale's paws gripped the sides of his head as he tried in vain to cover his ear holes.

'Aaargh! Yes, yes!' screamed Scale. 'Just tell me in as few words as you can, I beg of you!'

'You will find me the Head of the Baphomet.'

As the demon's dreadful voice filled the cavern, Scale noticed Josh running for cover. He narrowed his eyes. Every student of the Dark Arts had heard of the Baphomet, a powerful demon whose specialities were war and pestilence. The Baphomet had witnessed the dawn of time and possessed a dreadful gift for crossing the lines between hell and earth. Even Lucas Scale knew that the chances of finding such a thing were minimal – it had, after all, been missing for centuries. But then an idea began to boil in his ugly old head.

If anyone could find the Baphomet Head, Scale believed he could. If – no, when – he located it, he would hold the demon to ransom. He would hand over the Baphomet Head on his terms only.

The demon roared impatiently, making Scale fall to the floor, again clutching his misshapen head with his paws.

'I will do as you ask,' said Scale, when he had regained control of himself.

He saw or thought he saw something shift under the scarlet cowboy hat. It was wet and shiny, almost like a mouth but so hideous Scale couldn't be sure. Knowing the demon would be up for some sport, he took a deep breath and told it of his own plans for chaos and destruction in Temple Gurney.

'My aim is to finish this town and the people in it,' said Scale, his eyes downcast. He didn't want to see that . . . that terrible hole where the demon's mouth ought to be ever again.

'I believe our plans have something in common,'

went on Scale. 'I think it is time for this world to come under . . . er . . . shall I say, under new management?'

The demon made a horrible gurgling noise, which Scale took to mean it was laughing encouragingly.

'I have a few tricks up my sleeve to ensure that a certain pair of terrible boys – you'd think them human, more human than you or I – will return to this dreary little township,' spat Scale, forgetting in his excitement to be afraid. 'When I've finished with them, I would like to trade you my soul for theirs; two for the price of one.'

The demon gurgled again and Scale shuddered inwardly, trying not to visualise what was underneath its hat. Then, before it floated back into the tunnels, it took something from one of the many pockets on its duster coat and handed it to the werewolf. A slow grin crept over Scale's dreadful face and turned into wheezy laughter. The demon was keen to do business with him.

When he was alone again Scale opened his paw-like hand and held up a little cloth bag tied up in a bow with green string. Then he skipped around the caves, kicking up his bandy legs in glee. When the time came, it wouldn't be Scale's soul beholden to the demon. It would be the souls of Nat Carver and the Wolven creature, Woody.

CHAPTER 4
WHAT LIES BENEATH

'You've *seen* him,' hissed Woody, 'you've seen Scale.'

Around the time that Lucas Scale was enduring a visit from his demon, Nat Carver was shovelling egg and bacon into his mouth as though it was his last meal on death row.

At Woody's words he stopped shovelling abruptly, his fork poised in mid-air.

'How did you know?' Nat sighed, leaning back in his chair, his appetite suddenly a thing of the past.

'Well, *duh*,' whispered Woody, scooping egg yolk from his chin, 'you might as well have it tattooed across your forehead.' He checked over his shoulder to see if anyone was listening. 'And you've been acting even weirder than usual.'

'Yeah,' admitted Nat reluctantly, 'I've seen him.'

'I thought we were in this together,' hissed Woody.

'I don't think it's actually *him*,' said Nat, in a low voice, 'it's almost like he's a ghost – kind of, like, see-through.'

Woody looked as though he were going to puke. 'I thought we'd be safe here,' he said shakily. 'You said—'

'He'll never give up,' said Nat. 'Scale is the reason we joined *NightShift*, remember?'

'What d'we do now?' asked Woody.

'We wait,' said Nat grimly. 'See what he really wants.'

'We know what he wants,' said Woody, his eyes huge. 'He wants to kill us.'

'Yeah, he does,' hissed Nat fiercely, 'but, you know what, we've beaten him twice. He soon legged it when he saw me shift for the first time.'

'I s'pose,' said Woody, his voice reluctant, 'but his demon—'

'We don't know for sure the demon even exists,' interrupted Nat.

'Then,' asked Woody, 'how did Scale cheat the silver bullet?'

Nat hesitated, 'I dunno,' he admitted, 'but if Scale did do a deal with a demon, maybe . . . maybe he's somehow outwitted it.'

'Or,' said Woody, dismally, 'maybe they're still working together.'

After their rather miserable breakfast, Quentin Crone asked the boys to join Alex Fish in his office. Nat tried to forget about his conversation with Woody, and gazed around the room. It seemed to change every time you were in it. There was always something different to see: an object or painting that you'd never noticed before. Hardly any natural light filtered through the mullioned windows, so it was always gloomy – almost creepy – but also sort of cosy at the same time. In sharp contrast to the grotesque stone statues and gargoyles adorning the fireplace and mantelpiece, the elderly sofas were strewn with comfy cushions and throws that were big enough to snuggle down in when the fire went out, which it did with annoying regularity. On the walls there were some horrible paintings of people being eaten by dragons or being chucked into fiery pits, but the tapestries, although faded over the centuries, were fabulous in their detail, and the boys could look at them for hours.

There was one twelfth-century tapestry in particular that both Fish and the boys were always drawn to. It was a depiction of King Richard the Lionheart of England, but what made it extra special were the twelve white wolf-like creatures gathered around the monarch in a protective circle: the King's Wolven. Behind them rose the majestic hill of Glastonbury Tor with the church of St Michael at the summit. It reminded Nat of his flip back in time when he rode alongside Richard during the Third Crusade, surrounded by a pack of a dozen Wolven.

Having scoffed a packet of custard creams, Woody was standing before the enormous fireplace, peering at something intently. Etched in stone beneath the gargoyles were the words *QUIS NON OCCIDIT, CONFIRMAT.*

'What's that mean?' asked Woody, curiously.

'*"WHAT DOESN'T KILL YOU MAKES YOU STRONGER,"*' translated Fish. 'It's Latin. Catchy, huh?'

'Did Crone have that done?' asked Nat, curiously.

Fish shook her head. 'See?' she said tracing the words with her finger. 'It's quite faint. Some old Templar dude dreamt it up, like centuries ago.'

Nat frowned. 'How old is the *NightShift* organisation then?'

'It's a bit of a mystery,' admitted Fish, 'even the

boss doesn't really know.'

Nat was really puzzled now. 'I thought Crone had set it up,' he said, 'you know, after all the wild stuff that happened with the Proteus project and everything.'

'No,' said Fish, looking surprised. 'A bloke by the name of Freddie Alton was in charge before Crone. Unfortunately, all his nightmares came true during the time he was here. It sent him completely round the bend.'

'So who's Mr Crone's boss?' asked Woody.

Fish shrugged. 'I don't know. Not even *he* knows. Or at least if he does, he's not telling me.'

'Isn't that a bit weird?' persisted Nat. 'I mean, who pays us?'

'Look,' said Fish, running her fingers through her spiky black hair, 'all I know is that *NightShift* isn't government. It's funded by what the boss calls private means. Questions aren't really encouraged. I get the feeling—'

She stopped talking abruptly as the old wooden door opened and Quentin Crone came through backwards, trying to balance a tray laden with doughnuts and piping hot chocolate. Woody drooled unashamedly, and even Nat (who was usually more restrained) felt his mouth flood with saliva. He licked his lips greedily; he was beginning to feel more like a werepig than a werewolf.

Crone plonked the tray on his desk and smiled at them. His hair was flopping more than usual and he looked harassed and tired.

'Dig in,' he said. 'We just have time for a quick celebration. Agent Carver and Agent Woody, both of you have graduated with honours.'

Fish whooped and clapped. Quentin Crone patted both Nat and Woody on the back then folded his tall body into his chair by the fire.

'Before we move on to the next phase,' he said, crossing his long legs, 'you will be pleased to know that Martin Clough . . . er . . . also known as the Bakerloo Beast . . . is being assessed. He denies any knowledge of Scale's plans, or any association with Scale's alleged demon friend.'

'D'you think he's lying?' asked Nat.

Crone shrugged. 'Our people have pointed out to him that if he can prove he was possessed by Lucas Scale, he'll probably get away with a few hundred hours of community service, or possibly even rehabilitation at an expensive London clinic.'

'That's one unlucky dude,' said Fish, gravely. 'He's gonna have a hard job proving anything about someone as slippery as Scale.'

Everyone munched on a doughnut, lost in their own thoughts about Lucas Scale.

Crone broke the silence. 'Time for the final part of your training,' he said to Nat and Woody, and pointed to the floor. 'Are you ready?'

'There's more secret stuff down there than Area 51,' said Alex Fish, her beady eyes shining behind her specs.

Nat didn't know if he was ready for this or not, but curiosity got the better of him. 'Isn't Area 51 where the American government keeps all the dead aliens?' he asked.

'Apparently so,' agreed Quentin Crone, 'but as Alex mentioned, our collection of . . . ahem . . . oddities is reputed to be somewhat superior in content to that housed by our American friends.'

Nat was experiencing a major goosebump situation. Even the most experienced *Nightshift* agents talked of 'going downstairs' in hushed tones, unconsciously wiping their sweaty palms on their clothing. Since they met, Fish had often hinted about the strange stuff stored in the cellars beneath their feet and Nat remembered a certain magical key reputed to have belonged to Queen Cleopatra. It had once helped Nat and Alex Fish out of a very tight spot, but he found it hard to imagine what else could be down there.

'Talking of secret stashes,' said Fish, narrowing her eyes, 'I wouldn't mind betting my best pair of Jimmy

Choos that the missing Templar gold ended up in Area 51, or somewhere like that, and the US government's been using it to fund all sorts of dodgy stuff.'

Nat and Woody exchanged furtive smiles. If Alex Fish knew that Woody had already discovered the legendary Templar gold, she would have a pink and blue fit. He had stumbled upon the priceless hoard purely by accident and the boys had made a pact never to tell a living soul where it was.

When the final doughnut had been dunked, the door to Quentin Crone's office was double-locked and bolted from the inside. The faded carpet was rolled away and the ancient trap door beneath it was carefully opened.

The first thing the boys noticed was the cool updraught from the dark hole that now gaped hungrily in the middle of the floor. The second thing was the smell. It was the sort of smell (if you had been unfortunate enough to smell it before) that you would associate with things long dead: a crypt smell, the dry smell of old bones. Worse still, there was the cloying stink of ancient vampire, the unmistakable fartzy smell of the undead.

'We're not going to close the door on top of us, are we?' asked Woody, his flashing eyes and flaring nostrils betraying his anxiety.

'Stick together,' smiled Crone, reassuringly.

'There's a good few miles of storage under here.'

'Ready?' asked Fish, raising her eyebrows.

'Don't touch anything,' instructed Crone, 'and stay close to me.'

The boys didn't need to be told twice. They stuck like glue to their new boss down the seventy-seven steps that led into the dimly lit depths. When they reached the bottom both boys gasped. The cavernous space underneath Middle Temple Lane looked impossible. It was like being taken on a school trip to the maddest museum ever. As far as their eyes could see – which was further than any human eye – beyond the numerous display cases, there were crates and boxes piled up to the ceiling. There was an atmosphere about the place which demanded solemnity.

Crone touched Nat's arm, making him jump. 'This room was carved from the rock almost 800 years ago,' he said. 'And all those boxes have something incredible inside, something that very few people have ever seen.'

'Is there like . . . *dangerous* stuff?' asked Woody, looking at the nearest crate distrustfully.

'Is there like . . . *dead* stuff?' asked Nat, already knowing the answer and eyeing the vast space.

'Some of the relics you will see are *extremely* dangerous,' said Crone, serious now, 'and some are indeed dead, but not in the true sense of the word.'

'I was afraid of that,' sighed Nat, 'I can smell . . . eurgh . . . I can smell vampires.' He shivered, not with fright, but because it had got increasingly chilly since they had stopped moving. They followed Crone to a row of coffins, each lit from above by a single, eerie blue bulb.

Ohherewego, Woody two-wayed to Nat, *thisiswhereitgoesallscary.*

'A family of typical ancient vampires,' said Fish, briskly, leaning on the largest coffin. 'Commonly known as the undead, as you two know probably better than anyone else in the modern world. Our agents discovered them unliving in the basement of a butcher's shop in Hackney.'

Nat glanced at Woody, and could sense they were both feeling uncomfortable, because they could hear them. The vampires were still whispering inside their silver- and lead-lined coffins. Both boys realised the undead had heard them approach and could sense the wolf in their unseen visitors. Nat felt reassured by the massive chain and padlocks that secured them, knowing from past experience that he was safe from the bloodsuckers as long as no one fed them fresh blood to restore them fully to unlife again. But he couldn't stand the sound of their voices. He played a Lady Gaga 'earworm' in his head to block out their sly whisperings, and he could sense that Woody was as relieved as he was when Crone moved away.

True to his word, their boss showed them samples of the dreadful, the wondrous, the terrifying and the just plain weird. Like the restless, mummified feet of St Vitus, still dancing inside their box, which considering the gentleman had been dead for several hundred years was no mean feat, if you'll excuse the pun.

Not for the first time since all the craziness had begun, Nat felt increasingly unreal, as though all of this was happening to someone else. If anyone had told him a year ago that he would possess supernatural powers, be able to shape-shift into a large Wolven creature and be shown all of these astonishing international secrets he would never, *ever* have believed them. Woody was obviously beginning to enjoy himself, since he was venturing further away from Crone and Fish and sniffing out interesting artefacts for himself.

It would take us years to look in all these crates, Nat thought, as they walked through the avenues of boxes. Woody was slightly ahead of him now, but stopped abruptly in front of a smallish wooden box.

'What are those funny markings?' asked Woody.

Nat stared at the box and froze. It was about the same size and shape as one of his nan's hat boxes except that, as far as he knew, his nan didn't have the official insignia of the Nazi party stamped on the side of hers.

The hairs on the back of Woody's neck rose as though he could sense the power of the iconic shape.

'Those markings are called swastikas,' replied Quentin Crone. 'For centuries the swastika was a sacred symbol for many ancient religions, but unfortunately, since World War II, it will always be a reminder of terror and great suffering to the human race.'

Woody sniffed it gingerly, then pulled back quickly. 'Whatever's inside is alive,' he said. 'It . . . it sounds like hissing . . . like snakes.'

Nat saw Quentin Crone and Fish look at each other nervously.

'What's inside?' he asked softly.

'I'm afraid it's something rather terrible,' said Crone, apologetically. 'It's a head. The severed head of the Gorgon, Medusa.'

Nat went pale. 'And the noise Woody can hear is her hair. She has snakes for hair.'

Crone looked pleased. 'You know your Greek mythology, Nat, I'm impressed.'

Nat didn't let on that he had seen a rather good horror film about the Gorgon and actually had no idea it was a Greek myth. 'How come it's ended up here?' he asked.

'It was recovered from northern Germany after the war,' replied Crone. 'Heinrich Himmler, the second most powerful Nazi after Hitler, was said to have been awfully keen on the supernatural, especially if it could be used for evil.'

'Obviously, due to *NightShift's* strict health-and-safety guidelines, no one has actually ever opened the box,' explained Alex Fish, 'but it's been thoroughly scanned and tested.'

Woody cocked his head quizzically. 'Eurgh, snakes,' he muttered. 'Why does it have snakes for hair?'

'Apparently,' piped up Fish, 'Medusa was a real babe. Then she had a falling-out with someone called Athena who was jealous of her, and Athena gave her a reverse makeover – turned her hair into snakes and made her face really shockingly ugly.'

'So ugly,' continued Crone, 'that whoever gazes on the Gorgon is turned to stone.'

'So it wasn't a myth at all then,' said Woody, wrinkling his nose, 'it was true.'

'We thought the head was dormant,' said Crone, his brow creasing worriedly, 'but if you two can pick up some sign of activity, it sounds as though the snakes are still potent, even after all this time.'

An awful image had formed inside Nat's head of what might be going on inside that box and he didn't want it there at all. Suddenly, he felt really afraid. All this stuff buried down here for centuries was creepy. To start with, he had felt excited – privileged even – to be shown such amazing things. But some things should never be shared with anyone, and the Medusa with her snaky hair and shocking face ought to be destroyed.

For the first time in weeks Nat admitted to himself that he was missing his family. His parents, especially his mum, had been bitterly opposed to Nat and Woody having any further dealings with Quentin Crone and *NightShift*. In the end, they had been persuaded there was no choice. With more evil on the horizon thanks to Lucas Scale's devil dealings and the ever-increasing werewolf phenomenon, Nat and Woody's supernatural talents were more valuable than ever. Nat's parents were touring the country with *Carvers' Twilight Circus of Illusion* and he was relieved. Whenever they spoke on the phone, he never offered any information about his *NightShift* training and his parents never asked. It was better that way – what they didn't know wouldn't hurt them.

Nat's feeling of dread persisted long into the evening. Knowing all that stuff was stored below them was bound to be unsettling, but it wasn't just that making him so uncomfortable. He couldn't quite put his finger on it. When he managed to drift off (despite Woody's snoring) his sleep was thin and riddled with exhausting nightmares.

'Nat . . . hey, wake up!'

Someone was shaking him. Ugh, he felt terrible.

'Hey . . . you were dreaming,' said Woody, half amused, 'sounded like a bad 'un.'

Nat blinked, confused. 'Uh? Oh, God, yeah, it was. Nightmare.'

'Must have been,' yawned Woody, 'you were shrieking like a girl.'

Nat tried to remember what his dream had been about. He had been back at his grandparents' house in Temple Gurney, back in his old loft bedroom with its bookshelves and posters. Something in the room was making him feel disorientated and sick.

'Sorry,' he said. 'It was like I couldn't breathe.'

'You're lucky you haven't had any dreams about that Medusa,' said Woody. 'Every time I close my eyes, I can see it.'

'Thanks for waking me,' said Nat, suddenly very sleepy. 'G'night.'

'Night,' said Woody, softly, but Nat was already asleep.

CHAPTER 5
FIRST BLOOD

A few nights later, and under the cover of a shrouded moon, two dark figures stole across the ruined landscape of Helleborine Halt. One of them was looking forward to his first meal as a fully fledged werewolf. Josh Firkin, now covered in thick, light-brown fur, had the orange, fevered eyes of a hunter. He appeared nervous and over-excited, his lithe body twitching with unspent energy and youth. The other was Lucas Scale, a travesty of a wolf – a freakish horror.

Due to past, unwise experimentation, Scale had lost the ability to shift properly. Most of his life was spent as half-wolf, half-man. His orange eyes were often hidden by polarised glasses, his teeth pointed low to his chin and his awkward body shape, twisted and bow-legged, meant he needed a cane to help him walk. Changing shape gave him more strength, but although he succeeded in shifting from two legs to four, he appeared as a stringy, mottley-fleshed horror and often walked upright, which just looked plain wrong.

It had been raining for most of the day and it felt unpleasantly humid in the East Wood. There was a bitter, rank smell, which rose like a particularly foul gas from the leaves that lay rotting on the woodland floor. Lucas Scale ran with a weird, listing gait thanks to his bandy legs, but Josh Firkin, wild with the woodland sounds of scurrying creatures in the undergrowth, dashed ahead howling joyfully. Scale could feel his belly rumbling and gobbets of drool streamed from his mouth as he imagined the hot blood of his intended prey. He had three tricks planned tonight, partly for training and partly for sheer demonic entertainment, and each one was more ambitious and daring than the last.

Josh Firkin waited for his master, his nostrils flickering in and out, crazy with hunger and excitement.

Scale was thrilled by the youngster's enthusiasm, but he would need to keep Josh fairly calm and sane for the later stages of his plan, so he decided to check he still had control over him. He purred a few silky words into his ear and Josh's eyes dimmed till he was slightly less eager to rip everything to shreds. As for Lucas Scale, he was panting with anticipation. His first marvellous trick was bound to lure Nat Carver and his white pal back to Temple Gurney.

As they emerged from the wood, Scale led Josh to a smallholding owned by a man named Herb Goodwill. Herb's paddocks were home to his expensive collection of rare breeds of sheep – some of them a gift from the Prince of Wales himself. A superb location in Scale's opinion and, what's more, a convenient stone's throw away from Temple Gurney Primary School, which made it just about perfect.

The poor sheep didn't stand a chance. In a frenzy of greed, the werewolves dispatched the entire lot. What they didn't eat, they lobbed over the boundary wall, so parts of the animals decorated the alleyway leading to the primary school with gory ribbons.

'This'll be an interesting talking point in the little darlings' assembly tomorrow,' muttered Scale through a mouthful of nails, as he hammered the severed head of a ram to the wall below the school clock. It was just after three o'clock in the morning.

Josh Firkin's senses didn't know what had hit them. The second place Scale had brought him to that night was a large country estate in the East Valley, overlooking the Bristol Channel. All Josh was aware of was the wonderfully exotic smell, tainted by an overpowering stink of cat urine. He followed Scale eagerly, negotiating with ease the high walls guarding the estate.

Lucas Scale willed his new recruit to stay calm. It was imperative Josh didn't go mad and cause a situation that might lead to irreparable damage. After all, it wasn't stupid sheep they were dealing with here. On cue, two smaller, dark shapes came hurtling out of nowhere. Guard dogs!

The two Dobermans stood about as much chance as the sheep had. Not used to being the underdogs, they realised too late that they were outclassed by the werewolves, and pure shock passed between them as Scale and Josh, now working as a team, flashed their teeth. One managed to scoot out of the way and run screaming in the opposite direction, but the other made a fatal mistake. It skidded on the wet grass straight into Lucas Scale's jaws.

With the coast clear, Scale took Josh around the back of the farmhouse and out towards the orchards. Scale was highly respectful of the animals he planned to use for his next outrage. He cocked his awful head to one side and grinned horribly, his fangs glinting in the weak moonlight. He could hear the low growls of the animals inside as they too sensed something was . . . *different*.

They were part of a private collection that belonged (although not for much longer) to a crusty old retired rock star. Scale had done his homework well. Earlier he had tripped the alarms and disabled the security lights by biting through the connections. He had received a hefty electric shock and scorched his mouth quite badly, but a fried tongue was a small price to pay for success. Inside the ornate building were four white tigers ranging from 400lbs to almost 1000. In fact, if Scale were to stand beside them – not that he had any intention of doing so – he would have looked like a kitten, albeit a very ugly one. Letting them out would be easy. To avoid being their first victim, Scale intended to lay down plenty of fresh meat for the tigers to munch on. He felt entirely on top of the situation.

'Ooooooooooh oooh ooh ooh ooh!! Ah ah ah ah ah!! OOOh OOOOh OOOh!! WEEEEEEEEEEEE!!'

Scale nearly had an accident of the sudden toilet kind. What in the world was that hellacious noise? It sounded like a cross between the world's loudest vuvuzela and a colony of rabid elephant seals. His head snapped back at Josh, whose wolfish face looked equally horrified.

The racket carried on. 'OOOh OOOOh OOOh!! WEEEEEEEEEEE!!'

It was relentless. Then he relaxed. If he had been in human form he would have laughed. *Of course!*

He slunk as smooth as oil to the source of the noise, with Josh following at his heels. Housed in a large enclosure were six creatures, almost as large as infant humans. They had sensed the intruders and were shrieking like banshees. Baboons. Lucas Scale circled the enclosure, fixing them with his molten eyes. Josh watched in wary admiration as the baboons abruptly stopped their unholy screeching. Seconds later, they were curled up together in a large heap of monkey limbs and tails, fast asleep. Scale gave himself a mental pat on the back, and went back to the matter in hand.

The smell of wee increased, making Josh's eyes water as they got nearer the big cats. At first when their cage door swung open, the tigers were confused, but soon the scent of the bait made them forget everything else. The enormous male tiger flicked his tail and growled, revealing powerful teeth. Then they all fell on the meat. Scale was beside himself with excitement.

When they're hungry again they'll seek their own prey,

he thought to himself, as he told Josh to follow him. He wondered idly if the townsfolk of Temple Gurney were good at running away really, *really* fast.

Josh Firkin showed no signs of tiring and Scale was glad. The hardest task lay before them, and Scale was a little nervous about it.

Their final port of call that night was St Myrddin's church, which lay at the crossroads between Temple Gurney and Temple Cross. Scale climbed clumsily over the ancient wall surrounding the churchyard, and Josh went after him, sniffing the air with disappointment.

All the new werewolf could smell were the remains of the dead, and he wondered why he had been brought to this old bone-yard. He watched inquisitively as Lucas Scale fished out a small cloth bag tied at the neck with green string. Scale fumbled at the string with his gnarly old paws and Josh waited impatiently as he sprinkled a dark powder on some of the newer graves. There was something weird about the powder; it was blacker than anything Josh had ever seen, and when it fell onto the graves, it looked as though the earth was sucking it in greedily. Then, when the bag was empty, his master melted into the shadows once more, and Josh followed like a faithful puppy.

CHAPTER 6
I SEE DEAD PEOPLE

'I see dead people,' said Joe Wedlock gloomily.

His daughter looked up from her Marmite toast in surprise. 'I know, Dad,' she said. 'That's because you're a funeral director.'

'I don't mean *that*,' said Joe, morosely. 'I buries 'em and then . . . I sees 'em up and about again.'

Twelve-year-old Harmony Wedlock stared at her dad. 'You mean . . . ?'

Joe nodded. 'I saw Mrs Brimble last night. Just a glimpse like, but I could tell it was her.'

'How?' asked Harmony, her blue eyes wide.

'Because,' said Joe patiently, 'she had that blinkin' awful red hat on, the one she used to wear on Sundays.'

'Hang on a mo,' said Harmony, 'was this after you left the Slaughtered Sheep, or before?'

'After,' admitted Joe, uncomfortably, 'but there's no mistaking that red hat. It was her all right.'

'But,' protested Harmony, 'wasn't Mrs Brimble's funeral before Christmas?'

Her father nodded grimly. 'Ar. But I reckon since we had so much snow and ice, she's proberly only just thawed out.'

Father and daughter looked at each other across the breakfast table in dismay.

Harmony bit her lip. 'Dead people don't usually get up and walk about, not even in Temple Gurney . . . unless . . .'

Her dad shook his head miserably. 'She wasn't the only one I saw.'

Harmony reached across and felt his forehead. 'Hmmm . . . I don't think you've got a temperature.'

'I saw Mrs Wring,' said Joe stubbornly, 'and Miss Bessant who used to run the post office. I think we'd better let Bill Beechgood know. Looks like it could be vampires at work again.'

'Sounds more like zombies,' sighed Harmony. 'Pass the juice, please, Dad.'

Herb Goodwill hadn't been so outraged since the government had proposed a ten per cent tax on cider. During the night, something had massacred every single one of his rare sheep. There were bits of sheep strewn across the path, blood and innards dripping down the walls and off the fence. The attacks on the sheep had been savage: their heads had been bitten or in some cases chewed off and placed deliberately (almost artistically) up and down the path. Herb thought it looked like something that weirdo artist Damian Hirst would have been proud of.

Miss Boo (short for Boudicea) Sedgemoor, the headteacher at Temple Gurney Primary School, had dealt with the incident in the same calm way she always dealt with the unexpected, and marshalled the children through the carnage, taking care not to get any blood on her new suede shoes. She was a tall woman, with tiny, dolphin-like teeth and unfortunate two-toned hair that looked as though a large bird had dropped a poo on it.

'That's right, children, be *brave*,' she trilled. 'Careful, Adam. Don't walk in the . . . oh! Too late, darling. It'll wash off. Oh, Sebastian! Matthew . . . don't . . . don't *touch* it . . . !'

How proud she was of her small charges as they walked in single file, clutching their lunch boxes and singing the school song in high (but slightly shaky) piping voices.

'Of course,' she reported to Bill Beechgood as he helped her remove the grisly head of the ram from beneath the clock, 'my children aren't just *any* children. These are Temple Gurney children.'

Sergeant Bill Beechgood hadn't been altogether surprised when things started to kick off again. He had been born in the little cottage he still lived in, and although he was an extremely efficient police officer he had refused promotion so he could keep watch over the townspeople of Temple Gurney, most of whom he had known all his life. Like many residents of the unusual little town, he had been born with a sort of sixth sense – a heightened awareness of VERY BAD THINGS – because, as he knew, there were many bad things that happened in the world, especially nowadays.

When Miss Boo had telephoned him, he had known straight away what he was dealing with. There were no SOCOs (Scenes of Crime Officers) – or CSIs if you're American – no yellow-and-black police tape, no backup. There was diddly squat. Just Bill Beechgood and his constable, who would have to learn not to puke if he was going to stay on *this* beat. *What*, thought Bill Beechgood, *would be the point*? He knew ruddy well who had done this. And there was only one person in Temple Gurney with whom he could share the news, the rest were in London. At *Night-Shift*.

While Sergeant Beechgood was on the phone having a lengthy conversation with Quentin Crone, Tom Davis, the landlord of the Slaughtered Sheep, was getting ready to open up for lunch.

Since his son Teddy had disappeared, Tom had run his pub with a heavy heart. Sure, Teddy had been unruly and mouthy. Some would have said he was prime prison material and Tom, in his more sober moments, would probably have agreed. But Teddy was his son, and he hadn't laid eyes on him for almost a year. With his wife gone too, it was all Tom could do to carry on running the pub, for it had been a hard winter and many of his old customers had moved away. Temple Gurney was almost a ghost town these days. He still had a few punters, although he wasn't getting many through the doors after dark.

He was just emptying some change into the till, when an unexpected THUMP made him look up. The thump had been loud, and it had come, so far as Tom could make out, from the locked door. Then there was another THUD and Tom grinned slightly.

'All right, Skinner,' he called. 'Hold your horses.

You're five minutes early.'

Then – and you'll know this noise if you have a cat – there was a curious, scratchy, pishy-pashy sound as though enormous paws were sliding and kneading at the wooden door, trying to get in. Tom Davis frowned and stopped what he was doing. The noise stopped. He glanced at the clock. There was another THUD and lots of scuffling as though Skinner had been joined by a few of his cronies, keen to have a jar or two.

'All right, all right,' he said, as he opened up the counter hatch. 'I'm here now.'

Tom Davis disabled the alarm and pulled back the locks. It was a shame really that Lucas Scale wasn't there to see the look of sheer disbelief on the landlord's jowly face. But disbelief gave way to terror when the tiger, which was very hungry (and slightly bewildered), sprang at him with only one thing on its mind.

At just past midnight, Harmony Wedlock got out of bed to open her window. What she saw gathered in the front garden knocked the wind out of her. Standing silently, looking up at her, were the reanimated dead of Temple Gurney.

There were about twenty of them (some well past their sell-by date from the look of them). Among them were Mrs Brimble, complete with hideous red hat, and Junie Wring, who had babysat regularly for Harmony and used to plait her hair and give her hot Ribena before bed. Harmony had loved her and cried for days when she died. But now Junie Wring was staring hungrily at Harmony, as though she would like to eat her up. Miss Bessant from the Post Office was there too, and although when alive she wouldn't say boo to a goose, she stared back through the same dead, hungry eyes as all the others gathered on the Wedlocks' front lawn.

Harmony thought the worst thing – the creepiest thing – was the way they all stood there. Not moving, just looking. She shut the window carefully and yelled for the only person you can in these situations: 'DAAAAAAAAAAD!'

CHAPTER 7
TWISTED FIRE STARTER

'*If you go down to the woods today, you're sure of a big surprise,*' sang Lucas Scale in a surprisingly good tenor. Even so, hearing it blast through the underground chambers of their new property about two hundred times was enough for anyone and Josh Firkin kept his head buried under his pillow, trying unsuccessfully to block it out.

Scale felt as pleased as a pig partying in a pool of particularly pongy poo. He knew that having set various cogs in motion, Temple Gurney was on the edge of chaos, and pretty soon all his preparation and hard work would pay off. He also knew that before too long Helleborine Halt would be searched again by men in suits from Whitehall. But there are many and varied underground places for a wolf to hide, and Scale had struck gold in the form of a disused underground reservoir.

During the past few days he had been particularly busy restoring communications to the outside world. Opportunities for recruiting more werewolves were surprisingly low in Temple Gurney – only the families who had been born and bred there had stayed since the rumours about the Proteus affair began. And they had kept their doors barred and rarely ventured out after dark. But Scale had managed to track down some of the rogue werewolves he had recruited in the past, and with a little hypnosis they had been more than happy to join him in the underground reservoir.

He was ahead of his agenda and one step nearer to luring the Wolven brats back to Temple Gurney. The only thing he hadn't done was to start the search for the Baphomet. The demon had projected an image of the relic for Scale to memorise, and although Scale had once seen a dusty old drawing of it and was used to the grisly, the revolting and the terrible, he had recognised the Baphomet Head as something that was the very epitome of evil.

But before he carried out the demon's orders, there was something else that needed to be done, and this he would do alone, without the assistance of Josh Firkin. It was something personal, private. Scale was going to barbecue Nat Carver's grandparents.

Above him the moon was a vague, misty disc, but Scale's supernaturally enhanced eyes enabled him to pick his way through the trees to a small clearing. His car, a nondescript model of indeterminate colour, was hidden in a tumbledown building. Scale felt happier than he had for weeks and regretted he was no longer able to whistle a tune. His wolf mouth was entirely the wrong shape for that, or to pucker up for a kiss – not, he considered wistfully, that anyone would want to kiss him. But damn, he felt good.

Earlier he had made Josh break into a farm building and steal two cans of petrol. Now he loaded them, along with dry bracken and branches from the woods, into the boot then loped bandily around to the driver's seat, banging the door shut behind him.

'AAAAARGH!' Bellowing loudly, he flung open the door in agony, tears of pain spurting hotly from his orange eyes. He'd absent-mindedly trapped his flattened tail in the car door and crushed it again. Still whimpering, he started the engine, his good mood not quite so good anymore.

He drove haphazardly through the fog without headlights, relying on his special sight, along the rough track towards Temple Gurney. As he had hoped, there were no other cars about. His target was the second cottage on the left in Camellia Lane and he was delighted to see there was no light inside, which must mean they were in bed. With the moon hidden behind clouds, the front garden of 11 Camellia Lane was in shadow and Scale stole up the path. The gate shut behind him with a loud clunk and he stopped abruptly, but when no one appeared he relaxed and crept closer to the house. Opening the petrol cans made his nostrils flare in protest, but nothing was going to stop him now.

Working quickly, Scale splashed petrol around the wooden window frames. To be extra sure that no one could leave the house, he piled the bracken and wood at the base of both the back door and the front entrance. When he had finished, he inspected his handiwork and was pleased to see how thorough he had been, despite his haste. He didn't like to admit it to himself, but he was scared of the Carver boy's grandmother. She had got the better of him more than once, and he had no wish to see the old witch ever again.

He jabbed at his pockets with a paw-like hand then cursed up a storm. He had forgotten to bring a box of matches.

Scale was still trying to calm himself when he heard a clicking noise behind him. He spun round in alarm. All he could see was the blue and yellow flame of a lighter getting closer to his face, and he felt some of his fur singe.

'Allow me.'

The lighter clicked shut and an after-image flickered in Scale's eyes for a second.

'Here.' The lighter was pressed into Scale's hairy hand. 'Keep it.'

Recognition dawned on Scale's raddled features. 'I know you,' he growled.

'You should do,' said Teddy Davis, white teeth shining in the moonlight. 'You *made* me.'

They watched the house burn together.

Back in Middle Temple Lane, Nat Carver was having another vivid nightmare about his grandparents' house in Temple Gurney. It should have been a comforting dream – he had loved his old bedroom in the attic of Camellia Lane. In the dream he could make out his *Doctor Who* posters and the bookshelves that Granddad Mick had made. But somewhere at the back of his consciousness he was aware that recurring dreams – in his case anyway – were usually a warning.

His head ached and his throat felt dry and

scratchy, his eyes were sore and it was so hot. This was the part of the nightmare where he would get out of his dream bed and bang his head on the dream shelves. But there was something else happening tonight – there were tendrils of smoke curling under his bedroom door like ghostly fingers.

These aren't nightmares, thought Nat as he ran over to the window. *It's really happening!*

CHAPTER 8
IONA DE GOURNEY

Nat half ran, half fell into Woody's room.
Woody glanced up in surprise at the sweaty,
wild-haired boy in front of him. 'Where's the fire?'
asked Woody. Then he saw the expression on Nat's
face.

'What's wrong?'

'That's just it,' cried Nat. 'There *is* a fire! I've just
seen it. It's—'

'Slow down,' soothed Woody, 'take a breath and
tell me what's going on.'

'It's my nan and granddad,' said Nat. 'I . . . I think they're *dead*.'

When Nat and Woody burst into Quentin Crone's office, he was already taking a phone call from the crime scene. Crone's complexion was an unhealthy grey as he listened to Bill Beechgood, and the boys stood waiting in agonised silence, their hands shaking. When Crone finally put the phone down, Nat thought he was going to be sick.

'I don't know how much you two have sensed, but Sergeant Beechgood can confirm that no human remains were found at Camellia Lane,' said Crone.

Nat felt his legs buckle under him. 'Is he *sure*?' he asked.

'Positive,' said Crone firmly. 'What's more, Iona de Gourney has confirmed that Apple and Mick were nowhere near their house when the fire was started.'

Seeing Nat's stricken face, Crone put his arm round him, drawing Woody close at the same time. The boys clung to him gratefully.

Oh lord, thought Crone. It was at times like this that he struggled with his conscience. It was, after all, because of him that Nat and Woody continued to be in danger from malignant forces. It was he, Quentin Crone, who had been responsible for them joining *NightShift*.

'Was it deliberate?' asked Nat, blowing his nose.

Crone nodded. 'I'm afraid it seems that way.'

'Nan was always scared that Scale would do something like this, and now he has,' said Nat bitterly. 'They should have moved away, I should've insisted.'

'It wasn't your responsibility,' said Crone. 'Anyway, we don't know if it *was* Scale yet.'

'Who else would do something as . . . as *horrible* as that?' growled Woody.

'It *was* him,' said Nat, dully. 'It's like he's haunting me. He's always at the back of my mind, always in my nightmares.'

'He wants you,' said Woody. 'He's doing this stuff 'cos he's trying to lure you back home to Temple Gurney.'

'I think he wants us *both*,' said Nat. 'But even if you don't come with me, I've got to go. I've got to make sure Nan and Granddad are safe.'

'Whoa! Let's just see how things develop,' said Crone. 'It may be rather soon—'

'If Nat goes, I'm going too,' vowed Woody.

After a miserable lunch, Quentin Crone received the news he had been waiting for. A coded telephone call confirmed Nat's fears: Scale had been responsible for the fire.

Crone slipped quietly from the offices to keep an

appointment with a valuable friend to *NightShift*: Lady Iona de Gourney. It took him just a few minutes to reach his destination and, as he walked, he was hoping that the Temple Church would be quiet at this time of day.

He was pleased to see only a handful of tourists inside and, as always, Crone's mood was lifted a little by the beauty and calm inside the church. No matter if it was cloudy outside, the ancient interior always appeared to glow with an unearthly, soft radiance. Today especially, Crone was struck by the quality of the light and, despite himself, he felt a shiver of excitement. The atmosphere seemed to thrum with the spirits of the long-dead Knights Templar – the legendary warrior monks of medieval times who designed and built this church. Quentin Crone was not a particularly fanciful man, but as he gazed around the circular building he could have sworn their power was seeping into his bones.

He spotted her easily. Iona was standing apart from the other visitors, apparently contemplating the effigies of the Templar Knights who lay frozen in stone at her feet.

When he approached her, she looked up at him, her face shining in the golden light of the church.

'Iona,' he said softly.

'I was just thinking how beautiful these are,' said

Lady Iona de Gourney, gesturing to the stone knights. 'They always look to me as though they're going to spring into action.'

Quentin Crone seemed solemn, despite his pleasure at seeing Iona again. 'Yes,' he agreed, kissing her lightly on the cheek, 'it does rather look as though they're waiting for the call to arms.'

'For the final battle,' said Iona. 'Is that why you called me?'

Crone nodded. 'I need your help.'

Iona saw something like desperation in Crone's eyes and was fearful. Anyone who cared to glance their way would have seen a handsome, slightly stooped man in a well-cut suit in earnest conversation with a woman who looked as though she had stepped out of a storybook or off the set of an historical film.

'You said on the phone that Nat had a premonition about the fire?' asked Iona.

Crone nodded. 'He dreamt he was back at Mick and Apple's house in Camellia Lane. His bedroom was ablaze.'

Iona grimaced. 'Poor Nat, what a burden he carries.'

'He's seen Scale too,' said Crone. 'Some sort of astral projection.'

'A trick he learned from his demon no doubt,' shivered Iona. 'Lucas Scale is killing Temple Gurney. It's a ghost town. People are leaving in droves, and at night . . . at night across the valley, I can hear howls again.'

Crone sighed, long and hard. 'Lucas Scale started the fire. He did it to lure Nat and Woody back to Temple Gurney.'

Iona frowned. 'You *know* it was Scale? I mean, it's just the sort of dreadful thing he would do, but did Nat have a vision of him?'

'I know it was Scale who set the fire,' said Crone, grimly, 'because Teddy Davis has just told me it was. He was with him when he did it.'

Iona made a choking noise. 'Well I guess that makes perfect sense,' she said. 'The last time I saw Teddy was when *West Country Round-Up* showed pictures of him on television. He was crying, if I remember rightly.'

'He's . . . er . . . he's working for me,' said Crone, sounding a tad sheepish.

'Teddy Davis is a *NightShift* agent?' blurted Iona loudly, then lowered her voice as she realised people were staring. 'I don't know if that's an awfully good idea, Quentin. Isn't he a bit hot-headed to be of any use to *NightShift?*'

'He was in the Special Forces for some months,' Crone assured her. 'Unfortunately he went AWOL because he didn't like getting up early. I tracked him down and he agreed to go undercover.'

Iona still looked doubtful. 'But if Teddy Davis can testify as to what Scale has done, why not send half-a-dozen *NightShift* agents to bring him to trial? Surely you have enough on him to destroy him? Teddy must know where he's holed up by now.'

'When you hear what he's already found out, you'll understand why,' said Crone. 'And . . . erm . . . Nat and Woody don't know about Teddy. Not yet, anyway.'

'You *must* tell them,' urged Iona, 'and sooner rather than later. They'll sense it before too long anyway.'

Quentin Crone rubbed his chin and sighed. 'I just thought it was better Nat didn't know, for the time being, that Teddy Davis stood by and watched Lucas Scale burn his grandparents' house down.'

'Even so, they need to know,' said Iona. 'I'll break it to Nat if you don't want to.'

Crone smiled at her and nodded gratefully. 'Teddy is in an extremely sensitive situation,' he said. 'He had to make it look good otherwise Scale might have been suspicious. He'll show no mercy if he finds out Teddy is an informer.'

Iona winced. 'I'll do anything to help, but just how bad is it?'

Crone looked uncomfortable. 'Just about as bad as it can get,' he told her. 'The intelligence I've just received from Teddy Davis is devastating. Lucas Scale isn't working alone any more. He's been busy making more wolves to help him in his bid for power. Even worse, instead of Scale losing his soul to the demon he conjured, he's done another deal with it. He's promised to find something for it – an ancient relic which will prove catastrophic to the survival of the human race. If Scale and his wolves find it, I need to take it away from him, to continue to guard it.'

Iona stared at him. 'But do Nat and Woody need to be involved? I thought you made a promise to Nat's mum and dad that he would never be put in danger again.'

'I did,' said Crone miserably. 'But this . . . this thing Scale is after will need supernatural skills to sniff it out. No one at *NightShift* is better equipped than Nat and Woody to find it. And I have to remind you that basically, apart from Teddy, they're all we've got!'

'So although Lucas Scale is aiding and abetting a demon, he still has his own agenda,' said Iona, almost as though she was talking to herself. 'He still wants his revenge on Nat and Woody, but he wants a piece of whatever action the demon is planning too. Do you know what this relic is?'

Crone glanced round to see if there was anyone nearby. 'It's been called many things but you will know it by the name the Templars gave it,' he replied in a low voice. 'The demon wants Scale to find the Baphomet Head.'

Iona gasped, her green eyes luminous. 'Then it's planning something unspeakable.'

Crone nodded. 'History proves that whenever an emissary from hell – like Scale's pet demon – stays on earth for any length of time, something terrible happens in the world: World War I, World War II, Kosovo, the Rwandan civil war, the invasion of Iraq, the list goes on and on.'

'But no one knows where the Baphomet is, or even if it still exists,' said Iona.

'According to Teddy, Scale already has some leads,' said Quentin Crone. 'And if the Baphomet Head does still exist, my job is to make sure that Nat and Woody find it before Lucas Scale does.'

Nat and Woody were over the moon to see Iona at the *NightShift* offices. Nat wasted no time in asking her about Apple and Mick.

'Where *are* they? Do my mum and dad know what's going on? Do they know where Granddad and—?'

'Don't worry,' soothed Iona, her lips twitching into a smile. 'As far as Apple and Mick are concerned, you mean *when* are they, not *where*.'

Nat gasped. 'They've *flipped*?'

Iona's eyes sparkled. 'They're currently on a Viking settlement, teaching irrigation and knitting. The year is around 1016. They're having a smashing time.'

'How do you *know*?' asked Nat, suspiciously. He'd had experience of flipping backwards and forwards in time and it didn't always go smoothly. Sometimes you flipped even if you flippin' well didn't want to, and sometimes it made you puke till you went blue.

'Oh, you know your nan,' said Iona vaguely, 'she can travel anywhere.'

'Well *no*, actually,' said Nat. 'I thought I did. But since all this Wolven stuff happened, I've been a bit busy. She's . . . she's always been kind of—'

'Magic,' smiled Iona. 'She's *magic,* your nan.'

Fish's beady eyes widened. 'Is she, like . . . a witch?' she asked, trying not to appear nosy. She'd heard a thing or two about Apple Smith.

'She's not like one,' said Iona, dryly, 'she is one.'

What a blumming family! thought Fish. *The grandmother's a witch; the grandson's a posh type of werewolf; both of 'em can travel in time. Whatever next?*

'They don't know about the fire then?' asked Nat.

Iona shook her head. 'No point in spoiling their break. They've been restless since you two have been gone. After all that's happened in Temple Gurney, so many of their friends have moved away.'

'So what exactly *has* been going on?' asked Nat, curious but a bit frightened at the same time. It was bound to be something bad.

'Chaos,' said Iona, simply. 'Bill Beechgood is pretty sure lycans are responsible for the massacre of Herb Goodwill's sheep, but we need your opinion and your Wolven skills to confirm it. As for the missing tigers, it's very likely they'll be hiding in the woods, and will stay well away from the town. Quentin has arranged for Bill to swing by tomorrow so you can do a little investigating. But . . .' she hesitated, 'there are worse things than dead sheep and escaped tigers.'

CHAPTER 9
STUFFED

**Temple Gurney
Welcome to our Town!
Please Honour our Wildlife**

The last time Nat had seen the sign welcoming visitors to Temple Gurney, someone had scrawled 'Twinned with the Moon' on it, in thick marker pen. Now the writing had almost vanished and there were just a few ghostly marks underneath.

It was a lovely day – the kind of day when you'd expect to hear the buzz of lawnmowers and to see people out and about enjoying the weather. But spring had been late this year, and Nat noticed there were none of the usual tubs of cheerful summer flowers lining the roads in welcome. It was as if no one had bothered, or maybe the plants were scared to show their heads above the safety of the soil. The only vehicles they passed were a couple of tractors and a removal lorry as yet another family left their home without looking back. As Iona drove through the streets, Nat thought he had never seen so many FOR SALE signs, and even the houses without signs had their windows boarded up to stop anyone (or anything) getting in.

The High Street looked shabby (no one had bothered with hanging baskets here either) and there were no tables and chairs outside the little bistros and cafes. Instead, there were posters with the black-and-white photographs of the latest batch of missing boys flapping lazily in the wind. There were no old men playing chess in the market place as there usually would be on such a warm day. Apart from a very odd-looking old lady in a hideous red hat, who lurched drunkenly along the pavement, the place was completely deserted.

At Temple Cross, there was a sign plastered across the door of the *Slaughtered Sheep* public house: CLOSED UNTIL FURTHER NOTICE.

Woody, a nervous traveller and a slave to sick bags, always felt marginally better when he travelled in human form. He'd been in the front passenger seat with his head out of the window all the way down the M4. When Iona's Mercedes reached the gates of Meade Lodge, he shifted, leaving a pile of empty clothes, and ran the rest of the way on four legs, hugely relieved to be out of the confines of the car, which in his opinion was the worst form of travel ever invented.

Fish, on the other hand, was enjoying herself. Nat had told her all about the first time he and Woody had met Iona, and now she was actually going to Lady de Gourney's house. It was the first time she had ever been inside the home of a sorceress and she was already madly impressed by Lady Iona's unusual sense of fashion – who'd have thought the medieval look would work so well? As she followed the Mercedes slowly up the winding drive to Meade Lodge, she was so excited she almost forgot to breathe.

'It's a *castle*!' she said to herself. 'It's got a blumming turret and everything!'

Inside, she was even more impressed. She followed Nat and Woody into Iona's enormous living room, which she supposed must have been a real banqueting hall in medieval times. There was a fireplace cut into the stone wall at the far end of the room, which was roughly the same size as Fish's entire apartment, and she could just imagine the lord of the manor feasting here, hundreds of years ago. The room was cool, but the air inside seemed spiked with an assortment of gorgeous summer smells: spicy ginger and turmeric, a whiff of lavender and jasmine, honeysuckle and passion flower. Hundreds, probably thousands, of books lined the walls on shelves that reached up to the ceiling. In the hearth, she spied two beautiful Siamese cats dozing.

Nat watched in amusement as Fish stroked the nearest one then pulled her hand back with an expression of puzzled distaste on her sharp little face.

'Eurgh,' she grunted under her breath.

'Stuffed,' grinned Nat. He had been caught out the same way on his first visit to Iona's house. Then his grin turned to dismay. *Hang on a minute, there was only one cat there before. That must mean . . .*

'It's Clawdia,' said Iona, gently. 'I'm sorry Nat, she *was* old. At least I was able to do her the honour of stuffing her myself.'

'Er . . . right,' said Nat, not sure how to react to that sort of information. But despite his sorrow at the little cat's death – Clawdia had been his constant companion during his recovery from Lucas Scale's near-fatal attack – he had to smile when he saw the horrified expression on Fish's face.

Later, after an enormous dinner of roast chicken

with sausage and onion stuffing, fresh green beans, crispy roast potatoes with rosemary and garlic, and mashed golden swede with butter and pepper, followed by a nice light rhubarb sorbet, even Nat and Woody were stuffed. They followed Iona into her garden where they sat under the pergola and watched her menagerie of rescued animals wandering in the late afternoon sun. Nat couldn't help noticing that despite the lack of flowers in the rest of Temple Gurney, Iona's garden was bursting with colour. There were some flowers he recognised, but some, he knew from experience, were not only from another world, but another time.

Alex Fish thought it was about time they discussed the plan.

'Before we left the *NightShift* HQ you said there were worse things than tigers,' she said to Iona. 'What did you mean exactly?'

Iona's face darkened. 'Five teenage boys have been reported missing over the past few months, which sounds to me like Scale's work – more lycans he's corrupted,' she said. She never called shape-shifters werewolves; she thought it wasn't politically correct. 'And there've been reports of people being terrorised by the deceased.'

'Zombies?' asked Fish, her beady eyes gleaming.

Iona frowned. 'I do hate that term. I'd much prefer

these unfortunates were called 'living impaired' or 'life challenged'. But yes, Scale's pet demon enabled him to raise the dead as well as the undead.'

'So the demon is part of this?' asked Fish.

'I'm afraid it is,' said Iona.

'Flippin' *Nora*,' shivered Nat. 'Anything else we should know about?'

Iona took a deep breath. 'You already know that the demon helped Scale to acquire certain skills like astral projection and possessing other people's minds and bodies?'

'Like he did with Crescent,' said Nat.

'And the eye,' added Woody. 'That was terrible. He used it to spy on us.'

'But we still beat the pants off him,' pointed out Fish, with a satisfied grin.

'But we knew he would come back again,' said Nat. 'He's never going to rest until he . . . until he's got rid of me.'

'And me,' said Woody, in a small voice.

Iona fiddled with her long curly hair. 'Unfortunately, it's not just Scale we're up against,' she said. 'He's in the middle of something huge.'

'Go on,' said Fish.

'Scale's not just out to get me and Woody, is he?' asked Nat.

Iona shook her head. 'We know he's planning to

help the demon with something so devastating it could – will – mean the End of Days, the end of the world as we know it.'

Alex Fish put her hand to her mouth in shock. 'Like the prophecy in the Bible?' she asked.

'Armageddon,' said Iona. 'Scale was just playing with us before. The double agent working for *Night-Shift* has intelligence that proves Scale is helping the demon bring about global annihilation—'

'Hang on a minute,' butted in Fish, 'who's this double agent? First I've heard of it.'

Iona hesitated. 'It's . . . it's someone Nat and Woody have had dealings with, someone Quentin has used to infiltrate Scale's den and report back with his findings.'

'Someone we know?' frowned Nat. 'But – oh no – you mean Teddy Davis, don't you?'

Iona nodded. 'He's supposed to be recruiting more werewolves as *NightShift* agents.'

'So what has *Agent* Davis found out so far?' asked Fish, scathingly. She didn't like the sound of Teddy Davis at all.

'As I was saying,' said Iona, patiently, 'Scale's demon needs something to act as a trigger for its global control plan. It needs Scale to find a powerful ancient artefact which has been missing for hundreds of years. You have to find it before Scale does.'

* * *

As the darkest hour fell on Temple Gurney, more dead rose from their graves. The remaining townsfolk lay in their beds with their doors double-locked and listened to the strange howls from the East Wood, which seemed to be getting louder and nearer every night. Nat Carver lay in his bed thinking about Teddy Davis. And Alex Fish sat by her window, deeply worried. This double-agent business was a surprise and why hadn't Crone told her? When Fish had called him he hadn't been available, as though he was avoiding her. She just hoped like mad the boss knew what he was doing.

CHAPTER 10

THE BOYS ARE BACK IN TOWN

Herbie Goodwill, no longer the proud owner of rare and expensive sheep, eyed Nat and Woody with undisguised suspicion. Nat couldn't really blame him. If they hadn't been accompanied by Sergeant Bill Beechgood, the farmer wouldn't have given them the time of day. He was a tall, sturdy man who smelt of hard work, ancient aftershave and Werther's Originals.

'Chuffin' 'eck, Bill,' grunted Herbie with a scowl, 'I've heard of work experience, but you'm 'avin a laugh.'

'These boys have had experience of this sort of thing,' said the policeman shortly.

The farmer glared at first Woody then Nat. Nat could read what he was thinking – *Noshoesscruffylittlebuggerswhatgoodaretheygonnabewasteofmytime* – and glanced across at Woody, who looked faintly amused.

'C'mon, then,' said Herbie and trudged across the paddock.

'All my sheep, gone, just like that,' he said almost to himself. 'I s'pose I just need some paperwork for the 'surance.'

Nat nudged Woody, who had his nose high in the hair to sniff the atmosphere, his nostrils flickering in and out at an alarming speed. Worst of all, his eyes were glowing slightly in the overcast light. Nat could tell by Herbie Goodwill's face that he had noticed too, and was thinking that Woody was a right weirdo.

Fish was following her own enquiries, but she had given them strict instructions on how to behave. 'Herbie Goodwill has no idea about *NightShift* and what we do,' she'd said. 'He thinks you're from Environmental Health. If either of you go Wolven, it'll freak him out and you'll have blown your cover.'

Nat nudged Woody again, this time more roughly, and gave him a look. It was too late, though. Herbie Goodwill had backed away slightly and moved closer to Sergeant Beechgood for reassurance.

Nat and Woody looked sadly at the empty paddock. Bill Beechgood had cleared away the sheep parts, but there were still splashes of dried blood everywhere you looked. Nat closed his eyes and tried to blank out the sounds around him. The day was fraught with noise. Whatever had killed the sheep had upset the birds and other animals on the farm, and there was unease everywhere.

'We need more hush,' said Bill. 'They're trying to find out what happened here.'

'I told you what happened,' said Herbie, angrily. 'They escaped tigers come and killed 'em.'

Nat and Woody had seen, heard and smelt all they needed.

'I just need to have a word with my . . . er . . . my associates,' said Sergeant Beechgood.

The farmer made a harrumphing noise as if to say *associates, my arse*, but there was something about the boys that made him feel less annoyed. The quiet way they had examined the blood and listened so carefully convinced him that maybe they were doing something useful after all.

'I just want my 'surance money, is all,' he repeated.

'Ar,' said Bill, 'you'll get it, don't worry.'

When they were safely out of the farmer's way, Bill asked the question.

'Tigers?'

'Nope,' said Woody, ''fraid not. Much worse. Scale, and at least one other.'

Bill Beechgood *was* afraid. He sighed. 'I just needed confirmation, like.' He thought about the dripping ram's head nailed under the school clock. 'It'd have to be a ruddy clever tiger to figure out how to use a hammer and nails.'

While Bill took yet another statement from Herb Goodwill, Nat and Woody were invited into the farmhouse for a cup of tea and a slice of cake. Herbie's mother, Mrs Nellynora Goodwill, was a very old lady, who smelt of root vegetables, horse liniment and Fixodent.

Nat felt her staring at him as he sipped his tea.

'You got the sight, don't you?' she blurted out, a tremor of excitement in her voice.

'Sorry?' asked Nat, blushing.

'Second sight,' said Mrs Goodwill, showing her false teeth. 'I got it, and my ol' dad had it too.'

'Er . . .' began Nat.

'Oh, don't 'ee worry,' said Mrs Goodwill, tapping the side of her nose with a grubby finger. 'Your secret's safe with me. And your friend's. What's his story?'

Nat and Woody looked at each other nervously.

Mrs Goodwill patted both their hands. 'There's summat wild about 'ee both,' she said looking from one to the other. 'I can't quite work it out yet, but while I do, I'd like to tell 'ee a story. It happened to my old dad, years ago now.'

Woody brightened. 'Oooh good, I love stories. Is it a ghost story?'

'No, Lord love 'ee!' cackled Nellynora. 'Much more interesting than a ghost story.'

Sensing their hunger, she cut them each another slice of cake and snorted with glee when Woody drooled on the table.

'It happened afore I was born, just after the Great War,' she said, settling back in her chair. 'In those days not many people had cars in Temple Gurney, and my dad was one of the first 'uns to have one. One moonless night, he was coming down the main road from Temple Cross when he knocked summat over in the road. Well, he got out of the car and there in the middle of the road was a lovely fat hare, she was a beauty – a white 'un, but she was all concussed like. You don't see too many hares nowadays, not white 'uns like that, anyways. Our dad picked 'un up and wrapped 'un in his shirt so he didn't get blood all over his nice seats and brought 'un back, thought it would do nicely for his tea.

'Well, when he gets 'un home, she were breathin''

and sittin' up blinkin' and lookin' as though she were gonna make it through. Our dad, he had a change of heart. He wrapped 'un up and put 'un in front of the fire and went up to bed. Next morning, he comes downstairs and you'll never guess what?'

'The hare had changed?' asked Woody, his eyes flashing topaz in excitement.

Nellynora Goodwill's bright button eyes gleamed back at him. 'Ar, she'd changed all right! Changed into a liddle girl.'

'What happened then?' asked Woody, still chomping on his cake.

'She disappeared,' said Mrs Goodwill, wistfully. 'He never saw 'un again. Except . . .'

''Cept what?' asked Woody, eyes agog.

Nellynora got up creakily from the table and hobbled across to the Welsh dresser. She picked up something and put it in front of Nat and Woody. It was a wooden hare, beautifully carved in ash and polished to a rich lustre.

'Years later,' went on Mrs Goodwill, 'when our dad retired, he found this on the doorstep.'

'It was like a thank-you!' breathed Woody. 'That's a brilliant story!'

Mrs Goodwill looked at them both with merry eyes, satisfied at Woody's approval. 'That what you two are then?' she asked mischievously. 'Shape-shifters?'

'Er . . . er. . .' stammered Woody.

'Oh, don't 'ee answer me if 'ee don't wanner,' smiled Mrs Goodwill. 'I've lived in Temple Gurney all my life an' I'm used to keepin' secrets.'

Nat and Woody smiled politely. They trusted this funny old lady, but neither of them knew what to say.

''Ee got the wolf in 'ee,' cackled Nellynora Goodwill, '*that's* what 'tis!'

Nat gulped. 'Well . . .'

'Oh, I wan't bein' rude,' said Nellynora hastily. 'Wolfs bin round these parts since – well – *forever*. You specially,' she pointed at Woody, 'reminds I of a young man who courted I when I were a girl. You got the same look as 'ee.'

Nat panicked. He two-wayed Woody: *donttellheranything*.

Woody's eyes shone. '*Really?*' he said. 'Where did he live?'

Whatpartofdonttellheranythingdidn'tyouunderstand? sent Nat, crossly.

'In the woods,' answered Nellynora Goodwill. 'There was a bunch of 'em – white 'uns.'

Woody gasped. 'Wolven!'

Nellynora nodded. 'Disappeared, all of 'em.'

'Do you know where they went?' asked Nat excitedly, not caring that they'd blown their cover.

'Them with babbies went far away – across the

Channel I think,' said Nellynora, her wizened face creasing even more with the effort of remembering. 'But the young 'un who courted I, he said he was off to London. I always regretted not goin'.'

'Oh,' said Woody, his eyes glowing, 'it sounds like a different clan.'

'See, I've kept that secret all my life,' said Nellynora, proudly, 'but I can tell 'ee, you'm like them, brave and special like. Think you can save Temple Gurney from all these bad things? That's what you'm here for, isn't it?'

Nat nodded. 'I don't suppose you've seen anyone that's er . . . died lately, have you?'

Nellynora Goodwill thought hard as she gummed her cake. 'I think I may have as it happens,' she said. 'Guinevere Brimble. She passed over just afore Christmas and I swear I seen 'un walkin' down the High Street the other day.'

'You're sure it was her?' asked Nat, feeling cold.

Mrs Goodwill nodded. 'Ar. Had this funny way of walkin – sort of like 'un was drunk. That and the red hat 'un always wears, no one else's got an atrocity like that hat.'

Nat and Woody looked at each other unhappily. It seemed Iona had been right. The 'living impaired' were on the rampage in Temple Gurney.

CHAPTER 11

THE SECRET OF THE BAPHOMET

Lucas Scale gave Teddy Davis a horribly toothy smile.

'Welcome to my new home,' he said. 'Allow me to introduce you to . . . ahem . . . I suppose you could call him your little brother.'

Josh Firkin looked up disinterestedly from his computer game and scowled at the tall, well-built young man with blond hair and polarised sunglasses. Josh still had a lot to learn about the werewolf condition, but he knew this stranger wore expensive shades to hide his fiery orange eyes. He scowled at Teddy Davis, and carried on playing.

'Yeah, nice to meet you, an' all,' growled Teddy.

Josh didn't bother to reply, he just lifted his lip in a snarl.

'Now boys, play nicely,' giggled Scale. 'And Josh, where are your manners? Hand Teddy a snack, there's a good lad.'

Josh put down his console reluctantly and picked something small and pink out of a glass dish from the table. 'Mouse?' he growled.

'Uh, sure,' said Teddy.

Ungraciously, Josh flicked him one and Teddy caught it deftly. His first thought was that it was a sugar mouse, but then it wriggled. He glanced at the dish. Inside squirmed dozens of naked, blind baby mice. Teddy swallowed a gulp.

'Go ahead, Master Davis,' purred Scale, 'fill your boots.'

Teddy groaned inwardly. If he ate this the odds were his belly would rebel, and if he puked it would look bad in front of Scale. Hiding his revulsion, he tossed it into his mouth and chewed.

Scale seemed satisfied and he and Josh greedily finished the rest of the dish. Teddy tried to block out the sound of the tiny bones being crunched, and concentrated on his surroundings, keen to feed back as much as he could to *NightShift*. He was shocked, but he couldn't help feeling impressed at the operation Scale had built in such a short time at the disused reservoir.

'Of course, staffing levels will have to improve,' said Scale. 'There's only eight of us here, and five of those are pups.'

'Pups?' asked Teddy, puzzled.

'New recruits,' said Lucas Scale, rubbing his paws together with glee. 'Josh has been a busy boy, although they're not quite house-trained yet.'

Teddy tried to look enthusiastic, but his heart sank. The youngster was clearly under Scale's spell. Teddy was very careful not to look straight into Lucas Scale's eyes; he had been drawn in by their hypnotic powers once before. Scale was making up for lost time, using Josh to hunt out and recruit new lycans. But he was right – he would need more if he wanted to be able to carry out his plans.

After Lucas Scale had shown off his new communications systems, he dropped a bombshell.

'Vis-à-vis the recruitment situation,' he said in a low voice, his orange eyes glinting wickedly, 'you, dear Teddy, will be in charge of the human resource programme.'

Teddy Davis nearly passed out on the spot. He knew exactly what Scale meant and he had no intention of turning anyone into a werewolf by biting them. He swallowed hard and pulled himself together, hoping that Scale hadn't noticed.

'Oh, right,' he said, trying to sound cool, 'great.'

'Of course,' said Scale, curling his lip, 'this wouldn't be necessary if someone had done their job properly in the first place . . .'

Oh, here we go, thought Teddy, rolling his eyes, as Scale went off on one of his bitter rants about the failings of the original Proteus project. '. . . *and* I would have had all the werewolves I needed by now, *and* they would have had the Wolven DNA. It's all down to Dr Gruber's inability to grasp the basic understanding of decent leadership.'

Oh, get over yourself, thought Teddy, *and what about the small matter of being totally outclassed by two kids?*

Scale shook himself like a dog, smoothing the fur that had tufted unflatteringly around his head.

'Sounds like you got it all under control,' said Teddy smarmily.

'Come and sit down, take the weight off,' purred Scale, pointing to an uncomfortable-looking chair. Teddy froze. All at once he was back in the place where he had first laid eyes on Scale, at the edge of the East Wood. Scale had known he would be there – had been waiting for him. And Teddy had fallen under his spell. That was the last time Teddy had been human. But Scale did appear to trust him. And he was obviously very pleased with himself at the moment. Teddy just had to hide how terrified he was.

'It's always a risk making a deal with a demon,' admitted Lucas Scale, 'but for me it's really paid off, I can thoroughly recommend it.'

'But, like . . . isn't the price you pay too expensive?' gulped Teddy. 'Even for you? You'll lose your soul.'

'Ah,' grinned Scale, 'that's where you're wrong. The demon *needs* me, in case you'd forgotten.'

'No, I hadn't forgotten,' said Teddy. 'What is it again? I mean, the thing it wants you to get hold of.'

'The artefact I told you about is an ancient relic,' said Scale, 'a relic which has certain demonic qualities itself. What we're looking for is the Head of the Baphomet.'

Teddy was still acting dumb to get more information. 'Sorry, yeah, I sort of remember. Who is he?'

'A very important demon, my dear,' purred Scale, rubbing his gnarly old paws together. 'The demon Baphomet was slain long, long ago in the Dark Ages, by a knight serving King Arthur. According to certain writings of the age, the head was severed from its body but still the two parts refused to die.'

'Ugh,' shuddered Teddy, 'sounds like a load of old cobblers if you ask me.'

Scale roared, making Josh drop his game and

Teddy break out in a cold sweat.

'But I didn't ask you, did I?' he raged, pushing his terrifying face close to Teddy's. 'Listen and you may learn something useful!'

Teddy cringed, but more from the unfortunate stink of Scale's breath than anything else.

'The knight, Caradoc, tried to destroy the parts by burning them,' continued Scale. 'But it was like a cockroach – whatever he tried to do, it was indestructible; it refused to die. So, Baphomet's body was buried, supposedly harmless without its Head, and the Head was put under lock and key and interred in the deepest vault at Bath Abbey. It was said that the Head of the Baphomet held so much power it could open the gates of hell and release Lucifer himself.'

'I s'pose that's why your demon wants it.' Teddy shuddered inwardly. 'But why can't it go itself?'

'Teddy, Teddy, *Teddy*,' sighed Scale, 'if only it were that simple. My demonic friend, whose name I'm afraid I cannot pronounce, is unable to exist for long periods outside the Hellmouth. That is one of the reasons the demon is so keen to acquire the relic – the Baphomet's Head has the power to make things more comfortable for the demon and its kind on earth.'

Well, that's great news. Not, thought Teddy.

'Anyway,' continued Scale, oblivious to the dismayed look on Teddy's face, 'the Baphomet's Head disappeared centuries ago from the abbey.'

'So it'll be like looking for a needle in a haystack?'

'Not quite,' said Scale. 'It seems the Head of the Baphomet turned up again like a bad penny in the thirteenth century. Apparently it had been in the possession of the Knights Templar. When the order of knights fell out of favour, one of the crimes they were accused of was worshipping an idol instead of God, and wouldn't you know, it turned out to be the Baphomet.'

'But it could be anywhere in the world,' protested Teddy. 'Where are we supposed to start?'

Scale grinned. 'It'll be fun,' he said, 'like a treasure hunt.'

'Yeah, but . . .' started Teddy weakly.

'Don't fret, boy,' said Scale. He shuffled over to the fax machine and retrieved a pile of papers, which he thrust into Teddy's hands.

Teddy read the fax header. 'It's from the Vatican.'

'Well done,' said Scale sarcastically. 'I take it you know what the Vatican is?'

Teddy glowered. 'Course I do. It's where the Pope lives.'

Scale snorted. 'The papers you hold in your hands are facsimiles of the confessions of the Knights Templar, just before they were burnt at the stake in the year thirteen hundred and seven,' he said, his eyes flashing feverishly. 'The document emerged a few years ago when it was found in the Vatican's secret archives.'

'Don't tell me you've got a mole on the inside of the *Vatican*?' marvelled Teddy, impressed despite the seriousness of the situation.

Scale ignored him. 'Luckily for me, this document holds the key to the whereabouts of the Baphomet Head.'

Teddy lifted the top page, and tried to hide a smirk. 'Speak Italian do you?'

Scale grabbed the pages and howled in ugly frustration. Teddy waited while he had another tantrum, then asked the obvious question.

'What does this Baphomet dude look like then?' asked Teddy.

'There are many different descriptions,' admitted Scale, still glowering at the foreign words on the pages, 'but many ancient writings describe it as half man, half goat, most people's understanding of Lucifer.'

'Nice,' winced Teddy. 'And this was what the Knights Templar were worshipping?'

Scale giggled creepily. 'They weren't worshipping it, my dear, they were guarding it.'

CHAPTER 12
BRAINS

Harmony Wedlock first spied the two boys from the window of her dad's funeral parlour: *Wedlock and Wedlock Funeral Directors Est. 1820 – No job too small.*

The Wedlock family had been caring for Temple Gurney's dead for almost two hundred years and Harmony had been looking forward to taking over from her father, Joe, when he retired, although she had to admit to herself it didn't seem likely now. She knew it was probably a bit weird to want to be a funeral director when she grew up – most of her friends wanted to win *Britain's Next Top Model* or *The X Factor* – but she thought that undertaking was a wonderful job, a privilege in fact. Her dad had taught her to respect the dead, to wash them and lay them out in their funeral clothes, clean and set their hair and put make-up on them; and she found it all quite good fun. Not in a disrespectful way, of course. Joe's professional pride was second to none and he liked his clients to look as good as – if not a whole lot better than – they had in life. But all that had changed; something had happened to make a mockery out of the whole procedure. The dead were not content to lie in their graves. Someone was operating them like puppets.

Harmony stood on tiptoe, trying to see where the two strange boys had gone. They must be out-of-towners, because she was sure she had never seen either of them before. They looked out of place, somehow, not quite of this world. One of them had longish white-blond hair and a kind of wild, out-of-doors look about him; the other was more serious-looking, taller, with black hair. Harmony estimated they were both around her age, and neither of them wore any shoes, which she thought was very odd indeed. She turned the sign on the door to read *Closed* and slipped out onto the now-deserted High Street.

* * *

Despite their Wolven skills, Nat and Woody were so deep in conversation that they had no idea they were being followed as they walked towards Camellia Lane. After lunch, they had left Iona and Fish in the library at Meade Lodge, searching through medieval documents for any clue that would help them locate the Head of the Baphomet. Meanwhile, Nat and Woody had been dispatched to the blackened site where Apple and Mick's cottage once stood.

Despite being prepared, Nat felt his breath hitch in his chest as they turned the corner into Camellia Lane. The scorched remains of number eleven stood out like an ugly black scar. All that was left was the shell. The once-lush, fluorescent grass and all his grandmother's carefully tended flowers were gone, and the stench of petrol was everywhere.

'Can you smell *him*?' asked Woody, his nostrils flaring out.

'Oh yeah,' said Nat, grimly. 'His stink is lurking behind the smell of petrol, but I can almost taste it. Scale was here, definitely.'

'Hey! D'you get that?' sniffed Woody. 'I'm gettin' a whiff of someone else, too. It's faint, but I've smelt it before.'

'Yeah,' said Nat, his face stricken, 'I can smell it too. I can smell Teddy Davis.'

Having followed the two boys at a safe distance, dipping behind abandoned vehicles now and then, Harmony watched from behind a postbox as they went through the gate of 11 Camellia Lane. A thought crossed her mind: perhaps they had started the fire.

She wondered whether she should go and fetch her dad, or Sergeant Beechgood, but decided against it. Her dad was making plans for the family to leave Temple Gurney and packing the stuff they would need for their stay at Cousin Sheila's. And Harmony was glad, because every night the dead came nearer, and she knew it wouldn't be long before the late Miss Bessant or the late Junie Wring came calling. She slipped from the safety of the postbox and froze.

Standing about two metres away, tail flicking lazily from side to side, was the biggest tiger she had ever seen in her life.

Harmony's intestines turned to ice. The tiger stared at her with unblinking yellow eyes, the pupils small pinpricks in the bright afternoon sun. Harmony hardly dared breathe. The tiger yawned widely, showing humongous white teeth. She risked a glance to her left then to her right, but in her terror, she wasn't able to think straight, let alone work out where she could run to. *Is it real?* she wondered. It reminded her of her favourite book of all time, *The Tiger Who Came to Tea*. Perhaps that was what it wanted. Harmony felt an inexplicable bubble of laughter rise in her throat. The tiger looked so out of place in Camellia Lane, she thought – hoped – it might be some sort of crazy mirage.

The tiger carried on staring. *Like it's got all the time in the world to mess with my head,* thought Harmony. She seemed to remember hearing somewhere that you weren't supposed to stare at dogs because it was a challenge to them and they didn't like it, but did that also apply to tigers? She didn't know, so she tried backing away. The tiger tossed its head and moved forward. Harmony stopped, not wanting to encourage it to get any closer. She was way too scared to cry, and even if she was able to get her mobile phone out of her pocket, nine times out of ten you couldn't get a decent signal in Temple Gurney. She wondered if there'd be enough of her left for her dad to bury if the tiger ate her; and that made her feel sorry for herself and reminded her of Mrs Brimble and co, and she began thinking how unfair it was for someone of her tender age to be stalked by zombies and then eaten by a flamin' tiger.

The tiger started to growl. Harmony felt the deep resonance vibrate in her chest. She didn't know how her legs were still holding her up, they were shaking so badly. When the tiger stepped forward again Harmony made the decision that saved her life. If she was going to die, she wasn't going quietly. No siree.

'Yaaaaaaaaaaaaaaaaaah!' she screamed, waving her arms like a demented windmill. 'Get lost you old tiger! Yeeeeeeeehaaaaaaaaaaaaa!'

The tiger tossed its head again and roared – not like a lion would roar, but in a series of short, shouty chuffs. It sounded to Harmony like it was trying to shout back.

'Yah! Go on, get outta here,' shouted Harmony, encouraged by the uncertain look on the tiger's face. Then she gasped in horror. It was getting ready to spring. It was over for her. She was cat food.

She closed her eyes, waiting for the tiger's teeth to latch on to her throat and bring her down, the way she'd seen them do to deer or zebras on the Discovery Channel. The growling had changed into a louder, rumbling, throaty sound that reminded Harmony of a jet engine.

Then she heard a voice shouting, 'Run!'

'Wha—?'

She snapped open her eyes, and for the second time that day she couldn't believe what she was seeing. The tiger was still there, but its attention wasn't focused on her any more. In the narrow lane there was another creature, and the tiger was starting to back away. Harmony had never seen anything like it, and judging by the expression on the tiger's face it hadn't either. *Oh, flamin' heck*, she thought, *what is going on?*

The creature baring sharp teeth at the tiger was like a wolf, but it was enormous – larger than any wolf she had ever seen in pictures. Its luxuriant white coat shimmered in the sunlight. To Harmony, now in deep shock, the wolf creature didn't look real.

It's beautiful, thought Harmony dreamily, *with gorgeous, strangely glowing eyes*. Then she had a horrid thought. *Has it really saved me, or does it just want to eat me itself?*

'Quick! Over here!'

Harmony snapped out of her thoughts and saw one of the boys she had been following. She had forgotten all about them. It was the dark-haired one, and he was waving to her impatiently from behind what was left of the garden wall.

'Come *on!* You haven't got all day.'

Harmony didn't know how she found the strength to move her legs, but one last look at the tiger gave her the kick up the pants she needed. She stumbled towards the boy, and he dragged her over the brick wall, grazing her legs as he did so.

'Thanks,' said Harmony, breathlessly. 'I thought I was a goner.'

The tiger didn't stick around for very long. There was something not quite right about this white creature and its strange smell, and it wasn't worth fighting it for the young human. After pulling back its lips and showing its teeth in an annoyed grimace, it finally turned tail. Woody watched in reluctant admiration as it sashayed back down Camellia Lane, refusing to run away.

When he was satisfied it had gone, Woody trotted back to Nat and the strange girl. He plonked himself down in the shade of the garden wall and rested his nose on his paws.

'Is . . . is it . . . is he some sort of lycan?' asked the girl, timidly.

'Yeah. Um, yeah he is,' answered Nat, taken off guard. 'But how do you know about lycans?'

'Duh,' said the girl, and grinned. 'I live in Temple Gurney.'

Nat grinned back. His human senses were jangling after the discovery that Scale hadn't been alone when he destroyed his grandparents' house, not to mention Woody's encounter with the tiger. But his Wolven senses were telling him this girl, whoever she was, was a friend. She knew stuff. She understood that things aren't always what they seem. At the same time, Nat realised he was tired of secrets and lying and covering things up. He smiled at her. She smelled of bubble gum, grass and pancakes, and had a snub nose, long, brown hair parted sensibly in the middle, and legs that were too skinny.

Nat held out his hand. 'I'm Nat Carver, and the one with the fur is called Woody.'

The girl's brown eyes widened slightly. 'I've heard of you,' she said, 'you're like a legend.'

Nat looked embarrassed.

'I'm Harmony Wedlock,' said Harmony, 'and I'm very pleased to meet you.' She pointed at Woody. 'Can I stroke him?'

'Be my guest,' said Nat with a laugh.

Two hours and forty minutes later, Harmony's head was reeling. The calm, blue-eyed kid didn't just have a shape-shifter for a sidekick. He'd also told her he was an agent for a weird organisation called *Night-Shift,* which according to him, hunted and removed malignant supernatural beings, like vampires and ghosts. So, while Woody dozed in the hot sun, she told Nat about the zombies, and then she admitted she'd been following them to Camellia Lane.

'You were *stalking* us?' said Nat, not knowing whether to be annoyed or not. 'What on earth for?'

Harmony blushed. 'Not exactly stalking. That makes me sound like a lunatic. But you're strangers, and in Temple Gurney, strangers usually mean trouble.'

'So, how long has all this zombie stuff been going on?' asked Nat.

'My dad saw the first one a few days ago.'

'Red hat? Funny, lurching walk?' asked Nat, arms outstretched, zombie style.

Harmony nodded. 'Ugh, that'll be Mrs Brimble,' she said, goosebumps breaking out on her arms and legs. 'How can something like this happen? It's horrible!'

Woody expressed his disgust by cracking open one topaz eye and showing his teeth.

'Sounds like magic, voodoo magic,' said Nat. 'These dead old-age pensioners have been brought back to life by a powerful magician or demon. It's just the sort of thing Lucas Scale might be involved in.'

'Who's he?'

Nat suddenly realised he'd been telling Harmony a great deal, possibly more than he should. 'You don't want to know,' he said.

'But the zombies don't do anything, they just sort of stand there,' said Harmony. 'Dad says if we close the curtains and ignore them, they'll get fed up and go away. And what I don't understand is, if this Lucas Scale person is behind it, what's the point?'

'It's just the sort of thing that appeals to his sick

sense of humour,' said Nat. 'He'll be able to control what's left of their brains and send them after the living.'

'So, it's not like a virus then?' asked Harmony. 'They can't make new zombies by biting people, can they, like vampires?'

'No, but they're kind of relentless. They might be slow, but they're really strong. You can't get rid of them easily. They've a nasty habit of reanimating themselves unless you destroy all their moving parts. They do have one thing in common with vamps, though – the daybreak can kill them. But if Scale makes them attack at night, you'd only be able to hold them off for so long.'

'And then what?' asked Harmony, half knowing the answer already.

'They'll want to eat your brains,' said Nat, dolefully.

Woody picked up a chilling mental vision of having his skull cracked open with a spoon, and a zombie pensioner dipping in its bread-and-butter soldiers as if his brain was a runny boiled egg. Harmony Wedlock stared in horror at Nat.

'They'll be back at midnight,' she said, her eyes suddenly filling with tears, 'but my dad refuses to leave until the weekend. He's burying his head in the sand. Please, *please* would you help us?'

CHAPTER 13
SALT

Following Nat's frantic call to Meade Lodge, Alex Fish arrived at the undertaker's with bin liners, balls of string, a few sacks of salt and at least ten pairs of industrial-strength rubber gloves. She was clearly on a mission to show off her legendary zombie-bashing skills and Nat was dismayed to see that her tendency to behave like a control freak was as strong as ever. Harmony and her parents couldn't take their eyes off her, and Nat and Woody had to admit that she looked fairly amazing, even for Fish. She was dressed in a shiny black catsuit, her spiky hair was gelled rigid and she had even swapped her specs for contact lenses.

Although Joe Wedlock seemed very impressed with Fish (Nat suspected her outfit had something to do with it) he was worried about her choice of weapons, or lack of them.

'Erm . . .' he began timidly, 'wouldn't some sort of gun be more useful than bin liners and string? Or an axe, maybe?'

Fish glanced at him. 'I've dealt with this kind of thing before, sir,' she said. 'I do know what I'm doing.'

Nat nodded reassuringly. 'She took down a bunch of zombies in Highgate Cemetery,' he said.

'Single-handed,' added Fish, trying to sound modest, but not quite pulling it off.

Lucas Scale had watched with interest when the earth had first spat out Temple Gurney's dead. At that point, as the demon had warned him, they had been confused and kept trying to go back into their coffins, which had kept Scale amused for some time. But dark magic will spread like the plague, and soon there had been enough reanimated dead to form organised groups.

The zombies had begun to get hungry. They hung

about on street corners and front gardens, staring greedily into houses. During the day, they hid in the East Wood where the cooler air slowed down their decomposition. It took Scale longer than he'd planned to figure out how to command them to break down the doors and get rid of the rest of the town's cretinous population but now, by Lucifer, he'd done it! He rocked in his chair, eyes at half mast, a trickle of drool dripping lazily down his shirt as he concentrated on leaving his earthly body.

The clock ticked steadily in the hall. Just before it struck eleven, Woody's hackles rose like a stiff fan, and he growled softly. Alex Fish crossed the kitchen floor and peeked through the blinds. She gasped. Standing silently on the Wedlock's front lawn was a crowd of dead people, their fevered eyes staring out from blackened, rotting sockets.

'OK,' said Fish, looking flustered for the first time. 'There's . . . there's a few more than I had anticipated.'

'Where d'you want these bin bags?' asked Nat.

'When they break through,' said Fish, 'which they will soon because they'll be starving, we're going to shove these over their heads. It disorientates them, and they're usually too stupid to figure out how to pull them off. We'll need more salt, though. I didn't bring nearly enough.'

'There's sacks of rock salt in the cellar,' offered Joe Wedlock. 'We use it for the pavements in the icy weather.'

'Brilliant,' said Fish. 'That should give us all we'll need, weapon-wise.'

She and Nat dragged the sacks up to the ground floor and shook great piles of salt across the floor, under the windows and inside the doors. By the time they had finished it looked as though there had been a heavy fall of snow. Then they gathered up all the coat hangers they could find, and hung yet more bags of salt from the ceilings.

Harmony said, 'I know what that's for. I saw a horror film where demonic entities couldn't get into someone's house because the salt was like a magic charm – it warded off evil.'

'Not quite,' said Fish, her eyes gleaming. 'Have you ever seen the effect salt has on slugs?'

'Eurgh,' said Harmony. 'Do you mean we're going to *melt* them?'

'That's the idea, dude,' said Fish, with a wink. 'Now, Nat. I need you to shift, like, asap.'

Whoa, wait a minute, thought Harmony. *What's this? Shift? Nat never mentioned he was a flipping shape-shifter as well. Things are getting wilder and wilder!*

*   *   *

Having gone upstairs to change in private, Nat pulled off his clothes and folded them neatly on top of the cistern in the bathroom, already concentrating on his shift. He stood for a while, trying to get into the zone, then balled his fists and squeezed his eyes shut, willing his body to change with all his might. *One, one thousand, two, one thousand*, he counted to himself. *Yeeeees! Here we go!*

He could feel his body temperature rising and his heart start to pump faster, getting ready to circulate the Wolven cells around his system. His face began to push out and shift into the shape of a canine muzzle. Pins and needles fizzed in his hands and feet, and then everything stopped abruptly.

Nat waited. And waited. Nothing was happening. *Uh oh*, he thought, *I could be in a lot of trouble.*

Woody heard it before everyone else: a low, groaning sound as if words were being formed inside the wind, despite the calm night. Then came a *KERAACK!* followed by the sound of the letterbox being forced open.

'Oh.My.God,' said Harmony Wedlock. 'They're breaking in!'

And that's when the lights went out.

While Lucas Scale's earthly body twitched and drooled in his favourite rocking chair, his astral body floated above the dark houses of Temple Gurney. If anyone had witnessed the phenomenon, they would have assumed they were seeing the ghost of a dead person, not the twisted spirit of a bad wolf. Scale noted with satisfaction that one of the tigers had made a den on top of the bus shelter by the Co-op. There was evidence of a bloody carcass lying half in and half out of the shelter, but regrettably he didn't have time to check whether the kill had been human or not. He was headed to the undertaker's to see the outcome of his marvellous zombie joke.

When the Wedlocks' house was plunged into darkness, Joe Wedlock and Harmony were standing in the hallway, bin bags poised, Woody was behind the front door and Alex Fish was worried. Nat had disappeared, presumably because his change was taking longer than he had anticipated. But she needed him now.

The front door was caving in under the weight of the zombies, and everything was going mental. As the lurching undead creatures spewed through the doorway like a dangerous dark tide, they brought with them a wet, yellow smell that seeped into everything they touched.

I thought zombies were supposed to be thick, Harmony thought, gagging as their stench hit her nostrils and trying desperately to make out what was happening. *But they can't be that stupid – somehow they've found a way to turn the power off. And what on earth am I supposed to do with this bin bag?*

As her eyes adjusted to the meagre light of the moon, she could see that some of the zombies were in a worse state than the newly buried. Their clothes were now little more than dirty rags, ruined by water and mud seeping into their coffins deep underground. Worms and earwigs had been busy, too, nibbling their flesh into strips that hung from their bodies.

Suddenly Harmony was grabbed from behind and pulled backwards by Fish, as the unlucky zombies in the front line hit the salt with their bare feet. They moaned and shrieked in hate and agony as the salt stuck to their damp, decomposing flesh, making nasty hissing sounds at it sucked the last of the moisture out of their bodies. Harmony watched in horror as they seemed to sag and melt from the feet upwards. The stinking viscous fluid that pooled around them glowed a bright green, and Harmony's world began to go grey.

'Don't just stand there!' yelled Fish, realising in dismay that she had greatly underestimated these pensioner zombies. 'They're everywhere, help me!'

With enormous difficulty, Harmony pulled herself

together, realising that for the second time that day her life was under threat. *It's like being in an X-Box game*, she thought to herself. She bit the inside of her cheek so hard it drew blood, but the pain helped her focus.

Agent Fish had produced an enormous knife from her belt and was slashing wildly at one of the bags hanging from the ceiling. Before a grain could be wasted, Harmony sprang forward and started guiding the stream of salt. Working together, Fish slashing and Harmony directing, they targeted a glistening waterfall on to the heads of the fallen zombies, shrivelling and melting their faces as if they'd been attacked with hydrochloric acid.

Harmony glimpsed a similar scene of team zombie-bashing through the kitchen doorway as her dad worked alongside Woody, who was knocking the zombies to the floor with his enormous paws, while Joe dragged them through the salt and shoved them roughly out of the back door. As she backed away from the writhing bodies in horror, Harmony was glad about one thing: the zombies no longer possessed any human traits at all. As she scanned the gooey, stinking mess on the hallway floor, she saw that even the faces of the zombies not affected by the salt were unrecognisable, their expressions no longer able to show any emotion except greed. Harmony scooped up handfuls of spilt salt, taking care to throw a pinch over her left shoulder for luck, and poured more onto their bodies, feeling terrible about their pain but at the same time wishing they would stop their unearthly wailing.

She felt a tap on her shoulder. Harmony spun round and screamed. She could just about make a red hat.

'*Brains*,' said Mrs Brimble in a gravelly, grating voice.

'Come on then, you, Mrs Brimble!' shouted Harmony, shrugging off the grasping hands of the late Guinevere Brimble. 'Come and have a go if you think you're hard enough!'

Mrs Brimble pulled her lips back in a terrifying grimace and her gums shone pinkly in the moonlight, like those of a newborn baby.

'Ha!' shouted Harmony. 'You've lost your choppers! Whatcha gonna do? *Gum* me to death?'

Mrs Brimble's toothless jaws were clamping together threateningly and she pounced on Harmony, her cold, stinking fingers like a vice around her neck. As Harmony fought for breath, Alex Fish grabbed a frying pan and smacked it around Mrs Brimble's head. There was a loud DONG! and Guinevere Brimble's hat flew off. Fish watched as the zombie pensioner lurched after her hat, temporarily forgetting all about Harmony.

Fish quickly assessed the situation. As far as she could see, the only place the pensioners had breached was the front door. Thanks to the salt on the floor, the first unwelcome visitors had been stopped in their tracks, while the others were injured wherever the salt from the ceiling had made contact with them. Fish was satisfied most would be melted in around thirty minutes.

A pair of slack-jawed zombies had climbed over the writhing bodies on the floor, escaping the salt, as Mrs Brimble had. They shuffled towards Fish and Harmony in the same lurching manner, their hands stretched out before them.

'*BRAAAAAINS!*' they screamed in unison, and Joe Wedlock appeared from the kitchen and realised with an awful sick dread that Harmony was trapped in the corner.

'Get off my land,' said Joe, half-heartedly.

'Brains?' said one, cocking its head to one side and licking what was left of its lips.

Not piggin' likely, thought Woody as he catapulted through the kitchen door, only to see Mr Wedlock leaning over his daughter, bravely trying to protect her from the pair of gnashing horrors. Woody took a flying leap and knocked the two zombies over. They landed heavily, and Woody noted with satisfaction that in the fall, various limbs had fallen off or were now hanging grotesquely from glistening threads of gristle. Harmony dumped half a bag of rock salt over their heads and the two unfortunate zombies melted into green goo.

It was then that Woody realised he hadn't seen Nat since he went upstairs to shift. Everything had happened so quickly in the chaotic darkness, and Woody had a sudden sick feeling in his innards that something bad had happened.

Whereareyou? he two-wayed. *AreyouOK?*

There was something wrong, but Woody was distracted by more zombies lurching through the hole where the front door had been. Before they knew what had hit them, Joe Wedlock had deftly shoved bin bags over their heads, spun them around dizzily as if playing a macabre game of Blind Man's Buff and doused them with salt.

When the last zombie had been salted, Alex Fish stepped over Mrs Brimble's red hat as it slithered in the mess of green slime and checked outside. She allowed herself a shaky sigh of relief. They had won!

Chapter 14
Shift Happens

As Nat Carver was experiencing his worst nightmare, Lucas Scale's body, still sitting in his rocking chair where he had left it, began to shiver and shake as though he was plugged into the electricity mains. His orange eyes rolled up in his head exposing the whites, his teeth became fixed in an awful grin. His astral self had suddenly been catapulted back to his earthly body just as things were starting to get interesting. And it wasn't a pleasant feeling. For a full ten minutes Scale's body shifted, popped and jerked, and for a finale, his nether regions let off clouds of noxious green gas that smelt like Brussels sprouts.

Bugger, Scale thought when he was able to sit still, *back too soon!* It would have been so good to see the outcome of his wonderful trick, but his body had been jerked back just as the zombie pensioners had bashed the Wedlocks' door in. At least he could be sure of one thing: come tomorrow morning, the squitty little Carver boy and his fluffy sidekick would be sticking their goody-two-shoes *NightShift* noses into the case of the dead undertaker and his family, and Scale and his werewolves would be lying in wait! He would have been as mad as a boiled owl if he'd known that Nat and Woody were already there. Unfortunately for Lucas Scale, he had an awful lot to be mad about that night, he just didn't know it yet.

Josh Firkin was fed up and bored with just his computer for company. It was hot in the underground reservoir, and as he paced his room an unbearable feeling of restlessness drove him to move faster and faster till he broke into an oily sweat. He started to bounce off the walls, hitting his shoulder hard as he propelled himself across the floor.

Yay, it's like a Haribo buzz! thought Josh, his blood fizzing and popping in his veins as his heart pumped faster, getting ready to be slugged with the sudden surge of adrenalin which would build up as his shift started.

His head jerked back and his eyes stared at the ceiling as they turned molten orange, his nose and mouth merged to make a snout, his muscles bulged and stretched and his body began to morph into a rather gangly young wolf. When his change was complete, he scrambled up through the skylight, out onto the top of the grassy roof, and set off for Temple Gurney.

As Josh loped towards the High Street, it suddenly struck him that part of the problem with being a creature of the night was that he still lived in the most boring town in England. Temple Gurney was the sort of backward place where people still pointed at aeroplanes. *It's like living in the armpit of the world,* he thought gloomily as he padded towards the derelict-looking High Street. As part of his ongoing lycan training, Scale had shown Josh how to scare the townsfolk by poking his head through their kitchen windows and giving them a quick flash of his teeth, but since there weren't that many people left to scare, even that had lost its novelty value. Privately, Josh thought that being a werewolf wasn't anything like Lucas Scale had cracked it up to be. In fact it was stupid and boring. He was being bossed about by Teddy Davis and he was bitterly disappointed by a lack of the action that Scale had promised him.

His train of thought was abruptly interrupted as his finely tuned wolf ears caught the sound of human shouts and a weird sort of humming noise travelling on the slight night breeze from the sea. He stopped dead in his tracks and turned his snout upwards to sniff the air. His flared nostrils picked up a cocktail of smells: the sulphur-like stink of ozone from nearby Diamond Bay and the unmistakeable pong of rotting flesh. *Dead people!* There was no other smell like it in the world.

Curious, Josh slunk towards the source of the noise, still sniffing excitedly at the charged air. As the unlovely smell of mould and old bones mingled with the pungent smells of the living, Josh broke into a run, keeping low to the ground and staying in the shadows so the humans couldn't spot him. He was surprised when he turned into the High Street and saw the mob of elderly people pushing and shoving, all trying to get inside a house. *Heeey! This is good,* thought Josh. *This is exciting!*

He crept, commando style, towards the source of the racket, his ears pricked in anticipation of some fun at last. Then he pounced, scattering the shambling zombie pensioners across the road just for the hell of it. They proved to be poor sport, too easy to catch and tasting ranker than a dead seagull. Josh watched them with dark glee as they lurched back through the gate, moaning and chuntering about brains.

When he got bored of the chasing game, Josh slipped like a dark shadow through the alley behind the house, keen to see who was making the row inside. He waited for a while, crouched beneath a back window, cringing back when the yard was suddenly flooded by electric light. His enhanced hearing could make out most of what was being said inside. There appeared to be a number of people present. But then he recognised a voice he used to know, and it made him remember what it had been like to be a human boy.

Alex Fish glanced at her watch. Melting the zombies had seemed to take hours and hours, but to her surprise, it had only taken about twenty minutes. Getting the power back on was easy enough – one of the old horrors had been canny enough to flick it off at the mains. But getting Harmony and her dad to recover from their ordeal would take considerably longer. Now that the excitement was over, Fish could see that both of them, and particularly Joe, looked as though they had aged twenty years in those twenty minutes. She doled out the rubber gloves and helped clear up the melted pensioners, shovelling the gloopy gunge into the bin bags and tying them with the string, ready to take down the tip. By the end of it, both Wedlocks were covered in gore and their faces were dazed and confused, while Fish, to her immense satisfaction, still managed to look as fresh as a black dahlia.

Nat steeled himself to look in the mirror.

OK, breathe, he told himself. He leaned on the sink for support, knowing that whatever he saw was going to be much worse than he suspected. He closed his eyes to mere slits to lessen the shock, but it didn't help.

At first he thought Lucas Scale had projected himself again, but then he realised the awful apparition staring back was himself. *He was a monster!*

'Oh . . . noooo . . . I can't . . . AAAAAAhhhhhhh- hoooooooooowwwwwww!'

As soon as Woody heard Nat's anguished cry, he sprang up the stairs and flung himself at the bathroom door. Locked! In panic and frustration, Woody morphed into human shape, not caring a fig about his nakedness even though he could hear Fish running up behind him.

'Nat, are you in there? Was that you?' shouted Fish, pushing past Woody and banging on the door.

'Let me in!' yelled Woody. 'Are you in trouble?'

'Yeah,' came Nat's voice, shakily, 'you could say that.'

It was Nat, but sort of not, thought Fish. He sounded shocked and scared. 'What's going on?' she asked, her voice sharper than she intended.

'I'm . . . I'm stuck.'

'You're *stuck*?' cried Fish. 'Open the door!'

'No,' came Nat's voice. 'Go away.'

He's crying, mouthed Fish to Woody.

'Aw c'mon Nat,' wheedled Woody. 'It happens to the best of us, used to happen to me all the time!'

'Still no,' came the voice from behind the door.

'Nat, I need a towel or somethin',' said Woody desperately. 'I'm naked in front of Fish.'

There were a few moments of silence, before the bathroom door opened a tiny sliver. 'Just you,' came Nat's unsteady voice. 'Just you, Woody.'

When Woody slid through the door, Nat was staring at him with bright topaz eyes.

'Well,' said Nat, 'have you ever looked like this?'

Woody struggled hard not to show his friend how shocked he was by his appearance. Nat's features were stretched halfway between man and beast. His head had been pulled badly out of shape – his forehead was low like a wolf's – but the rest of his face was human shaped, which made him look oddly Neanderthal, and his ears were massive hairy objects which stuck out at odd angles. And then there was his mouth. It was too big for his boy-sized face and his teeth were elongated, ending in sharp points.

'Erm, it's not *that* bad actually,' lied Woody. 'I've seen worse.'

Nat took a deep breath. 'I'm sorry,' he said tiredly. 'I s'pose you can let Fish in, she's going to see me like this sooner or later.'

'You sure?' asked Woody, grabbing a towel and hastily tying it around his waist.

When Fish saw Nat she had braced herself for the worst. 'It's really not that bad,' she gushed. 'I bet it's just a temporary hiccup. After all, it's happened to Woody a couple of times!'

No one could accuse Alex Fish of being a cheerful person – she was way too cool to be jolly. But to Nat, who knew her very well, her fake, upbeat voice confirmed all his fears that he did indeed look like a horror-film extra.

'I feel terrible,' he said. 'My head feels like it's going to explode.'

'Nothing acts faster than Anadin,' said Woody helpfully, making Nat smile for the first time. Which was a mistake. The effect was devastating. Fish had seen some bad stuff in her time as a *NightShift* agent, but nothing had prepared her for the shock of seeing someone she counted as one of her best friends turn into a monster. She gasped and reeled away from him as though he had suddenly pulled a gun on her.

'Not that bad, eh?' said Nat, bitterly. 'I guess I know now what you really think.'

'Nat, I'm so sorry,' said Fish, feeling terrible, 'it's just that—'

'It's OK,' interrupted Nat. 'I need something for my headache.'

Fish put her hand on his arm and squeezed. 'What you need is Iona,' she said, firmly. 'And when we get back to Meade Lodge you'll be impressed with the progress Iona and I have made in the hunt for the Baphomet.'

CHAPTER 15
BITTEN

Just after Harmony's dad opened the kitchen window to let out the smell of evaporated zombies, Josh Firkin, nimble as a Slinky, poured himself through the tiny gap. Josh's keen nostrils picked up a smorgasbord of delights, and he was curious as to why he could smell humans *and* wolves. What was especially puzzling was that the wolf smell was different from anything he had smelt before. Josh was used to being around werewolves. After all he lived with several others, including that ultimate stinker Lucas

Scale. But the smell he was getting from the mystery wolves was just that: a smell, not a vile reek.

Josh pricked up his ears and sniffed. His keen hearing had picked out at least three humans talking – one male, two females – and two . . . well . . . they *sounded* human, but Josh's senses told him they were no more human than he was. The familiar voice he had heard earlier wasn't among them though, and he was glad. He didn't want to be reminded he had once been a boy. Josh shook his head impatiently to clear the images of his mum and little sister, and forced his thoughts to turn to his empty stomach. He couldn't resist a peek in the fridge and was busy finishing off all the food (including the packaging) when he sensed someone behind him. Banned from the bathroom and the drama of Nat's failure to shift properly, Harmony had heard Josh's greedy noshing noises and had gone into the kitchen alone to investigate. Sadly, in one small moment, that decision was to change her life for ever.

Josh Wedlock pulled his head out of the fridge and spun round, all blazing orange eyes and unchewed food tumbling from his gaping mouth. As Harmony gazed uncomprehendingly at this new horror, Josh forgot all about being a werewolf and was delighted to see someone who had been in the same tutor group since Year Seven.

Harmony! How you doin'? Josh thought he was speaking, but of course, with no human voicebox, the words just spilled out of his jaws as a jumble of short growls.

Harmony had no way of knowing that this enormous brown wolf had once been her friend Josh Firkin. People – especially young boys – had a habit of going missing from Temple Gurney but no one knew why. So she had no reason to suppose this terrifying beast was him.

'Stay back,' she whispered, unable to speak properly.

Josh, still forgetting he was a werewolf, tried to speak again. All that came out was, 'Grrrrrrrrr?'

Harmony looked desperately around her for a weapon, but couldn't see anything obvious. Her mind was screaming *HELP! DAAAAAAD! NAT! ANYBODY!* But all that came out of her mouth was a weak, wheezy moan.

Josh cocked his head to one side and whined. *Course! No wonder she's frightened, she probably doesn't recognise me!*

He moved towards her in what he hoped was a reassuring manner, but that just made it worse. She opened a drawer and started flinging stuff at him, and caught him hard on the nose with a plastic spatula, which hurt more than you would think.

The quicker Josh advanced, the quicker Harmony edged away until, reaching the doorway, she whipped round and belted into the hall. Josh, programmed to behave like a wolf, gave chase. Harmony slipped on the polished floor and would have banged her head badly if Josh hadn't grabbed her hand in his mouth to steady her.

Harmony cried out in terror and pain, and Josh released his hold, confused. She sat heavily on the floor and shunted away from him on her bottom, nursing her hand close to her chest and staring at the werewolf in shock.

'What have you done?' she asked, then keeled over in a dead faint.

Uh, God, what have I done? thought Josh, as he looked down at his former classmate's unconscious body. He nudged her with his nose, but she was out cold. He sniffed at her hand and his heart sank. There was a lot of blood. That meant he had broken the skin.

More to the point, it meant that Harmony Wedlock would become a werewolf.

Given the fact that part of Josh Firkin's job was to recruit new wolves for Lucas Scale, you might think he would see this as a *good* thing. The truth of the matter was:

In his old life Josh had liked Harmony Wedlock, and although being a werewolf had its fun points, a life serving Lucas Scale wasn't so wonderful.

He remembered Scale telling him that never, under any circumstances, was he to recruit girls. Josh couldn't remember why this was (he hadn't really been listening), but he was sure it was a good reason.

He whimpered. This was bad!

He sniffed at Harmony again, pawing her body miserably and wondering what to do next. But not for long. Joe Wedlock was coming up from the cellar. As he entered the kitchen all Joe saw was a large wolf pawing over the body of his beloved daughter and, staining the floor, blossoms of her red, red blood.

'HARMONY!'

Josh Firkin couldn't mistake the raw mixture of grief and rage on Joe Wedlock's face. He no longer had a choice. He turned, claws scrabbling on the slippery flooring, and threw himself at the kitchen window, ripping his leg on the jagged shards of broken glass as he escaped into the early dawn.

They found Joe Wedlock cradling the unconscious body of his daughter when they came downstairs. Fish no longer looked so glamorous in her black cat-suit but more like a real cat that had been dragged backwards and forwards through a hedge many times. Woody was paler than usual and was still wearing a pink bath towel, while Nat had found a checked baseball cap and matching scarf hanging behind Harmony's bedroom door. He had hidden as much of his unlovely features as he could manage, but knew he was unlikely to fool anyone.

But Joe Wedlock hardly noticed.

'Help me,' he pleaded. 'Harmony . . . she . . . she's been bitten. Look.'

Fish examined the serrated edge of the bite on Harmony's hand. 'Werewolf?' she asked grimly.

Woody sniffed the bite. 'Yeah, not too much pressure, just a flesh wound but—'

'That's all it takes,' said Fish. 'How long has she been like this?'

'I don't know,' cried Joe. 'The wolf was pawing at her when I found her. Will she die?'

Nat bent down. 'Help me get her into the car,' he said urgently. 'We need to get her to Meade Lodge. As fast as we can.'

Josh Firkin, now in human form, shimmied through the skylight and tiptoed naked through the chilly corridor to his living quarters. He could see the back of Scale's tatty head poking up from the back of his rocking chair, and – what luck – no sign of Teddy Davis. Josh felt dizzy with relief. Now, if he could just get to his bedroom and get his clothes on, no one would even—

'AAAAAAAaaaahaaaaaaaawooooooh! Whhhho-wwwwwwaaaarooooooh!'

Josh froze. *Oh brilliant!* The cacophony of howls was coming from the furthest part of the reservoir, which was home to the newly recruited werewolves. He must have woken them up, and now they were going to wake Scale. The mighty sound was magnified as it travelled through the tunnel and into the main body of the building. Scale's head jerked as he started to wake up.

Josh Firkin held his breath and scuttled crab-like past Scale's chair into his own corridor. He pulled open his door, crept behind it and pressed his back against it, panting hard. His heart was threatening to beat out of his chest, so he stayed there for a few moments with his eyes closed. When he opened them again, he realised he wasn't alone.

Teddy Davis was sitting on Josh's bed. In the darkness, Josh could see Teddy's orange eyes glowing like embers.

'Where d'you think you've been?' asked Teddy.

'Er, nowhere,' said Josh, breezily. 'I've just been, er, checking everything's all right, you know, just . . . checking.'

'What's that on your mouth?' asked Teddy, dangerously. 'Looks like blood.'

Josh wiped his mouth roughly with the back of his

hand. 'Uh, nosebleed.'

'Really?' said Teddy. He got up from Josh's bed and took hold of his arm. He narrowed his eyes as he raised Josh's hand to his nose. Josh noticed with fascination how large Teddy's nostrils were.

'Human,' snarled Teddy. 'This is human blood. Whose is it? And don't you dare lie to me.'

'I don't know what . . .' tried Josh, but he knew it was useless. Teddy Davis wasn't as stupid as he looked. Teddy moved as though he were going to grab him around the throat, but Josh managed to sidestep neatly away.

'I-I didn't mean it,' stammered Josh. 'She-she was running away and I just—'

'*She?*' Teddy's pale face got considerably paler. 'You stupid, stupid little squit,' he spat in Josh's face. 'Don't you know the rules?'

'What rules?' asked Josh. 'I wasn't going to recruit her. I know girls are rubbish at being werewolves. She fell over and I—'

'Shut up!' growled Teddy. 'Even Scale won't recruit females. Still, they rarely survive an attack. Whoever she was, she'll probably be dead by lunchtime.'

Josh stood mute and nude, tears forming in his eyes. 'But it was just a scratch,' he said. 'She won't die from that, surely?'

'Then that's even worse,' said Teddy with a curl of

his lip. 'She'll be like us. I hope you're satisfied.'

'Wh-what if he . . . Scale . . . finds out?' stammered Josh.

But Teddy didn't answer him. He just stood there with a terrible look of dread on his face. Josh turned round slowly, already knowing what he would see.

Lucas Scale had heard everything.

CHAPTER 16
CLUES

'There's nothing else I can do,' said Iona de Gourney, gently. 'It should have worked by now, but the process is starting already. I'm so very sorry.'

'But Nat said . . .' began Joe Wedlock, desperately.

'When Scale attacked Nat, he was very lucky,' said Iona. 'We had a medic on site who gave him a transfusion of Woody's blood within forty minutes of the attack. The Wolven cells destroyed the lycan cells.'

'I'm sorry, Joe,' said Fish, miserably. All her

confidence and bravado had shrivelled up and died. 'I let you down, we were too late.'

'What happens now?' whispered Joe, staring down at his daughter. 'She won't die will she?'

'I'll stay with her,' said Iona. 'And Mr Wedlock, I have no intention of losing her.'

'I think I need to stay too,' said Joe, 'see for myself, if that's all right.'

Lucas Scale liked people to be scared of him. The terrified look in Josh Firkin's eyes made his wormy heart sing, and the uncomfortable look in Teddy Davis' was disturbing but intriguing.

Young Josh has nothing else to hide, thought Scale. *I heard it all from behind the door.* But there was something about Teddy that was making Scale suspicious. He would have to see.

'You are sure the Carver boy and the Wolven were present in the undertaker's house?' he asked a still terrified Josh.

'Yeah,' nodded Josh, anxious to please. 'I didn't actually see 'em, but I could smell wolf an' I could hear 'em.'

'Had to be them,' said Scale, a faraway look in his awful eyes. 'Couldn't be anyone else.'

No prizes for guessing where they are now, he thought. *Oh, to be a fly on the wall in Mistress de Gourney's house.*

The next couple of days were tough for everyone at Meade Lodge. Iona and Joe took turns with Fish and the boys to look after Harmony, so someone was always with her as she sweated out her change. Luckily Harmony was strong and her body was able to withstand the ordeal, but Iona prayed her mind would prove equally resilient.

It seemed to Nat they'd been staying at Meade Lodge for weeks, because so much had happened. He had almost forgotten why they had come to Temple Gurney and what they were looking for.

Though Iona's priority was naturally Harmony, she was encouraging about the dreadful state poor Nat found himself in. 'I'm hopeful there'll be a charm or reversal spell I can do to make you shift properly,' she promised. 'I'll do some research and see what I can come up with. In the meantime, Fish can show you what we've found out regarding the whereabouts of the Baphomet. It's all looking very encouraging.'

This suited Alex Fish. She felt as though they had spent far too long faffing about. There were two leads she wanted to follow up. Itching to get on with it, she took the boys to the big banqueting hall at Meade Lodge, to trawl for information about her best lead – some guy called Rydian, the keeper of the Baphomet.

The hum from the bank of computers and the

heady smell of spices made Nat feel weird. His head still ached and it felt heavier than usual. Once or twice he caught Fish's eye and knew by her guilty expression that she'd been staring at him. Typically Woody didn't seemed fazed by Nat's new look at all, for which Nat was very grateful.

'Right,' said Fish, brisk again and keen to start work. 'This is what Scale and his demon are looking for.'

She passed some pictures she had downloaded from the internet to Nat and Woody.

'Eurgh,' gasped Woody, 'horrible. '

'We found loads of drawings and descriptions of the Baphomet,' said Fish, ignoring the face Woody had pulled. 'Obviously no photographs, 'cos no one living in our century has actually seen it. As far as we know, anyway.'

Nat studied one of the pictures Fish had handed to him. It was easy to see why Woody had shuddered at it. There was something so primitive and monstrous about the winged creature with the body of a man and the head of a goat that it was hard to imagine such a thing could be real. Its head was topped with a sort of spiked golden helmet, and the empty-looking yellow eyes made Nat certain that if this creature did exist, it was capable of bringing about the end of the world before it had its breakfast. Just looking at it on the page made him uncomfortable.

'Nat,' said Fish, 'you're not saying anything, what's up?'

Nat had gone pale. 'I . . . sorry. Woody, can't you feel that?'

'What?' asked Fish, puzzled.

'It's like someone just walked over my grave,' he shuddered.

Woody stared at him. 'Is it one of your feelings?' he asked. 'You know, like something bad is gonna happen?'

'Something bad did happen,' said Nat.

They all thought about Harmony, who was sleeping fitfully as she became hairier by the hour.

Nat shook himself. 'OK, sorry, we know what the Baphomet Head looks like now, so where do we start looking?'

Fish gave him a quick smile. *Good old Nat*, she thought, relieved he wasn't taking his own bad luck to heart.

She settled down on one of the squashy sofas. 'One of the accounts tells us that the Baphomet Head was guarded for the two hundred years of the Crusades by trusted Knights Templar monks. When they were arrested and put on trial for a number of things – including worshipping the Baphomet and turning their backs on God, which was like really bad criminal behaviour in those days – there was no sign of the

Head. And we know now that the Templar dudes were guarding it from falling into the wrong hands, not worshipping it at all.

'In Sir William de Gourney's later chronicles, Iona found some mention of the Baphomet, but it wasn't until the fourteenth century that Sir Will's great-great-grandson, Hugh de Gourney, takes up the story properly. As one of the last Templars, Sir Hugh knew all their secrets. He logged the Baphomet Head as being shifted out of France in around 1312 and being given to this hermit dude called Rydian to look after. Thirty-six years later, Rydian was tricked into giving the Head to an emissary from hell: a demon. Before Rydian and his men could recover it and send the demon back to hell, one third of the population of Europe had died from a mysterious, but deadly illness.

'That'd be the Black Death,' said Nat, grimly.

'Maybe the Head was buried with Rydian when he died,' suggested Woody.

'You're thinking along the same lines as me,' said Fish, spiking up her hair. 'According to Sir Hugh's chronicle, Rydian was a typical hermit, living on his own and devoting his life to prayer and the fight against evil. It's likely that no one else wanted the responsibility of becoming old Baphomet's guardian when Rydian popped his clogs. So we find the dead dude and we find the Baphomet. Obviously, the first thing we've got to do is locate the grave. And that's where we've been lucky. Look at this.'

Alex Fish pulled on a pair of thin, white gloves. Then she placed a book bound in soft brown leather and embossed in golden medieval illuminations on the desk in front of her. She carefully opened it at a page marked with a leather bookmark.

If Nat hadn't felt so bad, he would have been thrilled at seeing such a book again. The last time he had anything to do with a chronicle of this kind he had been flipped back to the Middle Ages; he was wary of touching it in case he found himself there again. But Nat's feeling of reluctance was soon replaced by awe, as Sir Hugh had obviously inherited his great-great-granddad's skill with the quill, and both boys peered at the beautifully vivid drawings. They looked as fresh and colourful as they must have done hundreds of years ago.

'Sir Hugh had awful trouble translating a lot of the Hermit's documents,' said Fish, 'cos they'd been written in the old Saxon language, not French or even Latin as was usual then. But there were a few mentions of Rydian living in a cave.'

Even with his new scary face, Woody could tell Nat was disappointed.

'But Britain is riddled with caves,' Nat said. 'How

will we know which one Rydian lived and died in, or whether he was ever there at all?'

'Wait a minute,' grinned Fish. 'Look at this entry here.'

Nat and Woody peered over her shoulder to where she was pointing.

'It says here that Rydian the monk lived in *terra totae aestatis*, and that, according to Iona's translation, is Latin for "the land of all summer", which is what Somerset was called in those days,' said Fish, eagerly. 'More importantly, if you look here, and here, there're more clues.'

Despite his first disappointment, Nat began to catch Fish's excitement. The hairs on the back of his neck rose when he saw what Sir Hugh de Gourney had drawn.

There were two figures, one unmistakeably Wolven in origin, the other a boy. And a boy whose face was hidden, his head covered with what looked very much like a checked baseball cap.

'What does it mean?' breathed Nat.

'Iona thinks it pretty much means that you and Woody must have flipped sometime while you were searching,' said Fish her eyes sparkling. 'How cool is that?'

'We've, like, become part of the legend, you mean?' said Woody, not understanding.

Fish nodded. 'Sometime in the past, hundreds of years ago, a story was passed around about two travellers from the future who would be the new guardians of the Baphomet Head. A story that became a legend.'

'How does the legend end?' asked Woody, who was scared to know but had to ask.

'That'd be too easy,' grinned Fish. 'See? If that drawing *is* supposed to be you two, and I'm sure it is, you're both described as searching in the land of all summer. And look at this bit – *Regius Alfredis villa aestival!*'

Nat and Woody looked blank.

'*Regius* refers to the king,' said Fish. 'This says that the old king of Wessex, King Alfred, had his summer palace at Cheddar Gorge.'

'So Rydian lived at this summer palace?' asked Nat.

Fish shook her head. 'Iona checked all the timelines and old Alf's palace would have been practically a ruin in Rydian's time, but look *here* . . .' Fish carefully turned more pages. 'Further on there's a map of where it used to stand. It shows an ancient chapel, which according to this has a small network of caves behind. Great for a hermit-type dude.'

'We'll need a copy of the map,' said Nat, adjusting his scarf.

'You're going *now?* asked Fish.

'No time like the present,' replied Nat.

'D'you need anything?' asked Fish.

'Just our noses,' grinned Woody.

If any of them had looked up at that point, they would have seen the grinning astral shade of Lucas Scale perched like a monstrous fly on the wall above them. He saluted them for their help and winked out like a light switch. Then his astral body floated back from Meade Lodge to the reservoir and slipped back into his gnarly old skin.

As soon as he was conscious, Scale rallied his wolves. He knew he was taking a chance on the new recruits, but all he really needed them for was their speed and strength. He knew from bitter experience that the Wolven scum were bigger and stronger, but if there were going to be a fight, at least the Wolven could be overpowered by sheer numbers. Scale watched Teddy Davis out of the corner of his eye. Since the day he caught him in Josh Firkin's room, he hadn't been quite so keen to share his plans with Teddy. Josh himself would need another session looking into Lucas Scale's eyes to ensure that he behaved himself in future. Still, at least Josh had given him valuable information about the whereabouts of the Wolven and their allies.

* * *

Teddy Davis felt alone and afraid. Suddenly, Scale seemed to be moving ahead in the quest for the Baphomet with frightening speed. Teddy hadn't been able to contact *NightShift* to warn Quentin Crone because he had no signal on his mobile, and he had no idea what was happening. The papers Scale had received from the Vatican had been hard to crack. No one in the underground reservoir could speak Italian, least of all Scale, but for some reason that didn't seem to matter. Scale had ordered Teddy to bring the new Hummer around from its hiding place in East Wood. The new werewolves were baying in their cells, and it seemed they were all going somewhere. Quite where, Teddy Davis didn't know.

CHAPTER 17

THE HERMIT'S CAVE

'Go safely,' Alex Fish said, as she dropped Nat and Woody by the side of the road. 'It's doubtful you'll find what we're looking for, but there might be a clue to prove that Rydian was here all those years ago. If there's a burial site, that'd be the best place to start looking.'

Nat nodded.

'I'll see you both at Iona's,' said Fish. 'The boss needs us back in London if the Baphomet Head isn't at Cheddar Gorge.'

153

'Why do we have to go back to London?' asked Nat.

'He's just covering himself,' replied Fish. 'If anyone can sniff out something that'll help us find the Baphomet, you two can. But if it's not in the cave, for everyone's sake, we need to be one step ahead of Lucas Scale.'

None of them could bear to think what might happen if Scale and his wolves got there first. And it was on this note that Nat and Woody set out towards the ancient ruins of King Alfred's summer palace, armed with just a photocopy of the ancient map. Fish shielded her eyes as she watched them climb the almost sheer face of Cheddar Gorge. Nat went first, his strange features hidden beneath the cap and scarf. Woody followed faithfully behind in Wolven form.

Nat felt his head ought to be on a swivel. As he and Woody made their way up the rocky gorge, he kept looking back, imagining he'd see Lucas Scale gaining on them, maybe with other wolves: bad wolves that Scale had recruited. Woody was panting like a steam train, his tongue lolling out of the side of his mouth.

When they reached the top, Nat took a look around him. The mighty Cheddar Gorge lay spread out a hundred and fifty metres below them, and apart from birdsong and a plane flying high everything was calm. He sniffed in the gorgeous scents of marjoram, wild thyme and firewitch, and the not-so-gorgeous whiff rising from the sheep poo that studded the grass. Standing there with Woody, the wind blowing gently through their fur, felt like being at the top of the world. Nat loosened the cap and scarf gratefully and flopped down beside Woody on the springy turf, spreading the map in front of him.

'According to this, we're sitting in the ruins of the summer palace now,' said Nat, 'Look, you can just about make out where the foundations must have been.' He pointed to the expanse of flattened turf. 'Can't see any sign of a cave or even a pothole, though. Can you?'

Woody was sniffing along the faint boundaries of where the ancient chapel once stood. It was weird to think that all those years ago people had lived in this royal palace, people who had been dust for centuries.

'I reckon . . .' began Nat.

But Woody had disappeared.

Readjusting his cap, Nat pulled himself up from his resting place and hurried to the place he'd last seen the Wolven. There was a sort of raised area in front of him, not quite a bank, but part rock, part grassy knoll. Nat felt the surface with his hands, trying to find a hidden hole or opening.

'OK, I give up,' he called. 'Where are you?'

There was a faint rustling and Woody wriggled out

of a small space just a little to the right of where Nat was standing. The opening was completely obscured by ivy and bindweed, and a bitter, damp smell invaded Nat's nostrils.

'You want me to follow you, right?' grinned Nat.

Seriousclaustrophobia.

Nat groaned. 'Tight fit in there?'

Woody chuffed. *Surething.*

Nat gritted his considerable teeth. Since all these wild Wolven adventures had begun, he'd had to do a great deal of squeezing into caves, crypts, underground passages, all things that would cause him to break out in the clammy, awful sweat of the claustrophobe.

'All right,' said Nat in a resigned voice, as he bent his head to follow Woody, 'but if Rydian did live here, he must have been a flipping dwarf.' Almost as an afterthought, he pulled the ivy across like a living curtain, to conceal the opening on the outer edge of rock. It was hard work stooping to avoid the low ceiling. If only he could still shift to four legs, it'd be easy to get along the tunnel to what he hoped would open up into a cave. Three hundred million years ago Cheddar Gorge and its spectacular caves had been created by meltwater floods as the permafrost repeatedly thawed and refroze, but Nat was pretty sure that this particular tunnel wasn't in the guidebook. It was damp inside the rock and smelt wet and seaweedy, but thankfully neither Nat nor Woody had any trouble seeing what was ahead of them.

'Wait,' hissed Nat, 'look at these!'

Woody reversed obligingly – the tunnel was way too narrow to turn around in – and looked with interest at where Nat was pointing.

'Cave paintings!' said Nat, excitedly. 'They must be thousands of years old, maybe, like, millions!'

Both Nat and Woody gazed in wonder at the black and red strokes on the limestone wall. They were intricately detailed drawings of the animals that roamed the land millennia ago. Pictures that no doubt told a story to the ancient people who once dwelt in the cave. Mammoth, deer and people with spears depicted what Nat supposed must have been a hunting party. Wolves, horses, eagles and beautifully drawn faces of adults and children sitting around a fire were all carefully etched onto the limestone. It was all too long ago for Nat to get his head fully around, but he could have stayed all day trying to find more. But Woody, mindful of the challenge they faced, nudged him with his muzzle.

'OK,' said Nat regretfully, 'you lead.'

Once more they set off downwards, both glad to feel a breeze coming from below. The path led them further and further into the earth, and to Nat's relief the ceiling began to get higher the deeper they got. Nat's Wolven vision kicked in when the last of the light from the entrance faded completely, and Woody finally led them into the cavern they hoped had been Rydian's.

An expanse of water shone with a bright green tinge and an assortment of majestic stalactites and stalagmites glowed deep purple. As Nat's eyes became fully adjusted to the darkness, he saw that the walls of the cave were completely covered from rocky ceiling to the stone floor with thousands of symbols and drawings.

'Hey, can you see what I see?' he said softly.

Woody made a snuffling affirmative sound that echoed scarily around the empty chamber. The two of them stood together in silence and gazed at the carvings. There were dragons and horses and shields and swords. There were fish and what looked like loaves of bread and crosses and men and women in medieval clothes. There were knights in armour, people burning, serpents and devils and . . .

The unmistakeable figure of the Baphomet. The horned creature with the head of a goat and the body of a man stared at them with fathomless, yellow, slanted eyes. Its gigantic wings were folded behind its body and it wore a spiked golden helmet on its head. Someone had painstakingly carved a perfect replica of the Baphomet into the limestone wall, and the horned goat creature towered over them in all its terrible splendour.

Nat felt the hackles on the back of his neck rise, and a familiar heat began creeping through his veins.

Yes! Oh, please, pleeeease let it be my shift! Nat prayed to himself, as he closed his eyes and *puuuushed* with all his might. But instead of the hoped-for shape-shift, he found himself still standing on two legs with his eyes fixed on the carving of the Baphomet, as if he were looking at a Magic Eye 3D picture. Woody chuffed politely as if to ask what on earth Nat thought he was doing, but Nat scarcely heard him.

As he focused on the carving, it shimmered and blurred. Then Nat smelt the sweet scent of incense and realised with amazement that he could see movement. A tall, muscular figure with long silver hair, wearing what appeared to be a dark cloak, emerged in his line of vision. Instinctively, Nat knew he was witnessing something that had happened long ago. They were in a time slip, but neither Woody nor the figure in front of him was aware of anything strange.

As Nat watched, the figure became clearer. He saw it had a grey beard and he guessed the garment was a monk's habit. Almost in slow motion, the monk began to chisel something in the soft limestone. Nat watched in a weird trance-like state as the man carved the face of the Baphomet.

Rydian had been here.

As Scale and his pack of seven followed the Wolven scent up the steep rocks of Cheddar Gorge, Scale could feel victory boiling in his innards. (Or maybe it was just wind.) When they got to the place where the ancient chapel had stood, it took no time to follow Woody's scent and locate the mouth of the hermit's cave. Josh Firkin made to enter and follow the Wolven, but Scale had a much better plan, simple but effective. He ordered his wolves to scratch up soil and rocks and block up the entrances to the smaller potholes near the ruined chapel. Nat Carver and his sidekick could do all the hard work of fetching out the Baphomet Head. Then Scale would snatch it from them, just like Abanazer in the tale of Aladdin.

When Nat found his voice again, he told an astonished Woody what he had seen in his vision.

'It's like a message from Rydian,' he gasped. 'Remember in Sir Hugh's chronicle? Somehow Rydian must have known we would come here looking for it, which means at some point we're gonna flip.'

Woody growled, which to Nat meant that he was distinctly unhappy at the prospect of time travel.

'It's fine,' reassured Nat, 'honest. I've done it twice and it was OK, apart from the passing out and the violent puking.'

Woody growled again, unconvinced. They continued to examine every cranny in the cave in search of bones or any other evidence that would lead them to the Baphomet Head.

'I reckon the cave goes further back,' said Nat. 'Listen. I can hear water trickling down from a stream, unless it's an underground stretch of the river.'

Woody gingerly put a paw into the green pool. It was shallow enough for him to wade through and he scrambled up onto the other side.

'Yeah,' said Nat, 'see? There's a sort of corridor made from rock.'

Nat followed Woody through the water to where the Wolven was now busy sniffing in the corners for a scent – any scent that would indicate a burial site. Sure enough, the rocky corridor opened out into another cave but Nat gazed around him in disappointment.

'The floor's solid rock,' he said. 'There're no gaps in the walls where anything could be hidden or buried. I don't know about you, but I don't think Rydian's bones lie anywhere near here.'

Woody chuffed in agreement and, satisfied they

had missed nothing, they began the long climb back the way they had come. This time Nat was leading, but as they reached the tunnel mouth, he stopped suddenly and put a warning hand on Woody's neck.

Uh Oh. Two things very wrong here!

When they'd been there before, Nat had pulled the ivy curtain across to camouflage the hole. But now it was open. And then there was the smell. He'd know that smell anywhere. Lucas Scale.

He put his finger to his lips and pointed. Seeing the picture forming in Nat's brain, Woody caught on immediately.

GOBACKNOW!

Woody didn't need telling twice.

CHAPTER 18
GOLD TEETH

'G et after them!' shrieked Lucas Scale.

The werewolves, keen to impress, jostled for position as they all tried to pile through the small opening at once, only to get firmly wedged. Scale's screams of fury could be heard from Charterhouse to Cheddar as he tried shoving them through from behind.

In the chaos, Nat lost his footing and he and Woody rolled at some considerable speed back down the rocky tunnel into Rydian's cave. With Scale's screams echoing through the air, Nat knew it was only a matter of time before the rest of the pack caught up with them. At the bottom, he ran after Woody towards the sound of water, hoping desperately there was a different way out. As they splashed their way through the pool, Nat knew that although the were-wolves didn't share their infra-red eyesight, they could still see better than humans, and if he was wrong about another entrance, he and Woody would be dead meat. In Nat's sights, Woody's body heat shone orange and Nat ran towards the warm glow, trusting that if Scale and his pack managed to untangle themselves and get into the cave, they wouldn't be able to see it too. The orange wolf shape stayed in front of him and Nat again felt a cool breeze on his face as he followed Woody through the freezing water.

Upthere, said Woody with his mind. *Jump.*

Nat squinted ahead and saw for himself what his friend was telling him. About a metre in front of them was a natural ledge, and beyond the ledge, a tiny pinprick of daylight.

'A tunnel,' said Nat, joyfully. 'Come on.'

AAAAAAAAAAAaaaaaaghoooooooooooowah!

'Noooo! They're through.' cried Nat. 'Go, go, go!'

Woody jumped up onto the ledge and Nat scrab-bled closely behind, trying desperately not to mind the closed-in space. It was half the width of the entrance tunnel and he'd thought that was small. A really horrible thought dawned on him. *What if . . . what if there isn't an opening at the end of the tunnel?* They'd be stuck like rats in a trap and Scale's wolves would drag them out and . . .

STOP! Nat caught Woody's thoughts, and forced himself not to panic. He bit his lip and followed Woody's tail. The Wolven was crawling now, dragging himself along by his long claws, while Nat's elbows and knees were being shredded by the loose rocks and jagged limestone.

'*AAAAAAAAAAaaaaahhhhooooorah!*' Another triumphant howl.

Woody's keen Wolven ears could hear the scrabbling sounds coming from the other end of the tunnel. Scale's pack was gaining on them.

He crawled faster, knowing he had to lead Nat out. Nat was struggling and Woody could feel his friend trying hard to block the bad thoughts from his mind and focus on escaping from this tunnel, getting away from the werewolves and out into the fresh air.

Despite Woody's hairy bulk in front of him, Nat sensed that the closer they got to the pinprick of light, the bigger it grew. After what seemed like hours, Woody's head finally popped through a tiny rabbit-like hole and breathed in a great gust of fresh air. It took a few seconds more for them both to squeeze their way through. Nat searched frantically for something to shove down the hole so they could stop the werewolves, but there was no time. They were close now – he could hear their breath and smell their meaty rankness.

'Run!' shouted Nat. 'Go on to Iona's without me if you have to.'

The ground outside the tunnel was steep and rocky, and as they half-ran, half-fell downwards, towards the grassy banks at the side of the gorge, Nat risked a look backwards and gulped. Two werewolves were already close behind, and they were flippin' *huge*. He craned his neck to see if there were more, and was horrified to see a threatening, slavering pack on the ledge just behind them, their orange eyes and teeth clearly visible in the late afternoon light. Nat briefly closed his eyes and prayed for a miracle.

He *puuushed*, in the hope that the miracle would be his long-awaited shift; if he could wolf out onto four legs, he and Woody would outrun the pack easily. But even as he pushed, his body stayed put in a terrible travesty of supernature, half-boy, half-Wolven.

STAYCLOSETOME. Woody's mindhowl tore through Nat's brain, jolting him out of his despair. He followed trustingly as Woody bounced down the rock-strewn route, nimble as a mountain goat. Nat knew he needed to erase any thoughts of their hairy pursuers from his mind and concentrate on the difficult climb down. He shadowed Woody, jumping into his pawsteps. Feeling like he was on a sort of pogo stick, he found himself smiling as he bounced after his friend. It was almost as though he were flying.

The werewolves fared much worse. Teddy Davis noticed, not for the first time, that Josh Firkin hesitated as the rest scrabbled through the narrow tunnel and out into daylight, and then hung back as they zoomed down the side of the gorge. Unable to brake with their paws, they skidded uncontrollably on their rear ends, sharp stones pricking the soft flesh, and flew past Nat and Woody down to the bottom of the ravine.

Mindful of Scale, who was yelling obscenities from above, Teddy Davis held back with Josh as far as he could. He wasn't sure if Nat and Woody knew that he was working as a *NightShift* agent. It could blow his cover if they saw him. If Scale suspected anything funny, Teddy would say he didn't hurry himself because Nat Carver had come out empty-handed. It was obvious he wasn't carrying anything at all, much less the Head of the Baphomet.

Teddy made another important observation. Since he had last seen Nat the boy seemed to have grown incredibly ugly.

* * *

Ooof!

Nat's landing was cushioned by Woody, and with Scale's banshee-like cries still ringing in their ears, they scrambled to their feet. Nat hurriedly adjusted Harmony's cap and scarf, grateful they hadn't been lost in the chase. They couldn't see the werewolves but they couldn't be far away and there was no time to lose. But if they tried climbing up the other side of the gorge, they'd be spotted immediately. And if they ran either way along the road they would be picked off like rabbits. Then a strange sound reached their ears, the massive rumbling of unmuffled engines accompanied by wild whoops and howls. Nat turned in confusion to Woody who was poised like a white marble statue, his ears pricked keenly, his nostrils twitching and flaring.

What now? thought Nat. But instead of the expected pack of werewolves thundering down the gorge, he was temporarily blinded by dozens of silvery halogen headlamps. What was more astonishing was that they belonged to a fleet of motorcycles ridden by unhelmeted gentlemen with bulging muscles. Before Nat and Woody could break away and run for the hills, they were completely surrounded by shiny Harley-Davidsons.

Despite the gravity of the situation Nat was

168

impressed. Most of the riders had flowing grey hair visible beneath bandannas and rude tattoos on their bare arms. On their chests, across assorted leathers, a slogan was emblazoned: **Hell's Angels – CHEDDAR**.

'Nat, right?' shouted the nearest Angel. He had a big golden smile, because most of his teeth were gold, and a necklace that appeared to be made from the teeth of a large carnivorous animal.

Nat stammered a yes and wondered what was coming.

'C'mon!' yelled Golden Teeth, checking behind him. 'They'll be on us if we don't get a move on!' He pointed at Woody. 'Your mate all right to run?'

Before Nat had a chance to reply, more howls, this time those of Scale's werewolves, bounced off the sides of the gorge, making the Hell's Angels itchy to get away. Golden Teeth grabbed Nat by the scruff of his neck and hoisted him onto the back of the thrumming Softail as the Cheddar Chapter of the Hell's Angels roared off down the gorge at full throttle.

Raw-bummed and shamed, Lucas Scale's werewolves slunk off into the cover of the lush countryside leaving Scale almost vomiting with rage and disappointment. He had seen for himself the image of the Baphomet carved into the side of the cave and, thanks to the information he had overheard while his astral body had been hanging like a fly on the wall at Meade Lodge, he had drawn the same conclusion as Nat and Woody. The monk, Rydian, had carved the Baphomet Head as a message or clue for the Wolven brats.

When he had calmed down, Scale licked his black lips contemplatively and frowned. The guardian of the Baphomet had known that somehow, in the twenty-first century, the Wolven would come looking. What was more, from the conversation between that known meddler (and his former employee) Iona de Gourney and the other brats, it appeared that the Carver boy had some talent for time travel.

This could be bad news, fumed Scale. *Very bad news indeed*.

'Yeeeeeehaaaaaah!'

Nat was on an adrenalin high. Not only had they outrun Scale and his pack of werewolves, he was thrilled to be on the back of Golden Teeth's Harley-Davidson, surrounded by Hell's Angels. At first he hung on for dear life, practically strangling Golden Teeth, his face pressed close to the biker's leather jerkin, which smelt of barley, tobacco and engine oil. Occasionally Nat glanced across to see a reassuring white blur as Woody galloped alongside, feeling the sheer joy of running with a pack – even if it was a pack of Softail Harleys.

When Golden Teeth was sure they'd left the were-wolves far behind, they cruised at a more sedate pace.

'Take you back to Meade Lodge?' shouted Golden Teeth over his impressive shoulder. 'Think you've had enough excitement for one day?'

'Please,' shouted Nat. 'You know Iona, then?'

'Yeah,' shouted Golden Teeth. 'She's a real mate.'

Blimey O'Reilly! thought Nat. *Who'd have thought Iona was mates with Hell's Angels!*

It was almost twilight when the band of motorcycles drew up outside Meade Lodge. Nat got off the Softail reluctantly and fixed his scarf tightly around his face.

'Shift trouble?' asked Golden Teeth sympathetic-ally. 'Bad luck mate, that's rough.'

'Yeah,' said Nat, 'tell me about it.' Then he frowned. 'How did you . . . ?'

Golden Teeth grinned and pulled off his wrap-around shades. His eyes were a pure, Day-Glo orange.

Nat's jaw dropped. 'You're all *werewolves*?'

The other bikers removed their shades too and Nat saw the answer.

'Lycans, if you don't mind,' grinned Golden Teeth. 'But we're the good guys. It's just that when we do right, nobody remembers, when we do wrong, nobody forgets.'

Chapter 19
Green Isle

Although it was past midnight when Alex Fish and the boys arrived back at *NightShift* HQ, the boss was still at his desk, as they knew he would be.

Crone tried not to make a big fuss about Nat's shifting predicament and how he was swaddled in a cap and scarf. Instead he squeezed Nat's shoulder encouragingly and gave him a smile. 'It'll sort itself out, I'm sure,' he said, falsely jolly.

I flippin' well hope so, thought Nat. Everyone was being really sympathetic, and that was nice of them, but he got the feeling they were thinking, 'Oooh, sorry for your trouble, but I'm so blumming glad it's not me.' Then he felt mean for imagining it.

Between them, he and Woody told Crone all about what had happened at the cave site and their narrow escape from Scale's band of werewolves.

'Did you see Teddy Davis?' asked Crone, anxiously.

Nat shook his head. 'All the wolves we saw were dark. I'd know Teddy anywhere with that blond pelt.'

Crone looked worried. 'I hope nothing's gone wrong. I haven't heard from him for days.'

'Maybe he's turned towards the Dark Side,' said Fish. 'From what I know about Teddy Davis, it wouldn't surprise me.'

Crone shook his head. 'I'm certain I can trust him,' he said, firmly. 'He's vital in feeding us information if Scale manages to find out where the Baphomet Head is before we do.'

'It's just a process of elimination,' said Fish, as they all drank hot chocolate with pink, white and green marshmallows floating on top.

'You mean we have to visit every place that Rydian travelled to?' asked Nat, aghast.

Fish nodded enthusiastically. 'The Baphomet carving confirms that Rydian was living in the cave for a while, but neither Nat nor Woody found any evidence of a grave site, so we can eliminate it.'

Nat popped another marshmallow under his scarf and into his strangely formed mouth. 'What about the drawing of me and Woody in Sir Hugh de Gourney's chronicle?'

'Yeah, we know that Nat's able to flip back in time,' piped up Woody, nervously, 'but *I'm* in the picture too. And *I* don't wanna flip!'

Crone steepled his fingers and thought for a moment. 'It certainly seems that the drawing is an indication that you *and* Nat were there at the time,' he agreed. 'And although obviously Rydian has been dead for centuries, if he did meet you both in the past, the carving was a message especially for you.'

'Exactly,' grinned Fish.

Crone passed them a piece of A3 paper. He had spent the last twenty-four hours searching the archives from the Templar vault for all the journeys made by Templar monks, and in particular by Rydian.

'This is a map I've put together of Rydian's travels, starting with his visit to the Holy Land,' he said, tracing the map with his finger. 'Quite clearly he travelled extensively: from the Holy Land to Glastonbury, from Glastonbury to Cheddar, Cheddar to the Templar headquarters here in London, to Somerset, York, Wales, Glastonbury, Stone Henge. Many of the sites are linked by holy lines, which as we know possess a certain spiritual power.'

'Dude got about a bit, seeing even bikes weren't invented,' said Fish, impressed. 'But if we need to follow in his footsteps, I only hope he didn't leave the Baphomet Head in the Holy Land, or it's gonna take us forever.'

'No,' Crone assured them, 'Rydian's travels abroad were when he was a young man. By all accounts he was getting on in years when he took over responsibility for the Baphomet. The last place mentioned is here. In London.'

It was three o'clock in the morning when Alex Fish, under cover of darkness, hurried through a quiet and deserted Middle Temple to the round Temple Church. Her heart was pounding. She had discovered something that everyone else had missed and hardly dared to hope she was right. If she was, it would mean their quest to find the Baphomet was over.

She paused at the great black door of the church and took from her pocket the Egyptian key she had secretly lifted earlier. She had used the key once before on the black crypt of the Vampire Queen. It had belonged to another Queen – Cleopatra – and it had the power to open any door in the universe. Fish pushed the key into the lock and turned it. The heavy door swung open on silent hinges.

Alex Fish ignored the bank of light switches and lit the candles in the ornate wall sconces instead. The moment of truth was approaching.

She knelt down and shone her torch onto the only tomb in the nave without an effigy of a knight on it. The tomb was an odd shape, like an elongated pyramid, with a faint inscription written down one side. Fish rummaged in her pockets for a pencil and unrolled a large piece of paper. Trying not to notice the way the gargoyles and grotesques flickered and capered evilly in the candlelight, she painstakingly took a stone rubbing from the side of the tomb. When she had finished, she stared at the imagery and the words, and rolled the paper up very carefully. Then she blew out the candles, locked the door with Cleopatra's key and made her way back to HQ.

She couldn't wait. She rallied Nat and Woody, who were both unable to sleep. Crone, realising that she wouldn't have woken him on a fool's errand, caught some of her excitement as they gathered once again in his office. Although it was still only five in the morning and Fish hadn't slept for twenty-four hours, the spikes on her hair were standing to attention and her sharp little face shone.

'I've found it,' she said. 'I've found Rydian's tomb.'
'Nooo!' chorused Nat and Woody. 'Where?'

Crone swallowed hard. 'Where?' he echoed, in a slightly squeaky voice.

'In the Temple Church,' answered Fish. 'I need you to help me look inside.'

Both Nat and Woody leapt to their feet.

'Whoah,' said Crone in a more normal voice. 'Before we go desecrating a medieval grave, I need you to tell me why you think it's Rydian's.'

'Here's the proof,' said Fish, proudly.

She unrolled the rubbing she had made and spread it out on Crone's desk. He gasped. On the paper was a clear imprint of the Baphomet Head, complete with spiked helmet.

'Can you decipher the words?' asked Fish, anxiously, 'it's like some crazy language.'

Crone screwed up his eyes and stared at the inscription for a few seconds. Then he chuckled. '"**Teacifnoc muem suno, tnuinever adiriv alusni ni ied mumod da inevlow muc**". It's Latin, but it's back to front.'

'What's it say?' demanded Fish.

Crone picked up a pencil and wrote it as it should be. *Cum Wolveni ad domum dei in insula virida reveniunt, onus meum conficeat.*

'Hey!' said Woody, rolling his eyes dramatically. 'Look, it says "*Wolven*"!'

It took minutes for Crone to translate. He took off

his reading glasses and smiled. 'You, my dear Alex, are a genius!'

'Never mind that,' cried Fish. 'What's it say in English?'

'When the Wolven come again to the house of God on the green isle, let my burden be done.'

'So what does that mean?' said Fish, looking a bit disappointed.

'I'm afraid I don't know yet,' said Crone, 'but it's a start!'

Crone wasn't finished with Alex Fish. Before he agreed to take them all for a peek inside the tomb, he wanted to know what had led her to believe it could be Rydian's.

'Good old-fashioned luck,' she grinned. 'I was looking at some old drawings of how the Templars liked to decorate their churches. They used to be a lot jazzier than they are now. All the walls would have been painted really bright colours and they would have had loads of flags and trophies and stuff all over the walls. I don't think they were a "less is more" type of outfit. Anyway, this book' – she heaved a heavy book, richly embossed with silver and gold foils, onto Crone's desk and carefully turned the pages – 'has a copy of a painting by some French dude of how the Temple Church in London looked in its full glory.'

Crone stared at the picture and, although he wasn't

usually a gasping man, he gasped for the third time that morning. The church had looked very different, as Fish had described. The walls were painted in reds and blues and oranges. But although the pictures were incredible, he still couldn't see why Fish had come to the conclusion that Rydian's tomb was practically on their doorstep.

'The map of Rydian's travels ended in London,' explained Fish. 'I started thinking about how important he would have been. After all, he did a favour for the Templar dudes dedicating his entire life to keeping the Baphomet safe. So why shouldn't they have honoured him by burying him here, in the English headquarters of the Knights Templar? But perhaps that would have been way too lucky. Then I noticed these.'

Crone and the boys followed her index finger as she pointed at the page. The columns supporting the nave were decorated with gargoyles, but not just any gargoyles. When they looked closer, they saw that the stone carvings were shaped like a monstrous horned demon with a spiked helmet – the Baphomet.

'But . . .' began Nat, confused, 'I've never seen them before.'

'After the war, the roof of the church was bombed and the main supporting pillars were replaced,' said Fish. 'They don't exist any more, that's why we missed them.'

'And the Baphomet features on the side of the tomb,' said Crone, almost to himself.

Fish produced a crowbar. 'Ready now?'

Crone nodded.

The tomb was empty.

No demon head of the Baphomet and not so much as a shin bone. When the lid was pushed back into place, they all walked despondently back to Crone's office.

'Should have known it would be too blumming easy,' fumed Fish, pacing the floor of the office. 'I was so sure we'd find something – at least another message or clue.'

'The message you found on the tomb is clue enough,' soothed Crone. 'When the Wolven come again to the house of God on the green isle, let my burden be done.'

Fish made a face. 'Well, house of God is a church, so it's got to be a church on an island. Could be any-where.'

'Let my burden be done,' mused Nat. 'When the Wolven come.'

Fish was still pacing up and down. She was beginning to make them all giddy. 'You think it's you, don't you?'

'Yeah,' said Nat, simply. 'Think about it. All the

clues point to Rydian meeting with me and Woody sometime in the past. Maybe he showed us, like centuries ago, where the Head of the Baphomet is hidden. What do *you* think?'

Fish had stopped pacing and seemed to have been struck deaf. And paralysed.

'Alex?' asked Crone. 'What d'you think?'

'Earth to Fish,' said Woody, amused.

'Oh man, oh *man*,' whispered Fish, turning round to face them, her eyes shining behind her specs.

She was standing in front of Nat and Woody's favourite tapestry, the one featuring King Richard and the ancient Wolven clan. She was clearly beside herself about something.

'Spill the beans,' said Crone, suddenly feeling very old and very tired. 'What's up?'

'Green Isle,' said Fish, almost to herself. 'Didn't your map mention Glastonbury?' she asked Crone. 'See, behind King Richard and the Wolven. That green hill behind them is Glastonbury Tor. But hundreds of years ago it was surrounded by sea and marshland. The ancients called it the Isle of Avalon.'

Nat grinned in delight. 'I've been there. And on the top of the Tor is the church of St Michael. That's it, the house of God on the green isle!'

* * *

In the underground reservoir, Scale felt the air shift and boil. His wolves shrank back into their quarters, their tails between their legs, as the atmosphere became polluted with dread and dark matter that rolled into every corner of their hideout like a rotten, stinking wave of sulphur.

The demon (whose name sounded like claws being dragged down a blackboard) was back.

When the dark matter cleared and Scale dared look, he saw the demon no longer in disguise, but in its raw form. It hovered above the ground, its image flickering like a broken television. It was like a boiled thing, a flayed thing, a bloody thing – something that had no business being above the earth. Its eyes were fire, its mouth a blackened, frayed hole. Lucas Scale's eyes hurt. He felt like bursting into tears for the first time in his life.

The demon no longer spoke with its screeching, terrible voice. Instead it sent blasts of pain through Scale's brain, which conveyed its displeasure much more effectively. Scale got the message. If the Head of the Baphomet wasn't found in thirty-six hours, Scale's soul would belong to the demon.

CHAPTER 20

MOONBATHING

Some people say they are drawn to Glastonbury Tor as though by an invisible magnet, and that's exactly how Nat and Woody felt as they followed Alex Fish up the legendary hill. The darkening air around them felt weird, as though it thrummed with ancient magic. Even Fish, who was human and therefore lacked any supernatural powers apart from red-hot female intuition, sensed the lure of something special. It was as though the atmosphere of the hill was wrapping itself around her with its energy and enchantment. In a few days, the Tor would be crawling with people celebrating the summer solstice, but this evening it was deserted. Mist was rolling in from the Somerset Levels, where ancient pilgrims would once have moored their boats, and gathering at the base of the Tor. From above, Nat could easily imagine what it must have been like hundreds of years ago: a tall, green island reaching skywards from the sea.

Nat was aware straight away that despite the electric feeling of excitement that magic will always generate, the place wasn't right. When he and Woody had been in Rydian's cave, Nat had felt different, as he always did when he sensed something big was going to happen. Then he had seen the vision of the figure he assumed to be Rydian the monk – the Keeper of the Baphomet. Admittedly his Wolven senses might have been heightened because he had felt the vibrations from Lucas Scale. He had known for sure that Scale and his wolves would have snatched the Baphomet away from them if they had found it that first time. But, disappointingly, Nat felt as though they had come to the wrong place.

By the time the three of them reached the top, it was 'dimpsey dark' as Apple would have described the twilight, and Nat felt a pang when he thought of his grandparents. He couldn't help wondering what his family would make of his new look, and felt sad, as though he was somehow to blame. *Must stop thinking about it*, he told himself and gritted his large teeth.

St Michael's tower, which was all that was left of the thirteenth-century church, looked creepy in the darkening skies. But although it was roofless, it did offer some shelter, and Fish thought it was a cracking place for them to pitch their tent. She, Nat and Woody stared down at the mist that was now totally obscuring the bottom of the hill. It was possible to imagine they were the only people left in the world as there was no visible light pollution from the town of Glastonbury. Just the three of them. Alone.

Nat shivered. It had begun to feel eerie. He could just imagine the sight of Scale and his wolves emerging from the mist and taking them by surprise.

'Is the Ag handy?' he asked Fish. His voice sounded flat and strange.

'Affirmative,' said Fish grimly, and patted her rucksack. 'Enough in this baby to fry their scabby brains if they try anything this time.'

Nat and Woody looked at each other, hoping what Fish said was true. When the tent was set up, Fish handed round flasks of hot soup and hunks of crusty bread and butter, as the boss always said that an army never marched on an empty belly.

'How're we going to do this?' asked Fish, when

they had eaten. 'Do you want to, like, just sit here and see if you get any, erm, visions, or have a sniff around, or what?'

'Nothin's coming to me,' said Woody, wrinkling his nose and looking disappointed. 'Nat?'

Nat shook his head. 'I got a hint of a horrible feeling that something awful used to happen here – not in the church but on this site.'

'Yeah,' shivered Woody, 'like human sacrifice or something.'

Fish made a face. 'Yeah, well I read on Wikipedia that the last abbot of Glastonbury Abbey and a couple of his monks were dragged up here and executed on the orders of King Henry VIII. It was really nasty. Apparently they were hung, drawn and quartered.'

'Ugh.' It was Nat's turn to shiver. 'Nice.'

'Not only that,' said Fish, with apparent relish, 'the abbot's executioners fastened his severed head over the door of the abbey and, I quote, "his limbs were exposed in four counties".'

Nat looked at Woody, who was clearly appalled.

'Maybe it's that,' agreed Nat, 'but I still don't think this is right. We've tried to pick up something in the tower, but there's nothing to indicate that old Rydian was ever even here, let alone the Baphomet Head.'

Woody sniffed the air. 'Nope,' he agreed, 'I'm gettin' nothin'.'

'I'm not giving up yet,' said Fish determinedly, 'and nor should you.'

Fish was beside herself with disappointment.

It had been interesting at first to watch Nat and Woody use their Wolven senses like psychic metal detectors, but after hours of finding nothing, not even a Roman pot or a Bronze Age brooch, they called it a night. At three in the morning Fish crawled into her sleeping bag in disgust, while Nat and Woody sat cross-legged outside the tent, munching their way through four enormous bags of salt 'n' vinegar crisps and discussing whether or not it was safe to eat the green ones. Afterwards, their bellies full, they lay on their backs, their faces raised to the velvety night sky, feeling the chilly glow of the moon on their skin and enjoying an unexpected but spectacular show of shooting stars burning across the sky.

At Meade Lodge, Harmony Wedlock had emerged safely from her first shift, and while Nat and Woody were enjoying the light show at the top of Glastonbury Tor, she was sitting in her pyjamas, feeling rather sorry for herself and stroking one of Iona's stuffed cats. Her dad and Iona were talking about her in hushed tones (or so they thought) in the kitchen, but Harmony could hear every single word with her new werewolf hearing. Her head buzzed with sounds she wouldn't normally have been able to hear, like the mice skittering and squeaking in the skirting boards. And who'd have thought that even the smaller creatures like the insects and moths nestling outside in the ivy could make such a flaming racket? Iona had told Harmony that she would learn to filter out all the stuff she didn't need to hear, and Harmony was hoping to control it sooner rather than later. It was all a bit too much, what with growing ears and a tail and all the other werewolfy stuff she had to be able to control.

When she thought she heard the soft fall of footsteps outside, she slid from the squashy sofa and peered out of the window onto the moonlit garden. It was some minutes before she caught sight of the owner of the footsteps and realised she had picked up the sound from much further away.

Whoever it was smelt female and wore a perfume that she hadn't come across before. It was mysterious, heady and sort of *dangerous,* and as Harmony inhaled it, she realised she wanted to meet whoever was wearing it. The person drew nearer and Harmony could see that she was swathed in a long black coat with a hood hiding her head and face.

Seconds after the female figure disappeared from her view, there was a single knock on the front door, followed by the faint rustling sound of two people embracing. Then the living-room door opened and Iona came in, followed by the tall figure wrapped in black. Harmony could feel the chill of the night still clinging to her visitor's coat, and shivered a little with the thrill of anticipation. Although the newcomer could hardly be described as normal (she was way too exotic), at least she looked human. And to Harmony, there was something about her that was startlingly familiar.

'Hey,' smiled the girl, bundling up her coat and chucking it casually on the floor. She wore a short, blue dress decorated with silvery moons and stars, black leggings and biker boots. Her pillarbox-red hair rippled down to her waist and as she removed her dark glasses, Harmony was so delighted she completely forgot her predicament and almost dropped the stuffed cat on the floor. She *knew* this girl!

'Oh,' she squeaked, 'you're . . .'

'This is Crescent,' said Iona, amused, 'although I can tell by your face you probably already know that.'

Harmony's eyes were threatening to pop out of her head. *Oh. My. God.* She couldn't believe it. Standing in front of her was Crescent Moon, who just happened to be the singer with the Howlers, who just happened to be Harmony's favourite band in the entire world. And here she was, in Iona's front room, in the flesh, her eyes glowing a soft orange. Crescent Moon was like her. She was a werewolf.

'How are you?' asked Crescent, lowering herself down onto the sofa next to Harmony. 'Iona tells me you're being really brave about all this.'

Harmony smiled at her idol shyly. *Suddenly, being a werewolf didn't feel so bad.*

When Iona had left the room, Crescent took Harmony's hands in her own and gave her a piece of advice that Harmony never forgot.

'You can embrace your condition as a gift and live a life of excitement and adventure,' said Crescent, her red hair glinting in the firelight. 'Or you can treat it as a terrible curse. If that's the path you choose, your life will be very lonely, and very miserable.'

'Thanks for being so honest,' said Harmony, bravely.

'S'true,' shrugged Crescent. 'I've been a werewolf since I was your age. It sucked at first, but now I wouldn't have it any other way.'

'How did you become one?' asked Harmony.

'That's a story for another time,' said Crescent. 'For now, you just need to know how to manage your shifts and remember to wear coloured contact lenses or sunglasses whenever you go out.'

'Iona said there aren't many female werewolves,' remembered Harmony. 'Why's that?'

Crescent shivered slightly. 'It's because girls aren't usually able to withstand the shock of being attacked. I guess you and me are made of strong stuff.'

'The last few days have been . . . difficult,' said Harmony, still stroking the rigid cat on her lap. 'The things I've seen – zombies, escaped tigers, Wolven . . .'

Crescent laughed, remembering her adventures with Nat and Woody and the vampire queen. 'Yeah, things always have a way of getting interesting whenever those two are around.'

Harmony was about to reply when the cat she had been absent-mindedly stroking suddenly shifted ever so slightly on her lap. After the strange happenings of the past few days, she'd been feeling nothing else could possibly astonish her. Now she watched, opened-mouthed, as the little cat stretched, flexed its claws and yawned as though it had been asleep for a very long time. It stood up, jumped from her lap and started to wash itself in front of Crescent.

'Hey Clawdia,' said Crescent, giggling at Harmony's expression.

'It's alive!' gasped Harmony.

'Yeah,' said Crescent, 'they do that if you keep stroking them for long enough.'

'B-but. . .' stammered Harmony.

'Clawdia is a witch's cat,' said Crescent, raising her eyebrows. 'What d'you expect?'

When she heard the sound of both girls laughing, Iona smiled at Joe.

'I think Harmony's going to be just fine.'

While Harmony and Crescent were bonding in the warmth of Iona's living room, Nat and Woody were stargazing on top of Glastonbury Tor. As they lay side by side, Woody stole a glance across at Nat and thought how strange his friend's unfamiliar profile looked in the bright light of the moon – his head so misshapen and cruelly twisted halfway through shifting from human to wolf. Nat seemed lost in his own thoughts, but Woody didn't try to tap into them – he respected Nat's privacy. Woody knew one thing, though, without needing to brainjack his friend. Nat was beginning to lose faith that he would ever change back.

'I don't know what to do,' said Nat, catching Woody's thoughts and breaking the silence. He turned his head to look at the Wolven.

'You mean about the way you look?' asked Woody, leaning up on one elbow so he could see Nat properly.

'Yeah,' said Nat, 'I can't go on like this, I just *can't*.'

'You look all right to me,' said Woody, loyally. 'Anyway, we don't know you'll be like it *for ever*.'

Nat tried to smile, but it came out all wrong, like a grimace. 'Thanks, but if I was going to change either way – like back to human shape or on to Wolven shape – I reckon it would've happened by now.'

Woody blew his cheeks out, the way he always did when he was stumped for the right answer. 'D'you want to hear a joke?'

It was Nat's turn to blow out his cheeks. 'Not really, your jokes are rubbish. No offence.'

Woody grinned in the moonlight. Telling jokes was his favourite thing. 'No, you'll love this one. It's really brilliant.'

'Oh, go on then,' sighed Nat, 'do your worst.'

'OK,' said Woody happily. 'What d'you call a wolf that howls at the moon in frilly knickers and a bra?'

'I don't know,' sighed Nat, 'Crescent?'

'Nope,' grinned Woody, 'an *underwerewolf*, geddit? Knickers and a bra, underwear.'

Nat shook his head in disbelief. 'That is *so* lame, even for you.'

Woody looked crestfallen, he had wanted to cheer Nat up, not make him worse.

'OK, this is really, really good,' he said. 'Have you heard the one about Wibble?'

'No,' said Nat, crabbily, 'and I don't want to either thanks, so don't bother.'

Woody ignored him. It was for Nat's own good, after all – he just didn't know it yet. 'Iona told me this one, and it was a real LMAO situation. Are you ready?'

'Mmm,' said Nat, disinterestedly.

'Right,' said Woody, getting comfy. 'The lord of the manor was a very old man who had a butler named Wibble. One day the old dude called Wibble and said, "Run me a bath, Wibble."

'"Yes, Sir," replied Wibble. "Will there be anything else, my lord?"

'"Yes, Wibble, please fetch my robe."

'"Certainly, Sir. Will there be anything else?"

'"Yes, Wibble, fetch my carpet slippers if you wouldn't mind."

'"Certainly, Sir. Will there be anything else, my lord?"

'"No, Wibble. If I need anything else, I shall call you."

'With that, the old dude lowered himself into the water and let rip a really loud fart. Five minutes later, Wibble returned with a hot-water bottle on a silver tray.

'"Here you are, my lord, your hot-water bottle."

'"I never asked for that," said his lordship.

'Wibble replied, "But you did, my lord. As you lowered yourself into the bath, I distinctly heard you say, *Whadabowdawadderboddlewibble*."'

There was silence for a few seconds then Nat howled. Literally. Woody looked at his friend, alarmed, then he realised Nat was laughing. It was infectious and for a few minutes the two boys were creased up with helpless laughter, which rang around the countryside.

'Oh, oh God,' said Nat, tears streaming down his furry cheeks, 'Iona told you *that*?'

'Yep,' grinned Woody, 'told you it was a good 'un.'

'Oh . . .' said Nat weakly, going off into howly guffaws again, 'that's the best joke I have ever heard and it's even better that Iona told it to you. I can't even imagine her saying "fart".'

'It's the way I tell 'em,' said Woody, happily, glad that he had made Nat forget about his predicament, if only for a few minutes. It was good to see his friend laugh again.

'Have you thought any more about what Nellynora Goodwill told us, back in Temple Gurney?' asked Woody, when they had stopped their fit of giggles for the fifth time.

'Yeah,' said Nat, 'and I bet you have too.'

'Thought of nothing else,' grinned Woody. 'As soon as we've found the Baphomet Head, I want to find those Wolven, Nat, I want that more than anything.'

In the morning, Nat and Woody stood together facing westwards. The Bristol Channel glinted gold and silver under wide blue skies, and Sheephome

Island rose mysteriously from the depths like a great humpbacked whale.

'My granddad took me there once in his boat,' said Nat, pointing out to sea. 'It's uninhabited now. It's a nature reserve and it's got this really cool ruined priory that—'

'*What*?' interrupted Woody. Nat stared at him. Woody had a really weird look on his face.

'What's the matter with *you*?' asked Nat. 'I was just saying that . . .'

Woody grabbed his arm. 'It's an island!' he cried excitedly. 'It's green and there's a holy building on it. "*When the wolven come again to the house of God on the green isle, let my burden be done.*" The Baphomet is there. I just know it!'

Chapter 21
Black Rock

Teddy Davis knew that his every move was now being watched. Ever since he'd been caught in Josh's room by Scale, he hadn't needed to be a brainiac to work out that Lucas Scale was keeping a close eye on him. Teddy knew that the wolf was waiting for him to make a mistake, and if that happened and he was exposed as a double agent working for *NightShift*, Scale would show no mercy. Teddy didn't like to think about it, but he was aware that Scale's way of dealing with traitors was to rip off their heads and pull their lungs out through the hole. Then – and this was the bit that Teddy really couldn't think about without feeling as though he was going to puke – Scale would give his tortured soul to the demon with the unpronounceable and brain-shrivelling name.

For all the above reasons, Teddy dared not contact *NightShift*. So he had no idea if Nat and Woody had discovered any more clues which might lead them to the elusive Baphomet Head. It was clear from their rapid departure from the gorge that they hadn't found anything there, apart from the images carved into the soft limestone of the cavern. And Scale had seen those too. But what had the Wolven been doing since then?

When the werewolves had seen Nat Carver scooped up by the enormous Hell's Angel and roaring off into the sunset in a cloud of smoke with Woody galloping alongside, it had been almost too much for Lucas Scale to bear. Since that moment, his behaviour had deteriorated so badly he'd taken to muttering in his rocking chair and snarling at anyone who dared come near.

Morale was lowered still further when the pups came back empty-handed from Abbas Combe. This village, Scale had been reliably informed by his demon, sported a church rumoured to have a Templar stronghold beneath the altar. When Scale's wolves had invaded the church just after evensong, they had menaced the vicar and the congregation but failed to find anything apart from a few ancient scripts, which were unreadable, and a couple of suits of rusty armour. And Scale's behaviour continued to slide into the realms of insanity and beyond.

To her absolute disgust, Agent Fish was instructed to go back to London after they abandoned the search of Glastonbury Tor, while Nat and Woody were given the job of continuing to look for the Baphomet Head.

'As you said yourself, Alex,' said Crone mildly, on her return, 'it's a process of elimination, and Nat and Woody are better equipped than you for finding hidden things.'

Fish pursed her lips but knew the boss was right. Without the benefit of Nat and Woody's Wolven gifts she would hold them up. Nevertheless, her expression remained hostile.

'I need you here,' said Crone, firmly. 'I have something to share with you. Something that concerns our agent.'

'I *knew* it,' said Fish, 'I bet he's double-crossed us and gone over to the dark side.'

Crone shook his head unhappily. 'I refuse to believe that,' he said. 'But I *am* worried that something terrible has happened to him.'

Fish stared at him aghast. 'Then I think you were wrong to send Nat and Woody without backup,' she said, coldly.

In Temple Gurney, the dark morning sky was threatening stormy weather as Nat and Woody left Iona at Meade Lodge and made for Diamond Bay. The obvious way to travel across the Channel to Sheephome Island would be to use the boat that belonged to Nat's granddad; and Nat crossed his fingers and hoped the *Diamond Lil* was still moored in the small harbour and that his granddad had left the keys in his usual hidey-hole.

Both Nat and Woody were relieved when they sighted her bobbing about on the choppy waves. They jumped aboard easily and Nat felt for the secret place under the door frame where Mick hid the key. As they stowed their wet-weather gear, Nat thanked his lucky stars he had listened to all Granddad had told him about piloting the little boat. He managed to steer the *Diamond Lil* clear of the bay and once they were chugging out to sea, he began to enjoy himself. But further out, the waves started to get bigger. Much bigger. Nat and Woody, neither of whom were good sailors, both turned an interesting shade of green.

Mick had told Nat that the funnel shape of this

part of the Bristol Channel, and the fact that it had one of the highest tidal ranges in the world, made it tricky to negotiate in any kind of boat. Although the *Diamond Lil* was a sturdy little vessel, she was being tossed about on the waves like a cork. The wind had increased and the spray from the sea made it difficult to see properly even with their enhanced eyesight. By the time they got to Sheephome Nat and Woody were wet through and shivering with cold.

The island loomed up in front of them, the cliffs black and impenetrable. A thick fog rose from the water so Nat couldn't see the jetty until they were about three metres in front of it; and, with jagged rocks at the bottom of the sheer cliffs, it took some effort and a great deal of luck to steer the *Diamond Lil* in the right direction and land her.

'I got the chills,' said Woody, looking miserable.

Nat's belly went cold. When Woody got the chills it was usually because he felt something bad was going to happen, a bit like Nat's own premonitions.

'Then we'd better get on with it,' said Nat. 'I don't feel too good about this either, but we should know more or less immediately if we're on to something.'

They jumped out of the boat, onto the rickety wooden jetty and hurried up the steps. At the top of the beach there was a concrete plateau and through the fog Nat could just about make out a ruined building. He remembered his granddad telling him it had been an inn something like a hundred years ago. It looked stark and unwelcoming in the dreary fog, and the cries of the seagulls above sounded eerie and mournful, only adding to the boys' anxious mood.

The eight reasons why Woody was suffering from the chills were about half an hour away, speeding along the Bristol Channel in a stolen RNLI lifeboat. They made quite a sight: a pack of werewolves, fur matted and bedraggled from sitting in the wet, all looking thoroughly fed up. It wasn't easy fitting them all in either, and the unfortunates who had to sit on the sides kept falling into the water. They were all in wolf form except for Lucas Scale, who insisted on steering. His face was frozen into a fearsome grin as he gritted his teeth and tried not to think about how wet and hateful the water was. The boat rode high, its powerful outboard engine weighing it down at the back, so it was difficult for even an experienced sailor to steer, let alone a crazed werewolf.

Scale was using his own process of elimination of Templar and religious sites to find the Baphomet Head. After his wolves' failure to find anything at Abbas Combe, it was pure bad luck for Nat and Woody that, as the nearest alternative site, Sheephome Island was next on Scale's list.

* * *

To make matters worse for Nat and Woody, it began to rain as they followed the steep zigzag path to the top of the island. A small wooded area of silver birch trees gave them shelter for a while, but it looked as though it would be wet for the rest of the day so they moved on. It was weird being the only people on the island. When there were day trips, wardens showed people round, but there didn't appear to be anyone about today and the small visitor centre was deserted. There were a few crumbling buildings dotted around and, because the island had been used as a lookout fort and barracks during both world wars, a number of abandoned and rusting gun emplacements still faced the sea as they had done in wartime. Although the mist was thinner on the top of the island, the wind blew and the rain lashed their faces, making it difficult for Nat to get his bearings.

'Are we lost?' shouted Woody, over the wind.

'Not exactly,' replied Nat, and pointed across the island. 'I think the priory's on the west side, I can remember it was quite a trek from the landing beach.'

'I think we better—'

'What?' asked Nat and froze. A shrieking howl was being carried across the island on the wind.

'I think we better run.'

Nat had already started running. But it looked as

if the werewolves had learned how to act as a proper pack. Obeying Scale's instructions, they spread out in a fan-like formation and came hurtling across the bracken, heading towards Nat and Woody, howling and yipping with excitement.

'Head 'em off at the point,' howled Scale. 'Remember, they must be taken aliiiiiiive.'

Nat didn't have time to think about anything as he pelted after Woody, the wind and rain blurring his vision as they ran. Both of them could smell the werewolves on the wind as they gained on them, a wet dog stink, and as Nat and Woody were on two legs the werewolves were at a distinct advantage.

CHANGE! Nat's mindhowl blasted through Woody's brain. *SAVEYOURSELF!*

But Woody had no intention of changing and leaving Nat behind. If Nat could have shifted, they would have had a chance, but on two legs he was too slow and they were hopelessly outnumbered.

Scale continued shrieking as they ran and Nat risked a quick glance behind. The worst was happening. The werewolves were getting closer and closer, and there was nowhere left to run.

'Ahaaaaaa,' came Scale's gleeful yell above the wind. 'Caught like rats in a trap.'

And so they were. Nat and Woody had run out of land. Scale watched as the pack of seven chased them to the edge of the island, where a World War II lookout post still stood. Grinning proudly, Scale made his way across the grassy plateau to join them. He was pleased with the pack, but he still wasn't sure he trusted them not to do something stupid, like eating both prisoners before they could impart any valuable information about the Baphomet Head.

Scale was delighted when he saw the state of Nat's face. The scarf and cap had blown away in the chase and his head was exposed.

'Oh ho ho,' he chortled. 'What have we here, Master Carver? I see you have a new look.'

Nat said nothing.

'No, I like it,' said Scale, pushing his face close into Nat's, enjoying the look of disgust as the boy got the full benefit of Scale's putrid breath. 'D'you know?' he continued, smirking. 'I think you look very handsome. If you'll excuse my vanity, I think you look rather like me. We could be father and son.'

'Get lost,' snarled Nat.

'Well excuuuse me,' simpered Scale, 'we are touchy today. Get out of the wrong side of the kennel, did we?'

Then Scale turned his attention to Woody. 'And Woody,' he said, 'we meet again. I was beginning to think you were avoiding me.'

'Go to hell,' said Woody.

Lucas Scale put his paws up in mock horror. 'Funny you should mention hell, because that's exactly where you two are headed.'

'What are you going to do to us?' asked Nat, coldly.

Scale's expression changed abruptly. 'I would have thought that was perfectly obvious,' he snarled. 'It's what you might call payback time. You will help me find the Baphomet Head, and then I will introduce you to a certain someone who has got the real hots for you.'

Nat had a pretty good idea what Lucas Scale meant. He was going to take them to his demon so that it could take his and Woody's souls instead of Scale's. Thoughts raced through his brain, mixing with Woody's as they both tried to fathom how they were going to get out of this deadly situation.

Quickly Nat itemised their options in his head so that Woody could see them. None of them were very tempting.

1. Attack the werewolves – *problem:* too many. He might have had a chance if he could still wolf out, but in his present state he and Woody would be ripped to shreds.

2. Go quietly and try to think of a way to escape when they were back on land – *problem:* they would have to help Scale find the Baphomet and maybe meet the demon.

3. Jump off the cliff – *problem:* strong currents.

Nat glanced surreptitiously behind him and felt his head go all weird and spinny when he looked all the way down to the rough sea. This earned him a slap round the face from Scale's enormous paw, which raked the side of Nat's cheek with his claws.

'Don't even think about it,' snarled Scale. 'You're too human to get very far.'

An odd feeling came over Nat. His head was still woozy and he couldn't hear anything properly, just a faint ringing like the sound of a wet finger rubbing the rim of a glass.

Oh my days, thought Nat, *I'm gonna flip!* The familiar taste of rosehips flooded into his mouth, and his last thought before he went was to grab Woody by his T-shirt. Before Scale could move a whisker both boys had been toppled backwards by the strength of Nat's flip and were plummeting into the coffee-coloured waters of the Bristol Channel. Not just off the cliff but off the edge of the world.

CHAPTER 22
FLIPPING

*B*limey O'Reilly, thought Nat, dismally. *Where am I? When am I? And where the flippin' heck is Woody?*

His instincts told him that he was in a time far, far earlier than the twenty-first century. It wasn't too much of a surprise. He had known this was coming, after all. The clues all pointed to both him and Woody flipping sooner or later. So here he was. He'd flipped, and he thought he'd hung onto Woody long enough to bring him too this time. *But, if that was true, where was he?*

Nat estimated he had still been in his own time when they'd both crashed into the water, and he was pretty sure that Woody had wolfed out as they fell, because he had felt Woody's teeth grabbing the neck of his shirt to pull him up to the surface. He had been dimly aware of the strong currents forming a sort of whirlpool pushing him down into the brown water again, like it meant business.

It had been late afternoon when Scale had caught up with them, and the weather had been wild and stormy. Whenever Nat was now, whatever year he was in, it appeared to be morning. Somehow he knew this was a younger world; the colours were more vivid, the air was cleaner – purer. He began to focus on his present situation. He was draped uncomfortably over a large seaweed-covered rock only a few metres from the shore, and the tide appeared to be on the turn. Tentatively, he put one foot into the brown swirling water and was relieved it was shallow enough to paddle to shore.

When he reached the muddy beach, he screwed up his eyes against the sunlight and looked about him. There was nowhere to go except upwards. Cursing the sharp stones on his bare feet, Nat stumbled painfully away from the mudbank. By the time he had staggered onto the scrubby grasslands, he was sweating, light-headed and sick to his belly. He fell to his knees.

'Ooooh,' he groaned and retched a couple of times before he trusted himself to stand up again. His legs weren't behaving themselves. They were wobbly and felt as though they were going to pitch him back into the mud. He stood still, the taste of rosehips still on his tongue. The Bristol Channel stretched out before him, glinting gold in the rays of the sun, but there was still no sign of Woody.

Nat stood for a while longer, hoping that he would see his friend scramble up to the beach, shaking the water from his fur.

Whereareyou? he called with his mind, now getting seriously worried. There was no reply and Nat reluctantly made his way further up the beach to some rough stone steps cut into the side of the cliff.

From his higher vantage point Nat spotted something that made his heart sink. There by the jagged rocks at the shoreline was a large white object being dragged in and out by the tide. Woody had been washed up like a piece of driftwood and was floating freely to the motion of the ocean.

'Woody!' yelled Nat and, forgetting his wobbly legs and sore feet, he stumbled back across the stones to where Woody lay.

Don't let him be dead, don't let him be dead, don't let

him be dead, prayed Nat. He pulled Woody's heavy body out of the water and flung himself on his knees. He was pretty sure Woody wasn't breathing. Nat pushed a wolf-like ear close to Woody's sodden chest. He couldn't even hear his Wolven heart beating.

'Woody!' Nat yelled again. 'Can you hear me?'

Nothing. Nat tried to remember what you're supposed to do when someone drowns. He rolled Woody over onto his back, which was difficult as his tail kept getting in the way. Then he prized open Woody's enormous jaws, taking care to roll his Wolven tongue out of the way so he wouldn't choke on it, and took a deep breath. He stuck his head in Woody's mouth and blew, pinching his nostrils at the same time. Nothing.

Nat took another enormous breath and blew into Woody's mouth again. He pulled back and shouted Woody's name. Still nothing; not a flicker of life. Nat fought the panic rising in his chest. What should he do?

Then he remembered seeing a TV programme about paramedics; they'd pressed a man's chest to get the heart started. So he pumped and pumped on Woody's Wolven body desperately. Just when Nat felt he had no more strength, he felt Woody's head move. Nat stood back to give him air and, to his joy, saw his eyelids flutter. Then he stood back further as at last Woody spluttered violently, bringing up what seemed to be half the Bristol Channel. When he'd stopped coughing up seawater, Nat was surprised to see Woody's fur bristle with indignation.

'What?' asked Nat. 'I had to do it!'

Dintwannaflipthoughfeelsick.

'You can't always plan magic,' shrugged Nat. 'I'm glad it happened. Scale would have fed us to his demon if we hadn't flipped, no messing.'

Woody's fur went back to normal. *Spose.*

'C'mon,' said Nat, feeling heaps better. 'If you're feeling a bit better, time to find out what's in store for us.'

There were signs everywhere that they had travelled through time. Nat recognised the beach they'd been washed up on as the one where they had moored the *Diamond Lil*, but there was no ruined inn or anything else to see, apart from a small wooden boat safely shored up at the top of the beach. The same zigzag path they had climbed in the twenty-first century led them up to an earlier grove of silver birch trees and they walked side by side through a fragrant wood carpeted with beautiful flowers. Nat was grateful for the feel of the soft grass soothing the cuts where the soles of his feet had been ripped by the cruel stones. When they came to the edge of the small wood, Nat could see the layout of the island had remained more or less the same, except obviously the lookouts and bunkers from World War II hadn't arrived yet. Instead, there was a series of buildings that certainly hadn't been there before. One of them looked like a house, but as they drew closer, Nat could see it was attached to a small church-like structure with a bell tower, a courtyard and a few low outbuildings. Deer and sheep grazed contentedly in the paddock adjoining the small house, and chickens scratched and clucked in the courtyard. There was something peaceful and welcoming about it. Both Nat and Woody felt they had come home.

They reached the courtyard and hesitated. Nat wondered if he should try to find a doorbell. His thoughts were interrupted by someone calling cheerily from the doorway.

'Good morrow, brothers.'

Nat, with Woody panting at his side, raised a hand in greeting and wished he didn't look such a fright.

The person who had hailed them was tall and muscular. *Not old*, Nat thought, though his hair and beard were white. Nat recognised him straightaway from the vision he had had at the gorge. It was the Templar monk. It was Rydian.

'Hi, er, good morrow,' said Nat weakly. 'Are . . . are you Rydian?'

'Yea, I am he,' said the monk, coming towards them. 'You seek me for the reason I see on your countenance?'

'Yeah, er, yea,' said Nat awkwardly. 'I'm Nat Carver, and this is Woody.'

The monk nodded. 'It is not just your troubled appearance upon which you seek advice?' he asked.

'No,' said Nat, simply. Then, as he smiled shyly up at Rydian, he glimpsed a familiar topaz light in his brown eyes. Nat stopped smiling and gasped audibly.

'You're Wolven!'

Rydian dipped his handsome head in acknowledgement and smiled.

'Tis true,' he said gently.

'We've come from the twenty-first century,' said Nat, realising he sounded like a bad sci-fi film. 'I mean, we travelled here from the future to get something. Something that will cause a war to end all wars, the end of the human race. You've left us clues – instructions – on how to find it: drawings at Cheddar caves and a message in a tomb at the Temple Church in London.'

Rydian looked fairly astonished at Nat's words.

'Oh, sorry,' said Nat, 'you won't have done it yet, left the clues I mean. That's to come.'

Rydian nodded thoughtfully. 'I have heard a prophecy that speaks of such strange phenomena,' he said. 'Pray come inside and tell me what it is that you seek.'

* * *

Rydian proved to be an excellent host. It was dark inside the priory, but candles were lit and food laid out in the form of delicious, oaty cakes and thick creamy milk. Woody shifted to human and borrowed one of Rydian's habits; and between them both boys told the monk everything, from when they first met, to Scale's demon and the race to find the Head of the Baphomet.

'I was elected to be the Keeper of the Baphomet Head,' said Rydian. 'The evil power it possesses is legion.'

'Do you know where it is?' asked Nat.

''Tis here presently,' said Rydian, 'in the vault.'

'Can we take it back with us, please?' asked Nat.

'If we can get back,' said Woody with a shudder. 'What if we're stuck here for ever?'

'It doesn't work like that,' said Nat, comfortingly. 'When I've flipped before the longest I've been gone is about twelve hours.'

'Don't leave me here,' said Woody. 'No offence,' he added, to Rydian.

'I will show you the Baphomet Head,' said Rydian gravely. 'If you can transport it safely, you may take it back to whence you came.'

Woody shook his head vigorously. 'No,' he said. 'We can't take it back.'

'Why on earth not?' demanded Nat. 'We can't just

leave it now we know where it is.'

'You've forgotten something really, really important,' insisted Woody. 'You can't fetch something from the past and take it to the future; it's against all the rules of time and space.'

'You've been watching too much flippin' *Doctor Who*,' said Nat, impatiently.

'It's actually true,' protested Woody. 'If you do that, you create a time paradox where a parallel universe is created and then there are two of everything which is normally OK but then you'd be talking about two Baphomet Heads and double the trouble and—'

'Stop,' said Rydian, 'who is this Doctor you speak of?'

'It's just Woody's favourite telly programme,' explained Nat.

'But . . .' Rydian looked completely baffled, like someone who has just had the offside rule explained to them.

'It's not important,' said Nat, 'but Woody's right. If we take the Head out of your century, it might cause all sorts of extra problems.'

'I know,' said Woody, brightly. 'What if we agree now that you're gonna hide the Head somewhere and you tell us where, and then our future selves can pick it up when we get back to our own time.'

'That could work,' said Nat, catching some of

Woody's excitement. 'And you must tell a man called Sir Hugh de Gourney to write about us in his chronicles. That bit's really important!'

'There's another thing that's important,' said Woody, nudging Nat, 'isn't there?'

Askhimaboutyourface.

Rydian caught Woody's thoughts and smiled sadly. 'I have known this to happen amongst our people,' he said, 'and it is true it may last for many years or, for some, until they die.'

Nat felt Rydian's words twist in his gut. Deep down he had suspected that his shift was never going to happen.

'But,' continued Rydian, 'I have heard tell of a sacred cure that I would take myself if my countenance became thus.'

Nat wasn't quite sure what Rydian meant sometimes, but he thought that 'countenance' meant face.

'St Michael's Abbey sits on a site of great power, the mighty isle of Avalon at Glastonbury.'

'We know it well,' said Nat, wryly.

'Below the great Tor, a holy spring fed from the sacred waters of the Underworld has been proven by our kind. On summer solstice, seek out the red water, drink only from the lion's head and immerse thyself in the pool.'

'Thank you,' said Nat. 'I'll do anything if I can just

change back.'

Mindful that he could flip at any minute, Nat wanted to make plans about the Baphomet Head.

'Wherever my life may take me, I will always be the Keeper of the Baphomet,' explained Rydian. 'It is written that I will die on this rock and that the Baphomet will stay with me.'

'You'll be buried with it?' asked Woody, trying not to shudder. 'Don't you mind?'

Rydian smiled. ''Tis my destiny. And when I am dead I will take its secret with me.'

'So,' said Nat, feeling uncomfortable talking about such things, 'where will you, er, your body be buried?'

'I will show you,' said Rydian his eyes twinkling topaz again. 'And we will look upon the Baphomet.'

'D'we have to?' asked Woody. 'I mean, we know what it looks like.'

'I think we need to,' said Nat. 'C'mon.'

Rydian led the way through the cool corridors until they reached an oak door set in a stone wall. From there he took them down a small stairwell into a narrow passage hewn out of the rock, where many domestic items were stored – stone jars, which Nat assumed contained food, and flagons of ale and mead. There were fruit and vegetables, too, and animal feed, all kept cool in the dark.

Rydian led them to a wooden box that looked like

a miniature coffin. Nat thought how weird it was to keep something so inherently evil alongside kitchen items like cheese and jam.

Rydian lifted the lid and placed his hands inside. He pulled the Baphomet Head from its resting place, closed the lid and placed the Head on top of the wooden box.

Nat was struck immediately by the sheer evil emanating from the Baphomet. You could see the sword wound that had severed it from its body. Although it was mostly bone, there was some evidence of skin and hair on the sides of its goatish face. Its eyes were closed, so the boys were spared the yellow glare they had seen in the medieval pictures, but it seemed to leak evil. Nat wished Rydian would put it away.

'It is dormant presently,' smiled Rydian, hearing Nat's thoughts. He could also hear a curious ringing noise, like a wet finger running around the rim of a wine goblet. The noise seemed to echo round the room. Woody leapt close to Nat and grabbed his arm.

'Rydian,' began Nat, but the taste of rosehips was already flooding his mouth.

Then he yelped in surprise as someone seemed to yank him backwards. He felt giddy again and tasted the bitterness of whatever lay beneath the rosehips. The last thing he was aware of was the warm, strong presence of Woody clinging to him with all his might.

Chapter 23
A Company of Wolves

It was dark and the rain was still falling hard, lashing down onto Nat's upturned face as he came out of the flip. The waves were like mini tsunamis crashing on the shoreline and sending spray high into the black sky. This time Nat didn't have to look for Woody because he could feel the heavy weight of him lying across his legs. He rolled over on the pebbles and pushed Woody away, feeling shaky, sick and extremely fed up.

Not for the first time since all this had started, Nat

wanted to go home. Not to Iona's, not to Middle Temple, but home to his mum and dad, wherever they might be now. It was like déjà vu only worse, for he knew they would have to climb back up the zigzag path, back though the silver birch wood and trace the ruins of the old priory, hoping upon hope that they would be able to find the Baphomet Head and get off the island before Scale and his wolves caught up with them again.

Woody was stirring, his body streaked with mud. He vomited a thin stream of brown water and sat up, looking as wretched and fed up as Nat felt.

'Here,' said Nat, handing Woody his T-shirt. 'Looks like the monk's habit couldn't flip with us.'

'I don't ever want to do that again,' Woody moaned, as he wriggled into the sopping T-shirt. 'It's just not right, travelling like that, it's . . . oh no, it can't be!'

'What now? asked Nat wearily.

'Oh Nat, I'm sorry,' said Woody. 'Look.'

Nat spun round in alarm and saw for himself what Woody had seen. He gave a terrible cry and ran towards the smoking, wrecked shell of the *Diamond Lil.* Not content with burning his grandparents' house to the ground, Scale and his wolves had set fire to his granddad's pride and joy. And with it had gone their chances of getting off the island.

Woody left Nat alone as long as he felt was necessary, but they needed to get moving. 'Look,' he said, touching Nat's shoulder, 'Scale's boat's still here. They must have missed the tides. We can take it and leave 'em stranded.'

Nat shook his head, his mouth set in a grim determined line, the spikes of his teeth clearly visible.

'If the tide's on the turn, we better get a move on,' said Woody.

Nat grinned suddenly, and Woody shivered inwardly. For a second there his friend had looked really frightening – vicious, even.

'Not without the Baphomet Head,' Nat said. 'C'mon partner, let's do it.'

Scale had almost chucked himself over the cliff after Nat and Woody when they had plummeted seventy metres off the side of the island. He pulled back at the last minute when he remembered the two things in the world that terrified the pants off him: bees, and being immersed in water. The Wolven would be pulverised by the waves and sucked underneath the roiling brown sea. So Scale had hung onto the rock feeling queasy at the sight and sound of the waves and waited for their bodies to reappear.

It was a wasted wait. The tidal range in this part of the Channel made it notorious for its currents, especially at the spring tide, and the opposing pull of the water caused freakish whirlpools that would suck you down and hold you in the mud until all you were fit for was a fish's dinner. By Lucas Scale's reckoning, Nat Carver was a sorry excuse for a Wolven; he was neither fish nor fowl. And the other one had been in human form when they fell – which meant they wouldn't have been able to use all their Wolven strength to save themselves. But instead of being pleased they were dead, Scale felt it had been a hollow victory. He felt cheated. Cheated of seeing the Carver boy and Woody suffer. The end had been way too quick.

Then he felt a cold chill of terror. Hadn't he promised their miserable souls to the demon with the unpronounceable name? *Damn and blast!* But he was pretty sure the Baphomet Head was here on the island. The wolves were scratching and digging with paws the size of shovels while he watched, huddled inside his coat against the strength of the wind. The demon would have to be satisfied with that.

The wolves struck demon gold not long after they had started excavating. As soon as they smelt bone they narrowed the search down to one spot; Scale made them all hang back in case the prize was damaged and did the last bit of digging himself. He cackled when he saw the miniature coffin and the unusual skeleton. *So the Keeper of the Baphomet was Wolven vermin*, he thought, and then he did a very bad and wicked thing. He leapt into the grave and hopped about in like someone doing joke Irish dancing.

A few of the less corrupt wolves, including Teddy Davis and Josh Firkin, thought this was bang out of order. Teddy Davis nearly blew his cover (what was left of it) and jumped on Scale then and there, but managed to stop himself. Time for that later. Lucas Scale held the wooden box up like a prize, his eyes flashing.

'This, my children, is the shape of things to come,' said Scale theatrically, his voice rising above the wind and the rain. 'With the demon on our side we will be the most powerful creatures in the world!'

There was no artificial light on the island so the boys had to rely on their enhanced eyesight and gaps in the cloud. Both boys felt better for getting moving, and their bodies warmed up with every step they climbed. Neither of them spoke. They just listened to each other's thoughts about the last twelve hours.

When they reached the wood they were glad of the rest from the driving rain and they stopped for a while, listening intently. There was the usual scurrying of woodland creatures and low calls from night birds, but there was also a whiff of corruption in the air: the yellow, fetid smell of a bad wolf.

'Plan?' whispered Woody.

'Like it always was,' Nat whispered back. 'We go to the place where the priory once stood, try to focus in on the underground vault, open Rydian's grave and grab the Baphomet.'

'That's what's so horrible about flipping,' said Woody, in a quiet voice. 'We only just met Rydian, spent some time with him, liked him and now he's dead.'

'Yeah,' agreed Nat, 'but don't forget he didn't die for ages after we met him.'

'Still horrible,' insisted Woody.

Nat couldn't argue with that.

They crept cautiously to where they had last seen the priory and checked the landscape for evidence of Scale. It was strangely silent. They ran to the incline and the flattened area of soft grass, and realised they were too late. A black hole gaped in front of them where the underground vault had been, heaps of earth had been excavated from the hole and all that lay in the grave was a skeleton. The skeleton of a large canine animal – a Wolven.

The Baphomet Head had gone.

'They got here before us,' said Woody, dismally.

'Looks like it,' said Nat. 'But where are they? They couldn't have gone back to their boat, we would have seen them.'

'My guess is they're holed up somewhere for the night,' said Woody. 'It's not exactly great weather for a boat trip.'

They stood and looked down at the open grave and the rain falling on Rydian's bones.

'D'you think that'll happen to us when we die?' shivered Woody.

Nat shrugged. 'I suppose I was expecting a human skeleton. It's kind of a shock.'

'Cover him up,' said Woody, suddenly. 'It's not right to leave him here like this.'

In silence, the two boys gently pushed the wet earth back in place. When it was done they stood there and took a few moments to remember Rydian as he had been a few hours ago to them, but centuries ago in the real scheme of time and space.

'We'll come back and get him,' vowed Nat, 'give him a proper burial in the Temple Church.'

'Listen,' hissed Woody. 'Can you hear something?

The boys stayed close to the trees, the ancestors of which had once formed a wind barrier for Rydian's vegetable garden, and listened intently. Peering through the trees, they could just see the old ruined inn by the landing beach. In the glassless windows shone flickering lights, as though candles had been lit inside.

'So that's where he is,' said Nat, his eyes glimmering in the darkness.

'Plan?' whispered Woody.

'Like it always was,' grinned Nat, enjoying the moment. 'Scale's done us a favour – his wolves did all the digging. C'mon, we're going to get the Baphomet Head.'

They jogged towards the path, rain obscuring their vision now they had left the shelter of the wood. When they got to the landing beach they pressed themselves close to the concrete walls below the inn. Nat beckoned Woody to follow him, and the pair moved up towards the front of the building.

Canyouhearthat? asked Nat with his mind.

Soundsrough, replied Woody. *Whatisit?*

The door of the inn was shut, so they went round the side and found a low window. Nat swallowed a gasp as he peered through. There appeared to be five or six sleeping werewolves, curled up together like the world's largest puppies. There was no sign of Lucas Scale, and Nat guessed he was wherever the Baphomet was.

Snoringwolves, Nat sent back, trying hard to overcome an awful urge to laugh out loud, not because he found it funny, but because he knew he had to keep quiet.

Thebox?

Idontseeitbutineedyoutostayhere, sent Nat firmly.

Before Woody could argue, Nat sat on the low sill

and, silently and gracefully as a gymnast, swung his legs over and lowered himself gently into the room full of werewolves. Woody didn't suffer any bad chills in his belly, but he did think Nat would have more chance of staying alive if he went swimming with great white sharks.

Nat hardly dared breathe as he felt his feet touch the floor. He eyed the sleeping shapes warily and crept forward on tiptoes towards the open door. He had to find the box. He stopped dead as the nearest wolf, a slender brown-haired youngster, began to run in his dreams, his four legs scratching the dusty stone floor. Nat let his breath go, and was just about to carry on when a shadow fell across the floor. The marrow froze in his bones. Framed in the doorway was a human figure who stared at Nat with eyes of orange fire. Then Nat realised whoever it was wasn't ugly enough to be Scale. He smelled familiar too. Like Teddy Davis.

Teddy put a finger to his lips and beckoned Nat to follow. They padded noiselessly across the room, and Teddy led the way down a narrow corridor. Nat caught the unmistakeable stink of Lucas Scale.

'Where is he?' hissed Nat.

'Scale thinks you're dead, drowned,' Teddy whispered back. 'What happened to your face, how—'

'It's a long story,' whispered Nat, 'just show me

where the Head is and we can all get out of here.'

Teddy beckoned again, and Nat had a horrible thought. *Suppose Teddy is a double agent, as Fish suggested, and he's leading me to my death?* He shook himself. He wasn't having any bad feelings. And if Teddy was a traitor to *NightShift*, he'd surely have raised the alarm by now.

Teddy pointed silently and pushed gently on a half-closed door, revealing Lucas Scale in all his evil glory as he lay skew-whiff on a low bed, snoring his head off. One paw was resting on the top of what appeared to be a miniature coffin. The last time Nat had seen it was eight hundred years ago, but it still looked in good shape.

Holding his breath, Nat crept softly towards the box, not daring to take his eyes from the sleeping werewolf. He put out his hand, gently picked up Scale's paw and lowered it carefully away from the box. He leant forward, taking care not to get too close to Scale's face, and picked up the wooden box, feeling the awful, dead weight of the Baphomet's Head.

CHAPTER 24
TEDDY

❦

Nat and Teddy sneaked out the way they came, not daring to breathe while Scale still snored.

They tiptoed once more past the sleeping bodies of the werewolf pack and made for the window where Woody was waiting impatiently, keen to get away. The box containing the Baphomet Head was heavy, but the sight of Woody's anxious expression turning to delight when he saw it gave Nat the strength to heave it over the window ledge and into Woody's outstretched arms. Nat and Teddy scrambled out after it, almost knocking Woody over in their haste to get out, both imagining being grabbed from behind by sharp teeth at any moment.

With Nat and Woody carrying the box between them, they all ran down to the beach as fast as they could, not daring to look back. Adrenalin always comes in handy if you need to run really, really fast, and the three boys hurried towards the stolen RNLI dinghy as quickly as the stony beach would let them, trying not to yelp as the stones and shingle shredded the soles of their bare feet. The dinghy was anchored where they had left the *Diamond Lil,* and for a moment Nat felt another wave of sadness wash over him at the loss of his granddad's boat.

The dinghy appeared to be keen to get away too. It pulled its mooring rope taut and strained as the tide turned. Nat hefted the wooden box into the boat and suddenly realised there was something crucial he hadn't considered. He had no idea how to drive the thing. Inside, it was nothing like the *Diamond Lil,* and Nat stood looking for a clue about how to start it.

'You got to pull up the anchor first,' shouted Woody over the roar of the waves. 'Then you got to yank the string.'

'Come on, *come on*!' shouted Teddy. 'We haven't got much time!'

But Nat could feel panic rising, threatening to overwhelm him. He was anxious to secure the wooden box so it didn't fall out on the way back to Diamond Bay, but the waves were making it difficult to keep his balance. It was Woody who pulled up the anchor and it was Woody who pulled the ripcord on the massive outboard engine. Nat thanked their lucky stars that his friend had watched the whole series of *Seaside Rescue* on the telly.

The sound of the RNLI dinghy roaring into life pierced Lucas Scale's brain like a skewer. He leapt from his bed as though possessed by the devil himself, and practically flew through to the sleeping werewolves in his haste and rage. It was obvious to him what had happened. Teddy Davis was gone, and so was the Baphomet Head! Scale's deranged screams woke the mess of werewolves on the dusty floor; they took one look at the state of their master and shrank back, yipping and whining in terror.

'Go fetch the box!' screamed Scale. 'He's stolen it and he's getting awaaaaaaay, you idiot bunch of mutts!

'AAAAAAoooooooooowooooooooooo!' The howls of the werewolves rang out their deadly warning.

'They're coming!' yelled Nat, now in serious panic

mode. Despite the engine roaring into life for a couple of seconds, it made a phlegmy splutter of protest and died.

'Yank it again,' shouted Nat. 'Quick! Tr—'

As the wind snatched his words away, Nat became aware of several dark shapes bounding down the beach towards them.

Oh, flippin' heck, he thought. *Now we're for it.*

'Choke,' shouted Woody to no one in particular. He found the button and pulled it out halfway, then glanced behind him, saw what Nat had seen and pulled it out all the way. He could hear Scale's lunatic screaming ringing in his ears, making him feel confused and clumsy, but he yanked the cord again and at last the engine started properly.

'Stay where you are!' ordered Lucas Scale's scream, sounding thin and weak in the wind. His initial shock at seeing Nat and Woody apparently still alive and uninjured, would have to wait. They had stolen the Baphomet Head!

'Yeah, right,' shouted Teddy Davis, who then scrambled to the back of the boat, where Woody was reaching out his hand. But as Nat turned the wheel, the boat whirled round in a crazy circle, ditching Teddy into the dark water. Everything blurred for a few seconds as Nat tried to get control of the unstable dinghy, while Teddy helplessly watched the boat spinning round and round.

When at last Nat managed to straighten up, he saw that Scale and his wolves had already entered the water and were way too close for comfort. Scale was up to his waist in the waves, his eyes burning like molten coals as he waded towards them. Nat realised they had run out of time and luck, there was no way they could get Teddy back on board before Scale got to them. He would kill them for sure and take the Baphomet. It seemed Teddy was thinking the same thing because he had shifted into an enormous blond wolf and was now heading towards Scale, his teeth bared.

'We gotta go!' shouted Woody. 'Come on!'

'We can't leave Teddy!' Nat yelled against the wind.

Scale was now less than a metre from the dinghy, Nat could smell him.

'Nat!' yelled Woody. 'We can't . . .'

As Lucas Scale's mottled paw stretched out to grab the side of the boat, Teddy Davis sprang forward and pulled Scale under the water. Woody grabbed the wheel from Nat and, harnessing the power of the engine, aimed the dinghy at the pack, scattering them. Then he turned it once more, this time in the direction of Diamond Bay.

CHAPTER 25
HARMONY

Following Nat and Woody's departure, with the Baphomet Head safely stowed in the bow of the RNLI dinghy, the werewolf pack regrouped. Teddy Davis loosened his teeth from the back of Scale's scraggy neck, glad that Scale had witnessed his valuable prize being whisked away from him. But now he had to fight for his life. Although he was bigger, stronger and younger than Scale, he would be no match for the pack.

'What are you waiting for?' Scale cried, his voice

235

sounding strangled and frightened.

To Teddy's surprise, the pack still hung back, showing no interest in going in for the kill. Instead they splashed around three or four metres away, their ears flat against their heads, whining and mouthing like natural wolves will do when they are distressed.

'Get him off me!' shouted Scale as loudly as he could manage. 'End him!'

Still the werewolves disobeyed and Scale felt sick with fear as Teddy dragged him under the hateful brown water again. Teddy Davis rolled him the way a crocodile does with its prey and Scale felt his world spin and his miserable life flash before him like a film. It was dark under the water but Scale, still spinning, became dimly aware that it had suddenly gone blacker than the blackest, darkest hole in a midnight coalhole. The presence of evil was all encompassing and Scale felt strength return to him as though something was breathing new life into him.

Then the dark lifted and Scale saw an object glinting like quicksilver in the muddy, swirling water. He made a grab for it and grinned. A timely gift from his demon!

His blond pelt was sodden and covered in blood when Scale dragged him from the water. But Teddy Davis was victorious even when he felt his lifeblood leave his body. There hadn't been much pain when Scale had stabbed him through his heart with the silver dagger, just a great tiredness and cold. As the sun came up he realised this would be the last dawn he would see. He used his remaining strength to shift just one more time, and looked straight into Scale's raddled orange eyes.

The last words Teddy ever spoke were to Lucas Scale. 'You lost,' he growled.

Scale had messed up badly and he knew it. Although the demon had helped him by sending him the silver knife, he would need to get the Baphomet back or he would feel the fires of hell sooner rather than later. The smell of Teddy Davis' blood still lingered, fuelling his anger, and the cold air was filled with the crazed howling of his werewolves, who had turned out to be useless wimps and would be punished severely.

Then the awful truth dawned on him. There was no boat. Like cats, werewolves can swim well enough if they have to, but they hate every soggy moment that the water permeates their fur.

But Scale was more scared of facing his demon without the Baphomet Head than he was of the coffee-coloured water of the Bristol Channel. He shucked himself impatiently from his suit, flinging it into the waves, which lapped at his twisted, gnarly old feet. Dressed in a pair of rather saggy underpants, he held his snout and plunged into the water, leading the disgraced pack on the treacherous two-mile swim back to Diamond Bay.

So it was that six werewolves dragged themselves from the water, seasick and exhausted and looking for another place to hide. They headed back to Helleborine Halt (in Scale's opinion the last place anyone would think to look for him) and he began to feel calmer. He was able to think again. He made himself focus on a new plan – one that would guarantee him getting the Baphomet back. Although Teddy Davis had been a traitor – even if he'd been spared having his head bitten off and his lungs being pulled through the hole as is usual – Scale was annoyed that he had needed to kill him.

'Could have held the demon off for a while with his soul,' he muttered to himself. He knew that the demon would appear to him soon, he could feel it in his scabby innards. 'Must have something prepared.'

After hours of scheming and planning (he even drew some rather childish diagrams of his new plan and pinned them on the wall) Lucas Scale began to get excited. This was really going to work! But first things first.

He threatened Josh with the same fate as Teddy if

he didn't cooperate fully. He needed him to pay a little visit to Mistress de Gourney and the girl whom Josh had accidentally changed into a female werewolf – Scale had found a use for her after all.

Harmony Wedlock's eyes gleamed pumpkin orange in the mirror. Other than this rather unsettling change, she looked normal. There was no sign of where the werewolf's teeth had punctured her skin, and with the help of green contact lenses the eye problem could easily be solved. Even the pain in her heart had gone since Crescent's visit. It *had* been bad, this thing that had happened to her, and her first change had been excruciating. Before Crescent came, Harmony had felt like an animal, *worse* than an animal – she was like a thing from a horror film, a monster, a killer.

Then Crescent had arrived and they'd sat together in front of the fire for hours, talking. Harmony had heard about all the good wolves – brave, proud lycans who would help her adjust to her condition. She'd learnt about the true ways of the wolf. And, after days of doubt that anyone could help her ever again, she'd felt calm.

Harmony turned away from the mirror and got into bed. Snuggling down into the quilt, she thought she heard something outside. A crunch on the gravel, a footstep maybe? She got out of bed and tiptoed to the window, noting how silvery and inviting Iona's garden looked in the bright light of the moon. She shivered. The moon had a power over her now, it would be easy to give in to it, shimmy through the window and run through the garden and into the East Wood. She shook herself, remembering what Crescent had taught her about self control.

CRAAACK!

Someone was throwing stones at her window.

Harmony lifted the latch and opened the mullioned window, feeling the cool air rush inside. Leaning out, she looked down into the garden and had the shock of her life.

'Wh-what're you doing here?' she gasped.

'Can you come down?' The moonwashed face of Josh Firkin gazed up at her.

'Where've you *been*?' hissed Harmony. 'The police've been looking for you for months. Your mum's worried out of her mind.'

'Come down and I'll tell you,' said Josh. 'Quick, we haven't got much time.'

'Hang on,' said Harmony, pulling on a jumper over her pyjamas. She was puzzled but excited to see Josh's familiar face. Like everyone in Temple Gurney, she had been dismayed when he had disappeared, and here he was standing in Iona's garden as large as life.

She jumped up onto the window ledge like a cat, shimmied down the drainpipe and landed gracefully on the gravel. Josh stood before her, his face half hidden in the shadow of the lodge. But Harmony could see it well enough to notice his eyes. They gleamed an unnatural orange in the darkness.

'Oh . . . you . . . you're a . . . ?'

Harmony's words shrivelled in her mouth. Another being slid out of the shadows grinning ferociously, a stinking wolf creature with molten eyes and an impossibly large mouth, filled with cruel, yellowing teeth. Confused and terrified, Harmony searched Josh's face for an answer. All she saw was guilt and regret.

'I'm sorry,' he whispered.

With the Baphomet Head safely underground at *NightShift* HQ in London, Crone called a special meeting in the recreation room for all agents.

'The efforts of Nat Carver and Woody to retrieve the Baphomet Head were successful,' said Crone, allowing himself a brief smile. 'The team sent to pick up Scale and his pack from Sheephome was unable to locate them, but they did bring back the bodies of our brothers, Teddy Davis and Rydian.'

Nat and Woody both wept unashamed tears for Teddy Davis and the monk whom they had known for such a short time, but with whom they'd shared so much.

Afterwards, they sat quietly in the courtyard, warmed by the morning sun.

'Not long now,' said Woody.

'Sorry?' asked Nat, blinking in the sunlight. He was wearing the cap and scarf again.

'Only a week to the solstice,' said Woody, excitedly, 'and then you get your face sorted.'

'I'm scared it's not going to work,' said Nat. 'What . . . what if it doesn't?'

'You have to believe in Rydian,' said Woody, gently. 'That's probably part of the cure – belief.'

Nat shook himself and grinned ruefully. 'Sorry,' he said, 'and thanks for not giving up on me. I know I'm being pathetic.'

'Well, yeah you are a bit,' said Woody, grinning back, 'but until you get your face back to normal, I s'pose I'll have to let you off.'

They both looked round as they heard footsteps, and the sound of someone slightly out of breath.

'*There* you are!' exclaimed Alex Fish. 'I've been looking for you. Something's come up. Something big.'

Nat looked up, his strange face weary in the sunlight. 'Then call *Ghostbusters,* we're having a break.'

'Harmony Wedlock has been taken.'

'What d'you mean, *taken?*' asked Nat.

'Lucas Scale took her,' panted Fish. 'He wants to exchange Harmony for the Baphomet Head. He sent us a CD with a ransom demand. If we don't comply with his instructions, he'll kill her the same way he killed Teddy Davis.'

Nat stood up, his eyes glowing. 'OK, what do we need to do?' he said urgently. 'We have to get the Head and—'

'There's no way,' Fish said sadly. 'The boss won't agree to handing over the Head.'

'Mr Crone should have acted sooner,' cried Woody, 'when we still knew where Scale was.'

'You can't be serious,' said Nat, 'we've got to get Harmony back. We can't just leave her.'

'Billions of people's lives are at stake if Scale gets hold of the Baphomet,' reasoned Fish. 'Harmony is just one person.'

Nat and Woody both stared at her, aghast.

'I meant,' went on Fish, hastily, 'that you can't negotiate with kidnappers.'

'You mean you *won't*,' said Nat, narrowing his eyes. 'We had to sacrifice Teddy to bring back the Baphomet Head, we can't do the same to Harmony!'

'I'm sorry, Nat,' said Fish quietly, 'but I'm with the boss on this one.'

CHAPTER 26
SNAKES AND STONE

'I know what you're thinking,' said Woody, a terrified look on his face, 'and I need to tell you that I think you're out of your tiny mind.'

Nat's face split into a toothy grin. The sort of grin that turned Woody's bones into icy jelly.

'We're going to get Harmony back,' Nat said grimly, 'and nobody needs to know how, until we've done it.'

'You're a bloody lunatic,' sighed Woody, shaking his shaggy head. 'It's way too risky.'

'Listen,' said Nat.

As Nat explained his plan, Woody's expression began to lose some of its unhappy look. Nat's plan was so dangerously outrageous and so unbelievably mental, Woody couldn't help thinking that it might work. And Nat was so enthusiastic that Woody even began believing that maybe, just maybe, they had a chance of pulling it off. Of all the hair-raising adventures they had found themselves in, this surely had to be the most ambitious. If it went wrong, they would be dead meat, and Woody found himself wondering if Iona would want to have them stuffed too and arrange them by her inglenook fireplace as grisly ornaments.

Nat waited until Crone had a site meeting at the Bloody Tower (apparently the ghost of Anne Boleyn was picking on tourists again) then he and Woody slipped inside his empty office feeling guilty, but excited. Nat rummaged amongst the files, found what he was looking for and whacked the CD that contained Lucas Scale's ransom message into Crone's computer.

They perched upright on the squashy sofas, bracing themselves for the sound of Scale's voice. There were a few seconds of distant muttering and microphone feedback and then it came. Scale's sly, wheedling tones were unmistakeable. It felt to the boys as if he were there, in the room, lurking somewhere in the shadows of Quentin Crone's office. The details were precise and quite brief.

'*Highgate Cemetery on Saturday night at 3.00 a.m. Westside. Bring the Baphomet Head and the exchange will be made. The Head for the girl. No further negotiation will be entered into. Tell no one.*'

'We'll do it for Teddy,' said Nat, suddenly, his strange face contorting with anger and then with sadness. 'He would have wanted us to rescue Harmony.'

Woody nodded. 'Saturday night, Sunday morning. We better start planning.'

They tried to act normally for the rest of the day while they worked out exactly what they were going to do. Once Quentin Crone returned to his office, they took it in turns to watch the door, but it seemed as if he was never going to leave. At last, well after midnight, Woody burst into Nat's room.

'He's gone,' he said. 'Come on.'

They hurried downstairs to Crone's office and rolled back the faded carpet to reveal the ancient trapdoor and the seventy-seven steps.

'We'll have to be quick,' said Nat. 'If Mr Crone comes back and sees all this open, we've had it.'

Woody swallowed hard. 'The quicker we go, the quicker we'll be back.'

'You first,' grinned Nat.

'No, I insist,' said Woody. 'After *you*.'

Nat took a deep breath and led the way, hurrying down the stone steps as fast as he could. At the bottom the boys scanned the dimly lit cavern in dismay.

'It's bound to be near the front, said Nat, 'with all the mega dangerous stuff. We'll have to separate.'

'I don't really want to split up,' said Woody, alarmed. 'I can hear whispering.'

'It's only the vampires,' said Nat, 'and they can't get out.'

Woody still looked unhappy.

'OK,' said Nat, 'you go and get the other one. At least we know where that is.'

Woody nodded reluctantly. 'Don't forget the Cleopatra key.'

'I'm on it,' said Nat.

As Woody disappeared from view, Nat took the Cleopatra key from its ornate box and shoved it deep into the pocket of his jeans. He hurried past the rows of display jars, hoping that the Baphomet Head would still be in its coffin-like box while it waited to be examined properly, and then categorised as HIGHLY DANGEROUS. Nat glanced at his watch. They had already been down here for ten minutes. He concentrated hard, trying to remember the Baphomet's dry, bitter smell. A few precious minutes later it came back to him, and feeling rather like a giant sniffer dog, he trained his nose on the scent his Wolven senses recognised.

There! There it was, on top of a metal crate which no doubt contained something equally hideous. Nat lifted the box down carefully, trying not to shudder too much as the Baphomet shifted inside. He carried the box to the end of the aisle and was relieved to see Woody had his hands full too.

'You ready?' asked Nat.

'Not really,' admitted Woody, shakily.

'Come on,' said Nat, 'we rehearsed this. We can do it.'

Woody nodded. 'Good luck, bro.'

Under the cover of darkness, and carrying the miniature coffin between them, Nat and Woody set off for Highgate Cemetery, using back streets and following Scale's instructions not quite but almost to the letter. *They told no one.*

It was raining, and as they made their way out of the City and into Highgate, they felt the head inside the box begin to stir. They hurried on, trying to ignore the creepy shuffling inside, thankful they couldn't see what was going on.

The cemetery was, of course, locked, but Nat had fished out the Cleopatra key and inserted it into the padlock. It made a satisfying click as it popped open.

'Here we go,' he said and grinned at Woody as the gates swung open. Woody hesitated. Nat's fur was standing on end, his wolfish features never more frightening than they were at this moment. Not for the first time since this had begun, Woody thought his friend looked more than a little like Lucas Scale.

And Lucas Scale was watching, Nat was certain. He could *feel* him. In front of them lay a sort of grass corridor with enclosed tombs on both sides, like miniature houses. With Woody walking closely by his side, Nat moved carefully along it, still holding the coffin and bristling with adrenalin. Up ahead, in a shaft of bright moonlight, shone the twisted shapes of trees and the pale, silvery headstones of yet more graves. Woody kept his eyes trained ahead, hoping like mad he wouldn't see any ghosts; he hated them, it was bad enough coping with what they had just been through at *NightShift* HQ, without interference from the dear departed, thank you very much.

'See anything?' hissed Nat.

'Nope,' replied Woody, before adding hopefully, 'maybe he isn't coming.' Then he remembered Harmony and what was at stake, and felt bad.

A movement beyond the trees made Nat stiffen, and he put a warning hand on Woody's arm.

'There,' he whispered, 'there they are. It looks like

there's a wolf with him as well as Harmony.'

'Never mind the flippin' wolf,' shivered Woody. 'What's that . . . that *thing*?'

Harmony Wedlock was soaked through, her feet were bare and her eyes were dull with pain and shock. Josh Firkin also seemed dazed, but loped behind his master like the little puppy he was again, having been forced to stare once more into Scale's molten eyes and submit to his control. Something else lurked alongside them, the same energy that Woody had spotted. It was enshrouded in the blackest mass of darkness that Harmony had ever seen, and her werewolf instincts assured her that she didn't want to see what capered and blazed inside. Whatever it was, Harmony knew it would suck all the goodness out of the world; all joy, hope, love and happiness would be vanquished if the thing inside the dark got what it wanted.

Nearby, high in the branches of an ancient cedar and armed with a crossbow, lay Agent Alexandra Fish. Quentin Crone hadn't been willing to trade with Lucas Scale, but he hadn't been willing to abandon Harmony Wedlock either. As *NightShift's* best markswoman, Agent Fish had been sent to kill Scale as soon as he showed in the cemetery and her crossbow was loaded with a single silver bolt, trained on his heart.

When Fish caught sight of Nat and Woody, she nearly fell off the branch.

Noooo, she thought, hardly believing her eyes. Crone had forbidden any trade with Scale, but instead of trying to kill him, the boys were going to give him the Head of the Baphomet! What was more, they were in her line of fire! She shifted her position slightly to see what was going on. There appeared to be some sort of face-off as Nat and Woody, with the Head of the Baphomet held between them, faced Scale, who held Harmony slightly in front of him, perhaps sensing the need for a human shield. Fish, her mouth dry, her pulse racing, felt sick. They were going to jeopardise everything.

Nat's first thought was that Scale looked madder, badder and more dangerous than he had ever seen him look before. He tried not to, but guessed that the unseen thing which lurked inside the black, flickering mass beside Scale was the demon Scale had done his devastating deals with.

'Ha,' spat Lucas Scale, breaking the heavy silence. 'So they've sent you both. Little wolves to the slaughter.'

His eyes flickered greedily over the wooden box which Nat and Woody had placed between them.

'*My* box,' said Scale.

'All yours,' agreed Nat. 'Send Harmony over.'

'The box first,' snarled Scale. 'You must think I'm an idiot.'

'When we step away from the box, send us Harmony,' said Nat, his voice strong and clear. 'Then you can open it to make sure the Baphomet is there, and we all walk away. Is that a deal?'

'I don't normally deal with impudent pups like you,' sneered Scale, 'but it sounds reasonable.'

Alex Fish watched, her heart in her mouth, as they all walked forward, Nat and Woody still holding the box between them, Scale still pushing Harmony in front of him. Fish raised the crossbow again, but again she couldn't risk a shot. She saw Nat motion to Woody, and they set the box down on the grass. Scale let go of Harmony and she rushed over to Nat.

Now Fish had her chance. As Scale knelt down in front of the box and flipped the catch, she raised the bow and fired.

For a split second a black mass of impossibly dark matter seemed to envelop Scale, just long enough for the bolt to be deflected from its target and whistle harmlessly through the air, embedding itself into the trunk of a tree. When Scale had recovered from the shock, he laughed heartily at Nat and Woody's equally shocked faces.

'Nice try,' he giggled. 'Come on down, my dear,' he called up to Alex Fish, whose white face was just visible in the branches of the cedar tree. 'Come down on your own, or I'll send my dear friend Josh to *drag* you down with his teeth.'

Nat and Woody held their breath while Fish abseiled smoothly down the broad trunk of the tree.

She shook her head in disbelief at Nat and Woody. 'I can't believe you've done this,' she said, sadly. 'You've just sealed our fate. The Baphomet was safe, hidden, and now this monster and his demon will see to it that the human race is doomed.'

Nat couldn't say anything. Instead he focused on the flickering blackness which must conceal the demon. The mass was getting lighter, and he saw Scale glance at it apprehensively. There was a noise like someone dragging their fingernails across a blackboard, and a dreadful apparition appeared in front of them, hovering a few inches from the floor. It blazed with an unearthly light; its eyes were flames, its mouth a loose, wet, hungry maw, although the temperature of the thing had to be around boiling point. Fish gave a haunted cry and tried to twist away, but to her horror, she was rooted to the spot by some invisible force. She forced her eyes to shut, her head turned as far from the demon as possible, her body shaking uncontrollably.

'Humans,' said Scale, pleasantly. 'What are they like, eh?'

Nat acted fast. He knew that he and the others would be able to take the sight of a demon in the raw, because none of them were human, including him. One way or another they were lycanthropes – *of the wolf*. But Alex Fish *was* human, and Nat couldn't take the risk that she would be turned mad. He flung himself at Fish, rugby-tackling her to the floor, so that the demon was out of her sight.

'Very gallant,' remarked Scale sarcastically. 'But let's get on, shall we. I still need to check the box.'

Nat glanced at Woody, no longer sure if this was going to work. With the demon hovering nearby, he didn't know if they would get away with it.

Lucas Scale's eyes gleamed as he leant over and sniffed the box. It gave off an old, old smell . . . an enchanted smell. Scale had been present at many rituals of the Dark Arts, and knew the smells of frankincense and myrrh, of the old days, the dark days, the bad days. And now he was on the brink of releasing something incredible, something that would lift him, propel him above the Nobel Prize winners, the scientists, the preachers and the philosophers. He would rule the world.

There was no wind in the cemetery. No small

animals scuttled in the undergrowth, no planes flew above, no ghost dared raise its head above its grave. All sensed something in the air – something prophetical – an end to the old world and the beginning of the new.

Lucas Scale ran his paws almost lovingly over the top of the heavy wooden lid. A malignant orange light danced in his eyes as he fumbled for the catch once again. Nat almost forgot to breathe as he watched Scale's clumsy paws scrabble at it.

Whatifhegetssomeoneelsetoopenit, came Woody's thoughts, as Scale appeared to have some trouble opening the last catch.

Nat closed his eyes. It was imperative that Lucas Scale opened the box himself. In the next few agonising seconds, Scale managed to snap the final clasp. The expression on his hideous face was one of triumph. His deal with the demon was done – he would hand over the Head and be free.

As Scale lifted the lid, a noxious green mist seeped out from the sides, and what was this? His triumphant expression was replaced by puzzlement bordering on confusion. There was a hissing noise, which sounded as though it was coming from inside the box, a noise almost like the serpentine hiss of snakes. No . . . not almost like – *exactly* like! And if that wasn't enough to make Scale slam the lid shut again, then the watchful, expectant look on Nat Carver's face should have been the final warning. But the box was open and for a second Scale thought he heard Teddy Davis' last words again. *You lost.*

The green mist became a haze shot through with a heady purple light that filled the west side of the cemetery. There was no horned head, there was no Baphomet, demon of the Underworld, instigator of war and pestilence. What lay inside was a monster: a monster with a crown of snakes for hair, a black tongue that writhed and forked and eyes that, if they locked their gaze with yours, would turn you to stone and . . .

He'd been tricked! And though he tried to shut the coffin lid down on the snakes that writhed and hissed in front of him, tried to pull his head away from the gaze of the Gorgon, Medusa, and cover his eyes with his gnarly paws, it was too late. He screamed in agony as his body began to calcify and stiffen.

Nat Carver and Woody watched in horror as the green mist expanded around Scale and the hissing snakes seemed to reach out towards him. They watched as Lucas Scale turned completely, and irreversibly, into stone.

The demon wailed in anger and frustration, the sky opened and hot rain poured from above. The more it screamed and capered, the more the Gorgon hissed and cursed. Then Woody closed his eyes and lifted the head of Medusa from the wooden box where another evil head had lain for centuries. He dragged it by its snake hair and threw it into the air. As the demon drew its cloak of dark matter around it, the head spun inside and disappeared with the demon into the darkness.

CHAPTER 27
THE TRUTH

I t was over, and although it had been a job well done there would be no celebrations.

Lucas Scale, turned to stone for eternity, was being prepared for his incarceration in the bowels of the *NightShift* HQ at Middle Temple. In fact, the preparation was quite simple: castors were fixed to the bottom of his feet so he could be moved around more easily for stocktaking and cleaning purposes. Nat thought that Scale would have been horrified at the indignity, especially as both sets of castors squeaked horribly. Alex Fish snorted with laughter when security wheeled him into place, making him stand with his face to the wall, but both Nat and Woody found it strangely sad.

'You know he would have killed you both if things hadn't gone so well,' said Fish bluntly.

Woody had shrugged. 'I s'pose you're right. But what a horrible thing to happen to anyone.'

'He got off lightly,' said Fish, suddenly grim. 'He escaped trial. Think what he did to poor Teddy.'

'I *do*,' said Nat, sadly. 'I think about it all the time.'

Now they were no longer under Scale's corrupt influence, the young werewolves were being given another chance because they had never killed anyone. A special *NightShift* training school was to be set up at Meade Lodge and they were offered a chance to become trained agents. When Harmony Wedlock and Josh Firkin heard about it, they were as keen as mustard to be included.

As for Nat – well, nothing had changed, or shifted. The summer solstice was approaching and he was due to travel to Glastonbury with Fish and Woody. Nat couldn't help but ask himself, *What if Rydian's suggestion doesn't work*? He was aware he was pinning everything on words spoken to him centuries ago by a Wolven who was now a pile of medieval bones in a coffin.

Nat hadn't spoken very much about it since their night on the Tor, but Woody knew he was dreading seeing his parents. And when Alex Fish announced that Nat's mum and dad were at *NightShift* HQ and demanding to see their son, Nat was adamant.

'I don't want to see anyone,' he said.

'But Nat, it's your mum and dad,' said Fish. 'What on earth am I going to say to them?'

Nat looked at her with flashing eyes. 'Tell them the truth.'

Fish stared back. 'Look, I'll just stall them. If Rydian was right, you'll be back to normal in a couple of days.'

Nat shook his shaggy head slowly, his head low. 'I don't think it's going to work.'

Fish swallowed. Nat was so brave – to see him like this was heartbreaking. But not even Woody could make him feel better. He was holding all of them at arm's length. She feared for his sanity if Rydian's cure didn't work.

Then Nat appeared to have made a decision. 'I'll just see my mum,' he said.

When Jude Carver walked into Crone's office, Fish had lit all the candles and the large room looked magical. Jude had been primed about Nat's appearance by Quentin Crone and Fish, but he turned out to be covered in a cap, sunglasses and a scarf, like an A-grade celebrity.

Jude was dismayed when her son withdrew from her hug.

Nat saw her stricken face. 'Don't . . . don't, Mum,' he said miserably. 'I'm sorry.'

'Oh Nat,' was all Jude could find to say, 'there's nothing to be sorry for. You're still my son, still Nat, whatever you look like.'

Nat made a choking noise and hugged her tight.

'Can I see you?' asked Jude softly. 'Would that be all right?'

Nat nodded and reached up to take his cap off. He heard Jude's sharp intake of breath as he removed his scarf and then, finally, his sunglasses. He looked up at her.

Jude smiled. 'D'you remember when Maccabee Hammer showed his true vampire self?'

Nat nodded. 'Course.'

'And it was OK, because he was still Mac under-neath?'

'I suppose so,' said Nat, doubtfully.

'Well, this is a bit like that,' said Jude. 'I can still tell it's you.'

Nat lowered his eyes. 'What if I stay like this?'

'I truly believe you won't,' replied his mum. 'There's good magic and there's bad magic. We've both seen what terrible things bad magic can do. Now we just need to trust in the work that good magic can do.'

'Yes, but—' Nat began.

'Shhh,' hushed Jude. 'If it doesn't work, we'll try something else, and keep on going until you shift completely.'

To Nat's surprise, he was beginning to feel better.

'Can I see Dad now?' he asked.

'You can,' said Jude, 'and you can see Apple and Granddad too.'

'They're back?' asked Nat, his strange face catching the candlelight.

'Back from the Dark Ages,' grinned his mum, 'and *very* worried about their only grandson.'

'D-does Granddad know about the *Diamond Lil?*' Nat stammered.

Jude nodded. 'He's sad about her of course, but he's so proud of you, Nat. When this has died down, he wants to take you and Woody to get another boat.'

'And we can call it the *Diamond Lil II,*' said Nat, feeling even happier. It would be sooo great just to do something normal again.

Over the next few days, *NightShift* HQ was strangely quiet following the buzz around Lucas Scale's stony demise. No one had seen Quentin Crone since the day Nat's family had arrived, and Fish couldn't get hold of him on the phone. The following evening, however, shortly before 8.00 p.m., Fish came into the boys' attic rooms and announced there was to be a special meeting in Crone's office in one hour. Her beady eyes shone with excitement.

'The boss won't tell me what it's about,' she said.

'Hope it's nothing awful,' said Woody. He had spent the day in Wolven form asleep under his bed.

Nat felt rested too, and glad to be back with his family. His dad and his grandparents were visibly shaken by his appearance and his nan cried a bit. Maybe it was the relief of Scale and his demon being safely out of the way for eternity, but the mood had lightened by the time Quentin Crone eventually appeared. There was a strange calm in the room, and once or twice Nat felt a familiar presence, as though someone was inside his head. Not in a bad way like Scale rummaging about in his brain, but more like one of his premonitions in reverse. As though something good was going to happen.

Crone's usually groomed appearance had gone badly askew. His face was ruddy with excitement, his smooth hair was sticking up in all directions and he had forgotten to put his tie on.

'Good of you to be here, Jude,' he smiled widely at Nat's mum. He was worried he was going to get the blame for Nat's unusual appearance, and was hoping she'd realise it would have happened anyway, even if he hadn't have been a *NightShift* agent. He pumped Evan and Mick's hands and gave a delighted Apple a smacking kiss on her rosy cheek.

'Something important has come up,' he said. 'I've got something I need to share with you. I was just going to bring them in and—'

He was interrupted by the door opening. Nat was aware of two very tall men entering Crone's inner sanctum. He had never seen either of them before, and yet they were so familiar he felt himself being drawn towards them, as though by an invisible cord. He glanced across at Woody, who had shifted to human form for the important meeting. He too had a slightly dazed look on his face.

'Erm, allow me to introduce two visitors from Her Majesty's office,' said Crone, who seemed to be having trouble breathing. 'Her Majesty's Chief Equerry, Sir Richard Wolven, and Her Majesty's private secretary, Sir Andrew Wolven QC.'

Both Nat and Woody laughed out loud, but not because they found the situation funny. It was the sort of laugh that bubbles up and break out in sheer joy and wonder.

The two men were dressed casually in the sort of clothes you might find in Marks & Spencer if you went shopping with your dad. But that was where the ordinary stopped and the extraordinary began. They were similar in looks and both of them at least two metres tall. Nat thought they looked a bit like Clint Eastwood in his younger days, when he played the tough cop, Dirty Harry. They were rugged and a little wild-looking, with longish silver hair and eyes that looked as though in some lights they would be topaz.

'This is who's been paying us?' breathed Fish, stunned.

'Not enough, it would seem,' said Sir Andrew, smiling. 'Agent Fish, I believe?'

Oh man, oh man, thought Fish and curtsied, then got up blushing furiously. 'Y-yessir.'

'Please, Alex,' said Sir Richard, courteously, 'there's no need. As you can see by her absence, we've left Her Majesty at the Palace this evening.'

'Blimey,' said Fish, and blushed again.

'You…you're Wolven,' said Woody shyly, 'aren't you?'

Both men inclined their silver heads.

'These gentlemen are our benefactors,' said Crone, who seemed to have recovered slightly. 'Until today, I had no idea that Wolven still served their monarch.'

'From the House of Normandy to the House of Windsor,' said Sir Andrew, with a slight bow. 'Her Majesty the Queen takes an active interest in matters of the supernatural.'

Everyone else seemed to have been struck dumb.

'Her Majesty is concerned for Nat, and the predicament he finds himself in,' said Sir Richard, breaking the awkward moment and looking straight at Nat. 'If I, or indeed Andrew, can be of any assistance, we would be pleased to provide you with anything you may need, either now or in the future.'

'Anything at all,' echoed Sir Andrew.

Nat swallowed. 'Thanks,' he said simply. 'I might have to take you up on that if I'm stuck like this for the rest of my life.'

Sir Richard Wolven inclined his head. 'I . . .' He hesitated and glanced at Sir Andrew, who nodded encouragingly. 'There is a need to make you aware of certain things,' he went on. 'It's about your past.'

You could have heard a pin drop in Crone's room. All eyes and ears were trained on Sir Richard.

'When you were bitten by Lucas Scale at the end of the Proteus project,' went on Sir Richard, 'Lady Iona thought you were going to die, and that the blood transfusion you received from Woody saved you from becoming a werewolf.'

Nat shivered, remembering that terrible night.

'The truth is, you wouldn't have died *or* become a werewolf,' said Sir Andrew. 'The blood transfusion you had from Woody didn't actually work, because *you didn't need it.*'

Jude Carver gasped. 'What do you mean?'

'There's Wolven blood running through your grandmother's side of the family,' said Sir Richard gently, 'has been for years. Your bloodline goes back almost as far as ours, but has been diluted through marriage to humans. You were a surprise, Nat.' He smiled kindly at Apple, who looked as though she was about to pass out.

'Stone me,' gasped Mick.

'For years Apple's family produced mainly girls, which tended to render the shape-shifting powers dormant,' explained Sir Andrew. 'Apple has gifts in healing and she understands the ways of animals better than any human. She also has powerful second sight. But you, Nat, are the first boy for generations, and you have inherited the entire Wolven gene, which overcame the taint of Scale's bite.'

No one said anything for what seemed like hours. Then Nat had a rather worrying thought.

'Did either of you know Nellynora Goodwill?'

Sir Richard's face lit up. 'Of course! She was just little Nell Bytheway when I knew her.'

Woody looked confused. Both Sir Andrew and Sir Richard looked way younger than Nellynora. He wasn't that good at estimating human ages, but he would have guessed that both the Sirs were a lot younger than Mick, who was Nat's *granddad*! 'But

Nellynora Goodwill has got to be in her nineties now!' he said, puzzled.

'Ten years our junior,' said Sir Andrew. 'She's still alive, then? Pretty little thing, if I remember correctly.'

Notnowshesnot, Woody two-wayed to Nat.

Sir Andrew and Sir Richard both caught Woody's thoughts and a clear picture of Nellynora Goodwill sitting in her kitchen back in Temple Gurney.

'Ageing can be cruel,' said Sir Andrew, raising an eyebrow at Woody.

'But . . .' began Woody.

'We Wolven live many years longer than humans,' said Sir Richard, gently.

Nat closed his eyes and groaned inwardly. Ordinarily, the thought of being able to live longer than humans would be well cool, but not if he was stuck halfway! Not only did he risk looking like a monster for the rest of his life, he was going to live longer than the average human because of his Wolven blood.

'So what happens now?' asked Nat.

'We continue with *NightShift*,' said Sir Andrew, 'and we hope we can rely on your help.'

Fish caught sight of Nat and Woody's faces, and she didn't like what she saw.

CHAPTER 28

CHALICE WELL, MIDSUMMER'S EVE

It was dusk when they arrived. The last of the sun had painted a pinky glow across the sky, and on Glastonbury Tor the ruins of St Michael's church shimmered like a mirage. They watched in silence as a steady stream of people carrying flaming torches snaked up the side of the great hill to celebrate midsummer.

Despite her fears for Nat, Fish couldn't help thinking that she had never seen anything so magical in her entire life. She found a place to park the car well away from prying eyes and glanced across at him. None of them had spoken much during the journey, each wrapped up in their own thoughts about what lay ahead.

'Ready?' asked Fish, her voice slightly husky as she tried not to cry. 'Remember, the place is heaving with all those pagan types. If they see you . . .'

'Let's do it,' interrupted Nat. His eyes were two pools of topaz light in the cramped confines of the car. 'Aren't you coming?'

Fish shook her head. 'This is for you, Nat,' she said, 'for you and Woody.'

Woody slipped out of the back seat and Nat hesitated before opening the passenger door.

'Wish me luck,' he said, turning his strange face towards her and trying to smile.

'With all my heart,' said Fish. She kissed him on his rough, hairy cheek.

'Whatever happens, promise me you'll come back.'

'Promise,' growled Nat, anxious now to get it over with.

Fighting tears, Fish watched as Nat and Woody made for the orchard and the hedged perimeter of the visitor centre. Only then did she allow herself to break down and cry.

Please, please let it work! Please let it be true!

*   *   *

As the boys approached the Chalice Well gardens, a weird metallic smell invaded their nostrils. Nat remembered Iona telling him that the source of the ancient spring was so rich in iron it left a red stain on everything it touched. Then she had shared with them the story about Joseph of Arimathea. It was said that when he was on a pilgrimage to England, he hid the chalice used at the Last Supper by his nephew, Jesus, in the well. Nat had been quietly thrilled. He thought that if legend said Uncle Joe of Arimathea had done such a thing, then he probably had. Because Nat of all people knew that, more often than not, legends and the old stories of long ago were mainly true.

Faith does funny things to some folk, especially if, like Nat, they're desperate. His mouth felt dry as he remembered Rydian's words: *Drink only from the lion's head and immerse thyself in the pool.*

By the time the boys found a way in to the Chalice Well gardens it was dark. They pushed through the thick hedges and sniffed the warm summer air appreciatively. The rich scents of honeysuckle and nightstock and the sweet tinkling sound of water added to the enchanted feel of the gardens. Despite their worries, both boys felt that the night air was charged with something amazing. They could feel it, but more importantly, they could *smell* it. *Magic*.

Silvered by the light of the swollen moon, the grass felt springy and lush beneath their bare feet as they followed the path towards the sound of water. Woody saw it first.

'*There!* There it is,' he exclaimed excitedly. 'The Lion!'

Set in the drystone wall was the stone head described by the monk, Rydian. Water gushed from its mouth and even by moonlight it was clear to see that Iona had been right, the water had a definite red cast. As it splashed on the stone, the droplets sparkled like rubies.

'Go on then,' said Woody, softly. 'What are you waiting for?'

'I don't know,' admitted Nat. 'I guess this is it. If it doesn't work, I don't have anywhere else to go.'

'It *will* work,' said Woody firmly. 'Rydian said it would.'

Nat took a deep breath and moved closer to the lion's head. He held his hands under the stone mouth and let the cool water run over them for a few moments. He could already feel the energy charging every hair on his face and body, making it crackle with static electricity. *This might actually work!*

He glanced at Woody and grinned. Woody's hair stood out in an electrified blond halo as he picked up

Nat's thoughts.

'Drink it,' urged Woody.

Nat wasted no more time. He got down on all fours and lapped the water like a dog as it splashed onto the stone below. As it slid down his parched throat, he could feel Woody's eyes boring into him, willing him to change.

'You've had loads,' said Woody anxiously. 'D'you feel any different?'

Nat shook his head. 'Nope. But Rydian didn't say how much I should drink.'

'Try the healing pool,' suggested Woody. 'You can always drink some more.'

Nat shook the water from his muzzle and followed his nose along the path toward the shimmering pool. It was true he didn't feel as though he was going to shift, but walking through the garden he did feel different – kind of calm and energised all at once, as though there were forces inside him at odds with each other, like two magnets pushing each other apart.

The healing pool was fringed by lush palms and Nat knelt down beside it. Reflected in the water, his face looked back at him. Was it imagination, or was it shorter, more human? Silently, he rose to his feet and stripped off his clothes, laying them carefully by the side of the pool. He looked down at his misshapen body, praying it would be the last time he would see himself this way.

Woody watched with bated breath as Nat dipped one hairy toe into the pool then seemed to shake himself impatiently. He waded in and lay down in the shallow water, immersing himself fully in its silky depths before coming up for air.

Nat closed his eyes, hearing nothing but the beating of his heart as he lay there letting the lapping water take him. At one point he opened his eyes and looked up at the stars, fixing on the brightest: Polaris, the Northern Star.

Nat felt the water rise up over his mouth and nose and for some strange reason he didn't feel scared. Memories of places and people fast-forwarded through his brain as the water seemed to pulse with energy and wash over his body. He remembered reading somewhere that when a person drowns they see their life flash before them in their last moments of consciousness.

This must be what it's like to drown, he thought calmly. Dream-like visions flashed through his brain: a baking-hot farmyard, a scruffy dog and a library full of strange books; rosehip cordial, the vermilion sun of a long-ago land and a medieval king; an underground room with specimens of dead creatures and a mad scientist; a silver caravan and a vampire's lair; old-lady zombies and a welcoming monk. Then the images whirled faster and faster until they scrambled in his brain: LucasScaleIonaCrescentSaffiMaccabee-HammerCroneRichardtheLionheartTeddyDavisOh-poordeadTeddyOpheliaScarletWOODYHarmony...

Afterwards, all Woody could remember was Nat lying in the healing pool, with the water gentle at first, then rising till it washed over Nat's whole body, as if someone had turned on a wave machine. It had a sort of hypnotic effect on him. Woody had shrieked like a girl (although he didn't tell Fish that bit) and covered his ears as the world seemed to explode around him. Deafening *Kerbooooms, craaaaaack-ack-ack-acks* and even *vizzzzzzzzzzz wheeeeeeeeeeez wheeeeeeeeeeeez* sounds filled the night sky and he ran for cover. Woody had never experienced fireworks, so he had no way of knowing that instead of the end of the world, it was just the pilgrims on the Tor celebrating the summer solstice.

When he plucked up enough courage to go back to the pool it was empty. Nat had disappeared!

CHAPTER 29

WOLVEN 4 EVER!

*W*here *the flippin' heck has he gone?* Woody peered into the reddish-coloured water, desperately trying to see what had become of Nat. He was just about to go back to the car and tell Fish the bad news that their best friend appeared to have melted, when he heard a familiar sound. It was faint but unmistakeable.

'AAAAAAAAHHHHOOOOOOOOOOAAAARR-WOOOH!'

Woody leapt to his feet. *Wolven?* Puzzled but excited,

he scooped up Nat's clothes and ran towards the sound, sniffing the air for traces of Nat's scent. He didn't have to search for long. Something pale and human-shaped appeared to be sitting beneath one of the enormous yew trees. Woody yelped in delight, for there, glimmering in the moonlight, was Nat, as bare-naked as the day he was born. It had worked!

'Welcome back,' cried Woody. 'But where'd you go? Your howl sounded like you were miles away!'

'I-I'm not sure,' stuttered Nat. His grotesque fangs had disappeared but his normal-sized teeth were chattering with shock. 'It was like when I flip, but I didn't get there. It was like drowning, no, *floating*, teetering on the edge of the world.'

Woody looked at his friend quizzically. 'Well, wherever you went it's made you look a whole lot better. I was worried you were stuck like that for ever.'

'I was a monster,' shivered Nat. 'I was like Scale.'

'You were slightly better looking than Lucas Scale,' said Woody, seriously, 'and not as evil. Or as mad.'

'Is . . . does my face look OK?' Nat asked.

'No, but it's back to normal,' laughed Woody. Then he fell silent. He wasn't sure what to say. Nat had made his feelings clear about the future at their last meeting.

Woody swallowed. 'What do you want to do now?'

'I want to go home,' said Nat, simply.

Woody handed Nat his jeans. 'We'll be back in a couple of hours.'

Nat shook his head. 'No . . . *home.* Back to my mum and dad's. I was, like, kind of hoping you would come too.'

Relief shone in Woody's face. 'We're really quitting?' he asked.

'Everything's different now,' said Nat. 'We beat Lucas Scale. Job done. It's over.'

Woody didn't say anything for some time. He would be glad to quit *NightShift;* he hadn't really wanted to join in the first place, he had done it for Nat. But something else was bothering him.

'You did howl, didn't you?' he asked anxiously, 'You *can* still howl, I take it?'

'I didn't say it *was* me,' said Nat, smiling wanly. 'There's magic in the air, can't you feel it?'

'I can smell it,' said Woody, his nostrils flaring in and out with alarming speed.

'I'm Wolven,' said Nat, liking the sound of his words, 'and not even magic can take away what I am. Anyway, we're a double act, remember. You're the freak and I'm the weirdo.'

'Can you still shift?' asked Woody anxiously. 'And if it wasn't you who howled, who was it?'

Nat's eyes glimmered with an intense topaz light.

'I think we're about to find out the answer to both your questions,' he said.

Woody saw with his mind what Nat could see and felt weak with relief. 'You still want to be Wolven!' he whooped excitedly. 'But . . . will it be for ever?'

'For ever,' said Nat, and smiled.

'AAAAAAAAOOOOWWWWWWWAAAAAAAAA!'

The howling came from the direction of the Tor. Nat and Woody stood waiting, heads slightly cocked to one side as they listened to the mysterious sounds coming from the foot of the magical mystery Tor.

Alex Fish heard the howls as she stumbled across the same meadow that Nat and Woody had passed through, grateful she had left her platform shoes at home. The magic was working on Fish too; her earlier grief and worries had all but vanished when the Wolven voices started. They were everywhere, bouncing and echoing across the countryside, filling the air with their joy. Whatever had happened was major, decided Fish. Man, oh man, she needed to see this.

The howls were getting nearer and nearer and suddenly she felt nervous. That wasn't Woody, or Nat either, Fish knew their Wolven voices, and anyway, this sounded like many voices. At least eight or more different tones and resonances.

'Blummin' Nora,' muttered Fish. 'How're they doing *that?*'

By the time she had pushed through the thick, spiky hedges, the howls had stopped and it was eerily quiet in the garden. Fish ran for the cover of the yew trees and tried to get her breath back. There was no sign of either Nat or Woody anywhere. A sudden movement to her left made her breath hitch in her chest. Not for the first time since this madness had begun, she wished she had Wolven infra-red eyesight.

Then she saw them. *Just like the tapestry in Crone's office!* A pack of King's Wolven, magnificently and dazzlingly white against the indigo of the midnight sky. It was difficult to count them as they were all gathered around something, tails wagging, chuffing and squealing gently to each other. Fish's eyes goggled behind her specs. She counted . . . *three* . . . *seven* . . . *thirteen*. And one of them was Woody. *So where,* she thought to herself, *is Nat?*

Fish edged closer. The ground mist was making it difficult to see them clearly. Then she saw him – the Grey Wolf. Nat Carver was no longer a monster, but a magnificent Wolven creature.

It had worked. Rydian had cured Nat!

Alex Fish watched as the King's Wolven, once thought to exist only in legend, began to wind their way towards the Tor. She stayed there for some time until she had seen the last Wolven tail disappear into the mist.

Seeyaboys, said Fish with her mind. *Dontforgetyourpromisenat.*

Then she grinned to herself and walked across the dewy orchard to her car.

ACKNOWLEDGEMENTS

Many thanks as always to all at the wonderful Chicken House, especially Chrissie and Nicki for their wise and insightful edits.

Thanks also to the following for their unfailing support and lots of laughs – Mum & Dad, Jamie, Mike and families, the Watkinsons (hey, Maddie!), the Ryes, the Williams', Anita, Des, Lita, Paul, Gloria and Alan.

Last but not least, to Phil, Dan & Frankie xxx